About the Authors

Debbie Macomber—Debbie's writing career actually started in childhood, when her brother copied—and sold!—her diary. She's gone on to a considerably wider readership since then, with over seventy books published and with devoted fans in every corner of the globe. Debbie lives in Washington State with her husband and she's a mother of four—two girls and two boys.

Barbara Bretton—With over eight million copies of her books in print, Barbara is a favorite with readers worldwide. In her decade-long career, this award-winning author has written thirty contemporary and historical novels, as well as numerous short stories and articles. Barbara lives with her husband in New Jersey.

Muriel Jensen—This bestselling author of almost twenty-five novels began writing romance fiction in the ninth grade. She realized she'd found her niche in life when her classmates started gathering around her desk every morning for the latest installment. Muriel is a mother of three and lives in Oregon with her artist husband.

Little Matchmakers

Debbie Macomber
Barbara Bretton
Muriel Jensen

Harlequin Books

TORONTO • NEW YORK • LONDON
AMSTERDAM • PARIS • SYDNEY • HAMBURG
STOCKHOLM • ATHENS • TOKYO • MILAN
MADRID • WARSAW • BUDAPEST • AUCKLAND

HARLEQUIN BOOKS

by Request—Little Matchmakers

Copyright © 1994 by Harlequin Enterprises B.V.

ISBN 0-373-20107-9

The publisher acknowledges the copyright holders of the individual works as follows:
THE MATCHMAKERS
Copyright © 1986 by Debbie Macomber
MRS. SCROOGE
Copyright © 1989 by Barbara Bretton
A CAROL CHRISTMAS
Copyright © 1989 by Muriel Jensen

This edition published by arrangement with Harlequin Enterprises B. V.

® and TM are trademarks of the publisher. Trademarks indicated with ® are registered in the United States Patent and Trademark Office, the Canadian Trade Marks Office and in other countries.

Printed in U.S.A.

CONTENTS

Need Dad. Tall, athletic. Mom pretty.
Call 555-5818.

THE MATCHMAKERS

Debbie Macomber

CHAPTER ONE

"DANNY, HURRY UP and eat your cereal," Dori Robertson pleaded as she rushed from the bathroom to the bedroom. Quickly pulling on a tweed skirt and a shell-knit sweater, she slipped her feet into black leather pumps and hurried into the kitchen.

"Aren't you going to eat, Mom?"

"No time." As fast as her fingers would cooperate, Dori spread peanut butter and jelly across bread for a sandwich, then opened the refrigerator door and took out an orange. She stuffed both items in a brown paper sack with a cartoon cat on the front. Lifting the lid of the cookie jar, she dug around and came up with only a handful of crumbs. Graham crackers would have to do.

"How come we're always so rushed in the mornings?" eleven-year-old Danny wanted to know.

Dori paused and laughed. The sound was low and sweetly musical. There'd been a time in her life when everything had fitted into place. But not anymore. "Because your mother has trouble getting out of bed."

"Were you always late when Dad was here?"

Turning, Dori leaned against the kitchen counter and crossed her arms. "No. Your father used to bring me a cup of coffee in bed." Brad had had his own special way of waking her with coffee and kisses. But now Brad was gone and, except for their son, she faced the world alone. Admittedly the rushed mornings were much easier to accept than the long lonely nights.

"Would you like me to bring you coffee? I could," Danny offered seriously. "I've seen you make it lots of times."

A surge of love for her son constricted the muscles of her throat, and Dori tried to swallow the dry lump. Every day Danny grew more like his father. Tenderly she looked down at his sparkling blue eyes and the broad band of freckles that danced across his nose. Brad's eyes had been exactly that shade of bottomless blue, though the freckles were all hers. Pinching her lips together, she turned back to the counter, picked up a cup and took her first sip of lukewarm coffee. "That's very thoughtful of you," she said.

"Then I can?"

"Sure. It might help." Anything would be better than this infernal rushing every morning. "Now brush your teeth and get your coat."

When Danny moved down the hallway, Dori carried his empty cereal bowl to the sink. The morning paper was open, and she quickly folded it and set it aside. There had once been a time when Danny had pored over the sports section, but recently he'd been reading the want ads. He hadn't asked for anything in particular lately, and she couldn't imagine what he found so fascinating in the classified section. Kids! At his age, she remembered, her only interest in the newspaper had been the comics and Dear Abby. Come to think of it, she didn't read much more than that now.

Danny joined her in the kitchen and together they went out the door and into the garage. While Dori backed the Dodge onto the narrow driveway, Danny stood by and waited to pull the garage door closed.

"One of these days," she grumbled as her son climbed into the front seat, "I'm going to get an automatic garage-door opener."

Danny tossed her a curious look. "Why? You've got me."

A smile worked its way across Dori's face. "Why, indeed?"

Several minutes followed while Danny said nothing. That was unusual, and twice Dori's gaze sought his eager young face. His look was troubled, but she didn't pry, knowing her son would speak when he was ready.

"Say, Mom, I've been wanting to ask you something," Danny began haltingly, then paused.

"What?" Dori said, thinking that the Seattle traffic got worse every morning. Or maybe it wasn't that the traffic got thicker, just that she got later.

"I've been thinking."

"Did it hurt?" That was an old joke of theirs, but Danny didn't have an immediate comeback the way he usually did.

"Hey, kid, this is serious, isn't it?"

Danny shrugged one shoulder in an offhand manner. "Well, I know you loved Dad and everything, but I think it's time you found me another dad."

Dori slammed on her brakes. The car came to a screeching halt at the red light as she turned to her son, her dark eyes rounded in shock. "Time I did what?" she asked incredulously.

"It's been five years, Mom. Dad wouldn't have wanted you to mope through the rest of your life. Next year I'm going to junior high and a kid needs a dad at that age."

Dori opened her mouth searching for words of wisdom that didn't come.

"I can make coffee in the mornings and all that, but you need a husband. And I need a dad."

"This is all rather sudden, isn't it?" Her voice was little more than a husky murmur.

"No, I've been thinking about it for a long time." Danny swiveled his head over his shoulder and pointed behind him. "Say, Mom, you just missed the school."

"Damn." She flipped on her turn signal and moved into the right lane with only a fleeting glance in her rearview mirror.

"Mom...watch out!" Danny shrieked just as her rear bumper barely missed the front end of an expensive foreign car. Dori swerved out of the path, narrowly avoiding a collision.

The driver of the other car blared his horn angrily and followed her when she pulled into a side street that would lead her back to the grade school.

"The guy you almost hit is following you, Mom and, boy, does he look mad."

"Great." Dori's fingers tightened around the steering wheel. This day was quickly going from bad to worse.

With his head turned around, Danny continued his commentary. "Now it looks like he's writing down your license plate number."

"Wonderful. What does he plan to do? Make a citizen's arrest?"

"He can do that?" Danny returned his attention to his flustered mother.

"Yup, and he looks like the type who would." The uncompromising, hard face that briefly met hers in the rearview mirror looked capable of just about anything. The deeply set dark eyes had narrowed into points of steel. The thick, equally dark hair was styled away from his face, revealing the harsh contours of his craggy features. He wasn't what could be called handsome, but his masculinity was blatant and forceful. "A man's man" was the term that came to mind.

"I recognize him," Danny said thoughtfully. "At least I think I do."

"Who is he?" Dori took a right-hand turn and eased to a stop in front of Cascade View Elementary. The man in the Audi 5000 pulled to a stop directly behind her and got out of his car.

"He looks familiar," Danny commented a second time, his wide brow furrowed in concentration, "but I don't know from where."

Squaring her shoulders, Dori reluctantly opened the car door and climbed out. Absently she brushed a thick swatch of auburn hair off her shoulder as she walked back to meet the tall formidable man waiting for her. Dressed in an impeccable three-piece suit and expensive leather shoes, he was all the more intimidating. His dark eyes followed her movements. They were interesting and arresting eyes in a face that looked capable of forging an empire—or at least slicing her to ribbons—with one arch of a brow. Dori was determined not to let him unnerve her. She indicated with her hand that Danny should stay by the car, but he seemed to think she'd need him for protection. She didn't, but couldn't take the time to argue with him.

"I don't appreciate being followed." She decided her best defense was an offense.

"And I don't appreciate being driven off the road."

"I apologize for that, but you were in my blind spot and when I went to change lanes—"

"You didn't so much as look."

"I most certainly did," Dori stated evenly, her voice gaining volume. For the first time she noticed a large brown stain on his suit jacket. The beginnings of a smile edged up the corners of her mouth.

"Just what do you find so amusing?" he demanded harshly.

Dori cast her eyes to the pavement. "I'm sorry. I didn't mean to be rude."

"The most polite thing you can do, lady, is to stay off the roads."

Hands on her hips, her hazel eyes sparking fire, Dori advanced one step. "In case you weren't aware, there's a law in Washington state against drinking any beverage while driving. You can't blame me if you spilled your coffee. You shouldn't have had it in the car with you in the first place." She prayed the righteous indignation in her tone would be enough to assure him she knew what she was talking about.

"You damned near caused an accident." He, too, advanced a step and a tremor ran through her at the stark anger in his eyes.

"I've already apologized for that," Dori said, knowing that if this confrontation continued she would come out the loser. Discretion was the better part of valor—at least that was what her father always claimed, and for once Dori was willing to follow his advice. "If it will smooth your ruffled feathers any, I'll pay the cleaning cost for your suit."

The school bell rang, and Danny hurried back to the car for his books and his lunch. "I've got to go, Mom."

Dori was digging around the bottom of her purse looking for a business card. "Okay, have a good day." She hoped one of them would; hers certainly didn't look promising.

"Don't forget I've got soccer practice after school," he reminded her, walking backward toward the front steps of the school.

"I won't."

"And Mom?"

"Yes, Danny," she answered irritably, the tight rein on her patience quickly slackening.

"Do you promise to think about what I said?"

Dori glanced up at him blankly.

"You know, about getting me another dad?"

Dori could feel the hot color creep up her neck and invade her pale face. Diverting her gaze from the unpleasant man standing beside her, she expelled her breath in a low groan. "I'll think about it."

A boyish grin brightened Danny's face as he turned and ran toward his classmates.

Searching for a business card helped lessen some of Dori's acute embarrassment. Another man would have said something to ease her chagrin, but not this one. "I'm sure I've got a card in here someplace."

"Forget it," the man said gruffly.

"No," she argued. "I'm responsible, so I'll pay." Unable to find what she wanted, Dori wrote her name and address on the back of her grocery list. "Here," she said, handing him the long narrow slip of paper.

He examined it briefly and stuck it into his suit pocket. "Thank you, Mrs. Robertson."

"It was my fault."

"I believe you've already admitted as much." Nothing seemed capable of cracking the granite facade this man wore like armor.

"I'll be waiting for the bill, Mr...?"

"Parker," he completed grudgingly. "Gavin Parker." He turned and retreated toward his car.

The name was strangely familiar to Dori, but she couldn't recall where she'd heard it. Odd. Danny had seemed to recognize him, too.

"Mr. Parker," Dori called out and raised her finger.

"Yes?" Irritably he turned to face her again.

"Excuse me, but I wonder if I could have another look at the paper I gave you."

The set of his mouth tightened into an impatient line as he removed the slip from his pocket and handed it back to her.

Quickly her eyes scanned the grocery list, hoping to commit it to memory. "Thanks. I just wanted to be sure I remembered everything."

The cold raking gaze of his eyes unsettled her, and by the time Dori was in her car and heading for the insurance office, she had forgotten every item. What an unnerving man! Just the memory of the look in his eyes was enough to cause a chill to race up her spine. His mouth had been interesting, though. Not that she usually noticed men's mouths. But his had been firm with that chiseled effect so many women liked. There was a hard-muscled grace to him...Dori put a bridle on her thoughts. How ridiculous she was being. She refused to give one extra minute's thought to that unpleasant character.

The employee parking lot was full when she arrived and she was forced to look for a place on the street, which was nearly impossible at this time of morning. Luckily, she found a narrow space three blocks from the insurance company where she was employed as an underwriter for homeowner policies.

By the time she arrived at her desk, she was irritated, exhausted and ten minutes late.

"You're late." Sandy Champoux announced as Dori rolled back her chair.

"I hadn't noticed," Dori returned sarcastically, dropping her purse in a bottom drawer and pretending an all-consuming interest in the file on her desk as her boss, Mr. Sandstorm, sauntered past.

"You always seem to make it to your desk on time," Sandy said, ignoring the sarcasm. "What happened this morning?"

"You mean other than a near car accident with a nasty man in a three-piece suit or Danny telling me the time has come to find him a new father?"

"The kid's right, you know."

Purposely being obtuse, Dori batted her thick lashes at her friend and smiled coyly. "Who's right? Danny or the man in the three-piece suit?"

"Danny! You *should* think about getting married again. It's time you joined the world of the living."

"Ah—" Dori pointed her index finger at the ceiling "—you misunderstand the problem. Danny wants a father in the same way he wanted a ten-speed bike. He's not interested in a husband for me..." She paused and bit the her bottom lip as a thought flashed into her mind. "That's it." Her eyes lit up.

"What's it?" Sandy demanded.

"The ten-speed."

"You're going to bribe your son with another bicycle so he'll forget his need for a father?" Sandy was giving Dori the look she usually reserved for people showing off pictures of their children.

"No, Sandy," Dori groaned, slowly shaking her head from side to side. "You don't want to know."

Her brow marred with a disgruntled frown, Sandy reached for a new policy from her basket. "If you say so."

Despite its troubled beginnings, the day passed quickly and without further incident. Dori was waiting to speak to her son when he trooped into the house at five-thirty, his soccer shoes looped around his neck.

"Hi, Mom, what's there to eat?"

"Dinner. Soon."

"But I'm starved now."

"Good, set the table." Dori waited until Danny had washed his hands and placed two dinner plates on the round oak table before she spoke. "I've been thinking about what you said this morning."

"Did it hurt?" Danny questioned and gave her a roguish grin, creating twin dimples in his freckled face. "What did you decide?"

"Well..." Dori paid an inordinate amount of attention to the cube steak she was frying, then said, "I'll admit I wasn't exactly thrilled with the idea. At least not right away."

"And now?" Danny stood at the table and studied her keenly.

She paused, gathering her resolve. "The more I thought about it," she said at last, "the more I realized you may have a valid point."

"Then we can start looking?" His young voice vibrated with eagerness. "I've had my eye on lots of neat guys. There's one who helps the coach with the soccer team who would do real good, but I don't think he's old enough. Is nineteen too young?"

This was worse than Dori had thought. "Not so fast," she said, stalling for time. "We need to go about this methodically."

"Oh, great," Danny mumbled and heaved a disgusted sigh. "I know what that means."

"It means we'll wait until after the dinner dishes are done and make up a list just like we did when we got your bike."

Danny brightened. "Hey, that's a great idea."

Dori wasn't nearly so sure as Danny rushed through his dinner in record time. The minute the dishes were washed and put away, the boy produced a large writing tablet.

"You ready?" he asked, pausing to chew on the tip of the eraser.

"Sure."

"First we should get someone as old as you."

"At least thirty," Dori agreed, pulling out a chair.

"And tall, because Dad was tall and it'd look funny if we got a really short guy. I don't want to end up being taller than my new dad."

"That makes sense." Again Dori was impressed by how seriously her son was taking this.

"He should like sports because I like sports. You try, Mom, but I'd really like someone who can throw a football better than you."

That was one duty Dori would relinquish gladly. "I think that's a good idea."

"And I think it would be neat if he knew karate."

"Why not?" Dori agreed amicably.

Danny's pencil worked furiously over the paper as he added this latest specification to the growing list. "And most important—" the blues eyes grew sober "—my new dad should love you."

"That would be nice," Dori murmured in a wavering breath. Brad had loved her. So much that for a while she'd thought she'd die without him. Even after all these years, the capacity to love another man with such intensity seemed beyond her.

"Now what?" Danny looked up at her expectantly.

"Now," she said and sucked in a giant breath. "Now that we know what we're looking for, all we need to do is wait for the right man to come along."

Danny looked doubtful. "That could take a long time."

"Not with both of us looking." She took Danny's list and placed it on the refrigerator with a large strawberry magnet. "Isn't it time for your bath, young man?"

Danny stood with obvious reluctance, shoved the pad and pencil into the kitchen drawer and headed down the hall that led to his bedroom.

Dori retired to the living room, took out her needlepoint and turned on the television. Maybe Danny was right. There had to be more to life than work, cooking and needlepoint. It wasn't that she hadn't tried to date. She had. Sandy had fixed her up with a friend of a friend at the beginning of summer. The evening had turned out to be a disaster, and Dori had refused her friend's attempts to match her up again. Besides, there hadn't been any reason to date. She was fairly content and suffered only occasionally from bouts of loneliness, usually late at night. Danny managed to fill her life. He loved sports and she loved watching him play.

But Danny was right. He did need a father figure, especially now as he moved into adolescence. Deep down Dori wondered how anyone could replace Brad. Danny had been too young to remember much about his father, as Brad had died when Danny was only six. Her own memories of that age were vague and distant, and she wondered how much she would have remembered of her father if she'd been in Danny's place.

The house was unusually quiet. Danny was normally in and out of the bath so quickly that she often wondered if he'd even given himself the chance to get completely wet.

Just as she was about to investigate, Danny ran into the room, clutching a handful of bubble gum cards. "Mom, that was Gavin Parker you nearly ran into today!"

Dori glanced up from her needlepoint. "I know."

"Mom—" the young voice was filled with awe "—why didn't you say something? I want his autograph."

"His autograph?" Suddenly things were beginning to add up. "Why would you want that?"

"Why?" Danny gasped. "He's only the greatest athlete in the whole world."

Dori decided to ignore her son's exaggeration. Gavin Parker might be a talented sportsman, but he was also rude and arrogant. He was one man she instinctively wanted to avoid.

"Here, look." Danny shoved a football card under her nose.

Indeed, the name was the same, but the features were much younger, smoother, more subdued somehow. The dark piercing eyes in the picture only hinted at the capacity for aggression. Gavin Parker's appearance had altered over the years and the changes in him were due to more than age. The photo that glared back at her was of an intense young man, filled with an enthusiasm and energy for life. The man she'd met today was angry and bitter, disillusioned. Of course the circumstances of their meeting hadn't exactly been conducive to a friendly conversation.

The back of the card listed his height, weight and position—quarterback. According to the information, Gavin had played for the Oakland Raiders, leading his team to two Super Bowl championships. In the year he'd retired, Gavin had been given the Most Valuable Player award.

"How did you know who he was?" Dori questioned in a light tone of surprise. "It says here that he quit playing football six years ago."

"Mom, Gavin Parker was one of the greatest players to ever throw a football. Everyone knows about him. Besides, he does the commentary for the Vikings' games on Sundays."

Every Sunday afternoon, Dori and Danny joined her parents for dinner. Vaguely, Dori recalled the games that had captured the attention of the two men in her life: her father and her son. Football had never interested her very much.

"Can we ask him for his autograph?" Danny asked hopefully.

"Danny," Dori said with a sigh, sticking the needle forcefully through the thick linen fabric, "I sincerely doubt that we'll ever see Mr. Parker again."

The young shoulders sagged with defeat. "Darn. Now the guys won't believe me when I tell them my mom nearly drove Gavin Parker off the road."

"I know you may find this hard to believe," Dori admitted softly, "but I'd rather not have the world know about our little mishap this morning, anyway."

"Aw, Mom."

"Haven't you got homework?"

"Aw, Mom."

Her lips curved and her resolve not to smile vanished. "The room seems to have developed an echo recently."

His head drooping, Danny returned to his bedroom.

The following morning in the early dawn light, Dori was awakened by a loud knock on her bedroom door. Struggling to lift herself up on one elbow, she brushed the wild array of springy auburn curls from her face.

"Yes?" The one word was all she could manage.

Already dressed in jeans, Danny entered the bedroom, a steaming cup of coffee in his hand.

"Morning, Mom."

"My eyes are deceiving me," she mumbled, leaning back against the pillow. "I thought I saw an angel bearing me tidings of joy and a cup of java."

"Nope," Danny said with a smile. "This is coffee."

"Bless you, my child."

"Mom?"

"Hmm?" Still fighting off the urge to bury her face in the pillow and sleep, Dori forced her eyes open.

"Do...I mean, do you always look like this when you wake up?"

Dori blinked self-consciously and again smoothed the unruly mass of curls from her face. "Why?"

Clearly uneasy, Danny shuffled his feet and stared at the top of his tennis shoes. "If someone were to see you with your hair sticking out like that, I might never get a new dad."

"I'll try to improve," she grumbled, somewhat piqued.

"Thanks." Appeased, Danny left, giving Dori the opportunity to pout in private. Muttering to herself, she threw back the sheets and climbed out of bed. A glance in the bathroom mirror confirmed what Danny had said. And her hair wasn't the only thing that needed a change.

By the time Dori arrived in the kitchen, she'd managed to transform herself from the Wicked Witch of the West to something quite presentably feminine.

One look at his mother and Danny beamed her a radiant smile of approval. "You look real pretty now."

"Thanks." She refilled her cup with coffee and tried to hide her grimace at its bitterness. Later, with the utmost tact and diplomacy, she'd show Danny exactly how much ground coffee to use. If she drank any more of this brew, she thought, she wouldn't need perms to curl her hair.

"Do you think we might see Gavin Parker on the way to school?" her son asked brightly as they pulled out of the driveway.

"I doubt it," Dori answered. "In fact, I doubt that Mr. Parker lives in Seattle. He was probably just visiting."

"Darn. Do you really think so?"

"Well, keep your eyes peeled. You never know."

For the remainder of the ride to the school, Danny was subdued, studying the traffic. Dori was grateful he didn't catch a glimpse of Gavin Parker. If he had, she wasn't sure what Danny would have expected her to do. Running him off the road again was out of the question. She felt lucky to have come away unscathed after the encounter the day before.

Danny didn't mention Gavin again that day or the next, and Dori was convinced she had heard the last about "the world's greatest athlete." But the first of the week she was surprised when a cleaning bill arrived in the mail.

The envelope was typed, and fleetingly Dori wondered if Mr. Gavin Parker had instructed his secretary to mail the bill. In addition to the receipt from a downtown dry cleaner, Gavin had returned her grocery list. Hot color blossomed in

Dori's cheeks as she turned the paper over and saw the bold handwriting. At the bottom of her list Gavin had added "Driving lessons." Dori crumpled the paper and tossed it into the garbage.

The sooner she ended her dealings with this audacious man the better. She had just finished writing the check when Danny sauntered into the room.

"What can I have for a snack?" he asked as he looked over her shoulder.

"An apple."

"Can I have some cookies, too?"

"All right, as long as you promise to eat a decent dinner." Not that there was much worry. Danny had developed a perpetual appetite of late. The refrigerator door opened behind her.

"Hey, Mom, what's this?"

Dori tossed a look over her shoulder at the yellow nylon bag Danny was holding up, pinched between forefinger and thumb. "Tulip bulbs. For heaven's sake, don't eat one."

Her son ignored her attempt at humor. "How long are they going to be in here?"

Dori flushed slightly, recalling that she'd bought them on special six weeks earlier. "I'll plant them soon," she promised.

With a loud crunch from a crisp red apple, Danny pulled up the chair across from her. "What are you doing?"

"Paying a bill." Guiltily she diverted her gaze to her checkbook, deciding to leave well enough alone and not mention to whom she was sending money. Another one of her discretion-and-valor decisions.

ON THE FOLLOWING SATURDAY MORNING, Dori came out of her bedroom and sleepily tied the sash of her housecoat. The sound of cartoons blaring from the living room assured her that Danny was already up. An empty cereal bowl on the table was further testimony. The coffee was made, and with a soft smile she poured a cup and diluted it with milk.

"You're up." Danny strolled into the kitchen and grinned approvingly when he noticed she'd combed her hair.

"Don't get hooked on those cartoons," she warned. "I want us to get some yard work done today."

"I've got a soccer game." Danny's protest was immediate.

"Not until eleven-thirty."

"Aw, Mom, I hate yard work."

"So do I," she said, although planting the tulip bulbs was a matter of pride to her. Otherwise they'd sit for another year in the vegetable bin of the refrigerator.

Twenty minutes later, dressed in washed-out jeans and a faded sweatshirt that had seen better days, Dori got the hand trowel from the garage.

The day was glorious. The sun had broken through and splashed the earth with a flood of golden light. The weather was unseasonably warm for October, and the last days of an Indian summer graced Seattle.

Danny was content to rake the leaves that had fallen from the giant maple tree onto the boulevard, and Dori was surprised to hear herself humming softly. The scarf that held her hair away from her face slipped down and she pushed it back with one hand, smearing a thin layer of mud across her cheek.

She was muttering in annoyance when Danny went into peals of excitement.

"You came, you came!" Danny cried enthusiastically.

Who came? Stripping off her gloves, Dori rose reluctantly to find Gavin Parker staring at her from across the yard.

"This damned well better be important," he said as he advanced toward her.

CHAPTER TWO

"Important?" Dori repeated, not understanding. "What?"

"This." Impatiently Gavin shoved a slip of paper under her nose.

Not bothering to read the message, Dori shrugged. "I didn't send you anything more than the check."

His young face reddening, Danny stepped forward, the bamboo rake in his hand. "You didn't, Mom, but I...I did."

Dori's response was instinctive and instant. "What?" She jerked the paper from Gavin's fingers. "I MUST TALK TO YOU AT ONCE—D. ROBERTSON" was typed in perfect capital letters.

"You see," Danny went on to explain in a rushed voice, "Mom said we would probably never see you again and I wanted your autograph. So when Mom put the envelope on the counter to go in the mail, I opened it and stuck the note inside. I really want your autograph, Mr. Parker. You were the greatest quarterback ever!"

If Gavin felt any pleasure in Danny's profession of undying loyalty, none was revealed in the uncompromising line of his mouth. From the corner of her eye, Dori caught a glimpse of a blonde fidgeting in the front seat of his car, which was parked on the boulevard. Obviously Gavin Parker had other things on his mind.

Placing a protective arm around her son's shoulders, Dori met Gavin's unflinching gaze. "I apologize for any inconvenience my son has caused you. I can assure you it won't ever happen again."

Taking his cue from the barely restrained anger vibrating in his mother's voice, Danny dropped his head and kicked at the fallen leaves with the toe of his tennis shoe. "I'm sorry, too. I just wanted your autograph to prove to the guys that Mom really did almost drive you off the road."

A car door slammed and Dori's attention was diverted to the boulevard. Surprise mingled with disbelief. It wasn't a woman with Gavin Parker, but a young girl. No more than thirteen and quite pretty, but desperately trying to hide her femininity.

"What's taking so long?" The girl sauntered up in faded blue jeans and a Seahawk football jersey. The long blond hair was pulled tightly away from her face and tied at her nape. A few curls had worked themselves free and she raised a disgruntled hand to her head, obviously displeased with the way the natural curls had sprung loose.

A smile lit her eyes as she noticed that Danny was wearing a football jersey identical to her own. "Hey, do you like the Seahawks?"

"You bet I do. We're gonna make it to the play-offs this year," Danny boasted confidently.

"I think so, too. My dad used to play pro ball and he says that the Hawks have got a good chance."

Approving dimples appeared on Danny's freckled face.

"Get back to the car, Melissa." Gavin's tone brooked no argument.

"But, Dad, it's hot in there and I'm thirsty."

"Would you like a glass of orange juice?" Danny offered enthusiastically. "Gosh, I didn't think girls liked football."

"I know everything there is to know about it and I throw a good pass, too. Just ask my dad."

Before either Gavin or Dori could object, Melissa and Danny were walking toward the house.

A delicate brow lifted in questioning. "I'll trade you one cup of coffee for an autograph," said Dori resignedly. A cup of Danny's coffee was poetic justice, and a smile hovered at the edge of her mouth.

For the first time since their dubious beginning, Gavin smiled. The change the simple movement of his mouth made in his austere expression was remarkable. Deep lines fanned out from his eyes and grooves bracketed his mouth. But the transformation didn't stop with his face. Somehow, in some way, the thick armor he wore had cracked as she was given a rare dazzling smile.

Unfortunately his good humor didn't last long, and by the time he'd followed her into the house the facade was back in place.

Melissa and Danny were at the kitchen table, sipping from tall glasses filled with orange juice.

"Dad—" Melissa looked up eagerly "—can Danny go to the Puyallup Fair with us? It's not any fun to go on the rides by myself and you hate that kind of stuff."

"I'm afraid Danny's got a soccer game this afternoon."

"I'm the center striker," Danny inserted proudly. "Would you like to come and watch me play?"

"Could we, Dad? You know how I love soccer. When the game's over we could go to the fair." Melissa immediately worked out their scheduling.

It was all happening so fast that Dori didn't know what to think.

"Mrs. Robertson?" Gavin deferred to her for a decision.

"What time would Danny be home tonight?" Dori asked, stalling for time. Gavin Parker might be a famous football player, but he was a stranger and she wasn't about to release her child to someone she didn't know. If she had to come up with an excuse, she could always use church the following morning and their weekly dinner with her parents.

"You have to come, too," Melissa insisted. "Dad would be bored to tears with Danny and me going on all the rides."

"Could we? Oh, Mom, could we?"

Needing some kind of confirmation, Dori sought Gavin's eyes.

Gavin said quietly, "It would make Melissa happy."

But not him. It didn't take much for Dori to tell that Gavin wasn't overly pleased with this turn of events. Not that she blamed him. The idea of spending an afternoon with two children and a dirt-smudged mom wouldn't thrill her, either.

Apparently seeing the indecision in her eyes, Gavin added, "It would solve several problems for me."

"Oh, Mom, could we?" repeated Danny, who seemed to have become a human pogo stick, bouncing around the kitchen.

"Who could refuse, faced with such unabashed enthusiasm?" Dori surrendered, wondering what she was letting herself in for. She gave Gavin the address of the nearby park where the game was to be played and arranged to meet him and Melissa there.

Granted a new audience, Danny was in top form for his soccer game. With boundless energy he ran up and down the field while Dori answered a multitide of questions from Melissa. No, Dori explained patiently, she wasn't divorced. Yes, her husband was dead. Yes, Danny and she lived alone. Danny was eleven and in the sixth grade.

Then Melissa explained that her parents were divorced and her dad had custody of her. She attended a boarding school in Seattle because her dad traveled so much. As the vice president in charge of sales in the whole northwest for a large computer company, her dad was real busy. In addition, he did some television commentaries for pro football games on Sunday afternoons, and she couldn't always travel with him.

Standing on the other side of his daughter, Gavin flashed her a look that silenced the girl immediately. But her father's censure apparently didn't intimidate Melissa for long, and a few minutes later she was prodding Dori with more questions.

Danny kicked two of his team's three goals and beamed proudly when Gavin complimented him on a fine game. A couple of the boys followed the small group back to the car, hoping one or the other would get up enough courage to ask Gavin for his autograph. Since even the discouraging look he gave them wasn't enough to dissuade the young boys, Gavin spent the next five minutes scribbling his name across a variety of slips of paper, hurriedly scrounged from jacket pockets.

The small party stopped at the house so that Danny could take another of his world-record-speed baths and change clothes. While they were waiting, Melissa watched Dori freshen her makeup. When Dori asked the girl if she'd like to use her cologne, Melissa looked at her as though she'd suggested dabbing car grease behind her ears.

"Not on your life. No one's going to get me to use that garbage. That's for sissies."

"Thanks, anyway," Gavin murmured on the way out to the car.

"For what?"

"I've been trying for months to turn this kid into a girl. She's got the strongest will of any female I've yet to meet."

Dori couldn't imagine Gavin losing any argument and was quick to conceal her surprise that his daughter had won this battle.

THE PUYALLUP FAIR was the largest agricultural fair in Washington state. Situated in a small farming community thirty miles southwest of Seattle, the fair attracted millions of visitors from all over western Washington and presented top Hollywood entertainment.

As a native Seattlite, Dori had been to the fair several times in the past and loved the thrill and excitement of the midway. The exhibits were some of the best in the nation. And the food was fabulous. Since Gavin had paid for their gate tickets, Dori treated everyone to hush puppies and cotton candy.

"Can we go to the rides now?" Melissa asked eagerly, her arms swinging excitedly at her side.

The crowds were thick, especially in the area of the midway, giving Dori reason for concern.

"I think I'd rather look at some of the exhibits before you two run loose," she said, looking at Gavin. His stoic expression told her he didn't care either way.

If Melissa was disappointed at having to wait, she didn't show it. Spiritedly she ran ahead, pointing out the displays she and Danny wanted to see first.

Together they viewed the rabbits, goats and pigs. Despite herself, Dori laughed at the way Melissa and Danny ran through the cow barn holding their noses. Gavin, too, seemed to be loosening up a little, and his comments regarding Melissa's and Danny's behavior were quite amusing, to Dori's surprise.

"Dad, look." Melissa grabbed her father's arm as they strolled into the chicken area and led him to an incubator where a dozen eggs were set under a warm light. A tiny beak was pecking its way through the white shell, enthralling everyone who watched.

The bee farm, its queen bee marked with a blue dot on her back, was another hit. Fascinated, Danny and Melissa watched the inner workings of a hive for several minutes. On their way out, Dori stopped to hear a ten-minute lecture from a wildlife group. Gavin and the kids weren't nearly as interested, but they all stood and listened to the plight of the American bald eagle.

From the animals' barns, they drifted to the 4-H displays and finally to the agricultural center.

Two hours later, Dori and Gavin sat drinking coffee at a picnic table on the outskirts of the midway while the two youngsters scurried for the rides.

"You don't like me much, do you?" Gavin's direct approach caught Dori by surprise.

It wasn't that she actually disliked him. In fact she had discovered she enjoyed his sharp wit. But Dori didn't try to fool herself with the belief that Gavin had actively sought her company. Having her and Danny along today simply made this time with his daughter less complicated.

"I haven't made up my mind yet." She decided to answer as straightforwardly as he'd asked.

"At least you're honest."

"I can give you a lot more honesty if you want it."

A slow smile crinkled around his eyes. "I have a feeling my ears would burn for a week."

"You're right."

A wary light was reflected in Gavin's gaze. "I've attracted a lot of gold diggers in my day. I want you to understand right now that I have no intention of remarrying."

What incredible conceit! The blood pounded angrily through Dori's veins. "I don't recall proposing marriage," she snapped.

"I didn't want you to get the wrong idea. You're a nice lady and you're doing a good job of raising your son. But he's looking for a father, so he's said, and you're looking for a husband. Just don't try to include me in your rosy little future."

Dori's hand tightened around the cup of coffee. Her eyes widened as she fought back the urge to empty the contents over his head.

The beginning of a smile worked its way across his face. "You have the most expressive eyes. No one need ever doubt when you're angry."

"You wouldn't be smiling if you knew what I was thinking."

"Temper, temper, Mrs. Robertson."

"Far be it from me to force myself on you, Mr. Parker." The derision in her voice was restrained to a bare minimum. Dori was amazed she'd managed that much control. Standing, she deposited her half-full coffee cup into a nearby bin. "Shall we synchronize our watches?"

He stared at her blankly.

"Three hours. I'll meet you back here then."

With his attitude, she'd enjoy herself far more alone. There were still a lot of exhibits to see. Remaining with Gavin was out of the question now. Undoubtedly he'd spend the entire time worrying that she was going to jab a ring through his nose.

Standing hastily, Gavin followed her, a perplexed look narrowing his eyes. "Where are you going?"

"To enjoy myself. And that's any place you're not."

Stopping in his tracks, Gavin looked stunned. "Wait a minute."

Dori jerked the strap of her purse over her shoulder. "Never." Rarely had a man evoked so much emotion in her. The worst part, Dori realized, was that given the least bit of encouragement, she could come to like Gavin Parker. He was a mystery and she always enjoyed a challenge. Melissa was an impressionable young girl, desperately in need of some feminine guidance. It was obvious the girl was more than Gavin could handle. From their conversation during Danny's soccer game, Dori had learned that Melissa spent only an occasional weekend with her father. Dori could only speculate as to the whereabouts of the girl's mother, since Melissa hadn't mentioned her. And Dori didn't want to pry openly.

"You know what your problem is, Gavin Parker?" Dori stormed, causing several people to turn and stare curiously.

Gavin cleared his throat and glanced around self-consciously. "No, but I have a feeling you're going to tell me."

Having worked herself up to a fever pitch, Dori hardly heard him. "You've got a chip on your shoulder the size of a California redwood."

"Would it help if I apologize?"

"It might."

"All right, I'm sorry I said anything. I thought it was important that you understand my position. I don't want you to go home smelling orange blossoms and humming 'The Wedding March.' "

"That's an apology?" Dori yelped.

People were edging around them as they stood, hands on their hips, facing each other, their eyes locked in a fierce duel.

"It's about the best I can do!" Gavin shouted, losing his composure for the first time.

A vendor who was selling trinkets from a nearby stand apparently didn't appreciate their bringing their argument his way. "Hey, you two, kiss and make up. You're driving away business."

Gavin tucked her arm in his and led her away from the milling crowd. "Come on," he said and inhaled a steady breath. "Let's start again." He held out his hand for her to shake. "Hello, Dori, my name is Gavin."

"I prefer Mrs. Robertson." She accepted his hand with reluctance.

"You're making this difficult."

"Now you know how I feel." She bestowed her most chilling glare on him. "I hope you realize that I have no designs on your single status."

"As long as we understand each other."

Dori was incredulous. If he weren't so insulting, she would have laughed.

"Well?" He was waiting for some kind of response.

"I'm going to look at the farm equipment. You're welcome to join me if you like; otherwise, I'll meet you back here in three hours." It simply wasn't a real fair to Dori if she didn't take the time to look at the latest in farm gear. It was a penchant that was a throwback to her heritage. Her grandfather had owned an apple orchard in the fertile Yakima Valley—often called the apple capital of the world.

Gavin brushed the side of his clean-shaven face and a fleeting smile touched the corners of his sensuous mouth. "Farm equipment?"

"Right." If she told him why, he'd probably laugh and she wasn't making herself vulnerable to any more attacks from this irritating male.

As it turned out, they worked their way from one end of the grounds to the other. Several times people stopped to stare curiously at Gavin. If he was aware of their scrutiny, he gave no indication. But no one approached him and they continued their leisurely stroll undisturbed. Dori assumed the reason was that no one would expect the great Gavin Parker to be with someone as ordinary as she. Someone over thirty, yet.

At the arcade, Dori battled to restrain her smile that hovered on the edge of laughter as Gavin tried to pitch a ball and knock over three milk bottles. With his pride on the line, the ex-football hero was determined to win the stuffed lion. An appropriate prize, Dori felt, although he could have purchased two for all he spent to win the one.

"You find this humorous, do you?" he questioned, carrying the huge stuffed beast under his arm.

"Hilarious," she admitted.

"Well, here." He handed the lion to her. "It's yours. I feel ridiculous carrying this around."

Feigning shock, Dori placed a hand over her heart. "My dear Mr. Parker, what could this mean?"

"Just take the stupid thing, will you?"

"One would assume," Dori said as she stroked the orange mane, "that an ex-quarterback could aim a little better than that."

"Ouch." He put out his hands and batted off invisible barbs. "That, Mrs. Robertson, hit below the belt."

She paused and bought some cotton candy, sharing its sticky pink sweetness with him. "Now you know what 'smelling orange blossoms and humming "The Wedding March"' felt like."

Masculine fingers curved around the back of her neck as his eyes smiled into hers. "I guess that did sound a little arrogant, didn't it?"

Smiling up at him, Dori chuckled. "Only a bit."

The sky was alight with stars and a crescent moon in full display before they headed out of the fair grounds and back to Seattle. The Audi's cushioned seats bore a wide variety of accumulated prizes, hats and leftover goodies. Both Danny and Melissa were asleep by the time they located the freeway, exhausted from eight solid hours of recreation.

Forty minutes later, Gavin parked the Audi in front of Dori's small house. Suppressing a yawn, she offered him a warm smile. "Thank you for today."

Their eyes met above the lion's thick mane. He released her gaze by lowering his attention to her softly parted lips, then quickly glancing up.

Flushed and a little self-conscious, Dori directed her attention to her purse, withdrawing her house keys.

"I had fun." Gavin's voice was low and relaxed.

"Don't act so surprised."

At the sound of their voices, Danny stirred. Sitting upright, he rubbed the sleep from his eyes. "Are we home?" Not waiting for an answer, he began gathering up his treasures: a mirrored image of his favorite pop star and the multicolored sand sculpture he'd built with Melissa.

Undisturbed, Gavin's daughter slept soundly.

"I had a great time, Mr. Parker." The sleepy edge remained in Danny's voice.

With her keys in one hand and the stuffed lion clutched in the other, Dori opened the car door and helped Danny out of the back seat. "Thanks again," she whispered, bending forward. "Tell Melissa goodbye for me."

"I will." Gavin leaned across the front seat so that his eyes could meet Danny's. "Good night, Danny."

"'Night." The boy turned and waved, but was unsuccessful in his attempt to hold back a huge yawn.

Dori noted that Gavin didn't pull away until they were safely inside the house. Automatically, Danny moved into his bedroom, not waiting for his mother. Dori set the stuffed lion on the carpet and moved to the window to watch the taillights fade as Gavin disappeared silently into the night. She doubted she'd ever see him again. Which was just as well. At least that was what she told herself.

"TIME TO GET UP, MOM." The sound of a loud knock against her bedroom door was followed by Danny's cheerful voice.

Dori groaned and propped open one eye to give her son a desultory glance. Mondays were always the worst. "It can't be morning already," she moaned, blindly reaching out to turn off the alarm before she realized it wasn't ringing.

"I brought your coffee."

"Thanks." Danny's coffee could raise the dead. "Set it on my nightstand."

Danny did as she requested, but instead of leaving as he usually did, he sat on the edge of the mattress. "You know, I've been thinking."

"Oh, no," Dori moaned. She wasn't up to more of Danny's budding insights. "Now what?"

"It's been a whole week now and we still haven't found me a new dad."

After spending the entire Sunday afternoon arguing that Gavin Parker wasn't husband material, Dori didn't feel ready for another such conversation. Someone like her wasn't going to interest Gavin. In addition, he'd made his views on marriage quite plain.

"These things take time," she murmured, raising herself up on one elbow. "Give me a minute to wake up before we do battle. Okay?"

"Okay."

Dori grimaced at her first sip of strong coffee, but the jolt of caffeine started her heart pumping again. She rubbed a hand over her weary eyes.

"Can we talk now?"

"Now?" Whatever was troubling her son appeared to be important. "All right."

"It's been a week already and other than Mr. Parker we haven't met a single prospective father."

"Danny." Dori placed a hand on his shoulder. "This is serious business. We can't rush something as important as a new father."

"But I thought we should add bait."

"Bait?"

"Yeah, like when Grandpa and I go fishing."

Another sip of coffee confirmed that she was indeed awake and not in the midst of a nightmare. "And just exactly what did you have in mind?"

"You."

"Me?" Now she knew what the worm felt like.

"You're a real neat mom, but you don't look anything like Christie Brinkley."

Falling back against the thick pillows, Dori shook her head. "I've heard enough of this conversation."

"Mom."

"I'm going to take a shower. Scoot."

"But there's more." Danny looked crestfallen.

"Not this morning, there's not."

His young face sagged with discouragement as he moved off the bed. "Will you think about exercising?"

"Exercising? Whatever for? I'm in great shape." She patted her flat stomach as proof. She could perhaps afford to lose a few pounds, but she wouldn't be ashamed to be seen in a bikini. Well, maybe a one-piece.

Huge doubting eyes raked her from head to foot. "If you're sure."

After scrutiny like that, Dori was anything but confident. But she was never at her best in the mornings. Danny knew that and had attacked when she was weakest.

As the shower spurted warm water, Dori's nylon gown slipped to the floor. She lifted her breasts and tightened her stomach as she examined herself sideways in the full-length mirror on the back of the bathroom door. At five-three she was a little shorter than average, but no pixie. Her breasts were full and she arched her back to display them to their best advantage. A bent knee completed her pose. All right, *Sports Illustrated* wasn't going to contact her for their swimsuit issue. But she didn't look that bad for an old lady of thirty. Did she?

By the time Dori arrived at the office, her mood hadn't improved. She was working at her desk and had begun to attack the latest files when Sandy walked in, holding a white sack emblazoned with McDonald's golden arches.

"Morning," her friend greeted cheerfully.

"What's good about Mondays?" Dori demanded, not meaning to sound as abrupt as she did. When she glanced up to apologize, Sandy was at her side, depositing a cup of coffee and a Danish on her desk. "What's this?"

"A reason to face the day," Sandy replied.

"Thanks, but I'll skip the Danish. Danny informed me this morning that I don't look anything like Christie Brinkley."

"Who does?" Sandy laughed and sat on the edge of Dori's desk, dangling one foot. "There are the beautiful people in this world and then there are the rest of us."

"Try to tell Danny that." Dori pushed back her chair and peeled the protective lid from the plastic cup. "I'm telling you, Sandy, I don't know when I've seen this child more serious. He wants a father and he's driving me crazy with these loony ideas of his."

The beginnings of a smile lifted the corners of Sandy's mouth. "What's the little monster want now?"

"Danny's not a monster." Dori felt obliged to defend her son.

"All kids are monsters."

Sandy's dislike of children was well-known. More than once, she had stated emphatically that the last thing she wanted was a baby. Dori couldn't understand such an attitude, but Sandy and her husband were entitled to their own feelings. Unless a child was wanted and loved, Dori couldn't see the point of bringing one into the world.

"Danny thinks I need to develop an exercise program and whip myself into shape," she said, her hands circling the coffee cup as she leaned back in her chair. A slow smile grew on her face. "I believe his exact words were that I was to be the bait."

"That kid's smarter than I give him credit for." Sandy finished off her Danish and reached for Dori's.

Dori had yet to figure out how anyone could eat so much and stay so thin. Sandy had an enormous appetite, but managed to remain svelte no matter how much she ate.

"I suppose you're going to give in?" Sandy asked, wiping the crumbs from her mouth.

"I suppose," Dori muttered. "In some ways he's right. I couldn't run a mile to save my soul. But what jogging has to do with finding him a father is beyond me."

"Are you honestly going to do it?"

"What?"

"Remarry to satisfy your kid?"

Dori's fingers toyed nervously with the rim of the coffee cup. "I don't know. But if I do marry again it won't be just for Danny. It'll be for both of us."

"Jeff's brother is going to be in town next weekend. We can make arrangements to get together, if you want."

Dori had met Greg once before. Divorced and bitter, Greg didn't make for stimulating company. As she recalled, the entire time had been spent discussing the mercenary proclivities of lawyers and the antifather prejudices of the court. But Dori was willing to listen to another episode of *Divorce Court* if it would help. Danny would see that she was at least making an effort, which should appease him for a while, anyway.

"Sure," Dori said with an abrupt nod of her head. "Let's get together."

Sandy didn't bother to hide her surprise. "Danny may be serious about this, but so are you. It's about time."

Dori regretted agreeing to the date almost from the minute the words slipped from her lips. No one was more shocked than she was that she'd fallen in with Sandy's latest scheme.

That afternoon when Dori returned home, her mood had yet to improve.

"Hi, Mom." Danny kissed her on the cheek. "I put the casserole in the oven like you asked."

In only a few more years, Danny would be reluctant to demonstrate his affection for her with a kiss. The thought produced a twinge of regret. All too soon, Danny would be gone and she'd be alone. The twinge became an ache in the area of her heart. Nothing could be worse than being alone. The word seemed to echo around her.

"Are you tired?" Danny asked, following her into her bedroom where she kicked off her shoes.

"No more than usual."

"Oh." Danny's lanky frame was at the doorway.

"But I've got enough energy to go jogging for a while before dinner."

"Really, Mom?" His blue eyes lit up like sparklers.

"As long as you're willing to go with me. I'll need a coach." She wasn't about to tackle the streets of Seattle without him. No doubt Danny could run circles around her, but so what? She wasn't competing with him.

Dori changed out of her blue linen business suit and dug out an old pair of jeans and a faded T-shirt.

Danny was running in place when she came into the kitchen. Dori groaned inwardly at her son's display of energy.

As soon as he noticed her appearance, Danny stopped. "You're not going like that, are you?"

"What's wrong now?" Dori added a sweatband around her forehead.

"Those are old clothes."

"Danny," she groaned. "I'm not going to jog in a prom dress." Apparently he had envisioned her in a skintight leotard and multicolored leg warmers.

"All right," he mumbled, but he didn't look pleased.

The first two blocks were murder. Danny set the pace, his knobby knees lifting with lightning speed as he sprinted down the sidewalk. With a lot of pride at stake, Dori managed to meet his stride. Her lungs hurt almost immediately. The muscles at the back of her calves protested such vigorous exercise, but she managed to move one foot in front of the other without too much difficulty. However, by the end of the sixth block, Dori realized she was either going to have to give it up or collapse and play dead.

"Danny," she gasped, stumbling to a halt. Her breath was coming in huge gulps that made talking impossible. Leaning forward, she rested her hands on her knees and drew in deep breaths of oxygen. "I don't...think...I... should...overdo it...the first...day."

"You're not tired are you?"

She felt close to dying. "Just...a little." Straightening, she placed a hand over her heart. "I think I might have a blister on my heel." She was silently begging God for an excuse to stop. The last time she'd breathed this deeply, she'd been in labor.

Perspiration ran in rivulets down the valley between her breasts. It took all the energy she had in the world to wipe the moisture from her face. Women weren't supposed to sweat like this. On second thought, maybe those were tears of agony wetting her cheeks. "I think we should walk back."

"Yeah, the coach always makes us cool down."

Dori made a mental note to give Danny's soccer coach a rum cake for Christmas.

Still eager to display his remarkable agility, Danny continued to jog backward in front of Dori. For good measure she decided to add a slight limp to her gait.

"I'm positive I've got a blister," she mumbled, shaking her head for emphasis. "These tennis shoes are my new ones. I haven't broken 'em in yet." In all honesty she couldn't tell whether she had a blister or not. Her feet didn't ache any more than her legs did, or her lungs.

The closer they came to the house, the more real her limp became.

"Are you sure you're all right, Mom?" Danny had the grace to show a little concern.

"I'm fine." She offered him a feeble smile. The sweatband slipped loose and fell across one eye, but Dori hadn't the energy to secure it.

"Let me help you, Mom." Danny came to her side and placed an arm around her waist. He stared at her flushed and burning face, his brows knit. "You don't look so good."

Dori didn't know what she looked like, but she felt on the verge of throwing up. She'd been a complete idiot to try to maintain Danny's pace. Those six blocks might as well have been six miles.

They were within a half block of the house when Danny hesitated. "Hey, Mom, look. It's Mr. Parker."

Before Dori was able to stop him, Danny shouted and waved.

Standing in the middle of the sidewalk, hands on his hips, stood Gavin Parker. He didn't bother to disguise his amusement.

CHAPTER THREE

"ARE YOU ALL RIGHT?" Gavin inquired with mock solicitude, battling back a snicker.

"Get that smirk off your face," Dori threatened. She was in no mood to exchange witticisms with him. Not when every muscle in her body was screaming for mercy.

"It's my fault," Danny confessed, concerned now. "I thought she'd attract more men if they could see how athletic she is."

"The only thing I'm attracting is flies." She ripped the sweatband from her hair; the disobedient curls sprang out from her head. "What can I do for you, Mr. Parker?"

"My, my, she gets a bit testy now and then, doesn't she?" Gavin directed his question to Danny.

"Only sometimes." At least Danny made a halfhearted attempt to be loyal.

There was no need for Gavin to look so pleased with himself. His smug grin resembled that of a cat with a defenseless mouse trapped under its paws.

"Aren't you going to invite me in?" he asked dryly.

Clenching her jaw, Dori gave him a chilly stare. "Don't press your luck, Parker," she whispered for his ears only. Hobbling to the front door, she struggled to retrieve her house key from the tight pocket of her jeans.

"Need help?" Gavin offered.

The glare she flashed him assured him she didn't.

With a mocking smile Gavin raised his arms. "I was just asking."

The front door clicked open and Danny forged ahead, running to the kitchen and opening the refrigerator. He stood at the entrance, waiting for Dori to limp in—closely followed by Gavin—and handed her a cold can of root beer.

With a hand massaging her lower back, Dori led the way to the kitchen table.

"Do you want one, Mr. Parker?" Danny held up another can of soda.

"No, thanks," Gavin said, pulling out a chair for Dori. "You might want to soak out some of those aches and pains in a long hot bath."

It was on the tip of her tongue to remind him that good manners forbade her to seek comfort in a hot bath while he still sat at her kitchen table. She couldn't very well abandon him.

Danny snapped open the aluminum can and guzzled down a long swig. Dori restrained herself to a ladylike sip, although her throat felt parched and scratchy.

"I found Danny's jacket in the back seat of the car the other day and thought he might need it." Gavin explained the reason for his impromptu visit. He handed Danny the keys. "Would you bring it in for me?"

"Sure." Danny was off like a rocket blast, eager to obey.

The front screen slammed and Gavin turned his attention to Dori. "What's this business about jogging to make you more attractive to men?"

Some of the numbness was beginning to leave Dori's limbs and her heartbeat had finally returned to normal. "Just that bee Danny's got in his bonnet lately about me remarrying. Rest assured you're out of the running."

"I'm glad to hear it. I'm rotten husband material."

A laughing sigh escaped as Dori's eyes met his. "I'd already determined that."

"I hung the jacket in my room," Danny explained to his mother, obviously wanting to please her. "It was real nice of you to bring it back, Mr. Parker."

For the first time, Dori wondered if the jacket had been left intentionally so Gavin would have an excuse to return. She wouldn't put it past her son.

Gavin held out his palm to collect the key chain.

"How come Melissa isn't here?" Danny wanted to know. "She's all right for a girl. She wasn't afraid to go on any of the rides. She even went on the Hammer with me. Mom never would." A thoughtful look came over Danny as if he were weighing the pros and cons of being friends with a girl. "She did scream a lot, though."

"She's at school." Gavin stood up to leave, the scrape of his chair loud in the quiet kitchen. "She thought you were all right, too...for a boy." He exchanged teasing smiles with Danny.

"Can we do something together again?" Danny asked as he followed Gavin into the living room. Dori hobbled at a safe distance behind them, pressing her hand to the ache at the small of her back. Who would have believed a little run could be this incapacitating?

"Perhaps." Gavin paused in front of the television and lifted an ornate wooden frame that held a family portrait taken a year before Brad's death. It was the only picture of Brad that Dori kept out. After a silent study, he replaced the portrait and stooped to pat the stuffed lion, now guarding the front window. "I'll get Melissa to give you a call the next weekend she's not at school."

"Not at school?" Danny repeated incredulously. "You mean she has to go to school on Saturdays, too?"

"No," Gavin explained. "She attends boarding school and spends the weekends with me if I'm not broadcasting a game. Things get hectic this time of year, though. I'll have her give you a call."

"Danny would like that," Dori said and smiled sweetly, assured that Gavin had understood her subtle message. Having Melissa call Danny was fine, but Dori didn't want anything to do with Gavin.

As Gavin had suggested, a leisurely soak in hot water went a long way toward relieving her aching muscles. Her parting shot to him had been childish, and Dori regretted it. She drew in a deep breath and eased down farther in the steaming water. Her toe toyed with the faucet. It felt sinful to be so lazy, so relaxed.

"The table's set and the timer for the oven rang," Danny called.

With her hair pinned up and her lithe—but abused—body draped in a thick housecoat, Dori ambled into the kitchen. Danny was standing in front of the refrigerator rereading the list of prerequisites for a new father.

"Dinner smells good. I'll bet you're hungry after all that exercise."

Danny ignored her obvious attempt to divert his attention. That kid was getting wise to her ways.

"Did you realize Mr. Parker knows karate? I asked him about it."

"That's nice," Dori hoped to play down the information. "I'll take out the casserole and we should be ready to eat."

"He's tall and athletic and Melissa said he's thirty-six—"

"Danny," she snapped impatiently, "no! We went over this yesterday. I have veto power, remember?"

"Mr. Parker would make a great dad," he argued.

Her glass made a sharp clang as it hit the table. "But not yours."

To his credit Danny didn't bring up Gavin Parker's name again. Apparently the message had sunk in, although Dori realized her son genuinely liked Gavin and Melissa. As for herself, she still hadn't made up her mind about Gavin. Melissa was a sweet child but her father presented another picture. No one exasperated Dori more than he did. Gavin Parker was arrogant, conceited and altogether maddening.

Another week passed and Danny marked off the days on the calendar, reminding Dori daily of his need for a new father. Even the promise of a puppy wasn't enough to dissuade him. Twice he interrupted her while they did the weekly shopping to point out men in the grocery store. He actually wanted her to introduce herself.

The date with Sandy's brother-in-law, Greg, did more harm than good. Not only was she forced to listen to an updated version of *Divorce Court*, but Danny drilled her with questions the following morning until she threatened to drop the new father issue entirely.

The next few days, her son was unusually subdued. But Dori knew the boy well enough to realize that although she had won this first battle, he was out to win the war. The situation was weighing on her so heavily that she had a nightmare about waking up and discovering a stranger in her bed who claimed Danny had sent him.

Monday evening, when Danny was supposed to be doing homework, she found him shaking money from his piggy bank onto the top of his mattress. She'd purposely given him a bank that wouldn't open so that he'd learn to save his money. He dodged her questions about the need to rob from it, telling her he was planning a surprise.

"That kid's got something up his sleeve," Dori told Sandy the following day.

"Didn't you ask?"

"He said he was buying me a present." This morning Dori had brought in the coffee and Danishes and she set a paper sack on Sandy's desk.

"Knowing Danny, I'd say it's probably a jar of wrinkle cream."

"Probably," she murmured and took a bite of the Danish.

"I thought you were on a diet."

"Are you kidding? With all the calisthenics and jogging Danny's got me doing, I'm practically wasting away."

Sandy crossed one shapely leg over the other. "And people wonder why I don't want kids."

The phone was ringing when Dori let herself into the house that evening. She tossed her purse onto the kitchen table and hurried to answer it, thinking that the caller was probably her mother.

"Hello."

"I'm calling about your ad in the paper."

Dori brushed an errant curl from her forehead. "I'm sorry, but you've got a wrong number." The man on the other end of the line wanted to argue, but Dori replaced the receiver, cutting him off. He sounded quite unpleasant, and as far as she was concerned, there was nothing more to discuss.

Danny was at soccer practice at the local park, six blocks from the house. The days were growing shorter, the sun setting at just about the time practice was over. On impulse, Dori decided to bicycle to the field and ride home with him. Of course, she wouldn't let him know the reason she'd come. He'd hate it if he thought his mother had come to escort him home.

When they entered the house twenty minutes later, the phone was ringing again.

"I'll get it," Danny shouted, racing across the kitchen floor.

Dori didn't pay much attention when he stretched the cord around the corner and walked into the hall closet, seeking privacy. He did that sometimes when he didn't want her to listen in on the conversation. The last time that had happened, it was because a girl from school had phoned.

Feeling lazy and not in a mood to fuss with dinner, Dori opened a package of fish sticks and dumped them on a cookie sheet, tossing them under the broiler with some French fries. She was chopping a head of cabbage for cole slaw when Danny reappeared. He gave her a sheepish look as he hung up the phone.

"Was that Erica again?"

Danny ignored her question. "Are you going to keep on wearing those old clothes?"

Dori glanced down over her washed-out denims and Irish cable-knit sweater. "What's wrong with this?" Actually, this was one of her better pairs of jeans.

"I just thought that you'd like to wear a dress for dinner or something."

"Danny—" she released an exasperated sigh "—we're having fish sticks, not filet mignon."

"Oh." He stuck his hands in his pockets and yanked them out again as the phone rang. "I'll get it."

Before Dori knew what was happening, he was back in the closet, the phone cord stretched to its farthest extreme. Within minutes, he was out again.

"What's going on?"

"Nothin'."

The phone rang and the doorbell chimed simultaneously. "I'll get it," Danny hollered, jerking his head from one direction to the other.

Drying her hands on a dish towel, Dori gestured toward the living room. "I'll get the door."

Gavin Parker stood on the other side of screen, the morning paper tucked under his arm.

"Gavin." Dori was too surprised to utter more than his name.

Laugh lines fanned out from his eyes as if he found something highly amusing. He had that cat-with-the-trapped-mouse look again. "Phone been ringing a lot lately?"

"Yes. How'd you know? It's been driving me crazy." Unlatching the screen door, she opened it, silently inviting him inside. What a strange man Gavin was. She hadn't expected to see him again and here he was on her doorstep, looking inexplicably amused about something.

Gavin sauntered in and sat on the deep, cushioned sofa. "I don't suppose you've read the morning paper?"

Dori had, at least the sections she always did. Dear Abby, the comics, Mike Mailway and the front page, in that order. "Yes. Why?"

Making a show of it, Gavin pulled out the classified section and folded it open, laying it across the coffee table. Idly, he moved his index finger down the narrow column of the personal ads until he located what he wanted.

A sick feeling attacked the pit of Dori's stomach, weakening her knees so that she had to lower herself into the maple rocking chair across from him.

"Are you in any way related to the person who ran this ad? 'Need dad. Tall, athletic, knows karate. Mom pretty. 555-5818.'"

It was worse, far worse, than anything Dori could ever have dreamed. Mortified and angry, she supported her elbows on the arms of the rocker and buried her face in the palms of her hands. A low husky sound slipped from her throat as hot flashes of color invaded her neck, her cheeks, her ears, not stopping until her eyes brimmed with tears of embarrassment.

"Daniel Bradley Robertson, get in here this minute." Rarely did she use that tone with her son. Whenever she did, Danny came running.

The closet door opened a crack and Danny's head appeared. "Just a minute, Mom, I'm on the phone." He paused, noticing Gavin for the first time. "Oh, hi, Mr. Parker."

"Hello, Daniel Bradley Robertson." Gavin stood up and took the receiver out of the boy's hand. "I think your mother would like to talk to you. I'll take care of whoever's on the phone."

"Yeah, Mom?" A picture of innocence, Danny met Dori's fierce gaze without wavering. "Is something wrong?"

Her scheming son became a watery blur as Dori shook her head, not knowing how to explain the embarrassment he'd caused her.

"Mom?" Danny knelt in front of her. "What's wrong? Why are you crying?"

Her answer was a sniffle and a finger pointed in the direction of the bathroom. Danny seemed to understand her watery charades and leaped to his feet, returning a moment later with a box of tissues.

"Do you people always use the hall closet to talk on the phone?"

Gavin was back and Danny gave his visitor a searching look. "What's the matter with Mom? All she does is cry."

The phone pealed again and Dori sucked in a hysterical sob that sounded more like a strangled cry of pain.

"I'll take care of it," Gavin assured her, quickly taking control. "Danny, come with me into the kitchen. Your mother needs a few minutes alone."

For a moment it looked as though Danny didn't know what to do. Indecision played across his freckled face. His mother was crying and there was a man with an authoritative voice barking orders at him. With a weak gesture of her hand, Dori dismissed her son.

In the next hour the phone rang another twenty times. With every ring, Dori flinched. Gavin and Danny remained in the kitchen and dealt with each call. Dori didn't move. The gentle sway of the rocker was her only solace. Danny ventured into the living room only once, to announce that dinner was ready if she wanted to eat. Profusely shaking her head, she assured him she didn't.

After a while the panic abated somewhat and she decided not to sell the house, pack up her belongings and seek refuge at the other end of the world. A less drastic approach gradually came to mind. The first thing she had to do was get that horrible ad out of the personals. Then she'd have her phone number changed.

More in control of herself now, Dori blew her nose and washed her tear-streaked face in the bathroom off the hall. When she moved into the kitchen, she was shocked to discover Gavin and Danny busy with the dinner dishes. Gavin stood at the sink, the sleeves of his expensive business shirt rolled up past his elbows. Danny was standing beside him, a dish towel in his hand.

"Hi, Mom." His chagrined eyes didn't quite meet hers. "Mr. Parker explained that what I did wasn't really a very good idea."

"No, it wasn't." The scratchy high sound that slid from her throat barely resembled her voice.

"Would you like some dinner now? Mr. Parker and I saved you some."

She shook her head, then asked, "What's been happening in here?"

In response the phone rang, its jangle almost deafening—or so it seemed to Dori, who tucked in her chin and cringed.

Not hesitating at all, Gavin dried his hands and walked across the kitchen toward the wall phone.

"Listen to him," Danny whispered with a giggle. "Mr. Parker figured out a way to answer the phone without having to argue. He's a real smart man."

Catching Dori's eye, Gavin winked reassuringly and picked up the receiver. After a momentary pause, he mocked the phone company recording. "The number you have reached has been disconnected," he droned.

For the first time that evening, the tight line of Dori's mouth cracked with the hint of a smile. Once again, she was forced to admire the cleverness of Gavin Parker.

Grinning smugly, he hung up the phone and sat in the chair next to Dori's. "Are you feeling okay now?"

She managed a nod, her jaw clenched. The confusion and anger she'd experienced earlier had only been made worse by Gavin's gloating. But now she felt grateful that he'd stepped in and taken charge of a very awkward situation. Dori wasn't sure what would have happened otherwise.

A finger under her chin tilted her face upward. "I don't believe you're fine at all. You're as pale as a sheet." A rush of unexpected pleasure shot through her at the impersonal contact of his finger against her soft skin.

His index finger ventured over the smooth line of her jaw in an exploratory caress. The action was meant to soothe and reassure, but his touch was oddly sensual and highly arousing. Bewildered, Dori raised her gaze to his. Their eyes met and held as his hand slipped to her neck, his fingers tangling with the auburn softness of her shoulder-length hair. Dori could see the gentle rise and fall of his chest and noted that the movement increased slightly, as if he too had been caught unawares by these emotions. His eyes narrowed as he withdrew his hand. "You need a drink. Where...?"

With a limp arm, Dori gestured toward the cupboard that held her small stock of liquor. As he poured a shot of brandy into a glass, Gavin demanded quietly, "Danny, haven't you got some homework that needs to be done?"

"No." Danny shook his head then hurriedly placed his fingers over his mouth. "Oh ... I get it. You want to talk to my mom alone."

"Right." Gavin exchanged a conspiratorial wink with the boy.

As Danny left the room, Gavin deposited the brandy in front of Dori and sat beside her again. "No arguments. Drink."

"You like giving orders, don't you?" Whatever had passed between them was gone as quickly as it had come.

Gavin ignored the censure in her voice. "I have an idea that could benefit both of us."

Dori took a swallow of the brandy, which burned a passage down her throat and brought fresh tears to her eyes. "What?" was all she could manage.

"It's obvious Danny is serious about this new father business and to be truthful, Melissa would like me to remarry so she won't have to board at the school anymore. She hates all the restrictions."

Dori sympathized with the young girl. Melissa was at an age when she should be testing her wings and that included experimenting with makeup and wearing the latest fashions. Nuns probably wouldn't encourage that type of behavior. Being cooped up in a convent school was obviously squelching Melissa's enthusiasm for adventure.

"You're not humming 'The Wedding March,' are you?" Dori asked.

Gavin gave her a look that threatened bodily harm, and she couldn't contain a soft laugh. She loved turning the tables on this impudent male.

"I've already explained that I have no intention of remarrying. Once was enough to cure me for a lifetime. But I am willing to compromise if it will help let up on the pressure from Melissa."

"How do Danny and I fit into this rosy picture?"

Eager now, Gavin shifted to the edge of his seat and leaned forward. "If the two of us were to start going out together on a steady basis, then Melissa and Danny would assume we're involved with each other."

Dori drew in a slow trembling breath. As much as she hated to admit it, the idea showed promise. Melissa needed a woman's influence, and all Danny really cared about was having a man who would participate in the things she couldn't. Dori realized her son was already worried about the father-son soccer game scheduled for the end of the season. For years his grandfather had volunteered for such events, but her dad was close to retirement and playing soccer these days would put a strain on him.

"We could start this weekend. We'll go to dinner Friday night and then on Sunday I'll take Danny to the Seahawks game if you'll take Melissa shopping." His mouth slanted sideways in a coaxing smile.

Dori recognized the crooked grin as the one he probably used on gullible young women whenever he wanted to get his own way. Nibbling her lower lip, Dori refused to play that game. She wasn't stupid; he was willing to tie up Fridays and Sundays, but he wanted his Saturday nights free. Why not? She didn't care what he did.

"Well?" Gavin didn't look nearly as confident as he had earlier, and that pleased Dori. There wasn't any need for him to think she'd fall in with his plans so easily.

"I think you may have stumbled on to something."

His slanted smile returned. "Which, translated, means you doubt that I have more than an occasional original thought."

"Perhaps." He had been kind and helpful tonight. The least she could do, then, was to be just a little more accommodating. "All right, I agree."

"Great." A boyish grin not unlike Danny's lit up his face. "I'll see you Friday night about seven, then."

"Fine." Standing, she joined her hands behind her back. "And, Gavin, thank you for stepping in and helping tonight. I do appreciate it. I'll phone the paper first thing in the morning to make sure the ad doesn't appear again and contact the telephone company to have my number changed."

"You know how to handle any more calls that come in tonight?"

Dori plugged her nose and in a high-pitched voice imitated the telephone company recording.

The laugh lines around his eyes became prominent as he grinned. "We can have a good time, Dori. Just don't fall in love with me."

So he was back on that theme. "Believe me, there's no chance of that," she snapped. "If you want the truth, I think you may be the—"

She wasn't allowed to finish as he suddenly hauled her into his arms and kissed her soundly, stealing her breath and tipping her off balance. With her hands pushing forcefully against his chest, Dori was able to break off the unexpected attack.

"Shh," Gavin whispered in her ear. "Danny's right outside the door."

"So?" She still wasn't free from his embrace.

"I didn't want him to hear you. If we're going to convince either of those kids, we've got to make this look real."

A pale pink spot appeared on each cheek. "Give me some warning next time."

Gently Gavin eased her away, studying the heightened color of her face. "I didn't hurt you, did I?"

"No," she assured him, thinking the worst thing about being a redhead was her pale coloring. The slightest sign of embarrassment was more pronounced because she was naturally pallid.

"Well, how'd I do?"

"On what?"

"The kiss." He shook his head as though he expected her to know what he was talking about. "How would you rate the kiss?"

This, Dori was going to enjoy. "On a scale of one to ten?" She allowed a lengthy pause to follow as she folded her arms and quirked her head thoughtfully at the ceiling. The time had come for someone to put this overconfident male in his place. "If I take into consideration that you are an ex-quarterback, I'd say a low five."

The corners of his mouth twitched briefly upward. "I was expecting you to be a little less cruel."

"And from everything you say, I don't expect your technique to improve with time."

"It might," he chuckled, "but I doubt it."

Danny wandered into the kitchen, whistling. "I'm not interrupting anything, am I?"

"You don't mind if I take your mom out to dinner Friday night, do you, sport?"

"Really, Mom?" Dori would willingly have given her son double his allowance not to have been quite so eager.

"I suppose," Dori said dryly. Gavin ignored her lack of enthusiasm.

"But I thought you said Mr. Parker was a—"

"Never mind that now," she whispered pointedly, as another flood of color cascaded into her cheeks.

"I'll see you at seven on Friday." Gavin rolled down the sleeves of his shirt and rebuttoned them at the wrist.

"It's a date."

Rarely had Dori seen Danny more pleased about anything. He quizzed her Friday from the very moment she walked in the door after work. As she drove him to her parents' place—they were more than happy to have their grandson for the night—he wanted to know what dress she was going to wear, what kind of perfume, which earrings, which shoes. He gave her advice and bombarded her with football statistics.

"Danny," she breathed irritably, "I don't think Gavin Parker expects me to know that much about football."

"But, Mom, it'll impress him," his singsong voice pleaded.

"But, Danny." Her twangy voice echoed his.

Back at her own house, an exhausted Dori soaked in the tub, then hurriedly dried herself, applied some makeup—why was she doing it with such care, she wondered—and dressed. She wasn't surprised when Gavin was fifteen minutes late, nor did she take offense. The extra time was well spent adding the last coat of pale pink polish to her long nails.

Gavin looked rushed and slightly out of breath as he climbed the porch steps. Dori saw him coming and opened the front door, careful not to smear the wet polish. "Hi." She didn't mention the fact that he was late.

Gavin's smile was wry. "Where's Danny?"

"My mom and dad's."

"Oh." He paused and raked his fingers through his hair, mussing the carefully styled effect. "Listen, tonight isn't going exactly the way I'd planned. I promised a friend a favor. It shouldn't interfere with our date if you don't let it."

"I'm not going to worry about it," Dori murmured and cautiously slipped her arms into the coat Gavin held for her. She hadn't the faintest idea what he had in mind, but knowing Gavin Parker, it wasn't moonlight and roses.

"Do you mean that?" Already he had his car keys out and was fiddling with them, his gaze lowered. "I ran into some minor complications at the office so I'm a bit late."

"I'm not concerned. It isn't like we're madly in love with each other." Dori was grateful Danny wasn't there to witness her "hot date." With Gavin she used the term "hot" very loosely.

While she locked the front door, Gavin sprinted down the porch steps and started the car engine. Dori released an exasperated sigh as he leaned across the front seat and opened the car door for her. With a forced smile on her lips, she slid inside. So much for gallantry and romance.

It wouldn't have shocked her if there were another woman waiting for him somewhere. What did surprise her was that he pulled into a local fast-food drive-in, helped her out of the car and seated her, then ordered hamburgers and milk shakes. She didn't know what he had up his sleeve or if he expected a reaction, but she didn't as much as blink.

"I did promise you dinner."

"That you did," she returned sweetly.

"Whatever else happens tonight, just remember I did feed you."

"And I'm grateful." She had difficulty keeping the sarcasm out of her voice. Good grief, where could he be taking her?

"The thing is, when I asked you to dinner I forgot about a ... previous commitment."

"Gavin, don't worry about it. For that matter you can take me back to my house; it's not that big a deal. In fact, if there's another woman involved it would save us both a lot of embarrassment." Not him, but the two women.

Gavin polished off the last of his hamburger and crumpled up the paper. "There isn't another woman." He looked shocked that she'd even suggest such a thing. "If you don't mind coming, I don't mind bringing you. As it is, I had one hell of a time getting an extra ticket."

"I'm game for just about anything." Fleetingly Dori wondered what she was getting herself in for, but learning that it involved a ticket was encouraging.

"Except that sometimes these things can go on quite late."

Now her curiosity was piqued. "Not to worry. Danny's staying the night with my parents."

"Great." He flashed her a brilliant smile. "As Danny would say, for a girl, you're all right."

He made it sound exactly like her son. "I'm glad you think so."

After dumping their leftovers in the garbage, Gavin escorted her to the car and pulled out of the parking space. He took the freeway toward Tacoma. Dori wasn't sure what he had in mind, but she wasn't turning back now.

Several other cars were parked outside a dimly lit part of the downtown area of Tacoma. Gavin stepped out of the car and glanced at his wristwatch. He hurried around the front of the car to help her out of the passenger side. His hand grasped her elbow as he led her toward a square gray building. The streetlight was too dim for Dori to read the sign over the door, not that Gavin would have given her time. They were obviously late.

They entered a large hall and were greeted by shouts and cheers. The room was so thick with smoke that Dori had to strain to see. The automatic smile died on her lips as she turned furiously to Gavin.

"I promised a friend I'd take a look at his latest prodigy," he explained, studying her reaction.

"You mean to tell me that you brought me to the Friday-night fights?"

CHAPTER FOUR

"Is that such a problem?" Gavin asked defensively, his gaze challenging hers.

Dori couldn't believe this was her "hot date" with the handsome and popular Gavin Parker. She'd never been to a boxing match in her life, nor had she ever wanted to. But then, sports in general had never interested her very much. Despite that, her "No, I guess not," was spoken with a certain amount of honesty. Danny would be thrilled. Little else would convince the eleven-year-old that Gavin was serious about her.

Following Gavin into the auditorium and down the wide aisle, Dori was surprised when he ushered her into a seat only a few rows from the ring. Whatever was about to happen she would see in graphic detail.

Apparently Gavin was a familiar patron at these matches. He introduced Dori to several men whose names floated past her so quickly that she could never hope to remember them. Glancing around, Dori noted that there were only a few other women present. In her gray-and-black crepe dress with its Peter Pan collar and the thin silk tie, she was decidedly overdressed. Cringing, Dori huddled down in her seat while Gavin carried on a friendly conversation with the man sitting in the row in front of them.

"You want some peanuts?" He bent his head close to hers as he asked.

"No thanks." Her hands lay in her lap, clutching her purse and an unread program she'd received at the door.

People didn't eat while they watched this kind of physical exhibition, did they?

Gavin shrugged and stood up, reaching for some loose change in his pocket. He paused and turned back to her. "You're not mad, are you?"

Dori was convinced that was exactly what he expected her to be. Perhaps it was even what he wanted. Her anger would be just the proof he needed that all women were alike. Based on everything that had happened between them, Dori realized Gavin didn't particularly want to like her. Any real relationship would be dangerous to him, she suspected—even one founded on friendship and mutual respect.

"No." She gave him a forced but cheerful smile. "This should be very interesting." Already her mind was fashioning a subtle revenge. Next time they went out, she'd have Gavin take her to an opera—one performed in Italian.

"I'll be back in a minute." He left his seat and clambered over the two men closest to the aisle.

Feeling self-conscious and completely out of her element, Dori sat with her shoulders stiff and squared against the back of the folding wooden seat. She was mentally bracing herself for the ordeal.

"So you're Dori." The man who'd been talking to Gavin turned to her.

They'd been introduced, but she couldn't recall his name. "Yes." Her smile was shy as she searched her memory.

"This is the first time Gavin's ever brought a woman to the fights."

Dori guessed that was a compliment. "I'm honored."

"He was seeing that blond beauty for a while. A lot of the guys were worried he was going to marry her."

A blonde! Dori's curiosity was piqued. "Is that so?" Gavin hadn't mentioned any blonde to her. If he was going to continue to see someone else regularly it would ruin their agreement. Gavin took her to the Friday-night fights, while he probably wined and dined some dizzy blonde on the sly. Terrific.

"Yeah," the nameless man continued. "He was seeing her real regular. For a while he wasn't even coming to the fights."

Obviously Gavin and this blonde had a serious relationship going. "She must have been really something for Gavin to miss the fights." Smiling encouragingly, Dori hoped the man would tell her more.

"He doesn't come every week, you understand."

Dori nodded, pretending she did.

"Fact is, during football season we're lucky to see him once a month."

Dori was beginning to wonder just how "lucky" she was. The man grinned and glanced toward the aisle. Dori's gaze followed his and she saw Gavin returning down the crowded center aisle, carrying a large bag of peanuts.

As soon as he sat down, Dori absently helped herself to a handful.

"I thought you said you didn't want any," Gavin said, giving her the sack.

"I don't," she mumbled, cracking one open with her teeth. "I don't even like peanuts."

"Then why did you grab them out of my hand the minute I sat down?"

"I did?" When she was agitated or upset, often the first thing Dori did was reach for something to eat. "Sorry," she said, returning the paper sack. "I didn't realize what I was doing."

"Is something bothering you?" Gavin's disturbed gaze was studying her. His eyes darkened as if he were expecting an argument.

Dori hated being so readable. She'd thought that sometime during the evening she'd casually bring up his liaison with this . . . this other woman who was jeopardizing their tentative agreement.

"Nothing's bothering me," she answered. "Not really."

His glittering eyes mocked her.

"It's just that your friend—" she gestured with her hand toward the row in front of them "—was explaining that you were seeing a blonde and..."

"And you jumped to conclusions?"

"Yes, well... it isn't exactly in our agreement." What bothered Dori most was that it mattered to her if Gavin was seeing another woman. She had no right to feel anything for him... except as far as their agreement was concerned. But her pride was on the line. If Danny heard about this other woman, she might slip in her own son's estimation.

"Well, you needn't worry. I'm not seeing her anymore."

"What's the matter," Dori taunted in a low whisper, "was she unfortunate enough to smell orange blossoms?"

"No." He pursed his lips and reached for a peanut, cracking it open with a vengeance. "Every time she opened her mouth, her brain leaked."

Dori successfully hid a smile. "I'd have thought that type was the best kind."

"I'm beginning to have the same feeling myself," he said dryly, his gaze inscrutable.

Feeling a growing sense of triumph, Dori relaxed and didn't say another word.

Soon cheers and loud hoots rose from the auditorium as the young boxers paraded into the room with an entourage of managers and assistants.

The announcer waited until the two men had parted the thick ropes and positioned themselves in their appropriate corners. Glancing at her program, Dori read that these first two were in the lightweight division.

Pulling down a microphone that seemed to come from nowhere, the announcer shouted in a clear, distinct voice. "Ladies and gentlemen, welcome to the Tacoma Friday-night fights. Wearing white trunks and weighing 130 awesome pounds is Boom Boom Bronson."

The sound echoed forcefully around the room. Immediate cheers and whistles followed. Boom Boom hopped into the middle of the ring and punched at a few shadows, to the delight of the audience, before he returned to his corner. Even when he was in a stationary position, his hands braced against the ropes, Boom Boom's feet refused to stop moving.

Then the other boxer, Tucker Wallace, was introduced. Tucker hopped in and out of the middle ring, punching all the way. The crowd went crazy. The man beside Dori stormed to his feet, placed two fingers in his mouth and pierced the air with a shrill whistle. Dori reached for another handful of peanuts.

The two fighters met briefly with the announcer and spoke with the referee before returning to their respective corners. The entourages formed again around each fighter. Probably to decide a strategy, Dori mused.

The bell clanged and the two men came out swinging. Dori blinked twice, stunned at the fierce aggression between the men. They may have been listed in the lightweight division, but the corded muscles of their abdomens and backs assured her that their stature had little to do with their strength or determination.

Gavin had shifted to the edge of his seat by the end of round one. The bell brought a humming silence to the room.

Dori knew next to nothing about boxing. She hated fighting, but the fierce competition between Boom Boom and Tucker seemed exaggerated and somehow theatrical. Despite her dislike of violence, Dori found herself cheering for Boom Boom. When he was slammed to the ground by Tucker's powerful right hand, Dori jumped to her feet to see if he was all right and could continue fighting.

"Oh, goodness," she wailed, covering her forehead with one hand as she sank back into her seat. "He's bleeding."

Gavin was looking at her, his compelling dark eyes studying her flushed, excited face as if he couldn't quite believe what he saw.

"Is something wrong?" Boldly her gaze met his and a shiver of unexpected sensual awareness danced over her skin. "I'm cheering too loud?" She'd become so engrossed in what was happening between the two boxers that she'd embarrassed him with her vocal enthusiasm.

"No," he countered quickly, shaking his head. "I guess I'm surprised you like it."

"Well, to be honest," she admitted. "I didn't think I would. But these guys are good."

"Yes." He gave her a dazzling smile. "They are."

The adrenaline pumped through Dori's limbs as Boom Boom fought on to win the match in a unanimous decision. At the end of three bouts the evening was over and Gavin helped her on with her thick woolen coat. The night had turned rainy and cold, and Dori shivered as they walked to the car.

The moment they were settled, Gavin turned on the heater. "You'll be warm in a minute."

Dori stuck her bare hands deep in her pockets. "If it gets much colder, it'll probably snow."

"It won't," Gavin stated confidently. "It was warm in the auditorium, that's all." He paused to snap his seat belt into place. Dori averted her face to check the heavy flow of traffic. They wouldn't be able to get out of their parking spot for several minutes, but there wasn't any need to rush. As much as she hated to admit it, she'd enjoyed the evening. Being taken to the fights was the last thing she'd expected, but Dori was quickly learning that Gavin was a man of surprises.

"Here," Gavin said, half leaning across her. "Buckle up." Before Dori could free her hand to reach for the seat belt, Gavin had pulled it across her waist. He hesitated, his eyes meeting hers. Their mouths were close, so close; only a hair's breadth separated them. Dori swallowed convulsively. Her traitorous heart skipped a beat, then hammered wildly. She stared at him, hardly able to believe what she saw in his warm eyes or the feelings that stirred in her own breast. A strange, inexplicable sensation came over her. At that moment, she felt as though she and Gavin were good friends, two people who shared a special bond of companionship. She liked him, respected him, enjoyed his company.

She knew when he dipped his head that he was going to kiss her, but instead of drawing away, she met him halfway, shocked at how much she wanted him to do exactly this. His mouth fit easily, expertly, over hers in a tender, undemanding caress. A hand smoothed the hair from her temple as he lifted his mouth from hers and brushed his lips over her troubled brow.

"Warmer?" he asked in a husky murmur.

Her body was suffused by an unexpected rush of inner heat, her blood vigorously pounding through her veins. Unable to find her voice, she nodded.

"Good." He clicked her seat belt into place, and with utter nonchalance, checked the rearview mirror before pulling onto the street.

Silently Dori thanked God for the cover of night. Her face burned at her own imprudence. Gavin had kissed her and she'd let him. Worse, she'd enjoyed it. So much that she'd been sorry when he'd stopped.

"I give you a six, maybe a low seven," she challenged evenly, struggling to disguise his effect on her.

"What?"

"The kiss," she returned coolly, but there was a brittle edge to her airy reply. Her greatest fear was that he might be secretly amused by the ardor of her response.

"I'm pleased to know I'm improving. As I recall, the last kiss was a mere five." He merged with the moving traffic that led to the main arterial, halted at a stoplight and chuckled. "A seven," he repeated. "I'd have rated it more of an eight."

"Maybe." Dori relaxed and a light laugh tickled her throat. "No, it was definitely a low seven."

"You're a hard woman, Dori Robertson."

Her laugh would no longer be denied. "So I've been told."

Instead of heading for the freeway as she expected, Gavin took several turns that led indirectly to the waterfront.

"Where are we going?"

"For something to eat. I thought you might be hungry."

Dori had to stop and think about it before deciding that yes, she probably could eat something. "One thing."

"Yeah?" Gavin's eyes momentarily left the road.

"Not another hamburger. That's all Danny ever wants when we go out."

"Don't worry, I have something else in mind."

Gavin's "something else" turned out to be The Lobster Shop, an elegant restaurant overlooking the busy Tacoma harbor. Dori had often heard about the restaurant but had never been there. It was the kind of place where reservations were required several days in advance.

"You were planning this all along," she stated as he drove into the parking lot in front of the restaurant. Her warm gaze studied the strong, broad face, with its thick brows and silver wings fanning out from the temples.

"I thought I might have to appease you after taking you to the fights."

"I enjoyed myself."

His soft chuckle filled the car. "I know. You surprised the hell out of me, especially when you flew to your feet and kissed Boom Boom."

"It's so different from seeing it on television. And I blew him a kiss," she said on a note of righteous indignation. "That's an entirely different matter from flying to my feet and kissing him. I was happy he won the bout, that's all."

"I could tell. However, next time you feel like kissing any athletes, you might want to try me."

"You must be joking!" She placed her hand over her heart and feigned deep shock. "You might rate me."

Gavin was still chuckling when he left the car and came around to her side. There was a glint of admiration in his eyes as he escorted her into the restaurant.

The food was as good as Dori had expected. They both had lobster and an excellent white wine, and following their meal, they sat and talked over cups of strong, hot coffee.

"To be truthful," Dori said, staring into the dark depths of her drink, "I didn't have much hope for our 'date.'"

"You didn't?" A crooked smile slid across Gavin's sensuous mouth.

"To my utter amazement, I've really enjoyed myself. The best part of this evening is not having to worry about making any real commitment or analyzing our relationship. So we can just enjoy spending this time together. We both know where we stand and that's comfortable. I like it."

"I do, too," Gavin agreed softly, finishing his coffee. He smiled absently at the waitress when she collected the money for their bill.

Dori knew it was time to think about leaving, but she felt content and surprisingly at ease. When another waitress refilled their cups, neither objected.

"How long have you been a widow?" Gavin asked.

"Five years." Dori's fingers curved around the cup as she lowered her gaze. "Even after all this time I still have trouble accepting that Brad is gone. It seems so unreal. Maybe if he'd had a lingering illness, it would have been easier to accept. It happened so fast. He went to work one morning and was gone the next. A year later I was still reeling from the shock. I've thought about that day a thousand times. Had I known it was going to be our last morning together, there would have been so many things to say. As it was, I didn't ever get a chance to thank him for the wonderful years we shared."

"What happened?" Gavin reached for her hand. "Listen, if this is painful, we can drop it."

"No," she whispered and offered him a reassuring smile. "It's only natural for you to be curious. It was a freak accident. To this day I'm not sure exactly what happened. Brad was a bricklayer and he was working on a project downtown. The scaffolding gave out and a half ton of bricks fell on him. He was gone by the time they could free his body." She swallowed to relieve the tightness in her throat. "I was three months pregnant at the time. We'd planned this baby so carefully, building up our savings so I could quit my job. Everything seemed to come crashing in all at once. A week after Brad's funeral, I lost the baby."

Gavin's fingers tightened over hers and he squeezed them as if to lend her strength. "You're a strong woman to have survived those years."

Dori felt her throat muscles constrict and she nodded sadly. "I didn't have any choice. There was Danny, and his world had been turned upside down with mine. We clung to each other, and after a while we were able to pick up the pieces of our lives. I'm not saying it was easy, but there really wasn't any choice. We were alive, and we couldn't stay buried with Brad."

"When Danny asked for a new father it really must have thrown you."

"That certainly came out of left field." Her eyes sparkled with silent laughter. "That boy thinks up the craziest notions sometimes."

"You mean like the want ad?"

Dori groaned and slowly shook her head. "That has to be the most embarrassing moment of my life. You'll never know how grateful I am that you stepped in when you did."

"If you can persuade Melissa to buy a dress, I'll be forever in your debt."

"Consider it done."

Strangely, her answer didn't appear to please him. He gulped down the last of his coffee, then scraped back his chair and rose to his feet. "You women have ways of getting exactly what you want, don't you?"

Dori bit back an angry retort. She hadn't done anything to deserve this attack. But fine, let him act like that. She didn't care.

As he held open the car door for her, he hesitated. "I didn't mean to snap at you back there."

An apology! From Gavin Parker! Dori stared at him in shock. "Accepted," she murmured, hiding her stunned reaction as she concentrated on getting into the car.

On the return drive to Seattle, Dori rested her head against the seat and closed her eyes. It had been a long difficult week and she was tired. When Gavin stopped in front of her house, she straightened and tried unsuccessfully to hide a yawn.

"Thank you, Gavin. I had a good time. Really."

"Thank you." He left the engine running as he came around to her side of the car to help her out. Dori experienced an odd mixture of regret and relief. She'd toyed with the idea of inviting him in for coffee. But knowing Gavin, he'd probably assume the invitation meant more. Obviously, since he'd left the engine running, he was ready to be on his way. Dori found she was disappointed that their time together was coming to an end.

With a guiding hand at her elbow, Gavin walked her to the front porch. She fumbled momentarily in her purse for her key, wondering if she should say anything. It hadn't slipped her notice that he'd asked her about Brad yet hadn't offered any information regarding his ex-wife. Dori was filled with questions she didn't want to ask.

She hesitated, her house key in her hand. "Thanks again." She didn't think he was going to kiss her, but she wouldn't object if he tried. The kiss they'd shared earlier had been pleasant, more than pleasant—exciting and stirring. Even now the taste of his mouth clung to hers. Oh no, what was happening to her? Dori's mind whirled. It must have been the wine that was giving her this lightheaded feeling, she decided frantically. It couldn't have been his kiss. Not Gavin Parker. Oh, please, don't let it be Gavin.

He was standing so close that all she had to do was sway slightly and she'd be in his arms. Stubbornly, Dori stood rigid; staying exactly where she was. His finger traced the delicate line of her chin as his eyes met hers in the darkness. Dori's smile was weak and trembling as she realized that he wanted to kiss her but wouldn't. It was almost as though he were challenging her to make the first move—so he could blame her for enticing him.

Dori lowered her gaze. She wouldn't play his game. "Good night," she said softly.

"Good night, Dori." But neither of them moved and he added, "I'll be by to pick up Danny about noon on Sunday."

"Fine." Her voice was low and slightly breathless. "He'll be ready." Knowing Danny, he was ready now. Her quavering smile was touched by her amusement at the thought.

"I'll bring Melissa at the same time," Gavin murmured, and his gaze shifted from the key clenched in her hand to her upturned face.

"That'll be fine." She moistened her lips. Not for anything would she make this easy for him. If they were going to kiss, he'd be the initiator.

He took a step in retreat. "I'll see you Sunday then."

"Sunday," she repeated, purposefully turning around and inserting the key in her lock. The door opened and she looked back at him over her shoulder. "Good night, Gavin."

"Good night." His voice was deep and smooth. She recognized the look in his eyes, and her heart responded while her nerve endings screamed a warning. Hurrying now, Dori walked into the house and closed the door. He hadn't kissed her, but the look he'd given her as he stepped off the porch was more powerful than a mere kiss.

THE NEXT MORNING the front door slammed shut as Danny burst into the house. "Mom! How did it go? Did Mr. Parker ask you any football questions? Did he try to kiss you goodnight? Did you let him?"

Dori sat at the kitchen table, dressed in her old bathrobe with the ragged hem; her feet rested on the opposite chair. Glancing up from the morning paper, she held out her arms for Danny's hug. "Where's Grandma?"

"She has a meeting with her garden club. She wanted me to tell you that she'd talk to you later." Pulling out a chair, Danny straddled it backward, like a cowboy riding a wild bronco. "Well, how'd it go?"

"Fine."

Danny cocked his head to one side. "Just fine? Nothing *happened*?" Disappointment caused his voice to dip dramatically.

"What did you think we were going to do?" Amusement twitched at the edges of her mouth, and her eyes twinkled. "Honey, it was just a date. Our first one, at that. These things need time."

"But how long?" Danny demanded. "I thought I'd have a new dad by Christmas, and Thanksgiving will be here soon."

Dori set the newspaper aside. "Danny, listen to me. We're dealing with some important issues here. Remember when we got your bike? We shopped around and got the best price possible. We need to be even more careful with a new father."

"Yeah, but I remember that we went back and bought my bike at the very first store we looked at. Mom, Mr. Parker will make a perfect dad." His arm curled around the back of the chair. "I like him a lot."

"I like him, too," Dori admitted, "but that doesn't mean we're ready for marriage. Understand?"

Danny's mouth drooped and his shoulders hunched forward. "You looked so pretty last night."

"Thank you."

"Did Mr. Parker notice how pretty you looked?"

Dori had to think that one over. To be honest, she wasn't sure Gavin was the type to be impressed by a new dress or the fact that she was wearing an expensive perfume. "Do you want to hear what we did?"

"Yeah." Danny's spirits were instantly buoyed and he didn't seem to notice that she hadn't answered his question.

"First we had hamburgers and fries."

"Wow."

Dori knew that would carry weight with her son. "But that wasn't the best part. Later we went to a boxing match in Tacoma."

Danny's eyes rounded with excitement.

"If you bring me my purse, I'll show you the program."

He bounded into the other room and grabbed her handbag. "Mom—" he hesitated before passing it to her, staring pointedly at her feet "—you didn't let Mr. Parker know that you sometimes sleep with socks on, did you?"

Dori could feel the frustration building inside her in turbulent waves. "No," she said, keeping her gaze level with the morning paper. "The subject never came up."

"Good." The relief in his voice was evident.

"Gavin wants you to be ready tomorrow at noon. He's taking you to the Seahawks football game."

"Really?" Danny's eyes grew to saucer size. "Wow. Will I get to meet any players?"

"I don't know, but don't ask him about it. All right? That would be impolite."

"I won't, Mom. I promise."

DANNY WAS DRESSED and ready for the game hours before Gavin arrived on Sunday morning. He stood waiting at the living room window, fidgeting anxiously. But the minute he spotted the car, Danny was galvanized into action, leaping out the front door and down the stairs.

Dori followed and stood on the porch steps, her arms wrapping her middle to ward off the November chill. She watched as Melissa and Gavin climbed out of the Audi. A smile fanned fine lines around her eyes at the way Danny and Melissa greeted each other. Like conquering heroes on a playing field, they ran to the middle of the lawn, then jumped up and slapped their raised hands in midair in a gesture of triumph.

"What's with those two?" Gavin asked, sauntering toward Dori.

"I think they're pleased about . . . you know, our agreement."

"Ah, yes." A dark frown puckered his brow as he gave her a disgruntled look and walked past her into the house.

Dori's good mood did a nosedive, but she turned and followed him inside. "Listen, if this is too much of an inconvenience we can do it another time." Somehow she had to find a way to appease Danny. The last thing she wanted was for Gavin to view his agreement to spend this time with her son as an annoying obligation. For that matter, she could easily take Danny and Melissa to a movie if Gavin needed some time alone. She was about to suggest doing just that when Danny and Melissa entered the house.

"Hi, Mr. Parker," Danny greeted cheerfully. "Boy, I'm really excited about you taking me to the game. It's the neatest thing that's ever happened to me."

Gavin's austere expression relaxed. "Hi, Danny."

"Mom packed us a lunch."

"That was nice of your mom." Briefly, Gavin's gaze slid to Dori. Although he offered her a quick smile, she wasn't fooled. Something was bothering him.

"Yeah, and she's a really great cook. I bet she's probably one of the best cooks in the world."

"Danny," Dori warned in a low breath, flashing her son an admonishing look.

"Want a chocolate chip cookie?" Danny directed his attention to Melissa. "Mom baked them yesterday."

"Sure." Gavin's daughter followed Danny into the kitchen.

Dori turned her attention to Gavin. "Listen, you don't have to do this. I'll take Danny and Melissa to a movie or something. You look worn out."

"I am." He jammed his hands deep inside his pants pockets and marched to the other side of the room.

"What's wrong?"

"Women."

Dori recognized the low murmuring that drifted out from the kitchen as the sound of Melissa talking nonstop and with great urgency. Whatever was wrong involved Gavin's daughter.

"In the plural?" Dori couldn't hide a knowing grin as she glanced toward the children.

"These are probably the very best cookies I've ever had in my whole life," Melissa's voice sang out from the kitchen.

Shaking her head, Dori broke into a soft laugh. "Those two couldn't be any more obvious if they tried."

"No, I suppose not." Gavin shifted his gaze and frowned anew. "Melissa and I had an argument last night. She hasn't spoken to me since. I'd appreciate it if you could smooth things over for me."

"Sure, I'll be happy to."

Gavin lapsed into a pensive silence, then stooped to pat the stuffed lion he'd won for her at the fair. "Don't you want to know what we fought over?"

"I know already."

As he straightened, Gavin's dark eyes lit with amused speculation. "Is that a fact?"

"Yes."

"All right, Ms Know-It-All, you tell me."

Dori crossed the living room and stopped an inch in front of him. "The next time you go out with another woman, you might want to be a bit more discreet." Deftly she lifted a long blond hair from his shoulder.

CHAPTER FIVE

"IT WASN'T MY FAULT," Gavin declared righteously. "Lainey showed up last night uninvited."

Dori's eyebrows arched expressively. How like a man to blame the woman. From the very beginning of time, this was the way it had been. It had started in the Garden of Eden when Adam blamed Eve for enticing him to partake of the forbidden fruit, Dori thought, and it was still going on. "Uninvited, but apparently not unwelcome," she murmured, doing her best to hide a smile.

Gavin rubbed the back of his neck in an agitated movement. "Don't you start in on me, too." His angry response sliced the air.

"Me!" It was all she could do to keep from laughing outright.

"No doubt I'm sentenced to a fifteen-minute lecture from you, as well."

Feigning utter nonchalance, Dori moved to the other side of the room and sat on the sofa arm. With relaxed grace she crossed her legs. "It wouldn't be fair for me to lecture you. Besides, I have a pretty good idea of what happened."

"You do?" He eyed her speculatively.

"Sure. This gorgeous blonde showed up..." She paused to stroke the side of her face as if giving the matter deep thought. "Probably with two tickets to something she knew you really wanted to see."

"Not tickets but—" He stopped abruptly. "Okay. You're right, but I was only gone an hour and Melissa acted like I'd just committed adultery or worse." His defensiveness quickly returned. Stalking over to stand by the television set, he whirled around, asking, "Are you mad at me, too?"

"No." Amused was more the word.

Gavin expelled his breath forcefully and looked visibly relieved. "Thank God. I swear this arrangement is sometimes as bad as being married."

"Even if I were upset, Melissa has scolded you far more effectively than I ever could."

The beginning of a smile touched his eyes, revealing tiny lines of laughter at their outer corners. "That girl's got more of her mother in her than I thought."

"One thing, Gavin."

"Yes?" His gaze met hers.

"Is this Lainey the one whose brain leaks?"

"Yeah, she's the one."

"So you went out with her again although you claimed you weren't going to?" She wanted to prove to him that he wasn't as stouthearted or strong willed as he'd wanted her to believe.

A narrowed look surveyed her calmly. "That's right."

"Then what does that make you?" Dori hated to admit how much she was enjoying this.

His level gaze was locked on her face. "I knew you'd get back at me one way or another."

Blinking her thick lashes wickedly, Dori gave him her brightest smile. It was obvious that Gavin was more angry with himself than with anyone else and that he didn't like his susceptibility to the charms of this blond bombshell. And to be honest, Dori wasn't exactly pleased by it, either, although she'd rather have choked than let him know.

"Don't worry, all's forgiven," she said with a heavy tone of martyrhood. "I'll be generous and overlook your faults. It's easy, since I have so few of my own."

"I hadn't asked for your pardon," he returned dryly.

"Not to worry, I saved you the trouble."

A barely suppressed smile passed over his face. "I can't remember Melissa ever being so angry."

"Don't worry, I'll talk to her."

"What are you going to say?"

Not for the first time, Dori noticed how deeply resonant his voice was. She shrugged one shoulder and glanced out the window. "I'm not sure, but I'll think of something," she assured him.

"I know what will help."

"What?" She raised her eyes to his.

He strode over to her and glanced into the kitchen. "Danny, are you about ready?" Before Danny had a chance to answer, Gavin pulled Dori to her feet, enfolded her in his arms and drew her so close that the outline of his masculine body was imprinted on her much softer one.

"Ready, Mr. Parker," Danny said as he flew into the living room with Melissa following sluggishly behind. Before Dori could say anything, Gavin's warm mouth claimed hers, moving sensuously over her tender lips, robbing her of clear thought. Instinctively her arms circled his neck as his fiery kiss burned away her objections.

"Gavin." The words vibrated from the emotion-charged tenseness of her throat. Somehow she managed to break the contact and, bracing her hands against his chest, eased her body from his. She was too stunned to say more than his name. The kiss had been so unexpected—so good—that she could only stare up at him with wide disturbed eyes.

"Danny and I should be back about five. If you like, we can all go to dinner afterward."

Mutely, Dori nodded her head. If he'd asked her to swim across Puget Sound naked, she would have agreed. Her mind was befuddled, her senses numb.

"Good." Gavin buried his mouth in the curve of her neck and Dori's bewildered eyes again widened with surprise. As he released her, she caught a glimpse of Melissa and Danny smiling proudly at each other. Dori had to smother an angry groan.

"See you at five." With a thoughtful frown, Gavin paused and ran his index finger down the side of her face.

"Bye, Mom," Danny interrupted.

"Bye." Dori shook her head to free her muddled thoughts and calm her reactions. "Have a good time."

"We will," Gavin promised. He hesitated, studying his daughter. "Be good, Melissa."

The brilliant smile she gave him forced Dori and Gavin to hide a tiny, shared laugh.

"Okay, Dad, see you later."

Gavin's astonished eyes sought Dori's and he winked boldly. Parents could do their own form of manipulating. Again, Dori had difficulty concealing her laughter.

The front door closed and Melissa plopped down on the sofa and firmly crossed her arms. "Dad told you about 'her,' didn't he?"

"He mentioned Lainey, if that's who you mean."

"And you're not mad?" The young girl leaned forward and cupped her face in her hands, supporting her elbows on her knees. "I thought you'd be furious. I was. I didn't know Dad could be so dumb. Even I could see that she's a real phony. Miss Peroxide was so gushy-goo last night I almost threw up."

Dori sat beside the girl and took the same pose as Melissa, placing her bent elbows on her knees. "Your dad doesn't need either of us to be angry with him."

"But..." Melissa turned to scrutinize Dori, her smooth brow furrowed in confusion. "I think we should both be mad. He shouldn't have gone out with her. Not when he's seeing you."

Throwing an arm around the girl's shoulders, Dori searched for the right words. Explaining his actions could get her into trouble. "Your father was more angry at himself than either of us could be. Let's show him that we can overlook his weaknesses and...love him in spite of them." Immediately Dori realized she'd used the wrong word.

"You love Dad?"

A shudder trembled through Dori. "Well, that word may have been a little too strong."

"I think he's falling in love with you," Melissa said fervently. "He hardly talks about you, and that's a sure sign."

Dori was unconvinced. If he didn't talk about her, it was because he wasn't thinking about her—which was just as well. She wasn't going to fool herself with any unwarranted emotions. She and Gavin had a dating agreement and she wasn't looking for anything more than a way of satisfying Danny's sudden need for a father. Just as Gavin was hoping to appease his daughter.

"That's nice," Dori said, reaching for the Sunday paper. "What would you like to do today?" Absently she flipped the pages of the sales tabloids that came with the paper.

The young girl shrugged and reclined against the back of the sofa. "I don't know. What would you like to do?"

"Well," Dori eased herself into a comfortable position and pretended to give the matter some thought. "I could do some shopping, but I don't want to drag you along if you'd find it boring."

"What are you going to buy?"

Remembering the way Melissa had watched her put on her makeup sparked an idea. "I thought I'd stop in at Northgage plaza and sample a few perfumes at The Bon. You can help me decide which scent your father would like best."

"Yeah, I'd like that."

Two hours later, before she was even aware of Dori's scheme, Melissa owned her first cosmetics, a new dress and shoes. Once Dori had persuaded the girl that it was time to experiment with some light makeup, progressing to a dress and shoes had been relatively easy.

Back at the house Melissa used Dori's bedroom to try on the new outfit. Shyly she paraded before Dori, her intense eyes lowered to the carpet as she walked. The dress was a lovely pink floral print with lace collar and cuffs. The T-strap dress shoes were white and Melissa was wearing her first pair of nylons. Self-consciously she held out her leg to Dori. "Did I put them on right?"

"Perfect." A sense of pride and happiness shone in Dori's bright eyes. Folding her hands together, she said softly, "Oh, Melissa, you're so pretty."

"Really?" Disbelief caused her voice to rise half an octave.

"Really!" The transformation was astonishing. The girl standing before her was no longer a defiant tomboy but a budding young woman. Dori's heart swelled with emotion. Gavin would hardly recognize his own daughter. "Come look." Dori led her into the bathroom and closed the door so Melissa could see for herself in the full-length mirror.

The girl breathed a long sigh. "It's beautiful," she said in a low, shaking voice. "Thank you." Impulsively she gave Dori a hug. "Oh, I wish you were my mother. I really, really wish you were."

Dori hugged her back, surprised at the emotion that surged through her. "I'd consider myself very lucky to have you for a daughter."

Melissa stepped back for another look at herself. "You know, at first I was really hoping Dad would marry Lainey." She pursed her lips and tilted her head mockingly. "That's how really desperate I am to get out of that school. It's not that the nuns are mean or anything. Everyone's been really nice. But I really want a family and a regular, ordinary life."

Dori hid a smile. *Really* was obviously Melissa's word for the day.

"But the more I thought about it, the more I realized Lainey would probably keep me in that stupid school until I was twenty-nine. She doesn't want me hanging around. If Dad marries her, I don't know what I'd do."

"Your father isn't going to marry anyone..." Dori faltered momentarily. "Not someone you don't like, anyway."

"I hope not," Melissa said heatedly. Turning sideways, she viewed her profile. "You know something else I'd really like to do?"

"Name it." The day had gone so well that Dori was ready to be obliging.

"Can I bake something?"

"Anything you like."

The spicy aroma of fresh-baked apple pie filled the house by the time Danny burst in the front door. "Mom!" he screamed as if the very demons of hell were in pursuit. "The Seahawks won. The score was 14 to 7."

Dori had been so busy that she hadn't thought of turning on the television. "Did you have a good time?"

"Mr. Parker bought me a hot dog and a soda pop and some peanuts."

Dori cast an accusing glare at Gavin, who gestured dismissively with his hands and grinned sheepishly.

"What about the lunch I packed you?"

"We didn't eat it. Mr. Parker says it's more fun to buy stuff at the game."

"Oh, he did, did he?" Amused, Dori found her laughing eyes meeting Gavin's.

The bedroom door opened a crack. "Can I come out yet?"

Guiltily Dori's gaze swung to the hallway. "Oh goodness, I nearly forgot. Sit down, you two. Melissa and I have a surprise."

Gavin and Danny obediently took a seat. "Ready," Dori called over her shoulder. The bedroom door opened wide and Melissa started down the hallway. Halting her progress for a moment, Dori announced, "While you two were at the game, Melissa and I were just as busy shopping."

Confident now, none of her earlier coyness evident, Melissa strolled into the room and gracefully modeled the dress, turning as she came to a stop in front of the sofa. Smiling, she curtsied and demurely lowered her lashes. Then she rose, contentedly folding her hands in front of her, ready to receive their lavish praise.

"You look like a girl," Danny said, unable to disguise his lack of enthusiasm. At the disapproving look Dori flashed him, he quickly amended his hastily spoken words. "You look real pretty though—for a girl."

Dori studied Gavin's reaction and felt her tension build at the pride that shone from his eyes. A myriad of emotions were revealed in the strong, often stern features. "This can't be my little girl. Not Melissa Jane Parker, my daughter."

Melissa giggled happily. "Really, Dad, who else could it be?"

Gavin stroked his chin as if he still couldn't believe his eyes. Slowly he shook his head, apparently speechless. "I don't know who's wearing that dress, but I can hardly believe I've got a daughter this pretty."

"I made you a surprise, too," Melissa added eagerly. "Something to eat."

"Something to eat?" He echoed her words and looked at Dori, who shrugged innocently.

Tugging at his hand, Melissa urged her father off the couch and led him into the kitchen. "Dori helped me."

"Not all that much. She did most of the work herself."

"A pie?" Gavin's gaze fell to the cooling masterpiece that rested on the kitchen countertop.

"Apple," Melissa boasted proudly, "your favorite."

Later that night, Dori lay in bed gazing at the darkened ceiling, her clasped hands supporting the back of her head. The day had been wonderful. There wasn't a better word to describe it. She'd enjoyed shopping with Melissa, particularly because the girl had been so responsive to all Dori's suggestions. Dori didn't like to think about the baby she'd lost after Brad's death. She'd so hoped for a daughter. Today it was almost as if Melissa had been hers. Dori felt such enthusiasm, such joy, in sharing little things, like shopping with Melissa. She loved Danny beyond reason, but there were certain things he'd never appreciate. Shopping was one. But Melissa had enjoyed it as much as Dori had.

Danny's day had been wonderful, too. All evening he'd talked nonstop about the football game and had obviously had the time of his life. Long after Gavin and Melissa had left, Danny continued to recount the highlights of the game, recalling plays with a vivid memory for every minute detail. Either the two children had superlative—and hitherto unsuspected—acting abilities, or their reactions had been genuine. Dori found it difficult to believe that the whole thing had been a charade. To be honest, she'd had her suspicions when Gavin first suggested this agreement, but now she believed that it could be the best thing to have happened to her in a long time—the best thing for all of them.

The following morning Sandy looked up from her work when Dori entered the office.

"Morning," Dori said absently as she pulled out the bottom drawer of her desk and routinely deposited her purse. When Sandy didn't immediately respond, Dori glanced up. Sandy was eyeing her speculatively, her head cocked slightly. "What's with the funny, bug-eyed look?" Dori demanded.

"There's something different about you."

"Me?"

"You and this football hero went out Friday night, didn't you?"

Dori couldn't help but chuckle. "Yes, to the fights, if you can believe it."

"I don't."

"Well, do, because it's the truth. But first he took me out for a four-star meal of hamburgers, French fries and a chocolate shake."

"And he's living to tell about it?"

Dori relaxed in her chair and crossed her arms, letting the memory of that night amuse her anew. "Yup."

"From that dreamy look in your eyes I'd say you had a good time."

Dreamy look! Dori stiffened and reached for her pen. "Oh, hardly. You just like to tease, that's all."

Sandy gave her a measured look and returned her attention to her desk. "If you say so, but you might want to watch where you walk, with all those stars blinding your eyes."

At about eleven o'clock the phone buzzed. Usually Sandy and Dori took turns answering, but Sandy was away from her desk and Dori automatically reached for the receiver.

"Underwriting," she announced.

"Dori?"

"Gavin?" Her heart responded, pounding like a jack-hammer gone wild. "Hi."

"What time are you free for lunch?" he asked without preamble.

"Noon." From the sound of his voice, something was troubling him. "Is something wrong?" Dori probed gently.

"No, not really. I just think we need to talk."

They agreed on an attractive seafood restaurant beside Lake Union. Gavin was already seated at one of the linen-covered tables when Dori arrived. She noticed that his eyes were veiled and thoughtful as he watched the maître d' lead her to his table.

"This is a pleasant surprise," she said to Gavin, smiling appreciatively at the waiter who held out a chair for her.

"Yes, well, I don't usually take this type of lunch break." There seemed to be a hidden meaning in the statement.

Gavin always managed to throw her off base one way or another. Just when she felt she understood him, he would say or do something that made her realize she hardly knew this man. Her intuition told her it was about to happen again. Mentally she braced herself, and a small sigh of dread quivered in her throat.

To mask her fears, Dori lifted the menu and studied it with unseeing eyes. The restaurant was known for its wide variety of seafood, and Dori was toying with the idea of ordering a Crab Louis when Gavin spoke. "Melissa had a good time yesterday."

"I enjoyed her, too. She's a wonderful child, Gavin." Dori set the menu aside, having decided on a shrimp salad.

"Once we got off the subject of you, Danny and I had a great time ourselves."

Dori groaned inwardly at the thought of Danny endlessly extolling her virtues. Gavin must have been thoroughly sick of hearing about her. She'd make a point of saying something to Danny later.

"Danny certainly enjoyed himself."

Gavin laid the menu alongside his plate and stared at her in thoughtful, nerve-racking silence.

Instinctively, Dori stiffened. "But there's a problem, right?" she asked with deliberate softness, fighting off a sense of unease.

"Yes. I think you might have laid on this motherhood bit a little too thick, don't you? Melissa drove me crazy last night. First Danny and now my own daughter."

Anger raged within Dori and it was all she could do not to bolt out of the restaurant. To Gavin's twisted way of thinking, she had intentionally set out to convince his daughter that she would be the perfect wife and mother. On the basis of nothing more than her visit with Melissa the day before, Gavin had cynically concluded that she was already checking out engagement rings and choosing a china pattern. "You know, I was thinking the same thing myself," she announced casually, surprised at how unemotional she sounded.

Gavin studied her with amused indifference. "I thought you might be."

His sarcastic tone was her undoing. "Yes, the more I think about it, the more I realize that our well-plotted scheme may be working all *too* well. If you're tired of listening to my praises sung, then you should hear it from my end of things."

"Yes, I imagine—"

"That's exactly your problem, Gavin Parker," she cut in, her voice sharp and brittle. "The reason Melissa responded to me yesterday was because that child has a heart full of love and no one who seems to want it." Dori fixed her gaze on the water glass as she battled back the rising swell of anger that threatened to choke her. "I feel sorry for you. Your thinking is so twisted that you don't know what's genuine and what isn't. You're so afraid of revealing your emotions that your heart has become like granite.''

"I suppose you think you're just the woman to free me from these despicable shackles?" he taunted.

Dori ignored the derision and the question. "For Melissa's sake I hope you find what you're looking for soon." She tilted her head back and raised her eyes enough to look full into his face with haughty disdain. "For my part, I want out." She had to go before she became so attached to Melissa that severing the relationship would harm them both. And before she made the fatal mistake of giving Gavin Parker her heart.

His eyes glittered as cold and dark as the Arctic Sea. "Are you saying you want to cancel our agreement?"

Calmly, Dori placed the linen napkin on top of her unused plate and stood, "I swear the man's a marvel," she murmured sarcastically. "It was nice knowing you, Gavin Parker. You have a delightful daughter. Thank you for giving Danny the thrill of his life."

"What are you doing?" he hissed under his breath. "Sit back down and let's discuss this like adults."

Still standing, Dori boldly met Gavin's angry eyes. Sick at heart and so miserable that given any provocation she would have cried, she slowly shook her head. "I'm sorry, Gavin, really sorry, but even a phony arrangement can't work with us. We're too different."

"We're not different at all," he argued heatedly, then paused to glower at the people whose attention his raised voice had attracted.

"Careful, Gavin," she mocked, "someone might think you're coming on a bit too—''

"Melissa's mother phoned me this morning," he announced starkly, and for the first time Dori noted the deep lines of worry that marred his face.

"What?" she repeated, her heartbeat accelerating at an alarming rate. She sat down again, her eyes wide and fearful at the apprehension in Gavin's expression.

"Our conversation was less than congenial. I need to talk to someone. I apologize if I came at you like a kamikaze pilot."

If, Dori mused flippantly. He'd invited her because he wanted someone to talk to and then he'd tried to sabotage their lunch. "What happened?"

"The usual. Deirdre's living in New York and is divorcing her third or fourth husband, I forget which, and wants Melissa to come and live with her."

Dori sucked in a shocked breath. She knew nothing about this woman. Until today she hadn't even known her name. But Dori was privy to the pain this woman had wreaked in Gavin's life. "Does she have a chance of getting her?" Already her heart was pounding at the thought of Gavin's losing his daughter to a woman he so obviously detested.

Gavin's laugh was bitter. "Hardly, but that won't stop her from trying. She does this at the end of every marriage. She has an attack of guilt and wants to play mommy for a while."

"How does Melissa feel about Deirdre? Does she ever see her mother?" She didn't mean to pry and she didn't want him to reveal anything he wasn't comfortable sharing. But the thought of this young girl being forced into an uncomfortable situation tore at her heart.

"Melissa spends a month every summer. Last year she phoned me three days after she arrived and begged me to let her come home. At the time Deirdre was just as glad to be rid of her. I don't know what happened, but Melissa made me promise that I wouldn't send her there alone again."

"I realize you're upset, but the courts aren't going to listen—"

"I know," Gavin interrupted abruptly. "I just needed to vent my frustrations and anger on someone. Melissa and I have gone through this before and we can weather another of Deirdre's whims." Gavin's hand gently touched hers. "I owe you an apology for the way I behaved earlier."

"It's forgotten." What wasn't forgotten was that he'd sought her out. Somehow, in some way, she'd reached Gavin Parker—and now they were on dangerous ground. This charade was becoming more real every time they saw each other. They'd thought they could keep their emotions detached and they were failing. More and more, Gavin dominated her thoughts, and despite herself, she found excuses to imagine them together. It wasn't supposed to work like this.

"You told me about Brad. I think it's only fair to let you know about Deirdre."

A feeling of gladness raced through Dori. Not because Gavin was telling her about his ex-wife. To be truthful, Dori wasn't even sure she wanted to hear the gory details of his marriage breakdown. But the fact that Gavin was telling her was a measure of his trust in her. He felt safe enough with her to divulge his deepest pain—as she had with him. "It isn't necessary," she said softly, their gazes holding.

"It's only fair that you know." His hand gripped the water glass, apparently oblivious to the cold that must be seeping up his arm. "I don't even know where to begin. We married young, too young I suppose. We were in our last year of college and I was on top of the world. The pros were already scouting me out. I'd been seeing Deirdre, but so had a lot of other guys. She came from a wealthy family and had been spoiled by an indulgent father. I liked him; he was a terrific guy, even if he did cater too much to his daughter— but he really loved her. When she told me she was pregnant and I was the baby's father, I offered to marry her. I have no difficulty believing that if I hadn't, she would have had an abortion. I went into the marriage with a lot of expectations. I think I was even glad she was pregnant. The idea of being a father pleased me—proof of my manhood and all that garbage." He paused and focused his gaze on the tabletop.

Dori realized how difficult this must be for him, and her first instinct was to tell him to stop. It wasn't necessary for him to reveal this pain. But even stronger was the feeling that he needed to talk—to get this out of his system.

"Usually people can say when they felt their marriage going bad. Ours went bad on the wedding day. Deirdre hated being pregnant, but worse, I believe she hated me. From the moment Melissa was born, she didn't want to have anything to do with her. Later I learned that she hated being pregnant so much that she had herself sterilized so there would never be any more children. She didn't even bother to tell me. Melissa was given to a nanny and within weeks Deirdre was making the rounds, if you know what I mean. I don't think I need to put it any more clearly."

"No." Dori's voice was low and trembling. She'd never known anyone like that and found it impossible to imagine a woman who could put such selfish, shallow pleasures ahead of her own child's needs.

"God knows I tried to make the marriage work. More for her father's sake than Deirdre's. But after he died I couldn't pretend any longer. She didn't want custody of Melissa then, and I'm not about to give up my daughter now."

"How long ago was that?"

"Melissa was three when we got divorced."

Three! The girl had never really known her mother. Dori's heart ached for this child who had never experienced a mother's love.

"I thought you should know," he concluded.

"Thank you for telling me." Instinctively Gavin had come to her with his doubts and worries. He was reaching out to her, however reluctantly at first. But he'd made a beginning, and Dori was convinced it was the right one for them.

THAT SAME WEEK, Dori saw Gavin two more times. They went to a movie Wednesday evening, sat in the back row and argued over the popcorn. Telling Dori about Deirdre seemed to have freed him. On Friday he phoned her at the office again, and they met for lunch at the same restaurant they'd gone to the previous Monday. He told her he was going to be away for the weekend, broadcasting a game.

By the following Monday, Dori was worried. She had trouble keeping her thoughts on her work. Every time she tried to concentrate, she wondered if she was falling in love with Gavin. It didn't seem possible that she could grow to care about him this quickly. The physical response to his touch was a pleasant surprise. But it had been years since a man had held her the way he did, so Dori had more or less expected and compensated for the physical impact of his lovemaking. The emotional response was what over-whelmed her. She cared about him. Worried about him. Thought about him to the exclusion of all else. They were in trouble, deep trouble. But Gavin had failed to recognize it. If they were going to react sensibly, the impetus would have to come from her.

Dori's thoughts were still troubled when she stopped at the soccer field to pick up Danny after work that Monday night. She pulled into the parking lot at the park and walked across the thick lawn to the field. The boys were playing a scrimmage game and she stood by the sidelines, proudly watching Danny weave his way through the defenders.

"You're Danny's mother, aren't you?"

Dori's attention was diverted to the lanky, thin man at her side. She recognized him as Jon Schaeffer's dad. Jon and Danny had recently become the best of friends and had spent the night at each other's houses two or three times since the beginning of the school year. From what she understood, Jon's parents were separated. "Yes, you're Jon's father, right?"

"Right." He crossed his arms and watched the boys running back and forth across the long field. "Danny's a good player."

"Thank you. So is Jon."

"Yeah, I'm real proud of him." The conversation was stilted and Dori felt a little uneasy.

"I hope you won't think I'm being too bold, but did you put an ad in the paper?"

Dori felt waves of color flood her face. "Well, actually Danny did."

"I thought he might have." He chuckled and held out his hand. "My name's Tom, by the way."

Less embarrassed, Dori shook it. "Dori," she introduced herself.

"I read the ad and thought about calling. As much as I'd hoped, it doesn't look like Paula and I are going to get back together and I was so damned lonely, I thought about giving you a call."

"How'd you know the number was mine?"

"I didn't," he was quick to amend. "I wrote it down on a slip of paper and set it by the phone, trying to work up enough courage. Jon spent last weekend with me and saw it and wanted to know how come I had Danny's phone number."

"Oh." Color blossomed anew. "I've had the number changed since."

"I think Jon mentioned that. So Danny put the ad in the paper?"

"All on his own. It was the first time I've ever regretted being a mother." Involuntarily her voice rose with remembered embarrassment.

"Did you get many responses?"

He was so serious that Dori was forced to conceal a smile. "You wouldn't believe the number of calls that came the first night."

"I thought as much."

They lapsed into a companionable silence. "You and your husband split up?"

Tom had a clear-cut view of life, it seemed, and a blunt manner. The question came out of nowhere. "No, I'm a widow."

"Hey, listen, I'm sorry. I didn't mean to be nosy. It's none of my business."

"Don't worry about it," Dori reassured him softly.

Tom wasn't like most of the men she'd known. He was obviously a hard worker, frank, a little rough around the edges. Dori sensed that he was still in love with his wife and she silently hoped they'd get back together again.

"Jon and Danny are good friends, aren't they?"

"They certainly see enough of each other."

"Could you tolerate a little more togetherness?" His gaze didn't leave the field.

"How do you mean?"

"Could I take you and Danny to dinner with Jon and me?" He looked as awkward as a teenager asking a girl out for the first time.

Dori's immediate inclination was to politely refuse. The last thing she wanted to do was alienate Jon's mother. On the other hand, Dori needed to sort through her own feelings for Gavin, and seeing someone else was bound to help.

"Yes, we'd enjoy that. Thank you."

The smile he beamed at her was bright enough to rival the streetlight. "The pleasure's all mine."

CHAPTER SIX

"MOM," DANNY PLEADED, following her into the bath-room and frantically waving his hand in front of his face while she deftly applied hair spray to her pinned-up curls.

"What?" Dori answered irritably. She'd been arguing with Danny from the minute he'd learned she was going out with Tom Schaeffer.

"Mr. Parker could phone."

"I know, but it's unlikely." Gavin hadn't been in touch with her since their Monday lunch. If he expected her to sit around and wait for his calls, then he was in for a surprise.

Danny's disgruntled look and defiantly crossed arms made her hesitate. "If he does phone, tell him I'm out for the evening and I'll return his call when I get home."

"But I thought you and Mr. Parker were good friends . . . real good friends. You even kissed him!"

"We are friends," she answered, feigning indifference as she tucked in a stray hair and examined her profile in the mirror. With a sigh of disgust she tightened her stomach—and wondered how long she could go without breathing.

"Mom," Danny protested anew, "I don't like this and I don't think Mr. Parker will, either."

"He won't care," she stated with more aplomb than she was feeling. Danny assumed that because she was going out on a weeknight, this must be some "hot date." It wasn't. Tom had invited her after their dinner with the boys and Dori had accepted because she realized that what he really wanted was a sympathetic ear. He was lonely and still deeply in love with his wife. She couldn't have picked a safer date, but Danny wouldn't understand that and she didn't try to explain.

"If you're such good friends with Mr. Parker, how come you're wearing perfume for Jon's dad?"

"Moms sometimes do that for no special reason."

"But tonight's special. You're going out with Mr. Schaeffer."

Dori placed her hands on her son's shoulders and studied him closely. The young face was pinched, and the deep blue eyes intense. "Don't you like Mr. Schaeffer?"

"He's all right, I guess."

"But I thought you had a good time when we went out to dinner Monday night."

"That was different. Jon and I were with you."

Dori knew that Danny wasn't terribly pleased that a high school girl from the neighborhood was coming to sit with him. He was at that awkward age—too young to be left completely alone, especially for an evening, but old enough to resent a baby-sitter, particularly when she was one of his own neighbors.

"I'll be home early—probably before your bedtime," Dori promised, ruffling his hair.

Danny impatiently brushed her hand aside. "But why are you going, Mom? That's what I don't understand."

Dori didn't know how she could explain something she didn't completely comprehend herself. She was worried that her emotions were becoming involved with Gavin. Tom was insurance. With Tom there wasn't any fear of falling in love or being hurt. Every time she saw Gavin her emotions became more entangled; she cared about him and Melissa. But as far as Gavin was concerned, the minute her heart was involved would be the end of their relationship. He'd made it abundantly clear that he didn't want any kind of real involvement. He had no plans to remarry, and the minute she revealed any emotional commitment he wouldn't hesitate to reject her as he had rejected others. Oh, she might hold on to him for a time, the way Lainey was trying to. But Gavin wasn't a man easily fooled—and Dori wasn't a fool.

The doorbell chimed and the sixteen-year-old who lived across the street came in with an armful of books.

"Hello, Mrs. Robertson."

"Hi, Jody." Out of the corner of her eye Dori noted that Danny had plopped down in front of the television. She wasn't deceived by his indifference. Her son was not happy that she was dating Tom Schaeffer. Dori ignored him and continued her instructions to the sitter. "The phone number for the restaurant is in the kitchen. I shouldn't be much later than nine-thirty, maybe ten." The front doorbell chimed again and Danny answered it this time, opening the door for Tom, who smiled appreciatively when he saw Dori.

"Be good," Dori whispered and kissed Danny on the cheek.

He rubbed the place she'd kissed and examined the palm of his hand for any lipstick. "Okay," he agreed with a sad little smile calculated to tug at a mother's heart. "But I'm waiting up for you." He gave her the soulful look of a lost puppy, his deep blue eyes crying out at the injustice of being left at the fickle mercy of a sixteen-year-old girl. The emphasis being, of course, on the word "girl."

If Dori didn't leave soon, he might well win this unspoken battle and she couldn't allow that. "We'll talk when I get back," she promised softly.

Tom, dressed in a three-piece suit, placed a guiding hand at the small of her back as they left the house. "Is there a problem with Danny?"

Dori cast a speculative glance over her shoulder. She felt guilty and depressed, although there was no reason she should. Now she realized how Melissa had made Gavin feel when he'd gone out with Lainey that Saturday night. No wonder he'd been upset on Sunday. Neither of them were accustomed to this type of adolescent censorship. And she didn't like it any more than Gavin had.

"Danny's unhappy about being left with a baby-sitter," she answered Tom half-truthfully.

With such an ominous beginning, Dori realized that the evening was doomed before it even began. They shared a quiet dinner and talked over coffee, but the conversation was one-sided and when the clock struck nine, Dori fought not to glance at her wristwatch every five minutes.

On the drive home, she felt obliged to apologize. "I'm *really* sorry..." She paused, then remembered how often Melissa used that word and, in spite of herself, broke into a full laugh.

Tom's bewildered gaze caught hers. "What's so amusing?"

"It's a long story. A friend of mine has a daughter who alternates 'really' with every other word. I caught myself saying it just now and..."

"It suddenly seemed funny."

"Exactly." She was still smiling when Tom turned into the street that led to her house. The muscles of her face tightened, and the amusement drained from her eyes when she noticed a car parked in front. Gavin's car. Damn, damn, damn! She clenched her fist tightly and drew several deep breaths to calm her nerves. There was no telling what kind of confrontation awaited her.

As politely as possible, Dori thanked Tom for the dinner and apologized for not inviting him in for coffee.

When she opened the door a pair of accusing male eyes met hers. "Hello, Gavin," Dori said on a cheerful note, "this is a pleasant surprise."

"Dori." The glittering harshness of his gaze told her he wasn't pleased. "Did you have a good time?"

"Wonderful," she lied. "We went to a Greek restaurant and naturally everything was Greek to me. I finally decided what to eat by asking myself what Anthony Quinn would order." Dori hated the way she was rambling like a guilty schoolgirl. Her mouth felt dry and her throat scratchy.

Danny faked a wide yawn. "I think I'll go to bed now. It's bedtime already."

"Not so fast, young man." Dori stopped him. Her son had played a part in this uncomfortable showdown with Gavin. The least he could do was explain. "Is there something you want to tell me?"

Danny eyed the carpet with unusual interest while his cheeks flushed with telltale color. "No."

Dori was convinced that Danny had phoned Gavin, but she'd handle that later with a week's grounding. "I'll talk to you in the morning."

"'Night, Mr. Parker." Like a rabbit unexpectedly freed from a trap, Danny bolted down the hallway to his bedroom.

It didn't escape Dori's notice that he hadn't wished her good-night. Hanging her coat in the hall closet gave Dori precious moments to collect her thoughts and resolve to ignore the distressing heat that warmed her blood. When she finally turned to face Gavin, she saw that a cynical smile had quirked up the corners of his stern mouth.

"Don't look so guilty," he challenged.

Dori's cheeks burned, but she boldly met his hard eyes, sparks flashing defiantly from hers. "I'm not." She walked into the kitchen and prepared a pot of coffee. Gavin followed her and she automatically took two mugs from the cupboard. Turning, her back pressed against the counter, Dori confronted his gaze squarely. "What happened? Did Danny phone you?"

"I thought we had an agreement."

Involuntarily, Dori flinched at the harshness of his voice. "We do," she replied calmly, watching the coffee drip into the glass pot.

"Then what were you doing out with a man? A married one, at that."

"Exactly what has Danny been telling you? Tom and his wife are separated. For heaven's sake, we didn't even hold hands." She studiously avoided meeting his fiery glare, angry now that she'd bothered to explain. "Good grief, you went out with Lainey. I don't see the difference."

"At least I felt guilty."

"So did I! Does that make you feel any better?"

"Yes!" he shouted.

Furious, she whirled around, tired of playing mouse to his cat. Her hand shook as she poured hot coffee into the mugs.

"Are we going to fight about it?" she asked as she placed his mug on the kitchen table.

"That depends on whether you plan to see him again." His face was impassive, as if the question were of no importance. Dori marveled at his self-control. The hard eyes that stared back at her were frosted with challenge, daring her to say she would be seeing Tom again.

"I don't know." She sat in the chair opposite him. "Does it matter?"

His mouth twisted in a faintly ironic smile. "It could. I don't particularly relish another frantic phone call from your son informing me that I'd better do something quick."

"Believe me, that won't happen again," Dori insisted, furious with Danny and more furious with herself. She should have known that Danny would do something like this and taken measures before she went out.

"So you felt guilty." His low, drawling voice was tinged with amused mockery.

"I didn't like it any more than you did." She expelled her breath and folded her arms in a defensive gesture. "I don't know, Gavin, our agreement is working much too well." With an impatient gesture she reached for the sugar bowl in the middle of the table and stirred a teaspoon into her coffee. "Before we know it, those two kids are going to have us married and living in a house with a white picket fence."

"You needn't worry about that."

"Oh, no—" she waved her hands in the air helplessly "—of course that wouldn't concern you. Mr. Macho here can handle everything, right? Well, you admitted that Melissa made you miserable when you saw Lainey. Danny did the same thing to me. I think we should bow gracefully out of this agreement while we can." Although Dori offered the suggestion, she hoped Gavin would refuse; she needed to know that the attraction was mutual.

"Is that what you want?" Deftly he turned the tables on her.

In a flash of irritation, Dori pushed back her chair and walked quickly to the sink where she deposited her mug. She gave a sharp sigh of frustration and returned to the table. "No, unfortunately I don't. Darn it, Parker, in spite of your arrogant ways, I've discovered I like you. That's what scares me."

"Don't sound so shocked. I'm a great guy. Just ask Danny. Of course, it could be my virility that you find so alluring, in which case we're in deep trouble." Chuckling, he rolled lazily to his feet and delivered his empty cup to the sink.

"Don't fret," she muttered sarcastically, "your masculinity hasn't overpowered me yet."

"That's probably the best thing we've got going for us. Don't fall in love with me, Dori," he warned, the amusement gone from his eyes. "I'd only end up hurting you."

Her pulse rocketed with alarm. He was right. The problem was that she was already halfway there. And she was standing on dangerously thin ice, struggling to hold back her feelings.

"I think you've got things twisted here," she told him dryly, "I'm more concerned about you falling for me. I'm not your usual type, Gavin. The danger could well be of your own making."

Her appraisal didn't appear to please him. "There's little worry of that happening. One woman's already brought me to my knees and I'm not about to let that happen again."

Dori forced back the words of protest, the assertion that a real woman didn't want a man on his knees. She wanted him at her side as friend, lover and confidant.

"There's another problem coming up I think we should discuss," he continued.

"What?"

He ignored her worried look and casually leaned a hip against the counter. "Melissa and I are going to San Francisco over Thanksgiving weekend. I'm doing the play-by-play of the Forty-niners game that Saturday. For weeks, Melissa's been asking me if you and Danny can come with us."

"But why? This should be a special time between the two of you."

"Unfortunately, Melissa doesn't see it that way. She'll be left in the hotel room alone on the Saturday because I'll be in the broadcast booth and I don't want her attending the game by herself. It *is* Thanksgiving weekend, as Melissa keeps pointing out. But I hate to admit that my daughter knows exactly which buttons to push to make me feel guilty."

"I don't know, Gavin," Dori hedged. She had planned to spend the holiday with her parents, but she loved San Francisco. Her mind was buzzing. She'd visited the Bay area as a teenager and had always wanted to return. This would be like a vacation and she hadn't been on one in years.

"The way I see it," Gavin went on, "this may even suit our needs. The kids are likely to overdose on each other if they spend that much time together. Maybe after three or four days in each other's company, they'll face a few truths about this whole thing."

Dori was skeptical. "It could backfire."

"I doubt it. What do you say?"

The temptation was so strong that she had to close her eyes to fight back an immediate yes. "Let...let me think on it."

"Fine," he answered calmly.

Dori pulled out a chair and sat down. "Have you heard anything more from Deirdre?"

"No, and I won't."

"How can you be so sure?"

The hard line of his mouth curved upward in a mirthless smile. "I have my ways."

Just the manner in which he said it made Dori's blood run cold. Undoubtedly Gavin knew Deirdre's weaknesses and knew how to attack his ex-wife.

"There's no way on this earth that I'll hand my daughter over to that bitch."

Until then, Dori had never seen a man's eyes look more frigid or harsh. "If there's anything I can do to help..." She let the rest fade. Gavin wouldn't need anything from her.

"As a matter of fact, there is." He contradicted her thoughts. "I'm broadcasting a game this Sunday in Kansas City, which means Melissa has to spend the weekend at the school. Saturday and Sunday alone at the school are the worst, or so she claims."

"She could stay with us. I'd enjoy it immensely." There wasn't anything special planned. Saturday she did errands and bought the week's groceries, and Danny had a soccer game in the afternoon, but Melissa would enjoy that.

"I was thinking more like one afternoon," Gavin said with some reluctance. "As it is, you'll hear twenty-four hours of my limitless virtues. Why ask for more?"

"Let her stay the whole weekend," Dori requested softly. "Didn't you just say we should try to 'overdose' the kids?"

GAVIN'S WARNING proved to be prophetic. From the moment Dori picked up Melissa at the Eastside Convent School on Mercer Island, the girl chattered nonstop, extolling her father's apparently limitless virtues—just as he'd predicted.

"Did you know that my father has a whole room full of trophies he won playing sports?"

"Wow," Danny answered, his voice unnaturally high. "Remember our list, Mom? I think it's important that my new dad be athletic."

"What else was on the list?" Melissa asked, then listened attentively as Danny explained each requirement. She continued to comment, presenting Gavin as the ideal father and husband in every respect. However, it hadn't escaped Dori's notice that Melissa didn't mention the last stipulation, that Danny's new father love Dori. Instinctively Melissa recognized it would be overstepping the bounds. Dori appreciated the girl's honesty.

As Melissa continued her bragging about Gavin, Dori had to bite her tongue to keep from laughing. Given the chance, she'd teach those two something about subtlety—later. For now, they were far too amusing. In an effort to restrain her merriment, she centered her concentration on the heavy traffic that moved at a snail's pace over the floating bridge. Friday afternoons were a nightmare for commuters.

The chatter stopped and judging by the sounds she heard coming from the back seat, Dori guessed that Danny and Melissa were having a heated discussion under their breaths. Dori thought she heard Tom's name but let it pass. With all the problems it caused, she doubted she'd be seeing him again. For his part, Tom was hoping to settle things with his wife and move back home for the holidays. Dori knew that Jon would be pleased to have his father back, and she prayed Tom's wife would be as willing.

Following the Saturday expedition to the grocery store, the three attended Danny's soccer game. To Melissa's delight, Danny scored two goals and was cheered as a hero when he ran off the field at the end of the game. Luckily they arrived back home before it started to rain. Dori popped the corn and the two children watched a late-afternoon movie on television.

The phone rang just as Dori was finishing the dinner dishes. She reached for it and glanced at Danny and Melissa who were playing a game of Risk in the living room.

"Hello," she answered absently.

"Dori, it's Gavin. How are things going?" The long-distance echo sounded in her ear.

"Fine," she returned smoothly, unreasonably pleased that he'd phoned. "They've had their first spat but rebounded remarkably well."

"What happened?"

"Melissa wanted to try on some of my makeup and Danny was thoroughly disgusted to see her behaving like a real girl."

"Did you tell him the time will come when he'll appreciate girls?"

"No." Her hand tightened around the receiver. Gavin was a thousand miles from Seattle. The sudden warmth she felt at hearing his voice made her thankful he wasn't there to witness the effect he had on her. "He wouldn't have believed it, coming from me."

"I'll tell him. He'll believe me."

Danny would. If there was anything wrong with this relationship, it was that Danny idealized Gavin. One day, Gavin would fall off Danny's pedestal. No man could continue to breathe comfortably so high up, in such a rarefied atmosphere. Dori only hoped that when the crash came, her son wouldn't be hurt. "Are you having a good time with your cronies?" she asked, leaning against the kitchen wall.

He chuckled and the sound produced a tingling rush of pleasure. "Aren't you afraid I've got a woman in the room with me?"

"Not in the least," she answered honestly. "You'd hardly phone here if you did."

"You're too smart for your own good," he chided affectionately. He paused, and Dori's blood raced through her veins. "You're going to San Francisco with us, aren't you?"

"Yes," she answered softly.

"Good." No word had ever sounded more sensuous to Dori.

She straightened quickly, frightened by the intensity of her emotions. "Would you like to talk to Melissa?"

"How's she behaving?"

Dori chuckled. "As predicted."

"I told you she would. Do you want me to say something?"

Gavin was obviously pleased that his daughter's behavior was running true to form. "No, Danny will undoubtedly list my virtues for hours the next time you have him."

"I'll look forward to that."

"I'll bet." Hiding her mirth, Dori set the phone aside and called Melissa, who hurried into the kitchen and picked up the receiver. Overflowing with enthusiasm, she relayed the events of the day, with Danny motioning dramatically in the background, instructing Melissa to tell Gavin about the goals he'd scored that afternoon. Eventually Danny got a chance to report the great news himself. When the children had finished talking, Dori took the receiver back.

"Have they worn your ear off yet?"

"Just about. By the way, I might be able to catch an early flight out of here on Sunday, after the game."

She hadn't seen Gavin since her date with Tom, and much as she hated to admit it, she wanted to spend some time with him before they left for San Francisco. "Do you need me to pick you up at the airport?"

"If you could."

"I'll see if I can manage it."

Before ending the conversation, Dori wrote down Gavin's flight number and his time of arrival.

Late the following afternoon, the three of them were sitting in the molded plastic chairs at the Sea-Tac International. They'd arrived early enough to watch Gavin's plane land, and Dori frequently found herself checking her watch, less out of curiosity about the time than out of an unexpected nervousness. She felt she was behaving almost like a love-struck teenager. Even choosing her outfit had been an inordinately difficult task; she'd debated between a wool skirt with knee-high black leather boots and something less formal. In the end she chose mauve corduroy slacks and a thick pullover sweater the color of winter wheat.

"That's Dad's plane now." Melissa bounded to her feet, ran to the floor-to-ceiling window and pointed to the 727 taxiing toward the building.

Dori brushed an imaginary piece of lint from her slacks and cursed her foolish heart for being so glad Gavin was home and safe. With the children standing at either side, her hands resting lightly on their shoulders, she forced a strained smile to her lips. A telltale warmth invaded her face and Dori raised a self-conscious hand to brush the hair from her temple. Gavin was the third passenger off the plane.

"Dad." Melissa broke formation and ran to Gavin, hugging him fiercely. Danny followed shyly and offered Gavin his hand to shake. "Welcome back, Mr. Parker," he said politely.

"Thank you, Danny." Gavin shook the boy's hand with all the seriousness of a man closing a million-dollar deal.

"How was the flight?" Dori stepped forward, striving to keep her arms obediently at her side, battling the impulse to greet him as Melissa had done.

His raincoat was draped over one arm and he carried a briefcase with the other hand. Dark smudges under his eyes told her that he was exhausted. Nonetheless he gave her a warm smile. "The flight was fine."

"I thought you said he'd kiss her," Danny whispered indignantly to Melissa. The two children stood to one side of Dori and Gavin.

"It's too public... I think." Melissa whispered back and turned accusing eyes on her father.

Arching two thick brows, Gavin held out an arm to Dori. "We'd best not disappoint them," he murmured. "We're liable not to hear the end of it for the entire week."

One hand was all the invitation Dori needed. No step had ever seemed so far—or so close. Relentlessly, Gavin held her gaze as she walked into the shelter of his outstretched arm. His hand slipped around the back of her neck, bringing her closer. Long fingers slid into her soft auburn hair as his mouth made a slow, unhurried descent to her parted lips. As the distance lessened, Dori closed her eyes, more eager for this than she had any right to be. Her heart was doing a drumroll and she moistened her suddenly dry lips. She heard Gavin softly suck in his breath as his mouth claimed hers in a slow, provocative exploration.

Of their own accord, her hands moved over the taut muscles of his chest and shoulders until her fingers linked behind his neck. In the next instant, his mouth hardened, his touch firm and experienced and unbelievably warm. The pressure of his hand at the back of her neck lifted her onto the tips of her toes, forcing the full length of her body intimately close to the unyielding strength of his. The sound of Gavin's briefcase hitting the floor barely registered to her numbed senses. Nor did she resist when he wrapped both arms around her so tightly that she could barely breathe. All she could taste, feel, smell, was Gavin. She felt as if she had come home after a long time away. He'd kissed her before, but it had never been like this, like a hundred shooting stars blazing a trail across an ebony sky.

Dori struggled not to give in to the magnificent light show, not to respond with every facet of her being. She had to resist. Otherwise, Gavin would know everything.

The grip of his hand at the back of her neck was painful, but Dori didn't object. If Gavin was experiencing the same overwhelming emotion as she was, he'd be just as confused and disarmed. He broke the contact and buried his face in her hair, mussing it as he rubbed his jaw over it several times.

"That kiss has to be a ten," he muttered thickly, unevenly.

"A nine," she insisted, her voice weak. "When we get to ten, we're in real trouble."

"Especially if we're in an airport."

Gavin's hold relaxed, but he slipped his hand around her waist, bringing her closer to his side. "Well, kids, are you happy now?"

"You dropped your suitcase, Mr. Parker." Danny held it out to him and eyed Melissa gleefully. He beamed from ear to ear.

"So I did," Gavin said, taking the briefcase. "Thanks for picking it up for me."

"Dori put a roast in the oven," Melissa informed him, "just in case you were hungry. I told her how starved you are when you get home from these things and how much you hate airplane food."

"Your father's tired, Melissa. I'll have you both over for dinner another time."

"I appreciate the thought," Gavin told Dori, his gaze caressing her. "But I *have* been up for the past thirty hours."

A small involuntary smile crept up the corners of Dori's mouth. She hadn't been married all those years to Brad without having some idea of the way a man thought and behaved away from home.

Gavin's eyes darkened briefly as if he expected a sarcastic reply. "No comment?"

"No comment," she echoed cheerfully.

"You're not worried about who I was with?"

"I know, or at least I think I do," she amended.

Gavin hesitated, his eyes disbelieving. "You think you do," he said with a sarcastic smile.

"Well, not for a fact, but I have a pretty good hunch of what you were up to."

"This I've got to hear." His hand tightened perceptibly around her trim waist. "Well?"

Both Danny and Melissa looked concerned. They were clearly disappointed that Dori wasn't showing signs of jealousy. Obviously, the two assumed Gavin had been with another woman. Dori doubted it. If he had, he wouldn't be so blatant about it with her. Nor would he mention it in front of the children.

"I'd guess that you were with some football friends, drinking beer, eating pretzels and probably playing a hot game of poker."

The smug expression slowly faded as a puzzled frown drew his brows together and hooded his dark eyes. "That's exactly where I was."

Disguising her pride at guessing correctly was nearly impossible. "Honestly, Gavin, think about it. I'm two months away from being thirty. I've been married. I know the way a man thinks."

"And men are all alike," he taunted.

"No," she said, trying desperately to keep a straight face. "But I'm beginning to know you. When you quit asking me if I'm concerned who you were with, then I'll worry."

"You think you're pretty smart, don't you?"

"No," she was forced to disagree. "Men I can understand. It's children that baffle me."

He continued to hold her close as they walked down the long concourse. Melissa and Danny skipped ahead.

"Were they a burden this weekend?" Gavin inclined his head toward the two youngsters.

"Nothing I couldn't handle."

"I have the feeling there's very little you can't handle."

Self-conscious now, Dori looked away. There was so much she didn't know, so much that worried her. And the main object of her fears was walking beside her, holding her as if it were the most natural thing in the world—as if he meant to hold on to her for a lifetime. But Dori knew better.

CHAPTER SEVEN

THE DISCORDANT CLANGING BELL of the cable car sounded as Dori, Melissa, Danny and Gavin clung precariously to the side. A low-lying fog was slowly dissipating under the cheerful rays of the early afternoon sun.

"When are we going to Ghiradelli's?" Melissa wanted to know, her voice carried by the soft breeze. "I love chocolate."

"Me too," Danny chimed in eagerly.

"Soon," Gavin promised, "but I told Dori we'd see Fisherman's Wharf first."

"Sorry, kids." Although Dori was apologizing, there was no regret in the shining brightness of her eyes. The lovely City of Saint Francis was everything she remembered, and more. The steep, narrow streets, brightly painted gingerbread houses, San Francisco Bay and the Golden Gate Bridge. Dori doubted that she'd ever tire of the subtle grace and beauty of this magnificent city.

They'd arrived Thanksgiving Day and gone directly to a plush downtown hotel. Gavin had reserved a large suite with two bedrooms that were connected to an immense central room. After a leisurely dinner of turkey with all the traditional trimmings, they'd gone to bed, Gavin and Danny in one room, Dori and Melissa in the other, all eager to explore the city the following morning.

After a full day of viewing Golden Gate Park, driving down Lombard Street with its famous ninety-degree curves, and strolling the water's edge at Fisherman's Wharf, they returned to their hotel suite.

Melissa sat in the wing backed chair and rubbed her sore feet. "I've got an enormous blister," she complained loudly. "I don't think I've ever walked so much in my life. There's nothing I want more than to watch television for a while and then go straight to bed." She gave an exaggerated sigh and looked toward Danny, who stared back blankly. When he didn't immediately respond, Melissa hissed something at him that Dori couldn't understand, then jabbed him in the ribs with her elbow.

"Oh. Me too," Danny agreed abruptly. "All I want is dinner and bed."

"You two will have to go on without us," Melissa continued with a look Joan of Arc would have envied. "As much as we'd like to join you, it's probably best we stay here."

Gavin caught Dori's gaze and rolled his eyes toward the ceiling. Dori had difficulty containing her own amusement. The two little matchmakers were up to their tricks again. "But we couldn't possibly leave you alone and without dinner," Dori said in a concerned voice.

"I'm not all that hungry." For the first time Danny looked unsure. He'd never gone without dinner in his life and lately his herculean appetite seemed likely to bankrupt her budget. For Danny to offer to go without a meal was the ultimate sacrifice.

"Don't worry about us—we can order room service," Melissa said with the casual ease of a seasoned traveler. "You two go on alone. We insist. Right, Danny?"

"Right."

By the time Dori had showered and dressed, Danny and Melissa were poring over the room-service menu like two people who hadn't eaten a decent meal in weeks. Gavin appeared to be taking the children's rather transparent scheme in his stride, but Dori wasn't so confident. They'd had two wonderful days together. Gavin had once lived in San Francisco and he gave them the tour of a lifetime. If Gavin had hoped that Melissa and Danny would overdose on each other's company, his plan was failing miserably. The two had never gotten along better.

After checking the contents of her purse, Dori sat on the end of the bed and slipped on her imported leather pumps. Then she stood and smoothed her skirt. Her pulse was beating madly and she paused to place her hand over her heart and inhale a deep, soothing breath. She felt chilled and warm, excited and apprehensive, all in one. Remembering how unemotional she'd been about their first dinner date only made her fret more. That had been the night of the fights, and she recalled how she hadn't really cared what she wore. Ten minutes before Gavin was due to pick her up, she'd added the final coat of polish to her nails. Tonight, she was as nervous as she'd ever been in her life. Twenty times in as many minutes she'd worried about her dress. This pink-and-gray outfit with its pleated front bodice and long sleeves ending in delicate French cuffs was her finest, but it wasn't an evening gown. Gavin was accustomed to women far more worldly and sophisticated than she could ever hope to be. Bolstering her confidence, Dori put on her gold earrings and freshened her lipstick. With fingers clutching the bathroom sink, she forced a smile to her stiff lips and exhaled a ragged breath. Dear heavens, she was falling in love with Gavin Parker. Nothing could be worse. Nothing could be more wonderful, her heart responded.

When she reentered the suite's sitting room, Melissa and Danny were sprawled across the thick carpet in front of the television. Danny gave her a casual look and glanced away, but Melissa did an automatic double take.

"Wow!" the young girl murmured in a low breath and immediately straightened. Her eyes widened appreciatively. "You're—"

"Lovely." Gavin finished for his daughter, his eyes caressing Dori, roving slowly from her lips to the swell of her breasts and downward. "An angel couldn't look any lovelier."

"Thank you." Dori's voice died to a whisper. She wanted to drown in his eyes. She wanted to be in his arms. A long silence ran between them and purposely Dori looked away, her heart racing.

"Don't worry about us," Melissa said confidently.

"We'll be downstairs if you need anything," Gavin murmured, taking Dori by the elbow.

"Be good, Danny."

"I will," he answered without glancing up from the television screen.

"And no leaving the hotel room for any reason," she warned.

"What about a fire?"

"You know what we mean," Gavin answered for Dori.

"Don't hurry back on our account," Melissa said, propping up her chin with one hand as she lay sprawled on the carpet. "Danny and I'll probably be asleep within the hour."

Danny opened his mouth to protest, but closed it at one fierce glare from Melissa.

Gavin opened the door and Dori tossed a smile over her shoulder. "Have fun, you two."

"We will," they chimed merrily.

The door closed and Dori thought she heard them give a shout of triumph.

Gavin chuckled and slid a hand around her trim waist, guiding her to the elevator. "I swear those two have all the finesse of a runaway roller coaster."

"They do seem to be a bit obvious."

"Just a bit. However, this is one time that I don't mind being alone with you." His hand spread across the hollow of her back, lightly caressing the silken material of her dress. Slowly his hand moved upward to rub her shoulder. His head was so close that Dori could feel his breath against the sensitized skin of her neck. She didn't know what kind of game Gavin was playing, but her heart was a far too willing participant.

At the whirring sound of the approaching elevator, Gavin straightened. The hand at her back directed her inside, and he pushed the appropriate button.

Inside the restaurant, the maître d' led them to a linen-covered table in the middle of the spacious room and held out Dori's chair for her. Smiling her appreciation, she sat, accepted the menu and scanned the variety of dishes offered. Her mouth felt dry, and judging by the way her nerves were acting, Dori doubted she'd find anything that sounded appetizing.

No sooner were they seated and comfortable than the wine steward, wearing a crisp red jacket, approached their table. "Are you Mr. Parker?" he asked in a deep resonant voice.

"Yes." Gavin looked up from the oblong menu.

The red-coated man snapped his fingers and almost immediately a polished silver bucket was delivered to the table. Cradled in a bed of ice was a bottle of French champagne.

"I didn't order this." His brow was marred by lines of bewilderment.

"Yes, sir. This is compliments of Melissa and Danny in room 1423." Deftly he removed the bottle from the silver bucket and held it out for Gavin's inspection. As he read the label, Gavin raised his thick eyebrows expressively.

"An excellent choice," he murmured.

"Indeed," the steward agreed. With amazing dexterity he removed the cork and poured a sample into Gavin's glass. After receiving approval from Gavin, he filled both their glasses and left.

Gavin held up his glass for a toast. "To Melissa and Danny."

"To our children." Dori's answering comment was far more intimate than she'd meant it to be.

The champagne slid smoothly down Dori's throat and eased her tenseness. She closed her eyes and savored the bubbly tartness. "This is wonderful," she whispered, setting her glass aside. "How did Melissa and Danny know how to order such an exquisite label?"

"They didn't. I have a strong feeling they simply asked for the best available."

Dori's hand tightened around the stem of her glass. "Oh, my goodness, this must have cost a fortune." Color flooded her face, blossoming in her pale cheeks. "Listen, let me pay half. I'm sure Danny played a part in this and he knows that I love champagne. It's my greatest weakness."

"You're not paying for anything," Gavin insisted with mock sternness. "The champagne is a gift and if you mention it again, you'll offend me."

"But Gavin this bottle could well cost a hundred dollars and I can't—"

"Are we going to argue?" His voice was low and warm.

Dori felt a throb of excitement in her veins at the way he was studying her. "No," she answered finally. "I'll agree not to argue, but under protest."

"Do you have any other weaknesses I don't know about?" he inquired smoothly.

You! her mind tossed out unexpectedly. Struggling to maintain her composure, she shrugged and dipped her gaze to the bubbling gold liquid. "Bouillabaisse."

Something close to a smile quirked his mouth as he motioned for the waiter and ordered the fish stew that was cooked with a minimum of eight different types of seafood. In addition, Gavin ordered hearts-of-palm salad, another uncommon delicacy. Taking their menus, the waiter left the table and soon afterward the steward returned to replenish their champagne.

Relaxing in her chair, Dori propped her elbows on the table. Already the champagne was going to her head. She felt a warm glow seeping through her, heating her blood.

The bouillabaisse was as good as any Dori had ever tasted; the wine Gavin had ordered with their meal was mellow and smooth.

While they lingered over cups of strong black coffee, Gavin spoke freely about himself for the first time. He told her of his position with the computer company and the extensive traveling it sometimes involved. The job was perfect for him since it gave him the freedom to continue broadcasting during the football season. Setting his own hours was a benefit of being part-owner of the computer firm. He spoke of his goals for the future and his love for his daughter; he spoke of the dreams he had for Melissa.

His look was poignant in a way she had never expected to see in Gavin. A longing showed there that was deep and intense, a longing for the well-being and future happiness of those he loved. He didn't mention the past or the glories he'd achieved on the football field. Nor did he mention his marriage to Deirdre. No comment was necessary; his reactions to his ex-wife had said it all.

Every part of Dori was conscious of Gavin, every nerve, every cell. Dori had never thought to experience such a spiritual closeness with another human being again. She saw in him a tenderness and a vulnerability he rarely exposed. So often in the past, just when Dori felt she was beginning to understand Gavin, he'd withdrawn behind a hard shell, where he kept his feelings hidden most of the time. The fact that he was sharing these confidences with Dori told her he'd come to trust and respect her, and she rejoiced in it.

The waiter approached with a pot of coffee and Dori shook her head, indicating that she didn't want any more.

Gavin glanced at his watch. "Do we dare go back to the suite? We've only been gone two hours."

The way she was feeling, there wasn't any place safe for her with Gavin tonight. She wanted to be in his arms so badly that she was almost anticipating the softness of his touch. She cast about for an excuse to stay. "They'd be terribly disappointed if we showed up so soon."

"There's a band playing in the lounge," he suggested smoothly. "Would you care to go dancing?"

"Yes." Her voice trembled slightly with renewed awareness. "I'd like that."

Gavin didn't look for a table when they entered the lounge. A soft, melodious ballad was playing and he guided her directly to the dance floor and turned her into his arms.

Dori released a long sigh. She linked her fingers at the back of his neck and pressed the side of her face against the firm line of his jaw. Their bodies were intimately close until Dori could feel the uneven rhythm of his heartbeat and recognized that her own was just as erratic. They made only the pretense of dancing, holding each other so tight that for a moment even breathing was impossible. Dragging air into her constricted lungs, Dori closed her eyes to the fullness of emotion that surged through her. For weeks she'd been battling her feelings for Gavin. She didn't want to fall in love with him. Now, in these few brief moments since he'd taken her in his arms, Dori knew that it was too late. Her heart was already committed. She loved him. Completely and utterly. But admitting her love now would only intimidate him. Her intuition told her that Gavin wasn't ready to accept her feelings yet or acknowledge his own. Pursuing this tiny spark could well extinguish it before it ever had a chance to flicker and flame.

"Dori." The raw emotion in his voice melted her heart. "Let's get out of here."

"Yes," she whispered, unable to force her voice any higher or make it any stronger.

Gavin led her off the tiny floor and out of the lounge and through the bustling lobby. He hesitated momentarily, as if undecided about where they should go.

"The children will be in bed," she reminded him softly.

The elevator was empty and just as soon as the heavy doors closed, Gavin wrapped his arms around her.

Shamelessly yearning for his kiss, Dori tilted her head back and smiled up at him boldly. She saw his eyes darken with passion as he lowered his head. Leaning toward him, she met his lips with all the eager longing that this evening had evoked. Gavin kissed her with a fierce tenderness until their breaths became mingled gasps and the elevator slowed to a stop.

Sighing deeply, Gavin tightened his hold, bringing her even closer. "If you were to kiss me like this every time we entered an elevator, I swear we'd never get off."

"That's my own fear," she murmured and looked deeply into his eyes.

He was silent for a long moment. "Then perhaps we should leave now, while we still can." His grip relaxed slightly as they stepped off the elevator.

No light shone from under the door of their suite, but Dori doubted that they would have any real privacy in the room. Undoubtedly Melissa and Danny were just inside the bedroom doors, eager to document the most intimate exchanges between their parents.

Gavin quietly opened the door. The room was dark; what little light there was came from a bright crescent moon that shone in through the windows. They walked into the suite, Gavin's arm around her waist. He turned, closed the door and pressed the full length of her body against it, his gaze holding hers in the pale moonlight.

"I shouldn't kiss you here," he murmured huskily as if he wanted her to refuse.

Dori could find no words to dissuade him—she wanted him so badly. The moment seemed to stretch out. Then, very slowly, she raised her hands to explore the underside of his tense jaw. Her fingertips slid into the dark fullness of his hair and she raised herself onto the tips of her toes to gently place her lips over his. The pressure was so light that their lips merely touched and their breath mingled.

Gradually his mobile mouth eased over hers in exquisite exploration, moving delicately from one side of her lips to the other. The complete sensuality of the kiss quivered through Dori and she experienced a heady sweep of warmth. A sigh of breathless wonder slid from the tightening muscles of her throat. The low groan was quickly followed by another as Gavin's mouth rocked over hers in an eruption of passion and desire that was all too new and sudden. She'd thought these feelings, these very sensations, had died with Brad. She wanted Gavin. She couldn't have stopped him if he'd lifted her in his arms and carried her to the bedroom. The realization shocked her.

His hands stroked the curves of her shoulders as he nibbled at her lips, taking small, sensuous bites. His long fingers tangled themselves in the soft strands of her hair, and he dragged his mouth over her cheek to her eyes and nose and grazed her jaw. She felt him shudder and held his head close as she took in huge gulps of oxygen, trying to control her growing desire. The need to experience the intimate touch of his hands and mouth flowered deep within her. Her breasts ached to be held and kissed. Yet he restrained himself with what Dori believed was a great effort.

"If you rate that kiss a ten, then we're in real trouble," he muttered thickly, close to her ear.

"We're in real trouble."

"I thought as much." But he didn't release her.

"Knowing Danny, I'd guess he's probably videotaped this little exchange." The delicious languor slowly left her limbs.

"And knowing Melissa, I'd say she undoubtedly supplied him with the tapes." Gradually, his arms relaxed their hold.

"Do you think they'll try to blackmail us?" she said, hoping to end the evening in a lighter vein.

"I doubt it," Gavin whispered confidently. "In any case, I have the perfect defense. I believe we can attribute tonight to expensive champagne and an excellent meal, don't you?"

No, she didn't. Dori was forced to swallow an argument. She knew that this feeling between them had been there from the time they'd boarded the plane in Seattle. Gavin had wanted to be alone with her tonight, just as she'd longed to be with him. Even the kissing was a natural consequence of this awakened discovery.

Deciding that giving no answer was better than telling a lie, Dori faked an exaggerated yawn and murmured, "I'd better think about bed; it's been a long day."

"Yes," Gavin agreed far too easily. "And tomorrow will be just as busy."

They parted in the center of the room, going in the opposite directions, toward their respective rooms. Dori undressed in the dark, not wanting to wake Melissa—if indeed Melissa was asleep. Even if she wasn't, Dori didn't feel up to answering the young girl's questions.

Gently lifting back the covers of the twin bed, Dori slipped between the sheets and settled into a comfortable position. She watched the flickering shadows playing against the opposite wall, tormenting herself with doubts and recriminations. Gavin attributed this overwhelming attraction to the champagne. Briefly she wondered what he'd say if it happened again. And it would. They'd come too far to go back now.

THE FOLLOWING AFTERNOON, Melissa, Danny and Dori sat in front of the television set to watch the San Francisco Forty-niners play the Denver Broncos. Dori was not particularly interested in football and knew very little about it. But she had never before watched a game that Gavin was broadcasting. Now she listened proudly and attentively to his comments, appreciating for the first time his expertise in the area of sports.

Frank Gifford, another ex-football player, was Gavin's announcing partner and the two exchanged witticisms and bantered freely. During halftime, the television camera crew showed the two men sitting in the broadcast booth. Gavin held up a pad with a note that said, "Hi, Melissa and Danny."

The kids went into peals of delight and Dori looked on happily. This four-day weekend was one she wouldn't forget. Everything had been perfect—perhaps too perfect.

Gavin returned to the hotel several hours after the end of the game. His broad shoulders were slightly hunched and he rubbed a hand over his eyes. His gaze avoided Dori's as he greeted the children and sank heavily into a chair.

"You were great," Danny said with unabashed enthusiasm.

"Yeah, Dad." The pride in Melissa's voice was evident.

"You're just saying that because the Forty-niners won and you were both rooting for them." Gavin's smile didn't quite reach his eyes.

"Can I get you something, Gavin?" Dori offered quietly, taking the chair across from him. "You look exhausted."

"I am." His gaze met hers for the first time since he'd returned. The expression that leaped into his eyes made her catch her breath, but just as quickly an invisible shutter fell to hide it. Without a word, he turned his head to the side. "I don't need anything, thanks." The way he said it forced Dori to wonder if he was referring to her. That morning, he'd been cool and efficient, but Dori had attributed his behavior to the football game. Naturally he would be preoccupied. She hadn't expected him to take her in his arms and wasn't disappointed when he didn't. Or so she told herself.

Melissa sat on the carpet by Gavin's feet. "Danny and I knew you'd be tired so we ordered a pepperoni pizza. That way, you and Dori can go out again tonight and be alone." The faint stress placed on the last word caused telltale color to suffuse Dori's face.

She opened her mouth to protest, then closed it. She certainly wasn't ready for a repeat performance of their last meal together, but she wanted to hear what Gavin thought. His gaze clashed with hers and narrowed fractionally as he challenged her to accept or decline.

"No," Dori protested quickly, her voice low and grave. "I'm sure your dad's much too tired. We'll have pizza tonight."

"Okay." Melissa shot to her feet, willing to cooperate with Dori's decision. "Danny and I'll go get it. The pizza place is only a couple of blocks from here."

"I'll go with you," Dori offered, not wanting the two children walking the streets by themselves after dark.

A hand stopped her, and Dori turned to find Gavin studying her. His mouth twisted wryly; his eyes were chilling. "What's the matter?"

She searched his face to find a reason for the subtle challenge in his question. "Nothing," she returned smoothly, calmly. "You didn't want to go out, did you?"

"No."

"Then why are you looking at me like I'd committed some serious faux pas?" Dori tipped her head to one side, not understanding the change in him.

"You're angry because I didn't hold up your name with the kids' this afternoon."

Dori's mouth dropped open in shock. "Of course not. That's crazy." Gavin couldn't honestly believe something that trivial would bother her.

But apparently he did. He released her arm and leaned back in the cushioned chair. "You women are all alike. You want attention, and national attention is all the better. Right?"

"Wrong!" She took a step in retreat, stunned by his harshness. Words failed her. She didn't know how to react to Gavin when he was in this mood and from the look of things, she expected it wasn't about to change.

Dori's thoughts were prophetic. Gavin seemed withdrawn and unnaturally quiet on the flight home early the next morning. He didn't phone her in the days that followed. Over the past few weeks, he'd taken the time to call her twice and sometimes three times a week. Now there was silence—deafening silence that echoed through the canyons of emptiness he'd exposed in her life. Worse than the intolerable silence was the fact that she found herself sitting by the phone, eagerly waiting for his call. Her own reaction angered her more than Gavin's silence. And yet, Dori thought she understood why he didn't contact her. And with further reasoning, she realized that she mustn't contact him. Maybe he thought she would; maybe he even wanted her to, but Dori wouldn't, couldn't. For Gavin was fighting his feelings for her. He knew that what had happened between them that evening in San Francisco couldn't be blamed on the champagne, and it scared the living hell out of him. He couldn't see her, afraid of what he'd say or do. It was simpler to invent some trumped-up grievance, blame her for some imaginary wrong.

Friday morning, after a week of silence, Dori sat at her desk, staring into space.

"Are you and Gavin going out this weekend?" Sandy asked, with a quizzical slant of one delicate brow.

Dori returned her attention to the homeowner's insurance policy on her desk. "Not this weekend."

"Is Gavin announcing another football game?"

"I don't know," she responded without changing her expression.

"Did you two have a fight or something?"

"Or something," Dori muttered dryly.

"Dori." Sandy's eyes became serious. "You haven't ruined this relationship, have you? Gavin Parker is perfect for you. Whatever's happened, make it right. This fish is much too rich and good-looking to toss back for another fisherman. Reel him in very carefully, Dori, dear."

A hot retort trembled on the tip of her tongue, but Dori swallowed it. Not once had she thought of Gavin as a big fish, and she didn't like the cynical suggestion that she should carefully reel him in or risk losing him. Their relationship had never existed on those terms. Neither of them was looking for anything permanent—at least not in the beginning.

Dori's mood wasn't much better by the time she returned home.

Danny was draped over the sofa, his feet propped up against the back, his head touching the floor. "Hi, Mom."

"Hi." She unwound the scarf from around her neck and unbuttoned her coat with barely repressed anger. Stuffing her scarf in the sleeve, she reached for a hanger.

"Aren't you going to ask me about school?"

"How was school?" For the first time in years, she didn't care. A long soak in a hot bath interested her far more. This lackadaisical mood infuriated her.

"Good."

Dori closed the hall closet door. "What's good?"

Danny untangled his arms and legs from the sofa and sat up to stare at her. "School is." He cocked his head and gave her a perplexed look. "You feeling sick?"

It was so easy to stretch the truth. She was sick at heart, disillusioned and filled with doubts. She never wanted to see Gavin Parker again, and she was dying for a word from him. Anything. A Christmas card would have elated her, a business card left on her doorstep, a chain letter. Anything. "I'm a little under the weather."

"Do you want me to cook dinner tonight?"

"Sure." Her willingness to let Danny loose in the kitchen was a measure of how miserable she felt. Last week at this time they'd been flying to San Francisco and Gavin had been sitting in the seat beside hers. A sad smile touched her mouth as she remembered how Gavin had reached for her hand when the plane sped down the runway ready for take-off. When she'd objected that she wasn't afraid of flying, he'd smiled brightly into her eyes, brushed his lips over her cheek and told her that *he* was afraid and that she should humor him. What a difference one week could make.

"You want me to cook?" Danny was giving her a puzzled look again.

"There might be a TV dinner in the freezer. Put that in the oven."

"What about you?"

Dori hesitated before heading down the long hallway to her room. "I'm not hungry." There wasn't enough chocolate in the world to get her through another week of not hearing from Gavin.

"Not hungry? You must really be sick."

Dori's appetite had always been healthy and Danny knew it. "I must be," she said softly, and went into the bathroom to run hot water into the tub. On impulse she added some bath-oil beads. While the water was running, she stepped into her room to get her pajamas, the faded blue housecoat with the ripped hem and a pair of thick socks.

Just as she was sliding into the fragrant mass of bubbles, Danny knocked anxiously on the bathroom door.

"Go away," she murmured irritably.

Danny hesitated. "But, Mom—"

"Danny, please," she cried. "I'm miserable. Give me a few minutes to soak before hitting me with all your questions." She could hear him shuffling his feet outside the door. "Listen, honey, if there are any cookies left in the cookie jar, they're yours. Eat them in good health and don't disturb me for thirty minutes. Understand?"

Dori knew she should feel guilty, but she was willing to bend the rules this once if it brought peace and quiet.

"You're sure, Mom?"

"Danny, I want to take a nice, hot, uninterrupted bath. Got that?"

He hesitated again. "Okay, Mom."

Dori soaked in the bath until all the bubbles had disappeared and the hot water had turned lukewarm. This lethargy was ridiculous, she decided, nudging up the plug with her big toe. The ends of her auburn curls were wet, but after brushing it, Dori left it free to hang limply around her face. The housecoat should have been discarded long ago, but it suited Dori's mood. The socks came up to her knees and she slipped her feet into rabbit-shaped slippers that Danny had given her for Christmas two years before. She seldom wore them but felt she owed her son an apology for repeatedly snapping at him. The slippers had long floppy ears that dragged on the ground and pink powder-puff tails that tickled her ankles. They were easily the most absurd-looking things she owned, but wearing them was her way of apologizing.

"Hi, Mom…" Danny hesitated when she stepped into the living room, concern creasing his young face. "You look terrible."

Dori didn't doubt it, with her limp hair, old ragged housecoat and rabbit slippers.

"Mr. Parker's never seen you look so awful."

"He won't, so don't worry."

"But, Mom," Danny protested loudly. "He'll be here any minute."

CHAPTER EIGHT

FOR A WILD INSTANT, Dori resisted the panic. "He's not
coming." She'd waited all week for him to call and heard
nothing. And now he was about to appear on her doorstep,
and she didn't want to see him. She couldn't face him,
looking and feeling the way she did. In her heart she was
pleading with her son to say that Gavin wasn't really coming. "I'm sure Gavin would phone first." He'd better!

"He did, Mom." Danny gave her a look of pure innocence.

"When?" Dori shouted, her voice shaking.

"While you were running your bathwater. I told him
you'd had a bad day and wanted to soak."

"Why didn't you tell me?" she cried, giving way to alarm.

The doorbell chimed and Dori swung around to glare at
it accusingly. Gripping her son by the shoulders, she had the
irrational urge to hide behind Danny. "Get rid of him,
Danny. Understand?"

"But, Mom—"

"I don't care what you have to tell him." She must be
crazy to make an offer like that, Dori realized.

The doorbell continued to ring in short, impatient peals.
Before either mother or son could move, the front door
opened and Gavin sauntered in. "What's the problem with
you two? Couldn't you see..." His words faded to a whisper as his gaze collided with Dori's. "Has anyone called the
doctor? You look terrible."

"So everyone's been telling me," she snapped, clenching
her fists at her sides. All week she'd been dying for a word

or a glance, anything, from Gavin and now that he was here, she wanted to throw him out of her house. Whirling, she stalked into the kitchen. "Go away."

Gavin followed her there and stood with his feet braced as if he expected a confrontation. "I want to talk to you."

Dori opened the refrigerator door and set a carton of eggs on the counter, ignoring him. She wasn't hungry, but scrambling eggs would give her mind something to concentrate on and her hands something to do.

"Did you hear me?" Gavin demanded.

"Yes, but I'm hoping that if I ignore you, you'll go away."

Whistling a carefree tune, Danny strolled into the room, pulled out a kitchen chair and sat down. His eager gaze went from his mother to Gavin and again to Dori, and they both stared back at him warningly.

"You two want some privacy, right?"

"Right," Gavin answered.

"Before I go, I want you to know, Mr. Parker, that Mom doesn't normally look like . . . this bad."

"I realize that."

"Good. I was worried because . . ."

"Danny," Dori hissed. "You're doing more harm than good."

The chair scraped against the linoleum floor as he pushed it away from the table. "Don't worry," he said, gesturing with his hands. "I get the picture."

Dori wondered how her son could claim to know what was going on between her and Gavin when even she didn't have the slightest idea. For that matter, she suspected Gavin didn't, either.

Taking a small bowl from the cupboard, she cracked two eggs against the side.

"How was your week?" Gavin wanted to know.

Dori squeezed her eyes shut and mentally counted to five. "Wonderful."

"Mine too."

"Great." She couldn't hide the sarcasm in her voice.

"I suppose you wondered why I didn't phone?" Gavin said next.

Dori already knew, but she wanted to hear it from him. "It had crossed my mind once or twice," she said flippantly, as she whipped the eggs with a vengeance such that they threatened to slosh out of the small bowl.

"Dori, for heaven's sake, would you turn around and look at me?"

"No!" A limp strand of hair fell across her cheekbone and she jerked it aside.

"Please." His voice was so soft and caressing that Dori felt her resistance melt away.

With her chin tucked against her collarbone, she battled down a mental image of herself with limp, lifeless hair, a ragged housecoat and silly slippers. She turned toward him, her fingers clenching the counter as she leaned against it for support.

Gavin moved until he stood directly in front of her and placed his hands on her shoulders. Absurd as it was, Dori noticed that his shoes were shined. Worse, they were probably Italian leather, expensive and perfect. A finger lifted her chin, but her eyes refused to meet his.

"I've missed you this week," he whispered, and she could feel his heated gaze resting on her mouth. It took all Dori's strength not to moisten her lips and invite his kiss. She felt starved for the taste of him. A week had never seemed so long. "A hundred times I picked up the phone to call you," he continued.

"But you didn't."

"No." He sighed unhappily and slowly shook his head. "Believe it or not, I was afraid."

His unexpected honesty allowed her to meet his gaze openly. "Afraid?"

"Things are getting a little thick between us, don't you think?" His voice rose with the urgency of his admission.

"And heaven forbid that you have any feelings for a thirty-year-old woman," she drew a sharp breath and held out a lifeless strand of auburn hair. "A woman who is about to discover her first gray hair, no less."

"Dori, that has nothing to do with it."

"Of course it does," she argued angrily. "If you're going to become involved with anyone, you'd prefer a twenty-year-old with a perfect body and flawless skin."

"Would you stop!" He shook her shoulders lightly. "What's the matter with you tonight?"

"Maybe this week has given me time to think. Maybe I know you better than you know yourself. You're absolutely right. You *are* afraid of me and the feelings I can arouse in you, and with damn good reason. You're attracted to me and it shocks you. If it hadn't been for the kids last weekend, who knows what would have happened between us?" At his narrowed look, she took another deep breath and continued her tirade. "Don't try to deny it, Gavin. *I* can figure a few things out for myself—that's the problem when you start seeing a woman whose brain doesn't leak. I've got a few live brain cells left in this ancient mind and I know darned well what's going on here. I also know what you're about to suggest."

"I doubt that." His brow furrowed with displeasure.

"It's either one of two things," she continued undaunted.

"Oh?" He took a step in retreat, defiantly crossed his arms and leaned against the kitchen table. His gaze was burning her, but Dori ignored the heat.

"Either you want to completely abandon this charade and never see each other again. This, however, would leave you with a disgruntled daughter who is persistent enough to have you seek out a similar arrangement with another woman. Knowing the way you think, I'd say that you probably toyed with this idea for a while. However, since you're here, it's my guess that you decided another mature woman would only cause you more trouble, given time. You're so irresistible that she's likely to fall in love with you. It's best to deal with the enemy you know—namely me."

His mouth was so tight that white lines appeared at the corners of his lips. "Go on."

"Option number two," she continued on a wobbly breath. "This one, I'll tell you right now, is completely unacceptable and I deplore you for even thinking it."

"What hideous crime have I committed in my thought-life now?" he inquired on a heavy note of sarcasm.

All week the prospect of his "invitation" had been going through her mind. Oh, he'd undoubtedly deny it, but the intention was there; she'd stake a month's salary on it. "You are about to suggest that we both abandon everything we think of as moral to sample marriage."

"Believe me—" he snickered loudly "—marriage is the last thing on my mind."

"I know that. I said *sample*, not actually commit the act. You were about to suggest that Danny and I move in with you. This, of course, would only be a trial run to see if things go smoothly. Then you'd call it off when things got complicated or life was disrupted in any way. My advice to you on that one is don't even bother suggesting it. I'd never agree and I'll think less of you for asking."

"Less than you already do," he finished for her. "Be assured the thought never entered my mind."

Dori could have misjudged him, but she doubted it. "Take a good look at me," she said and held out the sides of her ragged terry-cloth housecoat. Its tattered blue hem dragged on the kitchen floor. "Because what you see is what you get."

Gavin might not have been angry when he arrived, but he was now. "What I can see is that having any kind of rational discussion with you is out of the question."

Lowering her gaze, Dori released a jagged sigh. "As you may have guessed, I'm not the best of company tonight. I...I didn't mean to come at you with my fingers in the claw position." The apology stuck in her throat. She wished he'd leave so she could indulge her misery in private.

"I'll admit to having seen you in better moods."

She decided to ignore that. "As I said, it's been a rough week."

A long moment passed before Gaving spoke again and when he did, Dori could tell that he'd gained control of his anger. "There's a Neil Simon play at the 5th Avenue. Do you think you'll feel well enough to go tomorrow night?"

The invitation was so unexpected that it stunned Dori. The muscles of her throat seemed paralyzed, so she merely gave an abrupt nod.

"I'll pick you up around seven-fifteen. Okay?"

Again, all Dori could manage was a nod.

He turned to leave, then paused in the doorway. "Take care of yourself."

"I will."

Dori heard the living room door close, and she shuddered in horror at herself. What was the matter with her? She'd come at Gavin like a madwoman. Even now, she didn't know what he'd actually intended to say.

The recriminations and self-doubts remained with her the following afternoon. Perhaps because of them she splurged and had her hair styled at the local beauty parlor, a rare treat. Dori wanted to tell her stylist to do something new and exciting that would disguise her years and make five pounds instantly disappear. But she decided not to bother—the woman did hair, not magic tricks.

Dori couldn't recall any other date that had involved so much planning, not even her high school prom. She bought a fashionable jumpsuit that came with a fancy title: "Rhapsody in Purple." The label said it was sophisticated, dynamic and designed for the free-spirited woman, and for tonight, those were all the things she wanted to be. Reminding herself that it was the season to be generous and that she deserved some generosity herself, Dori plunked down her credit card, praying the purchase wouldn't take her over her credit limit.

At home, she hung the outfit on the back of her bedroom door and studied it. The soft, pale lavender jumpsuit had pleats, pads and puffs, and for what she'd paid, it should have been fashioned out of pure gold. The deep V in the back made it the most daring outfit she owned.

Dori had delivered Danny to her parents' house earlier that afternoon, so she was dressed and ready at seven. While she waited for Gavin, she searched the newspaper, looking for an advertisement for the play. He had told her it was a Neil Simon comedy, but he hadn't mentioned which one. A full-page blurb announced the title: *The Odd Couple*. Dori nearly laughed out loud; the description so aptly fitted her and Gavin. She certainly didn't know any odder couple.

Gavin was right on time, a minor surprise, and did a double take when Dori opened the door.

"Hi," she said almost shyly, holding her head high. Her dangling gold earrings brushed the curve of her shoulders.

"Hello..." For the first time in recent memory, Gavin seemed at a loss for words. He let himself into the living room, his gaze never leaving hers. "For a woman with dying brain cells and wrinkled skin, you look surprisingly good."

"I'll take that as a compliment," she said, priding herself on not rising to the bait. Any reaction from Gavin was good, she felt, and a positive one was worth every penny of the jumpsuit. "You don't look so bad yourself."

He straightened his tie and gave her another of his dazzling smiles. "So my innumerable female companions tell me."

That was another loaded comment best ignored. Dori reached for her handbag, an antique one beaded with a thousand minute pearls. She tucked it under her arm and smiled brightly, eager to leave. From past experience, Dori knew that they'd have trouble finding a parking space if they dallied over drinks.

Gavin hesitated as if he expected her at least to offer something, but she felt suddenly ill-at-ease, anxious to get to the theater and into neutral territory. "We should probably leave, don't you think?" she asked flatly.

Gavin frowned and looked toward her hall closet. "What about your coat?" he said in a lightly mocking voice.

"I don't need one." A woman didn't wear "Rhapsody in Purple" with a full-length navy blue coat. This jumpsuit was created for minks and ermine, not wool.

"Dori, don't be ridiculous. It's just above freezing out there. You can't go outside without a coat."

"I'll be fine," she argued. "I'm naturally warm-blooded."

"You'll freeze," he replied.

Grudgingly, Dori stomped across the room, yanked open the hall closet and threw on her winter coat. "Satisfied?"

"Yes," he breathed irritably, burying his hands deep within the pockets of his dark overcoat. Dori suspected he was resisting the urge to throttle her.

"I'll have you know I'm ruining my image," she muttered with ill grace, stalking past him and out the front door.

The seats for the play were excellent and the performers had received enthusiastic reviews. But Dori had trouble concentrating on the characters and the plot. Although Gavin sat beside her, they could have been strangers, for all the notice he gave her. He didn't touch her, hold her hand or indicate in any way that he was aware of her closeness. Nor did he laugh at the appropriate times. His mind seemed to be elsewhere—which pleased Dori immensely. Of course, her own concentration wasn't much better.

During the intermission, it became her goal to make him aware of her. After all, she'd spent a lot of time, money and effort to attract his attention. And she intended to get it.

Her plan was subtle. When the curtain rose for the second act, Dori crossed her legs and allowed the strap of her sandal to fall loose. With her heel exposed, she pretended to inadvertently nudge his knee. She knew she'd succeeded when he crossed his legs to avoid her touch. Part two of her plan was to place her hand on the common arm between their seats. Before he was aware of it, she'd managed to curl her fingers around the crook of his elbow. Almost immediately she could feel the tension drain out of him, as though he'd craved her touch, hungered for it. But that couldn't be. If that was how he felt, why hadn't he simply taken her hand? Gavin was anything but shy. This reluctance to touch her shattered her preconceived ideas about him and why he'd asked her out. When he'd admitted the night before that he was frightened, he hadn't been overstating his feelings. The revelation must have cost him a great deal, and she'd carelessly tossed it back in his face and then hurled her own accusations at him. He wanted to be with her, enjoyed her company, perhaps even loved her. Earlier he'd admitted that he'd missed her that week, and she'd cut him off with her fiery tirade. Now she wanted to groan and cry at her own stupidity.

Dori wanted to take him in her arms and humbly ask him to forgive her. She wanted to drop to her knees and plead with him to tell her what he'd really come to say. Regret, doubt and uncertainty all collided in her mind, drowning out the performers on the stage.

Oh, dear heaven! Could Gavin have realized that he loved her? Maybe. Even if he wasn't ready to act on his feelings, he had at least reached the point of discussing them. And she'd blown it. She'd taunted him in her outraged presumptions of a trial marriage, condemning him before he'd even spoken. Dori closed her eyes at the agony of her own thoughtlessness.

In that moment, when all the doubts crashed together in her mind, Gavin lifted his hand and closed it over hers, holding her slender fingers in his warm grasp.

Dori couldn't breathe; she couldn't move. An eternity passed before she could turn her face to him and see for herself the wonder she knew would be waiting for her. What she found nearly brought her to tears. His eyes were gentle and yielding in their dark depths, his look potent enough to bring her to her knees.

The play ended without either of them noticing and they applauded politely only because those surrounding them did. When the audience came to its feet, Gavin and Dori rose, but his hand continued to grip hers as if he didn't ever want to let her go.

Dori had never felt such deep communication with another person. If he admitted to being frightened, then so was she. Dori hadn't expected Gavin to come to her so easily. She loved him but had assumed it would take him far longer to acknowledge his feelings.

"The play was good," he said as he helped her into her coat. His voice was only slightly husky.

"Wonderful." Hers was overwhelmed by emotion. But if he noticed, Gavin gave no indication. It took all Dori had not to throw her arms around his neck and kiss him. A tiny smile bracketed her mouth, as she reflected that if he'd known what she was thinking, Gavin would have been grateful for her restraint.

The drive back to her house was accomplished in a matter of minutes. He pulled to a stop at the curb, but kept his hand on the steering wheel. "Is Danny with his grandparents tonight?"

Dori had the impression that he didn't ask it conversationally but out of a desire to be alone with her. Her heart pounded painfully. "Y-yes."

He gave her a funny look. "Are you feeling sick again?"

"No, I'm fine." Dori cursed the fact that life had to be so complicated. "Would you like to come in for coffee?" They both knew the invitation was a pretense. When Gavin took her in his arms, she didn't want half the neighborhood watching.

The car engine was still running and Gavin made an elaborate show of checking his watch. "Another time," he said softly, "it's late."

Ten forty-five was not late! If Dori was confused before, it was nothing to the myriad of bewildered emotions that went through her now. "You wanted to say something to me yesterday," she tried again, struggling to sound calm and composed. She forced a smile despite the catch in her voice. "I can't apologize enough for the way I behaved."

"One thing about you, Dori, you're completely unpredictable."

"You did want to tell me something?" she repeated.

"Yes." He paused and she noticed the way his fingers tightened around the steering wheel. "As I said, things are getting a little heavy between us."

"Yes," she whispered tenderly, her heart in her eyes.

"That was something I hadn't planned on."

"I know." Her throat constricted at the strong emotion she felt for him.

"In light of what happened in San Francisco..." He hesitated. "We reached a ten on that last kiss and even you said a ten meant trouble. Lord only knows where we'd progress from there."

"I remember." Who was he trying to kid? They both knew where they were headed and it wasn't the kitchen. She didn't know why he was hedging this way. Everything seemed relatively simple to her.

"Dori," he said hesitantly and cleared the hoarseness from his throat. "I've been thinking that perhaps we've been seeing too much of each other. Maybe it would be best if we cooled things for a while."

No words could have been more unexpected. All this time she'd been waiting to hear a profession of undying love and he'd been trying to tell her he wanted out. To her horror, her eyes filled with stinging tears. Fiercely she blinked them away. Her fingers curled around the door handle in her haste to escape. What a fool she'd been!

"Sure," she managed to stammer without disgracing herself. "Whatever you think is best." The car door swung open and she clambered out in such a frenzied rush that she was fortunate not to trip. "Thank you for the play. As I said before, it was wonderful." Not waiting for any response, she slammed the car door shut and hurried toward the house. The sound of his door opening and closing made her suck in a savage breath and battle for control.

"I thought you said you didn't want any coffee," she said, without turning around to face him. The porch light was sure to reveal her tears and that would embarrass them both.

"Dori, listen, I'm sorry. But I need some time to sort things out. Whatever is going on between us is happening too fast. Give me time to work things out."

From the distance of his voice, Dori guessed he was about halfway up the sidewalk. "I understand." She did, far better than he realized. She'd looked at him with adoring eyes and all the while he'd been trying to think of some way to dump her—or as he'd say, let her down easily. Her eyes blinded by tears, she ripped open her purse and searched hurriedly for the keys. "Don't worry, you've got all the time in the world," she muttered, clenching the house key between stiff fingers.

"A month. All I want is a month." The pause in his voice revealed his uncertainty.

"Take six," she returned impertinently. "Why stop there—make it ten." She wanted to laugh, but the noise that erupted from her throat was a dry, pain-filled sob.

"Dori." His shoe scraped sharply against the porch steps and then there was a tentative moment of silence as he stood there, looking up at her. "Are you crying?"

"Who me?" She laughed, sobbing again. "I'm only a few weeks short of being thirty, Gavin. Women my age don't cry. You don't want to see me again. Fine. I'm mature enough to accept that."

"Turn around and let me see your face."

Her chest heaved with the effort of not sobbing openly. She was such a fool.

"Dori, I didn't mean to hurt you."

"I'm not hurt!" she shouted and leaned her forehead against the screen door. Afraid another sobbing hiccup would escape, she covered her mouth with the palm of her hand. When she was finally able to catch her breath, she turned to face him. "I'm fine, so please don't feel obligated to stick around here. Danny and I'll be just fine."

"Dori, oh, Lord—"

"I'm fine," she insisted and wiped the tears from her face. "See?" Without another word, she turned back to the door, inserted the key and let herself into the house.

"DID YOU HAVE FUN with Mr. Parker last night, Mom?" Danny sat at the kitchen table with Dori who was sipping from a mug of hot coffee. Her mother had phoned earlier to announce that she could drop Danny off on her way to do some errands.

"The play was great." Dori felt frail and vulnerable but managed to give her son a wan smile. Her thoughts were darker and heavier than they'd been since she lost Brad. Danny would have to be told that her relationship with Gavin had come to a standstill, but it wasn't going to be an easy thing to do. "Did you have a good time with Grandma and Grandpa?"

"Yeah, but I'll be glad when you and Mr. Parker decide to get married because I'd rather be a family. Melissa and I could stay alone together and I wouldn't have to have a sitter or go to Grandma's house every time you want to go out."

"Danny, listen." Dori struggled to maintain an unemotional facade, although she felt as if her heart were breaking. "Mr. Parker and I have decided it would be best if we didn't see each other for a while."

"What?" Danny's mouth dropped open in utter disbelief. "But why? I thought you really liked each other. I thought you might even be considering marriage. Melissa was sure..." He let the rest drop as if he'd inadvertently divulged a top secret.

"No." She lowered her gaze and swallowed tightly. There was no choice but to give Gavin exactly what he'd asked for—time. She hoped and prayed that the budding love he felt for her would be strong enough to bring him back, but she couldn't depend on it. "Gavin isn't ready for that kind of commitment yet and this is something you and I must accept."

"But, Mom—"

"Listen," Dori implored, taking his small hand between her own. "You must promise me that you won't contact Gavin in any way. Sometimes adults need time to think, just like kids do, and we have to respect that. Promise me, Danny. This is important."

He studied her intently, finally nodding. "What about Melissa? Will we be able to see her?"

The two had become good friends and Dori hated to punish them for their parents' problems. "I'm sure some kind of arrangement could be made to have her over on the weekends that Gavin is broadcasting football games." For that matter, Gavin need never know, though she was certain Melissa wouldn't be able to resist telling him.

"You love him, don't you?"

Dori's smile was wistful. "Gavin Parker is a rare man and loving him is easy. But it won't be the end of the world if we never see him again."

Danny's eyes widened incredulously as though he found her words completely shocking. "But Mr. Parker was perfect."

"Yes," she agreed, "he met each requirement on our list, but there are lots of other men who will, too."

"Are you going to start looking for another father for me?" Danny rested his chin in the palms of his hands, his eyes forlorn.

Immediate protests crowded her mind. "Not for a while." Like Gavin, she needed time, but not for the same reasons he did. For her, it would be a waiting game. In a few weeks, she would know if her gamble had paid off. She was a fool to have allowed her heart to become involved; he'd warned her often enough. Now she was suffering the consequences.

In the days that followed, Dori was amazed at her strength of will. It wasn't easy, but when thoughts of Gavin invaded her well-defended mind, she efficiently cast them aside. He didn't make any effort to get in touch with her and she didn't expect him to. Whatever had happened with Deirdre had hurt him so badly that it was possible he would never risk committing himself to another woman. That was his and Melissa's loss . . . and hers and Danny's.

On Wednesday morning, as Dori stirred hot water into the instant oatmeal, she flipped through the pages of the paper. "Danny," she tossed over her shoulder. "Hurry, or you'll be late for school."

"Okay, Mom." His muffled voice drifted from his bedroom.

Setting his bowl on the table, Dori leaned against the counter and turned to the society page, looking for the Dear Abby column. At first she didn't recognize the people in the picture that dominated the front page of the society section.

Then her glance came to rest on Gavin's smiling face and her heart suddenly dropped to her knees. The oxygen became trapped in her lungs, making it painful to breathe. Some blond-haired beauty was grasping his arm and smiling up at Gavin adoringly. Dori knew the look well. Only a few days before she'd gazed at him in exactly the same doting way. She felt a knife twist in her heart as she read the accompanying article, which described the opening of the opera season with a gala performance of Bizet's *Carmen*. So this was how Gavin was using his time to sort through his feelings for her. It hadn't taken him long to seek out a woman with flawless skin and a perfect body. *Let him,* her mind shouted angrily. Foolish tears burned her eyes and she blinked them away, refusing to give in to the emotion.

"Mom, what's the matter? You look like you want to hit someone."

"I do?" Hurriedly, she folded the paper and stuffed it in the garbage can. "It's nothing. Okay?"

Danny cocked his head and gave her a lopsided look. "Mr. Parker told me that sometimes women can act weird. I guess this is one of those times."

"I'm sick of hearing about Mr. Parker all the time." She jerked open the refrigerator and took out bread for her son's lunch. When he didn't respond, she whirled around. "Did you hear me?"

Danny was paying an inordinate amount of attention to his cereal. "I suppose. Are you going to cry or something?"

"Of course not! Why should I? It's almost Christmas."

His spoon worked furiously, stirring the sugar into the cinnamon-and-raisin-flavored oatmeal. "I don't know, but when your mouth twists up like that, it always means you're real upset."

"Thanks," she returned flippantly.

The remainder of the day was as bad as the morning had been. Nothing went right. She mislaid a file. Her thoughts drifted during an important meeting and when Mr. Sandstorm asked her opinion, Dori hadn't the foggiest idea of what they'd been discussing. Sandy had given her a sympathetic look and salvaged a potentially embarrassing moment by speaking first. As a thank-you Dori bought her friend lunch, though she couldn't really afford it.

The minute she walked into the house, Dori kicked off her shoes and paused to rub her aching arches. Danny was nowhere to be seen and she draped her coat over the back of a kitchen chair, wondering where he'd gone now. He was supposed to stay inside until she got home. She took a package of hamburger out of the refrigerator, but the thought of coming up with a decent meal was almost more than she could face.

As she turned, she noticed the telephone. The receiver was off the hook. The cord stretched around the corner and disappeared into the hall closet. Danny. She crossed to the door and pulled it open.

Danny was sitting cross-legged on the floor and at Dori's intrusion, he glanced up, startled, unable to disguise his sudden look of guilt.

"All right, Daniel Robertson, just who are you talking to?"

CHAPTER NINE

"OH, HI, MOM," he managed awkwardly, struggling to his feet.

"Who is on the other end of the line?" She repeated her question, but already her mind was whirling with possibilities, all of them unpleasant. If it was Gavin, she was likely to do something stupid, such as grab the receiver and drone in a mechanical-sounding voice that the call had just been disconnected. The memory of his helpful little strategy produced a familiar twinge in her heart. Oh, Lord, she missed Gavin more than she'd ever thought possible. There was no point in trying to fool herself any longer. She was miserable.

"I'm talking to a girl," Danny admitted reluctantly, hot color creeping up his neck at being caught.

"Erica?"

"No." He lowered his gaze and reluctantly handed her the receiver. "It's Melissa."

Dori entered the closet, pushing aside their winter coats, and sat on the floor. For the past few days, she'd been cranky with Danny. She hoped this gesture would show him that she regretted being such a grouch.

Amused at his mother's actions, Danny sat across from her and closed the door. Immediately they were surrounded by a friendly darkness. "Hello, Melissa," Dori murmured into the receiver. "How are you?"

"Fine," the thirteen-year-old answered seriously, "I think."

"Why the 'I think' business? It's nearly Christmas and there's lots of things happening. A young girl like you shouldn't have a care in the world."

"Yes, I know." Melissa sounded depressed, but Dori didn't know how deeply she should delve into the girl's unhappiness. Where Gavin was concerned—and that included his relationship with his daughter—Dori was particularly vulnerable. She loved Gavin and felt great affection for Melissa.

Danny was whispering furiously at her from his end of the closet.

"Excuse me a minute, Melissa. It seems Danny has something extremely important to tell me." She placed her palm over the receiver and glared at her son in the dark. "Yes, Danny."

"Melissa's got a mother-daughter fashion thing at her school and she doesn't have anyone to bring."

Dori nodded knowingly. "Danny says that your school is having a fashion show."

"My home ec class is putting it on. I sewed a jumper and everything. It's almost as pretty as the outfit you helped me buy. The teacher gave me an A on it."

"Congratulations. I'm sure you did a good job to have rated such a high grade." Already Dori knew what was coming and she dreaded having to turn the girl down. But with the way things stood between her and Gavin, Dori couldn't very well offer to go.

"I sewed it superbly," Melissa admitted with a charming lack of modesty. "It's the best thing I ever made. Better even than the apron, but then I had to take the waistband off four times. I only made one minor mistake on the jumper," she continued, her voice gaining volume and speed with each word. "I sewed the zipper in backward, you know, so the tab was on the inside. I thought it was all right, it still went over my head and everything, but I had to take it out and do it over again. I was mad at myself for being so dumb." She paused to draw in a giant breath, then hurried on. "Will you come and pretend to be my mother? Please, oh, please won't you, Dori? Everyone has a mother coming, except me."

"Oh, Melissa." Dori's shoulders slumped forward as she sagged against the wall. "Honey, I don't know." Her stomach started churning frantically. She hated to refuse the girl, but Gavin was likely to read something unintended into her acceptance.

"Dori, please, I won't ask anything of you ever again. I need a pretend mother for just one night. For the fashion show."

The soft, pleading quality of the girl's voice was Dori's undoing. She played briefly with the idea of suggesting that Melissa ask Lainey, until she recalled the girl's reaction to the blatant blonde. Despite her misgivings, Dori couldn't ignore the yearning in Melissa's request. "I'll do it on two conditions," she agreed cautiously.

"Anything." The young voice rose with excitement.

"First, you mustn't tell any of your friends that I'm your mother. That would be wrong. As much as I wish I had a daughter like you, Melissa, I can never be your mother."

"Okay," she agreed with some reluctance, slightly subdued. "What else?"

"I don't want your father to know that I've done this." Gavin would be sure to see more in this simple act of kindness than there was. "Okay, Melissa?"

"That's easy. He won't even need to know because everything's taking place at the school and he never goes there on weekdays. And I promise not to tell him."

"Then I guess all I need to know is the date and time."

"Next Monday at seven-thirty. May I talk to Danny again?"

"Sure." Dori handed the telephone receiver back to her son and got awkwardly to her feet, hitting the top of her head on the rod positioned across the small enclosure. "Ouch," she muttered, as she gingerly opened the door, seeking a safe passage out.

A few minutes later Danny joined her in the kitchen where Dori was frying the hamburger. "That was real nice of you, Mom."

"I'm happy to do it for Melissa. She's a very special young lady." Gavin loved his daughter—that Dori didn't doubt—but she hoped he appreciated her, as well.

"Melissa was real worried about the fashion show. I thought it was tough not having a dad, but I guess it's just as bad without a mom."

And without a husband, Dori thought. "I'm sure it is," she replied smoothly. "Now how about if you set the table?"

"What are we having for dinner?"

Dori looked at the sautéing meat and shrugged. "I don't know yet."

"Aw, Mom, is it another one of *those* meals?"

ON FRIDAY MORNING, Dori overslept. Danny woke her almost twenty minutes after her alarm should have sounded.

"Mom," he murmured, rubbing the sleep from his face. "Aren't we supposed to be up? This isn't Saturday, is it?"

Dori took one look at the silent clock radio, gasped and threw back the covers. "Hurry and get dressed. We're late."

Feeling a little like the rabbit in *Alice in Wonderland*, Dori dashed from one room to the next, exclaiming how late they were. Her shower rivaled Danny's thirty-second baths for a new speed record. She brushed her teeth with one hand and blow-dried her hair with the other. The result was hair that looked as if it had been caught in an egg beater and a toothpaste stain on the front of her blouse.

"Should I buy lunch today?" Danny wanted to know, shoving his arms into a sweatshirt and pulling his head through to gaze at her inquisitively.

"Yes." There was no time to fix it now. "Take a dollar out of my purse."

Danny returned a minute later with her billfold. "All you've got is a ten-dollar bill."

"Oh, great." As she slipped her feet into soft leather pumps, her mind raced frantically. "What about your piggy bank?"

"But, Mom . . ."

"It's a loan, Danny. I'll pay you back later."

"All right," he agreed with all the charity of an ill-tempered loan shark.

"Hurry now. I'll get the car out of the garage."

Dori was parked in the driveway, revving the cold engine, when Danny ran through the garage. He slammed the door shut and climbed into the car.

"I got the dollar."

"Good." She looked over her shoulder as she backed out of the driveway. Traffic was heavy and driving took all her concentration.

"Mom," Danny said after a few minutes, then cleared his throat. "About that dollar."

"Danny, good grief, I'll pay you back tonight. Now quit worrying about it." She slowed to a full stop at a traffic light.

"But I'm going to need it. It's almost Christmas and I can't afford to be generous."

Dori paused to think over his words before turning to stare at her son. "Did you hear what you just said?"

"Yeah, I want my money back."

"Danny." She gave him an incredulous look. Her son couldn't afford to be generous because it was Christmas? The time of the year when love and human goodness were supposed to be at their peak. A low rumbling sound escaped from Dori's throat. Then she began to giggle. The giggles burst into full laughter until her whole body shook and she had to hold her side to keep from laughing harder. Still engrossed in the pure irony of his statement, Dori reached over and hugged her son. "Thanks," she giggled, "I needed that."

"It's not that funny," Danny objected, but he was laughing, too. He brushed the hair off his forehead and suddenly sobered, his hand still raised. "Mom, look, it's Mr. Parker. He's in the car right beside us."

Unable to resist, Dori looked over at the Audi stopped next to her. Her laughter fled as she recognized Gavin. He hadn't seen her and Danny, or if he had, he was purposely looking in the opposite direction. Just when she was wondering what, if anything, she could do, Gavin's eyes met hers. Dori's heart gave a wild leap and began to thump madly as the dark, thoughtful eyes looked straight into hers. Stunned, she recognized an aching tenderness in his face. She saw regret, doubts, even pain. She wanted to smile and assure him that she was fine but that she missed him dreadfully. She wanted to ask him how he was doing and about the picture in the paper. Ten other flighty, meaningless thoughts came to her all at once and she didn't have the opportunity to voice even one. A car horn blared impatiently behind her, and Dori glanced up to notice that the traffic light was green and she was holding up a long line of commuters.

"That was Mr. Parker, wasn't it?" Danny said as she stepped on the gas and rushed forward.

"Yes." Her throat felt dry and though earlier there had been laughter Dori now felt the compelling need to cry. Swallowing the urge, she took the next right-hand turn for Danny's school. A quick look in her rearview mirror revealed Gavin traveling forward, as if seeing each other this way was an ordinary, everyday occurrence. Perhaps he did regret their relationship, perhaps she'd read him wrong from the start and it hadn't meant a thing. But Dori couldn't allow herself to believe that. She had to trust her instincts and hold on to her heart. Otherwise it hurt too much.

Saturday and Sunday passed in a blur of vague anticipation. After seeing Gavin on Friday morning, Dori had half expected that he would call her during the weekend. She should have known better than to try to second-guess Gavin Parker. He did things his own way and although it hurt, Dori loved him exactly as he was. When and if he ever admitted to loving her, she would never need to doubt again. That was how Gavin was. She knew with absolute certainty that when he loved, it would be a complete and enduring love, a love to last a lifetime.

The only bright spot in her disappointing weekend was a phone call from Melissa, who wanted to be sure Dori would attend the Mother-Daughter Fashion Show as she'd promised. During the conversation, the girl casually mentioned that Gavin was in L.A. to broadcast a football game.

Monday evening, Dori dressed in her best professional suit, a charcoal gray two-piece with black pinstripes. She wore a white silk blouse and a small red bow tie that added a touch of bright color to the suit. Danny had agreed to submit to the humiliation of having Jody from across the street come to baby-sit. He was vociferous in letting Dori know that this was a sacrifice on his part and he wanted her to tell Melissa all about his unselfishness.

A light drizzle had begun to fall when Dori pulled into the school parking lot. She was surprised by the large number of cars. Dori had assumed Melissa was exaggerating a bit when she'd declared that she would be the only girl there without a mother. This was, after all, a boarding school and there were bound to be several girls whose mothers hadn't been able to attend.

Melissa was standing just inside the doorway of the large auditorium, waiting for Dori. A smile brightened her intense young face the moment she caught Dori's eye. Rushing to her side, Melissa gave Dori an excited hug and handed her a program.

"Is this the world-famous creation, designed by the renowned Melissa Parker?" Dori inquired with a proud smile. The corduroy jumper was a brilliant shade of dark blue with a frilly robin's-egg-blue blouse underneath.

"Do you like it?" Melissa whirled around, holding out the sides of the skirt in Hollywood fashion. Sheer delight created large dimples in each of her round cheeks. "I think it turned out so pretty. I didn't make the blouse, but you probably guessed that already.''

"It's wonderful.''

Taking her by the arm, Melissa escorted Dori down the middle aisle of folding chairs. "I'm supposed to seat you right here.''

"Where are you going?'' Dori glanced around her curiously. Only a few mothers were sitting near the front and it looked as though these seats were reserved.

"Everything's almost ready so I have to go backstage, but I'll be back later.'' She started to move away but abruptly changed her mind. "The choral group is singing first. They really aren't very good, but please applaud.''

"I will,'' Dori promised, doing her utmost to maintain a serious expression. "I take it you're not singing.''

"Only if I want to offend Sister Helene.''

In spite of herself, Dori chuckled. "Well, break a leg, kid.''

Another mother was seated next to Dori a few minutes later and they struck up an easy conversation. It would have been very easy to pretend Melissa was her daughter, but Dori was careful to explain that she was there as a friend of the Parker family. Even at that, Dori felt she was stretching the truth.

The fashion show began with the introduction of the school staff. Then Dori applauded politely at the end of the first series of songs presented by the choral ensemble. Melissa might not have had a finely tuned musical ear, but her assessment of the group wasn't far off. Nonetheless, the applause was enthusiastic.

Following the musical presentation came the fashion show. Dori straightened in her chair as the announcer, a young girl about Melissa's age, stepped forward to the microphone. Obviously nervous, the girl fumbled with her papers and her voice shook as she started to speak.

Melissa in her navy blue jumper was the fourth model. With natural grace, she walked down the middle aisle, turned once, holding out the skirt with one hand, and paused in front of Dori to display the even stitches of her hem. The mothers loved it and laughed outright.

At the end of the fashion show, the headmistress, Sister Helene, approached the front of the room to announce the names of the students who had made the honor roll for the semester.

"Ladies," the soft voice instructed, "when your daughter's name is read, would you please come forward to stand with her."

When Melissa's name was called out, the girl came to the front of the auditorium and cast a pleading glance at Dori. Her heart pounding, Dori rose from her seat to stand behind Melissa. She noticed that all the mothers with honor-roll daughters came from the first few rows; this was the reason Melissa had escorted Dori to the front. She wished Melissa had said something earlier. But then, it wouldn't have made any difference.

Dori's smile was proud as she placed her hands on Melissa's shoulders and leaned forward to whisper in her ear. "Daughter or not, I'm extremely proud of you."

Twisting her head, Melissa looked up at Dori, her expression somber. "I wish you were my mother."

"I know," Dori murmured quietly, the emotion building until her throat felt swollen with the effort of not crying. Still, she had to brush a stray tear from her cheek and bite her lower lip to keep from sobbing out loud.

The final names were read and there was a round of applause. "What now?" Dori whispered.

"I'm supposed to seat you and bring you a cup of tea and some cookies. Our home ec class made them. They're pretty good...I think. I was doing the sewing...not the cooking." She led Dori to her seat. "I'll be back in a jiffy."

"Fine." Dori crossed her shapely legs and with nothing to do, scanned the program for the fifth time. Her gaze rested on Melissa's name. This child could easily take the place Dori had reserved in her heart for the daughter she'd never had—and never would.

"You enjoyed that little charade, didn't you?" Gavin's voice taunted. Dori turned in shock as he sat down in the vacant chair beside her.

The words ripped through her with the pain of a blunt knife. Her program slipped to the floor and she bent forward to retrieve it. The auditorium seemed to roll beneath her chair and it took Dori a moment to realize it was only her nerves. Fixing a stiff smile on her lips, she straightened, forcing herself to be calm.

"Hello, Gavin," she said with a breathlessness she couldn't control. "What brings you here?"

"My daughter." Heavy emphasis was placed on the possessive pronoun to produce a not-so-subtle reminder that she was an intruder.

"Melissa invited me," Dori said in an attempt to explain her presence. "It's a Mother-Daughter Fashion Show." The minute the words were out, Dori knew she'd said the wrong thing.

"You're not her mother," he replied in a remote, impersonal tone that made her blood run cold.

"No, and I hadn't pretended to be her mother, either."

"That's not the way I saw it. Melissa's name was called and you hurried to the front like every other proud matron."

"What was I supposed to do?" she whispered angrily, her hands clenched in her lap. "Sit there with Melissa giving me pleading looks?"

"Yes," he bit back in a low controlled voice. "Did you think that if you maintained a friendship with my daughter we'd eventually resume our relationship? That's not the way it's going to happen. I asked for some time and you're not giving it to me. Listen, Dori, this isn't any easier on me." He paused and raked a hand through his hair. "Your coming here tonight makes things damned impossible."

A weary sigh came from deep within Dori. Gavin assumed the worst possible explanation for what she'd done. Perhaps he was looking for a reason to hate her and now he had all the excuse he needed.

"I've fended off a lot of women bent on ruining my independence," he said harshly, "but you're the best. You know I love my daughter. She's my weakest link."

Unable to bear any more of his sarcasm, Dori stood. "You've got it all wrong, Gavin. Melissa is your strongest point. You're arrogant, egotistical and so damned stubborn you can't see what's right in front of your face."

"Dori, what's wrong?" Melissa approached her from behind, carefully holding a cup of hot tea in one hand and a small paper plate of cookies in the other.

Dori took the delicate cup and saucer out of Melissa's shaking fingers. Not knowing exactly what to do with them, she handed the cup to Gavin. If he wanted to play mother, then he could drink the weak tea and eat the stale cookies.

"Daddy..." Melissa choked with surprise and turned stricken eyes to Dori. "I didn't tell him, honest."

"I know," Dori assured her.

"What are you doing here...I didn't tell you about...the tea...this is supposed to be for mothers and..." The words stumbled over her tongue in her rush to get them out.

"Sit down," Gavin ordered. "Both of you."

As they seated themselves, he dragged his chair around so that he was facing them both. Dori felt like a disobedient child but refused to give in to the sensation. She had done nothing wrong. Her only motive in attending the fashion show had been kindness; she had responded to the pleas of a young girl who desperately wanted a mother so she could be like the other girls. Dori had come for Melissa's sake alone, and the fact that Gavin was the girl's father had almost deterred her from coming at all—despite what he chose to believe.

"I think you'd better tell me what's going on." His eyes challenged Dori in that chilling way she hated.

"I believe I've already explained the circumstances," she inserted dryly. "However, it seems that you've added two and two and come up with five."

"Dad," Melissa demanded with open defense, taking note of Dori's unapologetic tone, "what are you doing here? This isn't for fathers—you're the only man here."

"The notice came from the school about the fashion show," he explained haltingly, glancing around him. "I have every right to come to my daughter's school any time I darn well please."

"But it doesn't give you the right to say those kinds of things to me," Dori stated calmly and drew together the front of her suit jacket. People sitting nearby were beginning to give them unwanted attention.

Gavin's features hardened and a thick brow was raised derisively in her direction. Without looking at his daughter, he instructed, "Melissa, get Dori another cup of tea."

"But, Dad—"

"You heard what I said."

Reluctantly, Melissa rose to her feet. "I'll be back in a couple of minutes." She took a few steps toward the rear of the auditorium, then turned to Dori again. "They have coffee, if you'd rather have that."

"Either one is fine," Dori answered with a smile and a reassuring wink. She probably wouldn't be around to drink it, anyway.

Gavin waited until his daughter was out of earshot. "This whole situation between us has got out of hand."

Dori crossed her arms and leaned back in the hard folding chair, suddenly weary.

"We had a nice thing while it was going, but it's over. You broke the rules," he said accusingly. "Any attempt on your part to drag it out will only be painful for the kids." His voice was tight with impatience. "I'm seeing someone else now," he explained. "Melissa hasn't met her yet, but she will soon."

Dori drew in a ragged breath and found she couldn't release it. It burned in her lungs until she regained her composure enough to slowly exhale. "I believe that." She didn't know how she could remain so calm when every breath was a struggle and every heartbeat caused pain. Deep down, Dori had realized that Gavin would do something like this. "I'm only surprised you waited so long. I scare you to death, Gavin, and you're running as fast as you can in the opposite direction. No doubt you've seen any number of airhead blondes in the past week."

"You think you know me so well." He eyed her coolly. "This time you're wrong. I saw what was happening with us and came to my senses in the nick of time."

Dori marveled at her self-control. Even though the whole world felt as if it were dissolving around her, she sat serenely, an expression of apparent indifference on her face. Whatever Gavin might say, she still tried to believe that eventually he would recognize that he loved her. All she had were her hopes. He was thickheaded enough to deny his love for her all his life. Dori didn't know what made her think she could succeed where so many others had failed.

"If you expected to shock me with your sudden interest in blondes, you haven't. I know you too well."

"You don't know me at all," he answered, though a deep frown marred his brow.

"From the beginning, I've found you very easy to read, Gavin Parker." Inside, Dori was convulsed with pain, but she refused to allow him to glimpse her private agony. "You love me. You may not have admitted it to yourself yet, but you do and someday you'll recognize that. Date all the blondes you like, but when you kiss them, it'll be my lips you taste and when they're in your arms, it's my body you'll long to feel."

"If anyone loves someone around here, it's you." He spoke as though the words were an accusation.

Dori's smile was infinitely sad. "Yes, I'll admit I love you and Melissa."

"I told you not to fall in love with me," he said bitterly. "I warned you from the beginning not to smell orange blossoms, but that's all you women seem to think about."

Dori couldn't deny his words. "Yes, you did, and believe me, I was just as shocked as you when I realized that I could fall in love with someone so pigheaded, irrational and emotionally scarred." She paused to fight the ache in her throat. "I don't know and I don't even want to know what Deirdre did to you. That's in the past, but you're wearing all that emotional pain like a cement shroud."

"I've heard enough." A muscle flexed in his strong jaw.

Letting her gaze fall, Dori tried to blink back the burning tears. "If you've found someone else who can make you happy, then I wish you the very best. I mean that sincerely, but I doubt you'll ever find that elusive contentment. Goodbye, Gavin. I apologize, I truly do, for ruining a promising agreement. With someone less vulnerable than me, it might have worked."

His gaze refused to meet hers. For all the emotion revealed in his eyes, she could have been talking to a man carved in stone. Without a word he was going to allow Dori to leave. Her heart had persisted in hoping that somehow she'd reach him and he'd stop her.

"You're not leaving, are you?" Melissa spoke from behind, setting the china cup on the seat of the beige metal chair. "I brought your tea."

"I can't stay." Impulsively she hugged the girl and brushed back the thick bangs that hung across Melissa's furrowed brow. "Goodbye." Dori's voice quavered with emotion. She wouldn't see Melissa again. Coming this evening had been a terrible mistake.

Melissa clung to her, apparently understanding what had happened. "Dori," she begged, "please . . . don't leave. I promise . . ."

"Let her go," Gavin barked, causing several heads to turn.

Instantly, Melissa dropped her hands and took a step in retreat. Dori couldn't have borne another moment without bursting into tears. With quick-paced steps, a forced smile on her face, she hurried out of the auditorium. Once outside, she broke into a half trot, grateful for the cover of darkness. She desperately needed to be alone.

By the time Dori pulled into her garage, the tears were making wet tracks down her face. She turned off the engine and sat with her hands clenching the steering wheel as she fought to control her breathing and stem the flow of emotion.

A glance at her watch assured her that Danny would be in bed and, she hoped, asleep.

The baby-sitter eyed Dori's red face curiously but didn't ask any questions. "There's a phone message for you on the table," the teenager said on her way out the front door.

Dori switched on the kitchen light and smiled absently at the name and number written neatly on the message pad. She reached for the phone and punched out his number, swallowing the painful lump that filled her throat.

He answered on the third ring. "Hi, Tom, it's Dori Robertson, returning your call."

"Hi, Dori," he began awkwardly. "I hope I'm not bothering you."

"No bother." She looked up at the ceiling and gently rubbed her burning eyes. "I had a school function to attend for a friend, but I'm home now."

"How are you?"

Dying, her heart answered. "Splendid," she murmured. "Getting ready to do some Christmas shopping. Danny's managed to hone down his Christmas list to a meager three hundred items."

"Would you like some company? I mean, I understand if you'd rather not, feeling the way I do about Paula."

"I take it you two haven't managed to patch things up?"

"Not yet," he said with an expressive sigh. "About the shopping—I'd appreciate some advice on gifts and such."

"I'd be happy to go with you, Tom."

"I know you've been seeing a lot of that ex-football player."

"I won't be seeing him anymore." She choked down a sob and covered her mouth with her hand to keep from crying.

"How about one night this week, then?"

"Fine," she managed, replacing the receiver a minute later, after a mumbled goodbye. Leaning against the wall, Dori made a sniffling attempt to regain her composure. Crying like this was ridiculous. She'd known from the beginning what she was letting herself in for. It wouldn't do any good to cry about it now.

When she wiped her eyes free of tears, she found Danny standing in the doorway of the kitchen, watching her.

"Oh, Mom," he said softly.

CHAPTER TEN

DANNY SAT AT THE KITCHEN TABLE spreading colored butter frosting over the gingerbread men. His look was
thoughtful as he added raisin eyes and three raisin buttons.

The timer on the stove went off and Dori automatically
reached for the padded oven mitt.

"You know, Mom, I don't like Mr. Parker anymore.
Melissa either. I thought she was all right for a girl, but I was
wrong."

"The problem is, Danny, we both love them very much
and telling ourselves anything else would be lying." For
several days Danny had been brooding and thoughtful.
They'd had a long talk after the Mother-Daughter Fashion
Show, and Dori had explained that they wouldn't be seeing
Gavin or Melissa again. Surprisingly, her son had accepted
that without argument.

"I don't love anyone who makes my mom cry," he insisted.

"I'm not crying anymore," she assured him softly, and
it was true, she wasn't. There were regrets, but no more
tears.

Licking the frosting from his fingers, Danny examined the
"new father" requirement list posted on the refrigerator
door. "How long do you think it'll be before we start looking again?"

Dori lifted the cut-out cookies from the sheet with a
spatula and tilted her head pensively to one side. "Not
long." Gradually, her pain-dulled senses were returning to
normal. Dating again would probably be the best thing for

her, but there was a problem. She wanted only Gavin. Loved only Gavin.

When she finished scraping the cookies from the sheet, Dori noticed that Danny had removed the requirement list, strawberry magnet and all, and taken a pencil from the drawer. Then he'd carried everything to the table. Wiping her floury hands on her apron, she read over his shoulder, as his pencil worked furiously across the bottom of the page.

"I'm adding something else," Danny explained needlessly, "I want a new father who won't make my mom cry."

"That's thoughtful, but, Danny, tears can mean several things. There are tears of happiness and tears of frustration, even angry tears. It isn't a bad thing to cry, but sometimes good and necessary." She didn't want to explain that the tears were a measure of her love for Gavin. If she hadn't loved him, it wouldn't have hurt nearly as much when they'd stopped seeing each other.

"Mr. Parker wasn't a very good football player, either," Danny complained.

"He was terrific," Dori countered, "and you know it."

"I threw away all the football cards I had of him, and his autograph."

He said it with a brash air of unconcern as though throwing away the cards had been a trivial thing. But Dori knew better. She'd found the whole collection of treasures—the cards, the autograph and the program from the Seahawks football game he and Gavin attended—in the bottom of his *Star Wars* garbage can and rescued them. Later, he'd regret discarding those items. He was hurt and angry now, but he'd recover. Next autumn, he'd be pleased when she returned the memorabilia so he could brag to his new junior-high friends that he had Gavin Parker's autograph.

"While the cookies are cooling, why don't you bring in the mail."

"Sure, Mom."

Usually Dori could count on Danny's good behavior during the month of December, but lately he'd been even more thoughtful, loving and considerate. She was almost beginning to worry about him. Not once had he nagged her about Christmas or his presents. Nor had he continued to pursue the new father business. Until today, he'd said nothing.

The phone rang as Danny barged into the kitchen, tossing the mail on the counter. He grabbed the receiver and answered breathlessly.

A couple of minutes later he turned to Dori. "Mom, guess what, it's Jon. He wants to know if I can come over and play. He's real excited because his dad is moving back in and they're going to be a real family again."

"That's wonderful. Tell Jon that I'm very happy for him." Dori wasn't surprised. From the thoughtful way Tom had gone about choosing Christmas presents for his wife and family, Dori realized how deep his love ran. He'd never mentioned why he and his wife had separated, but Dori was pleased to hear that they'd settled their problems. Did she dare hope that Gavin would recognize all the love waiting for him and return to her? No man could kiss and hold her the way he had and then cast her aside without regrets. Paula had her Christmas present and Dori wondered if she would ever have hers.

"Can I go over and play? I'll finish decorating the cookies later."

"Don't worry about it. There are only a few from the last batch and I can do those. Go and have a good time."

"Thanks, Mom." He yanked his coat from the closet and blew her a kiss, something he had taken to doing lately instead of giving her a real kiss. Her son was growing up, and she had to learn to accept that.

"Think nothing of it," she called lightly. "And be home in an hour." The last words were cut off as the back door slammed.

Dori watched Danny's eager escape and sighed. Her son was growing up, maturing. She used to look at him and think of Brad, but now she saw that Danny was becoming himself, a unique and separate person.

"No need to get melancholy," she chided herself aloud, reaching for the stack of mail. At a glance she saw it consisted of bills and a few Christmas cards. She carried them into the living room, slouched onto the sofa and propped her slippered feet on the coffee table. The first envelope had a return address she didn't immediately recognize and curiously she ripped it open. Instead of a card, there was a personal letter written on notebook paper. Unfolding the page, Dori's gaze slid to the bottom, where she discovered Melissa's signature.

Dori's feet dropped to the floor as she straightened. After the first line, she bit her bottom lip and blinked rapidly to clear away the ready tears that sprang to the surface.

Dear Dori,

I wanted to write and thank you for coming to the mother-daughter thing. Dad showing up was a real surprise and I hope you believe me when I tell you that I didn't say anything to him, like I promised. Really, I didn't.

Dad explained that I shouldn't bother you anymore and I won't. That's the hardest part because I really like you. I know Deirdre is my real mother, but I don't think of her as a mother. She's pretty, but I don't think she's really very happy about being a mother. When I think of a mother, I think of someone like you who buys groceries in the Albertson's store and tosses the oranges into the cart like a softball pitcher. Someone who lets me try on her makeup and perfume even if I use too much at first. Mothers are special people, and for the first time in my life I got to see one up really close. Thank you for showing me how I want to love my kids.

I feel bad that things didn't work out with you and my dad. I feel even worse that Dad says I shouldn't ever bother you again. I don't think I'm even supposed to be writing this letter, but Sister Helene said I could. It's only polite to properly thank you. I did promise her I wouldn't sign up for choir next year. Just kidding! Anyway, Dad refuses to let me talk about you or Danny. He doesn't seem to have time for me right now, but that's okay because I'm pretty mad at him anyhow.

I'd like to think of you as my mother, Dori, but I can't because every time I do, I want to cry. You told me once how much you wanted a daughter. I sure wish I could have been yours.

Your almost daughter,
Melissa

Tears clouded Dori's eyes as she refolded the letter and placed it back in the envelope. This was one lesson she hadn't ever counted on learning. This helpless, desolate feeling of hurting to the marrow of her bones, of grieving for a man incapable of commitment. Yet there was no one to blame but herself. He'd warned her not to fall in love with him. The problem was, he hadn't said anything about loving his daughter and Dori did love Melissa. And now, instead of two people facing Christmas with heavy hearts, there were four.

Gavin Parker could take a flying leap into a cow pasture and the next time she saw him—if she ever saw him again—she'd tell him exactly that. How long would it take him to realize how much his women loved him? Let him be angry; she was going to answer this letter. And maybe in a few months, when it wasn't so painful, she'd visit Melissa at the school and they'd spend the day together.

Dori's gaze rested on the gaily trimmed Christmas tree and the few presents gathered about the base. This was supposed to be the happiest time of the year. Only it wasn't.

Not for Danny or Dori. Not this year. The stuffed lion
Gavin had won for her sat beside the television, and Dori
couldn't resist the impulse to go over and pick it up. Hugging it fiercely, she let the soft fur comfort her.

When the surge of emotion subsided, Dori took out stationery and wrote a reply to Melissa. Afterward she felt
calmer and even a little cheered. Later that night, after
Danny was in bed, she reread it to be certain she'd said everything she wanted to say and decided no letter could ever
relay all the love in her heart.

Dearest Melissa,

Thank you for your sweet letter. I felt much better
after reading it. I know you didn't tell your father
about the fashion show, so please don't think I blame
you for that.

I'm going to ask you to do something you may not
understand right now. It's important that you not be
angry with your father; he needs you now more than
ever. He loves you, Melissa, very much, and you must
never doubt that. I care about him, too, but you'll have
to love him for both of us. Be patient with him.

Later, after the holidays, if Sister Helene thinks it
would be all right, I'll come and spend a day with you.
Until then, do well in your studies and keep sewing.
You show a definite talent for it—especially for stitch-
ing hems!

You will always hold a special place in my heart,
Melissa, and since I can't be your mother, let me be
your friend.

Love,
Dori

Dori was grateful that December was such a busy month.
If it had been any other time of the year, she might have
fallen prey to even greater doubt and bitterness. Every night

of the following week there was an activity she and Danny were expected to attend. She was with family and friends but had never felt more alone. She felt as if a vital part of herself was missing, and there was—her heart. She had given it to Gavin. And now she was caught in this limbo of apathy and indifference. After he'd panicked and run from her love, Dori had thought she could just take up where she'd left off and resume the even pace of her life. Now she was painfully learning that it would be far longer before she found her balance again. But she would, and that was the most important thing.

At the dinner table two days before Christmas, Danny stirred the mashed potatoes with his spoon and cleared his throat as if to make a weighty pronouncement. "Mom, did you know that this is Christmas Eve's eve?"

Dori set her fork aside to give his words serious consideration. "You're right," she said with a thoughtful look. As she remembered, she'd been about his age when she'd made the same discovery.

"And since it's so close to Christmas and all, I thought maybe it would be all right to open one of my presents."

Dori didn't as much as hesitate. "Not until Christmas morning. Waiting is half the fun."

"Aw, Mom, I hate it. Just one gift. Please."

One practiced look silenced him, and he concentrated on slicing his roast beef into bite-sized pieces. "Are we going to Grandma and Grandpa's again this year?"

They did every year. Dori wondered why Danny asked, when he knew the answer.

"Yes, just like we did last year and the year before that and the year before that and..."

"I get the picture," he mumbled, reaching for his glass of milk. He lifted it to his mouth, then paused, an intense, almost painful look edging its way across his young face. "Do you suppose we'll ever see Mr. Parker and Melissa again?"

"I don't know." A sadness tightened her heart, but she forced a strained smile to her lips. She hoped. Every minute of every hour she hoped, but she dared not say anything to Danny. "Why do you ask?"

"I don't know." He lifted one shoulder in an indifferent shrug. "It just doesn't seem right not seeing them."

"I know." Her throat worked convulsively. "It doesn't seem right for me, either."

Danny pushed his plate aside, his meal only half-eaten. "Can I be excused, Mom? I'm not hungry anymore."

Neither was Dori, for that matter. "Sure," she murmured, laying her knife across her own plate.

Danny carried his dishes to the sink and turned back to Dori. "Do you *have* to work tomorrow?"

Dori wasn't too thrilled at the prospect, either. "Just in the morning. If you like, you can stay home by yourself." Danny was now old enough to be left alone for more than an hour or two. Usually he preferred company, but on Christmas Eve he'd sleep late and then he could watch television until she got home around eleven-thirty.

"Could I really?" He smiled eagerly. "I'd be good and not have anyone over."

"I know."

The following morning Dori had more than one doubt. Twice she phoned Danny from the office. He assured her he was fine, except that he had to keep answering the phone because Grandma had called three times, too. Dori didn't call after that, but when the office closed, she made it to the employee parking lot and out again in record time. On the drive home, she had to restrain herself from speeding. Waiting at a red light, Dori was convinced she'd done the wrong thing in leaving Danny on his own. He wasn't prepared for this type of responsibility. True, he was by himself for an hour after school twice a week, but this was different. He'd been alone in the house for three and a half hours.

The garage door was open for her, and with a sigh of relief she drove inside and parked.

"Danny," she called out, slightly breathless as she walked in the back door. "I'm home. How did everything go?" Hanging her purse in the hall closet, she walked into the living room, faltered and stopped dead. Her heart fell to her knees, rebounded and rocketed into her throat. Gavin was there. There, in her living room. Dressed casually in slacks and a thick sweater, he was staring at her with dark, brooding eyes. Did she dare hope he'd come because he loved her? Her gaze sought Danny, who was perched on the ottoman facing Melissa, who sat in the nearby chair.

"Hi, Mom," Danny looked as confused as Dori felt. "I told them it was okay if they came inside. That was the right thing to do, wasn't it?"

"Yes, yes, of course." Her fingers refused to cooperate as she fiddled with her coat buttons. She was so happy and so afraid that her knees felt like cooked spaghetti, and she sank weakly into the sofa across from Gavin. "This is a..." Her mind went blank.

"Surprise," Melissa finished for her.

A wonderful surprise, her mind threw back. "Yes."

"They brought us Christmas gifts," Danny explained, pointing to the large stack of gaily wrapped presents under the tree.

"Oh." Dori had the impression that this wasn't really happening, that somehow she'd wake and find this entire scene only a vivid dream. "Thank you. I have yours in the other room."

A hint of a smile touched Gavin's mouth, but his piercing dark eyes studied her like a hawk about to swoop down from the skies to capture its prey. "Were you so sure of me?"

"No, I wasn't sure, but I was desperately hoping."

Their gazes held as he spoke. "Danny and Melissa, why don't you go play a game while I talk to Dori."

"I'm not leaving my mom," Danny declared in a forceful voice and sprang to his feet defensively. He crossed the small room to sit beside his mother.

Utterly surprised by his behavior, Dori stared at him, feeling an odd mixture of pride and disbelief.

A muscle moved in Gavin's rigid jaw when Melissa crossed her arms and looked boldly at her father. "I agree with Danny. We should all hear this."

Dori dropped her eyes to keep Gavin from seeing the laughter sparkling there. The kids were obviously going to stay to the end of this, whether they were welcome or not.

Gavin slid to the edge of his seat and raked his hand through his hair in an uncharacteristic gesture of uncertainty.

"I've been doing a lot of thinking about our agreement," he began on a note of challenge. "Things didn't exactly work out the way I planned them, but—"

"I'm not interested in any more agreements," Dori told him honestly, and immediately regretted interrupting him. Not for anything would she admit that it hadn't worked because she'd done exactly what he'd warned her not to do: fall in love with him.

Another long pause followed as he continued to watch her steadily. "I was hoping, Dori, that you would hear me out before jumping to conclusions." Speaking in front of the children was clearly making him uneasy.

Dori made a limp, apologetic motion with her hand. The living room had never seemed so small, nor Gavin so big. Every nerve in her body was conscious of him and she ached for the feel of his comforting arms. "I'm sorry. I won't interrupt you again."

Gavin ignored her and turned his attention to Danny instead. "Didn't you tell me once that you made out a requirement list for a new father?"

"Yes." Danny nodded his head for emphasis.

"Would you get it for me?"

Danny catapulted from the sofa and into the kitchen. Within seconds he was back thrusting the list at Gavin. "Here, but I don't know why you want to read it. You already know what it says."

"I think Dad might want to apply for the position," Melissa said, her eyes glowing brightly. "Dad and I had a really long talk and he feels bad about what happened and decided—"

"Melissa," he said flatly, "it would be best if I did my own talking."

"Okay, Dad." She leaned back against the cushioned chair and heaved an impatient sigh.

Dori's head was spinning like a satellite gone off its orbit. Her hands felt both clammy and cold and she clasped them in her lap.

Gavin appeared to be studying the list Danny had given him. "I don't know that I've done such a terrific job in the father department, but—"

"Yes, you have, Dad," Melissa inserted. "You've been really good."

Despite herself, Dori found she had to smile at Melissa and her "reallys."

"Melissa, please," Gavin barked and paused to smooth the hair he'd rumpled a few minutes earlier. The muscle in his jaw twitched again. "Dori." He said her name with such emotion that her heart throbbed painfully. "I know I don't deserve someone as wonderful as you, but I'd consider it a great honor if you'd consent to marry me."

The words washed over her like warm, soothing waters and she closed her eyes at the rush of feelings that crowded her heart. "Are you saying you love me?" she whispered, unable to make her voice any stronger.

"Yes," he answered curtly.

"This is for us and not because of the kids?" She knew that Melissa held a powerful hand over her father. From the beginning, both Melissa and Danny had tried to manipulate them.

"I want to marry you because I've learned that I don't want to live without you." His response was honest and direct.

"Then yes, I'll be your wife." Dori's was just as straight-forward.

"Okay, let's set the date. The sooner the better."

If he didn't move to take her in his arms soon, she'd embarrass them both by leaping across the room.

"I'm sorry, Mr. Parker, but you can't marry my mom," Danny announced with all the authority of a Supreme Court judge.

"What?" Dori, Melissa and Gavin shouted simultaneously.

Danny eyed all three sternly. "If you read my requirement list for a new father, you'll see that there's another requirement down there now."

Gavin's gaze dropped to the paper clenched in his hand.

"You made my mom cry, Mr. Parker, and you might do it again."

A look of pain flashed across Gavin's face. "I realize that, Danny, and deeply regret any hurt I've caused your mother. If both of you will give me another chance, I promise to make it up to you."

Danny appeared to weigh his words carefully. "Will you make her cry again?"

Frowning thoughtfully, Gavin studied the boy in silence. As she watched them, Dori felt a stirring of love and tenderness for her son and for the man who would become her husband.

"I hope never to cause your mother any pain again," Gavin muttered thickly, "but I can't promise she won't cry."

"Mom." Danny transferred his attention to Dori. "What do you think?"

"Danny, come on," Melissa said with high-pitched urgency. "Good grief, this is what we all want! Don't blow it now."

Danny fixed his eyes on his mother, unswayed by Melissa's plea. "Well, Mom?"

Dori's gaze met and held with Gavin's and her heart leaped wildly at the tenderness she saw. "Yes, it's what I want." They both stood at the same moment and reached for each other in a spontaneous burst of love and emotion. Gavin caught her in his arms and crushed her against his chest as his hungry mouth came down on hers. With a sigh of longing, Dori received his kiss, glorying in the feel of his arms around her. Coming to her and admitting his love and his need had been difficult for him, and she thanked him with all the love stored in her heart.

Twining her arms around his neck, she held him fiercely. She was vaguely aware of Danny murmuring to Melissa—something about leaving so he didn't have to watch the mushy stuff.

Gavin's arms tightened around her possessively, molding her closer to him while his hand slid up and down her spine, gathering her body as close as possible to his own. "Dear Lord, I've missed you," he whispered hoarsely against her lips, then kissed her again, harder and longer as if he couldn't ever get enough of her.

The sensation was so exquisite that Dori felt tears of happiness spring to her eyes and roll unheeded down her cheeks. "Oh, Gavin, what took you so long?"

Drawing back slightly, Gavin inhaled a shuddering breath. "I don't know. I thought it would be so easy to forget you. There's never been a woman in my life who has haunted me the way you have."

Her eyes shone with joyful tears as she smiled mischievously up at him. "Good." What she didn't tell him was that she'd felt the same things.

"Once I'd been in the sunlight, I couldn't go back to the shadows," Gavin murmured. He buried his face in her hair and breathed in deeply. "I tried," he acknowledged with an ironic laugh. "After Deirdre I didn't want any woman to have this kind of power over me."

"I know."

"Why is it you know me so well?"

Smiling happily, she shook her head. "I guess that comes from loving you so much."

"Everything happened just the way you predicted," he said with a look of chagrin. "No matter who I kissed, it was your lips I tasted. When I held another woman, my heart told me something was wrong, and I longed only for you."

"Oh, Gavin." She spread tiny kisses over his face. Her lips met his eyes, nose, jaw and finally his eager mouth. She didn't need to be told that these lessons had been difficult ones for Gavin. Surrendering his freedom to a woman had been an arduous battle between his will and his heart. But now he would find a new freedom in their love for each other. He had finally come to understand that, and she knew he would love her with all his strength.

Gently the side of his thumb wiped a tear from the highest arch of her cheek. "The worst part was seeing you in the car that morning with Danny." Dori heard the remembered pain that made his voice sound husky. "You looked like sunshine and were laughing as if you hadn't a care in the world. I saw you and felt something so painful I can't even describe it. You had me so tied up in knots, I wasn't worth a damn to anyone and there you were, laughing with Danny as if I meant nothing."

"That's not true," she said, her voice filled with tears. "I was dying inside from wanting you."

"You've got me," he said with an uncharacteristic humbleness. "For as long as you want."

"I love you," Dori whispered fervently, laying her trembling hand on his smoothly shaved cheek. "And I can guarantee you that one lifetime will never be enough."

Cradling her face between both his hands, Gavin gazed into her tear-misted eyes and kissed her with a gentleness that bordered on worship.

"I TOLD YOU it'd work," Danny whispered contentedly from just inside the kitchen.

"I knew it all along," Melissa agreed with a romantic sigh. "It was obvious from the time we went to the fair. They're perfect together."

"Yeah, your plan worked good," Danny agreed.

"We're not through yet." Her voice dropped slightly as if she were divulging a secret.

"But they're getting married," Danny argued in low tones. "What more could we want?"

Melissa's sigh came close to belligerence. "Honestly, Danny, think about it. Four is such a boring number. By next year there should be five."

"Five what?"

"People in our family. Now we've got to convince them to have a baby."

"Hey, good idea," Danny said eagerly. "That'd be great. I'd like a baby brother."

"They'll have a girl first. The second baby will be a boy for you. Okay?"

"I'd rather have the boy first."

"Maybe," Melissa said, obviously feeling generous.

Dear Diary—Mom's always grumpy at Christmas, but this year is going to be different.

Your friend,
Patty

MRS. SCROOGE

Barbara Bretton

Chapter One

More than anything in the world ten-year-old Patricia Mary Elizabeth Dean wanted a father. Oh, she knew all about Ronald Donovan, the Air Force captain whose name was on her birth certificate, but except for a dim memory of a tall man with red hair just like hers, Ronald Donovan was nothing more than a biological fact.

Patty knew all about biological facts and how marriage and babies didn't always go hand in hand the way they did in old movies and television sitcoms. She'd heard stories about the days when a young girl had to leave home if she became pregnant out of wedlock but those days were long gone by the time it happened to her mother Samantha. Sam stayed right where she was, in her parents' house in Rocky Hill, and finished her senior year of high school. Nine months pregnant with Patty, she marched up to get her diploma then marched back out of the auditorium and headed for the hospital in Princeton. Five hours later Patty was born, and it seemed that from her very first breath Patty had been looking for a man to be her father.

It wasn't as if she was lonely or unloved or anything like that. She had her mom, Grandma Betty and Grandpa Harry, and enough aunts and uncles to make writing thank-you cards at Christmastime a real pain in the neck. And, of course, there were a pile of nosy neighbors and well-meaning

friends who made sure Patty got home from school when
she was supposed to and that Sam's beat-up old Blazer
started up even on the coldest of winter days.

Patty was healthy, happy, and smart but she didn't have
a father and that one fact made the other facts seem not very
important at all. Her best friend Susan couldn't understand why Patty was so eager to have a father around the
house. "My dad is always telling me I can't stay up to watch
David Letterman," Susan complained just last week. "He
won't let me wear nail polish or get a perm or even think
about going to the movies with Bobby Andretti until I'm
twenty-one. You're really a whole lot better off with just
your mom, believe me."

Of course Patty didn't believe one single word of it. She
knew she was meant to be part of a *real* family like the ones
she saw on television. At night when she closed her eyes, she
dreamed of Cliff Huxtable and Jason Seaver sitting at the
head of the dining room table, carving the Christmas turkey while her mother proudly watched.

Not that Samantha Dean would ever just stand by and
watch, mind you. Patty's mom was as independent and
ambitious as they came. Sam had always managed to keep
a roof over their heads and good food on the table, even
while she juggled school work and taking care of Patty. The
one thing Sam wasn't very good at was finding a man to be
both husband and father, and so it was that Patty had decided to take over the quest.

And the moment Murphy O'Rourke walked into the
room to give his career-day presentation, she knew her
search was over.

Murphy O'Rourke wasn't handsome like a movie star,
although his sandy brown hair was shiny and his hazel eyes
held a friendly twinkle. He wore a brown polo shirt with a
corduroy sport coat that was frayed at the elbows—and
Patty couldn't imagine him sewing on those wimpy patches
Susan's dad had on *his* corduroy sport coat.

He wasn't too short—probably stood just about six feet. He wasn't all pumped up like Arnold Schwarzenegger or real skinny like Woody Allen. He didn't have a fistful of gold rings or ugly puffs of chest hair sticking out of his shirt, and his voice didn't go all oily when he talked to grown-up women. When Mrs. Venturella introduced him to the class he didn't try to be funny or cool or any of the thousand other things that would have been the kiss of death as far as Patty was concerned.

He smiled at them as if they were real live people and said, "Good morning. I'm Murphy O'Rourke," and something inside Patty's heart popped like a birthday balloon.

"That's the one," she whispered to Susan. "He's perfect."

Susan's round gray eyes widened. *"Him?"* The girl looked down at the fact sheet in front of her. "He hasn't even been to college."

"I don't care. He's exactly what I've been looking for."

Susan wrinkled her nose. "He's old."

"So's my mother. That's what makes him so perfect."

"I liked the fireman," said Susan. "Did you see those muscles!" The girl sighed deeply and fluttered her eyelashes, and Patty could barely keep from hitting her best friend over the head with her math notebook.

"The fireman was stupid," said Patty. "He didn't even understand the theory behind water-pressure problems encountered fighting high-rise fires."

"Patty, *nobody* understands things like that except you."

"The nuclear physicist from Bell Labs understood."

"Then why don't you think he's the right man?"

"Because he called me 'little lady' when he answered my question on the feasibility of nuclear power near major urban centers."

"But he was cute," said Susan. "He had the most darling red suspenders and bow tie."

"I hate bow ties."

Susan made a face. "Oh, you hate everything, Patty Dean. I think you're about the snobbiest girl I've ever—"

"Patricia! Susan!" Mrs. Venturella rapped her knuckles sharply against the chalkboard at the front of the room. "If your conversation is so fascinating, perhaps, you'd be willing to share it with the rest of the class."

Susan's cheeks turned a bright red and she slumped down in her chair. "Sorry, Mrs. Venturella," she mumbled.

Patty found herself staring up at the twinkling hazel eyes of Murphy O'Rourke and suddenly unable to speak.

"Patricia," warned Mrs. Venturella. "Don't you have something to say?"

Murphy O'Rourke winked at her and before she knew it, the words came tumbling out. "Are you married?"

All around her the class was laughing but Patty didn't care. This was important.

O'Rourke looked her straight in the eye. "No, I'm not."

"Do you have any kids?"

"No. No kids."

"Do you—"

"That's enough, Patricia." Mrs. Venturella turned to O'Rourke and gave him one of those cute little "I'm sorry" shrugs Patty had seen the woman give Mr. MacMahon, the phys ed teacher with the hairy chest. "I apologize, Mr. O'Rourke. Patricia is one of our advanced students and she has an active curiosity."

"I make my living being curious," he said, then crossed his arms over his chest and leaned back against Mrs. Venturella's desk. He looked straight at Patty. "Go ahead. Ask me anything you want."

"On the *newspaper* business," said Mrs. Venturella, with a stern look for Patty, who still couldn't speak.

"Do you make a lot of money?" Craig Haley, class treasurer, asked.

"Enough to pay my rent," said O'Rourke.

"Did you ever go to China?" asked Sasha D'Amato.

"Twice." He grinned. "And I was thrown out once."

Danielle Meyer held up a copy of the *New York Telegram*. "How come I don't see your name anywhere?"

"Because I quit."

Patty was extremely impressed: he didn't so much as bat an eye when Mrs. Venturella gasped in horror.

"What do you do now?" Patty asked.

"I'm a bartender."

The only sound in the classroom was the pop of Susan's bubble gum.

"Look," he said, dragging his hand through his sandy brown hair, "I didn't mean to misrepresent anything. When you guys called and asked me to speak at the school, I was still a reporter for the *Telegram*. This is a pretty new development."

"Why'd you quit?" Patty asked. If there was anything her mom hated, it was a quitter. She hoped Murphy O'Rourke had a good reason for giving up a glamorous job as a New York City reporter and becoming a run-of-the-mill bartender, or it was all over.

"Artistic freedom," said Murphy O'Rourke.

"Bingo!" said Patty.

She'd finally found her man.

MURPHY O'ROURKE had faced hostile fire in Viet Nam in 1971. He had stared danger in the face everywhere from the subways of New York City to the back alleys of Hong Kong to the mean streets of Los Angeles and never broken into a sweat.

He'd been lied to, cursed at, beaten up and knocked down a time or two but he'd never—not ever—encountered anything like facing sixty curious New Jersey schoolkids on career day at Harborfields Elementary School in Montgomery Township.

All in all, it made running naked down the Turnpike backward in a blizzard seem like a day at the park.

They asked him about passports and phone taps. They asked him about deadlines and drug busts and protecting his sources. Those kids had more questions than the White House press corps and he had a hell of a time keeping up with them.

Why had he let his old man talk him into this, anyway? His father had always been big on community participation and had agreed to this command performance a few months before the massive heart attack that laid him low. When Murphy stepped in to take care of things for Bill, he hadn't expected his job description would include a visit to Sesame Street.

Funny how quickly it all came back to you with the first whiff of chalk dust. The pencils and the rulers; the big jars of library paste and gold stars for perfect attendance; blackboards and erasers and the unmistakable smell of wet boots on a snowy morning. Of course today there was also the hum of computers and the friendly LCD glow of hand-held calculators, but except for a few different trappings, it was still the same.

School.

Even though it had been over twenty-five years since he'd been in the fourth grade, he found that a few things never changed. It wasn't tough at all to peg that dark-haired boy in the first row as the class wiseguy, or the pretty little blonde near the window as the class flirt. The clown and the jock and most-likely-to-end-up-at-trade-school were just as easy to pick out.

But that serious-looking girl with the bright red hair and big blue eyes—damned if he could figure out where she fit in the scheme of things. She didn't ask the usual questions about the glamorous life of a reporter. Instead of giggling when he told his best "I interviewed Tom Cruise" story, she asked him if he'd ever been married. Hell, even after he told her he'd never taken the plunge, she went right ahead and asked him if he had kids, and she never so much as blushed.

In fact she seemed more interested in knowing the details of his after-hours life than the details of his headline-making rescue of an Iranian hostage last year.

When Mrs. Venturella introduced the lawyer—"Anne Arvoti, divorce specialist"—Murphy breathed easily for the first time since he entered the classroom. He nodded at Mrs. Venturella, then was making a beeline toward the door when a small hand snaked out and grabbed him by the coat tails.

The red-haired girl with the ponytail. He should've known.

"You can't leave," she whispered, her freckled face earnest and eager. "There's a party afterward."

"I've got a bar to run," he whispered back, wondering why he felt like he'd been caught playing hooky and she was the truant officer.

"You have to stay," she insisted, clutching his coat more tightly. "I have to make sure that you—"

"Patty!" Mrs. Venturella's voice sounded to his right. "A bit more respect for Ms Arvoti's presentation, if you will."

He had to hand it to the kid. Her cheeks reddened but not for a second did she look away. "Please!" she mouthed, turning her head slightly so her teacher couldn't see. "You have to stay!"

Murphy hesitated. He hated schools. He hated school parties. He hated the thought of answering a thousand questions while he juggled milk and cookies and longed for a stiff Scotch. He had to get back to the bar and take over from Jack so the guy could grab himself some dinner. There was a meeting of the Tri-County Small Business Association at 7:00 p.m., then back to the bar for the usual late-night crowd. The last thing he had time for was playing Captain Kangaroo for a roomful of ten-year-olds.

But, damn it! This kid, Patty, was looking up at him with such unabashed eagerness that the rock that had passed for his heart for longer than he cared to remember thawed a bit.

"Christmas cookies, first of the season," she whispered, her blue eyes eager and bright behind her wire-rimmed glasses. "My mom made them."

"It's only December first," he whispered back. "Aren't you rushing things?"

"Christmas can't come soon enough for me, and, besides, I have a deal to offer you."

If there was one thing Murphy O'Rourke knew, it was when he had been bested. She was probably a Girl Scout pushing chocolate mint cookies. He could handle that.

"Why not?" he said, shrugging his shoulders and taking a seat near the blackboard. One cup of milk, a few Santa Claus cookies, and he'd be out of there.

Another hour. What difference could one more hour possibly make?

IT TOOK MURPHY exactly fifteen minutes to find out.

The kid was some piece of work.

"Fifty dollars," Murphy said, meeting her fierce blue eyes. "Not a penny more."

"Sixty-five dollars a tray," Patty Dean stated in a voice Lee Iacocca would envy. "Anything less and we'd be running in the red."

Murphy threw his head back and laughed out loud. "I don't think you've ever run in the red in your life. You're one tough negotiator."

"Thank you." She didn't even blink. "But it will still be sixty-five dollars a tray. My mother is an expert chef, and food doesn't come cheap."

"Does your father have you on his payroll? You're better at this than most Harvard MBAs."

He caught the swift glitter of braces as a smile flickered across her freckled face. "My mother will be glad to hear that."

"And your dad?"

She shrugged her bony shoulders. "I wouldn't know. The last time I saw him I was two years old."

"Two?"

"Yes," she said. "My long-term memory is excellent and I remember him quite clearly."

Murphy wouldn't have thought it possible but his battle-scarred heart again showed signs of life. He'd grown up without his mother, and he knew that the emptiness never left, no matter how old you got or how successful. "Yeah, well, then tell your mom she has one hell of a business-woman on her hands."

"Sixty-two fifty," Patty said. "Take it or leave it."

"Sixty-three," said Murphy, extending his right hand and engulfing the girl's hand in his. "Not a penny less."

Patty's auburn brows rose above the tops of her eye-glasses. "Sixty-three? Are you certain?"

"Take it or leave it."

"You're got yourself a deal, Mr. O'Rourke."

Patty gave him her mother's business card and promised that Samantha Dean would be at the Tri-County meeting later that evening to finalize the arrangements. Feeling smug and self-satisfied, Murphy grabbed an extra cookie and headed out toward his car in the rainswept parking lot.

It wasn't until he was halfway back to the bar that he re-alized he'd just made a deal with a ten-year-old budding corporate shark whose mother might take a dim view of handshake agreements with unemployed gonzo journalists who were now pulling drafts for a living.

And, all things considered, he wouldn't blame her one bit.

SAMANTHA DEAN stifled a yawn as the New Jersey Transit train rumbled toward the station at Princeton Junction. The railroad car was cold and damp and it took every ounce of imagination in Sam's body to conjure up visions of hot soup and a roaring fire. Before she knew it she'd be home with

Patty, the two of them snug in their favorite robes as they watched *MacGyver* and *Monday Night Football*.

"One more day," she said to her best friend Caroline. "Twenty-four hours and I never have to ride this blasted cattle car again."

"Speak for yourself," said Caroline, eyeing the handsome businessmen sitting opposite the two women. "I rather enjoy riding the train."

Sam resisted the urge to kick Caroline in her fashionable ankle. "You wouldn't mind a trek through the Sahara if there was a man involved."

"Try it some time," Caroline said, her dimples deepening. "You might find you like it. Men are pleasant creatures, once you tame them."

I'd rather tame a grizzly bear, Sam thought. At least grizzly bears hibernated six months of every year. She could never find time in her crazy daily schedule for a man, no matter how handsome. She turned and looked at her fluffy blond friend. "Do me a favor," she said, giving way to another yawn. "Why don't we just pretend you gave me matchmaking lecture number 378 and be done with it?" Caroline started to protest but Sam raised a hand to stop her. "It's not as if I haven't heard it all before."

Caroline leaned her head against the worn leather seat. Even at the end of a rainy, cold Monday she looked superb. If they weren't best friends, Sam just might hate the woman.

"You may think you've heard it all," Caroline said, "but I can tell you haven't paid attention. Patty needs a father, Sam."

Sam's jaw settled into a stubborn line. "Patty has a father," she snapped. "It's not my fault Ronald doesn't care that he has a daughter."

Caroline was as stubborn as Sam. "I'm not talking about Ronald Donovan and you know it. I'm talking about you, Sam. About your future."

"My future is fine, thank you. This time next month, I'll be open for business and from there the sky's the limit." For two years Sam had eaten, breathed, slept Fast Foods for the Fast Lane and she was finally on the eve of reaping the benefits of her backbreaking schedule of work and school and motherhood.

"There's more to life than your career, Sam."

"Easy for you to say. You have a career. Mine hasn't started yet."

"There's Patty," Caroline said softly, tearing her limpid blue-eyed gaze away from the man in the gray flannel suit across the aisle. "You should think about her happiness."

Sam's fatigue disappeared in a quick blaze of anger. "That's exactly what I'm thinking about, Caroline. Patty needs more than I could ever give her by waiting tables or typing envelopes. Fast Foods for the Fast Lane is my best hope."

Having a genius for a daughter wasn't your everyday occurrence. As it was, Patty was quickly outstripping the ability of Harborfields Elementary School to keep up with her. Unfortunately Patty's nimble mind was also quickly outstripping Sam's financial ability to provide tutors, books, and advanced courses her little girl deserved but didn't have.

Sam had no college degree, no inheritance to fall back upon, no friends in high places. What she had was a sharp mind, common sense, and the ability to turn the simplest of foods into the most extraordinary fare. With the area around Princeton booming with two-paycheck families and upscale life-styles, Sam realized that all the modern conveniences in the world couldn't compensate for the lack of a home-cooked meal made to order and ready when you were.

From that simple idea came her brainchild, Fast Foods for the Fast Lane, and with it the hope that she would be able to give Patty every chance in the world to achieve her potential.

The tinny voice of the conductor blared from the loudspeaker: "Princeton Junction, next stop!"

Caroline, elegant as always in her timeless gray silk dress, stood up and reached for her parcels in the overhead rack. "I should be imprisoned for grand larceny," she said, sitting back down next to Sam, her lap piled high with loot. "Three Bob Mackie beaded beauties and a Donna Karan business special and I didn't have to empty my bank account."

"I take it business is going well?" Sam asked, collecting her books and papers from the empty seat next to her. Caroline ran an offbeat boutique called Twice Over Lightly, where one-of-a-kind designer dresses could be rented for a night by New Jersey Cinderellas.

Caroline's broad smile told the tale. "It's going so well I can afford to wear the Schiaparelli to the Tri-County Masquerade Ball. Jeannie Tremont will be green with envy."

"No," said Sam, searching her briefcase for her car keys. "Absolutely not."

"Absolutely not what?" Caroline asked.

"I am absolutely *not* going to the Christmas party."

"Of course you are," Caroline said. "Don't be silly."

"I hate Christmas parties and I refuse to go to one where all the adults wear Santa Claus masks. I have better things to do with my free time." *Like eating, sleeping, and being Patty's mother.*

Caroline's elegant nose wrinkled in disdain. "Spare me your Mrs. Scrooge routine, Sam. It was old last year."

"I don't ask you to forgo your mistletoe, Caroline," Sam said evenly. "Don't go asking me to run around whistling 'Jingle Bells.'"

"You used to love Christmas," Caroline persisted. "You used to start decorating before Thanksgiving."

"I used to wear braids and watch *Leave It to Beaver*, too."

"You even celebrated Christmas the year you were expecting Patty and we both know what a rotten holiday that was. She's still waiting to set up the luminaria along the driveway on Christmas Eve."

"I was seventeen." Had there ever been a time when setting up those tiny white candles outside had seemed so wondrous, so important? "I didn't know any better."

Leave it to Samantha Dean to fall in love with a boy from the right side of the tracks. A high school romance with a girl from Rocky Hill was one thing; marriage to that very same girl was something else entirely.

There would be no marriage, said the illustrious Donovan clan, not even to legitimize the baby Sam carried. And so it was on Christmas Eve that Ronald was whisked away from the temptation and sent west where he ended up in the United States Air Force Academy, on the road to a bright and shiny future as a pilot.

And good riddance.

Sam had done fine by Patty up until now and, God willing, she would do even better once her catering business got rolling.

"You should get out more," Caroline continued, as the train rattled into the station. "Socialize. Christmas soirees are all part of doing business in this town, Sam."

"Well, the soirees will have to go on without me. I have ten weeks' worth of work and only four weeks to accomplish it. Believe me, I don't have time for Christmas."

"Everyone has time for Christmas."

Sam laughed out loud. "You don't even have time for the Tri-County meeting tonight."

"That's different. The store is open tonight and Jeannie has the evening off." She narrowed her eyes in Sam's direction. "I hope you're going."

Sam glanced out at the cold rain lashing against the train windows. "Not me. I intend to stretch out on the sofa and watch *Taxi* reruns while Patty tackles nuclear fusion."

"Not a very businesslike attitude, Sam."

"I'm not in business yet, Caroline."

Caroline waved her words away. "A mere technicality. You should be out there spreading Christmas cheer. I don't think you're being fair to Patty." Caroline looked altogether too pleased with her logic for Sam's taste.

"Just because I don't turn all warm and mushy when I hear 'Deck the Halls,' doesn't mean I'm going to deny Patty her fun."

"Well, thank God for that," Caroline murmured. "I would have kidnaped that girl for the holidays."

"Wait until I'm established," Sam said. "In a few years I'll have plenty of time for Christmas celebrations."

"I certainly hope so. Christmas is a time for miracles, honey, and there are few of them around these days. Who knows? Your big break might be waiting for you at the Tri-County meeting." Caroline patted Sam's hand. "You just have to believe."

"Oh, I believe," said Sam as the train stopped and the doors slid open. "I believe in peace on earth, joy to the world, and that not even Tom Selleck could tempt me to go to that meeting tonight."

Chapter Two

"No," Sam said, kicking off her wet Reeboks and collapsing into a kitchen chair. She'd been home less than fifteen minutes and already Patty was trying to push her back out the door. "Absolutely not."

Her daughter's bright blue eyes flashed with a spark of stubborn recklessness that Sam was all too familiar with. Nothing short of a world-class brainstorm would have kept Patty away from Monday-afternoon Math Club.

"But, Mom, I—"

Sam groaned and closed her eyes. "Not another word, kiddo. The only place I'm going tonight is to bed."

Patty's cheeks flushed with determination. "I promised you'd go to the meeting."

Wearily Sam braced herself and opened one dark brown eye. "That's what you get for making promises you can't keep."

"You have to go! I'll be humiliated if you don't."

"Then prepare yourself to be humiliated, Patty, because I'm not moving from this house." She stifled a yawn. "I may not even move from this chair."

"That's very unprofessional, Mother."

So it's going to be one of those nights, is it? Whenever Patty called Sam "Mother," Sam knew she was in for trouble.

"How can you be a small business when you don't go to small-business meetings?" her small and brilliant daughter reasoned.

"I'm not a small business yet, kiddo, and I never will be if I don't finish this last course." Loss Management and Customer Relations had turned out to be a combination of Abnormal Psychology 101 and Deficit Spending for the Soon-to-be-Bankrupt, while Food Preparation and You made Martha Stewart's elaborate arrangements look like leftovers. "What I need is warm food, a hot bath and a good night's sleep."

Patty's red brows knotted together over the bridge of her eyeglasses. "Test tomorrow?"

"A final."

"Scared?"

Sam opened her other eye. "What is this—*Invasion of the Body Snatchers*? You're the ten-year-old. You should be the one taking tests and I should be the one looking concerned."

Patty grinned and lifted the lid on Sam's favorite saucepan and the mouthwatering aroma of chili filled the tiny kitchen.

"I even left out the garlic," Patty said.

Sam had been a mother long enough to recognize a con job when she saw one, but there was something so wonderful about hot chili on a cold, wet evening that her maternal defense mechanism lowered.

"Did you remember to brown the meat?" Sam asked, weakening.

"Of course!" Her oh-so-grown-up little girl looked highly affronted. "And I mixed my own chili powder instead of using the bottled stuff."

Sam sighed. Although she prided herself on her Cordon Bleu-style of cooking, chili was her downfall and Patti knew it. "The spirit is willing," Sam muttered, "but the flesh is *very* weak. What's the catch, kiddo?"

Patty was the picture of innocence. "There's no catch."

"Patty." Sam's voice was stern as she struggled to hide her grin. Despite her genius IQ, Patty was transparent as plate glass, a fact for which Sam was forever grateful. It was one of the few advantages she had left. "You didn't volunteer me for another Christmas Party committee at school, did you?"

"I wouldn't dare," Patty said. "Not after the kids nicknamed you Mrs. Scrooge last year." Patty ladled some chili into a heavy white bowl and handed it to Sam. "I just think you should go to the meeting tonight, that's all."

The chili was warm, spicy, and downright delicious and Sam's defenses lowered yet another notch. "Any particular reason?"

Patty met her eyes head-on. "I think it's good business."

"What's his name?"

"Maa—aa! Why are you being so suspicious?"

"Because I'm a mother, that's why. The chili is terrific, kiddo, and I'm probably going to go to the darned meeting tonight but I think I deserve a straight answer, don't you?"

"Murphy O'Rourke," said Patty, sitting down at the table opposite Sam with her own steaming bowl of chili.

"What?"

"His name. Murphy O'Rourke."

"Oh, Patty!" Sam's spoon clattered back into the heavy white bowl. "You know how I feel about matchmaking. I don't have enough time for you much less a boyfriend."

"I'm not matchmaking," her daughter protested. "This is a business matter."

"You're making me nervous, Patty."

"He runs a bar in Rocky Hill and he lost his chef. I told him you could supply the food for the bar until he hires a new chef."

"Cook, honey. Bars don't have chefs." There was something very daunting about a ten-year-old child with the instincts of a Donald Trump. "I suppose you also negotiated a price."

She had. Sam whistled low. "That much?"

Patty nodded. "I probably could have asked fifty percent more but it's Christmastime."

"What does Christmas have to do with good business?"

"Really, Mother!"

"Oh, don't look so shocked, honey. I was only kidding." Each year she vowed to make an effort for Patty's sake, and each year it grew harder and harder to do. "How much did you say the job would pay?"

Patty told her again.

It was still impressive.

"And you wouldn't even have to work there," Patty continued, her voice eager. "You could make up the food here and drop it off at the bar on your way to the train."

"And school finishes up tomorrow," Sam said, warming to the idea despite her better judgment. With that amount of money for making a few hors d'oeuvres for a local tavern, she'd have time to get the store ready for its opening day, sleep late, Christmas shop and be able to pay her bills. It was too good to pass up. "What time did you say the meeting was?"

"Eight o'clock," said Patty, her small freckled face beaming with excitement.

"And he'll be there?"

Her daughter's red braids bounced as she nodded her head. "Yes. He promised to give you first chance at the job."

"All right," said Sam, giving in at last. "I'll go. If I'm going to be the Princeton corridor's number one entrepreneur, I suppose I'd better start entrepreneuring."

Patty leaped up and nearly vaulted the kitchen table in order to envelope her mother in a bear hug.

"You're the best mother in the world!" the little girl exclaimed in delight. "The absolute best!"

TWO HOURS LATER, the best mother in the world stood in the doorway of the meeting room and took stock of the crowd. Brooks Brothers, Savile Row, and a touch of the Talbot's catalog thrown in for good measure. Ivy League personified.

She glanced down at her flour-speckled sweater and trusty cords. Whatever had possessed her to be so cavalier about the Tri-County Small Business Association anyway? An elegantly coiffed woman in a navy suit and red shirt walked by with a nod of her head and instantly Sam felt two feet tall.

Eye shadow, thought Sam with a groan. *Gold earrings and lipstick and a clean sweater and that's just for starters.* Everything Patty had begged and pleaded for Sam to wear. As it was, she looked like a holdover from the Sixties. All she needed was a peace symbol embroidered on her pants pocket, love beads around her neck and a picket sign proclaiming her disdain for all things material.

Maybe she should pretend she was there to scrub the floors in the ladies' room. Judging by her appearance, that would be an easier sell than trying to convince these tailored wonders that she was one of them.

She stepped inside the doorway, keeping the wall firmly against her back. Where on earth had she gotten the idea that these meetings were casual? Well, there was no hope for it. Sam hadn't come all that way to slink out of there without accomplishing her objective. Sixty-three dollars for a tray of cocktail sandwiches wasn't something she could easily turn away from and, like it or not, Mr. Murphy O'Rourke would have to accept her the way she was or find someone else to do business with.

She eased into the crowd and scanned the stick-on name tags affixed to bosoms and pecs, feeling vaguely like an upscale pervert. Kaplan...Oliveri...DeSoto...Brennan... Everything but O'Rourke.

A tall, dark and handsome man in a sophisticated tweed suit approached. If this was Patty's business conquest, she would have to compliment her daughter on her good taste. He was positively gorgeous.

"Good evening," he said, white teeth gleaming.

Sam straightened her shoulders and wished she'd at least worn her hair down instead of in a ponytail. "Good evening."

"Still cold outside?"

"Freezing, but at least it isn't snowing."

Nodding, he drained a styrofoam cup of coffee. "The pot's empty."

"I beg your pardon?"

"The coffeepot's empty," he repeated. "I believe we could use more. The meeting's about to begin."

Sam arched a brow. "Then perhaps you should speak to someone who might be able to help you."

He had the decency to flush beneath his perfect tan. "I thought—I mean, aren't you—"

"No, I'm not."

His dark blue eyes traveled swiftly over her bedraggled form and she held her breath, praying he wouldn't call a security guard to evict her from the premises.

"I'm waiting for someone," she said, although it was really none of his business. "I *am* a member."

"I'm sure," he said, nodding, but it was obvious he had difficulty imagining an overaged street urchin being granted membership in such a hallowed institution.

Might as well go for broke, Sam. "You wouldn't happen to be Murphy O'Rourke, would you?"

"Afraid not," he murmured in a lock-jawed parody of all things Ivy then moved back into the crowd.

We need to have a long *talk, Patty,* she thought as she poured herself a tall glass of iced water and watched the Ralph Lauren sweaters mingle with the Laura Ashley dresses.

"Quite a turnout, isn't it?" asked a middle-aged man in aviator glasses.

"Quite," said Sam, feigning an air of privileged indifference. There were far too many prep school clothes at the Tri-County meeting for her taste. She'd spent a good part of her early adult life feeling second place to people whose claim to superiority was nothing more profound than being born in the right zip code.

Come on, O'Rourke, she thought, returning to her place by the double doors. She wanted to meet the man, solidify Patty's deal, and go home—preferably in the next five minutes, if possible. She scanned the smoke-filled room once again. Sam had checked the name tag of every man who even remotely matched her daughter's description of the elusive Murphy O'Rourke to no avail. In fact, not one of the men she'd approached had even heard of O'Rourke. Either Patty was playing an extremely unfunny practical joke or the mystery man had been stringing along a little girl who had been known to get more-than-a-little pushy when she was trying to make a point.

One day when Fast Foods for the Fast Lane was under-way she would belong here with the Stocktons and the Witherspoons and the Donovans, but this definitely wasn't the day. She was cold and wet and exhausted and positive she should have stayed home with a blanket and a hot-water bottle as she'd originally planned.

A white-haired woman took the podium, rapped sharply with her gavel, then launched into a series of public address announcements with a delivery flat as the Mojave Desert.

"Oh, no," muttered a male voice behind Sam. "I should've stayed home and watched the game."

A kindred spirit! Who would have imagined it possible? Eagerly she spun around in time to see a scruffy man in a battered trench coat blow into the room with all the grace and charm of the north wind. His black umbrella was inside out, his hair was wet and plastered to his forehead, and he was mumbling words not often heard in the environs of Princeton. Sam was surprised they'd let him in without fingerprinting him.

"Hold this," he said, pushing the cockeyed umbrella and a soggy sheaf of papers into her hands. "Damn coat's soaked."

Sam stared down at the umbrella and papers in shock. "Hold them yourself," she said, pushing them back at him.

"Come on," he said, his sandy hair dripping water into his hazel eyes. "Just let me hang the coat over the radiator and I'll take everything off your hands."

"You'll take everything off my hands *now*," said Sam, in the same tone of voice she used on Patty.

"Full of Christmas spirit, aren't you, lady?" he mumbled, but Sam noted he retrieved his belongings quickly enough.

"I suppose Christmastime is an excuse for bad manners these days." Who did this scruffy barbarian think he was, anyway? She owed Caroline an apology. Apparently there really was something to be said for dressing for success; she hadn't worked this hard and this long to be mistaken for a hatcheck girl.

He was grumbling under his breath about feeling like a circus juggler, and Sam turned to find another spot to wait for Murphy O'Rourke when a terrible thought struck her. Ridiculous. That scruffy looking specimen couldn't possibly be Patty's new business partner. Patty had described a tall and handsome man with money to burn. She took another look at the man in the worn corduroy jacket. Certainly no one would call him handsome. Attractive, maybe, in a somewhat battered kind of way with his large-boned build and the rugged face that had taken a punch or two in its day, but not even Patty could describe him as a hunk.

And as for looking like the proper Princetonian businessman—well, he had none of the sheen and polish of the men at the Tri-County meeting. No perfectly barbered coif for this man; his hair tickled his collar and flopped over his ears and looked as if it hadn't seen a stylist's scissors in a very long time.

But then, the man Patty had struck a deal with owned a bar not a barrister's office and this man looked exactly the way Sam imagined a saloon keeper should look.

And let's face facts, Sam, she thought as he met her eyes and flashed her a roguish grin. This was exactly the type of man Patty would think just terrific.

He appeared at Sam's elbow. "Any seats available or are you planning on a quick getaway?"

Sam gestured toward an empty row near the podium. "Be my guest. I'm waiting for someone."

"So am I."

That's what I was afraid of. She turned and looked up at him. "Murphy O'Rourke?"

He nodded. "Samantha Dean?"

She extended her hand. "I believe you and my daughter arranged a business deal today."

His grip was firm without being macho. A pleasant surprise. "The kid's sharp," he said, grinning. "I wouldn't want to face her at an arbitration table."

A man in the last row turned around and loudly shushed them.

"Look," Sam whispered, spirits sinking, "I don't think business deals made by a ten-year-old are binding. If you want out, I'll—"

The entire last row swiveled to glare at Sam and Murphy O'Rourke. Chastened, they found seats near the window and Sam struggled to stay awake during an interminable discussion of the Holiday Ball next Saturday night.

"If I snore, kick me," O'Rourke ordered, then closed his eyes.

Sam almost fell off her folding chair in surprise. All around them the most ambitious entrepreneurs in the region were exchanging business cards, setting up power breakfasts, and deciding whether the main arboreal theme for the masquerade ball should be mistletoe or holly. The air bristled with energy and, at least when they weren't discussing the Christmas party, Sam found herself itching for January first to roll around so she could be a real part of things.

Not O'Rourke. He was slumped in his chair, arms folded across his chest, head thrown back as if he didn't give a fig what any of Princeton's best and brightest thought about him. Sam was torn between admiration and horror. She had a healthy respect for clubs and associations and institutions, mainly because they had always seemed just beyond her grasp.

"All in favor of holly in the ballroom and mistletoe in the anterooms, signify by saying aye."

A chorus of *ayes* rang out. Sam withheld her opinion on general principle since she wouldn't be an official entrepreneur for another four weeks. Next to her, O'Rourke made a noise like a strangled moose.

"Ouch!" He leaned forward and rubbed his left ankle. "What the hell was that all about?"

"You snored," Sam said. "I'm saving you the embarrassment of public disgrace."

He inclined his head toward the podium. "Do you care about the dinner menu for the Christmas dance?"

"No."

"The wine list?"

"Not one bit."

His sleepy hazel eyes narrowed as he met hers. "How do you feel about the Giants?"

"True love," she said. "If you're a Jets fan, the deal's off."

"Mention the Jets at O'Rourke's and you buy drinks for the house."

"An admirable policy."

"How would you feel about ironing out our deal at the bar while we watch the game?"

He may not be a candidate for the cover of *GQ*, but Murphy O'Rourke was a man after her own heart. At least, in the business sense. "If we hurry, we might catch the end of the second quarter."

"You're okay, Samantha Dean," he said, flashing a devilish grin. "Let's go."

THE LOOK on Aunt Caroline's face was even better than a gift subscription to *Science Digest*.

"You've done the impossible," Caroline breathed, lowering herself into the rocking chair near the stereo.

"I know," said Patty, beaming with delight, as she handed Caroline a cup of hot tea then curled up on the sofa.

"The one meeting I skip and you convince your mother to go. How did you do it—hypnosis?"

"Money," said Patty proudly.

Caroline's perfectly lipsticked mouth dropped open. "You bribed your own mother? What kind of allowance do you get, girl?"

"I cut Mom a business deal."

"That does it," said Caroline, laughing. "Would you be my business manager, too?"

Patty felt happier than she had the day she won the Mid-Atlantic Science Fair with her work on water purification. Aunt Caroline wasn't one of those grown-ups who fell all over kids, pouring on the praise as if it was maple syrup. A compliment from her always had Patty walking on air for days.

Caroline listened closely as Patty told all about Career Day and Murphy O'Rourke and the saga of the sixty-three-dollar trays of food.

"And Mom couldn't resist," Patty finished up, her voice triumphant.

"Okay, Ms. Trump," said Caroline, leaning forward, "what's the catch?"

Patty felt her cheeks redden beneath the woman's knowing gaze. "There's no catch."

"Of course there's a catch."

Patty looked down at her feet which were stuffed into humongous bunny slippers. "Okay, so maybe I do have an ulterior motive," Patty said finally.

"Matchmaking again?" Her aunt shivered delicately. "You like to live dangerously, Patricia."

Patricia! How grown-up that sounded. How sophisticated. Leave it to Aunt Caroline to think of something so wonderful.

"You matchmake," Patty said, wishing she were wearing normal slippers. It was hard to be adult when your feet looked like Bugs Bunny. "Mom says that's all you ever have on your mind."

"Out of the mouths of babes," muttered Caroline, smoothing one pale brow with a manicured fingertip. "So what is he like?"

"Wonderful!" said Patty, forgetting that she was feeling sophisticated and worldly. "Perfect!" Just the thought of Murphy O'Rourke was enough to make Patty feel all Christmasy and happy inside, like the first snowfall of the season.

Caroline's blue eyes twinkled with delight. "I suppose he's handsome?"

For a second Patty couldn't conjure up a face to go with her romantic notions. "He's very...manly."

"Handsome?" Caroline repeated.

"Not exactly," said Patty as his image clarified. "He's kind of rugged."

"Uh-oh," said Caroline. "That bad, is he?"

"He's not bad at all," Patty said, leaping to his defense. She had an IQ in the top .05% percentile in the nation. Why couldn't she find the words to tell Caroline about the man she was certain would one day be her dad? "He was a foreign correspondent."

"I thought you said he owned a bar."

"He does now but he used to be a reporter."

"Does he look like he needs a shave?"

Patty nodded. "Five o'clock shadow."

"And he smokes?"

She thought about the pack of cigarettes tucked in his shirt pocket and the matches he'd cadged from Mrs. Venturella. "Camels."

"Last question," said Caroline, "and this one will tell the whole story—does he wear a trench coat?"

Patty's heart pounded wildly inside her chest. "An old one," she said, "and no hat." Murphy O'Rourke was the kind of man who laughed at the elements. In her wildest imagination she couldn't picture him as a little boy, all bundled up in galoshes and muffler and rain hat.

Caroline leaned back in the rocking chair and fixed Patty with a look. "Poor old Sam," she said, starting to laugh. "The girl doesn't stand a chance!"

Chapter Three

O'Rourke's Bar and Grill looked exactly the way a tavern in central New Jersey should look, and the moment Sam stepped inside, she felt at home. O'Rourke's boasted a great deal of gleaming mahogany, shiny brass, and enough beer mugs to keep the crew on *Cheers* happy for another eight seasons. A group of men well over voting age were clustered around a table near the old juke box, arguing loudly over great baseball teams of the past, while the football Giants played their hearts out on the big-screen TV mounted overhead.

The air smelled pleasantly of pipe tobacco, Old Spice and spirits, and Sam couldn't help but smile at the dark-haired waitress who scurried by, carrying a pitcher of beer and six glasses to the over-the-hill gang at the table. No hanging ferns and Perrier at this bar.

She peered around at the other customers. There also were no women. This was obviously that most sacrosanct of male establishments—the local watering hole—and she made a mental note to forget the watercress sandwiches on crustless pumpernickel in favor of ham and cheese on rye.

"Hang your coat on the rack by the door," O'Rourke said. "I'll get you a draft."

"Make it a hot chocolate and you're on."

The silence in the tavern was daunting as she strolled over to the coatrack. Murphy, the dark-haired waitress, and the Over-the-Hill-Gang all watched her as if she were a land mine.

"Hot chocolate?" Murphy O'Rourke sounded incredulous. "How about an Irish coffee?"

"I'm driving," said Sam. "Hot chocolate will be fine."

Murphy vaulted over the bar and rummaged noisily beneath the counter. "I don't see any hot chocolate back here."

The cluster of senior citizens found that highly amusing and they laughed along with O'Rourke.

Sam called up her friendliest smile. "How about a cup of coffee, then?"

"I don't think we have any," said Murphy, looking oddly uncomfortable behind the bar.

The waitress hit him on the arm with her tray. "Idiot! You can't make Irish Coffee without it, can you?"

His grin was sheepish. "I didn't think of that."

Not good, thought Sam. A saloon owner who didn't know the first thing about something as basic as Irish Coffee—and a saloon owner named O'Rourke, at that. No wonder he fell for Patty's spiel. He motioned for Sam to take a seat and she was about to claim a bar stool when the most elegant of golden agers rose to his feet and executed a courtly bow.

"We'd be honored if you joined us," he said.

"I'd love to," said Sam, glancing at O'Rourke who was still rattling around with the coffee pot, "but we have business to discuss."

"We have known Murphy since he was in knee pants. There is no business he cannot discuss in our presence."

Who would have figured the mercurial, devil-may-care man she'd met at the Tri-County meeting to be a part of a most intriguing extended family? She had to hand it to Patty; her daughter rarely befriended anyone ordinary.

"Forget it, Scotty." Murphy vaulted the bar once again then picked up two cups of coffee. "She's too young for you."

"Age is a state of mind," the older man pronounced in the lofty tones of a Princeton professor, "and I am in my prime."

His peers broke into hoots of laughter and a few clumsy, but amiable, jokes about snow on the roof and a fire in the furnace.

"Ignore them," said O'Rourke, leading Sam to a table on the other side of the room. "It's past their bedtime."

"Respect!" boomed the gentleman he'd called Scotty. "We are the only buffer between this establishment and bankruptcy court, my boy."

Sam's eyes widened. "Business isn't good?" *And you're willing to pay over sixty bucks a tray for sandwiches?*

"Business is booming," he said, sitting down opposite her, "but they still like to think they're the cornerstone of the bar."

Scotty winked at Sam and she chuckled. "Why is it I think they probably are?"

"You're a lot like your kid," said O'Rourke. "Blunt."

Sam nodded. "To a fault. It's a family trait."

He took a gulp of coffee then gestured broadly. "So what do you think of the place?"

"I think it's terrific. I didn't think bars like this existed anymore."

"They don't," said Murphy. "The fern bars are taking over the world."

The thought of ferns overtaking O'Rourke's made Sam laugh out loud. "A fern would choke on the cigar smoke in this place."

"Does it bother you?" he asked.

"Not a bit." Even if it did, she wouldn't have said so. Sam was blunt but she understood the rules. Everything about O'Rourke's was exactly as it should be—including the shroud of smoke settling over her shoulders. She gestured toward the old boxing photos on the brick wall next to her. "That's Joe Louis, isn't it?"

"My dad's a fight fan. You should see how many boxes of memorabilia he has stuffed in his attic."

She took a sip of the hot, surprisingly good, coffee. "It's nice of you to hang some of them up. Gives the place atmosphere."

"My dad'll be glad to hear that." He met her eyes. "It's his bar."

"What?" She couldn't keep her surprise from her voice.

"It's his bar," O'Rourke repeated. "I'm baby-sitting until he's back on his feet."

She leaned closer, her curiosity piqued. "What happened to him?"

"Heart attack." O'Rourke's voice lowered and he looked away for a split second. Just long enough for Sam to see both fear and love in his hazel eyes. "Guy doesn't even smoke."

"How is he? My uncle had a heart attack two years ago and he's back out there running eight miles a day."

"Pop's more the recliner-chair-and-remote-control type, but he's almost one hundred percent."

"And you're the resident barkeep?"

O'Rourke raked his shaggy brown hair off his forehead and grinned. "I can pull a draft with the best of 'em. Just don't go getting fancy on me."

The thought of Murphy O'Rourke fixing a piña colada, complete with the pineapple spear and paper parasol, was comical. "Judging by your clientele, you're safe. They look like a sturdy, all-American brew crowd to me."

"Does that disappoint you?"

Sam's eyes widened and she looked down at her baggy sweater and cords. "Do I look like the Perrier-and-lime type to you?"

"No," he said, that smile of his back in place. "That's one of the things I like about you."

Sam listened while he told her about the long recovery period Bill O'Rourke was going through. Murphy's brother in Florida had tried to convince Bill to put the tavern up for sale but the older man was adamant that it stay open, even if a stranger had to come in and tend to things in his absence.

"And you put aside your own career to come take care of things for your dad?" Sam couldn't keep the admiration from her voice as visions of *Happy Days* and Richie Cunningham helping out at the family hardware store spun through her head. "I'm impressed."

O'Rourke grunted and downed his coffee. "Before you nominate me for the *Croix de Guerre*, I should tell you there wasn't any career to put aside. I've been unemployed for the past few months."

She instantly understood the worn elbows on his corduroy jacket and the deplorable condition of his raincoat. Poor man was down on his luck and probably thrilled to have a steady job to go to each morning. "A strike?"

"In a manner of speaking." His hazel eyes glittered with a challenge as he met her gaze straight on. "Actually I walked out."

"Out of what?" It wasn't difficult to imagine him staging a walkout at a steel mill or an automobile assembly plant. He looked like the kind of man who wasn't afraid of hard work. Unfashionable work that dirtied your clothes and blackened your hands.

"I walked out of the New York office of the *Telegram*."

She sprayed coffee clear across the table and onto the lapels of his sorry excuse for a jacket. "Very funny. You had me going there for a moment."

"I'm not joking. I was managing editor."

Sam had a sense of humor. She could go along with the joke. "And I suppose before that you were foreign correspondent for Reuters."

"AP," he said. "First Moscow, then London."

"You should be a writer, O'Rourke. You have a way with fiction."

"I *am* a writer but I deal with the facts."

"Being a bartender is nothing to be ashamed of."

"If I were a bartender I wouldn't be ashamed."

"Okay," said Sam, mopping up the spill with a cocktail napkin. "Have it your way. Let's talk about the sandwich trays."

"I'm not kidding, Samantha."

"I said I believed you, O'Rourke." She whipped a notepad out of her pocketbook and uncapped a felt tip pen. "Do you want heros or club sandwiches?"

"Heros." He gulped more coffee. "I walked out on the paper as a protest for artistic freedom."

"Turkey, ham, or tuna salad?"

"Aren't you listening to a damn thing I'm saying?" He glared at her. "I thought club sandwiches were usually B.L.T.s."

"Good tomatoes are out of season. How about roast beef?"

"Jeez . . ." He dragged a hand through his shaggy, still-damp hair. "Some of each, why don't you?"

Sam scribbled a few lines then looked back up. "With lettuce? Without lettuce? Pickles? Assorted condiments? Perhaps a side of cole slaw and—"

"Gimme a break, will you?" He yanked the pen from her hand. "I don't care if you make peanut butter and jelly sandwiches."

Her eyebrows arched. "At sixty-three dollars a tray, I'd make quite a profit." He couldn't be a businessman by profession because he would have run himself into the red in days with an attitude like that.

"You've already made quite a profit. That kid of yours drives a hard bargain."

"Like mother, like daughter," said Sam with a smile. "Condiments?"

He leaned across the round table and told her exactly what she could do with her condiments in a way that made her laugh. "You sure you never heard of me? Three appearances on *Night Line* with Koppel. Johnny Carson Show in 1986. A mention in *Time* and *Newsweek*—"

"I believe you, Murphy, I believe you!"

"*U.S. News* and *World Report*—"

"I admit your credits are impressive but I still don't know who you are." She patted his forearm much the same way she often patted her daughter's. "Don't be hurt. I've been so busy the last few years I only found out last week that Reagan's out of office."

"Sorry," O'Rourke said. "I'm having trouble adjusting to the civilian life. Unless you're a news junkie, there's no reason for you to know who I am."

"No apology needed."

"I sounded like a jerk."

"We all do sometimes."

"Turkey and tuna."

Sam blinked. "I beg your pardon?"

"The sandwiches. Turkey and tuna. Rye and whole wheat. Plenty of cole slaw and garlic dills, if you have them."

"You are one very strange man, O'Rourke." She grabbed the pen back from him and wrote down his order. "Pretzels? Peanuts?"

"We have a supplier."

They went over how many trays she would prepare, refrigeration requirements, delivery times.

"You know your stuff," he said, a note of admiration in his voice. "If you can cook, I've got it made."

"I'd better be able to cook," Sam said as she put the cap back on her pen and closed her notebook. "I intend to become rich doing it."

"Ambitious?"

Her jaw settled into its familiar granite line. "Extremely."

He leaned back in his chair, fingers tapping against the arm. "Your daughter's a lot like you."

"I know," Sam said, pride welling up inside her chest. "She believes she can have anything she wants, as long as she works for it." And, considering Patty's intellectual gifts, the sky was the limit.

"Do you believe the same thing?"

Sam thought about the rose-covered cottage and gingham apron she'd once believed would be hers, then contrasted it to the life she had now. "Yes," she said slowly. "I don't believe in setting limits on achievement." Truth to tell, she wouldn't trade the life she had now for any dream of the past.

His expression was warm and friendly and gently mocking. "Make a hell of a ham sandwich, do you, Samantha?"

"You better believe it!" Laughter, sudden and delighted, broke through her reserve. "The name's Sam, by the way."

He extended his hand. "Murphy."

They shook solemnly. Although she hated people who judged others by the force of a handshake, Sam couldn't help but note the assurance and strength in his grip.

"How would you feel about manning the grill a few nights a week until I hire a new chef?"

For a moment Sam was sorely tempted. "I love short-order cooking, but my schedule is packed between now and New Year's."

"Christmas shopping?"

Sam made a face. "Business. I'm opening my shop on New Year's Day."

He stared at her as if he'd seen a ghost. "No one opens a shop on New Year's Day. Everyone's home watching football and nursing champagne headaches."

"New Year's Day," she repeated, voice firm. "Think of how many football parties I can cater."

O'Rourke's grin faded. "What about your own party?"

"I don't have one."

"You go to a friend's house?"

Sam shook her head. "About the sandwiches," she said, looking to change the subject. "Maybe we should—"

"You have to go somewhere," O'Rourke persisted. "No one stays home on New Year's Eve."

"You must have been one heck of a reporter. It's none of your business, O'Rourke, but Patty spends the night at her grandparents' house and I usually work."

"I thought you were in cooking school or something."

"Catering firms go crazy during the holidays. I can pick up a month's wages with a few days' work and manage to keep the house warm in January as a result. Who am I to refuse?"

The twinkle in his hazel eyes was replaced by a laser beam of unashamed curiosity. "You hate Christmas."

"Don't be ridiculous!" *You're too good at this, O'Rourke. Go back to searching for Kremlin secrets.*

"It's written all over your face."

"That's fatigue."

"What about Patty? Kids live for Christmas."

"Patty does just fine at Christmas, don't worry."

"You decorate a tree?"

"Of course."

"You put up lights at the window?"

"Patty does."

"Do you send Christmas cards?"

"When I can afford the stamps."

The glitter in his eyes returned. "And you hate every minute of it."

"Damn right I do." Sam shoved her chair back and rose to her feet. "I'll drop off the sandwiches on my way to the train station tomorrow morning. Please have someone here to let me in. Seven-thirty, the latest." She turned to head for the door but he grabbed her wrist.

"Hit a nerve, didn't I?"

"I'm surprised you didn't recognize a closed door when you saw one."

"I didn't get to be a foreign correspondent by letting doors stay closed."

"Well, I have a news flash for you, O'Rourke—you're not a reporter anymore, you're a bartender in New Jersey and how I feel about Christmas is none of your business."

His own chair scraped against the floor as he stood up and faced her. His rugged features had lost the edge of humor and it occurred to Sam that she was alone in a bar with a group of men she knew next to nothing about.

"One question," he said, his voice gruff.

She swallowed hard. "Just one then I'm out of here."

"Does this mean you won't be making the sandwiches for us?"

"With what you're willing to pay me? You must be joking," said Sam. "A deal's a deal."

"You don't know how glad I am to hear you say that." O'Rourke broke into a crooked smile that was actually rather appealing, in an odd sort of way. "I'm glad Patty brought us together."

"So am I," said Sam. "I think it be will profitable for both of us."

"Yeah?" said O'Rourke as he walked her to the door. "I was thinking that it just might be fun."

He didn't help her into her coat or walk her out to the parking lot or do any of the things a gentleman usually did. He was gruff, opinionated, self-centered and a lousy dresser

but by the time Sam was halfway home she realized that
Murphy O'Rourke was also one hundred percent right.

Fun!

Who'd have thought it?

Chapter Four

"Forget it," said Murphy when he turned around to face the gray inquisition after Sam said good-night. "She'll be cooking for us. Nothing more."

"She's a fine looking woman," said Joe, helping himself to another pint of draft. "Not all painted up like the one you brought around last Christmas."

"I like them all painted up," said Murphy, flipping the sign to Closed—and wondering when they'd take the hint.

"She looks to be a woman of fine breeding," Scotty pronounced.

"Don't go reading anything into it, Scotty. Strictly business."

"That was an exceptionally long business conversation, my boy. Certainly bar food does not require so intense a debate."

Murphy stifled a yawn. "We had a lot to talk about."

"Ham and cheese is that interesting?"

"Get off my back, will you, Scotty?" Murphy's tone was good-natured but exasperated. "We were talking about her kid."

"Acquiring a paternal instinct at this late date?"

Murphy grabbed a bar rag and swabbed down the counter by the sink. "Patty's a genius."

"All parents believe their offspring to be genius calibre."

"This kid's the real thing, Scotty. Certifiably brilliant."

"A child after my own heart." Scotty narrowed his eyes in thought. "What, may I ask, is she doing in a mediocre school like Harborfields?"

"You were at Princeton too long, MacTavish. Not everyone can afford snot-nosed prep schools for their kids."

"What does her father do for a living?" Scotty was of the old school and believed the male of the species should shoulder the greater portion of life's burdens.

The question brought Murphy up short. "I don't know," he said after a moment.

"Single mother?"

"Divorced, I guess," said Murphy, although they hadn't touched on anything quite that personal.

"You didn't see fit to ask?"

"It never came up."

"This child," said Scotty, following Murphy back to the office where he kept the bar receipt books. "What was it about her that put you in mind of me?"

Murphy sat on the edge of the metal desk. "Brainpower, Scotty. The kid has it in spades. Would you believe I spent five minutes with her and ended up hiring her mother to cook for the bar?"

Scotty's laugh filled the tiny office. "I'm seventy-two years old, my boy. I'd believe just about anything."

Murphy gave him the *Reader's Digest* version of the business negotiations played out that afternoon.

"A thirty percent markup at least," said Scotty.

"Try thirty-five."

"This child is a natural resource," Scotty declared. "No doubt she could alleviate the deficit in the blink of an eye."

"She did a hell of a good job alleviating her mother's deficit."

"Obviously Samantha is a marvelous cook."

"I hope so," Murphy mumbled.

"You hope so?" Scotty's eyes widened behind his glasses. "You haven't sampled her wares?"

"I tried some cookies."

"And . . . ?"

"And nothing, Scotty. Christmas cookies. That's it."

"And you've hired this woman to handle the care and feeding of your valued customers?"

Murphy opened his mouth to speak but the retired professor was on a roll.

"This tavern provides more than libation for a thirsty traveler, Murphy. It's a haven for the lonely, a home for the homeless, a—"

"Give it a rest, will you, Scotty?" bellowed Murphy. "We're talking pizza and hamburgers here, not the salvation of the western world."

"The younger generation," said Scotty with a shake of his head. "You don't understand the value of a neighborhood pub."

Right again, Scotty. Murphy had spent his adult life running as far and fast from Rocky Hill as his ambition could carry him and the minute Bill O'Rourke was ready to take over again, Murphy would be on the next plane out.

FRANK GIFFORD was announcing the start of the fourth quarter of the football game when Patty heard her mother's Blazer chugging up the driveway. She leaped from the couch and peered out the window through a crack in the venetian blinds.

"Mom's home!"

"Is she smiling?" asked her Aunt Caroline, striking a carefree pose on the couch as if they both hadn't been waiting anxiously for Sam to hear all about her meeting with Murphy O'Rourke.

"I can't tell. She's up to her eyebrows in Shop-Rite bags."

"Your mother is a sick woman." Caroline stifled a yawn. "We sit up half the night waiting for her to return from an assignation with a foreign correspondent and she ends up pushing a cart at the supermarket. I'm ready to give up on her, Patricia.''

The more Patty heard the name, the better she liked it. Why didn't it sound so wonderful when Mrs. Venturella called her Patricia? She pulled the drapes across the front window and curled up opposite Caroline. "She's whistling. That's a good sign.''

"Knowing Sam, she might be whistling because she got a great deal on cauliflower.''

Patty couldn't argue that statement; the past few years, her mother had been more interested in business than anything else on earth except for Patty herself. But this time was different; Patty was certain of it. How could her mom meet someone as perfect as Murphy O'Rourke and walk away unimpressed?

"Hi, Mom!'' Patty trilled as Sam closed the front door behind her.

"Hello to both of you,'' said Sam as Patty jumped up to help her mother with the parcels. "I didn't know you'd still be here, Caroline.''

Aunt Caroline had no time for small talk. "How long were you at the meeting?'' she asked.

Patty's breath caught in her throat.

"Five minutes,'' said her mom.

"Five minutes!'' Patty knew her voice sounded all high and squeaky like a little kid, but she couldn't help it. "You couldn't have spent just five minutes with him!'' Murphy O'Rourke was exciting and smart and funny—everything that was just right for her mom. There was no way in the world they could have said everything that needed to be said in just three hundred seconds!

"Five minutes at the meeting,'' her mom repeated, her expression neutral.

Sam headed toward the kitchen with her parcels. Patty grabbed a bundle and followed after her mom, with Aunt Caroline close behind.

"C'mon, Mom," urged Patty as the grocery bag split and spilled the produce on the counter top. "Don't tease me like that."

"Patricia is right," said Caroline from the doorway. "She's too mature for such teasing."

"Patricia?" Patty's mom put two grocery bags down on the counter near the sink. "When did that happen?"

"Patricia is an elegant name, as befits this brilliant child," said Aunt Caroline in her loftiest manner.

Sam looked back at Patty. "What do you think about it?"

Patty shrugged, wishing the conversation would go back to what was really important: Murphy O'Rourke. "I like it. It makes me feel grown up."

Groaning, Sam unpacked two rolls of toilet paper and some hand soap from the first bag. "Make yourself useful, friend." She pressed the items into Caroline's arms. "Stash these in the back bathroom."

"Slave driver," muttered Caroline and disappeared down the dark hallway.

Sam turned back to her packages. Patty was almost beside herself with excitement, as if her skin had turned itself inside out and all of her nerve endings were dangling in the breeze.

"Do your homework?" Sam asked, her voice matter-of-fact.

"Hours ago."

"Did Caroline keep you from going to sleep?"

Patty shook her head. "I was staying up to see you." *Uh-oh.* From the way her mom's dark brows arched toward the ceiling, Patty knew she had made a strategic error. Time to retreat and regroup. She fiddled with a teaspoon resting alongside the stainless steel sink. "Did you meet Mr. O'Rourke?" she asked, as casually as she could manage.

Her mom nodded.

"Did you talk about the job?"

"All that money for so little work—it should be against the law!" Her mom shook her head in amazement. "You cooked up quite a deal for me, Patty."

Patty's spirits soared. "Did you . . . umm . . . did you like him?"

"He's not very good at business. I like that in a man."

"I think he's cute," said Patty, stepping out onto thin ice.

"Cute?" Her mom laughed out loud. "The man dresses like a bum."

Patty was highly insulted. Couldn't her mother see that Murphy O'Rourke was a free spirit? Free spirits didn't worry about three-piece suits and lace-up shoes. "I think he has style."

"Honey, that trench coat was the worst."

"It has character," Patty retorted. "Can you imagine, Mom, one time he left it on the Orient Express and they sent it back to him the very next day."

"No doubt," said her mother in that I-am-the-grownup tone of voice that Patty hated with all her heart. "The Orient Express has a reputation to consider."

Caroline came back into the kitchen, her coat slung over her arm. "Did I hear something about the Orient Express?"

Suddenly Patty didn't want to talk about Murphy O'Rourke any more. Her Aunt Caroline had a string of boyfriends, one ex-husband, and at least a dozen lovestruck suitors hoping for a chance to win her heart, and Patty would bet dollars to donuts that Caroline wasn't about to surrender her heart to any of them. She loved her godmother, but Caroline had a funny way of looking at men, almost as if they were windup toys and not real people.

Her mom didn't think like that, and Patty couldn't imagine Murphy O'Rourke being bossed around by anybody.

Patty raised up on tiptoe and peered into the grocery bag atop the microwave. "Three jars of dill pickles?" she asked, looking to change the subject.

Her mom grinned and removed a bread knife from the drawer near the sink. "Your Mr. O'Rourke requested them."

Was Patty just tired or were her mother's dark eyes sparkling with fun?

"Business, business, business," muttered Caroline, slipping into her coat. "I give up on you."

"Good," said Sam, slicing into a loaf of rye.

Good, thought Patty. This wasn't the time for Caroline to bring up the Christmas masquerade ball. Her mother could be real stubborn when she thought she was being tricked into doing something she didn't want to do. Grandpa Harry always said that Sam would rather be boiled in oil than be forced to change her mind.

"I'll pick you up at seven," Caroline said, hugging Patty then heading toward the back door.

"Seven!" Sam looked positively panicked. "Isn't that late?"

Caroline paused in the doorway. "Didn't I tell you? I'm driving in tomorrow morning. I have a stack of Carolina Herrera gowns to pick up from Old Frosty on East Sixty-third Street." Old Frosty was a society wife whose idea of fun was buying expensive designer dresses and never wearing them. Half of Aunt Caroline's stock was courtesy of Old Frosty. In fact, there were an awful lot of ladies like her who seemed to shop for a living. Patty couldn't understand it because there was nothing in the world she hated as much as being dragged into Macy's at Quakerbridge and forced to try on new clothes for her mom. Why anyone would think all that dressing and undressing was fun was beyond her.

Grownups could be very weird sometimes.

Her mom and Caroline talked for a few minutes, trying
to arrange their schedule, then Caroline decided it wouldn't
hurt to get a later start. She'd pick up Sam and her sandwiches, then ferry them over to O'Rourke's Bar and Grill at
seven-thirty. "Old Frosty can wait," Caroline said with a
laugh as she wound her scarf around her throat. "I want to
get myself a look at Patty's dr—" Patty almost fainted, she
was so scared. She faked a sneeze and sent a glass tumbling
off the tabletop and crashing to the floor. Anything to keep
Caroline quiet! Her aunt was about to say "dream man,"
she just knew it. If her mom got so much as the slightest hint
of matchmaking—well, Patty couldn't bear to think about
what would happen.

Patty jumped up to get the whisk broom and dustpan.
What a close call that had been! She didn't take an easy
breath until Aunt Caroline waved goodbye and hurried
outside to her car.

"Don't you think you should go to sleep now, kiddo?"
asked Sam after the car disappeared down the street. "It's
after eleven."

She bet "Patricias" didn't have mothers who told them
it was time for bed. "I want to see the Giant's win."

"Why is it I have the feeling you haven't paid one second's worth of attention to the game all night?"

Patty giggled—a very un-Patricialike thing to do—and
snatched a piece of American cheese from the stack on the
counter top. "Aunt Caroline doesn't like football. We talked
mostly."

"And why is it I have the feeling that you talked mostly
about me?"

Patty really tried to be honest all the time, and not telling
her mother the one hundred percent truth made her feel kind
of jumpy inside. She could just imagine what Sam would say
if Patty told her that Caroline had bought tickets to the
masquerade ball for both of them! The only thing that

would make Sam angrier was knowing that Patty was envisioning Murphy O'Rourke as a permanent feature around their maple kitchen table.

"Maybe I am tired," she said. She didn't even have to fake a yawn. "I suppose I'll go to sleep now after all."

"Sounds like a good idea to me," said her mom with a knowing look. "You wouldn't want me to find out you'd been matchmaking now, would you?"

Patty felt like she did when she played dodgeball at school: her stomach tightened and it seemed as if all the air had been pulled out of her lungs.

"Are you mad?" To her horror, tears burned against her eyelids and she prayed she wouldn't do something as stupid and childish as crying.

"I should be," her mother said, leaning against the counter and taking Patty's trembling hands in her own cool ones, "but for some reason I'm not."

It's Murphy O'Rourke! thought Patty, her heart tumbling and twisting inside her chest. *How can you be mad at me when you've met the man of your dreams?*

"Murphy is a nice man," Sam continued, "and the deal you made is a good one."

"I knew it!" Patty crowed, her tears forgotten. "I knew you'd like him. I—"

The look on her mother's face made Patty's words die off abruptly.

"I'll enjoy my association with him this week but that's as far as it will go."

"But, Mom, I—"

"I won't fall in love with him, honey."

"How do you know?"

"He's not my type."

"He believes in artistic freedom."

"No castles in the air, Patty, please!" Sam pulled her into her arms and kissed the top of her head. Sometimes Patty thought her mother would still be kissing the top of her head when Patty was fifty years old and a Nobel Prize winner. "How on earth did I ever give birth to such an impossible romantic? Just because you're smitten with Murphy O'Rourke doesn't mean I should be."

"He's perfect, Mommy," she said, forgetting that she was way too old to call her mother by a baby name, "he really is. If you'd only—"

But her mother wasn't listening to any of it.

"You're enough, kiddo, you always have been. It's the two of us together, the way it should be."

"I hate him!" Patty exclaimed, surprising them both. "He ruined everything!"

"Now don't you go blaming Mr. O'Rourke because your plans went haywire, young lady. The poor man has no idea what you're up to and I intend to keep it that way."

"I don't mean Murphy," Patty said, starting to cry for real. "I mean *him*."

Patty could feel her mother tense up. "Ronald?"

"My *father*. If he hadn't been such a creep you wouldn't be stuck all alone with me today."

Patty felt like running away when she saw the tears glittering in her mother's eyes. "Don't go feeling sorry for me," Sam warned, her voice low and tender. "The best thing that ever happened to me was having you." She chucked Patty under the chin and Patty forced a smile despite herself. "The second best thing was not marrying your dad."

Patty didn't often feel like a dumb little kid. She understood more about science and math and physics than most grownups three times her age ever would. But it was times like this when she knew there was a whole scary world of things out there that she might never understand, no matter how colossal her I.Q. or how formidable her vocabulary.

"But I thought you loved him," she managed, trying to make all these puzzle pieces fit together the way they did on television. "Grandma Betty told me all those stories about the way you met. She showed me the pictures of you two at the junior prom."

"I did love him, honey, but there are times when love isn't enough to make things work out the way you want them to." Patty actually felt a sharp pain in the center of her chest as she watched her mother struggle for composure. "I—wasn't the kind of girl the Donovan's thought was right for their Ronald."

"Because you weren't from Princeton?"

"Because we weren't rich. Because we drove old cars and my father didn't dress up and wear a suit to work." Sam stopped and her eyes closed for one long moment. Then she looked into Patty's eyes. "Yes, we loved each other, but not enough to matter."

Patty was beyond hearing anything but the pain in her mother's voice. "I hate him," she said again, her voice shaky and thin with rage. "He shouldn't have listened. He should have come to your house one night and asked you to marry him and you both could have run away and been happy."

"Oh, my little girl." This time Patty didn't object to being called a little girl because that was exactly what she felt like. "I'm happy now, don't you know that? I have you and I have Grandma and Grandpa and Caroline and all of our friends and family and in a few weeks we'll have the store. I don't need anything else, honey. I have everything I could possibly want right here."

Oh, how much Patty wanted to believe her mother's words.

But deep in her heart Patty knew there was still an emptiness in her mother's heart same as there was in hers. An emptiness that only a husband and father could fill.

Murphy O'Rourke.

It just had to be.

Chapter Five

Patty woke up sick the next morning. The little girl was cranky and demanding, and nothing Sam could do was enough to soothe the child's ruffled feelings. As much as she wanted to stay home with her daughter, there was no way on earth she could miss her last day of school.

"Thank God for mothers," she said to Caroline when her friend showed up to drive them both into Manhattan. "I'm twenty-eight and I still need to be rescued from time to time." Betty would be there in half an hour to take over.

Caroline offered to wait for Sam to get free, but it quickly became apparent that the trays of sandwiches would never fit in the tiny sports car.

"Go," said Sam, waving her friend on. "No reason for both of us to be late." It was bad enough that she was running behind; the last thing she needed was to cause Caroline to miss her appointment with Old Frosty.

It was eight o'clock when she whipped into the parking lot of O'Rourke's Bar and Grill. Her heart was thudding at an alarming rate, and she took a few quick, deep breaths before unloading the sandwich trays and making her way to the locked front door. O'Rourke was bound to be furious and she didn't blame him. This certainly wasn't the best way to gain a reputation for a fledgling company.

"I can explain," she blurted the moment he opened the heavy front door and ushered her inside the dark and quiet bar.

"Patty's sick," he said, his voice husky as if he'd just climbed out of bed, which judging by the hour wasn't hard to believe. "Her fever is down to 100.5."

"She called you?"

"She called me." He took the trays from her and set them down on one of the scarred wooden tables near the front. "She said I shouldn't blame you for being late." His grin was sleepy and surprisingly appealing. "She told me you were only doing your maternal duty."

Sam groaned and wished she had a less verbally precocious child. "Believe it or not, I didn't put her up to it."

"I believe you. I haven't forgotten you have yourself one smart kid."

Sam's eyes suddenly widened as she realized he was barefoot, shirtless and wearing a pair of sweatpants with a blown-out right knee. "You'll be the one with the fever if you don't cover up. Hasn't anyone told you winter's almost here?"

"I don't feel the cold," he said matter-of-factly as he closed the door. "I just rolled out of bed and down the stairs to let you in."

"You live up there?"

"For the time being." He smothered a yawn with the back of his hand. "How about some coffee?"

"I don't dare. As it is, I'll be lucky if I make my train."

"Patty said you have your final exam today."

Sam arched a brow. "Patty seems to have told you quite a lot."

"Afraid so." He laughed and Sam found she liked the sound. "You're twenty-eight, unmarried, a budding entrepreneur, a great mother, a rotten housecleaner, and an all-around swell person."

"I suppose you know my height, weight, and social security number, too." *We have to talk, Patty....*

He leaned against the bar and folded his arms across his broad chest. "About five-seven, maybe one hundred ten soaking weight."

"What about the social security number?"

"Give me five minutes on the telephone and I'll come up with it." He tilted his head a fraction. "So how close was I?"

"Five-seven and a quarter and too-close-for-comfort with the weight."

"You're too damned skinny as it is. You should gain a few pounds."

"I will," she said, casting a covert glance at her watch. "Wait until I open up the shop. Good food is one of my passions. I'll probably blimp up the first month."

"Big deal," he said, snapping his fingers. "If you're happy, what does it matter?"

"You're definitely a strange man, Mr.—"

"Murphy. I thought we settled that last night."

"Murphy. Most men judge a woman by the way she looks."

"Hey, don't get me wrong. I'm not saying you should turn into Roseanne Barr but ten pounds wouldn't hurt you."

"I'll keep that in mind."

"Besides, I didn't hire you to model clothes. I hired you to make sandwiches."

Laughter bubbled to her lips. "I think we should quit while we're ahead."

"I'm not known for my tact."

"Can't say I'm surprised." She adjusted her scarf and slipped on her gloves. "You do know what to do with all of this stuff, don't you?"

His brows slid together in an early-morning version of a scowl. Intimidating it wasn't. "What is there to do with sandwiches? You dump them on a plate and people help themselves."

"I wrote out all the instructions on a piece of stationery and taped it to the tray of ham and swiss."

"You're making me real nervous, Samantha."

"There's nothing to be nervous about." Men were terminally strange when it came to anything more complicated than a can opener and a microwave. "I made a few appetizers last night to practice for my final. Patty and I can't eat all of them so..." Her voice trailed off.

"Appetizers?"

"Nothing fancy. Just heat and eat. It's on the house."

"No way. What do I owe you?"

Sam thought about Patty and her killer business deal. "Believe me, you don't owe me a thing. You're paying me more than enough as it is."

He inclined his head in thanks and opened the door. "What about the trays?"

"I'll come back tonight after school to pick them up." A brisk wind whipped through the open door to the bar, and she saw gooseflesh form on his arms. "Put something on now, will you, please?"

He grinned and Sam found herself grinning back. She hadn't grinned in at least six or seven years.

"My male pulchritude too much for you, huh?"

"Definitely," said Sam as she turned to leave. "Especially this early in the morning."

"Later," said Murphy O'Rourke.

"Later," said Sam.

You're right about this one, Patty, she thought as she headed across the parking lot toward her Blazer. *A genuinely terrific man.* Murphy O'Rourke was funny and sharp and not all that bad looking without his shirt on. She liked his style and his bar and the way he treated women and children.

Too bad she wasn't interested.

MURPHY WATCHED SAM trot across the parking lot, her shapely rear end looking damn cute in those black pants. For a skinny woman, she had a surprising number of curves hidden beneath her loose clothing. Of course, he usually liked his women a bit on the *zaftig* side but Sam Dean wasn't half bad. There weren't many things Murphy liked before his first cup of coffee and to his amazement Sam had turned out to be easy on the nerves.

Who would've thought it?

He liked the way she seemed comfortable in her own skin, not looking for a way to be anyone other than exactly who she was. She seemed ambitious without being driven; sharp without being brittle; friendly without being pushy. She was the kind of woman you could kick back with and relax. Watch the game. Read the papers. Take to bed and—

No way. Some men liked long and lanky brunettes with small boobs and tight butts and eyes that glittered like onyx. Murphy would be the first to admit the combination had its charm, but he liked his women small, blonde and as big-breasted as possible. He also liked women who came unencumbered, and it wasn't hard to see Sam Dean came with quite a bit of baggage, including the delightful Patty. Although for some strange reason he couldn't imagine any man thinking of Patty Dean as an encumbrance.

He continued to watch as Sam climbed into her battered Blazer, revved up the engine, then zipped off down the road toward the Princeton Junction train station. He glanced up at the big round clock hanging near the door to the kitchen. In about nine hours she'd be back.

The thought made him smile.

"What's this?"

Murphy started in surprise and turned around to see his father, dressed and in an overcoat, poking the sandwiches on the top tray.

"Food," said Murphy. "Thanks to Earle and his sudden departure, we have a kitchen problem."

Bill O'Rourke grunted and peeled back the wrappings on a huge pile of perfectly sliced pickles. "Real fancy," he said with a sharp look at his son. "Who are you trying to impress?"

"Not you." He debated leaving it at that but his better instincts won out. "I hired a new caterer from Princeton Junction. She threw the appetizers in as an extra."

"Free?"

"Is that so hard to believe?"

"Nothing's free in this world, boy. Thought you were old enough to realize that."

Murphy was thirty-six years old. He'd traveled the world. He'd lived through a bad marriage and a worse divorce. He'd acquired a hide tough as shoe leather and a heart to match, but damned if his old man couldn't still find the right place to stick the knife.

"Sounds like you've been talking to Joey Boy again."

"Your brother is worried about my future," Bill said.

"And I'm not?" *Damn it. Don't let him bait you like this.*

"I didn't say that."

"Yeah, but I suppose little brother did."

"He thinks I should see a specialist in Florida."

"Princeton doctors aren't good enough?"

"He thinks I should slow down."

"Dr. Cohen thinks you aren't doing enough."

"He thinks I should sell the bar."

"And do what? Count your food stamps?"

His father's cheeks reddened. "Joey thinks I should retire. He thinks I should sell the bar and the house and—"

"Yeah, don't tell me. Move down to Florida and turn into a sunburned old man with nothing but time on his hands." Murphy waved his arms in disgust. "I've heard it all before."

"At least I'd have family down there."

Good going, Dad. Now you're bringing out the heavy artillery. "Carole and Jay and the kids don't count?"

Fooled you, didn't I, Dad. You thought I was going to count myself in, too.

"Of course they count," said Bill, sounding uncertain. "But *you* aren't going to be here forever."

"That's right," said Murphy, struggling to remember that his old man was still under a doctor's care, "and you're not going to be recuperating forever. Things will get back to normal soon enough."

He's scared. He's had a heart attack. Remember everything Dr. Cohen told you about cardiac patients. Don't blow up!

Bill folded the plastic wrap back over the appetizers, his fingers trembling with the effort. It was almost enough to make Murphy relent.

Almost, but not quite.

"Stein called last night," Bill said, meeting Murphy's eyes. "He says he wants you back on the paper."

"He says a lot of things," Murphy mumbled, "some of which are even true."

"He says he'll give you a raise."

"I'll tell him where he can stick his raise."

"He said you can have the city beat. The tri-state gubernatorial coverage. A Sunday spot on *Face the City*. Anything."

"Right. Anything but freedom of speech." Murphy stormed over to the coffeepot and poured himself a steaming cup. "Forget it."

Bill fumbled through his pockets and extracted a stick of gum that he unwrapped and folded into his mouth. "You come rolling in here, playing savior, and think you can make everything right, when you haven't bothered to come around in years."

Murphy threw his hands in the air. "Isn't it too early in the morning for venom, Pop?" It wasn't like he'd abandoned his father then come around looking for an inheritance.

"You wanted out from the minute you were born."

"Can you blame me? This wasn't exactly a happy home we had here."

"I'm not made of money," Bill said. "You can't live here forever."

Murphy, who had not only been paying his way but everybody's else's, looked up from his cup at the man who'd fathered him but never understood one damned thing about who and what he was. "You've said that before," he said quietly. "On my eighteenth birthday."

Both men fell silent. Murphy had walked out that day within half an hour of Bill's terse pronouncement. He swore Rocky Hill was history and so was his father; the only way he'd come back was in a chauffeur-driven limousine with money to burn. It had taken eight years of struggling but on his twenty-sixth birthday he'd pulled up to O'Rourke's Bar and Grill in a monster Caddy limo with a full bar in the back and treated his father and his brother to a day at the track. On him. All of it. Murphy was a fountain of money that day and not even the fact that it took him six months to pay off the bills was enough to sour the sweet taste of victory.

For one fleeting moment, he'd been someone in his father's eyes and in his brother's. There'd never been another moment like it.

He looked at his father. *And probably never would be.*

"Want some coffee?" he asked, reaching for a clean cup.

"I'm on my way out," said Bill, buttoning up his coat.

"Need a lift?"

Bill shook his head. "Tessie Gargan is picking me up on the corner."

"Going any place special?"

"Doc Cohen wants me in."

"Good luck," said Murphy. "Maybe you'll be kicking me out of here sooner than you think."

Bill paused in the doorway, his fair Irish skin flooded with color again. "Nobody's forcing you to stay, boy. You can go back to your fancy friends anytime you want."

"Yeah, Pop," said Murphy when the door slammed shut behind his father. "You're welcome."

But then he had no right to expect thanks. His father needed help. His sister couldn't provide it. His brother had bailed out to Florida and a ritzy law practice. Only Murphy remained; volatile, greedy, *unemployed* Murphy. And it was Murphy who came back to the place he'd struggled to escape from for so many years, only to discover that the more things change, the more they stay the same.

All his life, Bill O'Rourke had avoided emotions—both his own and those of his two combative sons. His heart attack back in October had changed many things but not that one basic part of Bill's personality and Murphy doubted if anything ever would.

CAROLINE COULD BE BOSSY, annoying and generally a pain in the neck, but she was one terrific best friend.

Who else would sit at the corner of West Fiftieth and Eighth Avenue in the pricey sports car piled high with designer gowns just so she could drive New York's newest cooking school graduate back home to New Jersey that afternoon?

"I owe you one," Sam said as she settled into the cushioned leather seat and rested her head back.

Caroline chuckled and switched on the stereo system. "Just you remember that when the time comes."

Soft, lush music filled the small car as the Jaguar inched its way toward the Lincoln Tunnel. Sam closed her eyes and let herself drift lazily along on a cloud of her friend's ubiquitous Chanel No. 5. Neatly stacked on the tiny back seat, padded with tons of tissue to prevent wrinkles, were three glorious Cinderella ball gowns, the latest acquisitions from Old Frosty. A pale tea rose with delicate seed pearls tracing the curves of the bodice. A red beaded gown made for grand entrances. And a magnificent, fairy tale of a satin dress in a sapphire blue so deep and luminous that the sight of it had made Sam almost weep with joy.

A sigh threatened to escape, and she quickly translated it into a yawn. All Caroline needed was to know how badly Sam would love to primp and fuss and dress to the nines and dazzle the denizens of Princeton at the masquerade ball; there would be no living with the pressure her best friend would put on her. Anyone—even Sam—could spare just one Saturday night to live a dream but the rock bottom truth of the matter was the hundred-dollar ticket fee might as well be ten thousand. Money—wouldn't you just know that would be the problem.

But, oh, how wonderful it was to daydream about it! Sam wasn't given to flights of fancy the way Patty was, but it seemed as if the ball gowns whispered stories with each rustle of satin and silk. Dazzling women and handsome men in all their splendor, waltzing on a shimmering marble dance floor to the strains of Strauss. Exciting flirtations behind the de rigeur white velvet masques. Caroline would look like a movie star in the Schiaparelli gown while Sam— Sam would what?

She closed her eyes more tightly and concentrated. It wasn't as if she had no imagination, after all. She was a world-class daydreamer, but try as she might Sam couldn't conjure up one single vision of herself in anything but baggy cords and a black sweater.

She could come up with an elegant upswept hairdo only to pan down to her trusty Reeboks and sweat socks. Or she dreamed up a pair of pricey Maud Frizon pumps with bejeweled buckles and teamed them with her ragged jeans. But even more horrifying was the image of herself all decked out in Old Frosty's finery but with a face devoid of makeup and her overgrown hair pulled back in a ponytail.

It was as futile an undertaking in her daydreams as it was in real life. She was plain Sam Dean, nothing more, who had a daughter to provide for and a future to plan.

PATTY'S GRANDMA, Betty Dean, glanced at the thermometer and smiled. "Down another half degree, Patty. I think you'll live."

"Can I have some more ice cream?"

"You had some at lunchtime."

"Please, Grandma. My throat's sore and the ice cream makes it feel better."

Grandma Betty pursed her lips but Patty saw the twinkle in her bright blue eyes. "Maybe."

Grandma bustled out of Patty's bedroom, leaving behind the smell of cinnamon and brown sugar, and Patty had little doubt a bowl of vanilla ice cream wouldn't be long in coming. Smiling, she nestled back under her covers and thumbed through the newest issue of *Time Magazine*. Not even a discussion of supply-side economics could pique her interest. She glanced at her watch. Back at school they were just starting math class, and Patty had been looking forward to a special project Mr. Berman had promised would keep her busy for a while.

Except for the vanilla ice cream, Patty hated being sick because being sick meant staying home from school. Oh, she wouldn't admit it even to her best friend, Susan, but she looked forward to school each morning the way other kids looked forward to summer vacation. She loved the feeling of excitement when she sat down in class and opened her book, even if that excitement wasn't quite as much fun as it used to be. It seemed the longer she was in school, the harder the teachers at Harborfields Elementary found it to keep ahead of her.

Lately, Patty had been spending a lot of time in the Rocky Hill library, checking out big fat books on physics and calculus and advanced methods of food production for the

Third World. The librarian said that pretty soon Patty would have to go to the big Somerset County library in Bridgewater. "Can't keep up with you, honey," the woman had said with a shake of her gray head. "Don't know if the whole state can for long."

Now and then she'd hear teachers whisper about special classes and what a shame it was a child so bright was languishing in a school like theirs, and a cold knot of fear would form in Patty's stomach and made her wish she could be like everybody else. She loved her friends and she loved her teachers, and she couldn't imagine going to school any place but Harborfields. Sometimes she would see her mother's face grow all cloudy and sad looking when she thought Patty wasn't looking, and Patty found herself scared and confused and angry that her mom had to work so hard for things other people took for granted.

If she had a father, it all would be different. She just knew it. When there was a father in the house, everything was better. Oh, she knew real families weren't like the old TV shows where father always *did* know best and mothers like Donna Stone and Margaret Anderson spent their afternoons planning their evening dinner menus. Real families weren't even like the Huxtables or the Seavers where both mom and dad went to work and the kids had keys to the house. Real families didn't always fit together the way they should; real families didn't always like each other; but real families stayed together forever and that was the one thing Patty wanted.

She loved going to Susan's and listening to Mrs. Gerard complain about Mr. Gerard's magazines scattered around the family room and the toothpaste tube left uncapped in the bathroom. Even though Patty was only ten years old and had never had a father of her own, she somehow knew that Mrs. Gerard's griping was a form of affection and she wished with all her heart she had a father around the house to scatter magazines around and leave toothpaste tubes uncapped and make her mother smile.

Murphy O'Rourke could make her mother smile.

The magazine slipped from her fingers and she closed her eyes. Grandma Betty was whistling in the kitchen and Patty could hear the low mumble of the television set tuned to *As the World Turns*. She didn't want to fall asleep. Any minute Grandma would be bringing in a dish of vanilla ice cream, but it was so cozy there tucked under the covers. From somewhere came the sound of a doorbell ringing and Patty wondered who would come calling in the middle of a regular day...

"Honey, I'm home!" Murphy O'Rourke, looking tall and handsome in his corduroy jacket and worn raincoat, stepped through the front door of their house in Rocky Hill.

"Darling!" Sam O'Rourke swept into the room, her full skirts billowing around her knees. *"Dinner is almost ready. I made your favorite—chili and spare ribs."* Sam's dark hair was swept off her face and fell below her shoulders in glossy ringlets. Her makeup was perfect. Her frilly white apron looked fetching against her pale blue dress.

Murphy tossed down his briefcase on the piano bench and pulled her into his arms. "Just think," he said, "if it hadn't been for Patty, we never would have met."

"Yes," said Sam with a delighted sigh. "We owe this all to our daughter. Patricia Dean O'Rourke, the youngest graduate in M.I.T.'s history...."

"No man is luckier," said Murphy.

"No woman is happier," sighed Sam.

And no dream had ever been better.

Chapter Six

"Five minutes," said Sam as Caroline turned off the engine and let out the clutch later that evening. "I'll pick up the empty trays, get a bit of feedback from O'Rourke, and we're on our way."

"Don't rush on my account," said Caroline, reaching for the door handle.

"You don't have to come with me." Sam swung her legs out of the low-slung car. "I'll be back before you know it." The very last thing she needed was Caroline's opinion of Murphy O'Rourke.

Sam crunched across the gravel driveway with Caroline's footsteps crunching right behind. Boisterous male laughter seeped through the walls of O'Rourke's Bar and Grill, along with the friendly blare of big-band music popular around the time of the Second World War.

"They sound like a happy group of campers," Caroline observed as they paused in front of the door.

Sam resisted the urge to smooth her bangs and refresh her lipstick. Mustering up a smile, she opened the door and ushered Caroline inside.

Her friend looked at the crowd and went pale. "Samantha, these men are seventy, if they're a day."

"I know."

Caroline's shock was almost comical. "How old *is* O'Rourke, anyway?"

Sam was about to answer when she heard footsteps behind her, then a male voice.

"Hi, Sam."

Both women turned as Murphy O'Rourke, clad in a putty-colored shirt and a pair of baggy cords, strolled up to them. He carried a bottle of Schnapps in one hand and a bar towel in the other.

"Caroline," said Sam with a wide grin, "this is Murphy."

He tucked the bar towel in his belt and extended his hand. "You're the one with the clothes shop."

Caroline shook his hand and shot Sam another quelling glance. "You've been talking about me?"

"Patty has," said Murphy. "She called to tell me you both would be stopping by."

Sam's face flashed with embarrassment. God only knew what else her voluble daughter might have told O'Rourke. "You might want to consider an unlisted number. Patty seems to have taken quite a liking to you."

He shrugged amiably. "It's mutual. She's some piece of work."

Sam warmed at his words. "That she is. She's always trying to set me up wi—" *Oh, no, Dean. Keep your foot out of your mouth for a change.* She gestured toward the busy saloon. "You're busy. Why don't you show me where the trays are and we'll be on our way."

O'Rourke's hazel eyes were friendly and disarmingly direct. "You in a rush?"

"We're going out to dinner."

"I hope you don't have reservations."

She blinked. "I beg your pardon?"

He inclined his head toward Caroline who—amazingly—was now perched atop Scotty's table and laughing uproariously with his companions. "I don't think she's in any hurry."

"So I see." Sam glanced again at her best friend. "It would serve her right if I took her Jag and aimed it for the Pizza Hut."

"Patty said it's a celebration." He led her toward the bar where she claimed a stool on the end. "Congratulations. What are you celebrating?"

"My last day of school. If I never see Manhattan again it'll be too soon. I hate that city."

His expression darkened, and she remembered that Manhattan had been his stomping grounds before he walked off the job at the *Telegram*.

"Sorry, Murphy. I have strong feelings about New York City and most of them aren't nice."

"New York's a great place if you're rich enough to enjoy it. Fortunately I was rich enough." He reached under the bar and pulled up a bottle of asti spumante. "How about a toast to your graduation?"

She hesitated a moment. "I haven't eaten yet today. I might end up with a lampshade on my head."

He grinned. "I'd offer you some food but they cleaned me out."

Her eyes widened. "They ate everything? Even those bacon-and-mushroom pinwheels?"

"Even the pinwheels. I'd thought this meat-and-potatoes bunch would turn their noses up at fancy stuff like that."

She ran her hand along the brass rail, admiring the old-fashioned workmanship that had gone into the bar itself. "The world's full of surprises."

"Like that kid of yours," he said, popping the cork on the asti spumante.

"Like that kid of mine." She cast another glance at Caroline who paid her not the slightest heed. "Genius doesn't exactly run in my family."

He reached over and pulled down two flute glasses from the rack. "What about her father's family?"

"If genius ran in their family, maybe they'd be smart enough to appreciate their granddaughter."

"Their loss. I can't imagine anybody meeting Patty and not liking her."

Of course it was much more complicated than that and they both knew it. Not the sort of thing you discussed with a man you barely knew.

She watched as he poured the Italian champagne into the glasses. Murphy O'Rourke had nice hands, large and well formed, with a dusting of sandy-colored hair. His nails were cared for but not manicured. Sam hated men who wore clear polish and had their hair permed every few weeks. From the looks of O'Rourke's mop, he rarely paid a visit to the barber, which was all right by Sam.

He handed her a flute of asti spumante, then raised his glass. "To your success."

She raised her own in answer. "To a wonderful future for all of us."

They touched glasses. Sam sighed in pleasure as the bubbly golden liquid slithered down her throat. Normally talk of Patty's father or grandparents was enough to send Sam into a black cloud of depression, equaled only by her own reluctance to admit someone as dear as her little girl could mean so little to her own flesh and blood.

There was something about O'Rourke that rattled her defenses and loosened her tongue. He was as straightforward as a mug of draft. He had told her he wasn't known for his tact, and his behavior had borne out that statement, but somehow Sam found his blunt talk refreshing, instead of abrasive.

"I should get going." Sam polished off the rest of the Italian champagne and thanked God she wasn't driving for her head was buzzing rather nicely at that moment. "I have to be home by eleven."

Murphy chuckled and shot her a curious look. "A curfew at your age?"

She made a face at him. "My dad's babysitting Patty. Eleven's *his* bedtime."

He looked down at the battered Seiko on his wrist. "You're running out of time."

"Don't I know it." Across the room, Caroline was bent over the checker board with the apparent concentration of a nuclear physicist on the verge of a big discovery. "I'm ready to eat your bar stools." She cast him a mournful look. "Do you have any pretzels?"

O'Rourke's hazel eyes twinkled with a wicked light. "You can do better than that."

"I can?"

He reached for Sam's hand and drew her to her feet. "Let's go."

"THEY'RE GOING to be furious," said Sam, ten minutes later as they took their seats at Tony's Pizzeria.

"No, they're not," said Murphy.

"We shouldn't have done this."

"Of course we should have."

"What about the bar?"

"Scotty will keep things running."

"Caroline will kill me."

"Do you care?"

A laugh escaped Sam. "Not at the moment." She sighed with pleasure. "You were right, Murphy. This pizza is fantastic!"

"Worth the walk?"

"Even in a blizzard!" Sam had grumbled as they walked the two blocks to Tony's in a bitter wind, but she had to admit it was worth it. "The question is—how do we get the rest of the pizzas back to the bar before they turn into popsicles?"

Murphy gestured toward a sign near the cash register. "Tony delivers."

She stopped, pizza halfway to her mouth. "You could have called in the order."

"Sure I could have." He sprinkled crushed red pepper on his slice. "But you have to admit it's quieter here."

It was also more private. There had been thirty pairs of eyes trained intently upon them back at O'Rourke's. Thirty pairs of ears straining to hear every word that passed between them. Not that their words were particularly interesting or intimate, but such avid attention had made Sam a bit uncomfortable, especially with Caroline's bright blue eyes following Sam's every move.

Murphy might be a well-known figure at Tony's, but Sam wasn't and she found herself delighting in her anonymity. She could eat and drink and laugh all she wanted and not one single member of her family was around to wonder what was *really* going on. Sure, Caroline would have a few questions but Sam was certain she could handle her friend's curiosity.

Her own curiosity, however, was something else again as she pretended to concentrate her attention on her pizza. Truth was, it was Murphy O'Rourke who had her wondering.

"Hot peppers?" asked Murphy, pushing the container toward her.

"No, thanks."

"Cheese?"

"Not right now."

That wonderful lopsided grin tilted his mouth. "Questions?"

She leaned across the table. "What are we doing here?"

"You don't like it?"

"I love it."

"Great. I thought you would."

"You should be back at the bar."

"I needed a break. I was ODing on cigar smoke."

She nodded and sat back in her chair, chewing thoughtfully. *So, what did you expect, Dean? A declaration of love?* He wanted to get out and stretch his legs and grab a bite to eat. There was no mystery in that, no hidden romance. She refused to acknowledge a twinge of disappointment and instead grabbed for the hot peppers and sprinkled them liberally on her second slice of pizza.

Tony was whistling behind the counter as he packed the six pies into their boxes. The savory smells of onion and pepperoni and sausage filled the air.

"Do you always treat your customers this well?" Sam asked after Tony's delivery boy staggered out to the truck, unable to see over the stack of boxes.

"Good customer relations," he said with a shrug. "Keeps 'em coming back for more."

"You're a nice guy, O'Rourke. Why don't you just admit it?"

"Nice guys don't make good foreign correspondents. Looks lousy on the resume."

She thought about a third slice of pizza, hesitated, then reached for it, anyway. "I thought you were a city beat reporter."

"That was my last gig. Before that I spent ten years in Europe."

No wonder his trench coat had looked so battered; it had served as the official costume of the peripatetic correspondent. Why that should make her feel sad was beyond Sam. "Footloose and fancy-free, I suppose."

"Footloose and fancy-free except for a three-year marriage."

"Kids?"

"Nope."

"Your wife didn't like to travel?"

"My wife loved to travel," O'Rourke said, "but she didn't like traveling with me."

Sam took a bite of pizza, cheese stretching out like a white rubber band, and studied him intently as she chewed. "Are you over her?"

"Completely." His look matched hers in intensity. "How about you—divorced?"

"Never married."

"Does he see Patty?"

"About as often as Mr. Spock has sex—every seven years or so."

Murphy's use of language was salty and right on target.

"I've called him that a time or two myself," said Sam.

"He's missing out on a great kid."

"Serves him right," said Sam, her tone angry. "Unfortunately Patty's missing out on having a father."

"Does she miss him?"

"It's not Ronald Donovan she misses. It's having a real, live, seven-days-a-week father."

He leaned forward, eyes focused squarely on her. It wasn't hard to see how effective a reporter he must have been; there was something vaguely intimidating in his body language and intensity that could force state secrets out of shadowy hiding places. "How do you feel about that?"

She shrugged, wishing they'd stayed back in the crowded, noisy bar where a conversation like this could never have gotten off the ground. "Patty's a born romantic, Murphy. She believes in love at first sight, happily ever after and Donna Reed."

His intensity softened, and she thought she saw something akin to understanding in his eyes. "Nothing so terrible about that, is there, Sam?"

"Only if you're ten years old and you really think it can happen."

"It happens sometimes."

"Maybe," said Sam, "but not to anyone I know."

He started to say something then stopped on the first syllable.

"Go ahead," said Sam. "Tell me I'm a cynic. You won't be the first."

"That's not what I was going to say."

"Don't tell me you agree with Patty."

"I'm too cynical, myself, for that." He looked over at Sam and an uneasy feeling built inside her stomach. "I almost wonder if Patty—" He stopped, shaking his head. "No. That's too ridiculous."

"What is?" How she managed to sound cool and collected was beyond Sam.

"Do you think she was trying to set us up?"

Sam started to choke on her pizza and she had to grab quickly for her beer before O'Rourke vaulted the table and began administering the Heimlich Maneuver.

"Stupid idea, right?" asked O'Rourke once she caught her breath.

"Stupid idea," she managed. *You're too good at this, O'Rourke. You should be back pounding the political beat.* Her little red-haired daughter was a born matchmaker. No one from the butcher at Shop-Rite to her pediatrician had escaped Patty's scrutiny. Sam liked to tease her, saying she had a Noah's Ark mentality but Patty truly believed in a couples—only world and had made it her business to see that Sam found her better half.

That Murphy could figure that out after only one meeting was frightening.

"So you're not looking for a husband?"

Sam shook her head. "Afraid not. I've been waiting so long to open my store that nothing short of an earthquake could tear me away from it."

"I still don't know exactly what kind of store you're opening. Is it a deli?"

Now this was territory she was familiar with. "Delis are for Rocky Hill, O'Rourke. I'm talking pure Princeton cuisine."

"I thought you were a takeout service."

Sam lifted her chin in a parody of the proper Princeton matron. "Upscale takeout service, thank you very much. Not a pastrami on rye to be found."

He made a face. "Not another pasta palace I hope."

"Pasta salads are trendy, O'Rourke. I thought you ersatz New Yorkers know all about being trendy."

"All I know is that spaghetti belongs on a plate with meatballs. Case closed."

Sam couldn't help laughing out loud. "You sound like my father. He thinks the only good chicken dinner comes straight from the Colonel's bucket."

O'Rourke grinned but maintained his position. "I think I'd like your father." He placed another slice of pizza on her plate then helped himself as well. "So how did you end up in the world of sushi and potato skins?"

"I'm a domestic creature. I grew up mixing brownies and making meat loaf suppers. It's the only marketable skill I have. Unfortunately you can't make a living slinging corned beef hash and chicken fricassee around here."

"So you're going where the market is."

"Exactly." She told him the location of her store and watched with satisfaction as his eyes widened with respect.

"I'm impressed," he said.

"So am I," said Sam. "I never thought I'd find a place so close to the railroad station."

"Hungry executives will fall out of the train and into your shop."

"That's the general idea."

His expression was comically sorrowful. "Now if you were cooking real food, I'd say you had a winner there."

Sam, whose own tastes ran more toward meat loaf than blackened red fish, shook her head. "Sorry, O'Rourke. Marketing 101—I intend to supply exactly what they demand."

"I think you're going to make a fortune."

"I hope so. Patty's the most important thing in my life. She deserves the best I can possibly provide."

He nodded as if he really understood. "I'm angling for another overseas spot with UPI. The minute my father's back behind the bar, I'm out of here."

"It looks like we both have our heads on straight, doesn't it?" asked Sam.

"We know what we want and how to go about getting it. Can't ask for more out of life than that."

"No," said Sam after a moment, thinking about the delights to be found in a warm restaurant on a cold winter's night with a man who could actually become a friend. "I don't suppose you can."

THE WALK BACK to O'Rourke's felt wonderful to Sam, sated as she was after the pizza feast at Tony's. The wind was fierce, and they walked quickly, with their heads down. They didn't talk, but then, they didn't need to. She felt as comfortable with Murphy as if she had known him forever.

Pizza seemed to have worked wonders with the crowd at the bar. Sam had expected a barrage of questions—especially from Caroline—but their return to O'Rourke's was greeted with nothing more than a chorus of praise for the pizzas.

She sat down at the bar and watched as Murphy got to work. O'Rourke's Bar and Grill did a brisk, steady business. Customers arrived and departed with the predictability of a train schedule and there was no one who didn't have a good word for Murphy. He really had grown up in the tavern, Sam thought, as she watched an elderly woman with sleek silver hair and a quick laugh chuck Murphy under his chin.

Many of these customers had known Murphy since he was a little boy, and Sam found their affection for the former foreign correspondent endearing. Not that the elder O'Rourke was forgotten, however; you had only to listen to

some of the stories told by the tavern regulars to understand just how sorely he was missed. Bill O'Rourke had
opened the doors in the late forties and those doors had remained open ever since. There seemed to be some talk
among the regulars about Bill being afraid of getting back
to the daily grind after his heart attack, but Murphy never
entered into these conversations. He just smiled and poured
another draft and said, "Isn't it great about those Giants?"

Sam wasn't inclined toward on-the-spot analysis. As a
rule, she was too busy to spend much time digging into psy-
ches—her own or anybody else's. But there was something
about Murphy O'Rourke that made her wish she'd be
around long enough to figure out what made him tick. She'd
never known an honest-to-goodness man of the world before. Why, he'd been to places she'd never dreamed of going. Bangkok. Peru. The deserts of Saudi Arabia. Sam had
been content to remain in the town where she was born, in
the neighborhood where she'd grown up, surrounded by
people who knew her as well as she knew her own daughter.

It wasn't hard to imagine O'Rourke tossing down his bar
apron and grabbing his trench coat the moment his dad
stepped back into the picture.

No, she thought, watching as he fixed an Irish Coffee for
Scotty, no matter how hard Patty wished for it, she'd picked
the wrong man this time around. Murphy O'Rourke wasn't
going to be around for the long haul. He probably had his
suitcases packed and at the ready so he could be on the next
plane out the minute his father was ready to take over the
bar again.

The rest of the evening sped by in a blur of laughter and
song. Caroline took over the upright piano in the back of
the bar room and before too long the old timers were raising their voices to tunes Sam remembered from vintage
World War II movies: "Don't Sit Under the Apple Tree,"

"Rum and Coca Cola." She closed her eyes and imagined she was at a U.S.O. dance, jitterbugging with a fresh-faced sailor who was on his way to battle....

"You're not singing."

She opened her eyes in time to see Murphy slide a mug of hot coffee across the bar to her.

"Thank your lucky stars," she said, holding back a yawn. "I could clear your bar in a matter of seconds."

"Maybe you should give me a few choruses of something loud and off-key. It's almost midnight. It's time some of these—"

"Midnight!" Sam leaped to her feet. "I have to go!"

"What happens now? Do you turn into a pumpkin?"

"No, but Caroline's Jag might."

"Can you fit those trays into a sports car?"

"Caroline said we'll tie them to the bumper if we have to." She extended her hand. "I've had a terrific evening."

"Sorry you missed out on the Pizza Hut?"

"Not a bit. You were right about Tony's—definitely the best place in town."

He shrugged in that offhanded way she was coming to know. "I couldn't let you starve, could I? There'd be no one to make the sandwiches for tomorrow."

"A practical man, Murphy O'Rourke." And a nice one. A cushy assignment like this would go a long way toward pushing Fast Foods for the Fast Lane into the black.

She hoped he took his time finding himself a cook.

THE BAR CLEARED OUT soon after Sam and her friend left. All except for Scotty.

"Need a ride?" Murphy asked, wiping down the bar and dumping ice down the sink. "I'll run you home if you want."

"I have my car," said Scotty.

Murphy eyeballed the coffeepot. "I think there's enough for another cup."

"Caffeine after midnight is my arch enemy, Murphy."

Murphy poured himself a cup and leaned against the bar. "Okay, friend, out with it. What's on your mind?"

"You're perceptive, my boy."

"Not particularly," said Murphy. "You're an open book."

"Has it occurred to you that the Masquerade Ball is this Saturday?"

"Big deal." The last thing on Murphy's mind was getting all decked out in a tux and plastering a velvet mask on his kisser.

"Caroline plans to attend."

"I hope she has a great time." He took a sip of coffee and battled down the urge to pour sugar into the deadly brew. He wondered if Sam was going to the ball and had the feeling Scotty had the answer, but he refused to give the professor the satisfaction. "Did she promise you a dance?"

Scotty sat up straighter, his tweeds fairly bristling with self-satisfaction. "The last waltz."

Murphy gave the man a friendly punch in the shoulder. "You old dog. Nice going. Next thing I know you'll be asking her to go as your date."

"That thought had occurred to me," Scotty said, "but unfortunately she is already spoken for." Scotty was receiving a special Princteon citizenship award and Murphy knew the dapper professor would have loved to show up with a beautiful blonde on his well-tailored arm.

"Too bad," said Murphy.

"Quite," said Scotty.

"You could take Angela."

Scotty flashed him a lethal look. Waitress Angela Fennelli and Edmund "Scotty" MacTavish were the proverbial oil and water. "To be truthful, I already have another prospect in mind."

Murphy threw his head back and laughed out loud. "You've been holding out on me." He straddled a chair across from Scotty. "Who's the lucky woman?"

"You are, Murphy my boy. You're going to be my date."

CAROLINE WAS STRANGELY QUIET on the way home and Sam would have been suspicious if it wasn't for the fact her friend had already said yes, she'd be happy to stop at the all-night Shop-Rite so Sam could pick up a few extra fixings for the tomorrow's sandwich trays and no, it wasn't a bother.

Caroline pulled her sports car right up to the front and waited while Sam ran in and grabbed a few cans and jars of goodies she knew Scotty and Joe and the others would enjoy. Hadn't Murphy said he was crazy about olives? She grabbed a can on her way to the checkout and chalked it up to customer relations.

"Thanks," said Sam as she folded herself back into the low-slung car. "I hope I didn't take too long."

"Not at all," said Caroline as she drove out of the parking lot. In profile she appeared to be smiling. "I hope you got everything you need."

Sam swiveled around in her seat and took a close look at her best friend. Bad enough she'd be going home to an irate father. The last thing she needed was a mysterious friend. "Okay, out with it. Let's get it out of the way."

Caroline batted her eyelashes the way she had at Scotty. "Whatever are you talking about?"

"Murphy."

"A lovely man," said Caroline, her tone bland. "He makes wonderful coffee."

"That's not what I mean."

Caroline glanced quickly in the rearview mirror. "Then perhaps you should be more explicit."

"The matchmaking," said Sam. "When is it going to start?"

"I'm not going to matchmake."

Puzzled, Sam leaned back in her seat. "Don't tell me you didn't like Murphy." Caroline and Patty were two-of-a-kind when it came to finding possible husbands for Sam.

"He was quite pleasant."

"But—?"

Caroline shrugged her elegant shoulders. "But I can see he plainly isn't your type."

"Why don't you think he's my type?"

"I would think that's obvious."

"Because he's a bartender?" Although Caroline was a product of Rocky Hill same as Sam, she tended to be class conscious.

"I thought he was a foreign correspondent."

"Yes."

"And a reporter for the *Telegram*?"

"Yes, he was that, too," said Sam, "but he's between jobs."

"Oh. So he's unemployed."

"He's not unemployed." *Shut up, Sam! You sound like you're defending the man.* "He's helping out with the family business."

"He's not for you."

"You're talking to the daughter of a plumber, Caroline. There's nothing wrong with running a bar."

"And you're talking to the daughter of a mechanic. You're not telling me anything I don't know."

"So what's the problem? Why aren't you pushing Murphy and me together?"

"Chemistry." Caroline cast her a quick glance but Sam couldn't read her expression in the dark car. "There isn't any."

"I resent that."

"Sorry, but it's true. He's just not interested in you."

Sam's jaw settled into that old stubborn line. "You mean, *I'm* not interested in *him*."

"You heard exactly what I said, Sam. He's not interested in you sexually."

"And how would you know?" Sam retorted. "You were too busy wooing the Over-the-Hill Gang to notice anything."

"I noticed," said Caroline in that maddeningly calm fashion. "*He* didn't."

"Hah! I think you're—" Sam stopped in mid-sentence. She had spent four hours in O'Rourke's company and he hadn't flirted, teased, flattered, conned, or tried to seduce her in any way, shape, or form. They'd talked and laughed and traded war stories but the one thing they hadn't done was look at each other the way men and women often did. "You're right," she said at last, sinking lower in her seat. "One hundred percent right."

To Murphy O'Rourke she was nothing more than Sam the Sandwich Maker. How depressing.

SAM STOOD IN THE DOORWAY fifteen minutes later and waited while her father climbed up into his truck, started the engine, then disappeared down the quiet, tree-lined street. There had been some difficult times along the way, but Sam doubted she'd be where she was today if it hadn't been for the unswerving love and support of her parents. It was thanks to them she had the house she lived in. If she could provide one-half of that solid foundation for Patty, she'd count her lucky stars.

Yawning, she stepped back inside and locked the door behind her. Of course, it would be wonderful if she'd been able to provide a father for her brilliant little girl, as well, but some things not even an eternal optimist like Sam could manage. She believed fervently in the importance of a stable home and strong family and knew that it was within her power to provide that for Patty. With her parents' help and Caroline's unstinting support, Sam had managed to keep a half step ahead of her daughter's growing needs.

At least, so far she had.

She tiptoed through the narrow hallway and inched open Patty's bedroom door. The little girl was asleep, her red hair unbraided and pulled into a ponytail atop her head. Her glasses rested on the nightstand next to a pitcher of water, a humidifier and a Mickey Mouse alarm clock that had been a present for her fourth birthday. Sam knelt down alongside the bed and pressed her lips carefully against her daughter's cheek and brow. Cool and dry, thank God. Her nostrils twitched at the smell of Vick's Vapo-Rub and she remembered many winter nights when she was the little girl in the bed with her own mother slipping into her room to check her progress.

Oh, she could give Patty love and tender care. She could give Patty support and encouragement and an extended family to lean on when the going got tough. Sam could give her child all those wonderful things that matter so much in the scheme of things. But Patty wasn't your average child and some of the things she needed went far beyond what Sam was able to provide—at least, right now. Princteon offered limitless opportunities for Patty to excel but the door to those opportunities was closed as tightly for Patty as they had been to Sam years ago. Money would open those doors and Sam aimed to earn enough to do so.

She placed a kiss on Patty's cool forehead then slipped from the room. For a moment she hesitated, forgetting her promise to her mother, and was sorely tempted to go back into the kitchen and dive into preparing some of the delicacies she had in store for the men of O'Rourke's Bar and Grill. She'd been running on adrenaline all evening and could more than likely put in a few good hours at the stove but the lure of a warm bath on a cold winter's night was too seductive to resist.

How wonderful it would be if she had *Bal à Versailles* to perfume the water and French soaps and candles twinkling next to the tub as she sipped a glass of wine. She ruefully watched her reflection in the bathroom mirror as she stripped out of her slacks and sweater. How wonderful it would be if she had black lace underwear to replace her sturdy white cotton briefs. How wonderful it would be if her dark hair shimmered with auburn highlights and curved rather than hung straight to the middle of her back.

Sighing, she settled into the warm water and rested her head against an inflatable bath pillow. No wonder Murphy O'Rourke thought of her as Sam the Sandwich Maker. Who could blame him? She was tall and skinny and as plain as a loaf of bread on a supermarket shelf. Anything she'd ever known about makeup and hairstyles and perfume had disappeared along with the notion of spare time. Sam was a mother and a home owner; she was a student and an entrepreneur and a daughter and a best friend. But a woman, a lacy-lingerie-full-eye-makeup-French-perfume type of woman? Sam wouldn't know where to begin.

Interest in that type of thing had disappeared along with her Christmas spirit quite a few years back, and Sam simply didn't have the time or the energy to try to recapture either one.

If her daughter were to achieve her full potential, Fast Foods for the Fast Lane had to get off to a running start with the New Year. There wasn't room in Sam's master plan for failure—not for her and not for her little girl. When Ronald Donovan walked out on her eleven Christmases ago, he'd left behind a very scared—and definitely pregnant—girl. Well, times had changed. Sam wasn't a girl any longer and she definitely wasn't scared. She had Patty and she had her dream and all she had to do was survive one more Christmas and she'd be on her way to securing her little girl's future and her own in the bargain.

Everything else would simply have to wait.

Chapter Seven

From the first moment Patty's eyes opened the next morning, she knew it was going to be a special day. Her throat didn't hurt and her eyes didn't burn. She wasn't coughing or sneezing or blowing her nose.

And best of all, it was nine o'clock on a Wednesday morning and she could hear her mom whistling an old Beatles song in the kitchen! Patty sat up and sniffed the air as she donned her glasses. Bacon, French toast, and hot chocolate. She tossed off the blankets and swung her legs out of the bed, searching the cold oak floor for her slippers then slipping her feet inside. Grabbing her robe, she jumped up and hurried into the kitchen.

It had been a long time since she and her mom had had time together right in the middle of a regular week and Patty didn't want to miss a single second.

"Just in time," said Sam, as Patty hugged her around the waist. "If the bacon didn't work, I was going to put hot chocolate in your vaporizer."

"I'm all better." Patty stood still while her mother pressed the back of her hand to Patty's forehead. "See?"

"You're staying in today, just to be on the safe side."

Grinning, Patty took her seat at the kitchen table and reached for her glass of orange juice. "I smell garlic and tomatoes."

"I've trained you well." Sam placed a plate of French toast and crisp Canadian bacon in front of Patty. "That's for your friend Murphy and his pals. I'll be taking their trays of food over at noon."

Patty's heart bounced from one side of her chest to the other. Just thinking about the possibilities made her dizzy with excitement. She took a sip of juice then looked over at her mother. "Did you have fun with Aunt Caroline last night?"

"We did." Sam sat down opposite Patty and poured herself a cup of coffee.

"Did you eat at the Pizza Hut?"

"Nope. We ended up at the bar."

Patty thought she'd fall off her chair in surprise. "You ate dinner at the bar? I thought they didn't have a cook."

Sam gestured toward the pots simmering on her six-burner stove. "They don't. Murphy ordered in pizza with the works for everyone." She overlooked the fact that they had eaten theirs in a more private setting. No sense raising Patty's hopes.

"Wow!" Patty breathed.

"Don't go getting excited, kiddo." Her mom reached over and ruffled Patty's bangs. "We're talking pepperoni pizzas for twelve, not a candlelight dinner for two."

Patty speared a slice of bacon with her fork. "It's a start," she mumbled.

"Look at me, honey."

Reluctantly Patty met her mother's eyes and she didn't like what she saw there one bit. Why did her mother have to be so darned stubborn about these things? Murphy O'Rourke was absolutely perfect. Even Aunt Caroline thought so, and that was before she'd even met him. "What?" she asked, knowing she sounded just like a spoiled little kid.

"It wouldn't matter if I fell head over heels for Murphy."

"I don't understand."

"Honey, I'm just not his type."

"I still don't understand." Her mom might not be glamorous but she was definitely pretty. Okay, maybe she didn't fill out a T-shirt the same way that Aunt Caroline did, but *Cosmo* said all men didn't like women with chests like overstuffed sofa cushions.

"Maybe I can explain." Both Patty and her mom swiveled around in their chairs in time to see Caroline stroll into the cozy kitchen.

"I didn't hear you ring the doorbell," said Sam as Caroline joined them at the table.

Caroline grabbed an empty cup and reached for the coffeepot. "The door was open."

Her mom muttered something about changing the locks but Patty and her aunt only laughed.

"Your mom was right, Patricia," said Caroline, picking up the conversational ball. "She isn't Murphy O'Rourke's type at all."

Patty felt her mouth drop open in surprise. "But, I—"

Her aunt's dark blond brows lifted a fraction of an inch. "You should have seen them together last night—they could have been brother and sister."

For one long and scary moment Patty was afraid she would burst into tears like a big, fat baby, but just as her eyes were filling to the danger point, she caught the briefest smile flash over her aunt's face and her breath stopped. There was still a chance!

Caroline leaned forward, her eyes never leaving Patty. "You understand about chemistry, don't you?"

"Sure," said Patty, shrugging. "Like between Sam and Diane on *Cheers* and Maddie and Dave on *Moonlighting*."

"Exactly," said Caroline. "When it's there, everyone knows about it and when it's not—" she paused dramatically "—well, when it's not, there's nothing on earth you can do to fake it."

"Oh, for heaven's sake!" Sam scraped her chair back and stood up. "I'm going down to the basement for supplies. I hope you'll be through with this nonsense when I come back upstairs."

She fairly bristled with annoyance, and Patty had to bite the inside of her cheek to keep from shouting "Hooray!" Reverse child psychology. How clever of her aunt to think of it.

Caroline turned innocent blue eyes on Patty's mom. "Whatever has gotten into you, Samantha?" she inquired sweetly. "It isn't like you're interested in Mr. O'Rourke, is it?"

"No," said Sam, a bit too quickly to Patty's practiced ear. "I'm just tired of being the topic of discussion around here. Why don't you two try to find *you* a husband, Caroline? That might be fun."

With that, Patty's mother stormed out of the kitchen, muttering something about eye shadow damaging brain cells.

"You were right," said Caroline the moment Sam was out of earshot. "They're so wrong for each other that they're perfect."

"Isn't he wonderful?" asked Patty dreamily.

Caroline's chuckle was warm and amused. "Well, he's not my particular cup of tea but he *is* wonderful, I'll grant you that."

"Do you think they like each other?"

"They were thick as thieves last night. Even sneaked out together for a while. They seemed like old friends."

"They did? Wow!" breathed Patty, her pulse racing. "Did they kiss?"

"No," said Caroline, wrinkling her nose. "In fact, I'm not even certain they realize they're the opposite sex. At least not yet."

Patty slumped back in her seat. "Then I don't understand, Aunt Caroline. You said they were—"

"Perfect for each other." She gave Patty's earlobes an affectionate tug. "You know it. I know it. It's just a question of getting them to know it."

Knowing about sexual chemistry and understanding it were two different things. It was easier to understand quantum physics then to understand why grownups acted the way they did. "Can't friends get married?" It seemed to Patty it would be a whole lot easier to spend fifty years with someone you actually liked being around and not just someone you liked to kiss.

Patty struggled with the concept, but her view of romance was limited to movie images of beautiful Technicolor people in beautiful Technicolor costumes. How romance would find her sweater-and-jeans mother was a puzzlement. Suddenly she brightened. "Is it like icing on a cake?"

"Yes!" Caroline's smile was brilliant. "The cake is just fine without the icing but what a difference it makes when you have it."

"But we still have to get them together, don't we?" Apparently making sandwiches was a good icebreaker, but it wasn't about to thaw a glacier like Sam.

"Easy!" Caroline snapped her fingers. "The Christmas Masquerade Ball."

"You know Mom hates parties even more than she hates Christmas. She'll never go."

"Deep down old Scrooge loves Christmas, Patricia, and she loves parties. She just keeps herself too busy to realize it."

"I don't know," said Patty, feeling extremely skeptical. "If she didn't have me, I think she'd pretend the whole thing didn't exist."

"Trust me, sweetie—under all that bluster, your mom is an old yuletide cheerleader from way back. She used to start counting the days before Christmas back around Labor Day."

Patty had to laugh at the thought of her sobersides mother keeping a Christmas countdown, but then she grew serious. "It's all because of my real dad, isn't it, the reason she doesn't like Christmas?"

Aunt Caroline was one of those rare adults who believed in being honest with kids, even if it wasn't always exactly what you wanted to hear. "Yes, that's how it started, Patricia, but that isn't all of it. The trouble now is she's been running so hard, for such a long time, that she's forgotten everything she used to know about fun."

"She's forgotten about Christmas?"

"She's forgotten everything that's good about it."

Imagine needing to remember how to enjoy Christmas. Being grownup didn't seem so wonderful to Patty when she heard things like that.

"She'll never go to the ball," said Patty firmly. "Never."

"She'll go," said Caroline.

"She can't afford it."

"She won't have to."

"She'll say she has nothing to wear."

"When her best friend owns a rent-a-dress shop? She'll never get away with that."

"What if Murphy O'Rourke doesn't go?" Somehow it was easier to imagine him ringside at an Atlantic City boxing match than fluttering around a dance floor dressed like a penguin in a tuxedo.

"Believe me, there's nothing to worry about."

Patty listened to her aunt's scheme to get Sam to the masquerade ball with growing delight.

"And if it doesn't work?" she asked Caroline when her aunt was finished speaking. "What then?"

Caroline turned her graceful hands, palms up, on the tabletop. "If it doesn't work, we sit back and let nature take its course. I don't think we have anything to worry about."

Sam's footsteps clattered up the basement steps and Patty gasped as Sam entered the room. Her mother's straight dark hair was swirled on top of her head in soft curls. A diamond tiara glittered amidst the silky tendrils. She wore a shimmering gown of sapphire satin that bared her shoulders and fit closely at the waist, then billowed out into a luxuriously full skirt that reached to the floor. Only the toes of her sparkly pumps were visible. Her mom wore makeup and lipstick, mascara and blush, and at her ears the largest pair of diamonds Patty had ever seen twinkled for all the world to see.

It was a miracle!

Patty blinked once, then twice.

It was a dream.

There stood her mother in her everyday jeans and sweater, her dark hair long about her narrow shoulders, her arms piled high with cans of whole tomatos and puree.

"Patty?" Sam asked, heading for the counter across the room. "Is something wrong?"

Patty shook her head and looked over at her aunt Caroline whose smile held a few surprises of its own.

"We can't miss!" mouthed her aunt and Patty prayed she was right because in less than seventy-two hours, the great makeover of Samantha Elizabeth Dean was set to begin.

You KNEW western civilization was coming to a bad end when men like Murphy O'Rourke and Dan Stein held business meetings over scrambled eggs, bagels and coffee-with-cream-two-sugars-make-it-decaf-would-ya-honey.

The waitress scratched her head with the eraser end of her pencil and sashayed back to the kitchen of the Colonial Diner on Route 1 as Murphy prepared to do battle.

"Okay, Dan, now that you've blasted hell out of your expense account, I'll cut to the bottom line—you're wasting your time."

Dan, sixty-two years old and sixty-two pounds over his fighting weight, glared at O'Rourke and lit up a Camel.

"It's my time to waste. We want you back, kid, and we're willing to spend big bucks to get you."

Murphy looked around at the red vinyl and white formica interior of the diner and guffawed. "Yeah, Dan. You're pulling out all the stops, aren't you?"

Dan grinned around his cigarette. "What's the matter kid—you got something against a power breakfast?"

"Somehow I don't think this qualifies."

"Hey, you take what you can get in this world. If I could get you out of this godforsaken backwater burg, I'd show you something that'd knock your eyes out." Dan took a long drag on his cigarette. "You do remember how to get to Manhattan, don't you?"

"All too well," muttered Murphy as the waitress deposited their coffee and orange juice. "Gimme another month or two and I might be able to forget it."

"You and your old man still at each other's throats?"

"So what else is new?" Murphy gulped down his oj. "Thirty-six years and counting. We're going for the North American record."

"How's he doing?" Dan Stein and Bill O'Rourke were the same age and had similar medical histories.

"Pretty good. He should be back behind the bar by the middle of January, give or take a few weeks."

Dan narrowed his eyes and gave Murphy his best managing editor's scowl. "You plannin' on going into business with the guy?"

Murphy groaned and leaned back in his booth. The red vinyl seat crackled with the movement. "One of us would be up for murder-one within a week."

"You goin' on unemployment?"

"Can it, will you, Stein. You're giving me indigestion."

"You're gonna get more than indigestion when I tell you the big boss is gettin' tired of waiting for you to come to your senses."

Murphy bit into his bagel with gusto. "Gianelli should've thought of that when we had the fight."

"You were out of line."

"The hell I was." Murphy and the publisher of the *New York Telegram* had butted heads over newspaper policy. Frank Gianelli had hired Murphy away from the foreign beat with promises of free license to explore the domestic political scene, only to turn the *Telegram* into a cross between the *National Enquirer* and the Morton Downey television show.

"He's willing to give in on a few issues."

"He knows my number. Let him call me."

"He's a proud man."

"So am I."

"He's also a stubborn man."

"So am I."

Dan drained his coffee cup and flagged down the waitress for a refill. "You've got yourself a safety net, haven't you?"

Murphy grinned. "Am I that transparent?"

"You jumping back on the foreign beat?"

"I've got some feelers out."

"I thought you'd had enough of living out of a suitcase."

"So had I." A few weeks back in New Jersey with his father had shown Murphy that while family unity was possible for some people, it wasn't possible for the O'Rourkes. His brother could make a phone call once a month and be praised to the skies. Murphy could roll up his sleeves and take over the bar and be ignored. "Let's say I've had enough of domestic tranquility to last me awhile."

When in doubt, hit the road. It seemed as good a way as any to cope with life.

Dan lit up another cigarette. "I think you can get what you want out of Gianelli if you'll meet him halfway."

"Not interested."

"We're talking long-term career move here, O'Rourke, not just a two-year gig in Paris."

"Don't knock what you haven't tried, Dan. Those two-year gigs in Paris make for some nice memories."

"Memories don't keep you warm in your old age."

Murphy arched a brow. "Oh, yeah?"

"Why shouldn't you settle down and pay off a mortgage like the rest of us?"

"If I could find a woman like Marion, I just might."

Dan threw his head back and laughed his husky smoker's laugh. "Find your own woman, O'Rourke. It's taken me forty years to get used to the one I've got."

Envy, white-hot and unexpected, flared deep in Murphy's gut. Thirty-year mortgages and forty-year marriages. Kids and college tuition. Graduation, weddings, christenings. The whole normal chain of events.

He didn't know a damn thing about any of it and probably never would.

Dan looked longingly at a stack of pancakes on the table across the way. "Think we talked enough business to satisfy the IRS?"

"I think so."

"You'll consider Gianelli's offer?"

Murphy nodded.

"How about some pancakes?"

Murphy grinned and flagged down the exhausted waitress. "I thought you'd never ask."

OVERNIGHT huge candy canes and strings of lights and plastic manger scenes had sprouted on every lawn and store Sam passed on her way to O'Rourke's Bar and Grill, as if Santa Claus had himself declared Christmas decorations mandatory in New Jersey. A giant elf, sporting a green costume and pointy-toed slippers with bells on the toes, stood in front of Ben's Hardware Store and waved at traffic. He

looked suspiciously like the accountant who'd danced attendance on Caroline at her last soiree.

Christmas. What a bizarre time of year. Perfectly sane
human beings did the strangest things. Sam pulled her
Blazer into the parking lot of O'Rourke's Bar and Grill at
one minute to noon.

"Murphy?" she called out as she entered the dimly lit bar.
"It's Sam, Murphy!"

No answer. How strange. She put the tray down atop one
of the wooden tables and glanced about. A camel's hair coat
was draped over a chair. Maybe Murphy was in the tiny
room behind the kitchen that served as an office.

Well, no matter. She'd finish unloading the Blazer first,
then go searching for him.

Sam turned and headed for the door when Scotty's
cheerful voice stopped her.

"Greetings, Samantha," he said, his intelligent face lit
with a pleasant smile. "What wonders have you wrought
this fine day?"

"No fair, Scotty! You'll have to wait and see."

He sniffed the air speculatively. "Do I smell Danish ham
and sweet gherkins on cocktail rye with a soupçon of Dijon
mustard for tang?"

"It looks like I'll have my work cut out for me if I want
to keep you surprised."

"Don't worry about him," came a voice from the entrance. "It's the boss you should be worrying about."

Both Sam and Scotty turned to see Murphy O'Rourke,
arms piled high with boxes, kick the door shut after him.

"Where do you want these?" Murphy pretended to stag-
ger beneath the load of food.

Sam stepped forward to help him. "Let me take this—"

He grunted something and moved past her. "Just point
out a place, why don't you?"

Sam pointed to the table where she'd placed the first tray.
"Right over there."

"We're going to have to renegotiate the price, Dean." O'Rourke's countenance was fierce. "There's a hell of a lot of food here."

Sam's back went up in defense. "Don't worry, O'Rourke. The extras are on the house."

"No way."

Her eyes widened in surprise. "I thought you were feeling ripped off."

"You're the one who should be feeling ripped off. You contracted to make sandwiches, not five-course meals."

"Consider it a rehearsal for my opening in January. I'm trying to perfect my techniques. Why let all these goodies go to waste?" True enough. There was a limit to how much she and Patty could consume, and besides, after the killer deal her daughter put together, she felt she owed O'Rourke and his clientele a few extras.

Scotty turned toward Murphy who was shrugging his way out of a leather bomber jacket. "How was your power breakfast?"

Murphy started to say something then glanced at Sam and caught himself. "In polite words, lousy."

Scotty, a gentleman to the tips of his manicured fingers, turned to include Sam in the conversation. "Our mutual friend's employer—"

"Former employer," grunted Murphy.

Scotty winked at Sam and continued, "His former employer saw fit to travel all the way from the city—"

"There's a big deal," said Murphy, tying on his apron. "All of sixty miles. The man will do anything to get out of Manhattan."

"His former employer came all the way from the city to talk to this pigheaded young man about furthering his career."

"What career? I'm a bartender now."

"Murphy has the opportunity to become managing editor of the *New York Telegram*."

Sam turned to Murphy, who was busy stomping around
the bar with the subtlety of a wounded buffalo. "Managing editor. I'm impressed."

"Don't be," said Murphy.

"He's in a snit," continued Scotty, unperturbed. "He
longs for the life of the foreign correspondent."

Of course he would, thought Sam. If ever a man looked
ready to run, it was Murphy O'Rourke.

"The offers aren't exactly pouring in." Murphy's tone
was gruff. "Apparently my time has come and gone."

It was an oddly vulnerable remark from a man who
seemed invulnerable to such things as insecurity, but there
it was. Sam found she liked Murphy O'Rourke more than
ever.

"I think you have a few good years left in you," she said
lightly, touching his forearm. "I wouldn't worry about it."

"You're a kid," said Murphy with a sudden twinkle in his
hazel eyes. "What would you know about it?"

"I'm twenty-eight, and I know more than you realize."

"Talk to me when you're on the downside of thirty-five.
It's a whole other world."

"It's what you make of it," said Sam, "no matter what
age you are."

"Bravo!" Scotty, who had been listening to their exchange, broke into spirited applause. "Give this woman a
drink on the house."

Sam laughed and shook her head. "I'll take a rain check.
I have work to do at my shop."

"How about coffee and a sandwich?" Murphy inclined
his head toward the trays resting upon the table. "I hear our
caterer does a damn good job."

"She's the best in the business," said Sam, "even if nobody's ever heard of her."

"That will change soon enough." He pulled out a chair
and motioned her toward it. "I'll bet you didn't eat breakfast."

"I made french toast, bacon, and hot chocolate."

"Yeah," he said with an answering grin, "but how much of it did you manage to get?"

"Would you believe black coffee and a sip of juice?"

"I'd believe it. Like I said, you're too skinny."

Sam shrugged and reached for a sliced chicken and tomato sandwich with dilled mayonnaise on pumpernickel. "I can see when I'm outnumbered. Are you gentlemen going to join me?"

Murphy grabbed the sandwich closest to him while Scotty searched out the Danish ham he'd zeroed in on when Sam arrived. Munching on his sandwich, he carried a pot of strong black coffee over to their table and pulled a container of cream from the small refrigerator behind the bar. Sam threw her cholesterol count to the wind and helped herself.

"The folly of youth," said Scotty with an envious sigh. "I remember the days when milk and cream and eggs were good for you."

"Don't remind me," Sam moaned. "Do you know how sad it is to have to turn out a reduced-fat, reduced-cholesterol, reduced-calorie version of beef stroganoff?"

"The only thing sadder is having to eat it," said Murphy, straddling the chair next to her. "Smoking's no good for you. Sugar can kill." He shot Sam a look. "Even sex isn't what it used to be."

"Speak for yourself," said MacTavish.

Sam nibbled on her sandwich and watched O'Rourke out of the corner of her eye. So sex wasn't what it used to be, hmm? Wouldn't she love to know the story behind *that* statement.

A charged silence filled the room and Scotty—bless him—jumped in.

"The average English high tea has probably lined the pockets of more cardiologists and dentists than a lifetime of steak dinners."

Murphy laughed but Sam could only sigh.

"High tea," she said dreamily. "What I wouldn't give for one afternoon at Claridge's."

Once again she found herself under Murphy's professional scrutiny. "You've never been to Europe?"

"I've never been anywhere," she said matter-of-factly. "I've gone as far east as Manhattan and as far west as Philadelphia."

"New Jersey born and bred?"

She nodded. "I can see my epitaph—'Here lies Samantha Dean, she lived and died in Rocky Hill and never knew the difference.'" The words were out before she could stop them and the biting edge to her tone of voice surprised herself as much as it surprised the two men. "Sorry. I didn't mean to sound like that. I'm actually very happy here."

"There is no crime in craving travel, my dear," said Scotty kindly. "It is a natural desire of the active mind."

"It's one of the reasons I became a foreign correspondent," said Murphy as he poured them all more coffee. "I wanted to get out of here more than I wanted anything else on earth."

"When I was sixteen I used to lie awake nights, dreaming of London and Paris and Rome and all of the other wonderful places that were waiting for me to discover them." She had also lain awake nights, dreaming of how wonderful it would be to see those glorious places with Ronald Donovan. Her dreams of Ronald were long over but she was pierced with a sudden, bittersweet yearning for all the other foolish dreams that had once seemed so important.

"And then you had Patty?" asked Scotty.

"Yes. And then I had Patty. Not even London could compete with that."

"You could still go," said Murphy. "Kids are portable."

How could she explain to the footloose O'Rourke that while kids were portable, she wasn't. Years ago she'd made up her mind to stay put and, despite this outburst, she did not regret her decision. Travel took both time and money, and at the moment both commodities were tied up in Fast Foods for the Fast Lane. "Who knows?" she said after a moment. "Maybe someday I'll get there."

"Go," said Murphy. "You owe it to yourself to see England."

"Yes," said Sam, "but I owe it to Patty to stay here." Patty needed continuity; she needed security and challenges and every single cent Sam could possibly spare for her future education. Trips to London, no matter how wonderful, were dreams for some distant future when Sam was a successful entrepreneur and Murphy O'Rourke was just a topic of conversation around the bar.

O'Rourke didn't say anything. He nodded his head slowly, his gaze never leaving hers. In his eyes she saw something close to respect and admiration. And even though his opinion shouldn't have mattered, her heart beat just a little bit faster.

Chapter Eight

Murphy wasn't quite sure how it happened, but by the time three o'clock rolled around, he was in one bear of a bad mood. Scotty, Joe and the rest of the crowd had taken a tray of sandwiches and a pile of appetizers and retired to a table near the exit. From time to time they cast such baleful looks at him that Murphy almost felt contrite.

Almost, but not quite.

He never should have let Dan Stein talk him into that little "power" breakfast at the diner. That had been a lousy idea from the word go, and if Murphy'd had half a brain, he wouldn't have given the die-hard New Yorker directions to Rocky Hill. Born and bred New Yorkers didn't believe there was actually life on the other side of the Hudson River; if Murphy'd used his head, he would have let Stein go on thinking exactly that. But, no. His damn curiosity had gotten the better of him and Murphy let himself be coerced into consorting with the enemy.

All he had to do was say no to the *Telegram*'s offer and mean it. Sounded simple enough. Why was he finding it so hard to stick with his decision? In any given day he found himself vacillating between the life of a foreign correspondent, going back to Manhattan and the *Telegram* and disconnecting his word processor and pulling draft beer for the rest of his days.

Talking to Samantha Dean, listening to her optimism about her future and that of her daughter, made him aware of a void inside himself that he hadn't known was there until that moment. Sam knew who she was, and what she was about. She understood where she was going, how to get there and what was expected of her once she arrived. And add to all that the awesome responsibility of a child with a potential as phenomenal as Patty's, and you had a woman who was pretty phenomenal in her own right.

In one day Sam Dean did more that was important than Murphy O'Rourke had done in his entire life, a fact his father had been more than happy to point out after Sam left for her shop. Bill O'Rourke had come in from his morning constitutional and taken an immediate shine to the friendly young woman. It had been a long time since Murphy had seen a genuine smile on his dour father's face but Sam Dean had managed to call forth not only a smile but an actual laugh, as well. Scotty told Murphy that it had taken all of his willpower to keep from leading the patrons of the bar in a loud "Hip hip hooray!"

Bill's smile had faded the moment Sam left for her shop, and before she backed her Blazer out of the parking lot, Murphy and his old man were engaged in one of their sniping sessions. Bill stormed up to his room to nap. Murphy stormed about the bar, bullying the regulars and eating enough for six fullbacks after a famine.

"Retirement is supposed to be a time of fulfillment and tranquility," observed Scotty as Murphy clattered glassware and trays behind the bar. "Your foul disposition makes me long for the halls of academe once again."

"Be my guest," said Murphy, glaring at the former mathematics professor. "I'll drive you."

"Why don't you go out and take a walk?"

Murphy glanced toward the window. "It's snowing out there."

"It might cool you off."

"I don't need to cool off."

"That, my boy, is a matter of opinion. I think you need a change of venue."

Murphy glanced at the empty sandwich trays stacked at the far end of the bar. "Maybe that's not such a bad idea."

"The walk?" asked Scotty.

"No. The change of venue."

"But you just said—"

"When you're right, you're right, Scotty." He untied his apron and tossed it near the sink. "Can you watch things for me while I'm gone?"

Scotty cast a scornful look at the ancient cash register and the beer mugs waiting to be filled. "I think the time has come to talk about putting me on the payroll. I am highly overqualified for this work."

"You're a pal, Scotty. I won't be long."

He grabbed his leather jacket, his car keys and the metal trays. Why not? he thought, as he headed across the snowy parking lot toward his rented car. She'd been knocking herself out these past few days making epicurean delights for the guys at the bar. She must have her hands full with Patty home sick and Christmas coming and getting her store ready to open in less than a month.

The least he could do was stop by Fast Foods for the Fast Lane, drop off the trays and save her a trip back to O'Rourke's that night.

It doesn't mean anything, he thought as he started the car and cautiously eased the vehicle out onto the slippery street. If he didn't get out of the bar for a while he'd probably deplete a month's worth of Scotch before the afternoon was out.

He slid to an off-angle stop at a traffic light. Damn weather. She didn't need to be out in it, risking her life. She had a daughter who needed her, family and friends who cared. He could imagine her with a husband and a few more kids with Patty's brains and her smile. Murphy grunted as he moved the car forward again. Nobody'd notice if he plowed into a snowdrift and stayed there until spring.

You're a coward, son. He heard his father's voice as clearly as if he were in the car alongside him. *Anytime life doesn't go your way, you're looking to back out.*

"Can you blame me?" he mumbled, his fingers gripping the wheel as the snow thickened. "Who wants to spend winter in New Jersey?"

He thought of Samantha Dean and a smile broke through his foul mood. He liked her. Nothing complicated about that. He liked her ambition, her devotion to her daughter, her straightforward manner and her offbeat sense of humor.

When he was seventeen he was a wiseacre kid with more bravado than brains.

When Sam was seventeen, she was a senior in high school—and the mother of a newborn baby girl.

Murphy couldn't imagine what a hash he would have made of a situation like that.

It didn't take a genius to know Sam was something pretty special. He enjoyed her company as much as he had enjoyed her daughter's at the Career Day seminar at the grammar school. He'd never given a lot of thought to having a woman for a friend before. Reporters in general, and foreign correspondents in particular, weren't known for their fidelity to members of the opposite sex. The life-style wasn't exactly conducive to forging lifetime commitments and Murphy hadn't been overly interested in finding an alternative. His one brief shot at marriage had been over before it had a chance to begin, and frankly he hadn't been devastated by the divorce.

He and his wife had been lovers but they'd never been friends. In fact, there had been a lot of women he'd enjoyed in bed but few he'd ever tried to enjoy once they got out. He and Sam were off to a good start, and for some reason that made him feel better than he had in a long, long time.

SAM HAD JUST FINISHED sealing twenty pounds of unbleached flour into two huge metal canisters and was about to arrange her spices in alphabetical order on the open shelves near the stove when she heard a knock at the front door.

"Sorry," she called out, pushing her hair off her face with the back of her hand, "we're not open yet."

The knock sounded again.

"We're closed! Come back New Year's Day."

"Sam! Open up."

She stopped and stared toward the front of the store. Murphy O'Rourke? "What are you doing here?" she asked as she ushered the snow-covered man inside and relocked the door. "How on earth did you find me?"

He presented the empty trays to her with a flourish. "I wanted to save you a trip," he said, brushing the snow off his hair with a quick shake of his head, "and it wasn't too hard."

"You reporter types are resourceful."

He glanced around the bright and airy storefront and whistled low. "You entrepreneur types are pretty resourceful yourself."

Sam beamed with pleasure. "Thanks, Murphy. It *is* shaping up pretty nicely."

"Nicely? This place is dynamite. You'll be turning the yuppies away in droves."

Her laughter was high and unforced. "That's the general idea." In the distance they heard the low rumble of a New Jersey Transit train pulling into the Princeton Junction station. "Some location, isn't it? They fall out of the train, tired and hungry, and into my shop to pick up their dinner."

He folded his brawny arms across his chest and nodded. "I have to hand it to you, Sam, you covered all the angles. I don't see how you can miss."

Sam crossed herself and grinned like a kid caught in the cookie jar. "From your mouth to God's ear. Unless I've missed my guess, Fast Foods for the Fast Lane is just what Mr. and Ms Commuter are looking for." Suddenly she realized she was clutching the empty food trays to her chest like a shield. "You didn't have to do this, you know. I was going to stop at the bar on my way home."

"I figured I'd save you a trip."

She nodded as she placed the trays down atop the Corian counter that had cost her an arm and a leg on sale. "And I suppose you just happened to be in the neighborhood."

His hazel eyes twinkled. "No," he said. "I wasn't anywhere close and I'll have you know, the only thing I hate more than driving, is driving in a snowstorm."

She ducked her head for a moment, feeling inordinately pleased that someone would go out of his way to be in her company. It had been a long time since she'd felt particularly likable and the sensation was as delightful as it was noteworthy. "The least I can do is give you the grand tour."

"Wait a minute," he said, turning up the collar of his jacket. "I have to get something from the car."

He was back in a flash, brandishing a snow-covered, but absolutely delightful, pot of Christmas cactus abloom with vivid pink flowers. A huge lump formed in Sam's throat.

"Murphy! I don't know what to say..."

"You don't have to say anything." He handed her the beautiful plant. "Good luck with your shop."

She buried her face in the blossoms, taking those extra seconds to blink away sudden and surprising tears. Composure regained, she cleared a spot on what would soon be her main counter.

"Looks good," said Murphy.

"It looks wonderful!" said Sam, wiping sawdust off the counter top. "I may rethink my color scheme."

"Don't go getting crazy. It's only a little plant, Sam."

"Yes," said Sam, meeting his eyes, "but it's special." She raised up on her toes and kissed his cheek. His after-shave was spicy and crisp and altogether appealing. "Thanks."

"So what about the grand tour you promised me?" He slipped off his leather jacket and draped it over a step stool near the massive chrome refrigerator. "As far as I can see, this is the whole shebang."

"My dear Mr. O'Rourke, this is only the merest hint of the wonders inside this shop." Sam gave him her best number-one-businesswoman look. "Why, you haven't even seen my stove yet."

"What are you waiting for?" He grinned and took her arm. "Lead the way."

There was really nothing all that special about a restaurant-size stove or an industrial-strength microwave but to Sam they were as thrilling as a brand-new, shiny red Porsche. At best her acquisitions had elicited no more than pleasant smiles from her family and friends, and she had expected no more than perfunctory courtesy from Murphy.

She was wrong.

"Will you look at these shelves?" he said when he swung open the double doors to the refrigerator and stuck his head inside. "You could fit three Thanksgiving turkeys in here and still have room for a side of beef."

The stove was greeted with a low whistle, followed by a thorough inspection of the center griddle, the warming oven, and all six burners. "Pilotless?" he asked as he fiddled with a dial.

"Of course," said Sam. "This is a first-rate outfit I'm running here."

He duly noted the wattage of the microwave, the water temperature of her dishwasher, and the beautiful baking pans that had cost her more than a sane person would have paid for them. She found herself eager to show him every nook and cranny of the kitchen, displaying her dazzling array of takeout containers before him as if they were a king's ransom in emeralds.

She couldn't remember the last time she had felt so exhilarated and confident over her prospects—or quite so happy to share them with a friend.

"I have to hand it to you," Sam said ten minutes later over coffee in the front room, where she could cast quick peeks at her beautiful Christmas cactus. "Not only did you suffer through the grand tour, you actually asked questions!"

"Reporter's training." O'Rourke popped a peanut into his mouth and took another gulp of coffee. "I'm always looking for a good story."

"Well, this is the one," said Sam proudly. "Mark my words—I'm going to make my name or know the reason why."

"I believe you."

She looked him straight in the eye, and to her surprise he didn't blink. "I think you really do."

She told him about her plans for Fast Foods, about the delivery service, and the FAX machine for jet-age orders, and the way she hoped to provide a superlative product and still make a superlative profit.

"A practical dreamer," said O'Rourke when she finally paused for a breath. "I never thought I'd meet one."

"What about you?" she asked. "Are you a dreamer, too?"

"Me?" His laugh was brittle. "I gave up dreaming a hell of a long time ago, Sam."

"I don't believe you," she said, touching his wrist then pulling away, embarrassed by her boldness. "I see it in your eyes."

"You're seeing too many years of sleepless nights, that's all."

Let it go, Sam. This isn't your business. O'Rourke was a rare find: a man who actually listened. Why not be satisfied with that and not expect him to unburden himself like a guest on Oprah or Phil Donahue. She cast about for a new topic of conversation. "How are you at installing water faucets?"

"Don't know the first thing about it." It was the cheerful admission of a man who didn't need to know and was glad of the fact.

She pushed her chair away from the table and stood up. "How would you feel about holding the flashlight for me?"

He pushed his chair away from the table and stood up across from her. "I think I can manage it."

"Come on," said Sam, heading for the kitchen. "I'll put you to work."

Two and a half hours later Sam had the faucets working, the garbage disposal running, and—thanks to Murphy—five perfectly matched utility shelves hanging proudly over her butcher-block worktable.

"You have hidden talents," she said, as she admired their handiwork. "You should have been a carpenter."

"It may come to that yet." His tone was jovial but she caught an undercurrent of anxiety.

"Don't worry," she said, in her best mother-knows-best manner. "You'll be back on the foreign beat before you know it."

He moved in front of her, hands on his hips, head cocked to the side. "Yeah?"

"Yeah. You're too good to stay unemployed for long."

"How would you know? You haven't read a damn word I've written."

"Call it feminine intuition," said Sam over his loud groan. "You wouldn't let yourself be anything but terrific."

He laughed and ruffled her hair the way she often ruffled Patty's and an oddly pleasant ripple of sensation tingled deep inside her stomach. "Come on, Sam. There's a blizzard out there. Let's hit the road."

Sam glanced out the plate-glass window and shivered. "Good grief! It really does look like a blizzard." She tossed Murphy his coat and grabbed for her own. "Beat you to my car."

They slipped and slid their way across the snowy driveway, their laughter mingling with the sound of tires spinning from the street beyond. The snow was already well past her ankles and Sam knew her slacks were headed for the rag bin but she didn't care as Murphy ducked behind his rented car and started to make a snowball.

"Throw that and you're a dead man, O'Rourke." She dived behind her Blazer and began pressing handfuls of snow into a big ball. "I have the best aim in all of Mercer County."

Splat!

A huge wet snowball found its mark on Sam's right shoulder.

Murphy, blast his hide, peered over the fender of his car. "What was that about having the best aim in Mercer County?"

She ducked as another snowball whizzed past her.

"Lucky shot!" Sam fell against the side of her Blazer, sputtering and laughing. It was hard to talk with a mouthful of snow.

"Give up?" called Murphy.

"Not on your life!" She scrambled behind the fender of her Blazer and went into overdrive as another missile landed just over her head. "You won't get away with this, O'Rourke!" In the blink of an eye she had an arsenal of snowballs lined up and ready to go. "Take this!" she called and fired one off in his direction.

The man was too smart for his own good and he neatly deflected her shot. "Give up, Sam!" he said, taking aim again. "No woman alive can beat me."

It was her turn to duck. His snowball caught the edge of her right shoulder. She remained undaunted, pressed against the fender, snowball at the ready.

"What's the matter, Sam?" he called. "Running out of steam already?"

The smug sound of male superiority had Sam seeing red, but she kept quiet and still.

"Hey, Sam! Are you okay?"

Still Sam said nothing. She waited.

"I know what you're trying and it's not going to work. I wasn't all-star snowball thrower on the Geneva beat for nothing."

Silence. Sam could taste imminent victory and it was sweet.

"Sam?" Murphy's footsteps crunched across the parking lot. Closer . . . closer . . .

"Bull's-eye!" Sam's cry shattered the stillness and she roared with laughter at the look of surprise on Murphy's snow-covered face. "Never underestimate the power of a woman with a mission!"

Murphy sputtered and blinked and shook his head free of the splattered snowball.

"You play dirty," he said, his hazel eyes bright against his snowy lashes. "I never would've figured you for the type."

Sam flashed him a triumphant smile. "That'll teach you for typecasting people. I play to win."

"All's fair, etcetera, etcetera?"

"That's right." Sam was feeling quite smug.

"You're sure about that?"

"Positive."

The next instant Sam found herself swept up into Murphy's strong arms and deposited soundly into a snowdrift.

It was his turn to laugh. "All's fair, Sam," he said.

With that Sam grabbed him by the right calf and, praying her self-defense training wouldn't fail her, flipped him right off his feet.

And right on top of her!

"You're right," Sam said as his torso sprawled across her legs. "I *do* play dirty!"

The expression on Murphy's face was priceless. "I'll give you fifty dollars to keep this to yourself."

Sam knew her eyes were twinkling with delight. "I'll let you know."

"You could ruin my reputation at the bar if you tell the guys you bested me."

"Remember that, next time you start a snowball fight with a defenseless woman."

He leaned up on one elbow and met her eyes. His shaggy sandy-brown hair fell across his forehead, and his face was ruddy from the snow and the winter wind. He looked rumpled, healthy and, all in all, quite appealing. Sam was surprised at exactly *how* appealing.

"I like you, Samantha Dean." His voice held a note of admiration.

Again she experienced that odd fluttering sensation deep inside. "The feeling's mutual, Murphy O'Rourke."

They stumbled to their feet, laughing and dusting the snow off each other's clothing. O'Rourke seemed to take an inordinate pleasure in brushing her derriere clean and Sam made certain she got in an answering message of her own. Murphy waited while she climbed into her beat-up Blazer and started her engine.

"See you tomorrow," said Sam through the open window as the wind-driven snow swirled all about.

O'Rourke leaned inside and placed a kiss on her cheek. "See you tomorrow." The kiss was chaste, swift and almost brotherly.

Sam was very still as he plodded through the snow to his car and wondered what life would be like if she were a small and curvy blue-eyed blonde. The idea quickly disappeared, but the sweet warm feeling of his lips against her cheek lingered as Sam drove home through the storm.

PATTY COULDN'T EXPLAIN how she knew, but the moment she woke up on Thursday morning she would have bet her Pound Puppy that something had changed.

Her mom had been real quiet last night, not at all her usual chatty self. It wasn't that her mom was unhappy exactly; it was more like she had something on her mind and couldn't stop thinking about whatever it was.

And now, at eight o'clock on a snowy morning, her mom was *singing* in the kitchen. It wasn't just that she was singing, it was *what* she was singing. Patty leaped out of bed and pulled on her slippers and robe. She eased her door open and slipped down the hallway toward the kitchen. Her I-hate-Christmas mom was singing "Jingle Bells."

Patty stood in the doorway, transfixed with wonder. Murphy O'Rourke. It just had to be....

"Are you going to stand there all morning, kiddo, or would you like some breakfast?"

Patty started as she realized her mom was talking to her.

"You were singing Christmas carols," said Patty, staring at Sam as if she were an apparition.

"I don't think so, honey." Sam flipped the pancakes one-two.

"You were," Patty persisted. "I heard you with my own ears."

Sam shrugged and reached for a breakfast plate. "And what if I was? That's all you hear on the radio these days."

Patty poured herself a glass of orange juice and helped herself to a Flintstone vitamin. "Am I going to school today?"

"Look outside, kiddo. School's closed."

Patty walked over to the window and peered through the yellow and orange curtains. "Wow!" Her breath left a moist circle on the glass. "Can I go sledding with Susan?"

"And be home sick another two days? Not very likely."

"Maa-a-a." Patty sank into a kitchen chair. "I'm getting bored being stuck in the house." She'd already finished volumes one through five of the remaindered encyclopaedia her mom had found at the book store.

"Who said anything about staying in the house?" Sam deposited a stack of pancakes on the plate in front of Patty. "I thought you could come with me to the store."

"Yuk." Patty poured maple syrup on her pancakes. "There's nothing to do there."

"Oh, really?" Her mother sat down opposite her and frowned at the river of syrup pooling on Patty's plate. "I thought you could help me paint."

What a boring day! Patty couldn't remember why she'd ever thought something special might happen. She'd just as soon work on her mathematical equation that proved the existence of the Star of Bethlehem than paint walls. No television or radio or—

"Did you hear what I said, Patty?"

"We're going to paint the store," she said, sounding as glum as she felt.

"I asked if you wanted to stop at O'Rourke's with me when I drop off the food trays." Her mother took a sip of coffee. "I could use some help."

Patty wanted to jump on the table and dance with delight but her aunt Caroline's words sounded inside her head. *Be cool, Patricia. If Samantha figures out what we're up to, it's all over.* "I guess I'll go." Perfect! She sounded as if she'd rather stay home and mope.

"We'll be leaving in an hour. Do you think you can be ready?"

Patty looked down at her pancakes and struggled not to smile. "Yeah."

"You don't have to go, Patty. I can come back and pick you up before we go to the store."

"That's okay, Mom. I'll be ready."

Nothing in the world could keep Patty away from seeing her mother and future father together for the very first time.

Not even a blizzard!

"THAT'S SOME KID you've got there," said Murphy O'Rourke as he helped Sam arrange the sandwiches and appetizers on serving platters. "Scotty usually doesn't like anybody under thirty-five."

"Then that makes them even," Sam said, reassembling a triple-decker B.L.T. on white toast. "Patty doesn't, either."

Her little girl and the cultured professor had hit it off like a house afire. The moment they were introduced Patty launched into a discussion of higher mathematics that left everyone else in the bar gasping for air. When she explained a concept even Scotty didn't know about, he smiled and said he bowed to a higher intelligence.

"Let us find a table away from the masses," said Scotty with a wink in Sam's direction. "I want to hear your theory on exponential equations."

Patty beamed with pleasure and Sam's opinion of Murphy went up yet another notch when he served the little girl hot chocolate in a beer mug, complete with a frothy head of whipped cream.

"Is there really that much to say about fractions?" Murphy asked, scratching his head.

"Beats me," said Sam. "I stopped understanding most of what Patty has to say about seven years ago. If I didn't have the stretch marks, I'd think she was an alien visitor from some advanced planet."

"How do you keep up with her?"

"I don't." Sam took a sip of Murphy's rich dark coffee. "I feed her, clothe her and love her, but I sure as heck don't keep up with her."

Murphy looked toward Patty. "Some responsibility."

"Tremendous responsibility," said Sam, "but I can't imagine what my life would have been like without her. She's the best thing that's ever happened to me."

A series of expressions flickered across Murphy's face, and even Sam, who wasn't inclined toward analysis, saw both affection and admiration in his eyes.

"You're a lucky woman."

"Yes," she said, glancing toward her daughter. "I am, at that."

It was a tender, sweet moment. The kind of moment you wanted to stretch on and on. The kind of moment that futures were built on. Unfortunately, Patty and Scotty chose that moment to burst into peals of laughter that rattled the rafters of the bar.

"I never knew math was that funny," said Murphy.

"Neither did I." Sam raised her eyebrows in the direction of her daughter but Patty paid no heed. "I think they're up to something." *No matchmaking, kiddo, I'm warning you. Friendship is every bit as wonderful as romance.* And maybe if she repeated that phrase often enough, she might believe it....

Murphy grunted and poured himself a tall glass of club soda with a twist of lime. "He probably told her about Saturday night."

Sam's heart did a funny kind of thud against her breastbone. "Saturday night?" *Please don't tell me about the Playboy bunny/astrophysicist/humanitarian you're taking out to dinner.*

"The masquerade ball." He took a long gulp of club soda. "You're going, aren't you?"

Sam shook her head. "Not this year."

"Why not? You belong to the association. You're opening your store in a few weeks. You should be there along with everybody else."

"Tell that to my bank balance and my wardrobe."

"I was hoping to see you there."

Sure, you were. I could sit down and have a drink with you and your beautiful blue-eyed blond date. "You'll have to settle for seeing me over my hors d'oeuvre trays tomorrow."

"Sounds good, but I won't be around tomorrow."

"Oh." *Don't sound so disappointed, Sam. What he does and where he does it aren't any of your business.*

"I'm going into Manhattan."

"I see."

"I have an appointment with UPI."

"An overseas assignment?"

"I'm hoping."

Sidewalk cafés. Elegant Frenchwomen with cheekbones to die for. Moonlight walks near the Champs d'Elysé.
"Good luck."

"I probably won't get the job. I'm still technically with the *Telegram*."

"I thought you quit the *Telegram*."

"Yeah, but there's a contract and they tend to get real touchy about things like that."

"I still think you'll get the job." Murphy O'Rourke didn't strike Sam as a man who lost out very often, not once he put his mind to something.

"You're an optimist."

"My biggest fault," said Sam. "I always believe people will get their fondest wishes."

"What about your fondest wishes?" He leaned closer; she could almost feel his intensity. "Will they come true?"

"I'm trying," said Sam, "but so far my fairy godmother hasn't found me."

"Too bad you aren't going to the party. Maybe your fairy godmother will be there looking for you."

"Right," said Sam with a rueful laugh. "And maybe she'll turn me into Cinderella."

TWO TABLES AWAY, Patty and Professor Scotty exchanged knowing glances.

"Cinderella!" Patty breathed softly. "It's so romantic. I can't wait to see her face."

"And I can't wait to see his," said Scotty. "This is a fine plan, my dear child. A fine plan."

"I knew the minute I saw Murphy that he was the one."

"I wonder how long it will take them to agree with our assessment."

"My mom can be real stubborn."

"Murphy has been known to dig in his heels."

"My mom thinks Rocky Hill is the best place in the world."

"Murphy was looking for a way out from the day he was born."

"She thinks marriage is forever."

"He's been divorced."

They looked over at Sam and Murphy who were engaged in intense conversation, their heads pressed close together over the appetizer tray like old friends exchanging intimate confidences.

Patty grinned at the older man. "I think they're a match made in heaven."

He patted her hand. "So do I, dear girl. So do I."

Chapter Nine

It struck Murphy halfway through his interview with the chief honcho of UPI on Friday morning that he should be a hell of a lot happier.

So far everyone liked him, from the secretaries to the cub reporters to the executives who wouldn't know how to file a wire story if their collective lives depended on it. Every time he turned a corner he bumped into a familiar face and fielded another invitation to have lunch or dinner or drinks ASAP.

They were going to make an offer. Murphy didn't have a doubt in the world that they would. Interviews at his stage of the game were strictly *pro forma* matters. Social exercises rather than business deals. Sometime between now and Christmas the phone would ring and this seriously intelligent man on the other side of the desk would make an offer that would be just shy of knocking Murphy's socks off.

It was exactly what he'd thought he wanted back when he stormed out of the *Telegram* office in late October. Why then was he finding it so damned hard to muster up any enthusiasm?

You've had things your own way all your life. Why should this be any different?

Leave me alone, Pop.

Getting ready to run again, boy?

I only came back for you, Pop. I wanted to help.

Some help. How can I relax when I know you got one foot out the door?

I'm only thinking of you. Dr. Cohen says you should be doing more.

And what do you care, Mr. Big Shot? You've been too busy running all over Europe to care what happens in Rocky Hill.

That doesn't make any sense, Pop. First you tell me I want out, then you tell me I'm taking the bar away from you. Which is it?

"Murphy?"

Murphy jumped at the sound of his name. "Yes?"

The chief honcho laughed politely. "I asked if you want to go up to the dining room for lunch."

"Sure," said Murphy, rising from his chair. "I'm in no rush to get back."

"The Dover sole is superb."

Murphy smiled as the other man rose. "I'll consider it."

He knew it wouldn't hold a candle to the hearty, delicious concoctions Sam Dean had been supplying the past few days.

"It feels like the old days on the Geneva beat, doesn't it?" asked the chief honcho as they headed toward the private elevator at the end of the hall.

"Sure does," said Murphy, his tone bland.

"Those were the days," sighed the executive.

No, thought Murphy in surprise. As good as those days had been they couldn't hold a candle to the fun he'd had in the snow with Samantha Dean.

Don't even think it, boy. You're everything that woman and her kid don't need. You'd only hurt them when you left.

Shut up, Dad. This time you're probably right.

IT WASN'T THE SAME without Murphy.

Sam was amazed to discover how much she missed see-

ing him Friday afternoon when she stopped off at
O'Rourke's to leave the trays of sandwiches and appetizers
for the gang. Not even Scotty's courtly manners and effusive praise for her daughter's brilliance could ease the void
Murphy's absence created.

Sam fumed all the way to Princeton Junction and her
storefront. Scotty had said that O'Rourke would send a
cousin around later to return the empty trays. What kind of
nonsense was that anyway?

*He's only being considerate, Sam. There's no reason to
get all bent out of shape.*

He had a life of his own. He had every right to spend the
day in Manhattan job hunting, if that's what he wanted to
do. What correspondent in his right mind wouldn't welcome a job offer from UPI? Just because her future was
there in New Jersey was no reason to imagine the Garden
State held any long-term allure for O'Rourke.

Her stint as chief cook for O'Rourke's Bar and Grill was
as temporary as his stint as bartender. In fact, someone was
interviewing for the spot that very afternoon. Soon his dad
would be back mixing drinks and a cook would man the
stove in the kitchen, and she and Murphy would go their
separate ways.

In just a few days Murphy had become part of her daily
life. She looked forward to seeing him, to talking to him, to
making him laugh with stories about her years in cooking
school and her tribulations raising a girl genius. He could be
sardonic and he could be silly and while he wasn't the polished, sophisticated man of her dreams, he possessed a
rough-and-tumble attractiveness that could be quite appealing.

The simple fact of the matter was she liked him. She liked
him a lot. It was wonderful to be around a man who found
the details of your everyday life as fascinating as Murphy
seemed to find hers. She couldn't think of too many thirty-

six-year-old men who would have been able to enjoy an impromptu snowball fight with the same zest that Murphy showed the night before.

"So where are you then, O'Rourke?" she said to the empty storefront. Why wasn't he back at the bar where he belonged, keeping Scotty and Joe and the rest of the gang company?

And, while she was asking questions he'd never answer, why was he taking another woman to the Tri-County Small Business Association's Annual Masquerade Ball?

WHEN SAM GOT HOME from working at the store, Patty and Caroline were seated at the kitchen table, chatting away like old ladies at a quilting bee, and Sam found herself annoyed that Patty hadn't seen fit to at least take something out of the freezer for dinner.

"Are you staying for dinner?" she snapped at her best friend.

Caroline's pale brows arched. "Such a gracious invitation, Samantha. It breaks my heart to decline."

Caroline stayed a few more minutes, and Sam managed to muster up enough enthusiasm to give the woman a quick hug good-bye.

"Are you okay?" Caroline asked before she disappeared down the driveway to her car. "You're not yourself."

"Don't I wish," Sam muttered, glaring at her beautiful blond blue-eyed friend.

"You're overtired." Caroline turned up the collar of her cashmere coat. "Get a good night's sleep. Everything will look brighter in the morning."

"Hah!" Sam shivered as a blast of cold air whipped around her shoulders. "A likely story."

"Trust me," said Caroline, winking at Patty. "I know what I'm talking about."

"What was that all about?" Sam asked the minute she closed and locked the door.

Patty's eyes were wide and innocent behind her glasses. "What was what?"

"That wink."

"What wink?"

"You and Caroline are up to something, aren't you?"

Patty looked away, her braids falling forward over her shoulders.

Sam sighed loudly and tugged at one of her daughter's plaits. "Don't encourage Caroline," she warned. "We made a pact not to exchange Christmas gifts this year and I, for one, intend to stick with it."

To Sam's horror, Patty's lower lip trembled. "I hate it when you say things like that."

Sam scrunched down next to her little girl. "You know our budget, sweetheart. I'd rather spend my money on—" She stopped, suddenly uncertain whether or not the Santa Claus issue had been satisfactorily resolved last year.

"That's all right," said Patty, her voice breaking. "I know Santa Claus is just a myth for children, and I know you want to get me presents but—" Her narrow shoulders shook as Sam gathered her into her arms.

"Don't cry, kiddo. I know I've done a lot of complaining about bills this year, what with the store and school and everything, but Christmas will be the same as it ever was. I promise you."

"I know," said Patty, her eyes glistening with tears. "That's the problem." She sniffled loudly. "I wish we could have the Christmas candles outside this year."

"The candles aren't free, honey. Besides, don't we have enough to do with decorating the *inside* of the house?" Their neighborhood had a long-standing Christmas tradition that Sam devoutly wished would disappear. Every Christmas Eve the residents lined their driveways and the street with tiny white paper bags. Inside each bag a fat white candle rested in a bed of sand. At dusk the candles were lighted and the flickering flames burned until well past midnight, ushering in Christmas with a festive—and Sam had to admit, lovely—way.

For years Patty had been begging Sam to let them join in the spectacle, but Sam had always been too broke to buy the supplies or too busy working until late on Christmas Eve to participate. And there was certainly no way on earth she would let her daughter, brilliant though she was, play with fire.

Sam knew she'd acquired the nickname "Mrs. Scrooge" from her family for her avid disinterest in all things Yule these past few years but she'd never imagined Patty had taken it so to heart.

"I don't think you're fair," Patty said, pouting.

"Just you wait until the store opens and we start to show a profit."

"I don't care about that."

"Sure you do, honey. Maybe we could even get you that computer you love so much."

"I don't care about some stupid computer." Patty pulled out of Sam's grasp. "I just want you to be happy!"

"I am happy, Patty." Where on earth had this come from? A second ago they'd been talking about the luminaria that lined the street on Christmas Eve.

"No, you're not."

"Of course I am! How could I be anything but happy with a daughter like you?"

"I won't be with you forever," said her brilliant, but painfully young, little girl. "One day I'll go off to college and you'll be all alone."

Out of the mouths of babes... Sam's heart twisted. It seemed as if Patty had been at the center of her life for as long as she could remember. She'd grown up just one step ahead of her baby daughter and found it impossible to imagine her life being any other way.

"Don't rush things, sweetheart. There's still plenty of time."

"I wish you were married," Patty blurted out. "I wish I had a father."

What point was there to reminding Patty that she did, indeed, have a father? Expensive presents at Christmas and birthdays did not a father make. Ronald Donovan was nothing more than a name on a birth certificate, tucked away in a safety deposit box and all but forgotten.

"You have Grandpa Harry and all of your uncles," Sam offered, removing Patty's glasses and drying them with the hem of her soft cotton sweater.

"But they don't belong to me."

"People don't belong to other people," Sam reasoned, although she knew all too well what her daughter meant. "There are an awful lot of people who love and care about you, Patty. That's not something to take lightly." She slipped the glasses back on her daughter's serious, freckled face.

Was that a twinkle she saw in her daughter's bright blue eyes? "I still wish I had a real dad living right here with us."

"I'm afraid you only have a real live mother and she'll have to be enough."

"I still wish you were married."

Sam laughed and shrugged her shoulders. "Well, sometimes, kiddo, so do I."

"Really?"

"Really." The years from seventeen to twenty-eight had disappeared in the blink of an eye. Sam felt as if she'd gone from schoolgirl to mother in an instant. Her life had been filled with caring for Patty's ever-increasing needs, earning a living, then the back-breaking job of school and starting a new business. Even if she had been interested in romance along the way, she doubted if she'd have been able to squeeze a man into her schedule.

Funny how Murphy O'Rourke had been able to fit right into her schedule, making himself a part of her routine as if they'd been friends for years instead of only a few short days. She thoroughly enjoyed his company, and Patty was positively smitten in a way that Sam had never seen before.

Admit it, Sam—you're pretty smitten with him yourself.

She blushed under her daughter's knowing glance. Fat lot of good it did, being smitten with Murphy O'Rourke. He thought of her as a funny-looking younger sister and nothing more. She wasn't his type, and nothing on earth was going to change that.

Besides, if she were going to get serious about a man at last, she certainly wouldn't pick a footloose and fancy-free foreign correspondent as her heart's desire.

No, she wanted a quiet and stable businessman whose roots were as firmly entrenched in central New Jersey as hers were. She wanted a man whose idea of high excitement was running down to K-mart for a new snow shovel.

And, more than anything, she wanted a man who thought tall, skinny brunettes with brilliant red-haired daughters were the answer to a single man's dream.

Murphy O'Rourke?

Not very likely.

Sam sighed and kissed her daughter's cheek. "C'mon, kiddo. Give me a smile. We're in this together, just you and me."

"Yes," said Patty, forcing an answering smile. "Just you and me."

MURPHY HUNG OUT in Manhattan for a few hours after his meeting with the chief honcho at UPI. He wandered in and out of some of his old favorite watering holes, half hoping to bump into some of his pals from the *Telegram*, but no dice. Apparently other men his age had more important things to do.

In fact, they were probably all hot on the trail of a story that would have won Murphy the Pulitzer.

You made your bed, son, now you have to lie in it.

"Shut up, Pop, will you?"

"Say what?" The young, muscular parking attendant glared at Murphy through his mirrored lenses. "You got a problem, man?"

"No problem," said Murphy as another steroid-happy attendant brought his rented car to a squealing halt two inches away from Murphy's midsection. "Just another wonderful day in the Big Apple."

Traffic on Ninth Avenue was backed up halfway to Wall Street, and Murphy had to maneuver his way around a water main break, potholes and sidewalk Santas to get down to the Holland Tunnel and take an alternate route back to the sanity of central New Jersey.

As it was, he snarled his way home and stormed into the bar a little after six with all the charm of Conan the Barbarian.

"Down, boy!" One of the regulars hoisted a wooden chair and aimed its sturdy legs at Murphy who considered biting them off and spitting toothpicks at the clientele.

"I take it your meeting was unproductive?" Scotty's tone was smooth and conciliatory.

"Mmmph." Murphy's tone was not.

"Traffic heavy?"

"Hmmph." *Good going, O'Rourke.* Prehistoric man was probably a better conversationalist. He wanted to complain about the traffic, about the crowds in the city, about UPI and the demise of expense-account lunches but, to his surprise, there wasn't anybody in that bar he could talk to.

Scotty would lecture him on responsibility. His old man, who was watching him from behind the bar, would tune him out with a quick "I told you so." Angela, the waitress, would snort and tell him about her sore feet and varicose veins.

Sam would listen.

The thought was there, full-blown, as if it had been waiting in some dusty corner of his brain for him to notice. Sam was strong and opinionated, it was true, but there was a warmth about her that intrigued him. She was independent and ambitious and all of those terrific things but she was also a woman and that was what called to Murphy that night.

He tossed his tie and his trenchcoat over the bar and grabbed for his leather jacket hanging on the wall hook. "I'll be back in a few hours."

His father looked up from counting swizzle sticks. "Unfinished business?"

"Yeah," said Murphy, heading for the door. "Unfinished business."

AS IT TURNED OUT, Sam was harder to find than the Holy Grail. Her telephone number was unlisted. He couldn't remember if she lived in big Rocky Hill or little Rocky Hill and once he got that straight he called her Dane instead of Dean. Finally he called on one of his pals on the local police force to at least point him in the right direction. An hour and a half after his quest began, he turned onto a quiet street of middle-aged frame houses with neatly fenced yards. Number thirteen, nineteen—there it was. Twenty-three Harvest Drive.

The house with the police car in the driveway.

IT WAS DEFINITELY one of those days.

First Murphy wasn't at the bar. Then Patty lured her into one of those deep, soul-searching conversations about wanting a father that invariably tore at Sam's heartstrings and called up all manner of maternal guilt. Now her cousin Teddy, a twenty-year man on the local police force, decided to stop by and drop a bombshell on her doorstep.

"Frank's getting married this weekend!" Sam's voice rose an octave in surprise.

Teddy, a big bear of a man, laughed as he gulped down a cup of coffee in the front hall. "I can't believe it, either.

Never thought he'd give me a sister-in-law, that's for darn
sure.''

Frank was Teddy's twin, equally big and equally jovial.
Sam couldn't count the times both men had pitched in to
help her and Patty over the rough spots. Frank operated a
hot-dog cart in mid-Manhattan, which turned into that New
York City perennial each Christmas—a roasted chestnut
stand.

"So what's the deal, Teddy? Does he need the wedding
catered?" The thought of turning out one hundred dinners
on short notice made Sam blanch but there wasn't anything
she wouldn't do for her cousin. She was already planning
her shopping list.

"He's renting Uncle Joe's restaurant."

Sam whistled. "I'm impressed."

"What he needs is—" Teddy stopped and peered out the
glass panel next to the door. "You expecting company?"

"No, I'm—oh, yeah. A delivery boy is coming by to return some trays."

"Pretty old delivery boy," said Teddy. "Looks kind of
rough around the edges, if you ask me."

"Murphy!" Sam leaped to the door and swung it open,
battling down a sudden rush of excitement racing through
her veins. "What are you doing here?" *Brilliant, Sam! Talk
about a gracious hostess . . .*

He waved the round metal trays overhead. "You need
these, don't you?"

Teddy broke in with a theatrical cough. "You know this
guy, Sammy?"

Her cheeks reddened as she ushered Murphy into her
growing-smaller-by-the-second front hall. "Teddy, this is
Murphy O'Rourke. His dad owns O'Rourke's Bar and
Grill."

"Know it well," said Teddy, extending his paw of a hand.
"Spent many a happy hour in there. How's your dad do-
ing-"

Murphy's hazel eyes widened. "Great. He should be back behind the bar full-time in a few weeks."

"Glad to hear it. I know he had a rough spell of it there for a while."

"I love small towns," Murphy grumbled, just loud enough for Sam to hear. He looked at Teddy. "And you're—?"

"Sammy's cousin. Teddy Dean."

Teddy looked from Sam to Murphy then back again, and she didn't like what she saw in his eyes. In the best of times her family was both curious and talkative. Murphy's visit would be common knowledge from Rocky Hill to Trenton and back before Murphy finished his first cup of coffee. That was, if he had come to stay.

She cleared her throat. "Teddy dropped by to tell me my cousin Frank is getting married on Sunday."

Murphy nodded politely, obviously unenthralled by the Dean family saga.

"And you'll work the stand Sunday during the wedding?" Teddy said, forcing his full attention back to Sam.

"What stand?" asked Murphy.

"A chestnut stand." Sam laughed at the expression on his face. "You know—'Chestnuts roasting on an open fire...'"

"You're kidding."

"Hell, no!" said Teddy. "Frankie's got the best location in Manhattan. Right near Rockefeller Center. Makes a mint, too, let me tell you."

Sam thought of the many kindnesses both cousins had showed her over the years. "Of course, I will."

"You can keep the profits."

She waved away his words. "That's my wedding gift to them."

"He'll be back on Monday morning, bright and early."

Murphy snapped back to attention. "He only needs one day off?"

Teddy shrugged his huge, uniformed shoulders. "He's in love but he's not crazy. There's time for a honeymoon after the holidays. Too much money to be made in December."

"What a family," muttered Murphy, and Sam gave him a sharp jab in the ribs with her elbow. "Do you all sell food?"

"Just about," said Sam. "What else do you do when you love to eat as much as our clan does?"

Teddy looked down at his ample belly. "Only our Sammy here can eat and not pay the price."

"I'm lucky," said Sam. "Fast metabolism."

"I think she could use a few pounds," offered Murphy, dodging Sam's elbow.

"So do I," said Teddy.

"I think it's time to call it a night," said Sam with a glance at Murphy. "Don't you have crime to fight, Teddy?"

As if on cue, Teddy's squad car erupted in a series of squawks. "I think I'm being paged." He hesitated, once again looking from Murphy to Sam.

"Good-bye, Teddy," said Sam, opening the door wide.

Teddy winked at Murphy then chucked Sam under the chin. "Good night, you two."

Sam closed the door after her cousin then bolted the lock with a flourish. She leaned against the jamb and wiped imaginary perspiration from her brow. "Sorry you had to meet Teddy so early in our friendship. He's quite a character."

"That squad car gave me a scare," Murphy admitted as she led him into the kitchen. "I was afraid something had happened to you or Patty."

"Impossible," said Sam, switching off the television and putting up water for coffee. "Patty and I have too many guardian angels hovering over us."

Murphy straddled a chair, his gaze never leaving her. She caught her reflection in the door of her microwave oven. No wonder. She looked rotten. The ubiquitous ponytail. No makeup. Cheeks smeared with cake flour; vanilla extract instead of French perfume. And for sheer glamour, there was nothing like a faded blue chenille robe and sweat socks.

If she had a brain she'd take the cake out of the oven and stick her head in there instead.

"Excuse me, Murphy," she said, inching her way toward the door. "I'm going to change my clothes."

"Why?" He looked genuinely confused. "You look fine to me."

Of course you do, Sam. He's looking for a cup of coffee, not a romantic encounter.

She turned back to the counter and fussed with coffee beans and filters as if kitchen chores were foreign to her. At that moment, everything felt foreign—the fit of her skin, her thoughts, the odd sensation of having a man like Murphy in her country kitchen on a cold winter's night. "How was your day in the big city?"

"Okay."

She caught the hesitation in his voice and turned around to meet his eyes. "That bad?"

He nodded. "That bad."

"I'm a good listener." The aroma of freshly brewed coffee filled the air, mingling with the smell of cinnamon and cloves.

He reached for her hand and drew her closer. "I need one tonight, Sam."

Her heart thundered wildly inside her chest. "Well, I'm here."

"I'm glad."

"So am I," said Sam. "Now tell me all about your day."

And, while you're at it, tell me who you're taking to the Masquerade Ball . . .

STRANGE.

Murphy was only halfway into the story of his rotten day in the Big Apple when it happened. His anger, his fatigue, the general sense of going nowhere fast vanished completely. He finished his story, camping it up to make Sam laugh, but the rage that had driven it was long gone.

She had a great laugh, Sam Dean had, full-bodied and unself-conscious, tinged with the innocence of childhood but all woman. Definitely all woman. He couldn't remember the last time he'd just sat in a real-life kitchen and talked with a woman who listened. Really listened. Sam was warm and attentive and not shy about telling him when he was acting like a horse's hind quarter—which apparently was a hell of a lot.

"More coffee?" He watched as she walked over to the refrigerator for the pitcher of milk. Amazing how many curves she had hidden beneath that shapeless robe. A clear picture of the way she'd looked running across the parking lot that first morning at the bar passed before his eyes and he grinned. Long slender legs leading into gently rounded hips with a waist he could span with his hands and—

She was looking at him curiously. "Was that a no, Murphy?"

"No—I mean, yes." What it was, was a groan. He had no business thinking about Sam like that. "I should be hitting the road. This is the bar's busiest time."

She didn't disagree, and he suddenly felt awkward and clumsy, as if he'd overstayed his welcome.

He followed her into the hall—doing his best not to imagine the way she looked beneath her robe—mumbling all sorts of apologies for barging in on her.

She tossed him his coat, her lovely face lit with laughter. "Good grief, O'Rourke! I can't stand it when you're humble."

"You probably had plans for tonight."

She looked down at her attire. "Right. I was going to sew up a gown for the Masquerade Ball."

"You're going?" Maybe wasting a Saturday night with a bunch of stuffed shirts would have a compensation.

"Afraid not."

"Any chance you'll change your mind?"

"On, maybe one in seven million."

"I'll be banking on it, Sam." *Stupid, sappy line, O'Rourke. Since when do you spout mush like that? This is Sam you're talking to, not some air-headed bimbo from the Upper West Side.*

"Have fun tomorrow," she said, tossing her ponytail back over her shoulder. Did she have any idea how graceful such a simple gesture could seem?

"I'd say I have a one-in-seven-million chance of that."

"Congratulate Scotty on his award."

He nodded. Her dark brown gaze moved from his chin to his mouth and back to meet his eyes. Her tongue darted out to moisten her lower lip and he had the urge to pull her up close to him and kiss her thoroughly.

Ridiculous! She'd probably laugh in his face and tell him he'd been out of circulation too long.

Which, all things considered, was probably right.

"See you Monday?" he asked, turning up the collar on his jacket and stepping out onto the cold front step.

"See you Monday," said Sam.

Head down against the wind, he ran toward his car and made his way back to the bar.

"You okay?" asked his father when Murphy took over.

"Fine," said Murphy.

"You figure out whatever was eating at you?"

"No," he said, "but somehow it doesn't matter anymore."

His problems were still there waiting to be solved, but for one evening Sam had made it all seem very far away.

Chapter Ten

"Mom."

Sam groaned and pressed her face deeper into her pillow. "Go away," she mumbled. "It's not even dawn yet."

"Mom, wake up."

"Have a heart, Patty. At least let me sleep until the sun comes up."

"Get up, you lazy wretch!" There was only one woman on earth with the sugar-coated voice of a martinet. "It's almost ten."

"Go home, Caroline. Go bother someone else."

"We're going to have to resort to drastic measures," she heard Caroline say through her still-sleepy brain.

I'm dreaming all of this, she thought, drifting back toward sleep. *This isn't really happening.*

"Maa-a-a!" Patty's voice was high with anxiety. "You absolutely must wake up this minute!"

"No," said Sam, squeezing her eyes closed as tight as possible. She was in the middle of the most delightful dream about Murphy and their unexpected time together last night, and she wanted it to go on and on . . . "I am not waking up. Not for anybody."

"But you're a mother." Patty sounded scandalized and Sam smiled.

"No, I'm not. I hereby resign the position until a decent hour."

"Sorry, kid." Sam felt a hand grip the edge of the blankets. "I didn't want to play rough with you but—"

With that, the hand executed a perfect snap of the wrist that sent the bedclothes flying to the floor, and Sam sat straight up, gasping in the cool morning air in the bedroom, as Patty and Caroline looked on, amused.

"This is barbaric." She grabbed for the blankets but Caroline kicked them out of reach.

"Rise and shine," said her best friend.

"It must be six in the morning."

"Nine on the dot," said Patty with a smug smile.

Sam fell back against the pillows and covered her eyes with her hand. "I need caffeine."

"At your service." Caroline stepped out of the room, then returned with a white wicker tray heaped with serving dishes. "Caffeine, carbohydrates and an egg."

Sam uncovered her eyes and leaned up on her elbows.

Patty scrambled across the mattress and sat by Sam's uncovered, icy-cold knees. "Merry Christmas from Aunt Caroline."

Caroline placed the breakfast tray over Sam's narrow hips and removed the lid on the platter of perfectly toasted blueberry muffins. "Say one word about not exchanging presents, Samantha, and you'll be wearing the eggs."

"But we promised!" Sam felt awash in pleasure, embarrassment and a touch of righteous dismay. "No presents until our businesses are in the black."

"Mine's been in the black for two years now, kiddo, and I refuse to wait any longer."

If only the muffins didn't smell so incredibly delicious. "I said only Patty gets presents this year."

"Oh, stop being so tedious, Ms Scrooge, and eat your damned breakfast!"

Patty giggled as Caroline sat down in the slipper chair near the window.

Sam uncovered the fluffy yellow eggs and lifted the lid on the china pot of English breakfast tea. "I do hate to waste food."

Patty poured the dark tea into Sam's cup and liberally sugared it. Sam didn't have the heart to tell her daughter that she hadn't used sugar in her tea for at least eight years.

"Aunt Caroline has a whole day planned for you."

Sam almost choked on her sip of tea as she turned to face her best friend. "What is Patty talking about?"

Caroline leaned back and stretched her legs out in front of her. "Luxury, Samantha. Pure, unadulterated luxury."

The sweet, fruity smell of the blueberry muffins proved to be too much for Sam and she bit into one greedily. The plump, warm berries burst with flavor inside her mouth. "I can deal with breakfast in bed," she said, with a sheepish smile.

Patty's small frame relaxed beside her, and her daughter cadged a piece of the second muffin. "There's more, Mom." Patty turned toward Caroline, who still looked as if she hadn't a care in the world.

"This is your day, Sam. Today your secret wishes will all come true."

Sam's cheeks reddened as she remembered one of more interesting dreams about Murphy. "You painted the store for me?"

"Something more personal than that."

"You paid my phone bill."

Caroline waved her manicured hand in the air. "Don't be ridiculous. That's small potatoes."

A tiny thrill blossomed way down deep, in a part of Sam's heart that hadn't seen daylight in a very long time. "The masquerade ball tonight?"

"The masquerade ball," said Caroline.

Sam's heart was thudding so wildly she could scarcely think. "I can't," she whispered. "My hair...my nails...I don't have a thing to—" *Murphy's going to be there!*

"Yes, you do." Caroline rose from the chair and disappeared into the hallway.

Sam grabbed Patty's hand to keep from spinning away in pure excitement as she heard Caroline's footsteps returning.

"Voilà!" Caroline called from just outside the bedroom door. "Instant glamour, at your service!"

"Oh, my God!" Sam's eyes swam with tears as she stared at the glorious sapphire-blue satin confection draped across Caroline's arms. "Old Frosty's gown!"

"Yours for the night, Cinderella!"

"But, look at me." Sam stared down at her work-roughened hands, her unpainted nails, the reflection of her unmadeup face in the mirror across the room. "I'm a disaster."

"After I'm through with you, you won't be."

"Please, Mom!" Patty gave her an awkward hug around the breakfast tray. "Please go to the ball tonight!"

Think of it, Sam! You've worked so hard for so long—what could possibly be wrong with having one night to really shine?

"There's so little time. I still have the food trays to make for O'Rourke's and—"

"Everything's been taken care of," Caroline broke in. "All you have to worry about is being beautiful."

"And I suppose you're my fairy godmother?"

"Yes. That's exactly who I am tonight."

Forget it, her mind warned. *He has a date.* It didn't matter what magic Caroline wrought, for even the strongest alchemy couldn't turn her into a cuddly blue-eyed blonde.

But her woman's heart was sending out some strong messages of its own. *Go! Smile and dance and have a won-*

derful time. Let him see you at your best, even if only to show him what he missed.

"I'll do it," she said, laughter bubbling through her apprehensions. "I'll go to the ball!"

Even if it meant watching Murphy O'Rourke having the time of his life with the type of woman Sam could never be.

PATTY THOUGHT her heart would burst through her chest as she looked at her beautiful mother glide into the room ten hours later, with Aunt Caroline fussing at her heels. There wasn't a model or movie star anywhere in the entire world who could possibly look as glorious as her mom did that very moment!

"Well?" Sam stopped before Patty and looked down at her. "What do you think, kiddo?"

"Wow!" Patty managed over the great big lump in her throat. "You look... oh, wow!"

"I think we're a success," her mom said to Caroline with a nervous laugh.

"You're beautiful," said Caroline who looked wonderful in a slinky beaded black dress that seemed to stay up through sheer willpower alone. "You look like a princess in a fairy tale."

"You're Cinderella," Patty said, touching the shimmering sapphire folds of the full satin skirt.

"Well, I'm certain I won't find Prince Charming at the Tri-County Masquerade Ball." Sam tilted her head slightly and Patty caught the delicate tinkle of her rhinestone drop earrings as her mother looked into the standing mirror Caroline had brought over. "I don't think I'd recognize myself in a crowd." She held the sequined and feathered white velvet mask up to her face. "A woman of mystery! Who would have believed it possible?"

"I would," said Caroline, smoothing Sam's Gibson Girl upsweep with one gloved hand. "I always knew the potential was there, didn't you, Patty?"

Patty nodded vigorously. She knew her mom was pretty, if disinterested in her looks, but never in a million years had she imagined that under Sam's baggy cords and shapeless sweaters and straggly ponytail hid movie star material! Maybe growing up had some advantages besides being able to start work on a Ph.D. Could Patty possibly have such a wonderful surprise in store for her in another fifteen years?

"Wow!" she said again. She would have to remember to apologize to her friend Susan. Apparently there were times when no other word would suffice.

"Well, well!" Grandma Betty came from the kitchen, wiping her hands on her apron. "I never thought I'd see the day!"

"Neither did I," said Sam as she pirouetted gracefully.

Patty sighed as the full skirt of the satin gown made wonderful swishy noises with each movement.

"You're beautiful, Samantha," said Grandma Betty, who would watch Patty until the baby-sitter showed up.

Sam's eyes sparkled like the rhinestones twinkling at her ears. "I *feel* beautiful," she said in a voice as soft as her shiny dark hair.

The doorbell chimed and everybody jumped in surprise. Patty leaped up to answer it, swinging the front door open wide.

"If the ladies are ready, their car awaits," said a tall gray-haired man in a chauffeur's uniform complete with cap.

"Come on, Cinderella," said Caroline as she draped a wrap about Sam's shoulders. "The coach has arrived."

Sam bent down in front of Patty, who was sniffling and smiling and feeling an awful lot like a very little girl in front of her oh-so-glamorous mother.

"You'll be good for your grandmother, won't you?"

Patty nodded, not trusting her voice. She was so happy, and so hopeful, that she thought she could just spin out into orbit under her own power.

Sam kissed her lightly on the forehead and Patty almost swooned. Instead of smelling like cinnamon and sweet cream, her mom smelled like Shalimar. Her everyday mother was now exactly the kind of woman Patty imagined a man would love.

She looked over at her Aunt Caroline who flashed her a thumbs up sign. Patty waved good-bye from the front door. A full moon splashed across the snowy street. Winter stars twinkled high in the sky while Christmas carols seemed to blossom all around. Had there ever been an evening so absolutely *perfect* for romance?

The limousine eased silently down the driveway and headed up the street toward her mom's destiny. Unless she missed her guess, her mom and Murphy O'Rourke didn't stand a chance tonight, which was one hundred percent okay with Patty because she knew way down deep in her heart that this was the answer to all of her dreams.

She ran for the telephone and dialed Susan's number.

"Hello?"

"Susan, it's Patty."

Her friend squealed with excitement. "Did they go? How did your mom look? Has he seen her yet? Did you get a ride in the limousine? Did it have a bar and a television and—"

"Susan?"

"Yes?"

"*Wow!*"

MURPHY GAVE a final tug to his bow tie, straightened his cummerbund, then headed downstairs to meet up with Scotty.

"Wooo-eee!" Joe and Frank whistled and applauded as Murphy made his entrance. "Will you look at Beau Brummel there?"

Murphy didn't dare look over at his dad who was tending bar tonight. Bill's rumbling laugh was enough.

"One word out of any of you bozos and you're history," Murphy growled as Scotty stepped forward. He turned to look at his educated pal. "And if you give me a corsage, I swear I'll—"

"A corsage?" Scotty's elegant brows lifted. "I had thought more along the lines of a simple nosegay to complement your eyes."

"I've been wondering who you're dating, Murph," called out one of the regulars from across the bar. "Robbing the rest home again, are you?"

His dad's deep laugh grew louder. "At least now I know why I don't have grandchildren from this one."

"I'm glad you jokers are having a great time at my expense."

"Philistines, all of them," said Scotty as he slipped into his topcoat.

Murphy grabbed for his own coat. "I'm getting the hell out of here," he mumbled, then made a beeline for the door with Scotty close behind.

It was only seven-thirty and already it was the worst night of Murphy's life.

THE LIGHTS WERE LOW. The music was grand and lush. Chandeliers twinkled like diamonds overhead; diamonds glittered like—well, like diamonds on the fingers of Princeton's old guard. The women were lavishly coiffed and expensively dressed while the men were suave and sophisticated in tuxedos and old-fashioned tails.

And, miracle of miracles, Sam fit right in. No, she more than fit in, she looked as if she belonged. The moment she stepped inside the grand ballroom she knew she was home free. Caroline's date had spotted the glamorous blonde immediately—even with the plumed and sequined mask in place—and before Caroline was spirited off into the crowd, she whispered "Break a leg!" and Sam was on her own.

She straightened her shoulders and held her head high. There was something to be said for dressing for success. She felt positively regal in this princess dress. The voluminous skirt rustled and the toes of her peau de soie pumps alternately appeared and disappeared with each step she took. Her shoulders were bare; the low neckline revealed a rather amazing amount of bosom for a woman used to wearing Arnold Schwarzenegger's cast-off sweaters.

How wonderful it felt to be the center of attention as she swept through the ballroom, a study in sapphire satin and nonchalance. Men watched her as she passed, their eyes glittering behind their black masks. Sam couldn't remember the last time she'd been the recipient of so many long and lingering looks. In fact, she was fairly certain she'd *never* been the recipient of so many long and lingering looks.

Unfortunately none of those looks belonged to Murphy O'Rourke.

Sam peered through her mask at each man she passed. Tall men. Short men. Fat men. Men with mustaches and beards and foreign accents. Either these masks were infinitely more concealing than she'd originally believed or Murphy was nowhere to be found. She scanned the room for beautiful blondes, assuming one of them was Murphy's date. Still no sign of him.

She accepted a flute of champagne from a waiter and declined an invitation to dance tendered by a tall, slender man with piercing dark eyes. *Where are you, O'Rourke?* she thought as she made her way across the room toward the French doors. *If I live to be one hundred, I'll never look this good again.*

The bubbles tickled her nose as she sipped her champagne. *All dressed up and no place to go.* The least he could do was put in an appearance so she could dazzle him! This was all Caroline's fault. Sam was about to search out her best friend and attach herself to Caroline's side like a burr when she heard a familiar voice.

"Good evening, Samantha. May I say you look especially lovely tonight?"

She spun around. "Scotty! It's so nice to see a friendly face."

The man pressed a kiss to her cheek. "I want you to meet my date."

Sam laughed. "Date! You've been keeping secrets." The older man took her arm and propelled her across the dance floor in the direction of the orchestra. "Who is she?"

"You're jumping to conclusions, Samantha," said Scotty in a cryptic fashion.

Her eyes widened behind her mask as they approached a man of medium height whose back was to them. Her cheeks flamed with embarrassment. "Oh, Scotty! I'm sorry...I mean I didn't...I never suspected that you were—"

The man spun around. It was Murphy O'Rourke.

Chapter Eleven

What on earth had happened to the rumpled, sloppy Murphy O'Rourke she thought she knew?

His sandy hair was beautifully barbered. His five-o'clock shadow was a thing of the past. His tux was tailored to fit his broad-shouldered frame and his shirtfront was snowy white and starched to perfection. Even his bow tie was exactly the way it should be.

"Murphy?" Her voice was wispy for it was hard to draw a breath. Her heart was beating so rapidly that she felt her pulse pounding in her ears, at the base of her throat, her wrists...

"Sam." She watched, enchanted, as the sparkle in his hazel eyes turned to something darker, more intense. "You're beautiful."

She ducked her head for a moment then remembered that this was a night for magic. "So are you."

"I thought you weren't coming tonight."

"I wasn't." She told him briefly about Caroline's surprise Christmas present. His eyes never left hers. A warm, tingly feeling blossomed inside her heart. "So here I am, the brand new, hundred percent improved version of Samantha Dean."

"I liked the old version, too," he said, taking her elbow and leading her toward the dance floor. "You looked pretty cute last night in your ponytail."

Sam's ponytail was now a thing of the past. She'd left it behind on the floor of the Shady Lady Hair Salon that afternoon. "I hope you didn't get rid of your corduroy jacket," she said as he took her champagne glass and deposited it on a side table. "I'm rather fond of it."

"This isn't me," said Murphy, gesturing toward his fancy clothes.

"And this isn't me, either," said Sam, motioning toward her glamorous garb. This was a fairy tale come true, complete with Cinderella and the handsome prince. She glanced down at her shoes, half expecting to see they had been transformed into glass slippers.

The lush sounds of romantic music from the Big Band era drifted over to where they stood. Sam longed to ask Murphy to dance but she couldn't summon up the nerve. How foolish! This was the same man she'd tumbled with in the snow just a few days earlier. The same man who had fallen across her legs and rubbed her face in the snow and kissed her on the cheek like a brother would kiss his kid sister. The same man who had sat at her kitchen table last night and made her laugh. She looked at him in his elegant clothes and wicked mask. Nothing had changed.

Yet everything had.

She knew it and, she suspected, so did he.

The music grew more poignant, more enticing.

Murphy cleared his throat. "Scotty's a matchmaker."

Sam swallowed hard. "So is Caroline."

His hazel eyes twinkled behind the mask. "Do you think we've been set up?"

"Oh, yes," said Sam, "and I think I know who's behind it all."

"Patty?"

She nodded. "Patty."

He took her hand then and drew her into his arms. "Remind me to thank the kid."

"Oh, I will." A deep sigh of pleasure rose up inside Sam as she went to him. His arms were strong as he held her close to his broad chest. He moved gently at first, his body barely swaying to the rhythm of the music, and it seemed to Sam—practical, down-to-earth Sam!—as if she'd been waiting all her life for this moment. The cut of the gown bared her back almost to the waist and a thrill of excitement shot through her as he rested his warm palm flat against the ridge of her spine. Her dangerously high heels made Sam closer to his height, and her temple brushed the strong curve of his jaw.

If only the orchestra would never stop playing....

THE FRENCH had a word for it, but then, the French had a word for all things romantic.

Coup de foudre. The lightning bolt.

The way Murphy had felt when he turned and looked at Samantha in that shimmering blue dress. The sight of her, tall and slender in that incredible gown, knocked the breath out of his lungs. For a long moment he couldn't think or speak or do anything but stare at her. Her arms and legs were long and finely made; her torso, gently curved. She held her head high; her slender throat was white and supple, encircled with a glittering necklace.

This was Sam. His friend Sam. The Sam who made sandwiches for the gang at the bar and laughed when he buried her face in a snowdrift. The same Sam who was mother and daughter and friend.

A few hours ago he would have sworn on a stack of Gideon bibles that their friendship would never be anything more than exactly that. Now, with her in his arms, he wondered how he could ever have been such a fool. The feelings that had thrown him for a loop last night in her kitchen hadn't been his imagination, after all. Whatever it was that made Sam *Sam*, had the power to mesmerize him whether she was dressed in a bathrobe or a satin gown. She was the most fascinating woman he'd ever met.

And the most desirable. Her skin was silk beneath his fingertips. Her hair held the scent of an exotic garden on a summer's day. The way her body fit against his made him rethink his position on Fate. She was an exotic stranger in his arms, and yet she was the same woman he'd come to know and care for this past week.

Murphy had waited thirty-six years and five months for a woman to sweep him off his feet and now that he'd found her, he wasn't about to let her go.

"LOOK AT THEM," said Caroline to Scotty as the happy couple danced past them. "They couldn't be more perfect together!"

"We should be quite proud of ourselves," said the professor.

"That we should."

Sam looked up at Murphy as if he were the sun and the stars. He looked down at Sam as if she held the keys to paradise. They glowed with delight and the newfound blush of discovery, and if Caroline wasn't so crazy about Sam she might have been envious.

"Murphy has always claimed he was not the marrying kind," said Scotty.

"Sam said she hasn't time for anything but Patty and her store."

She met Scotty's eyes and the two of them burst into delighted laughter.

"Shall we dance, my dear?"

"Charmed, Professor," said Caroline. They both knew it was only a matter of time.

"WE'VE BEEN DANCING for almost two hours," Murphy murmured against Sam's ear.

"I know," she whispered. "Isn't it wonderful?"

His grip tightened as he drew her yet closer to him. Her body went softer and more yielding, if that was possible. At that moment all things seemed possible. Boundaries and rules and her old ways of thinking no longer mattered. The shell around her heart had broken at last and she felt almost giddy with joy.

She was Sam and yet she wasn't. He was Murphy—and yet he was someone better, someone exciting and dangerous and potently masculine.

This couldn't be happening, and yet it was.

She sighed and rested her forehead against his shoulder.

Oh, it definitely was happening...

For the past week, Sam had thought of Murphy O'Rourke as a reporter, a bartender, a dirty snowball fighter, and a brand new friend. The one way she tried not to think of Murphy was as a man.

She knew he had problems with his dad and his brother, that a lot of people wanted to hire him to report the news, and that there was a soft spot in his heart for kids and damsels in distress. She also knew there was an ex-wife somewhere out there in the world and probably a good number of ex-girlfriends, as well, but none of it had made a lasting impression upon her.

Oh, sure, she'd felt a prickle of envy when she thought he'd be attending this party with some nubile young blonde but the moment she saw him with the not-so-nubile Scotty in tow, her envy vanished.

So did everything else, save for the overwhelming sense that she was exactly where she should be, and at the exact moment of time she should be there.

Don't get carried away, Sam, her internal censor warned. *This isn't any more real than that dress you're wearing or the* faux *diamonds around your neck.* Come midnight Cinderella would have to leave the ball and go home alone without Prince Charming because that was the way life really was.

Murphy's arms tightened pleasurably about her. He smelled faintly soapy, faintly spicy, altogether masculine and intoxicating. His body was warm and broad and wonderfully powerful and he had an athletic grace that translated beautifully to the dance floor. If her fairy godmother appeared before her and said this moment could go on forever, Sam would have pledged her undying gratitude.

She floated through the evening on a cloud of excitement. Caroline joined them at the front of the ballroom and they all applauded madly as the eminent Professor Edmund MacTavish received his award. Scotty was such a splendid fellow! Caroline was such a wonderful friend!

She looked at the handsome, debonair Murphy O'Rourke and practically melted right there on the spot. And to think she owed it all to her precocious daughter. Sam was awash with tenderness, with excitement, with gratitude and happiness and—could it be?—a sudden, inexplicable rush of Christmas spirit. Why, she even found herself joining in with the crowd as they sang a lively version of "Deck the Halls."

Scotty rejoined them and she, Murphy, and Caroline toasted the older man's health and happiness. The orchestra started up once again and Sam went into Murphy's arms as naturally as drawing a breath. Not that drawing a breath was an easy task, for his closeness was having the most de-

cidedly powerful effect upon the once staid and practical
Samantha Dean.

"It's getting warm in here," said Murphy, his eyes sparkling behind the mask that tradition decreed should remain
in place until the midnight hour.

She fanned herself delicately. "It certainly is."

He inclined his head toward the French doors across the
ballroom. "Maybe we need some fresh air."

She nodded. "I think we do."

He danced her across the room in the blink of an eye, and
before anyone could notice they slipped out onto the patio.

"Are you cold?" he asked.

"I should be but I'm not."

"It's almost time for the late-night supper." He traced the
line of her jaw with the tip of his index finger. "Are you
hungry?"

Sam shook her head. Let the others swarm into the dining room. She felt sorry for them. What was food compared with a moonlit winter night?

Tiny white lights glittered from the bare branches of the
trees beyond the patio. From somewhere far away came the
sounds of laughter and music and crystal glasses raised in a
toast.

"I know it's not midnight," said Murphy, "but I think
it's time to unmask."

She watched, spellbound, as he reached for his mask and
slowly removed it. She'd thought herself on familiar terms
with the planes and angles of his broad and masculine face
but she felt as if she were seeing him for the very first time:
those high strong cheekbones; the powerful jawline and
stubborn chin; the fleeting dimples and off-center smile;
those thick sandy lashes framing his hazel eyes. Why hadn't
she noticed what a beautiful man he truly was?

She lifted her hand to remove her own mask.

"No." His voice was deep, commanding.

Taking a step toward her, he brought his large hands to her face and slowly removed her sequined velvet mask. Sam felt as if she were losing the last of her defenses against him.

"Hi, Sam," he said in a dark and dangerous voice she hadn't heard before.

Her hands trembled and she found it impossible to speak. The world seemed far away, as if they were suspended somewhere in infinite time.

Murphy reached forward and brushed a curl away from Sam's eyes. Such a gentle touch from such a strong and powerful man. That gentle touch was Sam's undoing. She lifted her eyes to meet his. He lowered his head toward her. Sam's lips parted; her pulses quickened.

This is it, she thought wildly. This was the moment they'd been moving toward all evening, the moment she'd been waiting for....

"Excuse us."

They leaped apart. A middle-aged couple, looking delightfully guilty, emerged from the shadows. "Sorry," said the woman with a giggle. "Don't want to miss dinner."

The man did his best to look dignified but the smudges of crimson lipstick near his mouth undid his valiant attempts.

Murphy's stormy expression matched her wildly churning emotions. "The roads are clear," he said, his voice almost a growl. "We could take a drive."

"Patty," Sam whispered. "Her sitter goes home at twelve-thirty."

He glanced at his watch. "An hour and a half," he said, slipping out of his tux jacket and draping it across her shoulders. "I'll have you back on time."

She smiled up at him, feeling coddled and cosseted and almost lethally feminine. "I'd love a moonlight drive."

If either had feared that the intrusion of reality would tarnish the lustre of the evening, their fears were groundless, for once they were tucked into the velvet darkness of the rented car, away from the sharp winter wind and prying eyes, the world dropped away once again.

"Where are we going?" Sam asked as he eased the car out of the parking lot.

"Someplace quiet."

A frisson of nervousness made Sam's breath catch for an instant. It was so dark and they were so alone. He drove slowly along Route 206, past stores and old houses and huge wooded areas yet to catch the land developer's eye. Turning right on tiny Highway 518, he headed up the winding curves toward Rocky Hill. Christmas candles burned in living room windows and colored lights twinkled around doorways. There were huge candy canes and wreathes with big shiny red bows. She could almost swear she heard the lilting voices of carolers in the distance. Sam smiled in the darkness of the car. What a wonderful season.

She cast him a quick glance. *What a wonderful man . . .*

Murphy made a right, then a left, and suddenly Sam knew exactly where they were headed. Five minutes later he pulled alongside the bridge that overlooked one of the Delaware-Raritan valley canals.

"I forgot you grew up around here," Sam said as he helped her from the car.

"This has always been one of my favorite spots." He put his arms around her shoulders and led her toward the railing. "Even when I wanted nothing more than to get the hell out of New Jersey, I still loved it here."

"You know what they call it, don't you?" The wind whipped up from the icy water but for some strange reason she didn't feel a thing.

He grinned at her. "Make-out Point."

"You knew."

"I know a lot of things, Sam."

"I'm sure you do," she said, her words tossed back at them by the wind. "You *are* an ace reporter."

He drew her into the circle of his arms as he had when they danced. "I know something special is happening."

She caught the scent of his skin, and warmth spread through her limbs. "You're going to kiss me, aren't you?"

He ducked his head lower to look at her. "That's the general idea."

He was so close she could see the shadow of his beard beneath his ruddy skin, imagine the feel of his mouth against hers, the way he would—

"I think this would be a good time," she said, her gaze resting on his lips.

"So do I." His head dipped toward her and an instant later his lips found hers. At first the pressure was light, almost teasing, and she found herself intrigued by the combination of steel and velvet his kiss called to mind.

Time curled around them as the seconds passed and with each one, Sam found herself drawing closer to him, yearning for a deeper, more intimate contact. Desire was a silken cord, binding her to him in exquisite anticipation.

It was as if he read minds, for suddenly his lips parted and she gasped as his tongue teased the place where her own lips met, then gained entry to her mouth. The champagne had left behind a fruity taste that mingled with a flavor reminiscent of brandy that was Murphy's own.

"So, here we are," Murphy said when he finally broke the kiss.

"Here we are," said Sam, drawing his face toward hers for another kiss.

Moonlight spilled over them, adding to the magical feeling that had followed them all evening. The way the snow sparkled, the silvery sheen of the water passing beneath the bridge, the eerie and beautiful designs the icy branches of the bare trees made against the night sky—all of it became part of Sam as she stood there cradled in Murphy's arms.

"I wasn't planning on this," said Murphy.

"Neither was I."

"That doesn't seem to matter much anymore, does it?"

"Not a bit."

"We don't have a lot in common."

"No, we don't."

"That doesn't matter either, does it?"

She sighed with pleasure. "I'm afraid not."

"So now what do we do?"

"I was hoping you'd have a few ideas."

"I do." He kissed her cheek, her nose, her forehead, moving slowly, tantalizingly, toward her mouth. "Open for me, Sam."

A long, voluptuous shiver rose up from the tips of her sparkly high heels to the top of her head. She was pure flame, a wildly erotic mass of nerve endings sensitized beyond endurance as she parted her lips and drew him into her mouth. She slid her hands up his chest and over his shoulders, feeling his heat burning through the fabric of his shirt. Burning through her body as his fingers gripped her waist under his jacket that was draped over her shoulder, then spanned her ribcage, easing upward inch by fiery inch toward the satin-covered curve of her breasts. He broke their kiss. Lowering his head, he pressed his lips against the hollow of her throat as a low moan began to build inside her.

Sensations that had been new and wonderful when she was sixteen were even more miraculous now that she was old enough to know the fragility of a moment like this. There were times in life when the better part of valor was to give over to emotion.

He bent his head toward her. She lifted her eyes to his. Their lips met again and—

"Anything wrong, folks?" Sam and Murphy leaped apart as the bright beam of a flashlight found them. "Kind of cold to be standing outside."

Sam squinted into the light and saw a familiar face at the other end of the flashlight. "Teddy? Is that you?"

The beam lowered. "Sam? What the hell are you doing out here?" He aimed the light directly at poor Murphy. "Hey, O'Rourke. Glad to see you."

Sam didn't dare wait for Murphy to respond.

"We were on our way back now," she said, certain she would be forgiven this small white lie. "Patty's sitter wants to go home by twelve-thirty."

Teddy checked his watch. "Better motor then, guys. Times a-wastin'. Besides, you'll need your sleep for tomorrow."

Sam's mouth dropped open. "Oh, my God! The chestnut stand."

"Don't tell me you forgot."

"Almost," said Sam.

"Then it's a good thing I bumped into you, isn't it?"

"Definitely an act of Fate," said Murphy, his expression deadpan.

"I think it's time to call it a night," said Sam, with a glance in Murphy's direction. "I have a busy day ahead of me tomorrow."

"What time do we get started?" asked Murphy.

We?

"Frank will have the stand set up by 10.00 a.m.," said Teddy as if he and O'Rourke had been lifelong cronies.

"You're coming with me?" asked Sam.

"Seems like that's the only way I'm going to see you tomorrow, doesn't it?"

She nodded, struck dumb with surprise. He really was a most remarkable man.

"We'll bring Patty," he continued as Teddy walked them to their car. "She'd probably get a kick out of the store windows and the tree. I've been promising to take my sister's boy in this season."

"Great idea," said Teddy, clapping Murphy on the back. "Use Frank's parking spot near Radio City. I'll make sure he okays it for you."

The two men shook hands. "Do I have anything to say about this?" Sam asked.

"Not a hell of a lot," said Murphy, putting his arm around her right there in front of her cousin Teddy, the town crier. Poor Murphy. Little did he know that was practically a declaration of intent in the Dean family. "If that's what I have to do to see you tomorrow, that's what I have to do."

"Looks like I'm leaving you in good hands, Sammy. I'll call Frank and tell him his wedding's on for tomorrow."

Teddy made to leave then turned back, a puzzled expression on his face. "Sammy?"

"Yes, Teddy?"

"Did you do something to your hair? You look a little different tonight."

SAM AND MURPHY were still laughing when they pulled into her driveway ten minutes later.

"What can I say?" Sam managed between whoops of laughter. "The men in my family aren't terribly observant."

Murphy threw his head back and howled at that one. "He's a cop, Sam! The man's *paid* to be observant."

Sam held her aching sides. "He still can't tell his own twins apart."

"Identical?"

"Not really," said Sam, as her laughter returned anew. "One's a boy and one's a girl."

They laughed until tears came, until Sam was certain it was impossible to laugh anymore and continue to breathe. This was the Murphy O'Rourke she'd first come to know and like. Easy-going, quick to anger and quick to laugh, arrogant, opinionated and—

A man. He wasn't her brother or her father or simply her friend. Tonight the sexual chemistry Caroline had claimed they lacked burst fullblown into being. And as their laughter died, that chemisty reappeared in the quiet of the car.

"Come here." Murphy's voice was low and gruff.

"I have to go in."

"You will," he said, drawing her close to him on the bench seat. "But first we have some old business to settle. I'd like to kiss you once without interruption."

The kiss was longer, deeper, sweeter than the kisses that had come before. Sam felt as if she were floating freely through space and time on a cloud of pure, intense emotion, unlike anything she'd experienced before. And it wasn't simply desire flooding her senses, although that was a part of it. It was something much more complex—and much more dangerous.

"I have to go in," she managed at last.

"Coward," he said. He got out of the car and walked around to open her door.

It was a wonder she managed to walk up the steps, with her head so high in the clouds.

"Sleep well, Sam," he said at the door, after another long and luscious kiss. "I'll be back at eight."

Seven and a half hours, she thought as she watched him drive off down the street.

Her brain told her that Murphy O'Rourke wouldn't be around forever, that his type of man moved on long before life had a chance to get dull.

Her heart told her otherwise.

It had been ages since Sam had listened to her heart but it appeared she had no choice.

For the moment her heart belonged to Murphy O'Rourke.

Chapter Twelve

"Going out again?" said Bill O'Rourke the next morning.

"That's right." Murphy grabbed for his down jacket and heavy gloves. "How about you?"

"Eight-o'clock mass." Bill put on his hat and scarf and looked at his son. "You should try it some time."

So you're bringing out the heavy artillery today, are you? "No lectures today, okay, Pop? The sun is shining, the birds are singing. It's a great morning. Let's leave it at that." Scotty would be helping out at the bar during the day, and Murphy intended to be back before it got crowded in the evening. His father should have absolutely no cause for complaint.

"Are you seeing Samantha today?"

"I am."

"And you saw her last night?"

"That's right." Murphy zipped up his jacket. "Is there something you want to say, Pop?" *Not that I want to hear it, but at least we should get it out in the open.*

"You still planning to leave when I get back behind the bar full-time?"

"My plans haven't changed."

"Then leave her alone, son."

Murphy's jaw dropped. "What did you say?"

His father rested a hand on Murphy's forearm. "I said, leave her alone. This isn't the kind of woman you walk out on when the fun's over."

His pulse beat heavily in Murphy's right temple. "You're on dangerous ground now, Pop. I'd back off if I were you."

"No."

Murphy stared at his old man.

"You've walked away from people and places and things all your life, Murphy. You're not going to do it with that girl and her daughter. Not while I'm alive."

Murphy slapped his gloves against the palm of his left hand. "Where the hell is this coming from? Have you been talking to my beloved brother again?"

"I don't talk to anyone about it. I'm talking to *you* about it. She's a good kid, Samantha is. Don't go leading her on, then leaving her behind like you've left everything else in your life."

"You make me sound like a real nice guy, Pop. What makes you think you know anything about how I feel?"

"I know what I see, is all. I know what you've always done. She deserves better than halfway measures, Murphy. So does her kid."

On that Murphy was in agreement. Samantha deserved the love and security she'd never found with a man, and Patty deserved the seven-day-a-week father of her dreams. But life didn't always send to you exactly what you needed.

Then again, maybe it did. He thought of Sam and how warm and sweet she had felt in his arms last night, of how they had both seemed sprinkled with stardust, blessed with magic. That counted for something, didn't it?

"Be honest with her," Bill warned as he headed for the front door. "Tell her the way it is with you. Don't lead her on."

You know she doesn't understand the rules, Murphy thought. Another woman might accept the fact that things aren't always forever without being told. He doubted if Samantha Dean was one of them.

He looked at his father and wished there were a way to shatter thirty-six years of barriers and strife in a single instant. He wanted to tell Bill that he didn't know what would happen between Sam and him but he wanted the chance to find out. She made him feel different inside, hopeful and young, in a way he hadn't believed was possible.

"Want a lift to church?" he asked as they left the house.

"Walking's good for the heart," said Bill, turning up the collar of his coat.

"I don't mind driving," said Murphy, wondering why he was pushing the issue.

Bill started down the back stairs then stopped and looked back at his son. "You'll leave," he said sagely. "The minute the right job comes along, you'll be gone quicker than she can ask where you're going."

"You don't know that," said Murphy. "You don't know anything about it."

"Maybe not," said Bill with a shrug of his shoulders, "but I know you. You'll leave. Mark my words on that—sooner or later, you'll leave."

WHEN MURPHY O'ROURKE pulled into their driveway at exactly eight o'clock in the morning, Patty nearly swooned with delight. Not only was he handsome and funny and smart, he was punctual, to boot! The only thing that kept him from being absolutely perfect was the fact that his nephew was a whiney little six-year-old who cried for his mother the whole way through the Lincoln Tunnel.

At first she wanted to give the little boy her most withering grown-up glance and tell him he was acting like a baby, but then she suddenly remembered little Kevin might one day be her very own cousin and she reached over and held the child's hand in hers until they came out of the tunnel and into the bright sunlight of Manhattan.

Her Grandma Betty said New York City was a dirty and disgusting place where nobody in his right mind would go unless he absolutely *had* to. Patty had only been to New York City two times in her entire life—once to go to the circus, and, once to see *CATS* on a school outing—but each time she had found it thrilling!

Manhattan was exotic and loud and a million times more exciting on a sleepy Sunday than Rocky Hill was on New Year's Eve. Even the air smelled different in New York City. Eagerly she began to unroll the window only to have her mom's sharp voice stop her in her tracks.

"Keep that window up, young lady," Sam warned. "This isn't Rocky Hill."

As if Patty could forget! She held her breath as two men in torn pants and big, bulky overcoats approached the car and spit on the windows.

Next to her, little Kevin let out a shriek and covered his eyes. Patty stared out at the men as they wiped the spit off with rags made of torn T-shirts.

"Why are they doing that?" she asked Murphy who was reaching into his pockets.

"Money," he said, extracting a few coins. He unrolled his window the tiniest crack and handed each man some change.

"Are they homeless?" she asked. It was hard to imagine why else someone would want to make a living waiting for cars to come out of the tunnel so he could clean their windows.

"Some are, some aren't," said Murphy, heading across the intersection the second the traffic light changed to green. "They've been doing this since before I was Kevin's age. It's anyone's guess."

Patty twisted around in her seat and looked back as three more men joined the original two and pounced on a big black limousine stuck at the light.

There were so many things to look at, that she wished she had eyes in the back of her head so she wouldn't miss one single thing. She swiveled to face front, just in time to see her mom brush a lock of hair off Murphy's forehead and say something that made him smile in a way Patty loved. Perhaps an extra set of ears wouldn't be a bad idea either, preferably ears that could hear private whispers.

There was some real grown-up stuff going on up there and Patty would gladly give twenty IQ points to know what it was. Actually she had a pretty darned good idea of what was happening: sexual chemistry! She had tried really hard to understand the concept when her Aunt Caroline explained it to her earlier in the week but Einstein's Theory of Relativity had been easier to understand than the mysteries between men and women.

But now she knew. Not that she understood it any better than she did a few days ago, but Aunt Caroline had been one hundred percent about one thing: when you saw it, you knew it! The very air around her mom and Murphy O'Rourke shimmered. The way they looked at each other, the sound of their laughter—little things, yes, but somehow those little things seemed to add up to a lot more than Patty would have imagined.

She looked over at Kevin, who was busy blowing spit bubbles in the space between his missing front teeth.

She still thought Murphy was the most absolutely perfect man to be her father—even if it did mean being related to Kevin!

SAM HANDED OVER a bag of warm, fragrant roasted chestnuts to the smiling tourists from Akron, Ohio.

"And a Merry Christmas to you, too," she said, matching them smile for smile. "Don't forget to see the Lord & Taylor windows!"

"We promise," said the man. "You've been terrific."

She watched them stroll down the street, laughing and eating chestnuts. A street-corner Santa manned the other end of the block, and she grinned as the couple from Ohio dropped money into his red chimney. The tinkling of his bell and his merry "Ho! Ho! Ho!" floated back up the street, mingling with the noise of Sunday traffic and holiday shoppers.

What an absolutely splendid day this was turning out to be! It was no wonder Frank wanted to make certain his stand was there in its usual place, wedding or not, for Sam couldn't imagine a more glorious location to experience a New York City Christmas. That majestic symbol of Manhattan at Yuletide, the Rockefeller Center Christmas tree, was straight ahead, rising up in the middle of the concrete and glass like a twinkling, multi-colored jewel. Trumpeting angels, constructed of glittering white lights, lined the walkways of the Plaza as they had year after year, for longer than Sam could remember. She tilted her head and listened to the merry sounds of music rising up from the ice-skating rink and the equally merry sounds of laughter as eager skaters braved the cold.

How long had it been since she'd felt this way—happy, confident? Out there in the brisk winter air, breathing in the sights and sounds of the holiday season and loving every single minute of it.

Of course, seeing the look of pure bliss upon her daughter's freckled face went a long way toward accounting for the joyous feeling inside Sam's heart. Patty beamed with delight each time she looked at Murphy, and Sam had to admit her daughter's affection seemed to be reciprocated. Who on earth would have imagined the gruff Murphy O'Rourke would have such a tender heart? She hadn't been blind to the patient, loving way he handled his fractious little nephew, moving the boy out of his bad mood with a combination of straight talk and a good-natured sense of humor.

But then, neither had she been blind to the tenderness in his eyes last night. What a devastating combination of opposites he had presented to Sam: heart-melting tenderness blended with a fierce sexuality that set fire to her soul.

She'd lain awake for a long time last night, wondering if the magic they'd experienced was the product of satin dresses the color of sapphires, of opulent velvet masks and the shimmering romanticism of the evening. What about when she was just Sam once more, with her straight dark hair and favorite black sweater, and her penchant for denim rather than diamonds?

She smiled foolishly at the passersby as she thought of the look on Murphy's face this morning when he rang her doorbell. The look in his eyes was the same look she had seen the night before when he held her in his arms. It was for *Sam*, not for her wardrobe or makeup or jewelry anymore than the way her heart quickened at the sight of his slightly crooked grin had anything to do with tuxedos or perfectly barbered hair.

Who would have believed it?

Sam was falling in love.

MURPHY WAS MESMERIZED by the animated figures in the window at Lord & Taylor. One, in particular. A lovely dark-haired Gibson girl in a sapphire blue gown who looked uncannily the way Sam had looked last night at the masquerade ball. That beautiful, fine-boned face. The delicate limbs. The doe eyes with their vulnerable intensity.

He crouched down to look more closely at her and felt a tug on his sleeve.

"Murphy." Patty's solemn, bespectacled face popped up in front of his nose. "Kevin has to go to the bathroom."

Murphy blinked and looked down at the squirmy little boy holding onto Patty's hand. "Do you?"

Kevin nodded. "A lot."

Murphy dragged his hand through his hair. There was a lot less of it since his visit to the barber yesterday morning, and it felt strange to him. He thought for a second. "Okay. No problem. We'll go into Lord & Taylor." Made perfect sense to him.

"Macy's," said Patty. "The men's room is bigger."

Murphy laughed out loud. "And how would you know that?"

"My cousin James told me."

Kevin looked up at his uncle with big hazel eyes. "I want Macy's."

Murphy hadn't been a reporter all those years for nothing. These kids were up to something but since it was Christmastime—and he was definitely in a Christmasy mood—he led them up to Herald Square.

Macy's was jammed to the rafters with shoppers. In just the first two minutes he caught the assorted smells of Chanel No. 5, Brut, pine needles, and gingerbread, and that was just for starters. He heard Chinese being spoken on his left, Spanish on his right, and the particular blend of English known as Brooklynese all around him. He grinned, feeling right at home. *Only in New York....*

He followed a sales clerk's instructions and found the rest rooms with a minimum of trouble. That solved Kevin's problem and any problem Patty might develop in the near future.

"Okay," he said, when they met up at the water fountain between the two rest rooms, "now what? We can go back to Rock Center and hang out with your mom until she closes for the day. We can go to F.A.O. Schwarz and look at toys even Donald Trump can't afford. We can—"

"Santa Claus," said Patty. "I want to see Santa Claus."

"You're kidding."

She shook her head and her pigtails slapped against her shoulders. "This is Christmastime and I'm a kid, aren't I?"

"Sure you are, but I thought—"

"I have something to ask him," said Patty with a quick glance toward Kevin.

Murphy started to say something about still believing in St. Nick but he remembered his little nephew was the jolly fat man's number one fan. *You're okay, Patty,* he thought as he followed her to the toy department and Santa's workshop. He was the adult. He should have come up with the idea of visiting Santa Claus. But it had been Sam's remarkable little girl who'd thought of it. Her fifty megaton IQ may have been a gift from the gods, but her generous heart came straight from her mother.

The line to see Santa was long. He couldn't remember the last time he saw so many little kids in one place before. Kevin was hyper with excitement and Patty held the kid's hand and pointed out the different elves and, unless Murphy was sorely mistaken, seemed pretty excited herself as they moved closer to the chubby guy in the red suit who received visitors on his velvet throne.

Next to his niece and nephew, Patty was the first kid in years who actually got to him. He'd spent most of his life not even noticing the shorter members of the human population. They spoke another language. Ernie. Big Bird. Oscar the Grouch. Murphy hated feeling stupid and talking to kids usually made him feel that way within ten seconds. It wasn't until his sister had Kevin and Laurie, that he'd begun to feel comfortable with kids and, to his amazement, enjoy their company.

He'd felt comfortable with Patty instantly. She was smart and funny and almost fiercely independent but it didn't take a genius to see there was a little girl hiding behind that very adult persona. "You can't walk out on those two," his father had said that very morning, meaning Sam and her little girl. "Don't make promises you can't keep."

I'm not going to hurt you, kiddo, he thought as he looked at Patty's face, flushed with excitement as she sat upon

Santa's knee. *And I'm sure as hell going to do my best to make sure I don't hurt your mother.*

Patty whispered something to Santa and then, to Murphy's surprise, the two of them turned and looked straight at him. Patty whispered something else and her happy smile was warm enough to melt the snows outside. Santa Claus winked at him, then flashed Patty a thumbs-up sign.

Murphy had the strangest feeling his future had just been decided for him.

"BUT I CAN'T!" said Sam as Murphy knelt down in front of her.

"Sure you can." He took her foot and rested it on his lap.

"It's been years since I last did it."

"You know that old saying..." His large hands caressed her ankle and teased her calf.

"This isn't like riding a bike, Murphy."

"It's easier. You can let me do all the work."

"You mean, just go along for the ride?"

"Lean on me. I won't go faster than you can handle."

"I shouldn't."

"Of course you should."

"It's dangerous."

"Not if you're careful."

"You're tempting me, Murphy."

"That's the general idea."

"Oh, why not!" She threw caution to the winds. "Go ahead! Lace those skates up for me and let's join the kids on the ice."

WHAT A BEAUTIFUL CITY, Sam thought a half-hour later as Murphy guided her around the skating rink. Fun City. The Big Apple. The most glorious, glamorous place in the entire world at Christmastime and she was right there in the middle of the excitement.

"You're doing great, Sam." Murphy eased them into a gentle turn, all to the rhythm of a Strauss waltz floating from the loudspeakers. "Next thing you know, you'll be going for Olympic Gold."

Sam laughed then grabbed his hand more tightly as her feet threatened to slip out from under her. "I don't think Dorothy Hamill is in any danger. I'm just trying to stay off my keister."

"Hold on to me."

She looked up at him, her heart so filled with emotion she could scarcely breath. "That's what I intend to do."

PATTY AND KEVIN were over in the far end of the rink with the skating instructor.

"Now, start with your right foot and push off—"

Patty started to skate with the rest of the kids when her mom and Murphy glided gracefully by. "Hey!" said Kevin, who was holding her hand. "You almost tripped me!" Patty scarcely heard his words. All of her concentration was focused on the wonderful sight before her. Her mom's cheeks were rosy with the cold and excitement; her dark eyes glowed as she looked up at Murphy and laughed. She didn't look like the glamorous movie star who'd gone to the masquerade last night, but she looked young and pretty and—

In love.

Could it be?

And then Patty saw it, the one thing she'd been waiting all her life to see. Right there in the middle of the ice-skating rink at Rockefeller Center with the Christmas tree twinkling above them, her mom and Murphy O'Rourke kissed each other on the lips, and her cautious, careful mom didn't even care that a million people were watching them!

This was it, she just knew it. This was how it would be if she and her mom and Murphy were a real family, and this was just one of a billion Christmases they'd spend together.

"Come on, guys," said Murphy a few moments later when he and her mom skated up to Patty and Kevin. "We're going to the Automat for dinner."

"The Automat?" asked Patty. "What's that—a car-wash?"

"Where have you been keeping this kid?" Murphy asked Sam, giving a playful tug to one of Patty's braids. "The Automat's an American original. You haven't lived until you've had one of their tuna salad sandwiches on white bread."

Sam groaned. "My daughter's tastes are a bit more advanced than that."

"I know the Automat," Kevin piped up. "You stick money in and food pops out the window."

"You remember," said Sam, smoothing Patty's bangs. "Like in that Doris Day movie we saw a few weeks ago, the one with Cary Grant and the New York Yankees."

Twinkling angels with trumpets held high.

A glittering Christmas tree straight out of a fairy tale.

Ice skaters twirling by as gracefully as ballerinas while wonderful music wafted through the air.

Macy's and Lord & Taylor and a Santa Claus who actually made Patty wonder if she should rethink her position on the possibility of flying through the air with eight reindeer and a well-stocked sleigh; and now the Automat where you inserted your coins into a slot and instead of a game of Pac-Man, you found yourself with hot chocolate and a tuna sandwich!

She glanced at her mom and Murphy, who were both looking goofier and more lovesick by the minute. This was even better than she had planned.

Chapter Thirteen

"Murphy!" Sam giggled as Murphy maneuvered her into the kitchen at Fast Foods for the Fast Lane. "What if someone sees us?"

Murphy pinned her against the refrigerator and kissed her soundly. "The only way the crowd out there would notice is if the food runs out."

Sam leaned her forehead against his shoulder as a wave of pure pleasure rippled through her body. "Did you know they were planning this?"

Murphy shook his head. "Only thing I knew was to keep you away until they unloaded the supplies."

The masquerade ball had turned out to be only the beginning of the wonderful changes in Sam's life. Christmas was in the air, and so it seemed was magic. There was Murphy, of course, and the joy she felt each time she saw him— not to mention the look of sheer happiness on Patty's face whenever she saw them together. And if that wasn't terrific enough, her father, cousins Teddy and Frank and assorted uncles had commandeered the storefront to perform a little magic of their own. In the next three days they intended to transform her shop into a surefire winner with fresh paint, spanking new wallpaper, and a ceramic tile floor to die for. Sam had only to fill her cupboards and stock her refrigerator and she was ready for business.

She sighed deeply. "Can you believe it?" she said, looking up at Murphy. "I actually have time on my hands."

He waggled his eyebrows in a deliciously wicked way. "I can think of a number of ways to use that time, Samantha."

She lowered her gaze to his mouth. "So can I, Murphy."

SAM SOON DISCOVERED there was any number of delightful ways to spend her free time.

She made Patty country breakfasts then drove her to school each morning. Caroline took to stopping by on her way to work for coffee and conversation, and Sam could barely restrain herself from throwing her arms around her best friend and pledging eternal fealty. If Caroline had not railroaded Sam into going to the masquerade ball, Sam and Murphy might still be having snowball fights in the parking lot.

Not that they were suddenly above snowball fights, mind you. She and Murphy had enjoyed a down-and-dirty battle right in her front yard just the other night. The only problem was that even though she had time to spare, time alone with Murphy was almost impossible to come by. She had her responsibilities toward Patty and her family. He had the bar to take care of. By the time the bar closed well after midnight, Sam was calling it a day.

And so they found stolen moments for long and lingering kisses, but those moments only left her hungry for the taste and smell and feel of him. She had no experience at all in juggling a social life and a family life and the notion of staying out an entire night—even if her mother took care of Patty—was as alien to Sam as the notion of flying to Saturn under her own steam.

Her personal code of behavior had been formed a long time ago and she was comfortable with it. To his credit, Murphy didn't push her to give more than she could, even though she knew he wanted her as much as she wanted him.

She was an old-fashioned woman in a world that held little store in old-fashioned values. She had made love with Ronald Donovan because her heart and soul had belonged to him; because she'd believed she would grow old alongside him. As deep as her feelings were for Murphy, she couldn't delude herself into believing he would still be around when her hair started to turn gray. Paris called to him—and Beijing and London and other exotic cities around the world. She needed more than a few nights in his arms. She would rather never be with him than love him and then lose him to his career.

But in the darkness of her room, alone in her bed, her imagination soared. It was a simple task to conjure up the image of his bare chest as it had looked that first morning she went to O'Rourke's. Every muscle, from his stomach to his shoulders to his biceps, had been imprinted on her memory. She lingered on each one, ran her tongue along the tracing of vein at the bend in his arm, buried her nose where his arm met his shoulder, let her hands slide over his ribcage and down to the round, muscular buttocks.

She knew how he would feel as he covered her body with his. She knew how she would open for him, welcoming him with all her heart and soul. In the quiet heart of the night she could hear the sounds of passion, catch the hot, heavy scent of sexuality, taste herself on his lips—

But she needed more in the way of forever than he could possibly give and they both knew it.

And so they spent their time talking and kissing and talking some more, as the days before Christmas disappeared one by one. Central New Jersey had another snowfall, and if the weather stayed cold they planned to take Patty and Kevin ice-skating Sunday at the pond in Cranbury, a picture-postcard town not far from Rocky Hill.

With all that extra time, also came the opportunity to spend some of it at O'Rourke's with Murphy and the rest of the gang. Instead of carting the sandwiches and appetizers over there on trays as she had in the beginning of their arrangement, she began cooking right on the premises. Bill O'Rourke had settled on an ex-sailor named Donahue to be their full-time cook; he would begin the day after Christmas. Sam intended to take full advantage of her position of power while she could.

Scotty deemed himself her helper and they laughed and joked while Murphy tended the bar. She loved the brilliant professor. He had taken an interest in Patty, confirming what she'd been told since her little girl was old enough to form her first thoughts: Patty's potential was unlimited.

"I'd like the chance to work with her on some mathematical concepts," said Scotty one afternoon in the week before Christmas. "Perhaps after school?"

Sam hugged him and laughed at Murphy's raised eyebrows. "That's wonderful! I'll pick her up this afternoon, and we can put you two at a table in the back of the bar."

"Great," muttered Murphy, with a twinkle in his eye. "I can hear my father now—what the hell are you doing, boy? This is a bar not a nursery school . . ."

"You don't know me as well as you think you do," came a voice from the bottom of the rear staircase. "You bring that little girl of yours around later," Bill O'Rourke said to Sam, after he kissed her on the cheek. "Anything to keep this old Scotsman out of trouble."

Murphy turned away and Sam's heart went out to him. It hadn't taken her long at all to determine that the relationship between the O'Rourke men was complicated, to say the least. Murphy had grown up without the loving support of a mother, and the three men—Murphy, his father and his brother—each donned an impenetrable shield to protect himself from the pain that came with being a family.

And yet she had seen Murphy with her daughter and his nephew, seen the easy-going way he'd handled both their tears and their laughter, felt the warmth and affection that seemed as natural to him as breathing. He would make a tremendous father some day. It was no wonder Patty had been drawn to him from the start.

"Your burger's ready." She garnished the plate with a semicircle of pickle rounds and a sprig of parsley, then handed it to Murphy. "Eat up. You may never see its like again once Popeye starts work here." It was a brilliant burger, if she did say so herself, with two types of cheese melted over the top, sliced red onions, and three strips of perfectly-grilled bacon.

He forced a laugh and for an instant she saw through his gruff exterior and straight to the center of his heart.

"Thanks, Sam," he said. "I could get used to having you around.

Her own heart fluttered dangerously. "Sorry," she said, "but you wouldn't want to disappoint Mr. Donahue, would you?"

Murphy was more wonderful than she'd ever imagined a man could be. To think that ten days ago they had been strangers—the footloose reporter and the earthbound mother and entrepreneur. It never should have worked between them and yet it had, beautifully! He had become a part of her life in the blink of an eye, and with each day that passed she found it increasingly difficult to remember what her life had been like before she met him.

Life seemed brighter, happier, more filled with promise than it had since she was a teenager. Her entire family was still buzzing over the Christmas lights she'd strung in the blue spruce tree in front of her tiny house and the mistletoe and holly she'd scattered about her living room. "Don't you know it's Christmas?" she'd asked Patty when her little girl questioned the pine boughs draped across the mantel and the shimmering ornaments nestled amidst the greenery.

And Sam didn't have to look far to discover the reason for her metamorphosis. Murphy.

Sam's world lit up whenever Murphy O'Rourke entered the room. It was as simple as that.

The delivery man showed up with that week's shipment of beer, and Murphy, hamburger in hand, went off to take care of business. Bill O'Rourke, however, stayed behind.

"How are you feeling?" Sam asked, putting together a low-cholesterol sandwich for him. "I must say you're looking well."

"I'm getting there," said Bill, his lean face creasing in a smile, "but I'm worried."

"I would think that's natural after all you've been through the past couple of months."

He waved his hand in the air between them. "Not about that. I'm worried about you."

"Me? Why on earth would you be worried about me?" This was the happiest time of her adult life. Worry seemed as far away as the twenty-fifth century.

He gestured toward Murphy who was laughing with the delivery man on the opposite side of the bar room. "You like him, don't you?"

Sam, never one to mince words, nodded. "Very much."

"He likes you, too."

She felt her cheeks flame, the same way Patty's did. "I'm pleased."

Bill's hazel eyes, so like Murphy's own, clouded over with sympathy. "The thing is, he won't be around forever."

She touched Bill's forearm in a gentle warning to tread softly through treacherous waters. "Neither will I. I open my store on January first. We'll have to rearrange our schedules."

"That's not what I'm talking about, Samantha. He's been running since the day he was born and he's not about to stop running now."

"I understand that, Bill. I wouldn't ask that of him any more than he would ask me to abandon my catering shop." Especially not now, when she was on the brink of spreading her wings.

Bill, however, was deep in his own thoughts, caught up in an entire web of family history. "The offer came in."

Sam's breath caught. "I know about the *Telegram*." She'd met Dan Stein on one of his frequent visits down to the wilds of New Jersey to woo Murphy back to the Big City.

"Not the *Telegram*, Samantha."

"The foreign beat?" Her voice was a whisper.

"The foreign beat." Bill patted her shoulder awkwardly. "Looks like we might be saying good-bye to our boy before we know it."

THAT EVENING, Sam, Caroline and Patty sat around the dining room table. Newspaper clippings were scattered everywhere, along with photocopies of magazine articles. In a perfect example of bad timing, Patty had taken it upon herself to do some library research on her favorite topic: Murphy O'Rourke.

"Isn't it wonderful!" Patty's face glowed with excitement. "He's as famous as Bruce Springsteen."

"I wouldn't go that far," said Sam. But there was no mistaking the power of his prose. Murphy O'Rourke was a well-respected, hard-working member of the Fourth Estate.

"Look at this." Caroline slid a photocopy of a *People* magazine article toward Sam. "He was the main interview in this piece on the Iran-Contra hearings."

"And he was on *Nightline*," Patty sighed. "He met Ted Koppel!"

Only Sam's little girl could wax equally enthusiastic over The Boss and late night TV's version of Howdy Doody.

"He's brilliant," said Caroline.

"He's adorable," said Patty.

"He has what it takes to be the Walter Cronkite of the print world."

"He could be on television."

"He could be the White House correspondent."

"He could win a Pulitzer Prize!"

Sam looked at her daughter and her eyes filled with tears. *Oh, honey, don't you see what this means?* Murphy O'Rourke was all of those things, but the one thing he wasn't was a bartender in Rocky Hill, looking for a wife and daughter who wanted nothing more than to stay exactly where they were.

"YOU REALIZE my family's going to talk about this, don't you?"

"You mean they stop eating long enough for conversation?"

Sam laughed as she turned the Blazer into the parking lot of Quakerbridge Mall a few nights later. "We *do* think about food a lot, don't we?"

"Think about it? Did you see the pile of wrappers Teddy and Frank left behind yesterday? You'll turn a profit just from your family alone."

Sam zeroed in on a space near J. C. Penny's, then muttered something un-Christmaslike as a woman in a blue Volkswagen zipped in ahead of her. "This is disgusting. I think the nearest empty parking spot is in Pennsylvania."

"What do you expect, Sam? It's ten days before Christmas."

"I usually wait until Christmas Eve then run out and do all my shopping in one fell swoop."

"Great attitude, Scrooge."

She screeched to a halt in front of Macy's. "Did Patty tell you about that?"

His expression was blank. "Tell me what?"

"Scrooge. That's my nickname."

"You're kidding."

She shook her head and whipped into a parking space a cool hundred feet from the door. "I'm afraid my Christmas spirit has been conspicuously absent these past few years.''

''You seem pretty spirited to me.''

She glanced at him. He wasn't laughing. ''Sometimes it takes a swift kick in the seat of your pants to make you appreciate life again.''

He reached across and took her hand in his. ''I know, Sam.''

How handsome he looked in the dim light of the truck. The right side of his rugged face was in shadow; the left was illuminated by the refracted glow from the streetlamp. Sharp angles and planes; hazel eyes that warmed her with a look—had there really been a time when Murphy O'Rourke had been a stranger to her life?

Moments like these were dangerous, however. Moments like these led deeper into the darker terrain of the heart, a place where Sam had little experience.

''Come on, Murphy,'' she said, pulling her shopping list out of her pocket. ''Let's hit the mall.'' The only danger there was to her bank balance.

SAM WAS MANY THINGS: a terrific mother, beautiful woman and budding business genius in the making, but she was one lousy shopper. It took Murphy exactly six minutes and forty-five seconds to discover just how lousy.

''You need a plan,'' he said, forcing her to sit down on a bench in front of Hahne's. ''Give me your list.''

''Mind your own business, O'Rourke.''

''I won't have a chance if you keep us running around in circles all night. Let's attack this scientifically.''

''Spoken just like a man,'' she said, her dark brown eyes twinkling. ''I suppose you know everything there is to know about Christmas shopping.''

''I know how to get it done with a minimum of trouble.''

''I thought trouble was half the fun of Christmastime.''

''You're baiting me, Ms Scrooge.''

She batted her eyelashes at him. "Now whatever do you mean, Mr. O'Rourke?"

He grabbed her list and scanned it quickly, looking for his name.

Sam grabbed the list back. "Don't look at that!"

"I already did. I'm not on the list."

He must have looked embarrassingly dejected, because she laughed and kissed him, right there in the middle of Quakerbridge Mall. "I don't need a list, Murphy. I know exactly what I'm getting you for Christmas."

He grinned. "You do?"

"I do."

"Will I like it?"

She paused, obviously considering his question. "I'm reasonably sure you will."

"Animal, vegetable, or mineral?"

"Sorry, Murphy. It's a surprise."

He leaned over and whispered something in her ear and she blushed, but looked pleased.

"Amazing," she whispered. "How did you ever guess?"

"Wishful thinking, Sam," he said, counting the days until Christmas. "Wishful thinking."

IT WAS EIGHT DAYS before Christmas. Murphy was getting ready to take Sam and Patty to the McCarter Theater to see a Princeton theater group's version of *A Christmas Carol*. He was feeling a little like Scrooge himself. Dan Stein had called twice, pushing Murphy to take the job on the *Telegram* and issuing dire warnings about some "...young Turk..." who was ready, willing and able to take Murphy's place if he didn't make up his mind and soon.

And then there was UPI. They'd sweetened their offer again, tossing in perks that would make another man weak at the knees.

He reached for his tie and draped it around his neck. Although he must have tied a thousand ties in his life, his fingers fumbled for a second before mechanical memory took over.

Another man, however, didn't have Samantha Dean to consider. Another man didn't have a brilliant little girl with bright red hair to think about.

He stared at his reflection in the mirror as he straightened the knot and smoothed the collar of his shirt. He remembered the exact time and place when he bought that shirt. A stormy May afternoon in Paris with a Frenchwoman with laughing eyes by his side. Whatever happened to her? Did she walk beside another foreign correspondent now and show him the best places to eat and the best places to drink and the best places to buy his shirts?

He wanted that old life on the foreign beat.

He wanted the down-and-dirty excitement of working on the *Telegram* in New York City.

And, damn it to hell, he wanted the happiness he'd found right there in Rocky Hill, in the arms of his Sam.

Bill's warnings came back to him now, and for the first time he understood. Could he ask Sam to give everything up—everything she'd worked so long and hard to achieve—and fly away with him? Could he ask Patty to live the life of a gypsy, moving from city to city, hotel to hotel, while he pursued his dream?

The answer was in reach. He could smell it and taste it but he couldn't put his finger on it. Not yet. But it was there, waiting for him to figure it out, and he wasn't altogether sure he was going to like that answer once he found it.

"YOU'RE QUIET TONIGHT." Murphy smoothed Sam's dark hair off her cheek and kissed the curve of her jaw. "Thinking about the Ghost of Christmas Past?"

Sam closed her eyes for a moment. It was Christmas Yet To Come that concerned her. "The show was wonderful, wasn't it?"

"Patty seemed to think so."

"My little girl would like Christmas to last all year long."

"Sounds good to me."

Sam looked at him, at his beautiful hazel eyes. "I never thought I'd say this, but it sounds good to me, too. In fact, I wish this Christmas season would never end."

Say something, Murphy. Tell me you love me, that you can't imagine leaving me behind while you conquer London and Paris and Rome.

Of course Murphy said nothing like that. He couldn't, because those words weren't part of him. His heart was torn with love and fear and doubt, all the crazy, wild emotions he'd hoped he'd seen the last of. He wanted everything, Murphy did. He wanted lover and wife. He wanted home and adventure. He wanted everything, and he didn't know what he could give in return.

And of course Sam didn't pursue the answer, because deep in her heart she knew she didn't really want to know.

But it was there, hovering between them, like Marley's Ghost, and it wouldn't go away.

"BACK EARLY."

Murphy started at the sound of his father's voice and reached for the kitchen light switch. "Why are you sitting in the dark? We're earning enough money to pay the electric bill, Pop."

Bill was seated at the head of the kitchen table with a cup of warm milk in front of him. "I was thinking about your mother."

Murphy said nothing as he crossed the room toward the refrigerator. What he wanted was a Scotch, straight up. What he had was orange juice straight from the carton. He sat down next to his father and took a long gulp. "Anything in particular about my mother?"

Bill sighed and shrugged his shoulders. "Just that I loved her, and it wasn't enough to make a difference." Murphy's mother had died in an accident before Murphy was old enough to start school.

"You always loved her, didn't you?" Murphy asked. His questions surprised him. He usually did a 180-degree turn away from conversations like this.

"From the first moment."

"You gave up that job with the Navy to marry her."

His father's eyes widened. "How'd you know that?"

It was Murphy's turn to shrug. "I don't know. It seems as if I've always known it." He leaned toward his father. "Was it a hard decision?"

Bill looked at him as if he were speaking in tongues. "Hard?"

"Yeah." *Tell me, Pop. I need your help this time.* "Did you ever wonder if you made the right decision?"

"Never." Bill's eyes filled with tears. "Not even for a second."

Murphy fell silent. It seemed as if he'd been filled with questions and doubts his entire life, always wondering if something better, something more exciting waited around the next corner. Something that would finally make his father sit up and notice him.

"You're not for her," said Bill, breaking the heavy silence of the kitchen.

"I think you're wrong," said Murphy. "I can make her happy. I can take her places she's never been."

"She's not like you. She's making her life here."

"She won't have financial problems anymore. The pressure will be off."

"She's the marrying kind, Murphy. Make no mistake about that. She has a daughter and a family and a future to consider, with or without you. She got along fine without you all these years, and she'll be fine again, if you get out now."

Murphy looked down at his hands. He wanted everything. He wanted Sam and Patty and the life he used to have. "How the hell do I decide?" he asked his father. "How do I know the right thing to do?"

Bill O'Rourke looked at him long and hard. "Son," he said, his eyes sad and old, "if you have to ask, then you don't know the answer."

THIS WAS EVERYTHING Patty had ever wanted in her whole entire life.

It was six days before Christmas, and she was curled up in the back seat of her mom's Blazer, right next to a big beautiful fresh-cut pine tree that smelled exactly the way a Christmas tree ought to smell. Normally her mom insisted on a fake tree because it was easier and could be shoved away back in the basement with no fuss the second the holidays were over. Murphy, however, shared Patty's belief that Christmas meant tradition, and he led them over to a Christmas tree farm in Hopewell where she and her mom watched while he huffed and puffed and chopped one down especially for her.

Her mom had finally stopped being Mrs. Scrooge. Murphy was a part of both of their lives. Professor Scotty had volunteered his time and expertise to teach Patty the advanced theories only Princetonians of his caliber were privy to. Hidden away in her coat pocket were two matching keychains she'd bought at the mall, halves of the same heart, one inscribed "Mom" and the other, "Murphy."

Life was about as wonderful as it was possible to be, and she had Career Day at Harborfields School to thank for it! And although Patty was too old and too smart to believe in such things, the little girl part of her heart couldn't help but pray that the wish she'd whispered in the ear of the Macy's Santa Claus would come true on Christmas morning and she would wake up to discover that Murphy O'Rourke was going to be her dad.

"WHERE DO YOU WANT IT?" Murphy's voice was muffled from under the boughs of the pine tree.

"In the living room," Sam called, grabbing the bags of ornaments out of the Blazer and closing the tailgate. "Right near the picture window."

Patty climbed out of the back, looking green around the gills.

"Are you okay, honey?" Sam asked, feeling her forehead.

"My stomach hurts."

Sam chuckled. "It's no wonder after all those hot dogs you ate over at the Market Fair. Let's go inside and I'll make you a cup of tea." She followed her daughter into the house. "Go check on the Christmas tree," she told Patty as she headed toward the kitchen. "I don't know if Murphy's up to the Dean standards of holiday decorating."

Patty disappeared down the hallway toward the living room. Sam put the packages on the counter top and slipped out of her coat. Hot chocolate, that was the ticket. She'd make a nice pot of it and toast some bread and—

"Sam."

She looked up. Murphy stood in the doorway, an odd expression upon his face.

"Is something wrong?" She stepped from around the counter. "Patty. Is she—"

"Patty's okay. There's someone here to see you."

A man appeared at Murphy's side. A man with bright blue eyes and deep red hair and a smile she knew as well as she knew her own.

"Hello, Samantha. It's been a long time."

It was Ronald Donovan.

The father of her child.

Chapter Fourteen

Patty sniffled and reached for the tissue on her nightstand. She had cried her way through one entire box and was well on her way to using up a second one, since her biological father left a few hours ago.

If she lived to be an old lady with no teeth and a hearing aid, she'd never, absolutely *never* forget the look on her mom's face when Captain Donovan said he wanted to take Patty away with him.

He was a stranger! Oh, sure, she'd seen him once or twice when she was a real little girl but those visits hadn't amounted to more than a pat on the head and a present wrapped up by some clerk in the department store at Quakerbridge Mall. "Give me something little girls like," he would have said, taking out his wallet. "You be the judge." If she closed her eyes she could still see the chubby girl cherubs and little boy angels on that "Welcome, new baby!" paper wrapped around her birthday present.

Why didn't he just go away wherever it was he came from? Why should she be punished because he got married and had a little boy of his own and suddenly decided he wanted to be her father, too?

She wished she didn't have his red hair and blue eyes. She wished she looked just like her mother and could pretend that Captain Donovan never existed—just like he'd spent so many years pretending his own daughter had never existed.

"I can give Patricia things you couldn't hope to provide, Captain Donovan had said after Murphy said good-night. *The finest private schools, tutors . . . think about it, Samantha. Are you being fair to the child?"*

Patty buried her face in her arms as deep sobs wracked her body. Didn't anybody understand that she was just like other ten-year-old girls? Didn't anybody understand that being smart didn't mean she didn't want the same things all of her friends wanted?

She didn't care about private schools and tutors and the fancy clothes and computers that Captain Donovan thought were so important for her to have. She wanted to stay right here with her mom and Murphy O'Rourke and be part of a *real* family.

All of her friends had moms and dads and sisters and brothers and arguments over who got to use the bathroom next. That's what she prayed to God for each night. That's the wish she wished over her birthday candles and looked for in every fortune cookie she opened.

It wasn't that much to ask. Why didn't her mom and Murphy O'Rourke understand that all they had to do was get married and all of her wishes would come true.

MURPHY GULPED DOWN a whiskey back at the bar and ignored the questioning look on Scotty's face. He hated Air Force Captain Ronald J. Donovan, Jr. The moment he saw the guy standing there, tall and straight and arrogant in his dress blues, it had taken the better part of valor to keep Murphy from ramming his fist down the guy's throat.

"Who the hell does he think he is, showing up like that?" he growled, storming back and forth. "Who the hell shows up ten years later to claim his kid?"

It's not your business. She's not your kid. Sam's not your wife.

"He looks like a damn jerk," he said to Scotty without explanation. "Arrogant, smug. Who the hell does he think he is?"

Scotty opened his mouth to speak but Bill placed a hand on the man's shoulder and met his son's eyes.

"Can you do better for her, son? What can you offer her that he can't?"

"I don't know!" Murphy roared. "All I know is I can't stand what's going on."

He wasn't afraid Sam would run off with her first love. Donovan was married with a kid and a career and plans for the future—a future that included Patty. It was something else that ate away at his gut, something darker and more frightening. That terrible thought that maybe the best thing that had ever happened to him was slipping through his hands.

"You gotta make up your mind to get out of her life, boy. For once in your life don't do what's best for you."

"It's not that easy," Murphy muttered, pouring himself another whiskey. Sam had done a fine job, bringing up her kid before either Murphy or Ronald Donovan showed up at her doorstep. Patty was bright and funny and endearing, and any man who became her twenty-four-hour-a-day dad would be one lucky guy. "He doesn't want Sam. He wants their kid."

His father put an arm around Murphy for the first time in a good twenty years. "It's not your decision, son. You don't have the right to an opinion this time around."

SAM WAS DETERMINED that the presence of Ronald Donovan in their lives wouldn't change things, and she embraced wrapping packages and decorating the Christmas tree with almost missionary zeal. She whirled through the small house like a tornado, making certain she stayed one full step ahead of the panic that waited at the outer edges of her mind.

"Over there!" She pointed toward a bare branch near the top of the tree. "The silver angel goes right next to the sleigh bells."

Murphy, who had been oddly quiet that evening, looped an ornament hanger through the angel's wings and positioned it on the tree. "How's that?"

"Terrific." *Right word, Sam. Where's the spirit to go with it?* Things had been so wonderful these past few weeks. She wasn't going to let Ronald Donovan's belated interest in fatherhood ruin the happiness she'd found with Murphy—and she sure wasn't going to let him ruin Patty's Christmas.

Murphy turned away from the tree, and she felt his gaze on her. "Are you okay, Sam?"

"Wonderful!" She forced a laugh. "Back to work, O'Rourke. If we want to get this finished before Patty comes home from math class, we have our work cut out for us."

"Let's take a break."

She shook her head.

"Sam." He moved closer and took her hand. "How bad is it?"

She lowered her head so he wouldn't see the hunted expression she knew was on her face. "Awful. He wants Patty to live with him this summer."

He was quiet for a moment. "That doesn't sound so terrible. Yeah, you'll miss her but isn't this what you wanted for her?"

"No." The force of her word surprised both of them. "I want a father for her, Murphy, not a caretaker. She needs love, not an unlimited expense account."

"Then your answer should be pretty clear."

"It's not that simple." The truth was that Ronald was offering Patty more than a summer; he was offering her a world of possibilities. She blinked away tears of confusion, then looked up at Murphy. "He can give Patty everything she deserves, Murphy—tutors and computers and the best schools in the country. I can't give her anything more than Rocky Hill and an uncertain future."

Was she wrong or did he flinch at her words?

"I know all about uncertain futures," he said slowly, his words measured. "I still don't know where I'll be come New Year's." He didn't have to say the next words; they both heard them loud and clear inside their hearts: *Not much of a life for a child . . .*

"Ronald asked me how you figured in our lives."

Murphy's smile was quick and bittersweet. "And . . . ?"

"I don't know how, Murphy," she said at last. "Do you?"

They had friendship on their side; they had respect, and chemistry, and—just maybe—they had love.

The one thing they didn't have was one chance in a thousand to make it work.

"I'M SORRY," Sam said to Ronald on his fourth day in town. "Patty's still at school."

"I know. I want to speak with you, Samantha."

She stepped aside and motioned him into her house. Did the man sleep in his uniform? This was their third encounter and she had yet to see him in civilian clothes. No matter how hard she looked, she couldn't find the boy she'd once loved anywhere in the man who stood before her now.

"Coffee?" She led him into the living room and gestured for him to take a seat.

"Nothing, thank you." He stood at attention, and it took Sam a moment to realize he was waiting for her to sit down before he took a seat.

She toyed with the idea of never sitting down for the rest of her life, but decided not even Patty would be this silly, and she perched on the arm of the wing chair. "Are you still taking Patty to dinner the day after tomorrow?"

"Yes," said Ronald, sitting down on the center cushion of the couch. "Linda will be joining us."

"With the baby?"

He shook his head. "My family will watch him."

Okay. So much for conversational gambits. "What is it you want, Ronald?"

He reached into one of his pockets and withdrew a sheaf of papers with razor-sharp creases, then handed them to Sam. "The best school for advanced students in the country."

Sam's hand shook visibly as she accepted the papers and placed them in her lap. "I'll give this to Patty."

"I want you to read it."

"I'd rather not."

"It concerns Patricia's best interests."

"I think I'm a fairly good judge of Patty's best interests, Ron."

"Perhaps not when it comes to her future."

Sam stood up, anger heating her blood. "You've already missed ten years of her past."

"And I'm trying to make amends."

"I don't need your help."

"I'm not offering any help to you, Samantha. This is for my daughter."

"*My* daughter, Ron. You don't have any claim over her."

"You have a right to hate me."

"I don't hate you. You just don't figure in my life at all." *And I don't want you suddenly turning my daughter's life inside out.*

"Now that I have Linda and little Thomas, I understand what I've missed."

"How wonderful for you."

"I'm not looking to take Patricia away from you."

Sam couldn't speak as panic grabbed her by the throat and wouldn't let go.

"All I am asking of you, Samantha, is the right to give Patricia the things you cannot."

"Like what, Ron? Love? Security? A hometown?"

"An education."

She stopped. This was dangerous territory, the one area she'd yet to master. "She's too young to be sent away to school."

"That may be true for an average child, but there is nothing average about Patricia."

"Only her IQ is unusual, Ron. She's just a little girl."

Ronald stood up, six feet two inches of impressive Air Force blue. "That's the kind of thinking that will limit her horizons." He talked about the exclusive school in northeast Massachusetts that specialized in expanding the horizons of children as gifted as Patty.

I don't like this, Ron. I don't want you to make sense. I want to hate you and your wife and your baby and everything you have to say... The things he was saying were the same things she worried about late at night when her defenses were down and guilt rose swiftly to the surface.

"I want you to think seriously about it," Ronald said, heading for the door. His posture was ramrod perfect; she could have dropped a plumb line straight down from his scalp to his heels. "I would like to broach the topic with Patty at dinner."

"I'll read the brochure but I won't make any other promises. I only want what's best for Patty."

"As do I. You're still a very young woman, Samantha. You've had more than your share of responsibility. Perhaps you and your friend Mr. O'Rourke might have more time to explore your relationship if you didn't have the day-to-day work involved with raising Patricia."

Sam didn't bother to dignify that last remark with an answer. Raising Patty was the single most wonderful experience of her life. "As I said, I'll think about it."

"I can't ask for more than that, can I?"

"No, you can't." *Why then do I have the feeling you will?*

PATTY PRESSED HERSELF up against the kitchen door and listened as Sam walked Captain Donovan out to his waiting cab.

You've had more than your share of responsibility...you and Mr. O'Rourke...more time together without Patricia to care for...

Murphy hadn't come around today. Her mom had lost that Christmas glow, and the tree Murphy had chopped down for them stood forlorn in the corner of the living room, its glittering ornaments looking sad somehow and abandoned.

You know why, a little voice deep inside her whispered. Oh, they tried to hide what was going on, but Patty knew. Grown-ups always said things like "Love isn't always enough," and Patty had never really understood what that meant until now. She knew—she just *knew* her mom and Murphy were as in love as any two grown-ups could possibly be.

But still it wasn't enough to change things.

And it had taken her father, Captain Ronald Donovan, to make her realize that only she could make it all work out for her mom and Murphy O'Rourke.

"YOU'RE DOING the right thing," his father said as he took Murphy to the train station at Princeton Junction on the morning of December 23rd. "It's time you decided what you're going to do."

The choice was what it had been from the beginning, between Dan Stein at the *Telegram* and the chief honcho at UPI. The exhilarating daily grind of a New York daily versus the glamour—and often, loneliness—of the foreign beat. UPI had outdone themselves. It was hard to imagine what reason he could come up with to justify refusing their offer. Money. Position. Perks up the ying-yang. All Dan Stein at the *Telegram* was offering him was hard work, stress, and a 15 point byline.

There didn't seem to be much of a choice.

"You'll be okay at the bar?"

Bill nodded. "I've missed it. Besides we're closed tomorrow night for Scotty's party."

"I'll be back Christmas afternoon."

Bill nodded again. "Did you tell Samantha?"

"What is this—an inquisition?" He'd told Sam, but it seemed to him that his announcement barely registered. She'd looked at him with those big brown eyes and said nothing, and he'd felt as if he'd taken a slam in the solar plexus. "She has a lot on her mind lately."

"You're doing the right thing," said Bill as the train lumbered into the station.

Yeah, Pop. You've already said that.

MANHATTAN that afternoon was one big Christmas party. Murphy dropped in on some of his old pals at City Hall, then strolled over to Wall Street to schmooze with the guys who played Monopoly with real money on a daily basis. Everyone thought him crazy to ever have considered not taking the foreign assignment. "New York?" they said. "Who needs it? Only a lunatic would stay here when Paris calls."

New York was cold in the winter and hot in the summer. It was loud and dirty and often dangerous.

"You'll regret it," said Dan Stein over egg nog at the *Telegram* office. "Hook up with those guys and you'll get fat and soft and forget everything you ever knew about hard-hitting journalism."

"Right," said Murphy. "Like the *Telegram* is going to match their offer."

"Pretty close." Stein quoted a figure.

Murphy whistled. "I'm impressed."

"You should be," said the older man. "Some of that came out of my hide."

"It's tempting but I don't think I'm going to bite."

"You're making a mistake."

"Probably."

"What about that woman with the kid? What happened? I thought you had something pretty special cooking there."

"It's complicated," Murphy said, hedging. "We want different things from life." *How different, moron? You both want to be happy, don't you?*

"Some things you don't walk away from," said Stein. "But I don't suppose you're old enough to realize that yet."

Feeling older by the minute, Murphy popped in at the UPI party a little after six o'clock. He'd expected lights and music and laughter. Good food and better conversation. At the very least, he'd expected a crowd of people bent on having a good time.

What he found was a cleaning woman who looked at Murphy as if he'd escaped from a police lineup. "Everybody's gone home," she said, making sure her mop was between them. "Don't you have a home?"

He doubled back to the *Telegram* party. Maybe he could con Dan Stein into taking him out to dinner.

"Everyone is gone," said the night receptionist, her brown eyes kind and warm. Like Sam's.

"Did the party move some place else?"

She shook her head. He saw pity on her face. He hated pity. "I'm afraid they all went home."

"Dan Stein's not here?"

"Afraid not."

Murphy ducked into a telephone booth in the lobby and dialed Dan's home number. "Hey, Dan!" he said when his one-time boss picked up the phone. "How about you and the wife and I mixing with the hotshots at the Russian Tea Room? I know how you like blini and—"

Dan's voice was filled with compassion. Murphy hated compassion more than he hated pity. "We're having a Chanukah celebration tonight. You're more than welcome to join us, kid."

Murphy wanted to join them more than he'd admit even to himself. "That's family time," he said, keeping his voice light. "*Mazel Tov.* I'll talk to you in a couple of days."

The most exciting city in the world was quiet as the grave. Murphy made his way back to the Plaza through a light snowfall. Even the hotel seemed deserted. He went up to his room and ordered a room-service dinner. In his entire life, he couldn't remember a time when he felt more alone.

He missed Sam. That went without saying, for he missed Sam every second he was away from her. He missed Patty almost as much. That was no surprise.

The fact that he missed his father was. He missed Bill's bitching and moaning, his sometimes caustic wit, the nagging sense that they were on the verge of something good after so many years of causing each other nothing but pain.

He missed his sister and his niece and nephew.

And he missed the bar. His pal Scotty with the trenchant humor and steel-trap brain. Joe and Eddy and the other regulars who over the years had made O'Rourke's Bar and Grill into a second home. They were family, all of them, in the truest sense of the word. They were there for each other in hard times; when others turned away, they were still there. They'd been part of Murphy's life since before he could remember. When he swooped into town—hail! the conquering hero—they had opened ranks to let him in but never once did they let success go to his head. He could be O'Rourke the gonzo journalist bigshot away from Rocky Hill, but there in the bar he was Bill's kid.

It was nice to know you had a place in the world.

Tonight in that empty hotel room in that empty city away from everything that mattered, he realized the truth. If he took that job with UPI, this would be his life. He'd live from hotel room to hotel room, his entire world crammed into two battered suitcases and summed up on his passport. He'd been there before and, by God, he'd be damned if he'd be there again.

He'd had it all before, but it hadn't been enough. It still wouldn't be. He could see that now. The fancy career and the fancy salary and all the fancy perks that came with the package could never reach the part of him that only Sam had been able to touch.

And the answer was so damned simple that he could only wonder how it was it had taken him so long to figure it out.

He'd take Dan Stein's offer to return to the *Telegram*. He'd fight the traffic, ride the railroad, live in Rocky Hill the rest of his life—hell, he'd do whatever it was he had to do in order to hold on to Sam and Patty and the family they could form together.

"Some things you don't walk away from," Dan Stein had said earlier that afternoon, and finally Murphy understood exactly what his new/old boss had meant.

It was all there, waiting for him, right where he'd first started out thirty-six years ago.

AT SEVEN on the evening of December 23rd, Ronald came by to pick Patty up for dinner and Sam found it difficult to keep from wrapping her arms around her only child and locking her away in her little house in Rocky Hill.

But of course she didn't. She smiled and said hello to Ronald and kissed Patty good-bye. She even stood on the front stoop and waved as Ronald backed his rented car out of the driveway and disappeared down the street. A light snow had begun to fall an hour ago. "Drive carefully!" she called out before she went inside.

It was out of her hands now. She had read the brochures about the Grey Oaks School. She had digested the impressive paragraphs of information about the Rhodes scholar tutors and state-of-the-art equipment and five-star accommodations. Her eyes had skittered over the hefty price tag attached to this golden opportunity, for Ronald had been one hundred percent right when he said it was beyond her ability to provide.

God knew Patty deserved this opportunity. Just because Rocky Hill fit Sam to a tee, didn't mean Patty would spend her days in the sleepy, historic town. Sam had been an average student, with average needs and average desires—not a little girl with the potential to make a difference in this world.

I miss you, Murphy, she thought as she moved through her empty house. *I wish I could talk to you about this.* But she couldn't. Murphy had left this morning for Manhattan and wasn't expected back until Christmas Day. Right this minute he was probably at some fancy party, drinking champagne and eating caviar, up to his eyeballs in beautiful, brainless blondes.

Her whole world was crumbling around her feet. Ronald was there to woo her daughter away. Murphy couldn't wait to see Rocky Hill in his rearview mirror.

There would be no more long, lingering kisses in the dark. No more whispered fantasies. No more kidding herself that their worlds could possibly coexist and include Patty, as well.

Merry Christmas, she thought, slumping into the recliner and staring at *Wheel of Fortune*.

She'd been right about Christmas all along. It was only for fools looking for a broken heart.

And Sam felt like the biggest fool of them all.

BY THE TIME MURPHY left New York City on the morning of the twenty-fourth, it was snowing in earnest. Big fat flakes obscured his vision from the window of the train bound for Princeton Junction, and the snow showed no sign of letting up. When the train pulled into the station an hour later, at least five inches had fallen, and he considered himself damn lucky to find a cab.

He burst into the bar a little after noon. "Where's Sam?" he called out. "I have to talk to her."

"She left," said Scotty, who was playing a game of gin with Bill. "With the storm and everything, she thought she should get home to Patty."

"What the hell are you doing here?" Bill asked. Murphy peeked at his dad's hand. The old man had three aces sitting side by side. Talk about the luck of the Irish.

"I'm staying," said Murphy, tossing his bags down behind the bar. "I'm taking my old job on the *Telegram*. I'm going to live in Rocky Hill and commute on that lousy railroad if I have to. And I intend to marry Sam if she and Patty will have me. I know what those two need. They need *me*. Sam needs a man who loves her, and Patty needs a father who understands she'll be a genius for the rest of her life, but she'll only be a child a little while longer. I'll be damned if I let her lose the best years of her life!" He stormed over to his father and glared at the man. "If you have a problem with that, keep it to yourself, or you might find me working the bar until the end of my days."

"Don't even kid like that," Bill said. "Go find her. Tell me that my golden years will be peaceful."

"It's all your fault," Murphy ranted, waving a finger under his father's nose. "I'm the product of conditioning. I want a wife, and a kid, and a damn house in the middle of nowhere. Everything I swore I'd never want." He stopped waving his index finger and offered his hand in greeting. "Thanks, Pop. I don't think I'll be able to repay you."

"So what are you waiting for?" his father bellowed. "Go claim your wife."

Murphy disappeared out the door as a big smile appeared on Bill O'Rourke's face.

"You sly dog," said Scotty, shaking his head in amazement. "This is what you wanted all along, isn't it?"

Bill's smile grew wider and he put his cards on the table. "Full house," he said. "Looks like I won the game."

MURPHY WAS A SWEATY, miserable wreck of a man by the time he got to Sam's house. The snow was deep and treacherous. He hated driving in the best of times; this was a trip to Dante's hell. He would have driven through a blizzard, however, to see Sam again and tell her he loved her.

He plowed his way up the unshoveled driveway and stomped up the stairs to the front door. He rang the bell. No answer. He rang again. Still no answer. Her car was there in the driveway. She had to be home.

He tried the doorknob. It was unlocked. Once they were married, he'd have to make sure the doors were locked. "Sam!" His voice seemed to echo in the quiet house. "Sam! Where are you?"

He heard a noise and turned to see her standing in the archway to the hall. Her lovely face was whiter than the snow falling outside. In her hand she held her daughter's Pound Puppy with the torn-off right ear.

"It's Patty," she said, her voice trembling. "She's gone."

Chapter Fifteen

Murphy was beside her before her legs gave way beneath her. He put his arms around her and led her to the sofa then sat down next to her and tried to bring the circulation back into her hands.

"She's gone," Sam repeated, her brain as frozen as the street outside her window. "She's gone!"

Murphy's ruddy face blanched but that was the only indication of fear. "Back up, Sam. Tell me the whole story."

Her hands fluttered helplessly in the air before her and he captured them again between his. "I went to the bar to make lunch. Patty was watching television. She was in her pajamas and robe. I wasn't gone more than an hour—" Her voice broke and she lowered her head in despair. "Oh, God, Murphy!"

"Donovan." Murphy's voice was hard with anger. "If that son of a bitch has kidnapped her, I'll—"

"He wouldn't," Sam said. If she was sure of anything, she was sure of that. "He took her out to dinner last night. If he had kidnapping in mind, he wouldn't have brought her back home."

Murphy glowered in her direction. "Did she leave a note?"

"Nothing."

"Did she pack a suitcase?"

"I didn't look."

They jumped up and ran to Patty's room. As far as Sam could tell, her daughter had taken nothing but her book bag and a few dollars from her piggybank.

"Christmas shopping?" asked Murphy.

"She finished ages ago." Sam couldn't stop the tears from flowing as she met Murphy's eyes. "It's my fault. I thought I was doing the right thing. I want her to have every advantage in the world." The thought of her daughter's sad little face when she came home from dinner with Ronald tore at Sam's heart. "She wondered why you weren't here for the past few days. She thinks she's to blame. She probably thinks I want her to go away."

"Where would she go?"

"I don't know. We can call Susan. My mother. Caroline."

Murphy pushed her toward the phone. "Go ahead. I'll go next door and call my contacts." He hugged her close for an instant, and she felt his strength flow into her body. "We'll bring that girl home, Sam. You can count on it."

One more miracle, God, Sam prayed as she dialed Susan's number. *You gave me Murphy. Now please help us find my little girl.*

MURPHY'S WEB of contacts reached far and wide. Scotty and the crew set out in the blizzard to look for the little girl. He called Sam's cousin Teddy and alerted the local police force and beat reporters from the *Home News, Courier, Newark Star-Ledger* and the *Trentonian.*

"We'll find her," he said to a crying Sam, after he ran back to her house. "*I'll* find her."

"I'm going with you."

"No!" He sat her back down on the sofa and smoothed her silky hair back from her face. "Not this time. Stay here. She might come back on her own."

"Oh, God, Murphy... the storm! How will she find her way?"

"Trust me." His tone brooked no argument. "I wouldn't let you down. What kind of way would that be to start our future together?"

Future? Sam thought as he ran through the snow to his rented car. *What future?* "Murphy!" Her voice bounced off the snowdrifts and back to her as he disappeared into the storm.

MURPHY'S FINGERS clutched the steering wheel of Sam's four-wheel-drive in a death grip.

"Bad choice of words, O'Rourke," he muttered through the sweat dripping down his face. He'd been out there for hours and still no luck. Visibility was zero. He had no traction; the vehicle slid from side to side as if it were entered in an Olympic ice-skating event. Not even four-wheel-drive was enough to combat the icy undercoating beneath the snow. The only thing he hated more than the act of driving was driving in a blizzard.

Somehow it didn't matter.

He had to find Patty—and not just for Sam. He had to find her for himself, as well.

SAM FELT USELESS back at the house. She had never been good at waiting. She'd always been the type of person to leap into things feet first, rather than hold back and read the instructions.

She smiled despite her panic. That's how it had been with motherhood. She read the books and studied the manuals and asked her own mother a thousand questions, but when it came down to it, she trusted her instincts and she and Patty had done just fine.

Why hadn't she trusted her instincts this time? Ronald was wrong. She understood his position about sending Patty to the best schools possible, but this wasn't the time. She needed to be a little girl first and a genius second. She needed to be grounded in home and family before she faced the world beyond Rocky Hill.

She needed Sam and, God willing, she needed Murphy O'Rourke, as well.

Our future together. She was positive she'd heard him say those words, positive they weren't a figment of her imagination. Oh, dear God, was it so much to ask for, that she and Murphy have a future as a family—and that Patty be right there at the center of it, safe and strong and healthy.

But outside the storm was raging and her little girl was so—

"No!" Sam's voice was loud and strong in the quiet house. Patty was fine. She was probably at school or at the library or off with her Grandma Betty doing some last-minute shopping. *I won't think about anything else,* she vowed. *I absolutely will not!*

She glanced at her watch. Four o'clock. Out on the street her neighbors were setting up the luminaria. As soon as the sky grew dark, the candles would be lighted, turning the entire street into a fantasyland. From babyhood on, Patty had loved sitting on the front steps and watching for that magical moment—even though Sam had never mustered up enough enthusiasm or spare cash to participate herself.

"Come home, Patty," she whispered to the empty room. "It's Christmas Eve."

PATTY SHIVERED as the blizzard winds almost lifted her off her feet. How she wished she'd never left her house!

Last night Captain Donovan had made everything sound so clear and reasonable that Patty felt dumb for not seeing things his way. He didn't seem to understand that she was just a ten-year-old kid. She had the feeling that everytime he looked at her, all he saw was her stratospheric IQ, and that made her mad. She was so many other things besides, and he'd probably never know about any of them.

Not like Murphy.

But Captain Donovan had been right about one thing: her mom had given up an awful lot to give Patty a happy life. Now her mom had a chance to be happy, herself, with Murphy O'Rourke, but that just wouldn't be possible as long as Patty was in the picture. Murphy would never stay put in Rocky Hill. He wanted to go back to London and Paris. If Patty went to that sleep-away school in Massachusetts, her mom wouldn't have to work so hard. Maybe she could even go with Murphy on one of those backpacking-through-the-Alps adventures he was always talking about.

Her mom had done so much for her. It seemed to Patty that this was the least she could do for her mom.

Patty's intention to find Captain Donovan had been good but she hadn't counted on a blizzard of such ferocity, or buses that had stopped running long before she made it to the bus stop. And she sure hadn't counted on how awfully hard it was to see where you were walking when the wind blew snow into your eyes—and the tears were flowing freely.

A vicious gust of wind-driven snow swept down on Patty and knocked her to her feet at the side of the road—what road it was, she didn't know. She struggled to get back to her feet but another blast of snow and then another made it impossible for her to regain her bearings.

"Help!" Her cry seemed tiny and lost in the scream of the storm. "Help me, please!"

Oh, Mom... Murphy... where are you?

"ANYTHING?" Murphy had to yell into the receiver to be heard over the storm howling all around the telephone booth off Route 1.

Teddy's voice sounded faint and faraway. "Nothing yet, Murph, but we've got all cars out searching. She'll turn up."

Same story from Dan Stein's local contact and from Scotty and Caroline and the guys from the rescue squad. He hesitated calling Sam but it had to be done.

"I'm heading down toward the mall," he said, trying to sound more confident than he felt. "I bet she's there doing some last-minute shopping."

He hung up before Sam had a chance to hear the fear building inside his gut. Patty wasn't shopping at the mall. The mall was closed. The roads were damn near impassable and he hadn't seen a bus in hours. Every thought he had was nightmarish.

Murphy stumbled from the telephone booth and was struggling to make his way back to his car in the blinding snowstorm when he heard a noise. He stopped, tilting his head to listen. Nothing. Must be his imagination.

"Help . . . please help me . . . Murphy . . ."

You're going crazy, O'Rourke. Hearing voices . . .

"Murphy . . . I'm cold . . ."

His entire body jerked as if he'd run headfirst into a cattle prod. His heart hammered wildly inside his chest.

"Patty!" His voice roared out above the scream of the storm. "Patty, I'm here!"

Her voice was muffled, indistinct. He called upon Boy Scout training and Army boot camp and God in heaven to help him find her. The landscape was like an Arctic tundra. Snowblind, he pushed his way toward the voice in the distance.

And then he saw it. A tiny scrap of red in the ocean of whiteness. The curly pigtails of Patricia Dean.

"Murphy," she said, running into his arms. "What took you so long?"

Rough tough Murphy O'Rourke, meanest reporter in New York, lowered his head and cried.

"Is MOM GOING to yell at me?" Patty asked as Murphy eased the Blazer onto her street.

"Probably," said Murphy, wiping sweat off his forehead with his forearm. "It won't mean a thing, though."

"It's because she loves me, right?"

"You know it, kiddo. She loves you more than anything in the world."

Patty's lips curved into a smile. "She loves you, too."

Murphy almost ran off the road. "She tell you that?"

The little girl shook her head. "She didn't have to. Some things I just know."

"Yeah, well, let's wait and see." He and Sam had been on a rocky road the past week. She may have decided life with him didn't sound like such a good idea. Not that he'd pay any attention, mind you. He intended to become part of Sam's and Patty's family and he wouldn't take no for an answer.

The street looked like a Christmas card come to life. Snow blanketed everything and continued to fall. Yet, despite the blizzard conditions, candles still burned in front of one house on the entire block. Sam's house.

Next to him Patty clasped her hands together in delight. "My candles," she said in a hushed whisper. "My Christmas Eve candles!" She looked at Murphy, and the smile she gave him was pure little girl. "I think everything's going to be okay."

SAM WAS STANDING near the Christmas tree, looking out the front window when she heard the unmistakeable sound of her Blazer plowing its way up the snowy street.

"Oh, dear God, please," she whispered, her face pressed against the icy glass as she peered through the swirling snow outside. "Please bring my little girl home." The world was no longer the safe haven of her childhood; it was rougher and more dangerous. A place where little children's faces peered from milk cartons and families prayed for a miracle.

She waited, her heart pounding violently at the base of her throat, as the sound grew closer. Her legs trembled and her hands grew colder than the falling temperature. The endless hours of waiting, of praying, of lighting the candles and hanging the stockings and pretending there would be a happy ending on this holiest of nights had taken their toll and as the familiar vehicle approached, the roaring inside her head intensified, rivaling the sound of the storm.

She knew somehow that God was listening to her prayers, that He had sent Murphy O'Rourke into their lives for a reason—to love them and protect them and share the good times and the bad. The Blazer cautiously made its way up her driveway with Murphy at the wheel. Her eyes swam with tears. The passenger seat was empty. Or was it?

"Patty!" Her daughter's name was a cry from the heart as the little girl opened the car door and jumped out. Sam raced out of the house and flew down the snowy steps.

"I'm sorry, Mommy!" Sam hugged Patty so tightly the little girl's words were muffled against Sam's sweater. "I didn't mean to make you scared."

Sam tried to sound stern but managed only to sound relieved. "Where on earth were you going, Patty? What were you trying to do?"

Patty's bright blue eyes glanced from Sam to Murphy then back again to Sam. "Captain Donovan," she said, her voice little more than a whisper. "I wanted to talk to him. I thought ..."

Her words drifted away in the wind and Sam cupped her daughter's chin, forcing Patty to meet her eyes. "You thought what, honey?"

"You and Murphy. I thought that maybe if I went away to that school Captain Donovan talked about that you and Murphy could—"

She looked up at Murphy who was listening intently to the exchange. "There's nothing more important than you, honey. There's nothing on earth I care more about than your happiness."

"I thought maybe if I went away you wouldn't have to work so hard." Her cheeks reddened. "Maybe then you and Murphy could go anywhere you want."

Murphy crouched down near them. "Running away doesn't solve anything, Patty. You should have talked to us. Maybe we had the answer all along."

Patty's mouth dropped open. So did Sam's. *One more miracle, please, dear Lord, and I'll never bother you again . . .*

"The buses stopped running," Patty said, sniffling. "I only got halfway and then I got lost."

"Why didn't you call?" Sam asked, kissing her soundly and administering another bone-crushing hug. "Don't you know that I'm here for you no matter what?"

"I lost my money in a snowdrift," said Patty, "and then I tried to find my way back but everything looked all white and the same."

"Tell me about it," said Murphy, tugging fondly on one of Patty's braids. "If it weren't for this head of red hair, I might never have found her."

Sam looked over at Murphy, at that dear and handsome face, and saw her future reflected in his eyes. "I'll never be able to thank you," she said, wishing she knew the right words to convey the powerful rush of primal emotions taking root inside her heart. "I—"

"Mom," said Patty, once more her practical, brilliant little girl, "can we talk inside. It's *freezing* out here!"

"Come on," said Sam, smiling at her two favorite people in the world. "Let's get you guys warm."

A FEW HOURS LATER, Sam tucked the afghan around her sleeping little girl and kissed the top of her head.

"She looks like an angel, doesn't she?" She turned to Murphy who was sitting in front of the fireplace in the living room.

"You look like an angel," he said, motioning for her to sit down next to him. "I don't think I'll ever forget the way you looked when you saw Patty get out of the Blazer."

Sam snuggled up next to him and kissed him soundly. "I owe it all to you, Murphy. You saved her life."

Was she imagining it or did her hero actually blush. "I wouldn't go that far, Sam."

"I know you saved my life."

"Your life was just fine. You didn't need anyone to save you from anything."

She swallowed hard. This wasn't the time for anything less than total honesty. "You saved me from being lonely, Murphy. I didn't think I could fall in love."

He met her eyes. "Past tense?"

"Past, present and future. I love you, Murphy O'Rourke. God help me, but I do."

"I love you, Sam." Murphy's words were the first Sam heard as Christmas Day came to Rocky Hill. "I love you and I love Patty and the best present you could give me is to say yes."

"Yes," said Sam as love and happiness and hope filled her heart to overflowing. "Yes! Yes! Yes!"

He laughed and held her close. "You haven't heard the question yet."

She pulled away a fraction and looked up at him. "You're asking me to marry you, right?"

"That's right."

Her breath caught for an instant. "You won't be going overseas?"

"Not on your life."

"Your job—what will you do?"

He gave her a sheepish, but extremely self-satisfied grin. "Meet Murphy O'Rourke, managing editor of the *New York Telegram*, and stalwart citizen of Rocky Hill, New Jersey."

She laughed despite herself. "You mean, you'll be a commuter?" Dashing, dynamic Murphy O'Rourke riding New Jersey Transit!

"A commuter," he said, gathering her close to him. "Life is full of surprises."

"No more Paris nights and London weekends," she said softly. "Any regrets?"

He looked at Patty, sleeping, then met Sam's eyes. "Only that I didn't meet you a long time ago."

"We still have plenty of time, Murphy." She kissed him on the lips. "But not if you don't ask me officially."

Grinning he dropped to one knee before her. "Will you marry me, Sam?"

"Yes!" She threw herself into his arms. "I can't think of anything on earth I'd rather do."

THE SIGHT OF GROWN-UPS kissing usually made Patty giggle and look away.

But not tonight. She watched from under the afghan as her mom and her almost-dad kissed each other by the light of the fire and started to plan a lifetime of happiness for the three of them.

Two tiny packages rested under the tree, wrapped in shiny paper of gold and silver. Halves of the same heart. One inscribed "Mom." And the other inscribed "Murphy," but not for long. The day after Christmas she'd ask her mom to take her to the mall where she'd have the jeweler inscribe "Dad" right there for the whole world to see!

"You'll get your wish, Patricia," the Macy's Santa Claus had said. "I promise you!" And even though Patty was too old to believe in Saint Nick, she'd somehow known the man in red was telling the truth.

Mr. and Mrs. Murphy O'Rourke. How wonderful it sounded.

Patricia O'Rourke. How terrific it would look, written in her diary in her very best script.

The O'Rourke Family. Now that was the very best of all. Her mom had Murphy to love and Murphy had her mom, and Patty was lucky enough to have both of them as her very own parents forever and ever.

From the churches of Rocky Hill came the glorious sounds of the church bells tolling midnight as Christmas carols rang out up and down the quiet, snowy street. What a wonderful day it would be.

She sighed happily and closed her eyes. "Merry Christmas to all," she whispered as sugarplums began to dance inside her head, "and God bless us, every one!"

**Dear Santa—Are you really St. Nicholas?
If you are, we need to talk.**

**Love,
Frank**

A CAROL CHRISTMAS

Muriel Jensen

Chapter One

Carol Shaw walked the dark trail from the cafeteria to the dorm she supervised at Saint Christopher's Home for Children. One moment she was alone, lost in thoughts of other winters, other Christmases. The next, she felt the unmistakable pressure of a gun in her back.

"Don't turn around," a disguised but familiar voice commanded. "I've got a message from the boss."

She froze in her tracks. A bone-chilling wind whipped dead leaves around her feet. "What is it?" she asked.

"You're to report to HQ in one hour."

"Dinner's in an hour."

Pressure was applied to the gun, and Carol arched her back. "I don't question orders, I just carry them out. One hour. Don't be late," the menacing voice advised, "or I'll soak ya."

Carol turned to confront the messenger and take the yellow plastic water pistol from his hand. The boy of eleven in jeans and a lined denim jacket gave up his weapon without complaint. His dark blond hair stood up in moderately moussed spikes that were impervious to the strong wind. Devilish brown eyes smiled at her. Carol had a particular fondness for Frank, despite his vision of himself as a top-level secret agent with license to squirt.

"I've asked you not to carry this in the winter," she reminded the youngster, laughing as she pulled him along with her to the dorm. "You get the other kids all wet, then they catch cold. Put it away, please."

"Okay." He turned to run up the path backward, slowing his pace to keep just ahead of her. "Godzilla said . . ."

Carol groaned. "Frank, I've told you not to call her that. You owe the kitty a nickel."

"Sorry." Frank corrected himself with an exasperated expulsion of breath. "Mother Margaret said that she wants to talk to you about the Christmas bazaar. And about somebody visiting or something. And I don't think she meant Santa Claus. Do you know that Kathy still believes in him?"

"Why shouldn't she?" Carol asked. "I do."

Frank rolled his eyes, fell into step beside Carol and hooked his arm into hers. "I'm not talking about what good people do for one another and all that baloney," he said with a world-weary matter-of-factness that was so typical of him. "I'm talking about some old guy who comes along and gives you stuff for nothing, just because you're a good kid. I mean . . ." He indicated the other four children who shared their dormitory. They were coming up the path through the woods from the school, the hoods of their yellow slickers flapping in the wind. "The fact that us kids are here is proof that there's no such thing. Either that, or Rudolph never found his way through the fog to Saint Christopher's Home for Children."

Frank smiled broadly, a smile that tried to say he had no objection to having been abandoned by his father. Carol knew that pain and resentment were hiding behind the smile, but the facade kept him going, and she was reluctant to disturb it. A woman who did some of her own best work behind a mask of cheer, Carol understood the value of a measure of pretense.

"If you maintain that attitude," she cautioned him, smiling, "he's not going to make much of an effort to find you." Carol turned to one of the other children. "Nicky! How was show-and-tell?"

The four children, three girls and a boy, clustered around Carol and Frank. They all spoke at once, reporting the events of their day. Carol bent down to give six-year-old Nicky her complete attention. He was small and shy, and only just coming out of his shell after five months at the home.

"Did you find something to share?" she asked.

He pulled a white mouse out of his coat pocket and held it a fraction of an inch from Carol's face. The girls leaped back, screaming. Carol barely stopped herself from reacting in the same way. Only Nicky's soft dark eyes, filled with admiration and affection for the tiny, wriggling, pink-eyed creature made her hold her position.

"A gerbil?" she asked faintly, as he took her hand and put the rodent in it. She closed her other hand over Nicky's new pet, allowing just enough room for the small head to explore. She made a conscious effort to ignore the feeling of tiny claws on the palm of her hand.

"A mouse," he corrected. "His name's Kermit."

"Kermit is a frog," Dorcas, the oldest of the girls, pointed out. "That's a dumb name."

"He likes it," Frank said aggressively. "It doesn't matter what you think, Dorky!"

Frank's use of the hated nickname earned him the predictable reward. Dorcas swung her nylon backpack at his face with remarkable precision.

"That's enough." Carol hurriedly gave the mouse back to Nicky and pulled Frank and Dorcas apart. Plump cheeks flushed, glasses askew, both thick brown ponytails bristling, Dorcas seethed at Frank.

"You're not supposed to call me that!"

"Then don't act like a dork!" he countered angrily, straining against Carol's hand.

"Frank," Carol said firmly, "you owe the kitty another nickel, and Dorie, you *must* stop hitting. You have to clean up after popcorn tonight." Frank and Dorcas stuck their tongues out at each other, but subsided. The problem of the mouse remained.

"Where did you get Kermit, Nicky?" Carol asked.

"Kirby Mitchell from Saint Joseph's dorm gave it to me." He looked up at her, his dark eyes suddenly grave. "Those guys are leaving next week, you know. He can't take it with him where he's going."

Carol knew that many of the large institutions for housing homeless children had been abandoned long ago in favor of smaller foster homes, where they received more individual attention. But Saint Christopher's remained. Its function had changed from that of an orphanage, founded by the Sisters of the Trinity, to a large group home and school, still operated by the founding order. Now antiquated plumbing and wiring, and needed repairs too numerous to be economically feasible were forcing Saint Christopher's to close its doors, too. So the children in its care, like all the others, were to be moved to foster homes.

In the meantime, Carol had to deal with the five most difficult to place of the home's sixty children. They were frightened. They were losing friends, what little stability they'd had in their young lives and, in some cases, treasured possessions like Kermit.

"When I go," Nicky whispered, his lip quivering, "will you take care of him?"

A silence fell over the usually noisy group. They exchanged looks of dread, but no one spoke his or her fear aloud. Carol knew she would have to discuss the move with them again, but now was not the time. She wanted a long, quiet period that would give them an opportunity for questions and honest answers.

"Well, none of us is leaving until February," she said cheerfully. "That's two long months, during which we'll have Christmas and Saint Christopher's all to ourselves. We're going to have a ball!"

"Santa's gonna come!" Kathy, dark-eyed and earnest, spoke with anticipation.

"With presents!" Candy, Kathy's five-year-old sister, jumped up and down.

Dorcas pushed her glasses back into place and spoke with the air of displaced aristocracy that was her trademark. "We're going to make cookies and ornaments. My mom and dad always had a tree that touched the ceiling, and it was full of gold and crystal ornaments."

"You're full of..."

Carol forestalled Frank's critique with a warning look. "We'll need a cage for Kermit," she said before a new battle could begin.

"He's got one." Nicky reached down and pointed to a square, not very sweet-smelling structure. He held up a box of pellets. "And food."

"Good. Okay. Let's get Kermit settled, then we'll change and go to the playground."

Out of the home's uniform and dressed in play clothes, the children gathered in the kitchen, where Carol put out cookies and milk. Kermit was settled in a clean cage on the dresser in the boys' room.

"Let's play hide-and-seek instead of going to the playground," Kathy suggested, putting on a frayed blue down jacket. She pulled up her zipper, then turned to Candy, who was struggling with hers. Patiently Kathy lowered the zipper, removed the threads that were interfering with its operation, then zipped it up.

Kathy and Candy had already been in residence at Saint Christopher's for two months when Carol took the position of dorm mother in February. For nine months, Carol had watched in fascination as eight-year-old Kathy cared for her sister day in and day out with more skill and patience than most adults could ever possess. Seeing that Candy's needs were met had become second nature to the older girl. It was very clear that the mother who had died too young had taught her well.

Kathy and Candy were pretty, smart and well behaved, and every time prospective parents visited, Carol prayed that the girls would be placed. But finding a home for one older child was difficult enough; finding a home for two was rare. The idea that they might one day be separated was something she refused to even consider.

Candy jumped up and down, endorsing the suggestion that they play hide-and-seek.

"At home," Dorcas began, and Frank caught Carol's eye, then rolled his own toward the ceiling. Carol braced herself, preparing to withstand another of Dorcas's fantasies. "I had a computer to play with before dinner. My friend Denise used to come over every day."

"To your penthouse in the hotel," Frank said scornfully.

Dorcas gave him a withering look over her shoulder. "That's right. And when we were bored with the computer, we played in Central Park."

Frank snickered. "Too bad you didn't get mugged."

Choosing diversion over arbitration, Carol pulled the door open. "Last one to the flagpole is 'it'!"

There was a mad scramble. Carol was "it," but at least another quarrel had been averted. She closed her eyes and counted loudly to ten. Giggles from Candy betrayed the refuge she shared with Kathy behind the still-green rhododendrons that fronted the school. Dorcas was found crouched behind the twelve-foot-high statue of Saint Christopher that dominated the grounds.

Carol leaned against the flagpole, trying to decide where to look for the boys.

"Lost someone?"

Carol smiled at the approach of Sister Claire, who taught the primary grades. "We're playing hide-and-seek. I think Nicky and Frank have left the planet."

Sister Claire nodded seriously. "Frank must have perfected that jet pack he's always trying to put together to escape the KGB."

The girls giggled and the sister smiled. Young and "rad" as Frank described her, Sister Claire was a favorite among the children. A straight wisp of dark hair fell from her thin black veil, held in place by a band of starched white fabric. She wore the black long-sleeved blouse and calf-length skirt that were the habit of the Sisters of the Trinity. Around her neck hung a cross on a simple silver chain.

Her blue eyes widened in innocence. She pulled her gray wool coat around her. "Well, I guess I'll leave you to your search. I'm going to help Sister Celestine with dinner. With some of the staff already shipped out, we're a little short-handed."

Despite Sister Claire's religious garb and innocent expression, Carol decided that right now she was not to be trusted. They'd played Monopoly together enough times for Carol to know that the young woman was both clever and shrewd.

"You wouldn't have seen them, would you, Sister?" Carol asked, advancing slowly as Sister Claire backed away.

"Seen them?"

The girls followed Carol, giggling harder at the nun's response.

"Ask Sister again," Dorcas prompted. "She can't lie to you, 'cause it's a sin!"

Sister Claire's eyes widened with a mock horror that delighted the girls. Then she turned soberly to Carol. "Who were you looking for again? Oops!"

Backing away behind the shelter of the sister's skirts, Frank and Nicky fell over one another in a laughing pile.

Sister Claire turned around in feigned surprise. "Well, my goodness!"

The children laughed, their spirits warm again, despite the bleakness of their prospects and the wintry afternoon.

"We adults are supposed to stick together," Carol teased Sister Claire.

"Frank offered to fix my pencil sharpener if I helped him pull it off." She shrugged. "It was too good a deal."

"And you, a representative of the Church."

Sister Claire laughed. "I'm firmly convinced Frank's going to be pope one day—or a Mafia don—and when he is, I want to be on his good side. Got to run. See you at dinner."

"I want to be 'it!' I want to be 'it!'" Nicky ran to Carol, pulling on her arm. "Can I be 'it,' Carol?"

Frank rolled his eyes in disgust. "Nicky, what did I tell you about volunteering?"

Nicky obviously didn't see the problem. "But it's volunteering for something fun."

"Hiding is fun," Frank explained. "Being 'it' means you have to work and find everybody."

Nicky was still confused. "But that's fun."

Frank put a hand to his eyes and shook his head. "The kid's hopeless, Carol."

Carol bent down and kissed Nicky's cheek. "Okay, Nick. You're 'it.' Close your eyes." He obliged, and she turned him slowly around while the other children scattered. "Now count to ten."

As he began to tick off the numbers, his eyes scrupulously shut tight, Carol headed into the trees. Now that the six retreat cabins on the grounds were closed, she and the children used them often in their games of hide-and-seek. The closest cabin was hidden by the fat pines, but it was near enough to Nicky that it should occur to him immediately as a possible hiding place. Just as he shouted in a high voice,

"Ready or not, here I come!" Carol opened the front door of the cabin.

"WHICH CABIN?"

Mike Rafferty, seated between his brother and his friend in the cab of the pickup, consulted the note in his hand. "Cabin A. The one closest to the school," he read, "in the grove of pines at the bend of the drive. That must be it."

"Right." The man driving wore a blue baseball cap backward, and tufts of thick red hair stuck through the sizing hole. He turned the truck around with an alarming lack of caution and backed through the trees right up to the cabin's small, rough veranda. Pine branches whipped against the windows, and the porch shook as the back of the truck made contact with it. Mike braced a hand against the dashboard. "God, Slug. Watch what you're doing!"

Slugger Lund turned off the motor and set the brake, looking at his friend with a mockingly reprimanding frown. "Watch your mouth. This is a church."

"It's a children's home."

"Run by nuns. Same thing. Just because your sister runs this place doesn't mean you can talk like a heathen."

As Lund jumped out of the truck, Mike turned to his brother with a groan of exasperation, only to find that he had covered his eyes. "Relax, Rick," Mike said. "We're here."

"Are the trees still standing?" Rick asked without lowering his hand.

"Yeah."

"The cabin?"

"Well, the porch is slightly askew. And there's probably a dent in the back of the truck. But then," he added philosophically, "it's Slug's truck."

Rick lowered his hand and looked at his brother. "The trip here was worse than my worst memories of teaching you to drive. I don't think I've ever been in such fear of my life. You sure it's safe to keep company with this guy?''

"Will you mellow out? He's the best hitter in the American League and he likes me. What can I say?"

"I thought you were the best hitter in the American League?"

There was just a moment's pause before Mike replied. "I was. Now Slugger is. Did you come to help me move my stuff or to complain about the transportation?"

Rick stretched cramped arms, then reached for the door handle, giving his brother a wry smile. "I don't see why I can't do both."

As Slugger began single-handedly to pull a small refrigerator out of the back, Mike stopped him. "Let's go in and reconnoiter, so we don't have to move things around more than once." Slugger effortlessly pushed the refrigerator back.

He followed Rick and Mike into the cabin. The small living area was cold and dark, furnished with old, random pieces upholstered in a well-worn blue and beige fabric. They looked comfortable enough to the visitors, though they were neither chic nor eclectically charming. As most residents of the cabins stayed only a matter of days and ate in the cafeteria, the kitchen was minuscule and had no appliances.

Mike took a cursory look around the bedroom, while Rick inspected the drawers of a small dresser and tested the comfort of a chenille-covered double bed.

"This is almost as bad as the visiting team dugout at Shively Field," Slugger said, leaning an arm on Mike's shoulder. "The offer to stay with Beth and me still holds."

"Thanks, Slug, but I need the time alone."

"It's only the end of your career," Slugger said, with what was clearly intended as friendly encouragement, "not the end of the world." Slugger was always a little short of the baseline when it came to subtlety and finesse, his friends knew. He went through life like a big bear, alternately hugging and maiming them.

Rick turned from the center of the room, an angry criticism of the other man's tactless remark on the tip of his tongue. But Mike stopped him with a look. Mike understood Slug. After all the years of facing crowds that cheered you when you were up and shouted crude insults when you weren't, he appreciated the man's inability to pretend. It was just difficult sometimes to determine whether he meant to encourage or depress you. Mike turned him toward the living room. "Let's get the kitchen stuff first."

"Right."

"Ah . . . Mike?"

As Slugger headed out to the truck, Mike turned in response to the question in Rick's voice. His brother stood in front of the bedroom closet. One of its double doors was open.

"Yeah?"

Rick beckoned him over. "Look at what Saint Christopher's Home for Children is providing you in the way of closet fresheners."

Mike went to stand beside his brother and saw the only thing that could have brought a smile to his lips after the well-intended brutality of Slugger's remark—a woman. She was standing in a corner of the closet, one hand wrapped around the hanging rod, looking like some pomander sent from heaven.

Dressed in jeans and a green down jacket, she was average in height. Chin-length red hair lay in fluffy tangles around a startled face. Wide eyes of a color he could define only as khaki looked back at him.

Carol had thought moments earlier that the footsteps advancing through the cabin did not belong to the children. When she'd heard the deep men's voices, she'd been sure. While listening to their conversation with half of her attention, she'd applied the other half to wondering who they

were, what they were doing here, and considering the misfortune of having chosen this particular moment to hide in
the cabin closet. Then the closet door flew open, and the
time for wondering who they were was past.

She concluded immediately that the two men facing her
were brothers. They had the same deep brown, curly hair,
the same broad brow over dark brown eyes. The man who
opened the door had a ready smile; the one whom the first
had called Mike had a cautious, more thoughtful smile that
was just beginning to form. The closet opener had straight,
elegant features. Mike's were rougher, his face squared. She
was sure she hadn't seen either man before, but something
about both of them was unsettlingly familiar. Neither one
was what Carol had ever expected to encounter at the beginning of a grim December in this secluded outpost on the
Washington coast.

Neither man looked dangerous, and she was sure there
had to be a good reason for them to walk right into this retreat cabin, which had been closed for several months. But
until she knew their purpose, an air of authority was called
for.

"This is private property," she said. Then realizing that
speaking from the corner of a closet probably diminished
her dignity somewhat, she stepped forward. Both men
moved back to give her room.

"You're right," Mike replied, folding his arms. He was
more thickly built than the other man, more athletic in appearance. "And at the moment, the property happens to be
mine. You might explain what you're doing in my closet."

Carol let her suspicion show. "Yours?"

Mike nodded. "I've rented this retreat cabin for two
months."

"Saint Christopher's stopped offering retreats months
ago."

"That's true, but I have a little pull here." He smiled
down at her. "Mother Margaret is my sister."

That was it—the dark features, the height, the mien of self-possession that were so characteristic of the director of Saint Christopher's. Frank had said something earlier about Mother Margaret wanting to talk to her about a visitor to the home.

With a breath of relief, she dropped her suspicions and offered her hand. "I apologize. I'm Carol Shaw."

A large, warm hand engulfed hers. Its owner's careful smile broadened just a little. "Mike Rafferty." He indicated the man beside him. "My brother, Rick. About your being in my closet . . ."

"We were playing hide-and-seek," she explained, not realizing until the words were out of her mouth how silly they sounded.

The brothers exchanged a look. Mike's eyebrows went up, and Rick said with a shrug and a grin, "Hide-and-seek. Why not?"

Mike turned back to the woman. "Who was playing?" he asked.

"The children and I," Carol replied. "I'm a dorm mother. Since these cabins are empty, we run in and out of them all the time. We won't anymore, of course," she amended hastily.

Then, with the suddenness of a coastal storm, they were surrounded by children.

"Where have you been? You didn't come and find me! Who are these guys? Why is there a refrigerator in the living room?"

Mike counted five little faces clustering around the young woman. Three children were jumping up and down, and the other two were pulling on her. Personally, he'd rather face the crowd at Yankee Stadium during the World Series.

Then one of the children, a boy of ten or eleven, called his name. "Mike Rafferty!" He said it with an edge of awe, his eyes big and brown as he came to stand right in front of Mike and look up into his face.

The recognition stroked his ego, of course, but Mike felt charmed by something more than that. "And you're ... ?" He offered his hand.

The boy looked at it for a minute, then put his own hand into Mike's, a smile lighting his face as he began to pump. "Frank Kaminski. I live here."

"Well, I'm glad to know you, Frank."

Two dark blond eyebrows met in concern over a freckled nose. "How's the arm?"

Mike looked back at the boy for a minute, then smiled. He'd come here to try to put all that behind himself, but thanks to Slugger and this boy, it wasn't going to happen today. "I've got a few pins in it," he replied, flexing the arm in question. "But at least I've still got it."

Frank nodded sympathetically. "Tough break. You'd have broken the record next season."

Mike shrugged. "That's the way it goes."

Rick put a hand on the boy's shoulder. "You sound like a real fan, Frank."

"I know all his stats." Without waiting for encouragement, Frank went on to recite them. ".353 batting average last year, 52 homers, 131 ribbies and American League MVP. God!" he said, forgetting all Mother Margaret's entreaties that he switch to "gosh." "And I shook his hand. I can't believe it."

"I'm going to be here for a while," Mike said. "We'll have to get together sometime and talk baseball."

"Mike? Rick?" From the direction of the cabin's small living room came the sound of Mother Margaret's voice.

Rick stuck his head around the corner of the room and called, "In here, Meg!"

Mother Margaret, ruddy-faced and tall in her dark habit and veil, hurried into the bedroom, to be wrapped in Rick's bear hug and lifted off the floor. She was passed on to Mike, who hugged her, then kissed her soundly.

While greetings were exchanged and familial insults tossed back and forth, Carol tried to usher the children through the door and out of the cabin. But they ignored her whispered encouragements. They knew Mother Margaret as the fair but strict woman who ran the home with efficiency and dealt firmly with their transgressions. Now they stood and stared openmouthed as she laughed with these strangers, entranced by the high, musical sound.

But Carol was the one who had held her as she wept when the official document arrived, confirming the imminent closure of the home. She knew Mother Margaret was a loving, caring woman, bound only by the conventions of her vocation.

Mother Margaret reached for Carol, pulling her closer. "Mike and Rick—Carol Shaw, the best dorm mother at Saint Christopher's. Carol, these are my brothers, Mike and Rick, the bane of my childhood."

Mike exchanged a look with his brother. "Who threw whose bike in the river?"

"You ran over my doll with it," Mother Margaret reminded him.

"Meg," Rick said. "He was on the bike at the time."

She nodded, assuming a judicious air. "Justice is swift and without remorse."

"You'll get yours," Mike threatened, then turning his attention to Carol, he grinned. "Actually, we've just met. She was hiding in my closet."

Mother Margaret's eyebrows rose. "You were?"

"It's easily explained," Rick said helpfully. "She and the children were playing hide-and-seek. Actually, now that I've seen her, I think I'll stay a couple of months and rest with Mike."

Mike shook his head. "Not a chance." Then he smiled wickedly. "You get to ride home with Slug."

As Rick groaned, the man in question appeared in the doorway. "Hey!" he shouted. "I could use some help out here!"

Frank stared as if transfixed, his mouth open, his eyes on the man before him. "Slugger Lund! Oh, my *God*!" Belatedly remembering Mother Margaret's presence, he covered his mouth with both hands.

But her only admonition was a look of mild reproach.

"I could help," Frank volunteered hopefully.

"Well, come on." Slugger put an arm on the boy's shoulder and looked disdainfully at Mike and Rick. "You'll probably be worth two of each of them, anyway."

"I'll help, too." Nicky followed them from the room, trailed by the girls.

Rick rolled his eyes and fell into step behind the small parade. "I'm probably not needed, but I should keep up appearances. Nice to meet you, Miss Shaw."

Turning to follow her five young charges, Carol was stopped by Mother Margaret. "Wait for me, Carol. It's about time for our meeting, anyway. The children will be all right with my brothers until we're finished." She looked at Mike and ordered sternly, "Remember, you're not supposed to lift anything heavy, so let Rick and your friend handle the big pieces. And I want you all to join us for dinner in the cafeteria before Rick leaves."

Mike nodded meekly. "Yes, Mother Margaret."

His use of her title brought a smile to her lips. She tossed back the veil that had been disturbed during her brothers' enthusiastic greetings. "Good," she said. "It's time you learned a little humility. See you at dinner." She drew Carol out with her into the windy dusk.

Chapter Two

"His entire life has fallen apart." Mother Margaret walked around her large office in the building that housed the school, gymnasium and administrative center of the home. The laughing woman of a moment ago had been replaced once more by the director of Saint Christopher's, burdened with the distribution of sixty little lives.

Carol was beginning to realize that personal problems were also preying on Mother Margaret's mind. "An automobile accident a few months ago almost took Mike's arm. What it did succeed in taking was his career. At the peak of one of the most successful careers in recent baseball history, he was told that he can never play again. The pins in his arm just can't take that kind of strain."

"Frank recognized him right away." Carol shook her head, remembering the brawny body, the cautious smile. "I'm ashamed to say that I didn't. I've never paid much attention to sports. He said he's rented the cabin for two months."

Mother Margaret nodded, perching on the edge of her desk. She crossed her black-stockinged legs at the ankles and sighed. "He's only been out of the hospital a week, but he's been so plagued by news reporters and agencies offering to make him rich on endorsements that he needed a place to lie low for a while. Our mother's house in San Francisco was too visible—he'd have been found there in a minute. So Rick suggested bringing him here."

Carol frowned over that conclusion. "Aren't you afraid he'll die of boredom, Mother Margaret? No offense, but the Washington coast in December isn't exactly a tropical paradise with sunny days for lying on the beach. And unless he's an introspective man, there's not a lot to do here, except play with children." She smiled. "Fine for you and me, but for a former baseball star?"

Mother Margaret nodded. "Not ideal, perhaps, but available. He's supposed to do a lot of walking to build himself up again after his hospital stay, and we have some of the most beautiful trails in the state. He is used to living the high life in the public eye, so I'm not sure how he'll react to life here on a cliff on the edge of nowhere. But Rick told me that one of the offers he's considering is from a publishing company that wants his autobiography. This could be the ideal place to think seriously about it and even to begin to write it."

Waiting for Mother Margaret to explain why she was sharing all this information with her, Carol remained attentive. "Maybe we'll see you and your brother, Rick, in print also."

Mother Margaret's smile returned again. "I'll probably have to buy him off at some outrageous price, or be drummed out of the order and possibly the Church."

"The attempted murder of a boy on a bicycle could smear your record."

"He ran over my doll with it," the director explained once more.

Carol shrugged. "I understand, but will the pope?"

They laughed together for a moment, then Mother Margaret sobered. "As if having his career fall apart wasn't bad enough, a woman who was very important to him chose to leave him while he was in the hospital. I'm not sure which blow hurt him most. Carol . . ." She raised bright dark eyes and sighed. "I know you have enough problems of your own, but since everyone else is leaving next week except for a few of the staff and you, I thought perhaps you could help me keep an eye on him."

Carol's instinctive reaction was that keeping life running smoothly for the five children in her care already kept her busy every spare moment. And being moved away from Saint Christopher's early next year was going to be hard on them; she was determined to give them the best Christmas they'd ever had. But it occurred to her that Mike Rafferty probably felt as lost now as her charges did. There must be something she could do.

"My mother is very concerned," Mother Margaret went on, "that he chose to come here rather than spend Christmas with her. She thinks it's more than trying to get away from the telephone and the uninvited guests. She thinks he's hiding out."

That sounded understandable to Carol. "Maybe he has a right to a little wound licking. Must be hard to lose your career and your girl at the same time."

Mother Margaret folded her arms and looked at Carol with affection and admiration. "You, more than anyone, know what it's like to sustain a terrible blow and keep going, to turn all the anger and bitterness around into feelings that are positive and productive." She paused, then said gravely, "I think you're one of the bravest women I know. Having you to talk to would do him so much good."

"Mother, I..." Carol began to protest. The fear that had been forcibly folded into the dark recesses of her soul was making a small effort to break free. But she was too good at repressing it. She'd faked composure for so long. She folded her arms, lifted her chin, and the fear subsided. "I'm no paragon of survival. The children keep me going, otherwise I'd be in a rubber room somewhere. I'm not sure I have a lot to offer."

"That's because you don't realize the importance of what you've done." Mother Margaret stood and walked around her desk to take her chair. "Mike's a fair artist and has a lot of patience. I think we could put him to work, helping you and the children get Saint Christopher's booth ready for the bazaar. He has to be careful of his arm, but he could help you make ornaments and put up the tree in the gym, and it won't hurt to have extra help when you take the children to town."

"I'm sure the children will be thrilled to have his company. He's welcome to hang out with us, if he doesn't find us too dull."

Mother Margaret laughed; the sound was distinctly unsaintly. "Your group is anything but dull, Carol. Oh..." She shuffled some papers. "We're close to getting Kathy and Candy's release forms signed. Their uncle's the only living relative, and he's working on a fishing boat in Florida. The report says he sounded willing to sign the form. It was sent to him, and we're awaiting its return."

"What about the others?"

The signature that provided the formal release of a child by parents or next of kin was a required step before a child could be adopted. It was a detail that usually didn't cause a lot of concern, until a prospective adoptive family expressed interest in a particular child. But now that the children were leaving Saint Christopher's, Mother Margaret was making a special effort to see that they left with all their paperwork finalized. The children of Carol's group had been placed in the same dorm and were being held longer than the others, because their families couldn't be found to provide the signature. The court could be asked to intervene in such cases, so a formal release was unnecessary, but Mother Margaret was determined to make every effort to clear the children's path to easy adoption.

"Dorcas's mother escaped from prison almost a year ago and still hasn't been found. Frank's father's an alcoholic.

And Nicky's mother went back to Mexico." Mother Margaret sighed and shook her head. "How can you hope to find people who leave children when they move on, like someone might desert a cat?"

Carol shook her head. "I don't know. I wouldn't even leave the cat." Blind rage would follow if she allowed the thought to form that really followed Mother's question. How could anyone abandon a child? No. That was counterproductive.

"One more thing." Mother Margaret put a hand to her forehead, as though it were beginning to hurt. "Mr. Engbretson says your sink was clogged up again."

"Guilty." Carol rolled her eyes. "We were making candles, and Dorie's began to drip. Instinctively she carried it to the sink, not realizing that it wouldn't run through like water."

"He says it's the fourth time he's been called to your dorm this month."

Carol began to count. The front-room window, the wallboard in the boys' room, Frank's bed, the... That did make four. "He's right. But that's his job, isn't it? It's not as though the children do these things on purpose. Frank's just a little stronger than he realizes, and the rest are just kids. They act first and think later."

Mother Margaret nodded philosophically. "I know. But our job is to try to reverse that process and turn them into productive rather than destructive citizens."

"Yes, Mother. But I think someone failed in that duty with Mr. Engbretson. He's the crabbiest man I've ever dealt with."

"He's lonely," Mother Margaret said.

Carol grinned. "That's no surprise."

"Carol—"

"Sorry, Mother." Carol stood. "Anything else? The kids have probably talked your brothers and Mr. Lund into hysteria by now."

Mother Margaret made a shooing movement with one hand while she opened a manila folder with the other. Assured that Carol understood why Mike Rafferty was here and that she would do what she could to help, Mother Margaret's attention returned to orphanage matters. "No, go on. Thank you, Carol."

Despite the children's pleas that they be allowed to visit the sisters' table where the celebrities were seated, Carol kept a firm rein on their mobility and their enthusiasm during dinner in the noisy cafeteria. "They're family," she explained. "They need some time alone together. Mother Margaret doesn't get to see her brothers very often."

"I wonder what it's like to have a sister who's a sister?" Frank speculated.

Carol pointed to the untouched broccoli on his plate. "Probably just like having a sister who isn't. Eat that. I'll bet Mr. Rafferty and Mr. Lund eat their broccoli."

"Mike and Slugger eat steaks and milk shakes."

"I'm sure ball players need a lot of energy."

"Rick's favorite thing is pasta."

Carol smiled down at Frank. "Did you guys get any furniture moved while you discussed food?"

"Everything. Did you see Godz—Mother Margaret—" Frank corrected himself at Carol's quick look "—laugh? She didn't look like a nun anymore, except for the clothes."

"A nun is just a woman who's decided to live her life in a special way." Carol reached across the table to stop Nicky from making bubbles in his milk. "Mother Margaret is a very hardworking woman who cares for all of you very much."

Dorcas stabbed holes in her mashed potatoes. "Then why is she sending us away?"

"It isn't her decision," Carol explained, noting that she had her entire group's attention. "The home is old and not very safe anymore. The people who tell her what to do think it would be a good idea if you all lived with families rather than in a big, drafty old place like this."

"But it's not like being adopted," Dorcas argued. "Jenny Powell in Saint Joan's dorm lived in a foster home before she came here. She says kids come and go in it all the time. You get to like somebody, and they get moved away—or *you* do."

"I'm sure that happens sometimes." Carol knew it happened often, but she felt obliged to make the move sound as hopeful as possible, since she had no way of preventing it. "But many times kids get adopted into their foster family, or get to stay until they're grown."

Frank met Carol's eyes with a steady gaze. "Well, my dad's coming for me before we move. I know it."

"My mother's going to come for me in our limousine." Dorcas's voice was tight, but her plump chin was firm. "And Kathy and Candy and Nicky are all going to get adopted. None of us will have to worry about moving."

"Meanwhile," Frank said, putting a bite of broccoli into his mouth and making a face that brought the other children to giggles, "I'm going to eat this stuff, so that when I'm grown, I can play major league ball."

Carol encouraged them to eat, assuring them that she had firsthand information from Sister Celestine in the kitchen that dessert was cake and ice cream. As the children tucked into what remained of their vegetables, Carol watched them, feeling inadequate for the task that lay before her. She had to be strong to make them strong. They would not be able to handle the February move, if she didn't help them put their fantasies aside and face the truth. There was only one chance in a hundred that the younger children would be adopted before the move, and an even slimmer chance that Frank's father or Dorcas's mother would come for them.

She took comfort in the fact that she had two more months to deal with the situation, and she prayed that somewhere between now and then she would be inspired to find a solution.

"Pardon me."

Carol turned with a start as a long leg inserted itself between the table and the bench on which she sat. Suddenly she was face-to-face with Mike Rafferty, who sat astride the bench.

"Hi, Mike!" the children chorused.

He smiled at them, then turned his attention back to Carol. "Rick and Slugger are about to leave. Since the kids were so good about helping me move in, I want Slug to send something back to them. But I have to take a nose count. May I?"

"Of course," she replied, thinking absently that there was something so intriguing about that cautious smile. "But I'm sure they were happy to help without expecting a reward."

"Yeah," they confirmed, again in chorus. The denial wasn't entirely convincing.

Mike leaned his elbows on the table, almost huddling with the children who were now on their knees on the bench, leaning toward him. "I'm going to have Slug send you team shirts or hats. Which would you prefer?"

"Shirts!" "Hats!" The replies were simultaneous but indecisive.

Mike laughed. "Okay. A show of hands for shirts." The girls waved frantically. "And you guys want hats?" Frank and Nicky nodded, their faces alight at the prospect. "Okay. Thanks again for helping. See you around."

As he stood, Nicky reached across the table to stop him. "Hey, Mike."

"Yeah?"

"What about Carol? She didn't help move you in, but only 'cause Godzi—" Frank elbowed him in the ribs and he winced, his face reddening as the older boy glared at him. He glanced at Carol sheepishly. "'Cause Mother Margaret took her away to a meeting."

Carol saw Mike lower his eyes for a moment, as though to maintain his composure. She didn't have to wonder if he'd understood the children's private name for his sister. He leaned a knee on the bench and looked down at her.

"Miss Shaw?" he asked.

"It's Mrs.," Frank corrected him. "But we just call her Carol."

"Okay. A shirt, Carol?"

His brown eyes went over her swiftly, assessing her size. There was nothing remotely suggestive in the action, but Carol felt her cheeks grow warm. In the time she'd been at Saint Christopher's, she'd hardly seen a man besides Mr. Engbretson and Father Cunningham, who came on Sundays to say Mass. Being this close to Mike was making her wonder if she'd completely lost her social skills in the last year.

"That isn't necessary," she demurred quietly.

"Nicky thinks it is. A hat?" His eyes went to her hair and she found that easier to deal with.

"All right. A hat. Thank you."

"Okay, we're out of here. Bye, kids." Slugger grabbed Mike's arm and began to pull him away, waving at the children as he headed for the door. Mother Margaret followed with Rick, who turned to wave as the children called goodbyes.

"I can't believe Mike Rafferty is staying at Saint Christopher's," Frank said, watching them leave.

"Yeah," Nicky sighed. "I wish he could stay in our dorm."

"He can't, 'cause of Carol."

"What do you mean?"

"'Cause he's a guy and she's a lady," Frank informed him patiently.

"But we're guys," Nicky argued, "and Dorie, and Kathy and Candy . . ."

Frank rolled his eyes, obviously feeling the burden of his superior knowledge. "We're boys and they're girls. That's different. When men and ladies live in the same place, they have babies."

"No!" Dorcas leaned toward Nicky, apparently prepared to set him straight. "The man and the lady have to—"

Carol stood abruptly. "We have to carry our dishes to the kitchen and get back to the dorm to do our homework."

"But what do—" Nicky began.

"And then," Carol cut him off, "if we're very efficient and get finished early, we can watch *The Fox and the Hound*. I picked it up at the library today."

The children forgot the abruptly terminated conversation as they put their dishes in the kitchen, then walked back to the dorm in an excited cluster. Only Frank objected.

"When are you going to borrow *The Exterminator* from the library?"

Carol put an arm around his shoulders. "That might be a little hard on Nicky and the girls."

He sighed and paused at the cabin's small porch as the rest of the children hurried inside. He leaned against the rough pillar and looked up at the black sky. Not a star was visible through the thick cloud cover. "Do you ever wish you were somewhere else?"

Carol wrapped an arm around the other pillar and leaned her head against it. "In another time, maybe," she replied, "but not another place. I chose to be here."

There was an unusual thread of bitterness in Frank's voice. "Well, I didn't." He was quiet for a moment, then asked curiously, "You mean like the olden days, when you were little?"

"No. I mean like just two years ago, when everything in my life was perfect. We all like to hold on to those times, but they just don't stay perfect very long. Life takes all kinds of twists and turns, and you have to be ready for them."

"Like leaving here." He made a small sound of amusement in the dark. "It's funny, I don't really want to be here, but I don't want to leave, either. At least not to go to a foster home."

"I know," Carol replied softly. "Going someplace new is always frightening. But you're smart and friendly, Frank. You'll make friends in no time."

"I wish my dad would come."

Carol drew a breath for courage. "But if he doesn't, you can still go on, Frank. You'll just keep going, and when you're grown, you'll make a life for yourself just the way you want it."

"I'm gonna play for the Yankees, just like Mike."

"Perfect." Frank was strong and smart. Carol was convinced that he'd become a force to be reckoned with one day—if his father's rejection didn't drag him down. She put an arm around him and drew him into the cabin. "And I'll come and see all your games."

"REMEMBER to rest the arm and take your walks," Rick admonished his brother, as Mike tried to close the passenger side door on him. He pushed against it. "Will you listen? And give some serious thought to going home with me for Christmas. I can easily pick you up on the way."

"I'm staying," Mike insisted. "But thanks. You taking Paula home with you to meet Mom?"

Rick quirked his lips in an expression that combined disgust with amusement. "That's over."

Slugger, behind the wheel of the truck, laughed and shook his head. "Looks like neither one of you is scoring with the ladies."

Another hit. Mike didn't even let himself feel the hurt and judged that Rick's reaction, when he turned to Slugger with an irritated "Damn it, Slug!" was more in defense of his sibling than of himself.

Slugger was completely surprised by Rick's anger. "What?" he asked.

"Forget it, Slug," Mike suggested. "You drive carefully, hear? And thanks a lot. I owe you a favor." He leaned across his brother to shake his friend's hand. "And you take care, Rick."

"Sure. Bye, Mike."

Mike waved them off, then stood in the middle of the road until the truck's taillights were out of sight. Then he looked around at the quiet, shadowy darkness. This was what he wanted, he reminded himself—to get away from the critics and the fans and his well-meaning family to sort out his options for the future. He hadn't expected to feel lonely.

Up the road from his cabin was the dorm that Frank said he and the other children shared with Carol. Lights were shining, and there was probably activity inside, though he could hear no sound. He liked children, but in large numbers they scared him. They were so quick and so smart, and lately he felt as though he'd lost control over everything. They made him feel as though he couldn't keep up with them—as though he were getting old. In any other profession that would be a laughable thought at thirty-three. But in baseball it was a fact. Still, he'd have had a few good years left.

Hell. He turned back to the cabin, reminding himself that he'd resolved not to become morose. He wasn't here to brood, but to decide on a new direction. He flexed the arm that still hurt like the devil and walked up to the porch.

"Mike?"

He stopped with one foot on the porch steps, turning at the sound of the raspy voice. Frank emerged from the shadows into the dim light coming from the cabin's living room. He carried a plain white bowl heaped with something covered in plastic.

"All *right*," Mike said as the aroma of popcorn wafted to his nose. "Thanks, Frank. But are you supposed to be out?"

"Carol sent me. She's standing on the porch, watching me." Frank moved back a couple of steps, away from the bushes that surrounded the cabin, and pointed. Mike followed him and saw Carol standing under the dorm porch light. She was clutching a sweater around her.

"We always have popcorn after homework. Tonight she borrowed *The Fox and the Hound* from the library. I'd rather see *The Exterminator*, but she doesn't think the little kids could take it."

Mike nodded. "She's probably right. I've seen it. Thanks for running this over."

"Sure. Well..." Frank hesitated, then started back toward the dorm. "See ya tomorrow."

"Right." Mike waved in the direction of the porch and Carol waved back. He saw Frank clear the porch steps, then both of them disappeared inside.

Mike pulled the plastic aside and tossed a kernel of popcorn into his mouth as he went into the cabin. There was something about popcorn, he noted with surprise, that alleviated loneliness. Thoughtfulness from a pretty lady didn't hurt, either.

Chapter Three

Cold popcorn for breakfast didn't dispel loneliness as well as hot popcorn at night, Mike thought the next morning. There was the germ of an important truth there, he decided as he made his way along a narrow trail between tall, swaying pines. Meg had told him that the trail wound down the mountainside about a mile to a jutting cliff where the Cape Delancey lighthouse stood.

The wind moving through the pines made a loud, mournful noise. Crows glided effortlessly over the tops of the trees on the strong currents of air, calling to one another with strident sounds. He could hear the crash of the surf, though he couldn't see it yet, and he wondered why he'd thought the coast would be a place for quiet reflection. The noise was deafening.

"Morning!" a breathless voice called as a gray and yellow blur passed him, surprising him out of his reflections. His first thought was that one of the older children was running away. Before he could focus on the figure, it disappeared around a bend in the road, but red bangs visible under the cuff of the gray watch cap had identified the passerby as the children's dorm mother, Carol Shaw. *Mrs.* Carol Shaw, according to Frank.

"Morning!" he shouted back, but too late. As he continued to walk, he wondered what had brought her to this remote spot. Remembering how Meg was always complaining about the school's tight budget, he felt sure it wasn't the salary. A need to get away? A divorce? Or was she simply the brooding Brontë type who loved a stormy atmosphere and emotional upheaval?

As Mike rounded the bend, the path broke out of the trees, presented him with the spectacular view of boiling surf crashing against the tree-covered cliffside, then wound away into the mist. A guardrail on his left protected him from a forty-foot drop to the ocean as he continued to walk. A chilling wind whipped around him, and he pulled up his collar against it.

Looking ahead, he saw the path he was following lean out over the ocean in a shallow arc. In the bend of the arc stood a lighthouse, tall and white and steadfast, its light winking into the mist at measured intervals. Carol appeared from the ocean side of the lighthouse, starting back toward him at a steady stride. The broad yellow stripe across the chest of her jacket was the only color against the gunmetal gray of water and sky.

He watched her come closer and closer, her legs in their gray sweats well coordinated and steady, her arms pumping enough to give her momentum, but not enough to exhaust her. She was aiming for endurance rather than speed. No short-stop potential there, he decided, but she'd be good at center field.

About halfway between him and the lighthouse, she stopped, leaning forward with her hands on her knees. He noticed as he approached that her gloveless hands were bright pink. She straightened just as he drew close. Her smile and her eyes were bright, her cheeks a shade somewhere between the pink of her hands and the red of her bangs.

"Hi," she said as he paused beside her. She was breathless and stopped to swallow. "The kids missed you at breakfast."

"I overslept," he confessed. "Thank you for sending the popcorn over last night."

"You're welcome. The kids thought we should do something to welcome our new neighbor."

"They must be in school this morning."

She nodded, her breath coming more evenly now. "Candy goes only to afternoon kindergarten, but on Mondays, Wednesdays and Fridays, Sister Celestine bakes cookies and lets the small ones help. It gives me a chance to run."

He looked a little wan, Carol thought. He was such a large man, legs long, shoulders broad, that one presumed an underlying vitality. But looking into his face in the light of day, she could see a slight pallor and a faint sensitivity in his eyes, as though he were recovering from an illness or an emotional blow. She remembered that in his case there had been both.

He smiled. "Well, if the cookies are for lunch, I'll have to be sure to show up. I brought a stove with me, but no groceries."

"I'm taking Frank to town tomorrow afternoon to the dentist. You're welcome to join us and do your shopping." Wondering if that was too bold a suggestion after just having met him, Carol added quickly, "Or we could bring some things back for you." Mother Margaret had asked her to keep an eye on him, but she probably didn't mean a close eye.

"Thank you." His smile was broader than before. He looked down into her unusual khaki eyes and couldn't decide which of the possibilities he'd considered before applied to her—divorce or escape. She was very natural, if a little shy, and she seemed both curious about him and afraid to pry. Which was just how he felt about her. "Do you have to hurry back to Candy?" he asked. "Or can you walk with me to the lighthouse?"

She wedged a bright pink finger under the elastic cuff of her jacket sleeve and checked her watch. "I have about forty minutes. Come on. The view from there is magnificent."

"Wait." He surprised himself as well as her as he pulled off his lined leather gloves and handed them over. "Please," he said. "Put these on. If you go jogging in this kind of weather, you should wear gloves."

Carol slipped them on, feeling the warmth from his hands as her fingers burrowed inside the soft, thick lining. "Frank lost his, so I gave him mine," she explained, laughing as she discovered she was able to fold over the last two inches of the fingers. "That's something I'll have to shop for tomorrow afternoon. Thank you. I guess a good glove is something a ball player would never be without."

He glanced down at her and smiled as they followed the narrow path. "I won't have to worry about that anymore."

"Mother Margaret told me you had an accident," she admitted cautiously.

"I was on my way home from the airport, and came bumper to bumper with a pickup that had strayed onto my side of the road," he explained. "The lane wasn't big enough for both of us."

Carol stopped in her tracks, the full impact of the coincidence startling her into immobility. In an instant another image flashed through her mind—seat belts holding lifeless bodies in a lump of torn metal, ambulances whining, horrified bystanders. Fear, anguish and anger sent out cautious feelers from deep inside her. For a brief moment she let her feelings hold sway, frowning involuntarily at the mental picture.

"Carol?" Mike put an arm around her, frightened by her sudden pallor and sincerely afraid she might faint.

She smiled at him, dealing firmly with the negative emotions that tried every day to wear her down.

"I'm fine," she assured him, taking a deep breath of air. "I pushed myself too hard on that run." Suddenly becoming aware of the strength of the arm that was holding her, she changed the subject. "You seem to have full use of your arm."

Reluctant to let her go, he found that she took the decision out of his hands as she adroitly stepped forward, urging him with a look to follow her. "I do," he replied, suspecting that the look in her eyes had nothing to do with a hard run. "As long as I don't do anything strenuous with it, like pitch or swing a bat, or tag someone running at me like a locomotive."

They reached the curve of land on which the lighthouse stood, and Carol led him around it to the guardrail. The uniform gray of sea and sky seemed to enclose them as though they had stepped into infinity. Carol took a deep breath and closed her eyes. There was color in her cheeks again, and Mike felt himself relax. "I love it here. The air is so clean. For thousands of miles it hasn't touched anything but ocean."

Mike leaned his elbows on the railing beside her. "I'm so used to full dugouts and crowds in the tens of thousands that I find being this remote a little hard to get used to."

"If you get lonely," Carol suggested with a wry note in her voice, "all you have to do is join us in the cafeteria or on the playground. You'll get enough noise and activity to make Yankee Stadium seem like the Arctic. And with Christmas coming, the kids will be even more hyper than usual."

Mike frowned. "Aren't all the kids leaving next week?"

"All but mine." Carol looked out at the gray ocean, her eyes unfocused, seeing something else. "The powers that be thought it would be best to make the move now, so the children can spend Christmas in foster homes where they'll be treated specially, individually. But we don't have formal releases signed on my kids, and Mother Margaret wants to send them off ready for eventual adoption."

"Is it just coincidence that all the children lacking releases are in your dorm?"

She turned to face him, smiling. "We should be heading back. No, it isn't. I was hired to care for these particular children. Mother Margaret could see this coming and put them together in a dorm, so they'd at least have each other when the other kids left." She kicked a rock in her path with enough force to make it ricochet off the mountainside and fall over the other edge. It was a long moment before they heard the splash. "I wish I could take them all away to some magic island, where they could have all the things other kids have, and be guaranteed that they'll never have to move again."

"Permanence and security are important to everyone."

Carol tore off her hat with an agitated gesture, running her fingers through her hair as though needing the freedom it gave her. "There's no such thing as permanence and security," she said. "But nobody should have to learn that until he's grown."

She stopped in the middle of the path. Mike knew there was more to her statement than the simple consequence of their discussion. It meant something more to her. For a moment he thought she might tell him. Those unusual eyes rose to meet his, wide, vulnerable, beautiful. Then they fell and she pulled off his gloves. When she looked up at him again, she smiled, but he knew the gesture concealed something from him. "Thanks for the use of your gloves. I have to run back to get Candy. I'll send Frank for you about four tomorrow afternoon?"

"Fine. See you at lunch."

Her smile was regretful. "I have playground duty at lunch. Bye."

Pulling on his gloves, he watched her run up the trail, disappearing into the narrowing arch of trees. His gloves were warm and smelled faintly of roses. As he began to walk on, it occurred to him that his baseball career might be over, but life still had a challenge or two to offer him.

"YOUR FIRST DAY at Saint Christopher's must have gone all right. I didn't see you at all, except for meals." Mike sat on a small flowered sofa in the parlor of the convent that housed the sisters. The room was cheerfully decorated in pastels, with a large wooden crucifix over the doorway that separated it from the dining room. The sound of feminine laughter could be heard from another part of the house. Mother Margaret placed a tray on a small, dark wooden coffee table. She poured coffee from a china pot into two matching mugs. "I thought you might come and visit me."

"I wouldn't intrude upon an important personage like yourself," Mike teased. "I'm here to make some decisions, not to get in your way. And anyway, I was busy all day. I had a morning jog with Carol Shaw, lunch in the cafeteria with the kids from her dorm, and I spent the afternoon with Tom Clancy. I've been meaning to catch up with his books for months."

She looked pleased with his schedule. "Good. But you know you can pester me any time you like. I grew up with the burden of keeping you and Rick entertained. I can handle it."

Mike frowned at her as he accepted a cup of coffee. "Aren't nuns supposed to be compassionate and self-sacrificing and spiritually inspiring?"

"You're so naive." She poured her own coffee. "We take vows of poverty, chastity and obedience. There's nothing in there about being holy—well, there probably is somewhere, but I don't think it applies to one's younger brothers." She offered Mike a dessert plate covered with a paper napkin. Then she pulled the protective napkin away.

"Twinkies!" he exclaimed.

"Shh!" She looked surreptitiously toward the doorway, through which Mike could hear the sound of the other nuns' laughter. "It's my private stash. Some vices aren't easily turned away from. You, of all people, should understand that."

"And thank you again, Meg," Mike said, taking a Twinkie and halving it with one bite. He chewed and swallowed. "You know fame and fortune haven't changed me."

"That's the trouble," she said, nibbling on hers. "You were insufferable before fame and fortune struck."

"You're so good for my ego, Sis."

"I wouldn't think a celebrity would have to have his ego boosted."

"I'm not a celebrity anymore," he reminded. "I'm just an ordinary guy."

"Will you find that hard to deal with?"

Seeing the serious concern in his sister's face, Mike shook his head, grinning. "No. I can live without the adulation and the publicity." He brought the coffee mug to his lips and hesitated a moment before taking a sip. Then he leaned back into the corner of the sofa. "I am a little concerned about finding something useful to do that doesn't involve living on endorsements or getting involved in Rafferty Office Supplies. I love the family dearly, but I want to do my own thing."

Mother Margaret nodded. "I can understand that."

He gave her a grin. "Then I must have said it wrong. That's the first nice thing you've said to me all evening."

"What did you and Carol talk about?" she asked.

"The children," he replied, resting one Reebok-clad foot on the opposite knee. "And helping them escape to a magic island, where all their needs would be met."

Mother Margaret nodded thoughtfully, smiling. "We worked out that little scenario together one rainy Sunday afternoon while the children were playing in the gym. I got to be monarch, as I recall. Carol felt more suited to the duties of sheriff."

Mike laughed at the picture that came to mind. "We also discussed Saint Christopher's, and the purity of the air at the lighthouse. And she invited me to go to town with her tomorrow afternoon, when she takes Frank to the dentist."

Mother Margaret broke a second Twinkie in half, gave one piece to Mike and studied the other with pensive gravity. "She's a very special woman."

A moment passed, then Mike asked quietly, "Why is she here?"

Mother Margaret looked up, frowning. "What do you mean? She works here."

"Why? I can see that she loves working with the children, but it's such a remote spot for such a young and pretty woman. Did she have a bad marriage? Is she running away from something?"

"You're not doing either," she reasoned, "and yet you're here."

"For two months. She's been here almost a year, and probably would stay if you didn't have to close in February."

She looked away to pour more coffee, and Mike recognized the gesture as evasion. "Why don't you ask her? More coffee?"

He held out his cup. "Please. Because I don't know her well enough," he admitted, unembarrassed, "and I'm curious."

"Then ask her," she repeated. "Maybe she'd like someone to talk to about it."

He put his cup aside. "So she is hiding something."

"To some degree I guess we all are."

"Not me." Mike denied the suggestion with a laugh. "My life is front-page news. Or it was. And anyway, don't get philosophical with me. I find her intriguing and would like to know her better."

"Then the best way to do that—"

"—Is to ask her." He nodded as he stood. "Well, Sister sister, you've been such a lot of help this evening. Thank you so much. Need anything from town tomorrow? More Twinkies?"

She shushed him again as she walked him to the door. "Please. Consider my image. Did Carol mention that we have lots of plans for you, beginning next week?"

He put his hand over hers on the knob, his dark eyebrows lowering. "What does that mean?"

"A little of your artistic talent will be required, a little of your resourcefulness and your physical prowess."

Distrusting the sound of that, he put his left arm to his right shoulder and winced dramatically. "I have this bad arm...."

"Fortunately, pine and cedar boughs aren't that heavy." Her smile was merciless. "We're having a Christmas party the night before the children leave. We want it to be special. And Carol's kids will be the only ones here for Christmas, and we want everything to be festive for them."

He expelled a long-suffering sigh. "All right, but I draw the line at being Santa Claus."

"Mr. Engbretson's going to be Santa Claus."

"And I suppose there won't be a glass of eggnog to be had in this whole place."

She shrugged noncommittally. "I'm not sure, but the good and charitable are often rewarded beyond their dreams."

"Mmm." He sounded doubtful. "Then I can expect nothing. Is that what you're telling me?"

"Depends on how you deport yourself, my son," she replied with an affected air of sanctity. "Good night."

Laughing, Mike wound his way through the shadows and past Carol's dorm to his cabin. As he opened the door, his foot brushed something near the threshold. As he leaned down to see what it was, the aroma of popcorn rose to meet him. The plastic-covered bowl was still warm as he carried it inside.

"I *AM* SICK." Frank lay atop his bed, arms folded, lips set. "I can't be taken to town," he insisted, then added on a frail note, "I probably shouldn't even be moved."

Carol had taken his temperature and found that it was normal. Consulting the other children about how he had seemed during the school day led her to believe that the virulent attack of undisclosed symptoms had come on suddenly.

"He was fighting with Billy Miller in front of the chapel after school," Dorcas squealed from the doorway of his room. "Mother Margaret gave him a demerit for it. He's awful close to having to scrub pans in the kitchen."

"I'm gonna kill you!" Frank shouted, sitting up with renewed vigor and deadly purpose. Then seeing Carol's raised eyebrows, he lay back against the pillows and added in the same frail voice as before, "As soon as the pain stops."

"He's just chicken to go to the dentist," Dorcas diagnosed, adjusting her glasses and throwing a fat braid over her shoulder.

"What are you?" Frank demanded from his sickbed. "Dr. Dorky?"

As Dorcas took several steps toward his bed, determined to finish him before the doubtful illness did, Carol intercepted her. "Please take the other kids to Saint Joan's dorm. Mrs. McGinnis is going to keep an eye on you until we get back from town."

"But he—"

"Now, Dorie."

With a groan of disgust at the injustice of it all, Dorcas complied. Carol sat down on the edge of Frank's bed. "Mike was going to come to town with us."

He was silent for a moment, his eyes filled with speculation. Then he closed them weakly. "I wouldn't want him to catch this. With his bad arm, he might just . . . die."

Carol stood. "I see. Well, you just lie there and stay quiet."

Mike responded to the knock on his cabin door with a smile and the empty popcorn bowl. "Hi," he said. "Thanks again for sharing. I thought you were going to send Frank."

Carol beckoned him to follow her to the dorm. "Frank's had a terminal attack of novocaine nerves. I'm getting nowhere with him, but he might listen to you. Would you talk to him?"

They had reached the porch of the dorm, and Carol ran up the steps, turning to see that Mike remained at the bottom. When she frowned at him, he smiled. "I don't suppose this is the time to tell you that the last time I went to the dentist, Slugger and another teammate dragged me all the way."

"No," she said firmly, but with an answering smile. "Adults have all the same fears as children. The only thing that makes us different is that we put our fears aside to help them deal with theirs." Then without giving him an opportunity for rebuttal, she opened the door. "This way."

Mike followed Carol through a living room that was tidier than any room he had ever kept. The white walls were adorned with children's artwork and awards.

Frank lay on his bed in the fetal position, his arms crossed over his stomach as he moaned pathetically. Mike did notice that the moaning hadn't begun until he cleared the threshold of the room. With a hopeful crossing of her fingers, Carol left him to it.

Mike sat on the edge of the bed and put a hand to the boy's shoulder. "I hear you've contracted a terrible disease," he said gravely.

Frank nodded. "I'm leaving everything to you."

"Thanks, Frank." Mike turned him gently onto his back. "But I'd rather you stuck around so we could talk baseball. We haven't gotten to do that yet." He put a hand to the boy's forehead. "I think your temperature's coming down."

"I'm probably getting the chills."

Seriously fearing that playing along was going to get him nowhere because Frank was smarter than he was, Mike tried a different strategy. "Scared of the dentist, huh?"

"No, I'm sick."

"Don't blame you," Mike went on. "I hate the needle most of all. Thinking about it is enough to make me brush my teeth *four* times a day. You supposed to have a filling?"

"Yeah." The admission was full of despondency and dread.

"Had one before?"

"Yeah." Frank sat up, his expression belligerent. "So don't try to tell me it doesn't hurt, 'cause I know it does."

"It does," Mike agreed, leaning sideways to rest his weight on the mattress. "But it's only for about a minute. After that your mouth is numb and you don't feel anything. Hurts a little later, after you've come home and the numbness has worn off, but by then you don't care, because it's over and it's a lot easier to be brave."

"But that first minute's a killer. When he puts the needle in . . ." Frank mimed pressing the plunger on a syringe, his face distorted like that of a mad dentist. "Then he wiggles it all around. Ugh!" He shuddered.

Mike barely restrained himself from doing the same. "If you know it's going to hurt and you're ready for it, you can handle it. A man has to do what's right for himself, even when it hurts."

Frank's brown eyes studied him with moody suspicion. "Why is it right for me when it's going to hurt?"

"Have you ever seen an old man without teeth?" Mike asked.

Frank thought about that. "A friend of my dad's had false teeth."

"Did you ever seen him without them?"

"No."

"Well, they look sort of like this." Sucking in his lips so that they wrapped around his teeth, giving him the appearance of not having any, he banged them together, talking in a high, broken voice.

As Frank collapsed into guffaws of laughter, Mike dropped the role and said evenly, "We're not supposed to laugh at people like that, because losing teeth isn't funny, and they probably all wish they had brushed better and more often. But you know what's even worse than that?"

Still laughing, Frank gasped for breath. "No, what?"

"It's an eleven-year-old kid without teeth because he was afraid to go to the dentist. Let me see how you'd look."

Frank mimicked Mike's earlier facial expression, and they collapsed into laughter together.

Carol didn't know what she had expected. Listening from just beyond the doorway, she had thought Mike might encourage Frank to be brave by repeating some heroic baseball story, or by simply urging him to be manly and brave. Though his absurd imitation of a toothless old man had her laughing as hard as they were, she was touched, too, by the honest, easy, understanding encouragement he had offered.

Carol stood alone in the corridor while Mike helped Frank into his jacket. His accident might have ended his career, she reflected, and divested him of his celebrity, but it seemed to her that he still had all the makings of a star.

Chapter Four

"Ah cat eat fo free ahrs!" Frank bemoaned his fate as the dentist's assistant walked him into the waiting room. Carol rose from her chair, putting an arm around him. Frank loved to complain about things—bedtime, cafeteria food, the home's rules—but when it came to matters of personal pain or grief, he complained very little. Seeing him pale and wide-eyed, with a hand to his swollen cheek, made her frown in concern.

"He shouldn't chew on that for three hours," the other woman translated, then added with a reassuring smile. "He'll be fine, and he was very brave." As Frank rolled his eyes, appreciating but dismissing the praise, she said, "He can drink through a straw, but nothing too hot or too cold. Keep brushing, Frank, so you'll only have to come back for cleanings."

As Carol and Frank stepped out onto the street, Frank tried to smile, but only one half of his jaw responded. "Don't you hate people who are cheerful when you're not?" he asked, having to speak slowly.

Laughing, she squeezed his shoulders and began to walk toward the car. "Yes," she admitted. "But that's her job. The way most people feel about dentists, they'd never go beyond the waiting room if she came out acting grumpy."

"I guess. There's Mike!" The tone in his voice changed as he waved madly to the man sprinting across the main street toward them. A cloudy, winter darkness was already falling, and Mike, clad in jeans and a dark jacket, moved against its backdrop like a shadow. Waving back, he waited for them at the corner, the streetlight picking out his smile, his wind-tossed hair and the grocery bag he held in one arm.

Frank pulled away from Carol and ran toward him. Carol saw Frank talk excitedly and point to his jaw. Mike leaned down to inspect it, then nodded in commiseration and approval.

"The dental assistant even said I was brave," Frank was saying as Carol reached them.

"She said *very* brave," Carol corrected. As Frank basked in the praise, she looked at Mike over the boy's head and smiled. "I see your shopping was successful."

For a moment she thought he hadn't heard her. His eyes seemed to be roaming her hair, her mouth, her cheeks. When they met her eyes, he returned her smile, coming out of whatever private thought had claimed his attention. "I've got all the junk food basics. I'm supposed to be working on a book while I'm here, and I figured I'd need things to chew on while I'm thinking."

Frank stood on tiptoe to peer inside the bag. "Cheetos!" he reported with enthusiasm. "Ritz crackers, Milk Duds, sardines, macadamia nuts, cheese with little green things in it..."

"Jalapeño," Mike explained.

Frank raised his head out of the bag and settled back on his feet. "What's that?"

"Hot pepper."

"Wow." Frank's amazement was quiet but sincere. "It must be great to be able to eat what you want instead of the yucky stuff you have to eat to be healthy. I wonder what it's like to have cheese with pepper in it for breakfast instead of cereal?"

Carol started off in the direction of the car and Mike and Frank followed. "I'll bet even Mike doesn't do that," she said over her shoulder.

"Actually, I did once," Mike said. "It was on a red-eye from New York to L.A., and I hadn't eaten since lunch."

"What's a red-eye?" Frank wanted to know.

"A late-night flight."

"Wow."

Mike smiled at him. "I had cheese and crackers in my carryon, and Slugger and I chowed down at about four in the morning. It was two days before I could eat again."

"Wow."

The station wagon was in sight when a plump, white-haired woman, who was limping down the steps of a tiny church, spotted Carol and waved. Leaning heavily on a cane, the older woman made slow progress, so Carol met her halfway.

"How are you doing, dear?" Mike heard the sympathy in the question leveled at Carol and tensed in curiosity.

"I'm fine, Mrs. Curtis," Carol replied, her tone kind but firm, obviously intended to ward off further questions. "You're looking very well."

"Thank you, dear. It's so nice to see you smiling."

Even on such a brief acquaintance Mike knew Carol's smile was forced, and he watched it become more so as she reached a hand out to draw him closer, apparently still trying to divert the woman's attention from herself. "Mrs. Curtis, I'd like you to meet Michael Rafferty. He's spending some time with us at Saint Chris's."

"How nice." It was obvious that the name meant nothing to her, and Mike took her hand, enjoying the anonymity. "Well, you're a handsome devil."

"Mrs. Curtis is the housekeeper here at Saint Peter's." Carol pointed to the small church behind them. "Well... we're on our way home now...."

As Carol began to back away, Mrs. Curtis grabbed her, the cane tracing a lethal arc in the air as she wrapped that arm around her. Mike pulled Frank out of the way, just in time to avoid a possible beheading. When Mrs. Curtis released Carol, Mike was surprised to find the old woman's eyes wide and brimming with tears. "Day by day, dear," she said softly. "Time heals everything."

Mrs. Curtis disappeared into an old Cadillac parked at the curb, and Carol headed for the station wagon at a steady pace. Frank left Mike's side and hurried to catch up with her, putting his hand into hers. Mike watched him look up at her and wait for her to look back. It was a moment before she did, but he saw her smile and squeeze his hand. There was comfort offered and accepted there, and Mike felt a growing need to know why. Apparently Frank understood Carol's secret and the importance of handling it with sensitivity and silence. The kid was amazing.

Carol unlocked the passenger side door, letting Frank into the back seat. As she turned to walk around to the driver's side, she found Mike's body trapping her between the car and the door he held open. Unguarded, her expression was strained and anguished.

Mike sensed a plea for silence and swiftly changed tactics. Instead of asking her if she was all right, he smiled. "Why don't I drive home?" he suggested.

She looked back at him for a moment, her eyes registering his understanding. She returned his smile, but he saw that it required effort. "Because this old wagon doesn't have power steering, and you have to be careful of your arm. Just sit back and relax and nibble on your jalapeño cheese."

For four blocks the after-work traffic was thick. They sat at a red light and watched two men at work on ladders on opposite sides of the main street.

"What are they doing?" Frank wanted to know, leaning forward over the back of the front seat.

"Hanging the city's Christmas decorations," Carol replied, accelerating as the traffic began to move. "Buckle your seat belt, Frank." She glanced over at Mike, who was sitting on his belt, and grinned. "You, too, Mike. Mother Margaret's rules."

He quickly complied. "Don't tell her you had to remind me."

Relieved that she had survived the encounter with Mrs. Curtis, Carol felt bold. "That kind of favor ought to be worth something."

Mike's cautious smile spread even more cautiously. "What did you have in mind?"

"A bite of the cheese."

"You got it." He delved into his pocket, then into the bag.

"I didn't mean this very moment," she laughed.

"I don't want interest to accrue on this debt." Applying the small blade of his pocket knife to the packaging, he removed the plastic, then sliced off a small corner. Snatching a Kleenex from the box on the dash, he dropped the cheese onto it, then handed it over.

"I can't have any," Frank complained from the back seat.

Mike glanced at him over his shoulder. "You can stop by tomorrow, when you can chew again, and I'll let you try it." When he turned back to Carol, she was already fanning her mouth. Delving into the bag once more, he came up with a can of Pepsi. Pulling the tab, he handed it to her. "So, you're a sissy," he said.

She was silent for a long five seconds before a laugh erupted from her. "Yes, I suppose so. But you'd better hide that from Sister Claire—she'd love it."

"I can't believe it's gonna be Christmas!" Frank said, pointing out the window to the stores filled with toys, glittery clothes and gifts to tempt even the most controlled of shoppers. "I'm going to ask for Nikes, a Swiss Army knife, binoculars and a baseball."

Carol caught his eye in the rearview mirror. "I thought you told me just the other day that you don't believe in Santa anymore."

She saw his reflection shrug. "I don't. But somebody else might want to get me something."

Mike laughed. "That's the spirit, Frank. Cover all your bases."

Carol sent him a quelling glance. "That's not admirable."

"It's very practical," he replied, still laughing, "and you've got to admire that."

"Carol, look!" Frank spoke excitedly. "The new owner is putting lights up on your old house."

Mike looked out the window to see four simple, two-story houses in a row. The third one had window boxes filled with some hardy green plant, and a perfect picket fence that bordered the sidewalk, then marched in parallel columns between the neighbors on both sides and disappeared into the darkness at the back of the house. A man on a ladder was tracing the outline of the house with lights, while a woman standing on the lawn directed him. She held her sweater closed with one hand and gestured widely with the other.

Surprised to learn that Carol had lived in Pointer's Beach, Mike turned to her to remark on the fact, and found her gripping the wheel with unnecessary strength. Her pallor was bright in the dark interior of the car, her slender frame rigid against the small-town scene moving past her window.

"Carol..." Frank tried to call her attention to the house again as it disappeared behind them.

"I have to concentrate on the road, Frank," she replied with deliberate patience.

"It's going to look beautiful," he said.

She swallowed, and Mike saw the faintest shudder run through her. "That's nice," she replied.

"GOOD THING you've got groceries," Carol said as she pulled into the small garage behind the home's main building. Children streamed down the paths toward their dorms. "We missed dinner."

"I'm not very hungry," Frank said as he followed Mike out of the car. "And my mouth hurts."

"How about some juice?" Carol suggested, pulling him into her shoulder. "Or I could see if the cafeteria's got any Jell-O."

He leaned against her wearily. "No, thanks. I'll just wait until I can have something good."

As they followed the path that wound through the forest of evergreens to the dorms and cabins, Mike inhaled the cold night air. It was tangy with the fragrance of fir and salt and a suggestion of snow. It stung his eyes and nostrils and invaded his lungs with invigorating freshness. He suddenly felt restless, unwilling to go back to his quiet cabin and the solitude he'd thought he needed so much.

"Thanks for the ride to town," he said as they rounded a curve in the path. The dorm was in sight, though all its windows were dark.

"We were going anyway." Carol kicked a clump of tiny hemlock cones that lay in her path. "And Frank enjoyed your company."

Mike smiled in the darkness. "*Frank* enjoyed my company? That's the last bite of jalapeño cheese you'll ever get."

Her giggle surprised him. "That's the last bite of jalapeño cheese I'd want, thank you." Carol stopped suddenly, her eyes narrowing on the darkness surrounding the dorm that stood a few yards ahead of them.

"What?" Mike tensed beside her, putting a hand out to stop Frank.

"Someone's on the porch," Carol said.

A slim figure was outlined in the thin winter moonlight, sitting on the porch steps, staring up at the moon. Then the head was lowered in a gesture that spoke of burdens and doubt. Carol took another step forward and the figure rose, turning in the direction of the sound. The moonlight caught the gossamer sheen of a veil, and Carol expelled a laugh of relief. "Sister Claire!"

At the same moment the sister called, "Carol?"

"What are you doing here?" Carol asked, closing the distance between them. Then, remembering the impression she'd had of a great burden, she added softly, "What is it?"

Sister Claire came down the few steps, her smile bright, her customary vivacity in place. "Sister Cel sent me to tell you she's saved you dinner."

"Please tell her thank you, but Frank doesn't feel like eating, and I've got to get the other kids."

"Mrs. McGinnis says she'll bring them back after you've had dinner. They're doing homework with her dorm kids. I can stay with Frank." Sister Claire smiled down at the boy. "What do you say, Frank? Want to play rummy? My Rambo poster against your promise to fix the bad drawer in my desk."

"Ask for a handicap," Mike suggested to Frank. "After all, you've been medicated."

"Thanks, Mr. Rafferty," Sister Claire said wryly, accepting the dorm keys from Carol. "That could have been my edge." She indicated the grocery bag in his arms. "Do you want me to stash that until you've had dinner?"

He held the bag away as she reached for it. "I don't know. There's jalapeño cheese in it, and Carol already warned me to keep it away from you."

Now the wry look was turned on Carol. "Thank you. It'll be a cold day in that hot place when I mention your petitions in my prayers." With a look of affronted dignity she took the bag from Mike, turned with Frank to climb the steps, then asked, loudly enough for her voice to carry, "Do you keep crackers in the dorm?"

"LOOK INTO MY EYES."

Carol looked up from the fragrant, succulent stew Sister Celestine had kept hot for them and instinctively did as Mike asked. Absently halving the corn muffin in her hands, she noted that his eyes had tiny flecks of gold in them, like the path of some faraway galaxy. They were kind and quiet, and it was a moment before she realized she was staring. She lowered her eyes and reached for the butter knife. "Yes?"

He pushed the cube of butter toward her. They sat alone on opposite sides of an empty table in the empty cafeteria. There was a distant rattle of pots and pans in the kitchen. "Do I look like an elf to you?"

She looked up again and gave his handsome face a studious perusal, careful to avoid his eyes. Then she took a bite of muffin and shook her head. "Not unless you've had your ears bobbed." Her eyes swept the line of his shoulders in the thick white sweater. "And to the best of my knowledge, elves are very small creatures. Why?"

"Meg has assigned me to you," he explained, blowing upon a spoonful of stew, "to help you gather and put up fir and cedar boughs for the Christmas party. Sounds like elf work to me." With a dramatic wince he raised the arm that held the spoon. "And I have this weak arm."

She laughed. "Please. I've already dealt with one deathbed scene today. And anyway, you have a gift for elf work. If it hadn't been for you, Frank would still have an aching cavity, so accept your assignment with good grace. Frank will want to do all the cutting, and Mr. Engbretson said I can use his truck to carry the boughs back, so all you and your weak arm have to do is offer moral support…and help me keep five children within the sound of my voice in the woods."

"We could tie them to trees until we need them."

Carol shook her head. "Not an acceptable solution."

"That's odd," he said in surprise. "I distinctly remember Meg doing that to Rick and me."

Carol laughed again. "I'm sure you must have made her desperate. Actually, you'll love being with the children at this time. They get beside themselves with excitement, but instead of being annoying, their mood becomes infectious. You end up having more fun than you ever thought possible."

"I'm supposed to be resting," he reminded teasingly.

"Plenty of time for that when you get old."

He didn't feel old, Mike thought as he finished his stew and went to work on an apple cobbler that was redolent of nutmeg, cinnamon and butter. Days ago he'd felt over the hill, thrown away. Tonight he felt curiously alive, even guardedly hopeful. He still had no idea what to do with his life, his future, but at the moment, the need to make a decision didn't seem to be the burden it once was. He was content to let the days pass, to do his elfish duties—and to get to know this woman.

As his mind formed those thoughts, Carol looked up from her dessert, and he started guiltily, afraid she had read his mind. But she simply looked around at the empty, silent cafeteria and shook her head. "I haven't had so quiet a meal in . . . well . . . years."

Mike sipped the coffee Sister Celestine had brought. "Did you work with children before you came here?" he asked. That was just the right tone, he thought. Interest without prying concern.

Then she looked up at him and he saw in her eyes that, right tone or not, he wasn't fooling anyone. Their dusty-gold gaze swept his face, making it clear that she answered because she chose to. "Only my own."

So she had children. Before taking time to think, he asked, "Are they with their father?"

Her head came up slowly, and when she looked at him, he realized in surprise that eyes could scream. The pain in them was so naked, so strong, that it seemed to have a sound that rang over and over again in his ears. He couldn't remember ever regretting anything so much in his life as having asked that thoughtless question.

"Yes," she replied finally. She put down her fork, put her napkin to her mouth, then pushed her plate away, straightening her back. "They were killed last December in a car accident, on their way to the airport to pick up my father." She took a sip of coffee and her swallow was audible. "Dad had come from Denver to spend Christmas with us."

"God, Carol..." Mike reached across the table to cover her free hand with his two, but he had no idea what to say. He had never seen so much pain in a woman's face—in anyone's face. Her simple beauty seemed to make it that much uglier.

"Things were frantic in the insurance office where I worked," she went on, "and I wasn't able to get away. But Jon, my husband, was a self-employed carpenter. He gave himself the afternoon off." Her eyes were dry and unfocused as she thought back, her voice frighteningly detached. "Gale and Becky were out of school for the holiday break, and Jon took them along. They wore their Sunday dresses and I put ribbons in their hair." She paused to take a breath and swallow again. "They had pale blond hair like their father. They were so excited that their grandfather was coming."

"Carol, stop." Mike squeezed her fingers and became aware that her nails were embedded in the palm of his hand. He held fast to her, unaware of the pain. "I'm so sorry. I...I..." He'd wanted to know, he thought, hating himself, because he'd thought there was some dramatic, romantic story attached to her presence at Saint Chris's. He somehow hadn't expected her secret to be full of such gritty reality. Not knowing what else to do, he poured more coffee into her cup and placed it near her free hand.

She took a sip, swallowed, then drew a deep sigh. She had never lost control, but she'd been caught in the grip of a pain so terrible that he'd have preferred to see her weep, because then he'd have known that she was shedding it. But she remained so still, so dry-eyed, that he knew her telling him had only increased the pain, not eased it. Her eyes were quieter now, but he thought uneasily that she had only stored the grief.

"Actually, I'm fine," she said, her voice sounding normal, if a little weary. "I've learned to keep going. Having the kids to fuss over and laugh with has brought me further than I ever thought I'd be able to go. And your sister's been wonderful to me...." She gave him a smile that helped him relax a little. "So don't expect me to sympathize with you because she tied you to a tree." Realizing that she still held his hand, she drew hers away, a little embarrassed, then gasped at the sight of blood under her fingernails. "Mike—!"

She took his hand and turned it over, revealing the perfect scalloped cuts left by her fingernails in the pad of skin at the base of his fingers. Keeping a grip on his hand, she pulled him to his feet and started for the kitchen.

"Sister Cel has disinfectant and ointment."

He pulled against her. "No. I'm fi—"

She stopped and turned to him, her eyes firm. "We're going to the kitchen to put something on that."

For a moment she reminded him of a manager he'd had in the minors. But it was a relief to see the determination in her eyes rather than the pain. "Right," he said meekly and allowed her to pull him into the enormous white room.

Sister Celestine came to him immediately to examine, then to treat. She sprayed Bactine, waving away the sting with her hand when he winced.

"Frank was braver than that," Carol said, her side glance full of gentle humor. So she intended to push aside the sadness they'd discussed and reestablish the easy friendship that was growing between them.

"What happened?" Sister Celestine asked.

Mike glanced at Carol and saw her silent plea. He smiled at the solicitous sister. "I tried to steal her dessert. The lady's paranoically possessive."

"Next time," Sister Celestine suggested, "just ask for seconds."

"Thank you." Carol and Mike walked side by side down the dark path that led to the dorm and the retreat cabins. The night had grown colder and its delicious winter scents even stronger.

Mike put an arm loosely around her shoulders, feeling a need to let her know he was near, though he had no idea what to do for her. "For what?"

"For fibbing about your hand."

He laughed softly. "I don't know. I think I made you look a little unhinged."

"Sister Cel probably figured out what happened, and is discussing it with your sister at this very moment." Carol's voice was quiet and amused. "Everyone at Saint Chris's knows about my family and that I prefer not to talk about it. Being comforted always makes me fall apart, and I've worked too hard at becoming functional again to let that happen."

Mike let a small silence fall, then said carefully, "Maybe they think talking about it would help you."

"It doesn't," she said stubbornly. "It only makes it hurt more."

He had a theory or two about that kind of grief having to hurt for a while before it could heal, but now didn't seem the time to mention them. "Well, it was my pleasure to fib for you. But, to quote a wheeler-dealer I know, that kind of favor ought to be worth something."

They stopped at the dorm steps. "What did you have in mind?" she asked quietly.

He dropped his arm as she turned to face him. "Nothing at the moment. But I'd like the favor held in abeyance until I think of something appropriate."

As Carol considered that suggestion, the dorm door opened and Sister Claire appeared on the porch, carrying Mike's bag of groceries. She smiled sheepishly at him as they met in the middle of the steps. She reached into the bag as he took it from her and held up the package of cheese—now a half package. "I throw myself on your mercy, Mr. Rafferty. When I saw that it was opened, all I intended was a whiff. Unfortunately, I forgot how weak of character I am. I couldn't eat at dinner, and well, it smelled wonderful. Carol will replace it for you when she goes to town again. I'm so sorry."

Carol raised an eyebrow. "*Carol* will replace it for him?"

Sister Claire nodded. "A vow of poverty, remember? I haven't any money that doesn't come from Mother Margaret. Somehow I can't picture asking her for several dollars to pay back the cheese I stole from her brother."

"You're wrong, Sister." Mike grinned. "She wouldn't give you the money, but she'd probably applaud you for getting the better of me." He took the shrunken bar of Monterey Jack with jalapeño from her, gave it one mournful look, then dropped it into the bag. "Consider it a gift. Good night, ladies."

"What a nice man," Sister Claire said softly as she stood beside Carol, watching Mike walk away.

"Sister Claire," Carol said, taking her friend's arm and leading her up the steps. The sound of television and children's laughter could be heard inside the cottage. "You're so incorrigible. I often wonder what you're doing in the convent."

At the dorm door, Sister Claire smiled at her. There was something sad behind the gesture. "Sometimes, Carol, so do I."

Chapter Five

"Is it really necessary that they be up there?" Carol looked up into the branches of a tall fir. Frank sat astride one thick bough, sawing off some of the smaller offshoots around him. Nicky offered encouragement from a branch nearby.

Mike tossed an armload of branches into the back of Mr. Engbretson's battered truck, then came to stand beside her, following her gaze. "Of course not," he replied easily. "We could have easily trimmed from the bottom branches, but Frank and Nicky wouldn't have had half as much fun." He transferred his gaze to her face, his eyes warm and teasing. "I thought you knew all about kids."

"I never said that," she denied. "I also have no knowledge of orthopedics, so please don't let them fall. The girls and I are going to cut some holly across the road."

"Sissy," he accused.

"Elf!" she countered, laughing when he gave her a look of disgust.

"Wait." He caught her arm, stopping her. Reaching into the bed of the truck, he pulled out a large cardboard box. "Toss it in here and watch out for stickers. Did you bring gloves?"

She held up her bare hands. "The kids are harder to catch when I'm wearing gloves."

Pulling off his own, he slapped them into her hands, his eyes lively and curiously dangerous. "You're very flip today, Mrs. Shaw. Please wear those. I'll chase down all escapees today."

Carol dutifully put on the sturdy gloves and found them as warm and as ill-fitting as the woolen ones he'd offered her the other morning. But the heat they held from Mike's hands quickly warmed hers. As he turned around to check on the boys, she watched him. He walked back to the tree with the unconscious grace of a professional athlete. Clad in snug jeans and bulky sweater, his wide-shouldered, lean-hipped form moved with a beauty that spoke of years of discipline and exercise. On his curly dark hair was a blue baseball cap bearing the Yankees emblem, the bill pulled down to shade his eyes. For a moment she had a picture of him running into a catch, surrounded by a cheering stadium, and felt a stab of pain for him and what he had lost.

Mike turned, and finding her still behind him, mistook the direction of her concern. "I'll watch them," he promised. "Go on."

Calling the girls to follow her, Carol crossed the road and set to work. Giving Dorcas a second set of clippers, she worked until the box was half full, then handed the clippers to Kathy.

"This is the best Saturday we've ever had!" Candy jumped up and down, her breath puffing in the cold air like steam from a little engine. "When are we going to eat?"

"As soon as we have the truck full."

"Can't I cut some?"

"You're not big enough, Candy," Kathy said, tossing a sprig into the box. "Maybe next year."

Dorcas stopped to frown at Kathy. "We won't be here next year."

Kathy frowned back. "I forgot."

Unsure how far the girls wanted to go with this conversation on a day when they had set out to combine pleasure with work, Carol sent out a feeler. "You'll be getting ready for Christmas with your foster families. You might not be cutting holly, but I'll bet you'll be having fun."

Dorcas and Kathy looked at each other, then Dorcas gave a branch of holly a vicious snip. "Maybe I'll run away before I have to leave."

"If you do that," Kathy pointed out practically, "Santa won't come to you."

"I'll do it after he comes."

"He'll know you're thinking it," Kathy reasoned, "and he won't come!"

Dorcas rolled her eyes. "God knows what you're thinking, but Santa doesn't."

"He does, too!" Candy shouted.

Dorcas turned on the youngest member of their dorm with impatience. "How do you know?"

"Kathy said so."

"Kathy doesn't know everything."

Candy frowned at that blatant heresy. "She does, too!"

"Girls, let's not fight," Carol said reasonably. "Running away wouldn't be a good solution, whether or not Santa would know about it."

"Why not?" Dorcas demanded.

"Because even though you don't have a mother and father, there are lots of people here who love you. Do you have any idea how much we'd worry? The sisters and I and the other kids? And you'd be all alone."

Dorcas sighed and turned a look on Carol that ripped a little further at a heart already in shreds. "My mother knows I'm here, but if I move, how will she find me? When Saint Chris's closes, there won't be anybody here to tell her where I went."

Kathy, who believed everything she was told, answered with conviction. "If she's a millionaire, she'll be able to hire a detective, even ten of them. They'll find you."

Dorcas prodded a holly leaf with the tip of her clippers, her chin quivering dangerously. "Yeah."

"When she tries to find you," Carol said quickly, controlling her voice with difficulty, "she'll know what state agency to go to for help. They have your records on a computer that can bring your file up in a second. It'll tell them where you are."

Dorcas turned to Carol with a hope clearly so frail that Carol was tempted to encourage her with lies, to promise her whatever she wanted to hear. But the child had been disappointed too many times to be set up again. "If she comes looking for you, Dorie, she'll be able to find you. If she doesn't, your foster family will take good care of you, and if you try to like them, you'll be happy."

Dorcas nodded, only half convinced.

"And you won't have any trouble with Santa," Kathy added.

Dorcas squinted at Carol as the sun emerged from behind the clouds. "Do you think Santa knows what we're thinking?"

She shrugged. "I don't know. But I know if you were to run away, even if he wanted to bring you presents, he wouldn't know where to take them."

Kathy looked startled. "Doesn't *he* have a computer?"

"Who?" Mike appeared behind Carol's shoulder, and she took the coward's way out.

"Santa," she replied. "Do you think Santa has a computer?"

"Oh, everybody ha—" he began, as Carol turned her back on the girls to face him. She gave him the most fractional but insistent shake of her head.

"Everybody has a computer but Santa," he said, nimbly shifting gears. "Much too cold in the North Pole. The circuits don't work."

Carol began to relax when Frank, who had followed Mike over, asked, "You mean Santa doesn't have electric heat, or even an oil furnace?"

"Santa has only a fireplace," Mike replied. When Frank would have challenged him further, he said, his eyes speaking to the boy, "Trust me, Frank."

To Frank, distrusting Mike Rafferty was unthinkable. He nodded and let the matter drop. "We're starving. Can we eat now?"

"Sure," Carol replied. "Picnic basket's on the front seat."

As the children all felt called upon to retrieve it, Carol breathed a sigh of relief and grinned up at Mike. "Thanks. You're the best liar I've ever met."

He nodded humbly. "It's a gift."

"APPLE?"

Leaning on one elbow on a blanket Carol had spread out in the sun, as though it were July instead of December, Mike looked suspiciously at the bright red fruit held out to him. Then he reached for it. "Why, thank you, Eve. No snake?"

"Not on the Washington coast. At least not poisonous ones." Carol took an apple for herself, then closed the picnic basket. Sitting cross-legged several feet away from him, she watched the children chase each other across the sunny meadow. "Have you done any work on your book this week?"

"I've started a couple of times," he said, buffing the apple on the sleeve of his sweater. "But it's harder to write about myself than I thought it would be."

She turned to him in surprise. "But you've been so successful."

He nodded. "I've been very lucky, I know. But when I tried to do a chronological story, starting with my year in the minor leagues, all the work and the desire of that time of my life came back to me with such intensity. And all the fun."

He looked up at her, squinting against the sun as a low rumble of laughter escaped him. "Playing ball was a hell of a lot of fun. My life will never be like that again. I think I'm afraid to put the past on paper and prove to myself how much has changed."

"I know." Her eyes still on the children, she draped her arms over her bent knees and sighed. "I put away all my pictures of Jon and the girls. I can only cope with having lost them if I don't remember them."

Remembering the look in her eyes the night they'd had dinner in the empty cafeteria, he dug back into his past for one of the few episodes of real grief there. "My oldest brother was killed in Vietnam. He was my hero, strong and caring and funny—a man who should have lived to a ripe old age, enjoying things and letting people enjoy him. Instead it was all over in as long as it takes for a bullet to reach its mark." He rolled onto his stomach, studying the pure white heart of his apple, seeing Gil's face as it had looked in a photo he'd sent just before he died—grimy, shadowed by the branches stuck in his helmet for camouflage, his smile a little less bright than Mike remembered it, a little more knowing. "I thought I'd never get over waiting for him to come home. Rick took over all the things Gil did for me—helping, listening, shouting—but it was a long time before I stopped waiting for him. But one day I did, and suddenly it was all easier."

Mike saw Carol close her eyes for a moment before she turned to smile at him. The gesture seemed to be intended as thanks for trying to help, but in her eyes was a kind of sorrowful sympathy that puzzled him for a moment. He had to study her before he realized that she was wondering how the loss of a brother could compare with that of the man with whom she had made love, endured the joys and trials of life, and borne the children she had also lost. It occurred to him with shattering force that it didn't, it couldn't. In his own comparatively simple personal crisis, he was reaching out to her because she was warm, intelligent, beautiful and magically capable of disturbing his doldrums—only to find that she was in the grip of a grief beyond his grasp. God, he was having a hell of a time hitting what he was thrown lately.

Mike rolled onto his stomach, working on the apple. "So what are your plans after the home closes?"

"I don't know." Her arms over her bent knees, she stared into the distance, her profile a study in doleful acceptance.

"I've applied for another job."

"In Pointer's Beach?"

"No, with the government. Oof!" Carol exclaimed as Candy landed in her lap with a thud and an effusive hug. A mighty yawn followed the hug, and after several moments of being rocked, Candy was fast asleep. Carol settled her on her stomach on the blanket between Mike and herself. A few moments later Dorcas, Kathy and Nicky appeared, pink-cheeked and bright-eyed, needing more to eat.

As Carol passed out apples, Frank came to the blanket, tossing a baseball. "Mike, you want to play catch?"

Mike sat up, putting out his hand, and Frank dropped the ball into it. It was a comfortable weight, a satisfying hardness, a sudden crystal ball of sight and sound and buried memories. Under its spell he stood, dropping the ball from one hand to the other, smelling summer grass, dust and the odor of humanity, even in the out-of-doors. He heard the jeers as well as the cheers, though he'd been mercifully blessed with fewer of the first, and the ribald, profane encouragement of his teammates. He saw color, the blur of faces and the challenge of a pitcher pulling on his cap, stamping down the mound, waging his battle of nerves.

"Mike?" Frank asked. "Want to throw a few?"

Mike flexed his bad arm and felt the answering pain. He tossed the ball at Frank and sprinted for the middle of the meadow. "Let's go," he called over his shoulder. But Frank was already beside him, doing his best to keep pace, then heading away from him to the far edge of the grass.

Carol watched them square off across the meadow, biting back the caution that was on the tip of her tongue. Mike knew what he was doing. Even at that distance she saw him smile as Frank went into an exaggerated windup and sent the ball toward him in a swift, straight line. Mike nodded, calling, "Good one." Frank was beside himself with excitement and pride. The line of his body tensed as he waited for Mike's return pitch. It came without deliberate drama. A slight leaning on his right leg, a rearing back of his arm, then the sudden, quick snap that sent the ball forward like an arrow from a bow. Frank yelped as he caught it, laughing and shaking his right hand.

"Sorry!" Mike shouted, laughing, too. "Forgot you didn't have a glove."

The ball went back and forth between them for an hour. When they finally came back to the blanket, arm in arm, Nicky was asleep beside Candy, and Dorcas and Kathy sat back-to-back, making up stories about princes and castles and kingdoms by the sea.

Frank carried the picnic basket to the truck, while Carol lifted Candy into her arms and Mike took Nicky. Carol saw him wince as he settled the sleeping boy against his shoulder. "You can wake him, Mike," she said.

"I've got him," he said. "Coming?" His brief glance in her direction contained a flash of temper she'd never seen in him, a hint of belligerence completely unlike the man she was beginning to know.

The back of the truck filled with evergreen, juniper, cedar and holly, the "logging" party crowded into the cab, two layers deep. Frank held Nicky, Carol cradled Candy, and Kathy sat on Dorcas's knees, enduring her tickles with shrieks and giggles. Seduced by the children's laughter, Carol turned to Mike to share it and found him watching the straight half mile of road back to the home, oblivious to their merriment.

"Thanks for coming along to help us," she said, trying to lure him out of his mood. "I'll tell Mother Margaret what an exemplary elf you've been."

He pulled up in front of the dorm. "Please do that," he said, his mood plainly tightening rather than softening, though he remained gentle and courteous as he helped her with the children.

"Can't you stay for a while?" Frank asked, grabbing hold of the sleeve of his sweater.

Mike stopped and smiled, jabbing the boy gently in the ribs. "I promised Mr. Engbretson I'd get the truck back to him by two-thirty. I'll probably see you at dinner."

"MAYBE SOMETHING'S WRONG with him," Frank suggested anxiously over breakfast the following morning. "He didn't make it to dinner last night, either."

Eyes wide and luminous, Candy said with the innocence of a child, to whom a death in the family had come far too early, "Maybe he died!"

The four older children groaned and turned angry looks upon her. "Well," she began defensively, "he used to be sick!"

"I'm sure he didn't die, Candy," Carol said, passing her another cinnamon roll as she subsided into a pout. "But I'll bet he doesn't feel well, because of all the pitching he did yesterday."

Frank frowned, looking startled and a little guilty. "But he said he wanted to."

Carol nodded. "I know he did. But I think he knew it wasn't a good idea and did it anyway. His arm probably hurts a lot now."

Dorcas looked concerned. "Shouldn't we check on him?"

Frank shook his head. "Adults don't like kids around when they're sick." He frowned reflectively. "My father hated it."

Carol knew that in the case of Frank's father, "sick" translated to "drunk."

"Well, Carol could check," Dorcas said, "while we go to town with Sister Claire."

Carol had Sundays off, and the sisters shared the duty of caring for the children. Sister Claire took over after Mass and breakfast. She drove to town to the museum, the shops or the go-cart rides.

Entrusted with the children's wish that she assess the welfare of their friend, Carol headed for Mike's cabin. The day was overcast and cold, and she made a conscious effort to shake off the gloom that threatened to take control of her. She hated Sundays. Monday through Saturday, the needs of the children kept her busy from the moment she awoke to the moment she fell into bed at night, drained of every ounce of energy. But the one day Mother Margaret insisted that Carol have free every week threatened to undermine the defenses she had built around her memories. Little things came back to haunt her, threatening to let loose the ugly pain that she'd buried deep inside her. Without the demands of the children to occupy her, she heard her daughter's voices, saw her husband's face, remembered the morning she had kissed them all goodbye, her mind already worrying about the day she faced at work, the meal she was planning for her father. And then they'd been gone, snatched from her in an instant and leaving a void that appeared to stretch into infinity.

A shudder racked her, but with the strength born of desperation, she put those thoughts aside. She had promised the children she'd check on Mike. Remembering his mood when they'd parted company yesterday afternoon, she had a feeling he wouldn't welcome her interference, but it was something to do on a bleak and windy Sunday.

She knocked twice before he responded. He pulled the door open, his face pale and unshaven, a flannel shirt hanging open over gray sweat bottoms. His dark brows were pulled together in an unwelcoming V. "Hi," he said in the tone of voice usually associated with, "And stay out!" In one hand he held a tube of something that smelled medicinal.

When he didn't invite her in, Carol folded her arms and gave him a friendly smile. "The children missed you at dinner last night and at breakfast this morning."

"Did they?" His aggressive mood was still in place, supported by what Carol guessed must be considerable pain. "Just like Frank enjoyed my company to town."

Carol blinked. "Pardon me?"

He studied her for a moment, then snickered to himself, bracing his hand on the doorway. "Forget it. You may assure the children that my arm hurts like hell, but I will live."

Carol looked into his eyes, saw the grim need to be alone and nodded. So much for something to keep her busy on a Sunday. "Well," she said, "if there's anything I can do—"

"Where are they?" he interrupted suddenly. "The children," he added, when she looked perplexed.

She explained that it was her day off.

"Would you like a cup of coffee?" he asked, surprising himself as well as her.

She stared at him for a moment, then accepted. "Please."

Carol had been in the cabin dozens of times when it was empty, but it looked very different now with Mike's things strewn around it. Books and paper littered the coffee table and a sweater lay over the back of the sofa, but the small living area was quite clean. He went into the kitchen beyond and turned to ask, "Cream or sugar?"

"Just a little cream, please."

He was back almost immediately with two mugs of coffee, offering her the lighter of the two. She placed it on the coffee table and picked up the tube of ointment he had left there. "Sore arm?" she asked gently.

He sat down beside her, letting his head fall against the back of the sofa. "It was stupid," he said, closing his eyes. "I knew it. You knew it, though I appreciate your resisting the impulse to tell me. I wouldn't have listened."

"Did you get the ointment on it?"

He rolled his head to glance at her. "It's hard to reach, and it doesn't help that much, anyway."

Carol uncapped the tube and knelt on the sofa. "Where is it?"

For a moment Mike looked at her in surprise, then sat up and pulled off his shirt. He reached around to knead his shoulder with his other hand. "In the shoulder, then all the way down the right side of my back to my waist."

It was a beautiful back, Carol thought, despite the small network of scars that marred it. The shoulders were big and bulky. The shoulder blades that he'd pulled back, expecting a dab of the cold ointment, were covered with a braiding of taut muscle. His skin was the milky-brown color of her coffee. On his left shoulder was a beauty mark.

Taking a grip on his sound shoulder, Carol went to work rubbing in the ointment.

He had a fleeting thought about the sexual suggestion associated with massage, then smiled to himself as Carol's competent fingers rubbed deeply, vigorously, into his knotted muscles and began to smooth them out. For all the seduction in her touch, he might have been pizza dough. He began to feel relief almost instantly.

She molded the knob of his shoulder, then rubbed down his arm and up again. He groaned a little as pain loosed its grip on him and left only a dull ache in its wake. Gently Carol pushed his head forward and down and went to work on the tightness at the base of his skull. Finally her fingers gentled and slowed as she gave his back and shoulder a final rubdown. "Maybe you'll have to come to terms with the fact that you can't toss the ball anymore," she said, her voice as soft as the movement of her hands. "At least not without suffering for it."

"I know. Aaahhh." His head dropped even lower as his body relaxed. "A part of me keeps doubting that it's as bad as the doctor says. Until I try to prove that it isn't."

"You could take up hiking," she suggested lightly, "and carry your pack on your other shoulder." She drew her hands away and sat down again, wiping them off on a napkin before reaching for her coffee.

He straightened reluctantly, rotating his head from side to side, almost unable to believe that relief had come so quickly. "I'm beginning to think chess is all I'm good for anymore. You're very good at that."

"I did it regularly for my husband."

It was on the tip of Mike's tongue to ask her what he'd been like, but he resisted, respecting her need to keep her family locked away in her past. Yet something about her seemed to cry out for contact today, as though she was desperately holding a terrible loneliness at bay. It began to occur to him that she'd come to check on him as much to give her something to do as to please the children. "I'm supposed to help Mr. Engbretson get Christmas decorations down from the attic," he said instead. He took a sip of his coffee and sat back. "How'd you like to help us?"

There was both good and bad in his suggestion. The thought of rummaging through the attic with him was not unpleasant; he was fun to be with. Mr. Engbretson, however, was another story. She turned to face him, leaning an elbow on the back of the sofa as she drank her coffee. "Do you usually solicit help from sissies?"

He braced a foot on the coffee table and looked at her. "Pretty ones," he replied.

For a moment she stared back at him in confusion. She hadn't been called pretty in more than a year. She hadn't even thought of herself in physical terms for that long, because the emotional effort she had to expend on surviving had required all her energies and concentration.

"Your reward shall be in heaven," he added.

She pursed her lips. "You stole that line from your sister. The truth is, Mr. Engbretson and I don't get along very well."

"Oh?"

"He's always yelling at my kids. In fact, he's always yelling at everybody. Mother Margaret says he's old and lonely, but I think he's just crabby."

Mike nodded. "I can identify with being crabby. It keeps everybody away when you don't want to be hurt anymore. I tried it when I was in the hospital, but everyone in my family just yelled back at me. I got nowhere and finally gave it up. Maybe he just has no one to yell back at him."

"I'd be happy to oblige." Carol smiled, then sighed. "But your sister won't let me."

Mike glanced at his watch. "I've got to meet him in ten minutes." He turned a gaze on her that was filled with amusement. "Last chance to do the noble thing." He rubbed dramatically at his bad arm.

"All right," she relented, laughing. "I'll help, but if he says one nasty word to me, you're on your own."

He got to his feet and shrugged into his shirt. "That's two favors I owe you."

"I'VE GOT IT."

"You are not going to carry this down a whole flight of stairs. I'll take it."

An enormous box marked Rudolph seesawed back and forth between Carol and Mike as they argued over which of them owned freight rights.

"If you carry this," Carol said firmly, "you'll be in pain again tomorrow and probably do serious injury to your arm."

"This thing weighs as much as it would if the real Rudolph were in it, along with the other six reindeer." Mike had a firm look of his own. "You're not carrying it."

"Eight."

"What?"

"There are eight other reindeer."

"And they are probably multiplying at this very moment," Lars Engbretson said in his singsongy Swedish-laced English, "waiting for the two of you to get the box downstairs." Tall and spare, the sixty-seven-year-old man effortlessly took the box from them and carried it down from the attic to the third floor of the school. "Perhaps you could manage the lights!" he called over his shoulder.

Carol hefted a square, shallow box and found it fairly light. She handed it to Mike. "I can take the other two as well," he said.

"I'll take those," she insisted. "Then we'll come back for the candles, the ornaments and the wreath."

"God, you're a tyrant!" he grumbled good-naturedly, following her down the stairs.

"The other day I was a sissy," she said, leading the way down the corridor to the freight elevator Mr. Engbretson was holding open. "There's no pleasing some people." Dusting off her hands, she smiled at the old man, keeping the smile in place when he returned a frowning stare. "One more trip and we'll have it made."

"And about time," he said, taking the boxes from them and adding them to a stack on the floor of the elevator. "My coffee break began twenty minutes ago. You can meet me on the first floor with the last load. And be careful with it. Some of the ornaments in the box you brought down earlier are broken." He let the door close.

Carol turned to Mike. "Do you realize that we've been working like dogs for him half the morning and most of the afternoon, and he is holding us responsible for a delayed coffee break, broken ornaments and the propagation of reindeer?"

Mike burst into laughter. Hooking an arm around Carol's shoulders, he led her back up the stairs. "You're holding up very well," he praised her. "I'm proud of you. I think I detect a little sense of humor under his harrumph, don't you?"

She frowned at him as they reached the last of the Christmas decorations that lay clustered together on the floor of the attic. "I don't know. Working with him always puts my sense of humor out of commission, so it's hard for me to tell. You take the candles." Carol took the two, four-foot red plastic candles with their five-inch orange flames and handed them to Mike. "I'll carry the box and the wreath."

"Yes, Sergeant.' Mike saluted and took a giant candle in each hand. Carol frowned at him and picked up the box, then unable to pick up the large, plastic-wrapped wreath, put the box down again. Pulling the wreath out of its protective wrap, she tried to loop it over her arm, but found its hard foil leaves too prickly for comfort. Suddenly inspired, she put it on her head.

Grinning, Mike rolled his eyes. "Sergeants wear stripes, not laurel wreaths."

Carol lifted the box and started carefully down the stairs. "Follow me, soldier," she called. "You're in charge of summoning the transportation."

When the elevator door slid aside, Sister Claire stood there, one laced shoe crossed over the other as she leaned against the wall, whistling as she waited. She straightened, studying Mike with his two candles and Carol beneath her foil wreath. "Don't tell me, don't tell me!" she said, holding the door open as it threatened to slide shut again. "We're going to have a procession? Hold a coronation? Repel lightning!"

Carol stepped off the elevator and put the box down. "None of the above. Where are the children?"

"In the kitchen. Sister Cel is starting to bake for the party. I wanted to tell you that they'll be fine until after dinner, if you and Mike want to take off to town for dinner or something. I mean, Mother Margaret says you've been slaving away all day."

Mike turned to Carol, a little surprised to find her looking trapped. "I do owe you a favor," he said.

"There's always a lot to do on Sunday nights," Carol demurred, pulling the wreath off her hair, the clown in her very suddenly and inexplicably gone.

Sister Claire frowned. "But it's the other kids' last week, and with preparations for the party and all..."

Fear prodded at Carol. She'd had a wonderful day in Mike Rafferty's company, the nicest Sunday she'd had in more than a year. But the thought of dinner alone with him gave her a feeling that was close to claustrophobia. She had shut down too many senses, switched off too many sources of stimulation. It was fine to have him bombard her emotions with other people around. But across a small table from him in some intimate little restaurant, she wouldn't know how to handle it. "No, thank you, Sister Claire."

Mike watched the panic form and grow in her eyes and felt helpless to do anything about it. He wished fervently that he could do for her what she'd done for him—pulled him out of himself, forced him into all the things he hid away from whenever feelings of inadequacy threatened to swamp him. But her defenses were higher than his. Of course, he thought, she'd been hurt more deeply. A grim flash of insight brought home to him the fact that they were poorly suited. Carol Shaw needed a man who could take a firm hold of her and pull her out of that grief. At the moment, he didn't have a firm enough hold on himself to do it. He rubbed at his arm. "I've had it for today. Soon as I get this box to Mr. Engbretson, it's crackers and cheese for me and an early night." He smiled at Sister Claire, appreciating her offer. "A little more crackers than cheese."

The sister widened her eyes innocently. "You mean Carol hasn't paid you back yet?"

Mike remembered how he had felt when he'd awakened this morning, compared to the way he felt now. "Actually, she has. Just not in cheese. Thanks for helping, Carol. I'll get this box to Mr. Engbretson.''

In Carol's wary eyes, surprise was mixed with gratitude. He seemed to understand what she was feeling when she couldn't quite analyze it herself, except to know that it was cowardly. ''Sure,'' she said. ''See you.''

Mike watched Carol and Sister Claire walk away side by side, the sister looping an arm around her friend and squeezing. An ache made Mike run a hand absently over his shoulder as he watched Carol's bright head disappear into the twilight. Then he straightened, noticing something unusual about the pain. It wasn't in his arm, but in his gut.

Chapter Six

"If we do not pick up the pace," Mr. Engbretson said from the top of an eight-foot ladder, "these lights will be up in time to light the way for the Easter Bunny and not Santa Claus."

Mike, whose job it was to feed the string of lights up to the old man, had become distracted by Carol and her children running past on their way to the playground. The children called to him and he waved. Carol stopped for a moment, gave him a small smile, then hurried after the children, a green and white scarf trailing in the air behind her. He glanced up apologetically. "Sorry. Here you go."

Mr. Engbretson drew carefully on the string of lights and cradled it in the hooks that had served the same purpose for years. "Women are trouble," the old man philosophized, backing down the ladder. Mike helped him move the ladder and the box of lights several yards over.

"Were you ever married, Mr. Engbretson?" Mike asked, feeding up lights as the old man climbed the ladder once again.

"For forty-one years." Mr. Engbretson perched with youthful steadiness on the top rung of the ladder. "But she was trouble."

Mike frowned. "I'm sorry."

For three days Mike had worked closely with the older man, stringing lights and the greenery swags that the sisters had created from the evergreen branches he and Carol and the children had harvested. This was the first time he'd seen him smile. And one had to be watching to catch it—the barest pulling back of his upper lip over strong, square teeth.

"Trouble isn't necessarily bad, just trouble," he added.

"So you didn't mind forty-one years of it?"

Mr. Engbretson sighed. "Only that it was over. More lights."

When the main building of Saint Christopher's Home for Children was outlined in lights, Mr. Engbretson positioned Mike against the back of the statue of Saint Christopher in the middle of the courtyard and disappeared inside the building. Mike folded his arms against the cold while he watched twilight turn to darkness. Then the darkness was illuminated with a gaudy brilliance. The colors of the rainbow followed each other across the large square building, over the doors, over the cathedral windows that flanked them and into the surrounding bushes.

Children appeared from all directions, small shouts of surprise turning into a roar of delight and applause. Then silence fell almost as quickly as sound had begun. Nuns and children stared, and Mike caught an intensity of feeling drifting around him, though he didn't quite understand it. Then he felt a body brush against his and looked down to find Frank leaning against his arm. When he moved his arm to put it around the boy, Frank looked up at him, colored lights reflected in his eyes. "It's beautiful," he said quietly, heavily. "But it's the last time."

Mike held him a little closer, understanding now the edge of sadness under the festive excitement. Mr. Engbretson disappeared into the building once again, and everyone's attention shifted to the roof, as a life-size Santa and reindeer came to glowing life against the night sky. There were more squeals of delight, laughter and a buzz of anticipation; in the face of the classic symbol of promise, sadness was put aside.

"How'd your arm stand up to all that work?" Carol asked as she and the other occupants of her dorm materialized beside Frank. Under the direction of sisters and dorm mothers, the other children began to disperse.

Carol was dressed in jeans and the same green down vest in which he had first seen her, the green and white scarf wrapped around her neck. Her cheeks and the tip of her nose were red, her eyes bright with a desperate cheerfulness. It occurred to Mike that Christmas must be hell for her.

"Lars did most of the lifting," he said, turning to face her with Frank still tucked under his arm. "All I provided was moral support and conversation."

Her eyes widened. "Lars?"

"We're on a first-name basis."

"I'm impressed," she admitted. "How do you rate?"

Mike grinned. "I'm not a woman. Women are trouble."

Carol folded her arms. "Says who?"

"I think it's common knowledge." Mike crossed his other arm over the chest of Frank's jacket as the boy laughed. "It's Lars's theory that trouble isn't bad, just trouble. And though he had forty-one years of it with Mrs. Engbretson, he now misses it. Under that blustery exterior is a sensitive man."

"Hmm." Carol sounded doubtful. "Did Frank tell you that Mother Margaret would like to see you?"

Frank drew in air in a guilty gasp. "I forgot."

"You forgot!" Mike pulled Frank's watch cap over his eyes, then applied a punitive tickling that dropped him to his knees. In a second the other four children were part of the scramble on the cold, hard ground.

"Stop!" Carol whispered, laughing herself. Peeling the children away, she wedged her hands between Mike and

Frank, who were still locked in high-spirited combat. "Mike! Mother Margaret has rules against wrestling on the grounds."

Mike felt her hands on his shoulder through the thick sweater he wore and the thermal shirt underneath. As he stood still, surprised by her touch, Frank took advantage of the moment to shift his weight and give his opponent a strong push. Mike fell toward Carol, who was kneeling behind him. She sat back and took his weight squarely in her lap.

For a startled moment they looked into each other's eyes. Mike felt his pulse quicken and his mind cloud. Carol's khaki eyes seemed to lose their focus, and one emotion after another chased across them while he watched, unable to interpret them quickly enough. Even under the layer of down, her heart pounded in his ear. Her lips moved soundlessly, and Mike judged that panic was beginning to overtake her. To ward it off, he flung a dramatic hand over his eyes. "The enemy has a mighty warrior, my lady. Save yourself. We're being overrun." His eyes closed, Mike lay limply in her arms, awaiting her response. The children giggled.

"You make that difficult, my lord," she said finally, her voice filled with amusement, "with your weight pinning me to the ground."

"Ah." He sat up and sprang to his feet, reaching down to help her up. Then he took a gentle but convincing grip on Frank's throat. "Go!" he said to Carol and the other children, pointing to the cafeteria. "I will defend your escape."

"But I must go with them, brave knight!" Frank said in a strangled voice.

Mike pretended to throttle him. "Pray, tell us why."

"It is meat loaf night, knight," he replied with a telltale grin, "and I starve."

"Well, we can be reasonable." Mike released him, straightened Frank's jacket and brushed it off, then gave him a gentle push toward Carol. "Then you are charged with the lady's safety, and that of her court."

Frank raised an eyebrow; he'd imposed that duty on himself long ago. "Of course." The group turned toward the cafeteria, the children waving at Mike.

Carol paused a moment to look at him over her shoulder, the wind tumbling her bright hair. "*Adieu*, Sir Knight," she called softly.

He bowed. "Until tomorrow, my lady."

MIKE FOUND MEG in a far corner of the kitchen, jacket off, sleeves rolled up and the ends of her veil tied back with a clip as she leaned with grave concentration over a pan of iced cookies, decorating them with sugar Santa faces. Affection swelled in him. She was the smartest, strongest, most competent woman he knew, but she was woefully inadequate in the kitchen. The fact that she was here at all showed how much she loved the children and wanted the party to be perfect for them.

He cleared his throat. "A little off center there, Sis."

"You might help instead of criticize," she said without looking up. "All those on the counter beside me need faces." An endless sea of cookies stretched across the back of the kitchen.

Mike found a box of snowman faces and started several pans over. "Is this why you wanted to see me?"

There was a moment's silence. "Actually, no," she replied finally, wiping her hands on her serviceable white apron. "I have something for you."

Mike looked up from his army of snowmen. "Why does that make me suspicious?"

"Because your veneer of Christianity is so thin," she replied, giving him a look of disapproval over her shoulder. "Sister Cel!"

In response to Mother Margaret's call, the small, rotund nun appeared at Mike's shoulder with a steaming mug of some brown-speckled milky substance. She stirred it with a cinnamon stick as she handed it to him. "I made this especially for you, Mike," she said.

"Eggnog!" he said, taking it from her. The scents of nutmeg and cream assailed his nostrils. Holding the cinnamon stick, he took a sip and his eyes widened. "Alcoholic eggnog!"

Meg was beside him, pulling him toward a stool against the back wall. "Sister Cel made the nog and the Christian Brothers made the brandy. It's practically blessed. Sit down."

Mike took another sip, relishing the taste of the holiday brew as it began to warm his stomach. His suspicions resurfaced, however, as Meg paced back and forth in front of his stool, apron dirty now, veil still pinched back out of her way. She was going to ask him to do something he wasn't going to like. He braced himself, undermined by the knowledge that he had yet to stand firm against her in thirty-three years of sibling rivalry.

Meg stopped pacing and put one hand on his shoulder. "The eggnog is a special treat for you, because you've given so tirelessly of your time and efforts this week to help Mr. Engbretson."

"Thank you," Mike replied without expression. "What else?"

He noted that she tried to look innocent but, even in the garb of a nun, did not succeed. "Even Carol had a go-around with Mr. E for making you work so hard."

Thrown off guard, Mike came to attention. "She did? When?"

"Two days ago. He came to me in a real huff, telling me that all women were trouble, but that she was more trouble than most because she was always fighting for everybody else—her dorm kids and now you."

Mike grinned, his insides growing warmer, though he hadn't sipped the eggnog in minutes. "No kidding?"

"No kidding. Will you be Santa Claus tomorrow?"

His feeling of well-being was almost dispelled by her question, but not quite. "No."

Meg folded her arms over her apron, and flour and powdered sugar puffed around them. "Please?" she asked quietly. "Mr. Engbretson was going to do it for us. Now he's complaining of muscle aches and sore joints because he tried to take the burden of the work off you."

"Meg, all those little kids," he pleaded reasonably. "I won't know what to say to them, and they'll know I'm not real. They'll lose their faith in Santa, and it'll be all my fault." His reasonableness turned to censure. "And yours because you tried to set me up with eggnog. *Your* Christianity is supposed to go deeper than that."

"I'm desperate," she replied impenitently. "These children are leaving here day after tomorrow, and their feelings range from nervousness to terror. God will help them adjust to new surroundings, I firmly believe that. But I know that a good send-off from Santa will help them believe that, even in their shaky world, someone still loves them."

"Damn it, Meg . . ."

"Please?"

The vulnerability in her face was his undoing. Staunch in her faith and her own abilities, Margaret Rafferty was a veritable storehouse of resourcefulness and determination. But the machinery of bureaucracy was moving her children around, and she could do nothing to insure their happiness—except offer them this send-off from Santa. His mind already made up, Mike took a sip of eggnog and appeared to consider. "Is this eggnog a one-shot deal?"

Her reaction was calm, but he saw the twinkle in her eyes. She had eyes like Gil's—filled with goodness. "I can probably negotiate a few more for you at decent intervals."

He toasted her with his mug. "Ho, ho, ho," he said.

"AND I WANT pink leg warmers, a new bag for my ballet shoes, a Roger Rabbit doll and pearl earrings." The young lady on Santa's knee, eight or nine years old, had required a good three minutes to divulge her list. She had perched in Mike's lap without a qualm and hooked an arm around his neck like an old friend. But now she looked for his eyes in the tangle of fuzzy white hair, mustache and beard, her own expression gravely serious. "Do you think you can do it?"

The only rule Meg had laid down for his performance was "Don't promise anything." It turned out to be the only rub in an afternoon that had been more fun than he had ever thought possible. He wanted to make promises. He wanted to run out as soon as the party was over and buy every child everything he or she had asked for. But it wasn't practical. Carriages made out of pumpkins, and ponies that could fly were not that easy to come by.

"You're just a helper, aren't you?" the little girl asked, sensing a lower level of authority in his hesitation.

"Yes, I am," he admitted, "but I help Santa pack his toys, and I'll tell him how hard you work and how much you want to be a dancer." While helping Lars set up the tree in the gymnasium, he'd watched her at the far end of the room, being put through a barre routine by the gym teacher. He was pleased that in the midst of the demands of all the children at Saint Chris's, someone had noticed a gifted little girl. Meg, he knew, never missed a detail.

Convinced he had Santa's ear, the little girl kissed his cheek and jumped off his lap. "Thank you, elf," she said.

Resigned to that identity, Mike looked at the diminishing line of children and saw that Nicky was next in line, with the rest of Carol's kids lined up behind him. Nicky's eyes were wide and he backed up against Dorcas. She pushed him forward. "It's Santa, Nicky," she said. "He won't hurt you."

He backed up again, shaking his head. "No."

Kathy leaned out from behind Dorcas. "Nicky, you've got to go, or we won't get to."

"Nope," he insisted.

Frank fell out of line and tried to take his hand. "Come on," he said gently, "I'll walk you up."

But Nicky pulled against him, his eyes growing wider.

"What's the matter?" Carol asked, appearing with a plastic cup of coffee in her hands. Loudly, simultaneously, the children explained the problem. Mike watched her sink to her knees beside Nicky, the soft flare of a red woolen skirt puddling around her on the tarpaulin.

As the woman and the child talked quietly, Frank leaned an elbow on the paddle arm of the chair borrowed from the administration office to serve as Santa's throne. "So how's your batting average today, Santa?" he whispered.

Mike turned and found himself looking into a broad wink. "Think of this as a covert operation," Mike whispered back. "And if you blow my cover, I'll see that all Santa drops on you is reindeer—"

"I've got the picture," Frank interrupted, his eyes widening respectfully. "See ya, Santy."

"I THINK Nicky's ready, Santa," Carol said, rising to her feet, the skirt settling around her legs with a graceful swish.

Mike put out a hand. "I'd like to hear what you want, Nicky."

Holding Carol's hand, Nicky gave Santa a long, uncertain look and started for the three steps that led to the platform where he sat. He stopped suddenly at the bottom and hid behind Carol. "You tell him what you want first, Carol," he bargained, "then I'll go."

Carol tried futilely to pull him from behind her. "But adults don't usually ask Santa for things."

"Why not?" her dorm children demanded simultaneously behind her.

"You have to talk to him," Kathy pleaded. "If you don't do it, Nicky won't, and Santa has to leave at three." She pointed to the large clock over the basketball hoop. It was fifteen minutes of. "If you don't go, the rest of us won't get to talk to him."

Carol looked at Santa and noted a subtle sharpening of his attitude. It was impossible to tell what was going on behind that tangle of whiskers, but she thought she could see a most un-Santa-like wickedness in his eyes. Resigned to her fate, she climbed the steps.

Santa drew her onto his knee, one hand bracing her back, the other resting on the hands she had folded in her lap. "Have you eaten all your vegetables?" he asked.

Carol suddenly developed a problem keeping a straight face. But Nicky was watching with such wide-eyed intensity that she knew a lot depended on her performance. "Except for the okra," she replied.

When Santa inclined his head as though to scold, Dorcas came to her defense. "We all hate it, Santa. It's awful."

Santa nodded. "All right. You're excused from eating okra, but you've kept the dorm clean and made time for your jogging?"

A gasp came from the bottom of the steps, where Carol's kids were now clustered, listening. "He knows Carol jogs!" Candy was openmouthed.

"Of course." Kathy patted her little sister's shoulder. "Santa knows everything. God tells him."

"My elves," Santa continued, "tell me that you've been very kind to your neighbor and send him popcorn at night when he's all alone." Another gasp came from the bottom of the stairs. "Because you've been kind, and Santa loves boys and girls who are kind, you can have anything you want."

Seduced by the gentle sound of his voice, aware of his closeness and the warm, though fraternal, touch of his hands, Carol felt her mind resist an answer. Feelings long dormant claimed her attention. "I . . . don't . . ."

"There must be something you want," Mike prodded in his guise as Santa. "A ruffly blouse, a pretty bangle . . ."

"A purse," ever-practical Dorcas prompted in a loud whisper. "Ask for a new purse!"

Something about that feet-on-the-ground suggestion brought Carol back to awareness. "That's it, please, Santa—a purse. Mine is always full of the children's things and lives a very hard life."

"What color?"

Carol found Mike's eyes in the thicket of hair and eyebrows. "Brown or black, so the fingerprints and crayon marks don't show."

Santa nodded. "That's a very short list. What about something impractical, too?"

Carol smiled, and one of the hands under Mike's came out to pat his. "I don't need anything impractical. I'm a very practical lady. Thank you, Santa." Standing, Carol reached down the steps for Nicky and gently pulled him up. "Santa, this is Nicky, a very good friend of mine. He's done all his chores and eaten his vegetables."

Nicky allowed Santa to lift him onto his knee. "Except the okra," he admitted honestly.

"I don't like okra, either."

Nicky looked Santa in the face. "You don't? What about squash?"

"Acorn squash is okay. Spaghetti squash is yucky." Nicky made an ugly face, obviously in agreement. At the bottom of the stairs, the other children giggled. Nicky leaned back against Santa's arm and got down to business. "I'd like a tricycle, my own television, a Nintendo Power Pad . . ."

Dorcas confided that she wanted nothing for herself, because she was sure her mother's limousine would be delivering gifts on Christmas morning. Then she whispered into Santa's ear. "But could you bring me a necklace, so I could give it to Carol? One of those things that looks like a diamond. Rubik . . . something?''

"Cubic zirconia?" Santa asked softly.

"Yeah."

She looked so hopeful, and the thought was so selfless that Mike found it impossible not to promise. "You bet. Wouldn't you like something for yourself? In case the limousine is . . . late, or something?"

"No," she replied confidently.

Candy studied his beard thoughtfully while she knotted her fingers. "Um . . . a teddy bear that plays music, a new jacket, one of the those puffy things . . . you know?" When Santa looked puzzled, Candy launched into a lengthy description of something that could be green or pink or blue or yellow and had arms and legs that "hanged all over" and could look like a cat or a dog or . . . Mike tried to hold on to what he could of the description, praying that someone could interpret it for him later. "And a cow. A real one." She ended on a big sigh.

Santa squirmed. "A real one?"

"Yes," she replied, surprised that he thought to question her. "Because I like them."

Kathy wanted a new jacket and told him frankly, "I'm tired of blue." She leaned into Santa's shoulder to ask confidentially, "Did my little sister remember to ask for a jacket?"

"Yes, she did."

"Good. She's tired of blue, too. And did she remember a Puffalump?"

"A red, green, yellow, or blue thing with arms and . . ."

"Yeah."

"Yes, she did. What else would you like?"

"Well . . . it's kind of expensive."

Mike was beginning to have trouble swallowing. "Tell me."

"You know those baby dolls that look really real? They come with diapers and a diaper bag and a bottle? If you have any money left, could I have one of those?"

Bending Meg's rule, Santa nodded. "If I have money left."

"Thank you, Santa."

Mike watched Kathy walk down the steps, thinking that if she didn't get the doll, she'd very probably suppose that Santa had run out of cash and not be upset at all.

Suddenly the burden on Mike's knee was more noticeable than the others had been, the elbow leaning on his shoulder more companionable. Mike watched Carol lead the other children toward the table of cake and cookies.

"I'd like a regulation bat, Santy," Frank said, "and a ball signed by all the Yankees. After all..." He grinned broadly. "I didn't reveal your identity."

Mike nodded. "True."

"And it wasn't because I didn't want reindeer do dropped on me."

"No?"

"No." Frank leaned comfortably against Mike. "It's because they still believe, and that's important to little kids."

Mike looked into the cocoa-brown eyes. "That's important to everybody."

"I know." Though apparently wanting to agree, Frank didn't seem entirely convinced. "I don't believe in Santa Claus, but I believe my dad's going to come for me before I have to move."

Mike felt a new ache. "If he doesn't," he asked gently, tightening his hold, "you won't let it kill your belief that there's a great foster home out there for you, and that you'll have a great life and grow up to play for the Yankees, will you?"

The uncertainty Frank had lived with most of his life rose out of the depths of his eyes, but so did the courage with which he'd learned to counter it. Ever the schemer, he grinned at Mike and suggested, "I guess if I had a ball with all their names on it to help me remember . . ."

With a spontaneous hug and a laugh, Mike put Frank on his feet and stood. "I'll see what I can do. Save me a piece of cake. I'm going to get changed."

MIKE SAT in a deep, lumpy chair in Meg's office, the Santa suit folded into a box on the floor beside him, the scratchy, atrociously designed mustache and beard in his hands. Even two flights up, he could hear the high-pitched children's voices at the party in the gymnasium. He leaned back in the chair and closed his eyes, hoping he wasn't going to burst into tears. When he had learned his career was over, he'd felt angry, cheated, depressed—but he didn't remember ever feeling as truly helpless as he did at this moment.

One by one, trusting little children had sat in his arms and confided their dreams. He remembered Carol's children particularly because he knew them better. In one way or another, they'd all been betrayed, and yet Dorcas had asked for a present to give Carol, Kathy's thoughts had been for her sister, and Frank, living with his own pain, sagely understood them all. The injustice of it was building a fire in his middle.

"I think you're good enough to take that show on the road," Meg said.

Mike opened his eyes to see her sitting on the edge of her desk, black-stockinged legs and practical shoes dangling. Still leaning back in the chair, he looked at her moodily. "How do you do it?"

He didn't have to explain. She smiled at him gently as she shrugged. "When you work with people, or rather for people, one of the first things you learn is that you can't change anything. You can touch lives lovingly, hopefully, prayerfully, and you can make a subtle difference, but not a big change. You do the little things and trust God to handle the rest."

Angrily, he tossed the beard into the box. "I'm used to slamming homers, Meg. I've stolen bases, made impossible catches, and saved the game in the bottom of the ninth. Don't tell me to trust somebody else."

She raised an eyebrow. "God, Mike. Not 'somebody.'"

He gave her a dark look. "You know what I mean."

"Yes," she said, "but you don't know what I mean. What do you want to do, take sixty-five children home with you to Portland and raise them as your own?"

At that moment he did, but understanding the absurdity of it, he gave her a fractional smile. "I'll give thirty-two and a half of them to Rick."

Meg rolled her eyes. "A crueler fate than the state ever dealt them. Look, Mike." She rested her elbows on her knees and leaned toward him, her silky veil slipping off her shoulders. "You gave them each a few moments alone with one of their ideals. You listened and counseled and cared." She smiled at him, the gesture pure affection for once, without humor. "I heard you and you were wonderful. You did all you could be expected to do. It's a very imperfect world, brother mine, but it's doing the best it can for these children. And God is watching. Believe that."

He sighed, looking beyond her and out the window to a gloomy, darkening afternoon. "We had so much as kids."

For a moment her smile, too, was reflective. "I know. Love made us strong. But these kids are tougher than you think. Don't presume they won't make it because they didn't have everything we had."

Mike remembered Carol's kids and had to allow that that was true.

"Carol was looking for you," Meg said, slipping off the desk to walk around it and sit in her torn leather chair.

"She was?" Mike pushed himself to his feet, galvanized by a small stir of excitement.

Meg didn't seem to notice, involving herself in the papers on her desk. "Yes. And Frank said to tell you he'd saved you some cake. I have work to do."

Mike put both hands on her desk and leaned toward her. "Did you know that the kids call you Godzilla?"

She smiled at him blandly. "You have to expect that when you can eat the tops off buildings. They called Patton 'Old Blood and Guts.' Goes with the territory."

"But they love you."

"I know." The quiet heroism in her eyes humbled him. "I love them."

Mike leaned across the desk to plant a kiss on her cheek. "And I love you. Want me to bring you some cake?"

She patted her desk drawer and grinned. "Nah. Got my Twinkies."

NICKY AND CANDY met him halfway across the auditorium, each latching onto a hand as they led him toward their table. "You missed Santa!"

"He had this dumb beard, but he was cool."

"He's gonna bring me a cow!"

"Carol's getting a purse," Kathy announced as Mike took his place at the table. He noted that the children's faces were glowing, their eyes shining. He had helped them believe.

"Oh?" He turned to Carol as she pushed a cup of coffee and a paper plate toward him. "So you talked to Santa, too?"

"He knew all about her," Candy said, eyes enormous. "And you know what?"

"What?"

"She even got to sit on his lap!"

"No kidding."

"Nope. And you know what else?"

"What?"

"He said she could have anything she wanted 'cause she's been so good. Can I have the rose on your cake?"

Sister Celestine had catered to the children's love of frosting by decorating each square of cake with a large rose of red icing.

"Sure." Mike pulled her into his lap, tucked the tines of his fork under the rose and carefully removed it. Then he put it to her lips.

As Candy greedily ate the rose and the other children ran off to participate in the games that were beginning at the other end of the auditorium, Carol leaned toward Mike. "It's too bad," she said, "that there's no one to tell Santa how good he's been."

Mike turned his attention from Candy to Carol. Her eyes were warm and without the constraint that often filled them lately when she looked at him. "Oh, I imagine Mrs. Santa does that," he said.

Carol glanced at Candy, and finding her absorbed in devouring the rest of Mike's cake, posed the question, "What if Santa is a bachelor?"

A little mystified by the interesting turn in the conversation, Mike tried to remain casual. "Then I guess he has to count on his friends."

Carol nodded as though that were reasonable, then reached out a slim hand to squeeze his forearm. As Candy ate away at the cake, oblivious to everything but the elemental satisfaction of a sugary treat, Carol gave Mike a smile that would keep him awake that night. "You did well, Santa," she said.

Chapter Seven

The children were leaving. Sprinting the short distance from his cabin to Carol's dorm, Mike stopped, emotion clouding an already bleak and rainy day. Shifting the large cardboard box under his arm, he leaned against the rough bark of a fir tree and watched Meg and Sister Claire hug three children before putting them into a car that would take them to a foster home and a new life. One of the children, a girl with long blond hair, clung to Meg a moment longer. Mike recognized her as the ballerina. Suddenly it all became personal, and he sent up a silent prayer that she would get everything she wanted.

As the car drove off, another pulled up, and the routine began again. Mike turned away and covered the last few yards to the dorm.

"Hi, Mike." Frank came to the door with a smile that had none of its usual warmth. Still in pajamas and bathrobes, the other children knelt on the sofa and peered out the window at what they could see of the driveway. They were silent.

Carol came out of the kitchen, a cup of coffee in her hands. Her eyes brightened when she saw him, and he had to consciously resist the temptation to touch her. "I'm so glad you came," she said, hooking her arm into his and pulling him into the kitchen. "Do you have plans for today?"

He should work on his book, he should write to his mother, he should clean his cabin, Mike thought. "No," he replied.

"I thought I'd take the kids to town on the excuse of buying supplies for the Christmas crafts. I know they have to accept the fact they're leaving eventually, too, but spending all day watching the other kids leave doesn't seem healthy to me." Her small smile had an element of pleading. "Want to help me ride herd on them?"

He looked over at the lineup of children, looking smaller and more vulnerable in their night wear, and nodded. "Sure."

Carol sighed. "They don't even want to get dressed this morning."

"I remember feeling like that." Mike shifted the box to his other arm. "When things are too ugly, you think you won't have to face them if you stay in bed. Come on. I think I can help. Okay, team, listen up!" Mike moved to the coffee table in front of the sofa, and the children turned around with desultory interest. "We've got work to do. We're going to town today to buy supplies for the things we're making for the Christmas bazaar." The girls perked up, but Frank rolled his eyes and Nicky sighed. "To make sure we're all united in this endeavor..."

Frank narrowed an eye. "Say what?"

"To make sure we're all willing to work together," Mike simplified, yanking open the box, "we're going to town in uniform."

A cry of excitement rose from the group and they peered more closely. The open box revealed blue and white shirts and hats emblazoned with the Yankees emblem. Mike handed hats around, then checked the shirts for sizes and passed those out, too. "Okay!" He clapped his hands. "Let's get moving." As the kids dispersed with shouts and giggles to their rooms, Mike turned to Carol. He handed her a T-shirt, then put a hat onto her head, only to whip it off again as it fell to her eyebrows. He adjusted the sizing band and tried again, feeling the cool silk of her hair as he reached around her to pull it securely into place. Her khaki eyes, shaded by the bill of the cap and by a confusion that he was just beginning to recognize as interest rather than rejection, turned to dark gold. "Team bus leaves in five minutes, Shaw," he said quietly, "and you're still out of uniform."

It seemed to require an effort for her to pull her eyes away from his. "Right," she said finally and disappeared down the corridor to the bedrooms.

Mike watched her go, experiencing that same comfortable satisfaction he used to get from a strong grounder to center field. It wasn't over the fence, but it got him on base.

IT AMAZED MIKE that a full complement of ball players rowdy with postgame excitement and too many beers made less noise than five young children on a flimsy excuse for a field trip. The noise in the station wagon was cacophonous.

Mike leaned close to Carol's ear. "How do you concentrate on driving?" he asked loudly.

Carol kept her eyes on the road, so that he wouldn't notice that his breath in her ear was harder on her nerves than the noise. "They've got more steam than usual to let off today. Ordinarily they don't get this bad until we're almost to town, then I can pull over and threaten them with dire retribution."

The traffic on the narrow, curving road to Pointer's Beach was steady that morning, Mike noted, and despite Carol's apparent calm, he couldn't help but think that keeping her mind on her driving was more difficult than she made it look.

Mike glanced over his shoulder, just in time to see Dorcas and Frank start squabbling over an automobile bingo game the kids were passing back and forth. Outclassed by

Frank's superior strength, Dorcas bit his hand. Frank screamed theatrically, the sudden sound making Carol flinch.

"Okay, that's it!" Mike's shout was swift and loud, and silence followed immediately. Five pairs of eyes rounded under five baseball caps. "I want you to settle down," he went on more quietly. "Carol is controlling a couple of tons of metal, moving at fifty-five miles an hour through fairly heavy traffic. It would make it a lot easier for her if you keep your voices down."

"It was all Dorky's fault," Frank grumbled, sending his archenemy a dark look.

"Dorcas didn't scream like a banshee." Frank stiffened, hurt by the criticism from his hero. "Now that you've developed a man's voice," Mike went on, "you have to learn to be careful with it."

Frank relaxed in his seat, hurt pride salved. Mike turned back to face forward and caught Carol's glance of impressed approval.

Silence reigned for several moments, then from somewhere in the back a small voice whispered, "What's a banshee?"

WHILE CAROL AND FRANK deliberated over the right weight of paper to use in making origami doves, Mike followed the other children through the stationery store. With four of them heading down four different aisles, Mike decided there was more planning involved in the duty of keeping children in tow than he realized. He caught Candy just as her small hands reached for a display of glass paperweights on a shelf above her head. "Those are very breakable," he cautioned, pulling her hands down.

She looked up at him, her dark eyes hurt. "I just wanted to look at it."

"All right." He picked her up, settling her on his hip until she could see not only the paperweights, but all the china figurines that had been placed even higher.

Her delighted gasp made him look at the display a second time, trying to see it as she did. "Horses!" she exclaimed. "Puppies, kittens and..." She frowned over the long-legged bird.

"Os-trich," Mike said carefully.

"Ostrich," she repeated. "Uh-oh!" At the warning quality of her voice, Mike followed her gaze through the open shelf and into the next aisle. A vertical spinning rack of pens, erasers, other miscellaneous items, and one small boy on it, teetered dangerously. Mike counted it no less than a miracle that he reached the rack before it fell.

Nicky glanced at him sheepishly, his index finger looped over one of the rack's many lethal-looking hooks. "It spins," he said. "Like that thing at school only the big kids can use."

Mike removed Nicky's hand from the rack and kept it firmly in his own. "This is a display rack, not playground equipment. It's not for riding on."

He found Kathy and Dorcas leafing through mounted posters of rock stars. They clung together in a giggling swoon over an amemic-looking young man in black leather with a spike-studded wristband and an electric guitar.

"Well, it looks like you have everything under control." Carol appeared at his elbow, looking cool and pleased that he had all the children together in one place. "You manage them so well, *you* should be a dorm mother."

His hands full of children, Mike looked down at her with a seriousness that wiped the smile from her face. "I just saved you from having to purchase a broken fifty-dollar paperweight and from having a child hopelessly perforated by a runaway spinning rack. Unfortunately, I was too late to save these two from turning into rock groupies." Only the light deep down in his eyes gave him away. Carol's smile began to reappear. "If you leave me alone with them once more, I will report you to my sister, the chancery office and very probably the pope. Can we go now?"

Carol bit back laughter. "Only if you're sure you want to."

"Carol..."

"Right. Come on, kids. On to the yarn shop." When the boys groaned, Carol let the laughter free. "Mike, if you and the boys want to go to the sporting goods shop across the street, we could meet in half an hour at the car."

Frank and Nicky looked as though they'd been granted a last-minute reprieve by the governor. Candy clung to Mike's neck when Carol tried to take her. "I want to stay with Mike."

"Honey, he and the boys are going to look at baseball bats and fishing stuff," Carol tried to reason. "It'll be boring."

Candy clung a little harder. "I want to go."

"Let me have her," Carol insisted, knowing Mike needed the respite. "She'll be all right once you're gone."

"It's all right." He caught Carol's hand as she would have wedged it between him and the child. Candy's weight was curiously comfortable in his arms, her large limpid eyes offering a plea he found impossible to refuse. "We'll take her with us." He gave Carol's hand a small squeeze, then released it. "Meet you at the car in half an hour."

I'm flipping out, Mike thought as he crossed the street, flanked by Frank and Nicky, Candy still clinging to his neck like a charm. *I'm having a good time. Rick suggested that my head had been more affected by the accident than my arm was. I don't have to worry about what to do with the rest of my life. I'm walking a straight line to the state hospital.*

THE SMALL RESTAURANT smelled deliciously of mesquite-broiled hamburgers and greasy French fries. Carol inhaled deeply of the aroma as she and Mike and the children settled into chairs at a round table in the middle of the terrazzo floor. Mike removed his baseball cap and hung it on the back of his wooden chair. Frank and Nicky immediately mimicked his actions.

A potted fern hung above Frank's head. He reached up an arm to give it a spin. Mike caught his hand and brought it down again. "If it falls on your head," he cautioned, "you'll have a fern growing out your ears for the rest of your life."

The picture that idea presented apparently amused Frank and he laughed heartily, giving Mike a swipe on his shoulder with his fist. When Mike pretended to be in pain, Frank laughed harder.

"Everybody agreed on hamburgers?" Carol asked, scanning the menu.

"With onions."

"Without onions and pickles."

"Mayonnaise instead of mustard."

"None of that yucky pink sauce."

"And don't forget French fries. Lots of French fries. And ketchup."

Mike grimaced at Carol. "You got all that?"

She nodded confidently. "Piece of cake."

Nicky looked up from the menu that Carol knew he couldn't yet read. "Cake? We can have cake?"

Carol laughed. "No, it was just an expression. This place doesn't serve cake. But maybe we can stop at the bakery before we go home."

"I have to go to the bathroom," Candy announced. An immediate chorus of "me, too," led to the evacuation of the table.

"And remember," Carol cautioned firmly. "No playing with the toilet tissue, or the towel roll, or the air blower. I expect you back in five minutes." The children skipped off happily.

Mike watched Carol give the waitress their order, easily remembering who wanted what on their burger, and cutting the fries down to five orders rather than seven. "Candy and Nicky will never finish theirs," she explained to Mike. Then she smiled. "You're going to need three days in bed after this. Although you do display a natural aptitude for dealing with children."

He denied that with a laugh. "I haven't done anything but chase them down in time to avert disaster."

She matched his laugh. "That's parenting in a nutshell. They like you, and you make them feel comfortable about that by letting them know you like them back. That's a gift some people don't have."

"Actually," he said, leaning back as the waitress distributed Cokes around the table, "I have to admit that I'm experienced. I have two little nieces. They live in San Francisco and I don't see them often enough, but I'm crazy about them."

"Your brother Rick's children?"

"No, Rick's a bachelor. They're my sister Lorraine's. Her husband's an attorney."

"Another bachelor." She stirred the ice in her Coke with a straw. "What do the men in your family have against marriage?"

He frowned. "Nothing. Rick works twenty hours a day building his business, and until recently, I was living like a gypsy, from training camp to New York, back to Portland off-season. That's not conducive to permanent relationships."

Remembering what Mother Margaret had told her about the woman who left Mike at the time of his accident, she tried not to let it show in her eyes but, sensing that he saw it, she lowered them.

"It's all right," he said. "I've learned to read the pitch. It's taken me a while to come to the conclusion that Linda wasn't interested in as serious a relationship as I'd thought."

He sipped at his Coke, then inclined his head with a small laugh, apparently at himself. "The Raffertys are all emotional. I suppose, because I feel things strongly, I mistook beauty and passion and...I don't know...convenience, I guess, for love. When I was lying in the hospital with my professional life in ruins and she came to say goodbye, I thought I was going to die." He looked at Carol ruefully. "I had several World Series-quality bouts with self-pity at the time. Anyway, I'm beginning to see things differently."

"So your stay at Saint Chris's is accomplishing its purpose?"

He had to think about that. In point of fact, it wasn't entirely true. He had retreated to Saint Christopher's for quiet and relaxation, to clear his mind and plan his future. But if anything, his thoughts were more muddled now than they had been when he arrived. A weight seemed to have lifted from him. He smiled to himself as he recognized that weight as the choking burden of self-absorption. Looking into Carol's eyes and seeing her struggle bravely every day to regain her foothold in a world that had cut away the ground beneath her had made the dissolution of his career seem insignificant. Listening to the dreams of valiant little children, who kept going against odds that would have crippled many adults, had almost made him forget that he'd ever been anything but a stand-in Santa Claus.

"I'm no clearer on the future," he said finally, "but I like the present a lot better."

She gave him a heartfelt nod. "That's just what Saint Chris's did for me."

As the girls arrived back giggling and smelling of hand lotion, Carol looked in concern toward the rest rooms.

"I'll check on the boys," Mike offered, pushing away from the table.

At that moment, Frank emerged, a look of urgency on his face as he hurried toward them. He stopped at Mike's shoulder. "Can you come and help us?"

Carol stiffened. "What happened?"

Frank's expression changed from one of urgency to an air of reluctance. "Well ... Kermit got away."

"Ker ..." Carol exchanged a shocked look with Mike, then dropped her head into her hands. Visions ran through her head of patrons of the restaurant standing on their tables, while a nine-ounce white rodent escaped from the men's room and terrorized the establishment.

Mike patted Carol's shoulder as he passed her on his way to the rest room. "If I'm not back in ten minutes, send help."

Mike, Frank and Nicky returned to the table a mercifully brief ten minutes later. Nicky looked relieved, though subdued, and carried a large foam "to-go" carton in which air holes had been made. "Mike says I should put him in the car," he whispered to Carol.

Retrieving her keys from her purse, she handed them to him. "Good idea. The car's right out front."

As the boy disappeared, assuming an air of importance with the car keys in his hand, Carol looked across the table at Mike. He had a hand over his mouth, obviously making every effort to remain properly grave in the face of such a blatant infraction of the rules. Frank covered his mouth with both hands, but broke into hysterical laughter, anyway. Mike attempted to give him a quelling look, but failed miserably and dissolved into laughter himself. The girls followed, and Carol gave up all effort at maintaining order. She guessed it was probably important for children to know that certain actions defied condemnation every bit as much as they defied approval.

One lonely French fry remained on the plate sometime later when Candy scrambled out of her chair. Eyes closing sleepily, full belly protruding under her new T-shirt, she climbed into Mike's lap and cuddled against his shoulder. Carol watched him hold her close and say something quietly to her as she burrowed into his neck.

Carol glanced at Kathy, wondering if she objected to her little sister sharing her affection with Mike. But instead of the jealousy she expected, she encountered a wistfulness in Kathy's dark eyes, an obvious wish that she were still small enough to crawl into his lap beside Candy. Their father had died before Candy was born, Carol knew, and was probably no more than a blurred memory to Kathy. In the case of paternal love there was no such thing as not missing what one has never had—the need for the security a good father provided was too intrinsic, too elemental. Carol's heart ached for Kathy, and she suddenly found herself longing for her own father, who lived a vast thousand miles away.

"Well, hot damn, it if isn't Mike Rafferty!" A paunchy older man in jeans and a red parka stopped at their table and offered his hand to Mike, putting his other hand on Mike's shoulder to prevent him from standing. "No, don't disturb the little one. I'm Milton Boardman and this is my wife, Gert." A small gray-haired woman behind him nodded and smiled. "I been a fan of yours since you were a rookie. We're from L.A., so the Dodgers are my team, but I always kept my eye on you. You're one sluggin' son of a gun." He frowned. "Shame about your arm."

Mike shrugged. "That's the way it goes."

"Sayin' goodbye to a .352 battin' average can't be something you do lightly."

".353," Frank corrected.

Boardman patted Frank on the shoulder and looked around the table at Carol and the children in their matching T-shirts. Obviously concluding they were Mike's wife and children, he laughed heartily. "Looks like you put together your own team good enough to win the pennant."

The children were beaming at him, Mike noted, apparently delighted at being mistaken for his. For the moment it seemed a harmless fantasy, and he made no effort to correct the man. "And to take the series in four," he said.

"Can I have your autograph?" Boardman began to pat his pockets, then turned to his wife, who pulled a store receipt from her purse. Holding a lightly snoring Candy with one hand, Mike signed it with the other. From Mrs. Boardman's purse also came a camera. "May I?" she asked quietly. "With Milty?"

Mike turned to Carol, afraid that a photograph might be carrying the innocent deception too far. But she nodded. Boardman quickly added a chair between Dorcas and Nicky, put an arm around each of them and grinned at his wife, who ordered, "Now, smile everybody." There was a moment's stillness, a click, and a loud commotion as Milton gave each of the children a five-dollar bill, then said goodbye.

Ecstatic with their windfall, all the children began to talk at once as Mike and Carol stared at each other like the stunned survivors of a hurricane. "I guess that's what happens," she said finally, "when you keep company with a star."

Mike laughed softly. "Wasn't he great? I won't miss the national attention as much as I'll miss being appreciated by guys like Milton."

"Aw, I appreciate ya." Standing, Frank put an arm around Mike's shoulders. Then he held up his five-dollar bill and looked imploringly at Carol. "Now can we go shopping for fun stuff?"

THE CHILDREN talked incessantly all the way home, excited by the unusual outing, by Mike's company, and by the financial boon that meeting Milton Boardman had brought them. But the conversation stopped when Carol drove past the empty schoolyard. It was only mid-afternoon, but the sky was darkening and dead leaves skittered across the paving. The grounds were silent. The large stone statue of Saint Christopher protected no one; his children, except for the five in the station wagon, were gone.

Kathy began to cry. Carol parked the car, then opened the back doors for the children. Mike lifted Kathy into his arms and she clung to him gratefully, arms around his neck, scrawny legs in jeans wrapped around his waist. He started down the trail to the dorm. Carol lifted out Candy, who was sobbing in sympathy with her sister, and shepherded the rest of the children together. His mouth set in a grim line, Frank took Nicky's hand and glanced at Dorcas, who stood still, blue eyes unfocused and ready to spill tears. He pinched the sleeve of her jacket between his thumb and forefinger, pulling her along. "Come on, Dorie."

In the dorm, Carol flipped on all the lights to counteract the swiftly falling darkness and turned up the heat. "Take off your jackets," she ordered briskly, filling the teakettle with water. "We're going to have cocoa and talk about this."

"I don't want to talk about it," Frank said, giving the scarf around his neck a desultory yank. "I don't think any of us do."

Approval was muttered from the sofa near the window, where the other children had settled. Mike, still holding Kathy, though she was quiet now, sat on one of its arms. Carol turned on the burner under the kettle, then went to Frank and helped him pull off his jacket. "Ignoring the fact that we'll all be leaving here in a couple of months won't change it, Frank. But having the right attitude about it will make it a lot easier."

"I've moved four times," Dorcas said, leaning back against the sofa cushions, half in and half out of her jacket. "It wasn't ever easy."

Carol nodded. "I know, Dorie. But this is going to happen, and we all have to do our best to deal with it. Now get those jackets off, so you don't catch cold."

Feeling helpless, Mike helped Kathy remove her faded blue parka. "Isn't it weird," she said, glancing at him with eyelashes spiked with tears, "that you have to put a coat on to go outside so you don't catch a cold, then you have to take it off when you get inside so you don't catch a cold? Sometimes," she added with a philosophical sigh, "it seems like things are fixed so that they always come out wrong. I have to go to the bathroom."

As she disappeared, Mike gathered up jackets and hung them on the pegs by the kitchen door. Carol was adding cold water to steaming mugs of cocoa, the line of her shoulders stiff.

"You okay?" he asked quietly.

She looked over her shoulder with a grim smile. "Of course not, but it's my job to make sure that they will be."

"Do you want me to leave?"

"You don't have to stay."

"That isn't what I asked."

"I think you've been unofficially voted an honorary member of the dorm." She handed him the tray of mugs. "And another lap and an open pair of arms never hurt at a time like this."

Cocoa passed around, Mike perched on the arm of the big chair Kathy and Candy occupied, while Carol made a place for herself on the sofa between Frank and Dorcas, pulling in Nicky between her knees. Silence and the sweet smell of chocolate filled the small room.

"I'm not trying to tell you that moving away from Saint Christopher's is going to be easy for you." She smiled at Dorcas and patted her knee. "We all know it'll be hard, but the important thing to remember is that it won't be the end of the world—it's just another road, and you'll go down lots of different ones in your lifetimes. At first it'll feel uncomfortable and unfamiliar, and it's okay to be scared, even to cry a little."

From the depths of the chair, Kathy rubbed her damp eyelashes. "What about a lot?"

Carol smiled at her. "You can cry a lot, because sometimes that does make you feel better. But then adjusting to your new surroundings will be your responsibility. You can't expect your new families to do it all for you."

Dorcas sighed. "You're always talking about responsibility."

"That's because it's so important. Each of us has the job to get along in this world, and you're not excused from it just because you're a little kid, or because things have made it harder for you than for other people."

"Like not having parents," Frank said.

"Or," Dorcas interjected with simple compassion, "having your children die, like yours did."

Frank, ever caring and protective of Carol, leaned forward to glower at Dorcas. "Dorky, you're so stupid!"

"I am not!" she shouted back. "I only meant . . ."

Gently Carol pushed Frank back. She was pale, but her voice was steady. "No, she's not stupid. She brought up my children, because she knows that what I felt when they died relates to what I'm talking about." She put a hand on Dorcas's knees and drew her closer. "I wanted to crawl under the bed and never come out, because it was just too hard for me to live without them. And then Father Cunningham told me about your dorm needing someone to stay with all of you. If I had stayed under the bed instead of coming to be with you, I'd have missed so much fun. Instead of letting that be the end of the world for me, I started again with you."

"But now that's going to be over, too," Frank pointed out.

"Being together will be over, but not the willingness to go on. Because you guys are so brave, you helped me be brave. The only difference is that instead of being brave together, we'll have to be brave separately."

"That'll be a lot harder," Dorcas predicted.

"I know," Carol admitted. "That's what I was talking about. When you get to your new families, if you try to be helpful, and stick to the rules, and not be grumpy, they'll think you're pretty great, and they'll try to be as good to you as you are to them. Before you know it, you'll all be as friendly and comfortable together as we've been here. But you have to do your share to make that happen. That's your responsibility." When everyone nodded in agreement, Carol hugged Nicky, then put him on his feet. "Okay, then let's wash our hands and go to dinner."

As the children's voices dissolved into sounds of water splashing in the bathrooms, Carol gathered up the cups and took them into the kitchen. Her movements were quick and abrupt, as though her nerves were strung too tightly to allow the smooth coordination with which she usually moved. Mike took the tray out of her hands and pulled her after him onto the porch.

"What are you...?" she began to protest, but he stopped the rest of it with a hand over her mouth. Above his hand her eyes were brilliant and panicky. He'd seen that look before, the day she'd passed him jogging and he'd told her about his accident. Sympathy frightened her, he knew, because she had such a tight but fragile hold on her control.

He lowered his hand, then put both hands at her back and pulled her toward him. She resisted, but he held firm. "Relax," he said gently. "I don't want you to fall apart, or break down, or dredge up the past. I just want you to lean on me for a minute to rest. I can't believe that that little talk didn't cost you something."

She expelled a long, ragged sigh and inclined her body against his. It was a little like leaning on a wall, she thought—a warm, responsive wall—and at that moment the support was a welcome relief. His arms tightened around her as a cold wind swept past them.

"They're too young to have to go through so much," she said wearily.

He bent his head, resting his cheek against hers. "I know. It isn't fair. But you've done what you could to make them strong. Meg thinks they're tough and that we've got to believe they're better equipped than the average child to deal with what happens to them."

Her voice became aggressive, though she still leaned passively against him. "Well, I'd like it in writing."

Mike laughed softly into her ear. "My career is proof that even with a solid contract, there are no guarantees."

Now she leaned away, her arms looped loosely around him. "There's only faith that whatever happens, we're in good hands. Do you believe that?"

"Oh..." He looked into the darkness that surrounded them as he thought. "I'm not sure I did a month ago. Today I do."

She smiled, acknowledging the reason for that. "The children."

"No," he replied evenly. "At least, not entirely."

Carol looked into his eyes, wondering if she had correctly interpreted his meaning. Mike looked into hers, letting her see that she had. "You're quite a lady," he said. "It's difficult to be around you and not be affected by you."

Emotion rose in her eyes, alternating between fascination and fear. But before either could settle, the children trooped noisily through the dorm's living room in search of Carol. Reluctantly, Mike drew away. He accompanied Carol and the children to the cafeteria, still unsure whether she found his continued interest in her appealing or frightening.

Chapter Eight

Mike was staring at the stiff white paper folded into a triangle and trying to remember the next step in the construction of an origami swan, when he was struck on the forehead by an airplane. Also constructed of paper, the missile landed harmlessly on his half-formed bird. He looked up at the boy seated across the table from him and tried to look severe, but Frank's shoulders shook with silent laughter.

Mike glanced at the other end of the cafeteria table where Carol and the girls and Nicky were hard at work, a flock of perfect swans resting on the table between them.

"I can't do it," Frank whispered, grinning. "Let's go throw some balls."

Mike flexed the shoulder that was finally almost back to normal and tried to look firm. "We're supposed to be helping."

Frank looked at Mike's hopeless triangle and his well-executed but nonstandard airplane. "But we're not," he pointed out.

"Maybe there's something else we can do."

Frank looked disgusted. "Later they're going to bake cookies."

"Cheer up," Mike advised. "They'll need tasters, won't they? Oh . . . hi, Carol."

Carol had slipped onto the bench beside him and was examining the airplane that had landed incriminatingly on the table in front of him.

"Frank did it," he explained, quickly denying blame.

"Oh, right!" Frank picked up Mike's feeble attempt at origami in a gesture of feigned indignation. "Well, look at what he made. It doesn't even look like anything—except maybe goriami somebody made a mistake with."

"Origami," Carol corrected him. She took the sad triangle from Frank and glanced from it to Mike. "It's a good thing you two aren't being paid piecework."

Her mood was light and teasing, and her cheeks glowed above the deep cowl neck of a hunter's-green sweater. It turned the khaki color of her eyes almost to lime. Mike tried to remain unaffected, afraid to call up that curious duel in her eyes. "You never said anything about payment."

"Sister Cel is making cider and donuts for all hard workers to share at our afternoon break."

Frank licked his lips. "Donuts?"

Carol shook her head in dramatic regret. "I hate to see you two miss out." From her lap she produced a spool of narrow red ribbon, a ruler, a box of red foil stars and a hole punch. Reaching for the box lid that held the finished swans, she picked one up and held it between her fingers. "We need a hole here...." She indicated the topmost fold of the swan's head. "Ten inches of ribbon to thread through the hole, and a star on each side of the swan's head for an eye. Think you two whirlwinds can handle it?"

Mike raised an eyebrow. "Do you think you can just offer us a bribe and expect us to...?" He stopped in mid-sentence as Frank took the ribbon and began to lay it against the ruler, cutting at ten-inch intervals. "Frank!"

Frank continued working. "Donuts, Mike. Anything's worth donuts."

With a sigh Mike took a swan in one hand and the hole punch in the other. "Well, maybe we can be bought. Now you wanted a hole, right?'' He slid the punch down the neck of the paper swan.

"No!" Carol leaned across his arm to prevent him from putting an ugly hole in the wrong place. "Right on..." Pointing to the swan's head with her forefinger, she turned to him to see if he was paying attention. Their faces were inches apart, and she noticed for the first time the devilment in his eyes. As he became aware of her breasts against his arm, an entirely different form of devilment invaded his expression. "On top," she finished softly, her own fascinated gaze rising to meet his. Then she seemed to pull back. "You'd better do it right," she threatened, teasing again, "or there'll be no origami hall of fame for you, and no donuts."

"Grump," he accused as she went back to the girls and Nicky. There had been no fear in her eyes that time, he noted with satisfaction.

"I UNDERSTAND you were a big help with Carol's origami swans project," Mother Margaret said absently as she studied the sheet of paper that she'd wound into her ancient Smith Corona typewriter. Mike sat in the chair facing her desk, his feet propped on one corner of it. Suspicious of her compliment, he wasn't surprised when she looked at him over her shoulder and smiled blandly. "Of course, holes in heads are something you can relate to."

Mike gave her an exasperated grimace. "Takes one to know one, Sister Smarty. I'll have you know that all the swans I worked on have a distinctly artistic touch."

Mother Margaret nodded. "Dirty thumbprints. Carol told me that, too."

"Those were Frank's contribution. We were better at the cookie baking."

"Cookie *tasting* was the way I heard it."

"Well, if you already know all about it," he said archly, "why are we discussing it?"

She turned away from the typewriter to lean an elbow on the desk. Her veil fell over one shoulder. "Because I haven't seen much of you this week and I wondered how you were doing. Have you recovered from being Santa?"

Mike swung his feet to the floor, unable to come to a conclusion about that. "Sometimes. Carol tells me you have to put the injustices and the frustration aside and just help the kids deal with things the way they are—and that makes sense. The day the other kids left, she had a talk with her dorm about what their attitude should be when they move on. She was so logical. She didn't make it sound like a lot of noble claptrap, but just a practical plan for surviving. She made those five little kids, who've been banged around by life, believe that they could dig down inside themselves and find more courage, more resourcefulness, more kindness to offer the new people in their lives. I admired her for that, and I believed it, too."

"But?"

He stood and wandered to the window. The grounds were dark except for the lights from Carol's dorm and the Christmas lights that outlined the window in which he stood. "But then Candy crawls in my lap, or Frank gives me that hero-worshiping smile, or one of the other kids takes my hand and I . . ." He shook his head, pacing back to the chair. "I guess I'm not used to being unable to make some difference."

Mother Margaret watched him walk across the room and stop before a small Nativity set she'd placed on a sheet of cotton atop her file cabinet. "Kindness, caring, make a difference to every life you touch. Carol says the kids adore you."

He turned to her, his expression grim. "What good will that do them when they leave?"

"Having received kindness somehow helps you understand that you can give it. That's an important lesson for anyone, but for a young child it's particularly valuable. It sets them on the right road, and nothing can stop them from going all the way with it."

He came back to the chair and fell into it, sinking down and leaning his elbows on the arms, making a temple of his hands. "That's nun talk, Meg."

She leaned back in her chair, laughing. "When have you known me to be sanctimonious?"

"Never," he had to admit.

"Then believe me when I tell you that four of those five children have never had a father figure in their lives. Frank had one, but he was a drunk. You're being a friend to them. You help them and hold them and let them know you care. That softens up the hardness that begins to grow in a neglected child, so that love can take root there. I know caring about them and worrying about them cause you pain, but don't let that stop you. Think about what it's doing for them."

Mike sat up. "Moving kids around is a crummy system."

"It's a system in which people are doing their best dealing with problems that are practically insurmountable and situations in which someone invariably loses. Railing against it doesn't help."

"That's what Carol says." He grinned at his sister, got up and sat on the edge of her desk. "Interesting how we've both spent the past hour quoting her. What else did she say about me?"

Mother Margaret thought. "She said something about you and the children almost destroying a stationery store, causing pandemonium in a restaurant rest room—"

"That's not what I mean," he interrupted.

"Oh?"

He picked up her stapler and studied it as though he'd never seen one before. "Did she say anything about me . . . personally?"

"I told you she said the children love you. . . ."

He dropped the stapler and looked her in the eye. "Did she mention how *she* feels?"

Mother Margaret studied him closely. "No. Do you find it difficult to tell?"

"Very." He smiled, as close to embarrassment as Meg ever remembered seeing him. "I was comfortable with Linda, because we never went too deeply into what we felt ... probably because, as it turned out, there was nothing there. But Carol has me thinking, analyzing all the time."

"Have you reached a conclusion?"

"I don't think there is one yet. Her first reaction to me is always interest...." He smiled again, at himself this time. "The other night I even saw fascination in her eyes. I think she'd like to know me better, but then—" he frowned "—she becomes afraid. I see it develop in her eyes every time I'm close to her, and I don't know what to do about it. I suppose she's afraid to care for another man."

Mother Margaret nodded. "That was such a devastating blow, and in the healing process, a year isn't a very long time."

He nodded, understanding that. Then he glanced at her, trusting. "Do you think she could fall in love again?"

She spread her hands. "I'm not sure I have any nun talk to cover that, Mike."

"Oh, c'mon," he said, grinning. "Take a stab at it. I'm convinced that, deep down, you know everything."

"Okay, I'll tell you what I think." She put her hand over his where it rested on her blotter. "She's a woman capable of great love. We see it in her every day. But she's in terrible pain, Mike, and the man who falls in love with her will have to be gentle and patient. I imagine when she reaches out to someone, it will be because she's feeling again, but because she's holding in so much pain, that's what she'll feel. And she'll resist, blaming the man who loves her rather than the past she can't let go of."

Mike thought about that for a minute and decided that it made sense. He leaned over to kiss Meg's cheek. "See?" he said, getting to his feet. "I knew you'd know. See you in the morning."

"Mike?" Mother Margaret took an envelope from a basket on her desk and handed it to him. "Would you give this to Carol on your way back to the cabin? It arrived express mail late this afternoon, and I haven't been able to get over there with it."

Mike accepted the official-looking envelope with its U.S. Government return address. "What is it?" he asked, frowning at it.

"Mail," she replied. "Personal mail."

Directing a wry twitch of his mouth at his sister, Mike left her office with his delivery. The night was cold and fragrant with pine and the promise of snow as he sprinted for the dorm. Carol looked pleased to see him. "Come on in," she said quietly. "The kids are asleep. Want some coffee?"

"No, thank you." His voice was a little tight, a little cool. He felt aggressive and quarrelsome, then guilty as he recalled Meg's advice. He had no idea what this letter meant, but he had a feeling it was something he wouldn't like. He handed it to her. "Meg asked me to deliver this."

She took the letter from him, nodding as though she'd been expecting it. "My travel arrangements," she said, meeting his gaze with a defensiveness of her own. "Thank you."

"Sure," he said, folding his arms. "Where are you going?"

She pulled out a chair for him at the kitchen table then sat down, leaving an empty chair between them. "I have a secretarial position at the American embassy in Paris. I'm scheduled to arrive there February 15."

Less than two months, he thought, a feeling of panic closing in on him. She felt something for him, he knew she did, but she was looking at him with a ruthless sort of nonchalance. He was sure it was an effort to divert whatever objection he might have to her plans.

He got to his feet and walked to the sink, wanting to look out the window into the darkness. "The man who loves her," Meg had said, "will have to be gentle and patient." He'd been loved and treated kindly all his life—a basic gentleness was part of his makeup. But he'd been gifted and ambitious enough to go after a dream—patience was foreign to him. He took a deep breath, hoping that a few quiet moments and the darkness beyond the window would bring it to him. But all he saw in the window was Carol's reflection.

He turned around and leaned against the counter. "Don't you have to speak the language?" he asked calmly.

She smiled. *"Mais, oui. Mes parents étaient Canadiens."*

Mike raised an eyebrow at her flawless French. "And does that come with a translation, *mam'selle*?"

Her smile deepened. "My parents were French Canadian. My father is second generation, but my mother came from Montreal. I'm a genuine Canuck, so I'll have to work hard on my accent, or I'll be laughed out of Paris."

Mike didn't know if it was the soft, melodic roll of the few words in French, or the sudden darkening of Carol's eyes, but he felt himself relax as he went back to the table. He took the chair next to hers. "Why so far away?"

She shrugged, absently running a finger along the edge of the table. "I thought it would be good for me."

"Why?"

She looked up, apparently startled that he was persisting. "It'll be something new."

"I'm something new," he said, smiling at his own blatant self-promotion. Then his expression sobered and he added softly, "And what's old and familiar in your life, you'll carry with you, no matter how far away you get from that house with the picket fence."

Carol gave him a look filled with haughty indignation. It was intended to keep him at a distance, but he saw her underlying pain and looked back at her steadily. "You won't freeze me out, Carol, so stop trying. Maybe it's time you settled up with the past."

Her indignation fell away and her expression was suddenly all pain. It pulsed so strongly in her that he felt it. After a moment, she shook her head and smiled grimly. "The past refuses to settle with me."

"You need a few defenses on your side," he suggested quietly. "Perhaps someone in your present. Maybe some dreams for the future."

She looked at him a little pityingly. "You have such a simplistic view of things."

"Confrontation isn't complicated," he insisted. "Difficult, but not complicated."

Carol stood and went to the refrigerator, her hands quick, her movements catlike as she poured milk into a juice glass. "If you have such a clear perception of everything," she said without turning to look at him, "then you should be planning your own future instead of worrying about mine."

"That's what I'm trying to do."

Carol turned with a frown of perplexity, the glass of milk in her hand.

Mike shook his head, wondering if her confusion was genuine, or just another tactic to keep him at a distance. "My future seems to be moving to Paris," he said, pushing himself away from the table.

She shook her head with an air of finality. "No," she said, repeating the word a second time. "No." She didn't have to be specific. She was saying no to everything; the denial was clear in her eyes.

For a moment he found it chilling. Then he remembered what it had felt like to shoulder the bat and connect with the pitch, the collective breath of a packed stadium held while the fans watched the arc of the ball. It had always filled him with a sense of power, even more than the cheers had. He'd never know that moment again, but he was still the same man who had swung the bat. His arm couldn't hit a homer anymore, but the drive, the determination, the guts that had put him there were still part of his makeup. With a sense of surprise, he realized for the first time that the man he was could make it without baseball.

Carol was watching his face in confusion. He saw the denial in her eyes slip, edged out by a reluctant longing. He walked to the counter where she stood, stopping within a hair's breadth of her. Her eyes grew wide, startled and warily defensive. Her lips moved in preparation for further argument, but no sound came from them.

He leaned over her, the distance between them charged with enough tension to fill the Astrodome. She leaned backward. *No,* she thought desperately. *Don't touch me, don't hold me, don't make me feel.* A fear close to panic rose in her, and when he placed a hand on the counter on either side of her, she felt as though every valve in her heart had malfunctioned.

"Yes," Mike said simply, still not touching her. Emphatically, firmly, he repeated, "Yes." Then he turned away and was gone.

Carol stood alone in the kitchen, a hand to her chest as she gasped for breath. Images cluttered her mind, faces she'd turned away from for a year came into sharp focus— Becky with her angel face, Gale with the devil in her eyes, Jon with his loving smile. She put her hands over her eyes, silently screaming, *No! No!* But the memory of Mike's voice penetrated even the depths of her grief. "Yes," he had said. "Yes."

CONCENTRATING HARD, her tongue caught between her teeth, Candy clutched the dart. Then she heaved it at the wall of balloons at the back of the booth sponsored by the parents' club of Saint Peter's School.

Mike, holding her up on his shoulder, danced back and out of the way as the dart headed straight down.

"Ooow!" Frank, standing beside him, howled in pain. The other children gasped, and the two mothers tending the booth leaned over the counter, hands clutched to their mouths as Mike swung Candy to the floor.

Frank pointed to the dart that had landed harmlessly near his boot. He looked at Mike with a big grin. "Just kidding. Missed me by at least a quarter of an inch."

The mothers looked at one another, then at Mike. "Perhaps you and your children should try something less dangerous. Like the fishing booth."

Mike shepherded the children away, taking a firm grip on the sleeve of Frank's jacket. "That wasn't funny," he said, his pulse dribbling back to normal. "You scared all of us."

Frank looked penitent. "I'm sorry. It was just a joke."

"Jokes that scare people," Mike said firmly, "aren't funny."

"There's the fishing booth." Dorcas pulled Mike along as she led the way. In a moment all five children were standing in line, talking and laughing together while they waited their turn. Ahead of them, a plump little girl held a fishing pole and cast the line over a makeshift divider that separated the back of the booth from the front. A moment later her "fish" was caught, a small doll in a pink blanket.

Candy jumped up and down. "That's what I want to catch!"

Judging by the crowd in Saint Bridget's gymnasium, Mike estimated that the bazaar had drawn every resident of Pointer's Beach and many from other parts of the county. Streamers, balloons and flags fluttered over people packed shoulder to shoulder from one basketball hoop to the other. The bleachers against each wall were dotted with people eating hot dogs, children napping, industrious mothers and nuns finishing handwork projects to replace those that were being sold faster than they could keep up. The air was full of the smell of popcorn, German sausage, and curly French fries. Mike found himself smiling. It smelled a lot like a ballpark.

"Does that smile mean you're having fun?"

Mike looked down to find Carol at his shoulder, two hot dogs in her hand and one giant Coke with two straws. She was wearing a thick gold sweater, and her eyes looked as if they belonged to a black Persian cat. She had tried to avoid him since their discussion in the kitchen three nights before, but the children had made it impossible. She had finally accepted the inevitable with polite friendliness, but this was the first time since then that he'd seen a little of the old spark in her eyes.

"Sure." He looked around at the carnival atmosphere. "I'm a sucker for this kind of thing. Your shift over?"

Carol nodded. "Now Frank and Dorcas are supposed to help Sister Cel man the booth, and Sister Claire wants to take the little ones to a puppet show being held in the rectory. That'll give you and me a chance to have lunch. The kids have eaten?"

Mike nodded. "Continuously since we arrived."

"Have they given you a hard time?"

He laughed. "Not deliberately."

"What do you mean?" she asked cautiously.

"Well..." He counted off on his fingers. "At the booth where you ring the neck of a Coke bottle with a rubber donut, Dorcas's aim was a little off and she hit Father Cunningham in the head." Carol gasped. "He was very gracious about it, and one of the mothers ran for an ice pack. At the Wheel of Fortune, Nicky spun the wheel right off the stand. It took Mr. Engbretson and me a few minutes to nail it back together. At the darts and balloons booth..." Mike recounted the story and began to smile as Carol's dismay turned to laughter.

"You've had quite a morning," she said, trying to sound sympathetic, but failing. "I'm sorry."

Mike frowned. "I might believe you if you weren't laughing. And how were you doing while I was playing *Adventures in Babysitting*?"

"I'll have you know we sold flocks of origami swans, and Sister Cel's baked goods are almost sold out."

"So is that lunch you're holding in your hands?"

"Right." She handed him a hot dog. "I knew I couldn't carry the hot dogs and *two* Cokes, so we'll have to share a large one."

The notion of a drink with two straws was charmingly old-fashioned and innocently suggestive. He smiled, and she looked away, relieved to see Sister Claire working her way toward them.

"Whew!" Sister Claire emerged from the crowd, a three-foot purple bear in her arms. "All right, where are the little darlings," she asked, "and what am I being paid for this?"

"You volunteered," Carol reminded. "They're 'fishing.' Mike and I are going to have lunch in the bleachers, then I'll relieve you in half an hour."

"An hour will be soon enough," she said, shooing them toward the bleachers. "Mother Margaret's got the booth now, so all's well."

Mike took hold of Carol's elbow and led her away. She followed him halfway up the bleachers, then onto a bench he seemed to select with great care. "Why didn't we just sit in the bottom row?" she asked, settling beside him.

He rolled his eyes at her. "Don't you know anything? You have to be at least halfway up to catch the foul balls."

Carol looked at him with mock concern. "I think you've gone a little foul yourself, Mike. We are not at a ball game. I am not Slugger Lund."

His eyes went over her in a swift glance, then he took the Coke from her. "I know that," he said, a small undercurrent of appreciation in his tone. "I presume that straw with the lipstick on it is yours."

Carol nodded, for a moment unable to say anything. She'd taken him aside for the purpose of talking about their discussion the other night, and the futility of his intentions. But the subtle suggestion of his remark just now flustered her, as though she were an inexperienced girl on her first date. Usually she appreciated honesty, but somehow honesty from him always made her feel threatened. Perhaps she could unsettle him a little.

"That's precisely what I want to talk about."

He sipped at the straw, then handed the cup back to her. "Slugger or lipstick?" he asked.

"You and me," she corrected, carefully peeling paper from her hot dog. She looked up at him, her jaw set. "Or the impossibility thereof."

He smiled. "We're not going to get into one of those 'No,' 'Yes,' things again, are we?"

"No," she replied. "You're just going to listen to me and believe what I'm telling you. I do not want to become involved with anyone at this point. I have nothing to offer. Allowing yourself to become interested in me will gain you nothing." She sipped at the Coke and put it on the bench between them.

"I did not 'allow' myself to become interested in you," he said, repeating her word, "I didn't seem to have a choice in the matter. And, anyway, it's already too late. And what I feel is a little deeper than interest." He picked up the Coke. "It's liking of a serious nature, Carol, and I'm not looking to gain, I'm looking to give."

For a moment Carol was speechless. How did a woman fight being "liked" by a man who said he wanted nothing from her but the privilege of giving to her? Then all her old defenses came into play. She'd been hiding too long to forget how. "I'm going to Paris," she said stubbornly. "My plans are made. Maybe when your book is translated into French and you come to Paris to promote it, we can have lunch or dinner." Certain that she had discouraged him, Carol went back to eating her hot dog.

"How do you say, 'You're a pigheaded little so-and-so' in French?" he asked quietly.

"I WANT to go fishing again!" Candy pleaded, clutching her doll in its pink blanket. "Maybe I could get twins!"

It was late afternoon and the crowd was thinning. The children, however, showed no sign of slowing down.

"I don't think we'd better do that," Frank cautioned gravely.

Mike and Carol looked at each other. "Why?" they asked simultaneously.

"Because when Candy got a banjo the first time she went fishing, Kathy went back behind the curtain and told the lady to take back the banjo and put a doll on the hook."

Mike shook his head. "Is there anyplace we'd be welcomed back a second time?"

"Let's go to the Coke bottle booth. Priests are supposed to forgive ya and ..." Frank had turned and pointed in the direction of the booth as he spoke. Then he stopped suddenly, his mouth open, a chalky pallor making Carol reach for him in concern.

"Frank, what's the—?" But he hadn't heard her. He was staring into the crowd and his bottom lip began to tremble. Carol followed his gaze and spotted a red cap in the crowd that resembled the one Frank's father wore in a photograph the boy kept in his room.

"Dad?" Frank whispered, as though to himself. Then he said the word louder, almost in a scream. "Dad!" He took off at a run into the crowd.

Carol started after him, but Mike held her back. "Stay with the kids—I'll go."

It was a moment before Mike could spot him, winding his way through the lingering visitors like a snake in a flower garden. Still several yards behind Frank, Mike saw him skid to a stop behind a man in a gray tweed jacket with a red woolen cap on his head. Frank grabbed the man's arm and tugged him around. "Dad!" Frank cried, surprise and joy making his voice crack, turning his pallor to hectic color. Two feet away now, Mike saw the joy in the child's face die and the pallor return as the man in the cap bent down to him.

"Well, hello, son," the man said gently. "Lost your father, have you?"

Frank stared up at the stranger, a look of such complete devastation on his face that the man's brow furrowed.

Mike pushed his way forward and put an arm around Frank. "I'm sorry," he said to the other man. "He mistook you for someone else. Please excuse us. Come on, Frank." When Frank didn't follow and continued to stare up at the man, Mike took hold of his hand and pulled him to the gym's side exit. The cloudy late afternoon was cold and windy—a shocking change from the closeness inside. But Mike noted that Frank didn't seem to be affected by it. He continued to look stunned and disoriented.

Mike sat on a concrete planter that ran along the side of the building and pulled him close. "Take a big breath, Frank," he ordered quietly. "Come on, a big one. Good. Take another one." Frank breathed in obediently, his mind clearly still preoccupied with his mistake, his eyes betraying the torture of his disappointment.

Mike became aware that Carol and the other children were clustered around them, but he knew Frank had no idea they were there. For the first time since he'd discovered his mistake, Frank's eyes focused on Mike. "I've even forgotten what my father looks like," he said in a quiet, shaky voice.

Mike put both arms around him. "Sometimes when you want something really badly, your mind creates the picture you want to see."

Frank shook his head as one large tear coursed down his cheek. "He never said he was coming back for me," he admitted, his voice breaking. "I was just so sure he would."

Mike enveloped him in his arms as Carol sat down beside them, obviously fighting for composure. The children gathered closer in various stages of emotional reaction. Kathy sniffed and patted Frank's shoulder. "I'll get you some water." With Candy in tow, she disappeared into the gym.

Nicky squirmed closer to put an arm around Frank, unable to do anything in the face of his friend's distress but cry along with him.

Dorcas sat down on the other side of Mike. "It's okay, Frank," she said, her voice lacking its usual strident, busybody quality. She looked as stricken as the boy. "I know my mother isn't coming for me, because she's in jail. I made up all that stuff about Central Park and the limo and the computer and the Christmas tree with gold and crystal ornaments. The last year we didn't have a tree at all. I don't think she even knew it was Christmas. But it made me feel better to make believe." She patted his arm awkwardly. "It'll be okay. You'll be a grown-up before the rest of us, and then you can do whatever you want. It won't be so long."

"Here, Frank." Kathy returned with a glass of water and handed it over with maternal care, pulling Nicky out of his way. "Drink it slowly, so you don't get hiccups."

Frank drank, rubbed the heels of two grimy hands across his eyes and drew a deep breath. He looked around a little sheepishly at Mike, Carol and the other children. "Sorry about that."

Carol stood and, swallowing hard, gave him a quick hug. Then she held him at arm's length. "You don't have to apologize to anyone for being upset and hurt, even angry, because of what happened."

"I cry all the time," Dorcas said. "I just don't let anybody know."

"Me, too." Kathy shrugged and smiled. "Only everybody knows, 'cause I can never stop."

"Yeah." Nicky sniffled.

"Well, for now, everybody has to stop crying," Mike said, getting to his feet. "You know why?"

Candy tugged at the hem of his jacket. "I know."

He lifted her onto his hip, waiting for her to explain.

"YoubetternotcryI'mtellingyouwhy," she said importantly, all in one breath, then broke into song. "Santa Claus is coming to town!"

Mike laughed and hugged her while Carol delved into her purse and passed Kleenex all around. "That's true," he said, setting Candy on her feet. "Although I think Santa understands this kind of crying. But I thought since we've had such a busy day, we should end it by having spaghetti at that great little Italian place on the water."

As the children reacted excitedly, Carol frowned. "But Sister Cel might have planned dinner. Besides, the budget..."

"Dinner's on me," he said, then he turned to the girls. "Dorie, Kathy, would you go ask Mother Margaret if she and Sister Cel and Sister Claire would like to join us for dinner?"

The girls disappeared at a run and Frank frowned up at Mike. "So why do we have to stop crying to have spaghetti?"

"If you cry in your spaghetti," Mike replied, "the noodles get slimy. Ever try to fork a slimy noodle?"

Frank smiled reluctantly. "That's dumb."

"No, it's not," Nicky said gravely. "I bet that really happens."

Frank rolled his eyes, then put an arm around his friend's shoulder. "*You're* dumb," he said.

Nicky smiled, obviously understanding that the accusation was made with affection rather than scorn. "Yeah," he agreed enthusiastically.

By the time Mike helped Carol put the children to bed, they were so exhausted from the physical and emotional trials of the day that they were asleep before the lights were out. Even Frank slipped off with a weary smile on his lips.

"I'm glad you were there." Carol spoke quietly as she walked Mike to the door. He turned to face her and she leaned against the doorjamb, smiling gently up at him. "He really needed a man at that moment."

"I'm glad I was there, too. There was a time when I thought facing a good pitcher took courage. I don't think I'll ever forget those kids, mired in their own problems, doing their best to comfort him because they knew how upset he was. I wonder if kids who have it good care about each other as much."

Carol smiled again. "Your sister's theory is that we're all pretty great. It's just that some of us get more chances to show it off than others do. Kids who have it easy probably love their friends as much. They just don't have to prove it as often. Going to work on the book tonight?"

He shook his head, pulling the door open. A blast of cold air blew into the room, fluttering the papers on the coffee table. "I don't think so. Somehow, I seem like a very dull subject at the moment. You going to be all right?"

She nodded. "Of course. You?"

"I'm not sure," he replied with a sigh. "I'm seriously considering kidnapping you and the children and hiding you all at my place. Then maybe this feeling of helplessness I get every time one of the kids takes my hand or looks at me with that sweet affection, will go away."

Carol laughed. "Then you'd have your sister, the state of Washington and the French embassy on your case. You'd better think that over."

He grinned, his mood changing subtly. "I think it would be worth the risk."

Carol tried to look firm. "You've got to stop doing that."

He raised an eyebrow innocently. "What?"

"Teasing me."

"Why?"

"Because . . ." She looked at a loss for an answer. "Because there's no point in it. I told you . . ."

"I know, I know." He raised a hand to forestall any further denial. "But one day you're going to wake up and decide you want to live again. When that day comes, I want you to remember me."

"I'm going to Paris."

"We'll see."

He moved to step onto the porch, and she grabbed his jacket sleeve. "Mike, I mean it."

To her dismay, he took the hand with which she had stopped him and brought it to his lips. He smiled down at her indulgently. "If you get that far, I can be there in three hours on the Concorde. A little thing like the Atlantic Ocean can't stop me when I really want something. See you in the morning, Carol."

Chapter Nine

"Nnf?"

Sister Claire, her nose and cheeks bright red, grabbed Carol by the shoulders of her robe and shook her. "Snow!" she exclaimed for the third time. "It's snowing! Get something on and come out."

The children scrambled around her, pulling on hats and mittens as they ran outdoors with whoops of wild delight. Carol looked beyond Sister Claire to the transformation that had taken place while she slept. The ground was a thick carpet of white, and the trees wore the snow like long capes of some exotic pelt. Even Santa and his reindeer wore caps of it.

Something elemental in Carol responded and she backed away from the door. "Come on in," she called over her shoulder as she ran for the bedroom. "Give me five minutes."

It occurred to her as she hurried into old black jeans, a flannel shirt and her down vest, that she hadn't felt like this in a year. She was excited, she thought with some surprise. She was looking forward to being out in the snow like a giddy child. She stopped for a moment, startled by the absence of grief. Surely if she waited a moment, it would overtake her. She had lived with it so long that she felt naked without it, incomplete. Painful memories stirred inside her, but the feeling of devastation wasn't there.

"Will you hurry before it melts!" a voice from the living room shouted. Carol yanked a stocking cap onto her head and complied.

Following the shrieks of laughter, Mike reached the slope behind the administration building just in time to see a plastic toboggan fly past. He recognized the screaming, freckled face in the front as Carol's, and the veil flying out at the back as belonging to Sister Claire. The breath caught in his throat for a moment as they headed for the bushes that rimmed the slope, but the two women bailed out in unison just before the toboggan crashed. They pulled each other up, laughing helplessly. Mike heard himself laugh, as well.

"She seems to be having a good time. Who's responsible for that, I wonder?" he heard a woman's voice inquire.

He turned to see Meg. A plastic toboggan identical to the one Carol and Sister Claire had used was tucked under her arm. "It appears to be the snow," he replied. Then indicating her toboggan, he added with a grin, "Seems to be bringing out the child in everyone."

She dropped it at the top of the slope. "Want to take a run with me?"

He looked at the flimsy toboggan and then at his expectant sister. "The last time I was on a sled with you, you insisted on steering, and I got four stitches on my forehead."

"Well, you can't steer these," she reasoned, "and what's inside your head wouldn't notice one more bump, anyway. You can even have the front."

Mike took his place, offering her a backward hand as she slipped in behind him. "Generous of you. I get to absorb the bushes first."

"Be sure to spit out the berries," she cautioned as she pushed them off. "They're poisonous."

"Did you see that?" Sister Claire demanded, pointing down the hill as Mike and Mother Margaret sped past them.

Pulling the toboggan back up, she and Carol hesitated long enough to see Mike cover his face as the front of his sled flew into the bushes and stuck.

"Can we try yours?" Frank ran down the hill at them, spewing snow in all directions as he skidded to a stop. "The girls are hogging the other one, and Nicky and I can't get a turn."

"Sure. Here."

Sitting in the snow at the top of the slope, Carol and Sister Claire watched the toboggans go up and down, passengers changing, Mother Margaret teaming with the boys, Mike taking the girls down one at a time, then all together.

"I'm going to Seattle after the holidays," Sister Claire announced suddenly.

Carol turned to her, surprised that she hadn't mentioned her new assignment before. Every time Carol had asked where she'd be going when Saint Chris's closed, she'd been curiously secretive. "I didn't know the Sisters of the Trinity had a school there."

Sister Claire smiled thinly, meeting her gaze, then looking out over the snow. "They don't," she said. "I'm leaving the Convent."

Carol stared at her, speechless, then something brought to mind the time Sister Claire had been waiting for them on the dorm steps, the evening they'd come back from the dentist. On that occasion Carol had gotten an impression that her friend was burdened by something. Knowing what a difficult decision this must have been for her, she wished she'd made more of an effort to help.

"My dispensation has come through," Sister Claire went on. "I'm free to go on January 15."

"Are you sure it's what you want?" Carol asked gently.

Sister Claire sighed heavily. "Yes. Positive. For so long I was certain the Convent was right for me. But since coming here two years ago... I want children, Carol—my own children—not kids that continually pass in and out of my life.

I guess I'm just not the quintessential giver like Mother Margaret is. I...I feel as though the woman in me wants something more now—someone for me."

"Will you still teach?"

"I'm not sure what I'll do." Smiling, Sister Claire turned to Carol. "But I'm excited. I'll always be a spiritual woman, just not a nun anymore."

"Well..." Carol took her hand and squeezed it. "With me in Paris and you in Seattle, we'll be a far cry from our comfy little niche on the edge of the world here."

Sister Claire looked around her at the pewter sky and the beautiful snowy landscape. The air was filled with the children's laughter and their excited cries. She expelled a sigh that Carol found curiously contented, in view of what they'd just discussed. "I have been comfortable here. Because I love everyone here, I ignored all the little feelings and signs that I wasn't right for this life. I watched Mother Margaret bump up against hundreds of lives and send them spinning in a positive direction." She turned to Carol with an admiring shake of her head. "She thrives on that. Touch, heal, move on. But I've discovered that I can't be like that. I want to take hold of something permanent and grow old with it."

"Maybe you want to be in love," Carol suggested carefully.

Sister Claire nodded. "Yes, one day. But right now, what I want is to direct my own life in my own way. And someday have my own family." Realizing too late what she had said, Sister Claire turned to Carol apologetically. "I'm sorry. That was thoughtless."

Carol hugged her. "Of course it wasn't. Do you think it hurts me to hear about people wanting families, because I've lost mine?"

Sister Claire studied her consideringly. "I'm sure it must. But maybe it's time you gave some thought to building another one."

"With some Parisian?" Carol inquired and laughed, hoping to dodge the subject.

Undaunted, Sister Claire said, "Mike's a prince."

Carol sighed. "I know. But I'm not Cinderella."

"Feet too big?"

Carol elbowed her and groaned.

"Past too big?" Sister Claire tried again.

Before Carol could reply, she spotted Mike trudging up the hill with the toboggan. Then he was beside her, hair mussed, face ruddy, breath puffing out. Despite all her objections and denials, she felt a small stirring of excitement. The thought of sitting close to him in the sled, framed and sheltered by his strong legs, had an appeal that somersaulted in her stomach with a longing she hadn't known for ages. She looked up at him expectantly. He dropped the sled beside her and offered his hand.

Sister Claire grinned at her as she got to her feet. "There's your pumpkin, Cinderella."

"I'll take the front," Mike said as Carol began to settle there. "Those bushes are tough on the complexion." She scooted back, making room for him. The confines of the sled dictated that she wrap her arms around his middle and sit body to body. The subtle bite of his after-shave mingled with the sharp fragrance of the deep winter day. His down parka was smooth against her cheek, the thick scarf around his neck, nubby but soft against her temple.

For an interminable moment the toboggan didn't move. Carol sat with her arms around him, absorbing the sensations his closeness inspired until their impression was almost overpowering. She began to feel the tick of her pulse, the thickening of her heartbeat.

Mike was shamelessly prolonging the moment. He had great confidence that the day would come when she'd let him draw closer to her, but his faith that it would be soon was diminishing. Having her tucked around him in the sled was too beautiful a moment to throw away. He savored the feel of her trim legs around him, the pressure of her body leaning against his, the grip of her hands around his middle. There were enough clothes between them to fill a department store window, but his body was reveling in the sensation, as though they were both naked and touching.

"Anytime today would be nice," Carol said into his ear.

With a grin at himself for thinking she might let him enjoy this, he pushed off and the toboggan careened down the hill, snow flying, Sister Claire's cheer ringing in his ear.

IT WAS DARK before the sledding stopped. Sister Celestine made chili and corn bread for dinner and apple cobbler for dessert. The children chattered excitedly about Christmas being a scant four days away.

"It's still snowing," Kathy reported. In blue-footed pajamas she stood on her bed, holding aside the utilitarian beige curtain while she stared at the silent, drifting snow. "We'll be able to sled tomorrow, too, and the day after."

Carol tucked in an already sleeping Candy, then went to tug Kathy into bed. "I bet Santa did this for us," Kathy said as Carol pulled up her covers.

"Nature did it," Dorcas offered sensibly from the far corner of the room.

Not to be discouraged, Kathy folded her arms over the blankets and said gravely, "I think Santa did it—to kind of make up for not being able to give us everything we asked for."

Dorcas leaned on one elbow. "He hasn't even come yet. How do you know we won't get what we asked for?"

Kathy said quietly, "I never do. Do you?"

Dorcas hesitated a moment, then lay back. "No."

"He just can't do everything, even though he'd probably like to. So he sent snow instead."

Carol bent down to kiss Kathy good-night, holding her close for an extra moment because she was such a special, selfless child. Then she hugged Dorcas, holding her, too, for an extra moment because she was such a realist, and special in her own way.

In the hallway, Carol met Mike coming out of the boys' room. "Everything all right in there?"

Mike nodded as they walked together into the living room. "If you don't think about Frank's plan to motorize the toboggan tomorrow."

Carol smiled. "I swear his brain never rests." In the middle of the room she turned to him, her expression suddenly sober. "Do you remember what all the children asked for when they told Santa what they wanted for Christmas?"

"Everything down to Candy's real cow. Why?"

Carol rummaged through her purse and scanned the balance in her checkbook. "Because they're convinced they won't get it. Kathy thinks that Santa sent snow so they wouldn't be as disappointed." She frowned. Her funds would just stretch to cover the small things she had planned to purchase for them tomorrow afternoon, when Sister Claire would keep an eye on the kids.

Mike put his hands into his jacket pockets. "Well, they're wrong."

Carol looked up from the checkbook, questioning. "You don't think Santa sent the snow?"

He smiled. "Sure. But the kids are going to get what they asked for. You can help me pick it all out."

Carol stared at him, not entirely surprised by his generosity, but touched by it. She dropped her checkbook back into her purse, then sat on one arm of the sofa with a sigh. "Maybe it's not the right thing to do. They have many more Christmases ahead of them. When it never happens again, they'll be disappointed."

"Or they'll remember how great it was that it happened once."

Carol looked up at him, seeing his warm but cautious smile in place, and slowly rose to her feet. She put her arms around his neck and held him, her heart filled with affection for this man who had come to love her dorm children as much as she did. It was not patronizing caring for the sake of his own self-satisfaction, but a genuine, deep concern for them, their safety and their futures. She tightened her grip on him for a moment, then stepped back.

Mike was trembling. Controlling the urge to pull her back, to hold *her*, he felt overwhelmed by her expression of affection. He wanted to prolong it; he wanted it to be more than friendship. But the tie that bound them was fragile at best, and he dared not risk tearing it. "Tomorrow," he said, backing toward the door, "we're going shopping."

Chapter Ten

But the following day Carol had more serious concerns than shopping.

"The toilet won't flush," she explained to Mother Margaret shortly after 6:00 a.m. "And all the faucets are dry. I think the pipes have frozen."

Mother Margaret, in the very civilian garb of robe and slippers, pulled Carol into the convent. "We've got the same problem. I already have a call in to the plumber." She sighed, leading the way into the kitchen, where Sister Cel and Sister Claire, also still in night wear, sat over cups of coffee. "But I was hoping the problem didn't involve the cabins, as well. Want a cup?"

Carol raised an eyebrow. "Where did you get the water for that?"

Mother Margaret put a steaming mug in front of her and smiled teasingly. "You're not much of a pioneer, are you? Sister Celestine melted snow."

Carol smiled at her own lack of imagination, gratefully pulling the coffee toward her. "You'll have to forgive me. I was awakened rather suddenly by a little girl who was desperately dancing. A walk into the woods before your eyes are open is hard on the system. Fortunately, Mike arrived to lead the boys' expedition."

Mother Margaret took the chair opposite Carol and smiled confidently. "I'm sure we'll have the problem solved in no time. Have a Twinkie."

Carol looked in surprise at the plate in the center of the table, filled with Mother Margaret's private stock. "You're sharing?"

"Only to prevent us from divulging her vices to the children." Sister Claire bit into one with obvious relish.

Half an hour later the group around the table had swelled to include Mike and the children. A frantic Mr. Engbretson had called and been reassured by Mother Margaret that the crisis would soon be behind them. The plumber, however, could not validate her promise.

"It appears—" Mother Margaret cleared her throat as she hung up the telephone "—that pipes have broken all over town." She frowned into her coffee cup, a slight shade over her usually confident demeanor. "Because it's so close to Christmas, several of the plumber's staff are on vacation. He won't be able to get to us for four or five days."

A communal gasp rose from the group. Nicky sidled up to Carol. "When I have to go again, I won't be able to hold it for five days," he whispered worriedly.

Carol patted his shoulder, assuring him that he wouldn't have to. Visions of every resident of Saint Chris's moving into Pointer's Beach's one gas station crossed her mind.

Mike stood and reached for the telephone. "Get everyone packed, Meg," he said decisively, putting a hand over the mouthpiece. "We're moving to my place."

"We can't..." Mother Margaret began to protest.

"We can't stay here," he said, then into the receiver, "Hutton, it's Mike. We're going to have houseguests for a few days. Three nuns, five children, and a woman."

Mother Margaret rose, apparently gaining confidence in the plan. "Mr. Engbretson has nowhere to go."

"Add a man to that list, Hutton," Mike said into the phone, then with a small frown he asked, "Hutt, are you okay?'' He listened a moment, then answered patiently, ''Five children. Right. No, you heard me. Nuns. Three of them. And a man and woman. No, they're not together. Good. We'll arrive in three or four hours. Thanks, Hutton.''

Mike hung up the telephone and looked around the table. ''Well, we'd better get moving.'' The other sisters dispersed, and the children ran off toward the dorm, squealing delightedly.

''I'll have to call the mother house and tell them what we're doing,'' Mother Margaret said, a smile beginning to form on her lips. ''And then the plumber again.''

''Go ahead. Carol and I'll get the kids packed. We'll make a stop in town for breakfast and find a rest room somewhere that's working. Pack lightly. We won't have much room for luggage.''

Mother Margaret rolled her eyes as she picked up the phone. ''As though I had an extensive wardrobe.''

Carol followed Mike to her dorm, offering every argument she could think of. ''Mike, that'll be eleven of us under one roof.''

''Twelve. You forgot Hutton. I have lots of room.''

''Who'll cook?''

''Sister Cel will be with us, and Hutton takes care of my house.''

''Well, I can't come.'' She stopped in her tracks, tossing the dangling end of her scarf over her shoulder.

He turned to frown at her. ''Why not? I didn't hear Meg relieve you of duty.''

Why not? Carol asked herself frantically. Because it was dangerous. She didn't want to know any more about him. She was too interested in him already. She didn't feel emotionally strong enough to handle anything complicated.

''Well...since you'll all be under one roof, I won't really be needed.'' That was a lame excuse, but it was the best she could do. "Maybe I could use the time to visit my dad over Christmas."

Mike walked the few steps back to her and looked down into her eyes. "You are going to continue to care about me, whether or not you spend time in my home. Flying off in a panic isn't going to protect you from what's growing between us. And can you really bring yourself to leave these kids at Christmastime?"

That did it. Whatever panicky notions she might have entertained about escaping him and the prospect of four or five days in his home evaporated. She didn't want Christmas to come at all. She'd lost everything in her world last Christmas. The days of peace and love would be days of pain and wrenching memories for her. But she couldn't abandon her dorm children. Though she would happily sleep through the next week, she wanted things to be loving and festive for the children.

"The mother house will never agree to our going," she prophesied gloomily.

At that moment, a voice from the convent door shouted, "Mike!" Mike refocused his attention, and Carol spun around, to see Mother Margaret clutching her robe around her. She raised a thumb in victory. "It's okay. Stop by for us when you're ready!"

MIKE'S HOME was a sanctuary of English country coziness in the hills overlooking the Willamette River and the city of Portland that sprawled along both banks. During the drive from Pointer's Beach in the back of the station wagon, Carol had tried to decide whether his decor would be modern or rustic. She hadn't expected the warm comfort of big-flower-patterned furniture, pedestaled ferns, filmy curtains and French doors that led out to a covered patio.

The children and the nuns were speechless. Mr. Engbretson ran his hand along the molding in an archway, inspected the window frames, then squatted to look into a stone fireplace in the large sitting room. He seemed uncomfortable at being unable to find cause for criticism. Even Mother Margaret couldn't tease. "Mike, it's a beautiful place."

"Thank you. Lorraine helped me pull together the feeling of an English inn, where I spent a week several years ago."

A short, spare man in a dark suit appeared in the doorway. His shoulders were straight, his head of thinning white hair was held high, his attitude one of control and efficiency. Carol watched him look over the quiet group of nuns and children. His eyes widened slightly, and she got the distinct impression that he'd just quelled an urge to run in the other direction. Then his eyes fell on Mike, and he seemed to pull himself together. He moved into the room with quiet, almost martial grace.

"Hutton!" Mike pulled him into the large group and put an arm around his shoulder. Hutton was a good foot shorter than his employer. "Good to see you. We had a plumbing emergency at Saint Christopher's, and my friends here will be staying with us until it's over. I don't remember if you've ever met my sister, Mother Margaret."

"No, sir," Hutton replied, the elegant sound of British gentility in his speech. "I did attend little Erika's birthday party with you and met the rest of the family, but I seem to recall that Mother Margaret couldn't join us. And I don't believe she's ever been here to visit."

Mother Margaret offered her hand. "Hutton, I'm delighted to know that someone can deal with my brother day in and day out and remain civilized."

Shaking her hand, Hutton slid his boss a look. "There are moments when I bend under the effort, ma'am. Welcome."

Mike continued the introductions, then Hutton reported, "All the rooms are ready. Cots are set up for the girls in the downstairs guest room and for the boys in the den. The sisters can share the room on the corner upstairs, and the young lady can have the smaller one next to it."

Mike frowned. "There are only two beds in the corner room and three sisters."

"I've added a cot, sir," Hutton informed him with a raise of his eyebrows. "We've cornered the market on cots in this county."

Mike grinned. "Very good. Okay, kids. Go on and find your rooms." As the children dispersed with a whoop of excitement, Carol hurried to follow them, but Mike pulled her back. "I'm going to need you," he said. "Sister Claire, can you keep track of the kids this afternoon?"

"Of course."

"Good. In the basement there's a television, a VCR, a Ping-Pong table and a pool table. Movies are in the cabinet half of the entertainment center. Hutton usually keeps the bar down there filled with peanuts and chips and soft drinks."

"Right."

She went after them, and as Sister Celestine would have accompanied her, Mike pulled her back, too. "Hutton's going to need you, Sister Cel. Meg, you're in charge of calling the family and telling them where we are, so they don't worry about us."

Nodding, Mother Margaret turned away, then came back several paces, folding her arms and frowning up at her brother. "You seem to think I'm no longer in charge."

Mike reached out to pat her cheek. "And Rick always says *he* got all the brains. You're in charge of a rickety old place with faulty plumbing. I'm captain of this team, Meg. And, whatever you do, don't invite them over."

"I'll bring the bags in," Mr. Engbretson announced.

"I'll do that," Mike said, trying to stop him, but he lifted his chin.

"Are you thinking I'm too old to do it?"

"Yes," Mike replied, grinning as he looked at him levelly. "Last time you did all the work, I ended up being Santa Claus because of your aches and pains."

For the first time that Carol could remember, and probably in the recorded history of Saint Christopher's Home for Children, she guessed, Mr. Engbretson smiled. "Well, you're wrong. Just didn't want all those little beasties sitting on my knee, so I faked it."

Mike laughed. "Lars, that's a lie."

Then suddenly the smile was gone, and Mr. Engbretson's expression became soft and vulnerable—another first, Carol thought. He winced slightly, as though entertaining a painful memory. "You held them and listened to their wants, knowing what's behind them and what little lies ahead. Could you do it a second time?"

Mike looked back at him, understanding precisely what the older man felt. He slapped his shoulder. "Well, this Christmas is going to be different. Take the small bags. I'll bring in the others."

As Mr. Engbretson left, Hutton looked at Sister Celestine, who smiled at him beatifically. She probably outweighed him by seventy pounds. Hutton asked his employer softly, "Sir, what do nuns and children eat for lunch?"

Mike smiled and began to lead away the remaining threesome. "The same as other mortals, Hutt. Sister Celestine here is a treasure in the kitchen, and I'm sure she'll be more than happy to help you prepare lunch. Right, Sister?"

"Oh, yes, indeed."

They reached an enormous kitchen that was decorated in shades of blue with light wood accents; copper pots and pans hung from a lattice rack suspended from the high ceiling. Small-paned windows ran along the wall that abutted the patio, and snow now drifted past in whorls. The warmth of the room made the storm outside seem like nothing more than a beautiful display. Instead of being inconvenienced by it as they had been at Saint Chris's, they could simply watch it from this cozy shelter and enjoy it.

While Mike and Hutton showed Sister Celestine all the kitchen's conveniences, Carol began to grow optimistic about making it through this Christmas. The cheer that pervaded the house was difficult to ignore, the jocularity of the adults and the children thrown together in it, impossible to fight. Sister Celestine was tying back her veil, and Hutton was rummaging for an apron for her when Mike turned to Carol. "As I recall," he said, taking her hand and pulling her from the room, "we had a date to go shopping today."

SITTING BESIDE MIKE in a shiny red pickup, Carol watched the snowy scenery inch past as they slowly proceeded down the slick surface of the road. Watching the highway, Mike reached out to tug at her arm. "Come closer," he urged.

A score of clever remarks crossed her mind, but she couldn't voice one of them. The warmth of the holiday, the beauty of the snow, the knowledge that her dorm children were having a wonderful time, pressed in on her to fill her, too, with Christmas spirit. That left little room for doubts and cautions. She unbuckled her seat belt and obeyed.

A little surprised at her cooperation, Mike patted her knee, giving her a smile that melted all tension. A man who always looked ahead and analyzed the pitch, Mike forced himself to forget that sometime after the holidays he was going to lose her. For one afternoon he had her to himself, and she seemed as determined as he was to enjoy it. Pennants were won after carefully plotted campaigns, but games were won day by day, and so, he was just beginning to realize, was life. Long-range plans could be decimated in an instant. But a moment fully lived and enjoyed became a part of you and remained with you forever. Relaxing behind the wheel despite the conditions outside, he draped an arm across Carol's knees.

"MIKE, it must be ten feet tall!" Carol craned her neck to study the top of the blue spruce that Mike was walking around and surveying with a clinical eye. He examined the tag that hung from a branch halfway up. "Twelve," he said, then stepping back, nodded. "It's fat and even and beautiful."

She thought of the vaulted ceiling in his living room. "I'd put it right by the..."

"French doors," he finished for her, "in the living room."

She turned to him, surprised that he had read her mind. "Yes," she said, moving into his shoulder as he extended his arm toward her. "And fill it with colored ornaments—none of that thematic, one-color stuff."

"Right. We're going to need more ornaments. Don't let me forget."

Half an hour later, several shop assistants carried the tree out to the pickup, while Mike and Carol made several trips back and forth with a dozen ten-foot swags of greenery. They made a stop for ornaments and lights, then walked hand in hand into a covered mall that had been transformed into a Christmas fairyland. Animated angels and Dickensian carolers were everywhere, and the potted trees that set off a skating rink in the middle of the mall were trimmed with small white lights.

Mike led her into a toy store.

"Now, wait." Carol brought him to an abrupt halt and pulled him aside near a display of dolls. Puzzled by her tone, he waited for her to explain. "We brought all the presents we made for each other with us, and you've just spent a small fortune buying a tree and things to make the house look festive. Trust me—the kids don't want or need more...."

"Pardon me. Excuse me...." Mike raised both hands and she fell silent, folding her arms, prepared to resist what she knew would be an argument. "You're a little out of your league here, Mrs. Shaw. I know you're their dorm mother, but I—'' he indicated himself with a waggling of his thumb "—I was Santa Claus. I know what they want, and I know how badly they want it.''

Carol's eyes softened at the amusement and the sincere generosity she saw in his. "Mike, I know that, but toys are expensive and you've already..." She gestured widely with both hands.

He caught them, pulling them together and squeezing them. "Will you relax? Santa had a good season.''

"Santa broke his arm and spent weeks in the hospital.''

"Santa is insured.''

"Santa has to think about his future.''

"Santa's future," he said gently but quellingly, "is going to Paris. So let him enjoy Christmas, okay?''

Carol covered her face with both hands in frustration, then dropped them and looked at him, uttering a sigh. "Let me offer one more argument.''

Sighing, too, he folded his arms and waited.

"The sisters and I," she said patiently, "have tried hard to make the children understand that Christmas is not a commercial event.''

He nodded. "I agree completely. It's a time for love and sharing, so let's love them and share with them, and make their jaws drop on Christmas morning.''

Carol threw her hands up in despair. "I give up. *Tête de pioche!*''

Mike blinked. "'Scuse me?''

"Pigheaded guy," Carol translated. "Or literally, pickax head.'' She studied him a moment, thinking that he was easily the most generous-hearted man she'd ever met. Jon had been kind and caring, but very practical. He'd been generous with himself, but material things were hard-earned and carefully distributed. The thought came and went with an ease that startled her.

"You know, if I were you," Mike said gravely, "I'd be careful about insulting Santa in a foreign language this close to Christmas."

Carol put her arm through his and drew him toward the dolls. "I think the role has gone to your head. Well, if you're serious about this, Kathy must have asked for a doll."

"She did." Mike moved his arm to put it around her shoulders. She looped hers around his waist as they leaned back to study the top shelves. "She was specific about one with diapers, a diaper bag and a bottle."

"There." Carol pointed to a small one just above her head.

"No, there." On the top shelf was one the size of a healthy infant; all of Kathy's requirements were displayed through the plastic cover of the box. "It has designer diapers. Kathy would appreciate that." The box was so large that it had to be taken back to the truck before they could continue shopping.

Carol found him as difficult to deal with over the rest of the purchases. All the musical bears had to be tested to find the right tune for Candy, something cheerful but not lively enough to keep her awake. The color was important, also. Bears weren't supposed to be pink or lavender. It had to look like a genuine bear and play something akin to Mozart.

"Mike," Carol pleaded, "it's almost six. I imagine Hutton will be expecting us for dinner."

Pushing a tricycle back and forth, checking the rotation of the wheels, Mike glanced at his watch. "I'll take you out to dinner. We'll call and tell them not to wait for us. This should have a basket and a horn, don't you think?"

"HI, HUTT!" Mike stood in a phone booth at the outside entrance to the mall, Carol wedged in beside him. Outside, snow swept past in beautiful silence. "We're still shopping. You'd better not hold dinner for us."

"Very good, sir." Hutton's voice was a little louder than usual; he was apparently competing with some racket behind him. "Could I ask you to bring home more milk? Or better yet, a cow. Perhaps a herd?"

Mike smiled into the phone. "You holding up okay, Hutton?"

"Yes, sir. But the food isn't faring as well."

"Good man. We'll be home by nine."

"Goodbye, sir."

"What did he say?" Carol looked at Mike as he hung up the telephone. She hadn't room to move and barely room to breathe, yet somehow she'd never felt freer.

Mike read the look on her face and strove to keep the mood casual. For the first time since he'd known her, she looked as though the smile wasn't put there by conscious effort, but came from some source of pleasure deep inside her. Curiously, that impression put the same kind of smile on his own face, he knew.

"He sounds as though he's teetering on the edge," Mike replied. "We'd better have dinner, wind up this shopping and hurry to his rescue."

Carol looked perplexed. "Certainly the sisters are keeping the children under control."

"I'm sure they are, but Hutton's never been around children, and he's been around nuns even less. He's not very comfortable with strangers, unless they come from Hyde Park and ring for tea."

"How did you and Hutton end up together?" Carol asked as she carefully wound spaghetti onto her fork. They sat in a sea of red-checkered tablecloths and dripping candles stuck into old wine bottles. In the background, Dean Martin sang cheerfully of *"Amore."*

"He had worked for some friends of my mother who came here from England. About three years ago they went back, but he decided he'd prefer to stay in the United States. When my mother heard about it, she called me, because I had just bought the house. It's worked out perfectly." He snapped a bread stick in half and offered a piece to Carol. He glanced up at her with a grin. "Except that I can't make him stop calling me 'sir' and treating me like I'm next in line to the throne."

She accepted the bread stick and buttered its tip. "You can't buy that kind of devotion. You'll have to mention him in your memoirs. How's that coming, by the way?"

"A certain redhead and her little friends," he replied, frowning at her as he nibbled at his own piece, "have been a serious impediment to my progress."

"I'd apologize for that," she said, reaching for her wine-glass. Her smile was warm and easy, and a longing he'd kept in check all afternoon began to grow inside him. "But it wouldn't be honest. The children have enjoyed having you around so much. I was so worried about keeping their spirits up, once the other children left, but you were like . . . like an answer to prayer."

Mike dropped the bread stick onto his plate and pushed it aside. He pulled his glass of Chianti toward him and looked into it for a moment. Then he raised his eyes and asked, "And what do you pray for for yourself?"

She thought for a moment, turning the rim of her glass with her fingertips until her wine caught the glow from the candle. "Just the will and the ability to keep going," she said. Then she lifted eyes made molten gold by the candle flame and added softly, "Those haven't been quite as hard to find lately."

Mike felt his heart stall. His instinct was to reach across the table for her, but he knew it would be fatal to move too soon. He sipped the Chianti and let its full-bodied richness warm him. "That could mean it's time for you to take a turn toward the future."

Her smile became regretful. "I'm still trapped in memories. Please understand that I'm not moping, or agonizing, or enjoying the pain. I . . . we . . . all just loved each other so much."

He and Linda hadn't loved each other, but there was enough love in his family to light Yankee Stadium, so he had no trouble understanding that. All the same, Carol had taken a step or two toward him this afternoon, and he wasn't going to let her slip back. Meg had told him that the man who loved Carol would have to be gentle and patient. With a warming calm that settled over and into him, Mike suddenly knew that he was that man. Meg had just forgotten to mention that he'd have to be tenacious, too.

"What . . ." he asked softly, looking into her eyes, "if I insist on invading your memories?"

Carol reached across the table and covered his free hand with her own. "You can invade my present." She laughed softly and squeezed his hand. "You *have* invaded my present. But you can't do anything about my memories. They were formed before you, without you. They remain intact, whatever you do."

He turned his hand to catch hers in it. "Are you planning to live your life out with them, never adding new ones?"

As he spoke, Carol looked into his eyes and knew that she did have a store of new memories. Unbidden, she received a sharp recollection of Mike as she had first seen him, when he'd found her hiding in his closet and he'd peered in, smiling cautiously at her. Quickly her mind filled with images of him—running across the street against a darkening sky, the afternoon they'd taken Frank to the dentist, as Santa Claus with a nervous Nicky in his lap, helping the children when they'd cut the boughs in the woods, carrying Candy, holding Kathy, teasing Dorcas, reassuring Nicky, laughing with Frank. And then there were all the times she'd found him looking at her as he was now—in his eyes a grave desire, coupled with a gentle understanding and determined patience. Feeling began to rise inside her, and for the first time in a year she didn't fight it.

"Come on." Mike waved for the waiter and put a bill on the table. "We still have to find something for Dorcas."

"What about Frank?" Carol followed Mike to his feet.

"I've already taken care of that. Slugger's bringing it tomorrow. Who's going to explain to Candy that she can't have a real cow?"

AFTER THREE MORE TRIPS to the truck with jackets, toys, chocolate Santas, giant candy canes for the children, Pendleton woolen caps for Hutton and Mr. Engbretson, and gift packs of fruit and cheese for the sisters, Mike and Carol stood in the middle of the toy store hand in hand. It was three minutes to nine, and the clerks eyed them malevolently.

"We've got to make a decision," Carol said.

"Dorcas didn't ask for anything." Mike looked around despairingly. After three tours of the store, they were no closer to selecting a gift for her, and he felt a desperate need to find just the right thing. "All she wanted was a necklace, so she could give it to you. She said her mom's limo would be coming with toys for her."

"Now that she's shot her own hole in the myth about her mom and the limo, I think she'll be able to be more honest about other things, as well. Let's get her a doll." Carol pulled him over to the display from which they'd selected Kathy's. "A great big cuddly one."

Mike looked doubtful. "Do you think she'll like it? I mean...she's a great kid, but she's not..."

"Soft?" Carol asked. Then she saw it, a doll as tall as a two-year-old, with a pudgy face, a big smile and blue eyes that closed when you tipped her backward. She pulled it down and studied it. "Kathy's tried to get her to play dolls with her ever since I've been here, and she's never touched one. I think she's never had her own." She looked up at him, her eyes full of tears. She blinked back. "Let's get her this one. I have a feeling she'll love it."

Weighted down with their final purchases, Mike and Carol trudged across the almost empty parking lot. Several inches of snow covered the ground, and the white stuff flew at their faces as they headed for the truck.

"Whew!" Carol stopped in the middle of the lot, dropping her packages and flexing her fingers. Her nose and cheeks were red, her eyelashes tipped with snow. "I don't know how Santa does it. Carrying Christmas from place to place is exhausting."

Mike stopped beside her, gently setting the plastic bag containing Dorcas's doll on the snow. Removing his gloves, he dusted the snow from her bangs before it could melt into her eyes. "It's easier when your sleigh flies. You don't have to carry things to a truck."

She smiled at him, feeling absurdly warm despite the coldness of the night. "No wonder the kids are convinced you know everything."

He laughed. "I talk a good line."

"No, it isn't that." Carol surprised him by putting her hands at his waist, analyzing him as though from some clinical distance. "I know you have doubts about your future at the moment, but you're so sane about everything else. You see things as they are, pretty much with acceptance—except for the fate of the children, and no one could accept that with equanimity. You laugh and cry and care." She sighed and he saw the clinical distance leave her expression. It was replaced by a sudden intensity, a surge of feeling. "I like that about you, Michael Rafferty."

He didn't take a moment to think. If he did, he'd probably decide what he was about to do wasn't right for her, him, or whatever might become of them. So he simply wrapped his arms around her in the snow that was swirling under the beam of the parking lot light and kissed her.

Even through his thick parka and the sweater underneath, he felt her mittened hands climb his back and hold him. Her lips were cold when his own touched her, and he moved over them gently to warm them. She responded without the resistance or even the reserve he had feared. Her lips moved with his, teasing a little, caressing, exploring.

Carol wasn't sure what was happening. She felt as though she were a tightly wrapped package under whose taut twine Mike had slipped a knife. The knot that had confined her for a year came apart with a sharp snap. Feeling washed over her, the first emotion she'd felt in aeons that didn't involve pain. She felt aroused and soothed at the same time and yet didn't find the paradox confusing. It occurred to her in a deep corner of her brain that there was comfort in the reawakening of the emotional and sexual responses that made her a woman.

Mike felt her tremble in his arms and drew back to see if fear had invaded her response. But what he saw in her limpid eyes had more to do with excitement and satisfaction than alarm. He suspected that he might be imagining that reaction, because it was what he wanted to see, but when she stood on tiptoe and pulled his head down again, his fears were put to rest. She wanted this as much as he did.

He covered her face in kisses, pulling off her knit cap when it obstructed his path to her ear. She pushed his down collar aside and planted kisses at his neck, then raised her lips to his ear. His hair was thick and cold against her face, and she burrowed her nose in it, delighted in how male it felt.

He finally pushed her away and held her at arm's length. Their breath swirled around them in a sudden gust of wind. For an instant Carol looked intoxicated by what they had shared, then her eyes came to life and she looked more delighted than stunned. "My goodness," she said.

Mike laughed softly and reached for the packages. "A sleigh that flies isn't everything."

Chapter Eleven

Hutton's grip on composure was more desperate that it had been when Mike and Carol had left to go shopping.

"Kids okay?" they asked simultaneously when he confronted them in the living room. As though on cue, loud laughter issued from the basement.

"They're watching movies."

"The sisters?" Carol asked in concern.

"When I brought chips down, they were playing pool. It's your family, sir."

Mike turned away from the cupboard from which he was pulling cups. He frowned at Hutton. "What happened?"

"They're coming." He made the announcement heavily, squaring his shoulders with apparent trepidation at the very thought. "They're coming here. All of them."

Mike put a hand to his eyes and uttered a small sound of distress.

"Mr. Rick's coming day after tomorrow, your mother and other sister and her family will be arriving from San Francisco by plane that evening." Hutton's voice rose as hysteria began to battle with his British steadiness. "I recommended that they make motel reservations, sir, because there's not another cot to be had in all of western Oregon!" He swallowed and seemed to make an effort to calm himself. "They said they'd bring their sleeping bags."

"Don't fold on me, Hutton." Mike led the man to a chair and poured him a cup of coffee. "You're doing great, Hutt. There's a big bonus in this for you, I promise."

"I don't care about a bonus, sir." Hutton took a sip of coffee and visibly tried to pull himself together. "It's just that—well—children and nuns, sir! And Mr. Rick! And that Sister Celestine . . ."

Mike sat down opposite him, his expression fond and sympathetic. "Took over your kitchen?"

Hutton sighed. "No, sir. She's ever so sweet about asking me what I'd like her to do and keeping out of my way, but we fixed chicken and potatoes and vegetables for dinner."

"Yeah?"

Hutton shook his head sadly. "Her potatoes lyonnaise were superb. I thought she'd be just a cafeteria cook, but she's as good as I am."

Mike put a hand over his mouth as Hutton stared despondently into his coffee. Carol turned away from the mirth she saw in Mike's face before her own erupted. "Well, I'll tell you something, Hutt," Mike said, leaning toward him confidentially. "There's too much pepper in her stew."

Hutton looked delighted. "Really?"

Mike looked at Carol for corroboration, and she offered it falsely but without hesitation. "That's right, Hutton. It's just a pinch too much, but it is too much."

"Well." With new reason for living, Hutton got to his feet. "I think I'll check and see if they need anything downstairs. Anything I can do for the two of you first?"

Mike shook his head. "Not a thing."

Stiff-backed, with a new spring to his stride, Hutton disappeared down the steps.

Mike dropped his head onto his arms with a groan and Carol sat down beside him, laughing. "Think of what a great couple of chapters this is going to be in your book."

Mike lifted his head and shook it. "Is science fiction selling this year?"

"How many more people will that be?"

He paused to calculate. "Six. But it'll seem like sixty. My brother-in-law's a great guy. My mother and my sister are a lot like Meg. Rick's like keeping a tornado in a thimble, and two more little children are just what the noise level in the basement needs."

"Easy." Carol rose to put her hands on his shoulders. "You've got the same quality in your voice Hutton has. Just try to roll with it." Gently, Carol began to massage him. "Everything's going to be fine."

"You're lying," he said, closing his eyes as he began to feel himself relax.

"Lying to yourself as a method of self-help is very underrated." Carol pinched gently along the cords of his neck and into his hair. "You have to face the truth of the present, but it doesn't hurt to lie to yourself about the future. Aahh!" A little cry of surprise escaped her as Mike reached behind him for her wrist and, pushing his chair away from the table, swung her into his lap. Her arms went easily around his neck, and she found herself smiling rather than resisting. "You're stopping the flow of blood to your extremities," she cautioned, smoothing the hair she had mussed while massaging his scalp. "That undermines the effects of the massage."

He fastened his arms around her waist and planted a light kiss on her lips. "I'm less interested in blood flow to my muscles than I am in love flow to my heart."

Loud laughter rose once more from the basement, and Carol looked a little nervously toward the source of the sound. "Need I remind you," she whispered, "that your house is full of nuns and children?"

"That's close to what I had in mind when I bought it," he said, kissing her again.

"I don't understand."

"Wife and children. I was looking forward to the day when I'd have a wife and children."

She smiled ruefully. "It looks more like a butler and transient houseguests to me."

Exasperated but undaunted, he said plainly, "I'm trying to tell you, Carol, that I can see you here. I can see you and me . . . together."

For a moment, she put her cheek against his, then pulled away and said softly, "I can't, Mike."

Mike rubbed one hand up and down her spine, the other gently stroking her knee. "Carol, I know how much the past hurts you, but you've got to come out of it. Can't you make the effort for me?"

The moment the words were out of his mouth, he cursed himself for a fool. He tightened his grip on Carol, bracing himself for her to rise angrily to her feet. Instead, her arms simply fell away from his neck; her expression was less angry than world-weary, as though she had suffered more than he would ever understand.

"What do you know about making an effort?" she asked, her eyes level with his, their expression direct. "You're a born athlete with a wonderful gift. I know you didn't become a star by accident. It took hard work. But you had the physical and emotional resources to give you what you required. And when that was taken from you, you realized that suddenly you weren't as strong as you thought. You had to find a quiet place to heal your wounds and regroup. I lost my husband and my babies, Mike." The pain that was always at the back of her eyes strengthened, reaching for him with an intensity that made it his own. "I have dragged myself out of the nightmare every morning, then dragged myself to work with the children, because I understand that they've suffered very nearly what I have—and they're just babies themselves. Every brave, hopeful word I give them, every smile, has to be clawed up from deep inside me, because I don't feel courage and I don't feel smiles. Most of the time I want to crawl into bed and die myself." Carol swallowed and stood. He made no effort to stop her. She looked down at him and said quietly, "So don't tell me about making an effort. Good night, Mike."

Mike put his head in his hands and let the misery wash over him. What in the hell had possessed him to say that to her? How had he dared? Because he'd been thinking from his own point of view and not hers. Somewhere in the back of his mind had been the notion that he'd lost his career—certainly he wouldn't be required to lose Carol, too. Selfish, he thought angrily. And stupid.

"Are you all right, sir?" Mike looked up to see a weary-looking Hutton leaning over him solicitously. The butler's eyes went to the empty chair that Carol had occupied, then back to Mike. "Trouble with the lady?"

Mike nodded. "Trouble understanding the lady, Hutton."

Hutton grinned; it was a rare slip of dignity on his part. "You have the commiseration of every male in the world there, sir. You need a nip of my special reserve."

Mike didn't have to watch him reach into the cupboard to know what he was bringing down. They'd shared a tot of Hutton's Napoleon brandy the night Mike came home from the hospital. The brandy had helped him face Linda's empty closet and the long hours of pain in his arm without medication, from which the doctor had decided it was time to wean him.

Hutton poured a generous measure into a balloon glass and warmed it in his hands before passing it to Mike. It occurred to him that the brandy was the color of Carol's eyes after he'd kissed her.

"You've got to join me, Hutton," Mike insisted. "You're going to need it before this holiday is over."

"Yes, sir." The butler's agreement was hearty and immediate. He raised his glass. "To what, sir?"

"Oh..." Mike thought for a second. "To Christmas, Hutton. A time for love, miracles, elusive insights..." As he paused, another gust of laughter erupted from the basement. He smiled. "And children. To Christmas."

CAROL'S FIRST THOUGHT upon starting down the stairs was that she was in the wrong house. Mr. Engbretson was laughing. He stood on a ladder outside the long, wide staircase, passing a fat, fragrant garland through the balusters to Hutton, who sat on the stairs to receive it, wove it around the baluster and passed it back.

"You dogfaces took Normandy," Hutton was saying, "because our RAF Typhoons carpet bombed the hell out of our ground targets. The panzers couldn't move against us."

"I was wounded three times," Mr. Engbretson said, slinging an end of the garland over his shoulder as he worked, "and when I got home to Portland, I could not order a beer because I was too young. But I remember a nurse who didn't think so. She was..." He parted his hands to describe some feature, the nature of which remained unspoken as his eyes fell upon Carol. "Your mouth's open, girl," he said.

She closed it and folded her arms. "So is yours, Mr. Engbretson—in laughter. I just paused a moment to enjoy the sight."

"Is that so?" His shrewd glance acknowledged her riposte. "Well, I've made a friend here. Seems Archie and I were both at Normandy. Knowing we have memories in common has eased my heart—and freed my laughter." He raised an eyebrow at her. "Are you ever going to let that happen to you?"

Carol stared at him, or rather at where he had been, as he descended the ladder and moved it. She'd never thought he'd noticed her, except as the pest who called him when the children had caused some domestic disaster or other. To discover that he had not only noticed her but had obviously taken the time to analyze her was unsettling.

As she continued down the stairs, she saw that Santa's workshop could be no busier today than Mike's house was. The huge tree had been put up in the very spot they had discussed. Mother Margaret and Sister Claire were supervising the younger children's decoration of it, while Frank and Dorcas arranged a Nativity set on the room's glass-topped coffee table. As Carol drew closer and realized that the set was of porcelain, she got down to her knees between the children to examine the figures more closely. Every feature was beautifully detailed, the line and grace of each piece suggesting the set's considerable value. "Maybe we'd better put this up higher, where nothing can happen to it," she suggested.

Frank looked up, holding the figure of a sleeping sheep carefully in his hand. "Mike said to put it down low, so the little kids could see it."

Dorcas placed the infant Jesus between Mary and Joseph, then leaned back on her knees to study the tableau. "He said his mom always did that, so the kids could all touch it."

Carol studied the glossy finish of the figures, which was catching the rare, late-December Oregon sunlight, and said anxiously, "But this set is very expensive."

"Sister Claire mentioned that," Frank informed Carol, "but Mike said he trusted us to be careful."

"Okay." Carol got slowly to her feet. "Please do. I'm going to find a cup of coffee."

In the kitchen, Sister Celestine was fussing over Mike and Slugger, who were at work on omelets, sausages and toast. On the table between them lay a long white box.

"Well." Mike looked up from his conversation with Slugger to smile at her. "I hope you're not the one assigned to wake up Santa." He glanced at his watch. "You're punching in kind of late."

Carol shook her head, mystified. "I can't believe the kids didn't wake me. Good morning, Slug."

"They wanted to wake you, and he stopped them," Slugger explained. "Just so he could use it against you when you got up late. Nice guy. Well, thanks for the omelet, Sister Cel."

At the stove, Sister Celestine added ham and onions to a bubbling egg mixture, then glanced his way and waved.

Mike patted the box as he stood. "Thanks for getting the team to sign the ball. Frank'll be thrilled."

"Sure." Slugger pushed Mike back into his chair. "I'll see myself out. Merry Christmas, you guys."

"You, too, Slug."

As Slugger disappeared through the swinging doors, Mike went to the stove for the coffeepot and reached into the cupboard for another cup. He placed the cup in front of Carol, poured, then topped off his own coffee.

Sister Celestine brought Carol a steaming, fluffy omelet and a piece of grainy, dark toast. "Thank you, Sister," Carol said, admiring the beautiful plate with its thin slices of orange and pear. "I thought I'd missed breakfast."

Sister Celestine bustled away with Mike's empty plate. "When have I ever forgotten to save some for you?" she scolded over her shoulder.

Carol leaned toward Mike and whispered with a glance at Sister Celestine's back, "And you made me tell Hutton that she puts too much pepper in her stew. I feel like a traitor!"

Relieved that she didn't seem angry with him, Mike whispered back, "We saved a man's pride. I'm sure she'd understand."

Looking at him doubtfully, Carol tucked into her breakfast. Sister Celestine filled the dishwasher, then wandered into the other room while the machine sloshed and hummed away in the corner.

Carol looked up at Mike, sitting opposite her. He appeared relaxed, content to finish his coffee while she ate. He raised a questioning eyebrow as she continued to study him.

"I'm sorry I climbed all over you last night," she said hurriedly, before his good humor this morning could convince her that an apology was unnecessary. "I swore I'd never be one to wallow in my grief, yet I—"

"You don't wallow in it," he interrupted. "And I was presumptuous and stupid to take that attitude with you."

She poked at her omelet with the tip of her fork, pleased that he understood, but a little reluctant to let him assume the entire blame.

"I know you're just trying to help," she said, glancing at him with a shrug. "But it isn't that I'm not making an effort...."

"Carol, I'm so sorry I said that." He leaned forward, elbows on the table, his mug harbored between them. "I've resisted commitment for a long time, because you lose control when you love someone. Slug is two hundred and fifty-four pounds of line-drive eater, but all his wife has to do is look at him and he turns into a very large pile of putty. I didn't want that. I wanted to control myself so I could control the bat, so I could control my career." He sighed, curling his hand in for his coffee mug and taking a long drink. "Well, now that's all over, and I feel a little out of control. I don't know which way to turn." He put the cup down. Folding his arms on the table, Mike looked at her levelly. "Except that something instinctive in me keeps turning to you."

Carol pushed aside her half-empty plate and leaned toward him. "The present wasn't real to me until I met you. I mean..." She paused, groping for a way to explain. "I lived in it, I even functioned in it, but I wasn't aware of it. I was part of the past. Since you came to Saint Christopher's, I think and feel here and now. But the past still has a hold on me...." She paused again, putting a hand to her forehead in a gesture of embarrassed discomfort that made him smile. "And it wouldn't be fair to ask you to . . . wait around until I was ready."

"Depends," Mike said. He stood and carried his cup to the counter, then turned and leaned against it, facing her. "On whether or not I have to wait here while you're in Paris."

Carol picked up her plate and put it beside his cup. She stood toe-to-toe with him, her arms folded aggressively. In his charming, unobtrusive but all-pervasive way, he wasn't going to give her an inch. She was used to latitude from the men in her life, and she wasn't sure she liked this persistence. Then he smiled at her, his expression full of tenderness and a sweet indulgence that was still coupled with respect, and she decided that she liked it after all.

"I had made the Paris decision before I met you," she reminded him.

He nodded. "But now you've met me."

She smiled. "If this doesn't work out between us, I'm out a good job."

"That makes two of us," he said with a laugh. "We can ride the rails together instead of getting married."

Laughing with him, Carol fell into his arms; it felt so good to have him push her pain aside so consistently. She was finding it impossible to be unhappy around him, finding it difficult to remember the day that had lived with her like a dark burden for so long.

"Mike, Mr. Engbretson needs . . ." Frank burst through the swinging door, his eyes falling on the pair in each other's arms. Carol instinctively tried to push away from Mike, but he continued to hold her loosely.

"Needs what?" Mike asked.

Frank approached them slowly, looking from one to the other, his soft brown gaze sparked with interest, a smile forming on his lips. "Are you two doing what I think you're doing?"

Carol drew a strained breath, but Mike asked easily, "What do you think we're doing?"

Frank grinned at Mike and guessed. "Sucking face?"

Mike rolled his eyes. Grabbing Frank by his shirtfront, he pulled him toward them. Frank laughed, completely unthreatened.

"I kissed her," Mike said, putting an arm around the boy, his other arm still holding Carol. "Because we'd just shared a laugh over a funny thought. It felt good to be friends, so I kissed her. 'Sucking face' just doesn't cover it."

Frank nodded as though he understood. "But I bet I'm not supposed to tell the other kids."

"Kissing's kind of a private thing," Carol said, hugging him. "And your discretion would be appreciated."

He narrowed an eye. "Discretion?"

"A zipped lip," Mike translated.

"Got it."

"Good. Now, Mr. Engbretson wanted what?"

Before Frank could reply, there was a loud scream from the living room, followed by lusty crying and the babble of many voices talking at once. Carol and Frank followed Mike as he ran to investigate.

"Oh, no!" Carol groaned to herself as she saw everyone in the household gathered on the floor in front of the Nativity set. From the expressions on the children's faces, she concluded that one of the figures had been broken. Her eyes ran quickly over them and counted the Holy Family, three kings, three shepherds, several lambs, the donkey.

In the center of the large group, Kathy was trying to pull something from Candy's hands. Carol could see blood on them as the child wept and clutched them.

"Candy, give it to her!" Dorcas shouted, obviously upset. "Your hand's cut."

"It's all your fault." Kathy turned on Dorcas with maternal vehemence. "She wouldn't have dropped it, if you hadn't tried to take it away from her."

Dorcas gasped at the injustice of her accusation. "Carol said the pieces were very expensive. I just didn't want her to break anything."

As all the adults tried to coax the broken object from Candy's hand, Mike reached into the middle of the group and lifted the child out. She struggled, then realizing who held her, settled against his shoulder and sobbed. Carol gently pried her bloody fingers apart. In her little hands was the decapitated ox.

"She thought it was a cow," Kathy explained gravely, her eyes filled with tears. "She's sorry."

"There's nothing to be sorry about," Mike said firmly, "except that her hand's cut."

Hutton came over to inspect the injury. "Just scratches, really," he diagnosed. "Some Bactine will fix that right up."

For the second time that day, Mr. Engbretson shocked Carol. "And I have special glue," he said gently, going around to look into Candy's face, almost hidden in Mike's shoulder. "It will repair it so that it will look like it was never broken. Would you like to help me?" He held his hands out to her invitingly.

Candy lifted her head and looked at Mike, sniffling. "I broke it. I should help fix the cow, so she can give the baby Jesus milk and keep him warm."

Hutton reappeared with a bottle of Bactine and cotton balls. "We will fix your hand first," Mr. Engbretson said, taking her from Mike. "Then we will fix the ox."

"It's a cow," Candy disputed as he led her away, trailed by Hutton and Kathy.

"It looks like a cow, but it has different horns, see? And..." His lilting, accented voice drifted away as they filed into the kitchen. The rest of the group dispersed, except for Mother Margaret, who came to hook an arm in her brother's.

"Tell me the truth," Carol said softly to Mother Margaret. "Did you do a frontal lobotomy on Mr. Engbretson?"

"He's been forced into close contact with us, and has gotten to know the children in a way other than as a source of problems for him. Hutton has offered friendship, we've included him in our meals, and this house..." She looked around herself and nodded. "This house would soften the heart of an angry bear."

Mike smiled. "Thank you, Mother Gentle Ben."

Mother Margaret shook her head over his disrespect. "And I was just going to tell you what a prince you've become. How I admire the generous, thoughtful man you are, and how this wonderful house of yours is warming all of us, making this a truly memorable Christmas."

Stunned, Mike patted the hand on his arm. "Thank you, Meg."

"Don't thank me," she said, pulling away from him, "'cause now I'm not going to tell you that. Mother Gentle Ben, indeed!"

Chapter Twelve

Carol hung up the telephone, a frown on her face. Near her on the carpeted basement floor, Sister Claire supervised the children in the stringing of popcorn. "Still no answer?" she asked.

"No." Carol sank moodily onto a deacon's bench. "My father's a real stay-at-home. I don't understand it. I tried to call him yesterday before we left Saint Chris's, and I couldn't reach him. I hope he didn't try to call me and get worried when no one answered."

Sister Claire smiled. "Maybe his pipes froze, too, and he's moved somewhere else temporarily."

"No, they're more prepared for freezing weather in Denver than we are. And if that happened, he'd call me."

"If you keep trying, you're bound to reach him."

Carol glanced at her watch. "I promised to take the children skating after lunch. They need to let off some steam." She smiled fondly at the hardworking group on the floor. "They've been so good."

"Why don't I take them?" Sister Claire got to her feet and dusted off her skirt.

Carol blinked. "By yourself?"

Sister Claire looked affronted. "You don't think I'm capable?"

"It'll be like uncorking warm champagne."

"I'll bring Mother Margaret and Sister Celestine. They were just wishing this morning that there was time for some last-minute shopping. You can take over their gift-wrapping duties and keep trying your father at the same time."

"I'd feel guilty. You've watched them more than I have since we've been here."

Sister Claire shrugged, as though that detail were negligible. "That doesn't matter. Life's pretty disordered for all of us right now, anyway."

Remembering her disclosure of several days ago, Carol took Sister Claire's hand and pulled her down beside her on the bench. "How are you doing?"

She smiled and leaned an elbow on the back of the bench. "I'm confused, frightened, doubtful and wondering why on earth I decided to turn my life around in midstream." She toyed with the tip of her veil, then tossed it over her shoulder. "But I called a friend of mine who left the convent last year, and she says that's pretty normal. When I'm not worried about the future, I'm convinced I'm doing the right thing. But when I become concerned about supporting myself, making friends, being a productive human being without the support of a whole community of women working toward the same end . . . I get scared."

Carol squeezed her hand. "I felt a little like that when I was a young wife and mother in a new neighborhood. I was doubtful of my abilities, a little afraid of my awesome responsibilities. Then I met other young mothers, and I learned something valuable about women. We've promised to be as devoted to our families, as nuns are dedicated to a life devoted to God. We're not as organized as you...." She smiled. "And certainly not as holy...and we might not have such far-reaching effects, but we're as committed to helping each other as your community of sisters is. If you need help, make a friend of the woman next door or the one you work with. We're all in this together."

Sister Claire hugged her. "That's a comfort. I wish you weren't going to be all the way across an ocean."

Carol gave her a rueful grin. "I'm not sure I will be."

"What?"

"I don't know. I can't explain right now. Let me get my purse. You'll need money for this afternoon."

Carol ran upstairs, taking a moment to dial her father's number again. When the phone continued to ring unanswered, she replaced the receiver with a growl of frustration, then extracted several bills from her purse. At the bottom of the stairs she encountered the children and the sisters, already dressed for outdoors. She tried to pass the money to Sister Claire, but it was refused. "Mike already took care of it."

He stood on the fringe of the group, a cup of coffee in his hands. Carol turned to him with a sigh. "Must you fling money around with such abandon?"

Mother Margaret pushed the already loud group out the door. "Most eccentrics like to do that," she replied for him with an innocent smile. "We'll see you in time for dinner. We've got Sister Cel, and I think Hutton's going out, too. That means you two are in charge of dinner."

"No problem," Mike assured her.

Mother Margaret snickered. "And probably no dinner." Mike pushed her the last inch out the door and closed it. Hutton and Mr. Engbretson appeared from the direction of the kitchen, shrugging into coats, still in deep conversation about Normandy. Hutton came to an abrupt halt in front of Mike and Carol.

"You're sure you can spare me, sir?" he asked his employer.

Mike nodded. "I'm sure. How often can a man find *The Invasion of Normandy* at the local theater and watch it with a comrade who was there, too? You old soldiers have a great time."

"The kids voted on hamburger for dinner," Hutton said, then smiled indulgently. "Lucky for you, sir. They're all formed and on a platter on the bottom shelf of the fridge."

"Bless you, Hutt."

"I thought Lars and I would stop at The Benson for a drink on the way home."

"Great."

"Who'd have ever thought," Carol asked as Mike closed the door behind them, "that Mr. Engbretson and Hutton would have so much in common?"

"Maybe it's a case of opposites attracting, as long as there's a common ground somewhere. In their case it's Normandy. In our case it's gift-wrapping."

She smiled at him, her concern over her father fading a little as he joined his hands behind her head and bent down to give her a light kiss. She responded just as lightly and sincerely, and he raised his head with a satisfied sigh. "You did tell me you were going to give Paris a second thought?" he asked, his eyes scanning her features, as though he couldn't look at them long enough. "I didn't dream it?"

She put her hands at his waist. "I've decided to find a job closer to home."

"Thank you," he whispered, drawing her back into his arms.

"Thank you," she said softly, "for making home a place I no longer need to escape."

He kissed her again, deeply, lengthily, his hands wandering over her back and hip, his mouth eliciting a little groan from her as it followed her throat to the invitingly unbuttoned collar of her blouse.

Carol felt his strong back muscles under her hands, his warmth and energy and humbling tenderness, and pulled back while she still had the clarity of mind to do so. "We're supposed to be wrapping presents," she said, drawing a ragged breath. "The sisters are doing my job, because I promised to do theirs."

He nipped at her ear. "I didn't make any promises to anyone."

She wanted to push him away, but the puff of his breath in her ear felt wonderful. "Well...you shouldn't stop me...from...from keeping mine."

"Go ahead," he said, pulling back the short fringe of her hair to expose her neck to his nips and kisses.

Her head fell forward against his chest, and she let it rest there as she gathered her reserves. When he raised his head to apply his ministrations to the other side of her neck, she pushed against his chest, wedging a small distance between them. "We're wrapping presents," she said firmly, though breathlessly. "Where were the sisters working?"

He sighed. "They were working in the sitting room. Come on. I locked it so the kids wouldn't get nosy."

A large library table was littered with rolls of paper, ribbon, tape, scissors and gift tags. On the floor all around the table were some of the gifts they had purchased the night before. Stacked on a leather sofa were those that were wrapped, splashes of red and green and gold and silver foil. Carol looked at the daunting heap on the floor. "We've got our work cut out for us."

"Thanks to you. I'll get a pot of coffee. We're going to need it."

When Mike returned, Carol was carefully creasing the ends of the wrap on the box that held Kathy's doll. On her face was a preoccupied frown. Mike pulled a small end table beside her and put the coffee on it. "What's the matter?"

"Oh, I still can't reach my father."

"Sister Claire told me you were worried about him." He picked up a stuffed cow they'd bought for Candy and studied it doubtfully. "He's probably just out Christmas shopping. I'm sure there's no need to worry."

"But what if he's tried to call Saint Chris's? He'd have no way of knowing where I've gone." She taped the second end of her package and set it before her, smooth and perfect. "You'd better use tissue for the cow," she advised. "You can just gather it at the top and tie a bow around it."

When she telephoned again in a half hour and there was still no answer, her concern and her frown deepened. "I just don't understand it."

"Carol, he's a grown man. Maybe he had plans of his own—maybe he has a lady friend. Pass the tape."

Carol gave him a disgruntled glance and slapped the tape into his extended palm. "I know he has a lady friend, but he'd have called me if he was going to be away for more than a day. Have you got the pink ribbon?"

"Me?" he asked innocently. At the sound of his voice, she looked up to see that he had tied a length of it around his head, the tails of a big bow dangling past his ears. "Want to unwrap me for Christmas?"

She leaned toward him, her chin propped on one hand. "You look ridiculous."

He mimicked her action, leaning toward her until their faces were an inch apart. "I have no pride where you're concerned."

"And no scruples, apparently." She yanked an end of the ribbon until the bow gave, then set it aside.

"None. Want to chuck all this and make love with me?"

Carol realized with a start what an appealing suggestion that was. During the past few weeks his warmth had woven itself inside her, melting the cold memories, lighting all the dark places she had closed off a year ago. She felt ready to live again—and fell back against her chair as that knowledge struck home. She was in love with Mike Rafferty.

"What?" Mike asked in concern.

She studied him for a long moment, afraid to tell him, afraid to let loose something she wasn't sure she could control. Feelings rose and swelled inside her, invading the quality of her breathing, the smile on her lips, the quietness of her eyes.

Mike watched her face change. "What?" he asked again, concern diminishing, fascination growing.

Evasively she said, "Get back to work. I'm going to try my dad again."

With a groan Mike began to wrap the box that held Frank's bat and ball. He ignored Carol when she returned and fell moodily into her chair. "Well, when I do reach him, he's certainly going to hear from me."

"Poor guy."

"Well, he should keep in better touch."

"Carol . . ."

"He's always checking on me."

Mike patted the paper-covered table, searching for scissors. "Relax," he said absently. "I'm sure he's okay."

When Carol did not immediately retort with a concerned objection that he wasn't, Mike raised his head from the search for scissors and looked into her speculative khaki eyes. "What do you know about this?" she asked.

Startled by her question, he looked back at her guiltily, then shook his head with what he hoped was convincing innocence. "Nothing. He's *your* father."

Carol stood. "You're lying."

Finding the scissors, he took great care in positioning the box in the center of the paper, avoiding her eyes. "You mean, he's not your father?"

Carol took the scissors from him and put them aside, leaning against the table. "No. I mean you're not telling me the truth about this. Sit down," she added, as he tried to stand.

He obeyed and folded the ends of the paper around the box. "I did not have your father kidnapped, if that's what you're suggesting."

"What did you do?"

He rolled his eyes and abandoned the package. "When would I have had the opportunity to do anything? You've been with me constantly since we left Saint Chris's." He tried to stand again, but she sat on the edge of the table and put both feet on the knees of his jeans. He sat back with a long-suffering sigh.

"Just tell me this," she asked with disarming vulnerability. "Did he elope with Mrs. Golardo?"

Mike laughed. "No, he didn't elope with…" Then, as her expression changed from one of vulnerability to an air of shrewd satisfaction, he realized he'd been had. He closed his eyes and sighed.

"Where is he, Mike?" Carol asked.

He swatted at the calf of her leg. "That was rotten."

"Where?"

"On his way here. He had some shopping to do. He'll arrive tomorrow."

"What?" Carol jumped to her feet and looked down at him. "Why?"

"Because I sent for him." He rested his head against the back of the cathedral chair and looked into her uncertain expression. "I wanted you to have something besides a purse for Christmas."

Carol stared at him, speechless. All the feelings of a moment ago rose to constrict her throat and fill her eyes. "How do you always manage to do that?" she demanded at last in a whisper.

He stood, a little concerned by her reaction. He didn't see the delight he had hoped for. "Do what?"

"Find the thing I most need," she explained in awe, "whether it's a smile, or help with a chore, or something for the kids…or the sight of my father.…" She swallowed and sniffed impatiently. "And give it to me."

He saw it then in the depths of her eyes, a pleasure so profound that it hurt. He put his hands in his pockets, because he didn't want to risk making the wrong move. "I'd like to make that my life's work."

Carol took the few steps that separated them and put her hands at his waist. Resolutely, Mike kept his hands in his pockets.

Composed now, and truly sure of herself for the first time in a year, she drew a deep breath. "I love you, Michael Rafferty," she said, looking into his eyes.

Mike's hands came out slowly, in direct counterpoint to the quick burst of emotion in his eyes. He ran them gently up her arms, almost afraid to touch her and burst this fragile dream. "I love you, Carol."

The words seemed to form around her like a silken embrace. She let her forehead fall against his chest as the past gave her up with an almost physical release. She looked up at him, her eyes alight with the freedom his love gave her. "I'd like to show you," she whispered. "I'd like us to show each other."

He hesitated, his hands going around her to caress without confining. "As a thank-you?"

She shook her head, smiling gently. "No. Because I love you and you love me. Because there's something between us so warm and so alive—and I've been...asleep for so long."

Her reply fractured Mike's careful control; he swept her into his arms and headed for the stairs.

Carol got a vague impression of a large room, of frosty sunlight through a broad window that lighted the foot of a big bed and a tweedy carpet at its foot. But her awareness was focused on Mike and the single-mindedness with which he placed her in the middle of the soft bed and leaned over her. She framed his face with hands that were steady and warm, and smiled at him. "Hi," she said softly.

He nodded, understanding the sense of discovery she felt, the delicious newness there was in looking at each other as lovers. "Hello," he replied. "Welcome to my life."

She twined her arms around his neck and leaned up to kiss his lips. "I'm so happy to be here."

Holding her, Mike turned and fell onto the mattress, bringing her down with him. Slipping his hands under her sweatshirt, he pulled it up, distracted from removing it by the soft warm skin under his hands. He allowed himself a moment to stroke her waist and back, then met the obstruction of her bra and unfastened it. As his hands moved up to her shoulders, Carol relaxed against him completely with a little sigh. He drew the shirt and bra over her head and off her arms, a little surprised to feel his hands tremble. But he lost the ability to consider the reason when Carol began to unbutton his shirt and reach under his T-shirt—the tremor seemed to underlie every muscle in his body.

Mike sat up to let her toss aside his flannel shirt, then endured with a torturous sense of pleasure the inching up of his T-shirt with fingernails that skimmed his chest, his back and the sensitive underside of his arms. By the time the shirt was off, whatever shred of control he'd had over himself and the situation was gone. He was all emotion, all longing, all need.

In his eyes Carol saw the desire for her, all entangled with the love and warmth that were building their relationship, and thought that she had never felt so completely cherished. Jon had loved her with every particle of his being, as she had loved him. But in him there had never been this miraculous softness, this unguarded delight in her nearness. She recognized that without pain or guilt, then dismissed it completely as she put her arms around Mike.

He held her to his chest with a hand between her shoulder blades, the pearled tips of her breasts against his skin a sensation he clung to for a moment. Then he cradled her in his arm and worked the sweat bottoms and a pair of silky bikini panties down her legs and over the side of the bed. Reverently he swept a hand from her waist, past her hip bone and down a slender thigh to her knee. He felt her muscles react to his touch and looked into her eyes. "Is this happening?" he asked.

She ran a hand down his chest, pausing to stroke across his flat middle, where a sturdy belt buckle prevented further exploration. "It's happening," she replied with a little laugh. "My body doesn't believe it, either."

Yanking back the bedspread and blankets, Mike placed her against the pillows, then removed his jeans and briefs. Carol raised her arms to him and he went into them, feeling whatever defenses a man maintained when he made love to a woman go the way of his reason and his self-control. He was completely hers.

Carol took his weight with a murmur of contentment, closing her eyes as his hands began to explore her body with care and serious attention. They kissed and stroked, caressed and savored, until they trembled as one, yearned as one, ached to become one.

Mike rose over her, pausing long enough to look into her feverish eyes. "In a life that's been so full," he said in wonder, "it's as though there's been nothing until you—until this moment."

As he became a part of her, Carol gasped, knowing that they were now irrevocably one.

After that, she lost all conscious thought. Feeling, sensation overpowered everything. Held tightly to Mike, she became aware of every life force in her body, every pulse and rhythm in his. They seemed to form a whole as though created before time by some divine hand that had fashioned each only to fit the other. Their oneness made perfect music out of two simple songs, each out of tune until that moment.

It was a long time before they drifted down to a world whose reality had changed.

Locked together, lying on their sides, they looked into each other's eyes and saw themselves reflected, each a part of the other, each different yet each the same.

Carol removed one hand from Mike and put it to her small breast, as though doubting her own substance. Perhaps, she thought, amazed by how she felt, it was just that it had been so long.

Reading her mind, Mike took her hand, kissed it, and placed it back around his waist. "I can't explain it," he said. "Maybe it's just that when something is part of the design...when something is so right...it makes everything right. I feel as though I'm perfectly tuned for life now—as though there isn't anything I can't handle or do."

Carol leaned into him, absorbing the wonder, the consummate, bewitching delight of loving Mike Rafferty.

Later she awoke with a start, surprised to find Mike dressed, adding logs to a fire that blazed cheerily in a curved brick hearth across the room. She blinked and looked around, seeing the room for the first time. It was long and broad, occupying, she guessed, one entire corner of the large upper floor. Following the house's English country theme, the furniture was dark and massive, the spread and draperies colorful and soft. Around the room were photographs, trophies, framed awards and other baseball memorabilia.

Carol saw Mike get to his feet, dust off his hands and turn to the bed. She studied his eyes, wondering if what she remembered was part of a dream, or if the entire world had changed when they made love. Then she saw the same perplexity in his eyes, the same astonishment she felt.

He came around the bed to sit on its edge, wanting to look into her eyes and see love for him there. He felt as though their lovemaking had derailed his entire life—and yet he had no fear of the future, no doubt that this was right. Unless he had imagined the love in her eyes.

He saw that he hadn't. She held the blankets to her breasts, her pink cheeks and the vulnerable curve of her milky shoulders all the evidence he needed that he hadn't imagined anything.

He leaned forward to plant a kiss on her lips, deeming it wise not to involve his hands. "Want a shower?"

Carol caught a whiff of soap and after-shave. "You didn't wait for me," she accused him gently.

"If I had," he said with a grin, "the house would have been full of nuns and children again before we'd finished."

Her eyes widened. How could she have forgotten where they were? "What time is it?"

He glanced at his watch. "Almost four." He disappeared into a dressing room at the far end of the bedroom and returned with a short, white terry robe. "Bathroom's through the dressing room. Get a move on, and I'll get started in the kitchen."

"Kitchen?" She frowned, shrugging into the robe.

"We're in charge of hamburgers, remember?"

She'd forgotten that, too. With a little groan of alarm, she hurried toward the bathroom. Mike caught the belt of the robe and stopped her, pulling her into his arms. He waited for her to object, knowing she was beginning to worry about the children returning, but instead, her eyes softened and she leaned against him, waiting. He had to draw a deep breath to be able to concentrate on what he'd wanted to tell her.

"You've got at least half an hour. Take a long, slow shower. Relax..." he said, taking one more kiss and relishing the eager way she gave it, her body soft and trusting against his. Then he pinched her chin, trying to bring both of them back to reality. "And try not to look like that. Meg doesn't miss anything, and neither does Frank."

As he left the room, Carol wandered into the bathroom. "Like what?" she asked aloud as she went to the mirror over the double sink. Then seeing the unmistakable glow on her face, she turned away from the mirror and headed briskly for the shower. "Like that."

THE CHILDREN were apple-cheeked and beside themselves with excitement. "Sister Claire skated with us!" Kathy reported as Carol helped her off with her coat.

Frank began to laugh. "And she fell down trying to catch me. Sorry."

At the sister's playful glower, he abbreviated the story, but Candy felt it should be finished. "And this nice man went to help her, and she pulled him down, too!"

Now everyone was laughing, Carol and Mike included, and Sister Claire sighed over their betrayal. "I did my purgatory at the skating rink this afternoon," she said, turning to hobble toward the kitchen. "I'm sure I'm going straight to heaven when I die."

"And pray they don't put you on skates!" Frank called after her.

"Give her a break, will you?" Mike said, pulling the scarf from the boy's neck. "Did you have fun, Nick?"

"Yeah!" he replied enthusiastically. "When I fell, I fell on top of Sister, so I didn't even get hurt!"

"Good thinking," Mike praised, then frowned at something he saw on the boy's lip. "Is that blood?"

"Jelly donut," Dorcas replied, for once smiling with complete happiness. "We stopped at the bakery after skating. We had a great time. I bet even people who live around Central Park and drive in limos don't have as much fun as we did."

"It's not what you've got," Mike said. "It's what you do with what you've got."

Frank rubbed his backside. "I fell all over what I've got."

Dorcas giggled. "One time, Sister lost control and knocked over everybody who was standing around watching." Frank fell into hysterical laughter at the memory, and when Hutton and Mr. Engbretson arrived home, they found themselves drawn into the general excitement without knowing what had precipitated it.

Dinner was a quick affair; the children were anxious to see the tree lighted for the first time. Mike turned out the house lights, and everyone gathered around as he connected the cord that led to the tree. The "Oh!" that rose from everyone was one heartfelt, single expression of satisfaction from the motley group that had decorated the tree: nuns, children, a butler, a handyman, a former baseball star—and a woman finally free of pain.

"I can't see!" Candy complained, trapped in a throng of taller bodies. Mike reached down to lift her onto his shoulders. "Wow!" she gasped with such appreciation that the tension was broken and laughter took over again. Sister Claire began to sing in a clear alto, and the others joined in. They sang carol after carol, finally sinking to the carpet to sing even more. Over the children's heads, Carol caught Mike's eye, her heart so full of love and happiness that the words she couldn't say in front of everyone weren't necessary, anyway.

"I LOVE SINGING Christmas songs," Candy said as Carol tucked the girls in just before midnight.

"Christmas songs are called carols," Carol explained.

Candy giggled. "Just like you."

"And things that are sweet to eat," Carol said, playfully nibbling at her neck as the child laughed helplessly, "are named after you."

Kathy stared out at the moonbeam coming in through the window. "I wonder what Santa's doing right now?" she asked thoughtfully.

"Checking his list." Dorcas, ever practical, imagined his schedule. "Probably checking the reindeer, and I think you have to do something to the runners on a sleigh. Wax them or something."

Kathy propped herself up on her elbows. "You're sure he'll know where we are?"

Carol gently pushed her back, pulling up the covers. "I'm sure he will. There's no need to worry. Now, I want you girls to quiet down and go to sleep. Tomorrow's Christmas Eve, and there'll be lots of things for us to do. Mike's family is coming, and we're going to help him get ready for them."

"This is the best Christmas," Kathy said feelingly.

"Yeah," Candy agreed, settling into her pillow.

Even Dorcas's agreement was hearty. "Yeah!"

Carol went down to the boys' room and found Mike closing the door behind himself. He looked unusually pensive, unnaturally quiet. But when he looked up and saw her, he smiled with characteristic good humor.

"Something wrong?" she asked, touching his arm.

He looked to the end of the corridor, beyond which could be heard the voices of the sisters around the tree. "Yes," he whispered, pulling her into a shadowy corner. "I can't stand to see you and not touch you, to try to act as though the whole world is normal, when it's upside-down—or I am. We have to talk."

Carol put a hand over his mouth, stifling her own laugh. "Shh! I know, but there's too much going on right now, too many people and children around to talk."

He pulled her hand from his mouth and lowered his head. "Then just kiss me."

Her protest died on his lips as they covered hers with warm, playful mobility. He made no effort to be quick; the proximity of the sisters' laughter added spice to the danger of stealing a kiss. Carol finally pushed him away, gulping for air, a blush and smile stealing over her at his lack of decorum. She swatted at his arm. "Try to behave yourself," she chided with a sternness that didn't quite achieve its purpose.

"When you blush like that," he said into her ear, planting another kiss there, "I could misbehave on the convent steps."

With a groan Carol escaped into the boys' room, closing the door behind herself and leaning against it while her heartbeat rocketed. Frank's voice came out of the darkness, its sound both casual and wicked. "Been sucking face again, huh?"

Chapter Thirteen

Carol was kissed awake. Her first instant of awareness roused her out of a deep and cozy sleep to a state of revved pulse and tingling nerve cells, like some space-age vehicle accelerating from 0 to 60 in four seconds.

"Mike?" she asked breathlessly, her eyes still closed, as he sat up and brought her with him, wrapped in his arms. "What are you doing?"

"You're turning into a slugabed."

She tucked her nose into his throat with every appearance of settling there. "It's you," she said sleepily. "And this house. When you finally relax after a year of being uptight..." She yawned and resettled herself. "I guess you just go...a little overboard. Just give me five more minutes."

"Not a chance." Mike lifted her off the bed and set her bare feet on the cool carpet. She tottered dangerously, and he put a hand to her back to support her. "The kids are begging to open one present, and I don't know what to do."

Carol swayed against his hand. "Ask Mother Margaret."

"She and Sister Cel have gone for groceries."

"Sister Claire, then."

"She's begging to open a present, too."

Carol opened one eye and nodded, able to believe that. "I'll be right down."

"I'd better wait," he said, sitting on the edge of the bed. She went to join him, but he turned her around, sending her toward the closet with a slap on her backside.

She sent him a scolding look over her shoulder as she grabbed jeans and a turquoise sweater. "Won't everyone wonder what you're doing up here?"

"I told them I was coming to get you."

She snatched underwear from the dresser and headed for the bathroom. "But if you take too long, they'll get suspicious."

"Not a chance," he said dryly. "They're all already sure. We're only fooling ourselves by thinking we're fooling them. Could you pick up a little speed?"

They did look as if they knew, Carol thought five minutes later as she followed Mike into the kitchen, where the children and Sister Claire were finishing breakfast. Hutton gave her a smiling "Good morning," followed by a too-casual shift of his attention back to the hotcakes bubbling on the griddle. Mr. Engbretson, who kibitzed with him while leaning against the counter with a cup of coffee, studied her a little longer, finally giving her the smallest fraction of a smile before turning back to Hutton. Sister Claire blew absently into her coffee. The children seemed to find the idea of a developing relationship between Carol and Mike quite acceptable—and unworthy of discussion on a day filled with much more important considerations.

"So we thought if we could open just one present each," Frank was saying as Carol took a chair beside him, "we'll be angels for the rest of the day—or at least until it's time to open the other stuff tomorrow."

"You can open one small present now," Carol said, raising her hands to quell the feverish reaction she knew would result. "And you will be angels today, because we don't bargain with good behavior, right? We behave well because it's the right thing to do." As the children scurried off toward the tree, Sister Claire in the lead, Carol turned to Mike. "At least for most of us," she added, patting his cheek.

He caught her hand, laughter alight in his eyes. Mr. Engbretson cleared his throat, and Hutton began to whistle. With a long-suffering sigh, Mike rose and pulled Carol to her feet, going out to join the children.

Carol guided the children toward those packages that contained the color books and craft projects she'd bought specifically for this purpose. Their delight at something new was contagious, and soon Hutton and Mr. Engbretson were on the floor, helping Frank with his model B-51, Nicky with his puzzle and the girls with their coloring.

Shortly before lunch, Carol answered the doorbell, and was confronted with a pyramid of Christmas packages wearing jeans and Frye boots. She removed a square, foil-wrapped package from the top, and looked into eyes as dark as Mike's and a broad smile.

"Rick, right?" she asked. She'd seen him only briefly when Mike arrived at Saint Christopher's, and that seemed so long ago.

"No, Rick Rafferty," he said, moving forward. "Never heard of Rick Wright." His progress was stopped by a long, narrow package at the bottom of the stack, which was wider than the doorway. "No, no, don't touch anything," he ordered, as Carol's hand hovered around the dangerously teetering packages.

Carefully Rick turned sideways and crab-walked into the room. Mike appeared and hurried forward to lend a hand.

"Don't touch anything!" Carol warned, guiding Rick through the foyer to the dining room. Mike stepped back, watching his brother pass. "You sure you brought enough stuff?"

"There's more in the van. Am I near the tree?"

"A little to the left."

"Is there anything in my way?"

"Clear floor."

Rick opened his arms and let the pyramid of packages fall to the floor. With a little shriek Carol covered her eyes, expecting the tinkle of broken glass, the tearing of paper, the thud of things dented and smashed. But there was hardly a sound.

"Stuffed animals," Rick was saying quietly to Mike as Carol dared to look. "Hats, scarves, mittens, board games."

Mike shook his head despairingly. "For me?" he asked.

"What you need," Rick advised, "can only be accomplished by a good brain surgeon. Have I missed lunch?"

Rick kept up his patter through lunch and a cutthroat game of Pictionary that lasted most of the afternoon.

"I'm not teaming with you," Mike said when they were choosing sides, and his proximity to Rick would have made him his partner. He moved across the table to put a chair between Frank and Carol. Rick looked injured. "I play it for fun," Mike explained, "and you're always out for blood."

Rick rolled his eyes. "I like a competent, quick-witted partner. Where's Meg?"

"She's gone to the airport with Hutton to pick up Mom and Lorraine and everybody. I'll get you a sharp partner. Sister Claire!" Mike called over his shoulder. She was sitting on the floor with Candy and Nicky, who were working on a puzzle. "Keep up with her, smart a—"

Carol gave him a vicious elbow to the ribs. "Smart aleck," Mike said innocently. "I was going to say smart aleck."

"We don't have any money on this, do we?" Carol asked quietly half an hour later, when it became clear that the pairing of Rick and Sister Claire was proving disastrous for the rest of the participants.

"No," Mike whispered back, "but Sister is in danger of losing the two-pound block of Monterey Jack and jalapeño I bought her for Christmas."

"Did you really?" Carol smiled, her expression full of affection. "She'll be thrilled."

"Don't look at me like that, okay?" he pleaded under his breath.

"Like wha—?" Then she remembered her reflection in the mirror the afternoon before and aborted the question. She looked up to see Rick watching them, all silliness gone from him as he studied her and his brother with an eye that saw things hidden, even things unknown to the object of his scrutiny.

"You two might do a little better," Rick said, "if you paid more attention."

"They're in love," Frank added with all the candor of observant youth.

Carol groaned, and Mike turned to Frank with a look that began as stern, then changed at the delight on the boy's face. "Everybody knows," Frank justified himself, just in case. "And everybody thinks it's neat." When Mike still said nothing, the boy grimaced and hazarded a guess. "But I'm dead anyway, right?"

"Real close, pal." Mike handed him the hot pot that stood in the middle of the table. "You can redeem yourself by filling this up."

"Sure." Frank got up and passed behind Mike, exchanging a grin with Rick.

"Cute kid," Rick commented.

Carol leaned her hot face against Mike's shoulder and laughed. "That doesn't begin to describe him."

"THEY'RE HERE!" Kathy reported from the window as Hutton pulled into the driveway with Saint Christopher's station wagon. Rick herded the children out the door, and Mr. Engbretson followed to help carry suitcases. Mike and Carol paused a moment in the foyer for one last, private kiss.

"We've got to stop doing this," Carol said.

Mike frowned. "Why? Everybody knows now. Come on. You'll love my mother."

Mike was halfway out the door, already waving at Lorraine, when Carol's sudden stop brought him up short. The pain of her fingernails digging into his hand made him turn back to her. "Carol, what—?"

Her eyes were huge and horrified, and her face had gone deathly white. Her lips were parted and pulled back into a grimace as she looked beyond him to the driveway. He followed her gaze, wondering what had brought about such a reaction. Then he saw them. His nieces Erika and Patsy, three and five, were dressed in bright red jumpers over frilly white blouses. They stood together like two little holiday models in a store window, their pale blond hair in braids tied in fat, white bows. Suddenly Mike remembered what Carol had told him the night he'd learned about her family. *Her* little girls had been three and five with fine blond hair, and they'd been dressed to pick up their grandfather at the airport last Christmas. The last time she saw them, they must have looked much as Erika and Patsy did now.

Carol's first reaction at the sight of the girls had been a burst of joy. A miracle had happened. It *was* Christmas. Somehow her babies were back. She had taken a step toward them before the grimness of the intervening year rose up to strike her yet again. Those were not her little girls. They were someone else's, not hers to hold and rock and comfort. Her babies were gone. *Forever, Carol,* a voice inside her seemed to say. *Forever. When will you ever understand that?*

Suddenly she understood as she had never understood in the last year. It settled on her with the weight of an anvil on her chest. Jon was gone. Her babies were dead. And then it was as though a door opened, admitting every pain, every vicious fear, every cold and paralyzing memory she'd fought so long and hard to hold back. They ran at her like monsters in the night, ready to devour her.

She yanked herself away from Mike and ran for the stairs with a small scream in her throat. It seemed to amplify as she ran, growing louder and louder as she topped the stairs, raced down the hallway, gained the door to her room. Underlying the scream were the sounds of her name and pursuing footsteps, but they meant nothing. They were going to get her at last, she thought, with the fatality born of having one's last defense ripped away. She had lost.

By now the scream had grown high and interminable, and she turned frantically to find its source. "Becky!" she cried, running into her room. "Gale! Mommy's here! Mommy's here!"

"Carol!" Strong hands turned her around and shook her.

"I'm here," she cried again. "Don't cry, Mommy's here!"

"Carol, please!" Mike was holding her face, looking into her eyes, his own eyes tortured and filled with tears. Had he seen them, too?

She tried to pull away from him once more, but he held her firmly. "They're crying for me!" she screamed at him. "Let me go!"

"Carol, they're gone!" he shouted back. He shook her again, then, as she stopped to try to focus on him, said more quietly, "Your children are gone."

She fell against him in a paroxysm of weeping as horror met reality and came into focus, the one not very different from the other. "They must have cried for me," she sobbed. "I know they cried for me, and I wasn't there! Jon must have thought of me when the truck overturned right in front of him. He must have said my name."

Mike enveloped her in his arms, trying to wrap himself around her like a shield. He felt torn apart by her anguish. He wanted to soothe her and tell her that it was all right—he was there. But he understood that this release had been too long in coming.

"I should have died with them!" she cried as he pulled her with him onto the edge of the bed. "I *want* to be with them!"

"No," he said firmly. "What would the kids in your dorm have done without you? God kept you behind for a reason. You're doing what he wanted you to do."

She shook her head against him in an agony of pain. "I hear them crying all the time, Mike. All the time!"

He rocked her back and forth, holding tight. "I know it hurts," he said gently, "but listen to them. Then they'll rest. And you'll be able to rest."

She pushed at his chest. "No, I don't want to. I can't!" She felt herself on fire, a concentration of pain from head to toe. "The . . . the last day just lives in my mind and I . . . I can't . . . ."

Mike brushed back her hair and drew her against his chest despite her efforts to move away. "What did they say to you when they left for the airport?"

She closed her eyes. "What did they say, Carol?" he insisted gently.

She thought, her brow pleating at the memory. "Becky said . . ." She sobbed, mimicking a small child's voice. "'You look pretty, Mommy. I wish you could come.'" Then without prompting, she went on. "And Gale said what she always said. 'I love you, Mommy.' She looked over her shoulder at me and waved, and I . . . I told her not to get her dress dirty." She shook her head over the pain of the memory. "My last words to my baby were, 'Don't get your dress dirty.'" She pounded both fists against his chest. "How could I have done that?"

"Carol," he chided gently, "every mother in the world since Eve sends her children off with the same admonition. Don't let that torture you."

She stared into a corner of the room, her eyes still unfocused. "I wasn't there when they needed me."

"That's only true of the last moment of their lives, and there was nothing you could have done about the accident. They're in good hands now. They don't need you anymore. But your dorm kids do."

The dorm kids. Out of the waves of pain came images of the little faces that had kept her alive for the past year, like some emotional life-support system. With that thought she remembered that they'd be leaving soon, and the pain that was already unbearable grew still more intense.

"You wanted Christmas to be so special for them," Mike reminded her.

Yes, she had. They had done so much for her; she had wanted to do that for them. But at that moment she felt drained to the point of exhaustion, and the very thought of moving out of the room was abhorrent. She had to do it. Pain was subsiding now, leaving emptiness in its wake. That was easier to deal with. She leaned away from Mike and drew a shaky breath. "I'd better wash my face and go downstairs."

"Not yet." Mike stood and pulled her to the pillows, drawing the other end of the bedspread over her. He sat down on the edge of the bed once more, a hand braced on either side of her. "You need a little time to rest, a little time to take care of yourself instead of everybody else."

"But I..." She tried to sit up, but he pushed her back, holding her hands on top of the bedspread.

"I can't imagine the pain of what you've gone through, but I do understand the grieving process, and I know that you have to let it hurt before it'll heal. I think you couldn't face the pain, so you found a way to put it aside and go on by working with the children. It's worked so far, but you can't move into the future until you put the past away, and to do that, you've got to let it hurt."

"The pain is stronger than I am."

Mike bent down to kiss her cheek. "I've seen you in action. Nothing is stronger than you are. Now sleep."

"IS SHE OKAY?"

Mike looked up from holding a cold washcloth to his face and saw Rick, leaning against the doorway that led from his dressing room. His arms were folded, his eyes concerned.

Mike tossed the washcloth into the sink and dried his face and hands. "Yeah, I think so."

"Meg guessed what happened and explained everything to us." Rick studied his brother's face. "Are *you* okay?"

"I guess." Mike walked around him into the dressing room, taking a fresh sweater out of a drawer.

Rick followed. "Do you want to talk about it?"

Mike pulled the burgundy woolen garment over his head. "No."

"It took you all this time to make headway with her," Rick speculated when Mike's face emerged from the sweater neck, "and now you've been blown back again."

Mike stopped, the sweater halfway down his chest. He looked at Rick, first annoyed, then amused. He yanked it the rest of the way down and walked into the bedroom. "It irritates the hell out of me when you do that," he said.

"I'm a photographer. I read faces." Rick leaned back on the bed on one elbow while Mike combed his hair. "Putting that together with what Meg and the kids have told me wasn't too difficult. So am I looking at her as a sister-in-law?"

Mike tossed the comb on the dresser and turned to Rick with a bleak smile. "I'd like to think so, but I'm not sure. Can you get by without knowing for certain that my life is in perfect order?"

"Worrying about you is a habit of long standing."

"Do I look as though I require worrying over?"

Rick frowned. "You looked better yesterday."

"Yeah, well..." Mike walked to the door. "Yesterday Carol's past hadn't risen to punch me in the gut. I keep wanting her to get over it, but just now I saw what she suffered when her husband and children died, and I don't know how I'd deal with that kind of pain. Losing Dad and Gil was grisly, but now that I love her, I know that losing her would be like a kind of death.''

Rick stood and went slowly toward him. ''But she's alive, and she has to go on, and nobody can carry on in solitude. No matter how hard the past hit her this morning, if you love her, then she's got something to live for.'' He put a hand on Mike's shoulder and pressed. ''It'll be all right. Come on, I'll beat you at Pictionary.''

''You did that this morning.''

''Sister Claire's in great form now.'' He opened the door and pushed Mike through. ''I'll do it even better tonight.''

LAUGHTER RANG through the house. Carol smiled at the sound, unable to resent it. But her emotions were so raw, she wondered if she'd ever be able to laugh that way again, or to feel as she had only this morning—completely in tune with a man, willing to consider marriage and more children. The pain she'd lived with for so long had been replaced by a curious emptiness, a sort of limbo in which she felt very little.

A small knock sounded on the door; Carol was sure it was one of the children. She propped up a pillow and leaned against it, smoothing her hair. ''Come in,'' she called cheerfully. She had expected Frank, or possibly Kathy. Dorcas walked in, coming shyly across the room to stand at the side of the bed. Her ponytails were askew from playing.

''Hi,'' she said, putting a hand over Carol's atop the blanket. The gesture was very adult, very understanding. ''Are you going to come down for dinner?''

''Yes,'' Carol replied, hoping she'd be able to look at Lorraine's little girls without making another scene. ''I was just thinking about changing my clothes.''

''Hutton and Sister Cel made a turkey and all that stuff that goes with it.''

''Mmm.''

Dorcas sat on the edge of the bed, a small quiver in her bottom lip before she seemed to firm it. "Frank and me and the other kids made a deal not to talk about this as long as we're at Mike's, 'cause it makes us sad, but I guess it's okay to talk to you about it." She leaned toward Carol earnestly. "Pretty soon we're all going to be going to different places, and I . . . I wanted to say something, okay?"

Carol nodded. "Of course, Dorie."

"You used to make believe about your little girls, didn't you, like I used to make believe about my mom and all the stuff we had?"

Emotion rose to flood the emptiness, and Carol had to swallow carefully. "Yes, a little."

"Well, it's better if you don't," Dorcas said. "You have to get ready to live with new people—new foster families and new friends. Well, you won't have a foster family, but there's Mike. Like you told us, it's your responsibility to fit in."

Carol clutched at Dorcas's hand. "That's true."

"If you got married," Dorcas suggested, "you could have more little girls."

Carol nodded, unable to find a voice.

"Then, when we're all grown-up, we could have a re-onion at your house."

Carol cleared her throat. "Reunion."

"Yeah. Wouldn't that be fun?"

"Yes, it would." Carol tossed the bedspread aside and swung her feet to the floor. "I suppose right now, we'd better concentrate on being on time for dinner."

Dorie sighed. "There's only one bad thing about dinner."

Carol squared her shoulders. "What?"

"Okra."

She found herself with a smile she didn't know she had. "Oh, no!"

CAROL AND DORCAS reached the bottom stairs to find that the Pictionary game had become an arena of male rivalry. Mike and Rick, Mr. Engbretson and Hutton, Frank and Nicky, and a big, blond man who must have arrived with the contingent from the airport pored over new instructions.

"I think all the ladies are in the kitchen," Dorcas said quietly.

Mike looked up from the table, his eyes going quickly over her in an obvious attempt to assess her emotional state. Certain that she was under control, she smiled at him. He smiled back, preparing to rise.

But a young woman emerged from the kitchen and rounded the table to hook her arm through Carol's. She had shoulder-length dark hair, a trim body in a dusty-pink sweat suit, and a graceful height that Carol envied. "You don't want anything to do with them," the stranger said firmly. "They're now playing for sweat socks, or something. It's getting ugly. I'm Lorraine." She paused for breath. "The *youngest* of the Raffertys." She put special emphasis on the adjective.

Without looking up from the game, Rick said, "Only because raising her has aged the rest of us."

Mike laughed, giving him a congratulatory slap on the shoulder. "Good one, Rick."

Rick returned a thumbs-up, obviously pleased with himself.

Lorraine shook her head in disgust. "See what I mean? We think we've come so far, yet here we are in the progressive eighties with the women in the kitchen and the men behaving in disgusting, chauvinistic ways while waiting to be served."

As Lorraine led Carol and Dorcas past the table, the blond man put out his hand. "I'm motor-mouth's husband, Pat Walker."

"Don't be lured by that open, friendly manner," Lorraine warned as Carol shook his hand. "I was, and look what it got me."

Carol did just that, studying her clear complexion and beaming face, and guessed what had happened to her. "Happiness, contentment and fun?"

Lorraine looked over Carol's head at her grinning husband and brothers and dragged off her new friend to the kitchen. "You need a little educating. Mom?"

The kitchen was a cloud of steam, a collection of tantalizing smells, a stronghold of women in white aprons. A plump woman with the carriage of a diva emerged from the chatting, laughing group of nuns and children, wiping her hands on the skirt of her apron. She had permed gray hair and a smile that decimated the impression made by her square shoulders and formidable chest.

"Carol, this is my mother, Rita Rafferty. Mom, this is Carol."

The woman took Carol into a maternal embrace. Then she held her at arm's length and asked gently, "Are you all right?"

"Yes," Carol replied, insisting to herself that she would be. "I apologize for—"

Rita hugged her again, cutting off the apology. "Nonsense. Here." She handed her a potato masher and pulled her toward a bowl of steaming potatoes, to which milk and butter had been added. Rita wandered around the kitchen like a sergeant, assigning jobs and supervising their execution.

As Carol worked, Patsy climbed onto a stool beside her. "I like lots of butter," she said, apparently planning to sit and chat for the duration of the task. "I'm five."

Carol stared at her for a moment, air trapped in her lungs. The child was all pink cheeks, blue eyes and perfect baby teeth, and she waited for the pain to overtake her. It came, but more gently than it ever had before, just the bittersweet nudge of something beautiful that hadn't lasted long enough.

Lorraine put an arm around her daughter's waist and prepared to pull her off the stool, her expression anxious. "Darling, Carol is very busy. Why don't you... ?"

Carol put out a hand to stop the other woman, meeting her eyes, then smiled, amazed to find that it wasn't that difficult. "She's not in my way. Let her stay."

"But..."

"Please."

"All right." Lorraine hugged her daughter, then cautioned, "but don't try to tell Carol to put in marshmallows."

"Marshmallows?" Carol asked.

"We put 'em in sweet potatoes," Patsy explained gravely as her mother walked away, "but those are yucky. Mashed potatoes are yummy, so why don't we put marshmallows in those and make 'em more yummy? I keep asking Mommy to try it, but she never does."

Chapter Fourteen

"Want to come with me to pick up your father?" Already dressed in a blue down jacket, Mike intercepted Carol as she helped clear the table.

She looked at him in surprise. With all that had happened since Mike had told her he'd sent for him, she'd almost forgotten her father's impending arrival. She stood undecided for a moment, looking at the sea of dirty dishes.

"We can handle this," Lorraine assured her, stacking plates. "Go ahead. We'll have eggnog ready when you get back."

In the hall, Mike took her coat from the guest closet and helped her into it. Then he came around to face her, pulling up her collar with a care that was both gentle and possessive. "You feeling okay?"

She forced a smile, taking a step back out of reach. The hollow feeling inside her had left her confused and cautious. "I'm fine. Ready?"

Mike pulled the door open, letting her pass through it without touching her. He'd hoped that what happened that afternoon would turn her further toward him instead of away. But the look in her eye reminded him that this just wasn't his year. As he followed her out to his truck, he was also reminded of what Meg had told him. "Patience. Gentleness and patience." He unlocked the passenger side door, let Carol scramble up without helping her, because that would have involved touching her, and closed and locked her door. He gave his keys an exasperated toss as he walked around to the driver's side. If only patience weren't so damned hard to come by.

CAROL SPOTTED her father instantly in the long stream of passengers coming through the gate and went into his arms with a little groan of relief. In all the crises in her life, he remained the same—tall, strong, loving. She held him hard. "Oh, Daddy."

"Hi, baby," he said, holding her tightly in his embrace of rough tweed and gentle, paternal affection. "Are you doing okay? You look peaked."

Laughter and loud conversation drifted around them, and she drew him aside to introduce him to Mike. "I'm great," she said, deciding as he looked at her doubtfully that it was only half a lie. "And it's so good to see you. Dad, this is Mike Rafferty. Mike, my father, Charles Martin."

Mike extended his hand. "I'm pleased to meet you, Mr. Martin."

"Well, I'm delighted to meet you." Carol's father pumped his hand with enthusiasm. "Call me Charlie. I can't begin to thank you for taking care of my ticket. I don't think I've ever traveled first-class before."

"Please don't." Mike took his carryon and started for the baggage claim area. "From here on out, Charlie, the accommodations are strictly boot camp quality. How do you feel about sharing digs with two young boys, an itinerant photographer and a baseball has-been?"

Mike saw Charlie look him over with eyes a more definite green than Carol's but with the same capacity for close scrutiny. He finally smiled. "They retired your number. I think that saves you from ever being a has-been. Happy to share your digs."

The evening unfolded with a sweetness and a serenity Carol was surprised to be able to feel. Though still experiencing the hollow sensation from that afternoon, she absorbed the warmth and gentle insanity of the Raffertys, the wonder and excitement of the children as they opened gifts from the family, and her father's generous affection.

She noted that Mike carefully left her time for her father, keeping a distance that served to grant her privacy, yet left him close enough, so that she could simply reach out to him if she found it necessary.

The children were up by five on Christmas morning. Carol hurried into a sunny-yellow sweat suit that was a gift from her father, and ran downstairs to find the adults already clustered around the delighted children. Most of the Raffertys were still in nightclothes and robes, but Mike and Rick, who had apparently brought in wood for the fireplace, were dressed in jeans and old sweatshirts. The sisters were bustling around, pouring coffee, while Hutton and Mr. Engbretson worked together in the bright, warm kitchen.

Carol sat on the arm of her father's chair as the children identified and amassed their gifts from Santa.

When Frank opened his package and discovered a regulation bat and ball signed by each of the New York Yankees, his joy was indescribable. With the bat in one hand and the ball in the other, he threw his arms around Mike, who sat on the floor several feet away. "This is so great!" he said over and over again. He pulled away, his expression suddenly grave. "Whatever happens, I'll always have these, and they're so great." Emotion pulled at his lip, and he fell against Mike's shoulder once more. "*You're* so great."

Candy, on her knees in the colorful pile of discarded wrapping paper, looked at him in confusion. "Santa brought it," she reminded him, obviously wondering why he seemed to be thanking Mike. But Lorraine put another package into her hands, and she was distracted from the problem by the delight of yet another gift of her own.

Nicky was riding his trike around the dining-room table, and Kathy was sitting in Rita's lap in the rocker, rocking her doll, when Dorcas looked in confusion at the large box in her own lap. She turned to Carol and whispered, "I think something's wrong."

Carol went down on her knees beside her. "Why, Dorie?"

"Well, I asked for...for something little. I don't think this is mine."

Suddenly Mike was beside them, reaching far under the tree for a small, slim package. He handed it to Dorcas. "Here's a little package with your name on it."

Her eyes widened. The tag read, To Carol from Dorcas. She stared at it for a moment, then a small smile of satisfaction lighted her face. She handed the package to Carol. "This is *from* me, for Carol."

"Oh, sorry," Mike said innocently. "I must have misread the tag."

Carol remembered her discussion with Mike about Dorcas's request. She opened the package carefully, marveling at his thoughtfulness in fulfilling the child's wish for her—as well as having bought her a dozen other gifts, as he'd done for all the children, too.

When Carol pulled the tiny teardrop of crystal on its gold chain out of the box, Dorcas's mouth opened on a little "Oh" of pleasure.

Carol stared. She couldn't tell a diamond from cubic zirconia, but she could recognize a gold chain—and that made her suspicious of the beautiful bauble. Unwilling to make Dorcas suspect collusion, she didn't even turn to Mike. "Dorie," she said, clasping the chain around her neck, "this is the loveliest pendant I've ever owned. Thank you so much." She gave the girl a hug, holding her an extra moment for having thought of her at a time when avarice ran high in even the most generous of children. "Now let's see what you've got."

Returning her attention to the large package, Dorie shook her head in unrelieved wonder. "But I...I didn't ask for anything else!"

"Well, Santa sent it," Mike said, indicating the tag. "He must have wanted you to have something else. You'd better open it."

Carol guessed by the way Dorcas pulled slowly on the ribbon, carefully separated the tape from the paper, then put it aside, obviously savoring the experience, that opening presents wasn't something she had done often. She stared at the doll that was now visible through the plastic film on the lid, then removed the lid and stared a moment longer.

Carol feared she'd made a mistake. She'd just exchanged a worried look with Mike, when Dorcas reached inside the box and brought the beautiful, pink-cheeked doll to her shoulder, crushing her in her arms and rocking her with a happiness so profound that Carol had to draw a deep breath to retain her composure.

Suddenly, a hand holding a ball rested on Carol's shoulder, and a hand holding a bat rested on Mike's, drawing their two heads together. "If you two don't quit sniffling," Frank whispered, "you're going to blow Santa's cover for sure." Then he was off in response to a summons from Mother Margaret.

"He knows about you?" Carol asked.

Mike shook his head, watching the boy pick his way through children and packages to reach the other side of the room. "Is there anything he doesn't know about?"

THE NEXT THREE DAYS had a dreamlike quality. The children were as uninhibited and free as any who led normal lives in loving homes—because, for a brief period, that was just what they were doing with a loving extended family. Rita offered them grandmotherly love, and Charlie provided grandfatherly encouragement and support. Lorraine and the sisters spoiled them like doting aunts, and Rick and

Pat ran themselves ragged, tossing Frank's baseball, cheering Nicky up and down the driveway on his tricycle, guarding the matriarchy of little girls and their dolls from mischievous little boys. Hutton was a slave to their wishes, and Mr. Engbretson was kept busy repairing toy trucks that had never been intended to fly, and manufacturing puzzle pieces to replace those that went missing. At night there was seldom an adult lap without a child in it.

Carol had never hoped in her wildest dreams to be able to give them this kind of Christmas. Not only was it filled with the toys and gifts that lent the season its special excitement, but they were both giving and receiving the love that made the days magic.

Unaccustomed to so much free time, Carol wandered outside one cold afternoon, restless, while everyone was inside watching *White Christmas*. The snow was gone now, though the temperature remained in the low thirties, and she walked to the middle of the backyard, which offered a view of the busy Willamette River.

"Hi."

Carol turned at the sound of a familiar voice, but saw no one.

"Up here!" The voice called again. Carol raised her eyes and beheld a startling sight. Sister Claire sat on the roof of the garage, veil flying in the late-afternoon wind. "Come and join me."

It didn't occur to Carol to ask what she was doing up there. Sister Claire was a unique individual—and someone else who would be walking out of her life in the near future. Spending time with her suddenly seemed important.

Sister Claire pointed to her left. "There's a pretty strong trellis there."

Gingerly, Carol climbed the trellis. The gentle slope of the garage's shed-style roof made sitting easy. "Okay," she said, settling beside her friend. "What are we doing?"

"Getting a new perspective." Sister Claire, knees drawn up in the slacks all the sisters had been wearing since the arrival of snow, smiled at Carol. "You've been looking like you need a new slant on things, too."

Carol sighed. "It's a little frightening to find that the new life you thought you were building can be so undermined by the past."

"Do you have to let it undermine the present?"

"I don't think I have a choice."

Sister Claire shook her head, looking out at the horizon where the dark blue of dusk was already beginning to inch its way toward them. "There's always a choice."

Hearing the heaviness in her voice, Carol asked quietly, "Is that why you're leaving?"

There was a long pause. "Yes," she finally replied. "I had about talked myself out of it. This life has become comfortable, I know what's expected of me, and I love Mother Margaret and Sister Celestine. It's pretty certain we'd all have been sent on together." She sighed, shaking her head. "But since we've been here at Mike's, I know that isn't what I need to be doing. His family is so warm and wonderful and funny. There's such a generation of love in this house. It reaffirms my need to do that—build a family that's so strong, nothing can prevail against it."

It occurred to Carol that death could prevail against it, but she remained silent. And after a moment's thought she realized that that wasn't true—Jon and the girls still lived in her with such strength that she didn't fit anywhere else.

"But getting back to you—" Sister Claire stretched her legs out, moving carefully "—you and Mike are so in love, it's obvious to everyone."

Carol closed her eyes, turning up her face to the cold early-evening wind. "I thought so," she replied. "Then I made such a scene over Lorraine's girls."

Sister Claire turned to her impatiently. "You didn't make a scene, you expressed grief. That's allowed, you know. No one's asking you to be Wonder Woman. The fact that you still feel the loss of your husband and the children doesn't mean you can't love another man."

"With all due respect, dear Sister Claire," Carol said with a grin, "how would you know?"

The darkness was about to overtake them and a spindly, crescent moon was visible on the horizon. "Because it's scriptural," she said decisively. "Christ said, 'Love one another.' He didn't say 'Love one another when you're feeling secure,' or, 'Love one another when it's uncomplicated,' or, 'When you're not feeling pain, love one another.'" She forestalled Carol's protest by raising both hands, then lost her balance and quickly lowered them to steady herself.

"Could we get down?" Carol asked.

Sister Claire shook her head. "I was about to make a point. He didn't specifically mean romantically, but He didn't exclude it, either. Love that makes people strong, that makes babies who become productive, compassionate human beings, has got to be important. You have a right to have that again, Carol. Don't discard it because you can't see over the pain."

"What kind of wife would I be," she asked urgently, "with my heart caught in the past?"

Sister Claire looked at her as though she were one of the children. "Do you think Mike would let it stay there?"

The sound of male laughter suddenly erupted below them, accompanied by the slam of the back door. A light went on, dispelling the gathering shadows. Mike and Rick walked into the light, heading for the plastic-covered woodpile against the back fence.

The absurdity of their position on the garage roof made the women turn to each other and smother laughter. Both men turned, Mike looking around, Rick looking up. "Pardon me," Rick said conversationally, elbowing his brother, "but do you see two women sitting on the garage roof?"

Mike looked up, shading his eyes against the bright light. "Carol?" he asked in disbelief, then less disbelievingly, "Sister Claire. What in the hell...?" Rick elbowed him again and he stopped. He drew a steadying breath and went to the foot of the trellis. "I want you both down here right now."

Carol was pleased to comply. "We were just getting a different...ahh!" Halfway down the trellis, she felt hands grasp her waist and swing her to the damp grass. Before she could finish, Mike reached up again and brought down Sister Claire.

"A different what?" he asked, looking down on both of them, hands on his hips. "A different way to break your neck, a different way to give me a heart attack?"

Not knowing how to reply to that, a little surprised by his angry, authoritarian tone, Carol folded her arms and borrowed a device she had learned from dealing with the children. "It was Sister Claire's idea. I didn't really want to do it." Sister Claire reacted with a dramatic gasp of outraged innocence.

Mike continued to look down at them, his sense of humor battling with the fear he'd felt at seeing her perched on top of the roof. He ran a hand down his face in exasperation.

"I'd give it up and take them inside," Rick advised, obviously biting back a laugh. "I'll bring the wood in."

"I'll help." Sister Claire started after Rick as he headed across the yard.

"No..." Mike tried to stop her, horrified at the idea of a nun carrying wood.

"I've done it before," she assured him, shooing him toward the house. "Go on."

At the door, Mike held Carol back with a hand on her shoulder. She turned to look up at him expectantly, her eyes still amused. "A different what?" he asked.

"Perspective," she replied. "On life. Things."

"Us?" he asked. He still maintained that distance and she appreciated it. She squared her shoulders just a little to let him know that, for the moment at least, she didn't want him any closer.

She nodded. "Yes."

"And what did you conclude?"

"I didn't," she said. "You made us come down."

Mike followed her into the house, thinking that life in the major leagues had never been this complicated.

"MIKE, TELEPHONE!" Rick, flipping pancakes, handed the phone over his head to Mike, who stood beside him, frying bacon. Carol carried plates back and forth from the stove to the table and the horde of hungry children. In the dining room, the other adults lingered over fruit and coffee, awaiting their turn to eat.

"What?" Mike demanded into the receiver, putting a hand over his other ear to block out the noise from the kitchen table. Carol shushed the children and went to the stove to watch the pan of bacon. Mike swung the phone cord over Rick's head and sank onto a stool, as though what he was hearing sapped his energy. Carol looked at Rick, who shrugged.

After a long, one-sided conversation, Mike replied, "Sure. Tell them I'm interested and I'll call them back by the end of the week." He cradled the phone on the wall, a look of amazement on his face. He turned slowly to Rick and Carol. "They want me to manage the Portland Pilots."

"Wow!" Frank was beside Mike in an instant, apparently having eavesdropped. "Are you going to do it?"

"Yeah…" Mike was still unfocused. "Maybe. But I want to think about it before I give them an answer."

Carol leaned toward Rick and whispered, "We're not talking about airplane pilots, are we?"

He put an arm around her shoulders. "No. We're talking about the number two team in the American League. Mike could make them number one. Bacon's burning."

As Carol quickly pulled off the bacon to drain it on a paper towel, Frank ran into the dining room to spread the news. In a moment the kitchen was full of family, and all the friends who were now family, Hutton, Mr. Engbretson, her father. They were all as excited for Mike as he was—or should have been. Carol noted a slight withdrawal on his part, a little holding back of the all-out delight he must be feeling inside. Suspecting that she might be partially responsible for his reluctance to accept the offer wholeheartedly, Carol absented herself on the pretext of getting her father packed.

"I'm perfectly capable of doing that," Charles told her as he watched her make a neat stack of his shirts and pajamas. "You should be celebrating with the family." He studied her face as she ignored his protest, fitting the stack neatly into one side of the suitcase. "Or are you still holding on to Jon and the girls?"

Carol gave him a look of hurt surprise. She'd thought he would understand. "They're holding on to me, Dad."

"Carrie..." He took a sweater out of her hands and turned her around, holding her shoulders. "They're together in a place where there is no wanting. You, however, need a man to love you. You need to give your love to a man and to more children." He shook her gently. "Come alive, Carol. Mike Rafferty loves you, despite that look you always wear around him."

She frowned. "What look?"

"The look that says, 'Don't touch me. I'm fragile.' A lot of men would walk away, but he stays close, always within your reach. I guess you don't get to be MVP by being a coward. But that patience can't last forever."

"Daddy, the other day, when Lorraine and her family arrived..." She began to recount the incident with Lorraine's little girls.

"Rita told me about that," he said. "That must have been hard for you—they do look like...like Becky and Gale." He swallowed with obvious difficulty and Carol put her arms around him. He'd been an adoring grandfather; she didn't remember that often enough.

"It all came back as though it had just happened," she said into his shoulder. "How can I start over with Mike when I still feel like that? I'd kill his pleasure in everything a man and woman come together for."

"I think that was the grief you didn't let yourself feel a year ago when you should have." He held her away and looked into her eyes, his own filled with loving sympathy. "I kept waiting for you to turn to me for comfort, but you never did. You were determined to bury your grief with them, because you thought you couldn't bear it. You did the same thing when your mother died. You've confused courage with stoicism, but even you can't do that forever. It came out, as it needed to. I think you'll be all right now, as long as you don't close yourself off with the past."

That was almost precisely what Mike had told her. Did no one see it her way? "I just need a little time to think."

"Fair enough," he said, giving her a final squeeze before letting her go. "Just remember that there's a time to stop thinking and start acting. Don't wait too long."

CHARLIE LEFT that afternoon, and the Raffertys and Walkers the following morning. Rick offered to drive them to the airport, before driving himself back to Seattle. There were long hugs, tears, and addresses exchanged with the children, who promised to write and tell everyone where they were.

"I want to take them all home with me," Rita said tearfully to Carol, a hankie pressed to her nose. "But I wouldn't be able to keep up with them, and there's so much to be worried about today...."

Carol hugged her; the woman had been so kind to her. "They'll be fine, Rita, I promise you. Now, don't worry. Just write them, like you promised."

"You take care of yourself." Rick gave her a bear hug, then looked into her eyes with unusual gravity. "And I want you to take care of Mike. If you don't, I'm coming after you."

She smiled, trying to make light of his threat. "He takes pretty good care of himself."

"He used to," he said, still serious. "But I think those days are over for him." He hugged her again, then picked up his bag. "Don't forget."

After the others had left, Hutton and the contingent from Saint Christopher's stood in the middle of the silent living room, faces quiet, expressions uncertain. Even the children knew that Christmas didn't last forever, but the five days had been a very special time in their disrupted lives. For a little while love had been everywhere and had given purpose to every day.

The holiday came to an abrupt end that afternoon; the Pointer's Beach plumber called to report the pipes repaired and functioning at Saint Christopher's. Mother Margaret's announcement was received gloomily by everyone.

"You're coming back?" She stood on the threshold of Mike's room, and was surprised to find him packing.

"You bet," he replied casually, snapping his suitcase shut. "My rent's paid until the middle of February."

She walked into the room to sit beside his case. "Mike, what if she can't let herself love you? Will you be all right?"

"She does love me, Meg," he replied with convincing veracity. "I know that as surely as I know that I love her. One day she's going to turn around and realize that, and I'd like to be nearby. And I have a book to finish."

"And an offer to consider."

"Yes."

She smiled up at him. "Have I ever told you how proud I am that Mike Rafferty is my brother?"

"No." He gave her a dry look as he lowered the suitcase from the bed to the floor. "And if you do now, mountains will fall, floodwaters will rise and the ground will open to swallow all of us."

She stood, looking pleased with herself. "Ah, the satisfying implementation of power."

"Meg." He caught her arm as she would have left the room. "Maybe I do need to hear it."

"You won't record it or anything?"

"I promise."

She put her arms around him and held him. "Then I love you, brother mine. Don't give up. My money's on you."

He pulled away, grinning affectionately. "You don't have any."

She laughed wickedly. "I sold Frank my Twinkies."

SAINT CHRISTOPHER'S Home for Children was dark and still. Mr. Engbretson hurried into the main building to turn on the Christmas lights and those on Santa and his reindeer, but Christmas was over. The magic couldn't be recaptured. Reality had to be faced once again and, for the home's remaining occupants, it was too grim to be dispelled by colored lights.

Carol finally got the children to bed with promises of candy-making and a walk to the lighthouse the following day. They showed polite interest, but she had the feeling that it was more to make her happy than because they were enthusiastic. She came out to the kitchen to find Mike making coffee.

"Want something to go with that?" she asked chattily, routing through a large box of groceries Hutton had sent with them. "I think there are some croiss—"

"I just want to talk," Mike said firmly, putting the cups on the table. He pulled out a chair for her. "Please."

Carol took the chair and faced him as he sat, the strange emptiness she continued to feel making this easier to face than she'd expected. "You want to know if I'm still going to Paris."

He took a sip of coffee, as though he needed it. "Yes."

She sighed. "I think I have to."

He accepted her reply with a calm that surprised her. "You don't think our having made love changes anything?"

"I thought it had changed me," she said, pain rising in her, suddenly making the discussion not so easy. "Then I saw your little nieces and I reacted like my true self—like the woman I will always be—Becky and Gale's mother, Jon's wife."

"Carol," he said quietly, "you're using that as an excuse to slip back to where it's comfortable."

Her eyes widened at the word and her back stiffened. "Comfortable?" she repeated in a tone of disbelief.

"If you decide to love me," he said, leaning toward her, his mood and manner implacable, "you start all over again. You'll have the potential for a loving relationship with a man, more children, a happy family life. And with that comes the potential for more grief. I imagine the odds of that kind of horror happening to you again are slim, but they do exist."

The truth of what he said was there in her eyes. She didn't know it, but he saw it. "If you coach a baseball team," she said, her voice unsteady, "you'll always be in a plane or on a bus."

"All right," he said. "I'll get a job as a bank teller or a shoe clerk, if the thought of my traveling frightens you. That won't protect me from a hundred other things that could happen to me, but I'll do it for you. I'll do anything if you'll give me a chance to love you."

Her throat was clogged with emotion, her brain a maze of unclear thought and fiendish doubt. "I...I'm hollow inside, Mike. I thought I had something left to give you, but I was kidding myself. You need a whole woman...." She smiled, trying to pull out of the cloud that surrounded her. "A young woman without a troublesome past, so that you can start fresh."

"Carol." His quiet voice was scolding. "I can't start fresh—I don't want to. I come with a whole lot of baggage myself that I can't just shake off. I don't want a woman to play with, I want someone to live and love with. Won't you trust me and move ahead with me?"

This is it, Mike thought, *my last-ditch stand.* He could see the love for him in her eyes, but he could also feel the wall that had gone up the afternoon his nieces had arrived. Her brave step into the future had been badly shaken, and the pain had been intense. It stood between them now, palpable. But he'd endured enough pain himself to understand her reluctance to set herself up for more.

God, I want to, Carol thought, searching his eyes for some guarantee. His dark gaze was even, steady—as firm a promise as any woman could hope for. But she wasn't any woman. She'd lost everything once and was coming to the grim realization that she simply hadn't the courage to risk it again. Accepting cowardice, she lowered her eyes. "I can't."

A heavy silence lay between them for several moments. Then Mike got to his feet and reached across the table to cover her hand with his own. Her fingers were cold, but they turned to clasp his. "I won't bring it up again," he said quietly, "but I'll be here. If you change your mind..."

She looked up, her eyes round with concern. He let himself feel a moment's hope. "You won't stay away from the children because...of us?"

Hope shriveled. "Of course not. I've come to love them as much as you do. If you and I can't direct our love at each other, at least we can turn it on them and send them off with it."

As Carol stood and looked him in the eye, a little sigh of regret escaped her. Her voice was tangled in emotion. "I was a good wife and a good mother. But I don't think I'm good enough for you."

He shook his head, his expression also filled with regret. "I'd have enjoyed proving you wrong." He turned to the door. "Good night, Carol."

Chapter Fifteen

Sister Claire left on a rare sunny day in the middle of January, looking like a stranger in jeans and a red jacket over a pale blue sweater. Her hair was short and dark, a soft frame for the pretty features so long disguised by the severity of the habit. Mike, Carol, the children, Mother Margaret, Sister Celestine and Mr. Engbretson waited with her at the bus stop in Pointer's Beach. A Greyhound bus would take her to her sister's in Seattle. A bone-chilling wind negated the warming effects of the wintry sun.

"I'm expecting a letter from all of you by Valentine's Day," she said, swallowing hard and forcing a smile as the bus came into view several blocks down the street.

"Candy and I will make you a valentine," Kathy promised, close to tears.

"Me, too!" Nicky promised. Dorcas and Frank seemed unable to speak.

The bus drew closer and Mother Margaret took Sister Claire into her arms, holding her a long moment before letting her go. "Be happy," she said, her voice strained despite the careful control she seemed to have over her emotions. "Enjoy the world, Claire, but don't let it change you."

For a moment Claire was speechless, then she hugged her superior once more. "Thank you for everything, Mother."

Sister Celestine embraced her, admonishing her to eat properly.

"And don't try to fix things by yourself," Mr. Engbretson said with a gruff sniff. "You know how you are."

Mike handed her a business card. "This is my brother's number. He says he'll be glad to help you find a job. Just call him." He smiled. "I'll never have jalapeño cheese again without thinking of you."

She smiled, too. "And being glad you don't have to share it with me. I'm glad I got to know you."

One by one she hugged the children, coaxing them into smiles and reminding them to write. Then the bus pulled up at the curb, and the doors opened with a squeak and a whoosh of compressed air. Carol looked into her friend's eyes and saw that she and Claire stood on the same threshold, each still in the powerful grip of the past, each straining toward a new future. She took Claire into her arms. "Have a wonderful life," she said firmly. "I want to go to my mailbox in Paris and find a letter, telling me that you've got a great job and are dating a wonderful man."

Claire laughed and pulled away, holding Carol by the shoulders. Her eyes became grave; they had discussed Carol's change of plans. "Okay," she said softly, "but I'm sending the letter to Portland. If you want to read it, you'd better be in the right place. Bye."

In a moment the bus pulled away, proceeding on its route to the other small towns on the peninsula. The contingent from Saint Chris's waved as it turned onto the highway and disappeared.

The two sisters stared after the bus, Carol tried to comfort the weeping little ones, and Mike moved between Dorcas and Frank, pulling them close.

"We will have lunch at McDonald's," Mr. Engbretson declared with another sniff. "I will buy. Come along. Come along."

Carol followed with the little ones as Mike, the older children and the sisters fell into a parade behind them. She no longer questioned Mr. Engbretson's bursts of thoughtfulness and good humor. So much had changed during Christmas at Mike's house.

"THE CHILDREN have all been placed." Mother Margaret sat behind her desk, looking wearily across it at Mike and Carol, who sat in chairs facing her. "They're all going to different homes except Kathy and Candy, who will stay together." Mike closed his eyes and Carol sighed. "It's the best we could have hoped for," Mother Margaret assured them, passing a folder to Carol. "Here are some details about the foster families who'll be taking them in. They'll be picked up in five days. Our work here is almost finished."

Carol stood, her manner calm, stoic. "I'll tell the children. The longer they have to prepare, the easier it'll be for them."

Mike looked up at her, wanting to disagree with her, if only to get some reaction. They'd dealt with each other politely and carefully for the past several weeks, and he was on the brink of giving up hope that patience would gain him anything. He wanted to shake her—then he remembered how she'd looked the afternoon she'd first seen Patsy and Erika.

"I'd like a solution, too," she said, reading his eyes and his mind. "But sometimes there just isn't any." She turned and left the room.

Mother Margaret leaned back in her chair, studying her brother and the traces of pain around his mouth and eyes. It was different from the physical pain he'd carried when he arrived. "I warned you about her," she said softly.

He glanced up, toying with the seam of the right boot resting on his other knee. "I know," he said and sighed. "But I decided to take a chance anyway. I'm not sorry, and

I haven't given up. Maybe a little time in Paris..." he shrugged; despair gripped him when he thought about Carol being that far away. He drew a breath, steadying himself. "I'm sure she'll be pining for me within days."

Meg smiled at him with pity and affection. She picked up an envelope and passed it across the desk. "This was in this morning's mail."

Mike frowned, studying the New York return address. Inside the envelope was another, smaller envelope with a vaguely familiar name in the upper left-hand corner. Milton Boardman. Suddenly he remembered the tourist at the restaurant in Pointer's Beach. Smiling reflectively, he opened the envelope and removed a note written on lined paper.

Was a real kick to meet you, Rafferty. None of my friends believed me till I showed them the picture. Thought you'd like a copy. So I took guts in hand and called George Steinbrenner, who promised to send this on. If you're ever in Los Angeles, please look us up.

Best, Milton Boardman

Tucked into the note was the photograph of himself, Carol and the children in their Yankees shirts and caps, Milton in the middle with a big grin. There was a certain rightness to the photograph that cut Mike more deeply than any pain he'd ever experienced before. He stared at it for a moment, then handed it across for Meg's inspection. Her brows drew together and she sighed as she studied the picture.

"The kids had a great couple of weeks," she said, handing it back to him. "Some children never get even that. They're going to be all right."

"You keep saying that," he said.

She smiled, closing one hand over the cross that hung around her neck. "Because I believe it."

"DORCAS'S FAMILY is named Kirby and has a girl and a boy," Carol read from the notes as she and the children sat clustered on the sofa. She looked at Dorcas with a grin. "And a swimming pool."

"All right!" Frank was enthusiastic. His excitement was artificial, but Carol knew he was trying to bolster the moods of the other children. "What about mine?"

Carol riffled through the sheets of paper and scanned the brief biography of Frank's family. "Yours has a small wheat farm in a place called Sheridan. And you'll love this, Frank. They raise huskies."

He frowned. "What are those?"

"Sled dogs."

Nicky smiled thinly at Frank. "Maybe they'll take you for a ride. Maybe if I come to visit, I can go, too."

Frank glanced at Carol, knowing the likelihood of visits was slim. But he smiled at Nicky. "Sure. Even if you don't, I'll try to send a picture."

Dorcas, sitting beside Carol, leaned her head against her arm. "Will you send us pictures of Paris?"

"Of course. Every chance I get."

Kathy frowned. "How come you're not staying with Mike?"

Frank, who somehow understood everything, gave Kathy a warning look. "Sometimes grown-ups can't do what they want any more than we can. I don't think she wants to talk about it."

Carol reached across Nicky to touch Frank's knee. "Thank you, Frank, but I can talk about it. Mike and I are going to be friends. Just like we'll all be friends, always. But he's going to start a new job in Portland, and mine is in Paris. There would never be time for us to be together."

Dorcas absently pleated the folds of Carol's skirt. "It seems like there's never enough time for the right people to be together."

Nicky jumped up as a firm rap sounded on the door. "It's Mike!" he called unnecessarily as their friend stepped into the room.

Carol smiled, genuinely pleased to see him. His presence always had a steadying effect on the children. She even felt herself relax, knowing he'd come to share the burden of helping them accept the news. He smiled back.

Candy ran to him, her arms raised. He lifted her onto his hip. "Our family has four other little girls. We'll have lots of kids to play with."

"And my foster father is a doctor in Astoria," Nicky informed him, following him to the deep chair across the room where he sat with Candy. "If I get sick, I won't have to go to the hospital, 'cause he can fix me right at home."

Mike pulled the boy onto his other knee. He listened to Frank and Dorcas's descriptions of their foster families, admiring the courage with which they tried to look ahead. It was sobering to realize that these children were braver than he was. "I came to walk you guys to dinner," he said, "and tell you that Mother Margaret has given you the day off from school tomorrow."

Despite the crisis of moving, a day off from school was cause for delight. Frank grinned. "How come?"

"Well, it seems the sisters have a few things to get ready for themselves, since they'll be leaving right after you, and Carol's got to go to town to get some things she needs for her trip. So the six of us can ride the go-carts and eat ice cream while we wait for her."

The children's mood clearly lightened at the prospect, and there was conversation and laughter as they went to get their coats to go to dinner.

Carol rose from the sofa and Mike got to his feet. Half the width of the room remained between them. "Thank you for that," she said quietly.

He nodded. "Sure."

"WHEN DO YOU have to report for spring training?" Frank asked. Mike and the children sat at a round, white-topped table in a pink and white ice-cream parlor on Pointer's Beach's main street. It smelled of chocolate and butterscotch.

"March, I think," Mike replied, scraping his spoon across the top of a scoop of black walnut ice cream. The excitement he should have felt just wasn't there. The work would help him get from one day to the next—he knew that—but it was no longer his life's blood. These days his heart seemed powered by Carol's smile and the children's laughter, but there'd been precious little of either in the past few weeks. He dredged up a grin for the boy. "That's when I want you to start practicing. It'll still be cold, but your body warms up with the season. Come June, you'll be ready."

Frank grinned back, the heart of his smile as artificial as Mike's. "Maybe I'll play for your team someday."

Mike nodded. "I'll come scout your games when you're in high school."

"Candy and I'll come and cheer for you," Kathy promised.

"We're younger," Dorie reminded her. "We won't be out of foster homes yet."

Nicky, kneeling on his chair, looked up from his sundae with a strawberry mustache. "Frank says when he gets out, he's gonna come and get all of us."

Kathy frowned. "I think he'll have to be married."

Nicky shrugged. "He can marry Dorie."

Dorcas reacted instantly, crossing her eyes and putting both hands around her throat, as though she would prefer death by her own hand. Simultaneously, Frank shouted "Yuk!" with such emphasis that Nicky, beside him, almost fell off his chair. When he laughed and overbalanced, struggling to right himself, Mike reached out to lend a hand.

As he did so, a tiny blur of white raced up his arm and across the table.

"Oh, Nick!" Mike said, getting to his feet as the girls shrieked and jumped out of their chairs. "You didn't bring Kermit again?" The tables around them cleared amid oaths and more shrieks, as two young boys and a woman with two children scrambled to their feet.

"He wanted to come," Nicky replied feebly, crawling under the table in search of his pet.

"Anybody see where he went?" Mike followed the direction in which he thought he'd seen the mouse move. The route was confirmed a moment later, when there was a loud scream from somewhere beyond the half doors behind the counter. With a groan he followed the sound, the children running behind him.

CAROL GLANCED at her watch. Mike and the children were ten minutes late in picking her up. That wouldn't have been cause for concern in anyone else, but Mike was the most dependable, punctual man she'd ever met. He had a lot of other qualities, too, though it would do her little good to think any more about them—they'd been running through her mind for days.

Drawing in a deep gulp of biting early-February air, Carol looked up at the grim, gray sky and wondered how Claire was doing. She missed her gentle insanity even more than she'd expected to. A grimness to match the sky settled around her; in four short days, the special life she'd lived at Saint Christopher's Home for Children—and the special people who'd become part of that life—would be gone. She could write to the children, but it wouldn't be fair to intrude upon their adjustment to new lives by visiting, so she would probably never see then again. She had known it was coming; she had helped the children prepare for it. It was too late now to wish that she'd prepared herself a little better.

She drew another deep breath and squared her shoulders. She was good at this sort of thing when she put her mind to it. All she had to do was turn all sensors off and do what had to be done. But suddenly, unbidden, came the memory of an afternoon at Mike's house, when she'd lain in his arms and come alive again—so alive that since then all the old tricks she used no longer worked. She was no longer the grieving widow and mother who had turned aside her grief and become an automaton. She was a woman again, alive, aware, attuned to everything around her. Pain had come alive, too, but in the last few days she'd barely noticed it. She'd been most aware of a desperate deprivation every time she saw Mike and didn't touch him, every time he looked at her and couldn't make himself smile. She even found herself longing for the early days of their relationship, when she'd still been locked in her past but had had easy access to his warm, teasing friendship.

KERMIT IN ONE HAND, Nicky's hand in the other, Mike led the children hurriedly to the car. "Everybody in and buckle up," he ordered, his voice a little sharp after the twenty-minute search for Kermit with two young women standing screaming in the ice-cream parlor's sink. Once behind the wheel, he carefully handed the mouse to Nicky, who sat in the middle. "Please keep hold of him."

Nicky rubbed Kermit's head with a small fingertip. "I'm sorry."

"I know. It's okay." Mike concentrated on speaking quietly while looking over his shoulder to check seat belts. "But we're half an hour late picking up Carol, so let's all be on our best behavior, so we can get there quickly."

They were within blocks of their destination when Nicky held up Kermit to look into his pink eyes. "Do you think you'll like Astoria?"

"As long as they don't have a cat," Frank replied for Kermit.

"A cat?" Nicky turned to Frank, the ugly potential of such a possibility alive in his eyes. In his anguish, he slackened his hold on Kermit, who took immediate advantage of the freedom. "Kermit!" Nicky shouted, unbuckling his seat belt.

"What?" In fairly busy midafternoon traffic, Mike slowed, holding Nicky back in his seat with one arm while controlling the car with the other, watching the traffic and trying to figure out what had happened.

"I'll get him." Frank slipped to the floor of the car. "He's under the gas pedal! I've almost got him!"

Still holding Nicky in place, Mike glanced down at Frank, then up again—just in time to see a battered blue pickup pull away from the curb. Its driver didn't seem to notice the steady stream of traffic in the lane to which he sought entry. Hoping Frank had said that Kermit was under the gas pedal, and not the brake to which he was firmly applying his foot, Mike yanked Frank up and into Nicky's lap, leaning sideways to hold both boys in place. The station wagon slammed into the back of the pickup with a teeth-jarring crash.

CAROL HAD IMAGINED the sound of metal crashing into metal for a year; it was the sound track of her every nightmare. Even before she saw the blue pickup a block away lurch forward from the impact, her heart began to thud, and her mouth went dry. When she saw that the pickup had been struck by the station wagon from Saint Christopher's, her heart plummeted to her feet, and for one awful moment her blood froze. *No*, she prayed, pleading. *Not Mike and my dorm kids. Please!*

She ran the block in Olympic time, pushing aside people who were beginning to gather around the wagon, including the well-meaning man who was trying to open the driver's side door. She tore it open, pausing for a moment at the sight of Mike, leaning back against the headrest, his eyes closed. Blood poured from a gash over his left eye.

"He hit his head on the steering wheel," Dorcas said, her eyes wide as she leaned over the front seat. "He took his belt off to get Frank up...."

It occurred to Carol to wonder what Frank had been doing on the floor, but she was too busy rooting for a handkerchief to press against the gash to think any more of it. A quick glance into the front and back and the high level of squirming and explaining told her that the children were fine.

"Ah!" Mike grabbed her wrist, trying to sit up. "The kids..." he said, trying to push her away.

"They're fine." She pushed against him and found him momentarily too disoriented to struggle. "Just lie still."

He winced as she applied pressure. "Did I...squash Kermit?"

"He's fine, Mike! See?" Nicky held the struggling mouse under Mike's nose before Carol could stop him.

Mike opened one eye and gave the boy a tiny smile. "Good. I'm having him on a sandwich tomorrow."

Nicky giggled, unimpressed by the threat.

Mike tried to sit up again, this time applying more strength to the effort. Carol continued to resist, also applying more strength. "The kids should be looked at," he said, pulling the troublesome handkerchief from her grasp.

The whine of a siren became audible. "You're all going to be looked at," Carol said, reclaiming her pressure bandage. "You're probably even going to get some stitches."

"Carol, why are you sitting on me?" Mike asked testily.

"I'm not sitting on you," she replied. "I'm just holding you down with my knee."

He cautiously opened both eyes and squinted; cymbals crashed within his already formidable headache. But after careful focusing he was able to notice that she was flushed with concern; her movements were quick but gentle as she dabbed at his forehead. He felt a moment's elation that she was clearly so worried about him. Then he realized that it was probably just the shock of the crash. She'd lost everyone who meant anything to her in just this way. Though this accident was minor, it must have brought back all the old agonies for her once again. With a sigh, he closed his eyes and left her to her nursing.

WITHIN FIFTEEN MINUTES of Carol's call to Saint Christopher's, Mr. Engbretson arrived at the hospital to take the children home. Convincing the children to leave Mike took much longer. She finally had to promise that whatever time she got home with him, she would bring them in to see him.

"I'll leave you my truck," Mr. Engbretson told her as she walked them to the hospital's double glass doors. "We'll go back in the station wagon. It's pretty battered, but it seems to be drivable." He paused to look down at her in concern. "Are you going to be all right?"

She nodded. "Yes, of course. Please reassure Mother Margaret that Mike's going to be fine, too. I had a little trouble convincing her when I called."

Mr. Engbretson laughed. "She called the doctor herself. He told her four stitches and no problems."

"That's right." It was dusk as she stood on the top step to wave them off. "Thank you, Mr. Engbretson."

He paused two steps down, holding Nicky by the hand, and turned back to her, blue eyes steady. "You will call me Lars."

Knowing the honor was equivalent to being knighted, Carol nodded gravely. "Thank you, Lars."

HIS EYES CLOSED against the vicious headache, Mike sat in the poorly sprung truck's passenger seat and tried not to think. Carol looked the way he felt, pale and fragile and startled—as though it was hard for her, too, to believe that everything was over.

He felt the truck stop at the light outside of town. They started off again with a grinding of gears that stirred his headache further. "Clutch," he said without opening his eyes. Her unfamiliarity with a manual transmission was making the ride less than comfortable.

She made an impatient sound. "Who's driving this truck?"

"Evel Knievel?" he guessed.

"Ha ha," she said.

They bounced on in silence for several minutes more, then her voice penetrated the pain in his head again. "Do you still want to marry me?" she asked.

For a moment Mike said nothing—he doubted that he even drew breath. He sat up gingerly, leaned into the corner of the front seat and tried to focus on her. "I'm not sure I heard the question."

"Do you still want to marry me?" she asked a second time, still without removing her eyes from the road. He watched her lick her lips and swallow.

"Well, I don't know," he finally replied. "I thought you had nothing to offer me."

She sighed, appearing to concentrate on the stretch of road picked out by their headlights. "So did I. Until I saw the accident and..." Her voice broke. "I thought I'd lost you... and the kids. Just like the last time." She pulled off the road just before the climb into the hills, but it was a moment before she could turn away from the wheel to look at him. When she did, her eyes were large and moist and filled with pain.

Forgetting his own pain, Mike moved to the middle of the seat and took her into his arms. "I'm sorry I was responsible for your reliving that," he said.

"No." She surprised him by pushing him away, her unsteady lips firming. "The fear and the pain I felt weren't for Jon and my girls. They were for you and my dorm kids." She put her arms around his neck and looked into his eyes, her own even gaze underlining the importance of what she was telling him. "I loved my family so much, Mike, but I think I've finally assimilated the love and put the grief away. I love you. I want to marry you."

"Carol. God." He crushed her to him with a sense of disbelief. "Say that again. Right in my ear."

"I love you," she repeated gently against his temple. "I want to marry you."

He pulled away, his headache forgotten. "When?"

She looked a little reluctant. "Do you think four days is too fast? I'd like the kids to give me away before... before they go."

He nodded, still staring at her. A shaky hand went up to stroke her cheekbone. "What about Paris?"

She shrugged with a negligence that was completely convincing. "It was just someplace to go. Maybe we can visit it one day. I really don't care."

"I took the coaching job," he warned.

She smiled. "I know. I can go with you, can't I?"

Again he pulled her close, feeling life beginning to flow in his veins. "I'll make you happy. I promise."

"You've already done that. Just love me."

"Always. Forever."

"Mike?" She drew back, a question half-formed on her lips and spilling out of her eyes. He waited. When she tried several times and finally sighed without asking it, he held her loosely in his arms. "You can ask me anything," he said gently. "Just say it."

She looked at him, paused, then shook her head, turning to start the truck. "I'll ask you tomorrow. Tonight I just want to savor the fact that you love me and I love you."

Mike remained in the middle seat, an arm around her shoulders as the truck moved onto the road. He could savor that for a lifetime. He could wait until tomorrow to hear the question.

THE MORNING of their wedding came, and she was still unable to ask the question. They had called their families and received their blessings. Rick and Claire had driven together from Seattle to stand up for them. As Claire helped her adjust the light blue, broad-brimmed hat on her head, she tried to close her mind on the question, but it still kept forming.

She just couldn't ask that of Mike, when he was just finding his feet again after a major disruption in his life, when the future looked promising but uncertain. She was beginning to feel stronger every day, almost invincible, but she had no right to ask something so outrageous of him. Perhaps they could consider it later, when there would be more time.

She sighed, tugging at the peplum of her blue silk suit. Yes. That would be the sensible thing. Later. But the unspoken thought lay like a small wound in the heart of her happiness.

"You're very fidgety," Claire said, stepping back to look at her. "Bridal jitters?"

Carol smiled and shook her head. It was difficult to equate this glamorous young woman in soft pink, wearing a matching hat that was all flowers and fluffy veiling, with the nun who'd been such a good friend. "Just a little nervous," she said.

"I think you're doing the right thing."

Carol nodded. "I know I am."

From the back bedroom wafted the sound of quiet conversation, as Sister Celestine helped the girls dress for the ceremony. Carol noticed the absence of giggles, the subdued tenor of their talking. All the children had been delighted by the announcement of the wedding, but tomorrow they would all go their separate ways, and that heartache pervaded everything. Carol closed her eyes, thought for a moment, prayed, then pulled away from Claire's fussing hands and ran for the front door.

"I KNOW it is uncomfortable, but it will only be for a little while."

"Who ever decided that making a dumb knot around your neck made you look good, anyway?"

"It is the sign of a gentleman. Nicky does not mind."

"I think we look kind of neat, Frank."

"I think we look like we're gonna choke!"

In the living room of his cabin, Mike slipped into the tux jacket Rick held out for him. The argument went on in the next room as Mr. Engbretson helped the boys dress, but he tuned it out. There was a tension underlying Frank's voice that he recognized as pain. And at the heart of his own almost overwhelming happiness there was an answering pain. It was absurd to think that he could do anything about it right now. Carol's love made him feel like Superman, but he couldn't expect her to want to... That was stupid. She'd been through so much. She'd need time, his undivided attention—and his love.

"If you don't loosen up," Rick said, pulling the front of Mike's tux together and smoothing it over his shoulders, "you're going to send her running in the other direction. You look like you're going up against Orel Hershiser."

Mike expelled a breath and tried to force himself to relax. "Sorry." He took a step back. "How do I look?"

Rick studied him and nodded halfheartedly. "Well...for you, pretty good. But don't think I'm going to forget that you got the blue cummerbund and I got the pink."

Mike grinned. "You're supposed to match Claire, I'm supposed to match Carol. Tough luck."

"Your sympathy helps," Rick said dryly. He glanced at his watch. "There are forty minutes until the ceremony. Why don't you sit down and try to get yourself together?"

Pacing across the room, Mike ignored the suggestion. "I'm together. My together is just a little more physical than yours."

"If you faint at the altar," Rick warned, "I'm going to be mortified. And you'll lose hero status with Frank and Nicky."

Mike stopped pacing and turned to Rick with a look so grim that he was silenced. Then Mike moved to the kitchen. "You want a glass of water?" he asked over his shoulder. Putting a hand on the refrigerator door, his attention was diverted and he didn't hear Rick's answer. Pinned there with a magnet was the picture Milton Boardman had sent of himself and the seven of them around the table at the restaurant. Candy was asleep in his lap, and the other kids were all leaning in toward the center, grinning from ear to ear, happy, pretending that they were a family. Suddenly its rightness was too overpowering to ignore or even to treat with caution. He snatched the photo, sending the magnet flying, and ran past Rick to the front door.

"Where the hell—?" Rick began, then, seeing the photo in Mike's hand, smiled and shouted, "I'll get my own water!"

MIKE AND CAROL met in the middle of the leaf-strewn path that ran between her dorm and his cabin. They went into each other's arms in a mixture of laughter and surprise.

"What are you doing out here without a coat?" Mike asked, holding her away and rubbing his hands up and down her blue-silk-clad arms. Then his gentle scolding was arrested by the vision of warmth and color she made in the middle of the bare and drizzly landscape. "You are so beautiful," he whispered, as though he'd just made that observation for the first time.

She smiled, touched and a little embarrassed by the compliment. He looked big and handsome, and so filled with life and energy that for a moment she faltered in her purpose. Then he looped his arms around her waist. His hold was so tender, his gaze so kind, that she laughed a little with the sure knowledge that he would always love her in just this way.

"I wanted to find you," she said, resting the palms of her hands on his chest. "To... to ask you that question I never finished the other day." Then she looked puzzled. "But what are you doing out here?"

"I was coming to find you," he replied easily. "I have a question, too. But you first."

She would have preferred that he go first, but she nodded, eager to ask him before she lost her nerve. "Would you... could we... I mean, are you... a private person?"

He stared at her, trying to understand the question. For the past ten years he'd lived his life in the public eye, and the time that hadn't been spent there had been filled with the comings and goings of his nosy family and friends. Since his accident, his attempt to hide away to find himself had resulted in having his life taken over by nuns, children and this woman, who was now as much a part of himself as his heart.

"No," he replied, knitting his brow as he tried to read the reason behind the question in her eyes. "Why? Are you already considering separate vacations?"

She laughed softly, nervously. "No, I just wondered if you'd want to... to live alone."

"Alone?" He repeated the word, puzzled by it. "With you I would not be alone."

"Right." She tried to clarify the question. "But would you want *us* to be alone... I mean, together?"

"You're not making sense," he declared finally.

She closed her eyes and breathed out a gust of air that rippled the brim of her hat. She grabbed his hand and held it between her two. "Mike, what I want to say—" Her hand connected with something unfamiliar, and she pulled her eyes away from his to extract the photo from his hand. She looked down into the broad smile of Milton Boardman and into the faces of her dorm kids, grinning in their Yankees hats and T-shirts. She, Carol, looked for the first time in a year as though she belonged somewhere, and Mike, relaxed and proprietary, was clearly caring for all of them.

She looked up at him again, her khaki eyes brimming with love. "What was *your* question?" she asked.

Life fell into place around him, and he took a moment to relish the feeling. He smiled, realizing that there was no such thing as being in control; there was only reacting well to whatever happened. "I was wondering," he began, pulling her closer, looking at what the shadow of the brim of her hat did to the emotion churning in her eyes, "if you saw any reason why that picture shouldn't become reality. Now. Today."

"Not one." She pulled his face down and kissed him long and deeply. Then she pulled back with a small frown. "But now? Today? The ceremony's in about twenty minutes, and bureaucratic red tape..."

He turned her toward the dorm and headed for the administration building. "Go back inside. I'm going to see Meg and have her get things rolling."

"Mike..." She wanted to caution him that it would take time, that the wheels of the government turned slowly.

"I love you!" he shouted, sprinting up the walk.

"I love you, too!" she shouted back, thinking that even a bureaucratic government couldn't stand against such power.

MOTHER MARGARET looked at her brother in astonishment. "All of them?"

He nodded firmly. "All five."

"And Carol's in agreement?"

"Complete agreement."

She sat down and shuffled through papers. "Okay, but be prepared for it to take time. They might have to go to their assigned homes, and in a few weeks, after—"

"No." He leaned on her desk with both hands, his eyes dark. "We take them home to Portland with us tomorrow, or we all stay here until the question is resolved."

"But, Mike—"

"Call the bishop," he said straightening. "Call the pope, if you have to, and the governor. And call Patrick. Tell him to start working on the legal end."

Meg sighed. "I'll miss your wedding."

"We'll do it over for you on our first anniversary." He reached across the desk to kiss her cheek. "Get us our kids, Meg."

Meg dialed a number, smiling at Mike's back as he closed the door behind him. "Sure thing, Mike. Sure thing."

MIKE GAVE his responses clearly, so secure in Carol's love, so attuned to their mission that he was calm. The children behind them in the second pew, sober little faces turned toward them, were his now, his and Carol's, no matter who lingered over the decision or how long it took. He knew what he wanted now and was determined to have it.

As Carol repeated her vows, the past finally at peace within her, she felt more complete, more real, than she ever had before. She thanked God for the miracle of Mike and prayed that He would compound the miracle by making the children hers, too.

"I pronounce you man and wife," Father Cunningham said, smiling as he blessed them. "You may kiss the bride."

Mike looked down at Carol and saw everything he'd ever wanted in the world in her eyes as he bent his head. Carol felt the promise in his light kiss, and all the tenderness of his regard for her in the firm but gentle pressure of his hands on her arms. She drew a deep breath of contentment and took his arm, turning to walk down the sanctuary steps. Rick and Claire fell into step behind them, the children standing in the second pew, waiting to follow. Behind them Mr. Engbretson dabbed at his nose with a blue bandanna.

Then the double doors of the chapel opened and Mother Margaret stood in the opening, silhouetted against the gray February sky. Mike and Carol stopped, the entire wedding party coming to an abrupt halt behind them. The formality of the ceremony broke down as Rick and Claire, briefly apprised of the plan, flanked Mike and Carol to hear the results of Mother Margaret's efforts. Mr. Engbretson inched around the side, and Sister Celestine bustled through the children knotted in confusion behind the adults, all straining to hear.

"What's the matter?" Dorcas asked.

"Aren't we going to eat now?" Nicky wanted to know.

Sister Celestine turned to them with a finger to her lips. "Hush. We'll eat in just a minute."

Mike lowered his arm to catch Carol's fingers in his as he waited for Meg to reach them. He tried to assess what she was about to say by analyzing her expression, and found that he couldn't. She was wearing her children's-home-administrator's face, the controlled, philosophical look she always wore when she was trying to explain away the inequities of the system. He squeezed Carol's hand and braced himself.

"Everyone seems to think it's a good idea," she said quietly, smiling. "There are, however, procedures that have to be followed, regarding investigation of your characters and backgrounds which, in the interest of the children, can't be waived."

Mike felt Carol lean against him. "How long?" she asked, disappointment strong in her voice.

"A few weeks," Mother Margaret replied. Carol emitted a small groan, and the only word that occurred to Mike could not be said in a church. "Meanwhile," Mother Margaret went on, a broad smile suddenly taking over her face, "you have temporary custody for as long as it takes."

Carol screamed and Mike shouted; they pounced to include Mother Margaret in their hug. Claire jumped up and down, Rick took a weeping Sister Celestine into his arms, and Mr. Engbretson disappeared once more into his bandanna.

Kathy turned to Dorcas. "What's going on?"

Dorcas turned to Frank. "What's custody?"

Frank shook his head, a rare look of confusion in his eyes. "I don't know. Something to do with... parents and going to court."

The excitement gradually subsided, then everyone became aware of the children standing behind them in the middle of the aisle, watching in complete bewilderment.

"Well, come along, everyone." Mother Margaret shepherded Father Cunningham, Sister Celestine, Mr. Engbretson, the best man and maid of honor toward the door. She turned to smile at Mike and Carol. "We'll start the reception without you. Join us when you can."

"Aren't we gonna eat?" Nicky asked anxiously.

"Yes," Mike replied, shooing the children into a pew. "But we have to talk first."

Dorcas rolled her eyes. "We don't have to kneel again, do we?"

"No," Carol replied. "Just sit."

With the children ranged in one pew, Mike and Carol went into the one in front of it, sitting sideways to look over the back. Mike opened his mouth to speak, saw all the watchful little faces, and suddenly realized he didn't know what to say. He smiled at Carol. "You're so good at this."

"It was your idea," she reminded him.

"We got the idea simultaneously, as I recall."

Frank sighed. "Look, we've been through this before. Just tell us. Don't treat us like little kids. Are they coming for us early? Are we going to miss the reception?" He swallowed and seemed to straighten, angling his chin with just a hint of a man squaring his jaw. "Are you trying to say goodbye?"

Carol reached over the back of the pew to put a hand to the side of his face. "We're trying to say hello, Frank," she said, her voice heavy with emotion.

He looked at her blankly. "Hello?"

Deciding she needed help, Mike stepped in. "Nobody's coming for you. We're all going home to Portland together."

Kathy, her arm protectively around Candy, asked gravely, "For how long?"

"Forever," he replied. "We're going to adopt you."

Distracted from hunger by the sudden turn of the conversation, Nicky stood and moved into Mike and Carol's pew. "That means we're going to live together. All of us?"

Mike turned and pulled him onto his knee. "That's right. Would you like that?"

Nicky looked at the other kids, who were apparently still confused. Suddenly the forward pew was full of children. Kathy and Candy moved in beside Mike, Dorcas sat down next to Carol and Frank stood, leaning against the back of the pew in front of them.

Dorcas leaned forward to be able to see Mike as well as Carol. "You're kidding, right?" she asked gravely.

Carol put an arm around her. "We're not kidding, Dorie. We're going to be a family, all of us."

Dorcas looked from Carol to Mike as though still trying to assimilate the news. "And live where we lived at Christmas?"

"Yes."

"But..." She shook her head. "That wasn't real. That was like one of the dreams I used to make up. It's like—" her voice faded "—the stuff other kids have."

"It was real," Carol assured her, wrapping both arms around her. "Life won't always be as wonderful as it was at Christmas. It'll be kind of like it was here. Sometimes we'll have fun, sometimes we'll get mad at each other, sometimes you'll feel great and sometimes you'll feel gloomy. But we'll all be there, and you'll never have to move again until *you* get married.''

Kathy looked up at Mike, eyes and smile both glowing. ''I know it's real. You know why?''

He brushed the dark hair out of her eyes, so overcome with feeling that he hardly trusted his voice. ''Why?''

She knelt on the pew to hug him. ''Because Santa did it.'' Candy wriggled in between them, and since Nicky refused to abandon his position, Mike had to shift to make room for the sudden invasion of his lap. ''I didn't ask him when I talked to him in the gym, but I asked him at night when I said my prayers.''

Dorcas looked horrified. ''You're not supposed to pray to Santa.''

''Sister Claire said he used to be Saint Nicholas.'' Kathy frowned at Mike. ''That was okay, wasn't it? It worked.''

Mike nodded, holding her close. ''It was okay. Now, we're going to the convent for the reception, then tomorrow we're going home to Portland.''

''Aren't you supposed to have a honeymoon?'' Dorcas asked.

All the little bodies between him and Carol gave that question an edge of humor, but he answered seriously. ''Yes, we are. But we'll wait a couple of months for it. When we go, you'll stay with your grandmother.''

Nicky frowned. ''I don't have a grandmother.''

Dorcas poked his leg. ''You do now, silly—Rita. Now she's Grandma Rita.'' As though she still couldn't quite believe it, she looked to Mike for confirmation. ''Right?''

''Right. So we're all in agreement that this is a good idea?''

The reply was loud and unanimous. Mike set Nicky, Kathy and Candy on their feet, and Carol left the pew with Dorcas, gathering them around her. Frank, who had been very quiet during the discussion, remained in place at the end of the pew as Mike lifted the kneeler with his foot and prepared to leave. The boy's face was pale, his eyes wore a stunned look, his bottom lip was dangerously unsteady. Mike put a hand on his shoulder. "Are you all right?"

Frank swallowed and looked up at him. "Do you mean," he asked in a careful whisper, "that I'm going to be…Mike Rafferty's son?"

The awe with which he spoke the words made Mike understand, more than anything else had, the awesome responsibility he had undertaken—and the rewards that awaited him if he could just do it right. He took the boy into his arms and held him, then pulled away and smiled down at him. "I will be Frank Kaminski Rafferty's father."

Frank smiled back. "Wow!" he said.

They walked down the aisle, an army of seven, arms entwined, everyone talking at once. At the door of the church, Carol tugged Mike to a stop. He looked down into her face to see love, happiness—and another question. He turned to her, giving her his full attention.

She put her hands at his waist, her manner hesitant, appealingly embarrassed. He looped his arms around her and waited.

"Well…I was just thinking." She hunched a shoulder and moved a hand to trace the line of his lapel. "Claire and Rick seem to be good friends, Sister Cel and Mother Margaret are going on to Denver, we've got the kids…"

"Right. All nice and neat."

She shook her head. "Mr. Engbretson doesn't have anywhere to go."

Smiling, Mike bent down to kiss her. "He does now. He's going to stay with Hutton in the guest house and build a playhouse in the back, expand the patio, and work on a few other projects I have in mind. We talked before the wedding."

Carol stood on tiptoe to hug him. "I swear to you," she whispered fiercely, "that I will devote my life to giving you everything."

"God," Mike said, crushing her close, thinking how much his life had changed in two months. "You already have."

If you are looking for more titles by

BARBARA BRETTON

Don't miss these fabulous stories by one of
Harlequin's most renowned authors:

Harlequin American Romance®

#16393	BUNDLE OF JOY	$3.25	☐
#16493	RENEGADE LOVER	$3.50	☐

Harlequin® Promotional Titles

#83246	SOMEWHERE IN TIME	$4.99	☐
#83238	TO HAVE AND TO HOLD	$4.99	☐

(short-story collection also featuring Rita Clay Estrada,
Sandra James, Debbie Macomber)

(limited quantities available on certain titles)

TOTAL AMOUNT	$
POSTAGE & HANDLING	$
($1.00 for one book, 50¢ for each additional)	
APPLICABLE TAXES*	$_____
TOTAL PAYABLE	$_____
(check or money order—please do not send cash)	

To order, complete this form and send it, along with a check or money order
for the total above, payable to Harlequin Books, to: **In the U.S.:** 3010 Walden
Avenue, P.O. Box 9047, Buffalo, NY 14269-9047; **In Canada:** P.O. Box 613,
Fort Erie, Ontario, L2A 5X3.

Name: _____

Address: _____ City: _____

State/Prov.: _____ Zip/Postal Code: _____

*New York residents remit applicable sales taxes.
Canadian residents remit applicable GST and provincial taxes.   HBBBACK2

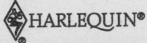

HARLEQUIN®

MILLION DOLLAR SWEEPSTAKES (III)

No purchase necessary. To enter, follow the directions published. Method of entry may vary. For eligibility, entries must be received no later than March 31, 1996. No liability is assumed for printing errors, lost, late or misdirected entries. Odds of winning are determined by the number of eligible entries distributed and received. Prizewinners will be determined no later than June 30, 1996.

Sweepstakes open to residents of the U.S. (except Puerto Rico), Canada, Europe and Taiwan who are 18 years of age or older. All applicable laws and regulations apply. Sweepstakes offer void wherever prohibited by law. Values of all prizes are in U.S. currency. This sweepstakes is presented by Torstar Corp., its subsidiaries and affiliates, in conjunction with book, merchandise and/or product offerings. For a copy of the Official Rules send a self-addressed, stamped envelope (WA residents need not affix return postage) to: MILLION DOLLAR SWEEPSTAKES (III) Rules, P.O. Box 4573, Blair, NE 68009, USA.

EXTRA BONUS PRIZE DRAWING

No purchase necessary. The Extra Bonus Prize will be awarded in a random drawing to be conducted no later than 5/30/96 from among all entries received. To qualify, entries must be received by 3/31/96 and comply with published directions. Drawing open to residents of the U.S. (except Puerto Rico), Canada, Europe and Taiwan who are 18 years of age or older. All applicable laws and regulations apply; offer void wherever prohibited by law. Odds of winning are dependent upon number of eligible entries received. Prize is valued in U.S. currency. The offer is presented by Torstar Corp., its subsidiaries and affiliates in conjunction with book, merchandise and/or product offering. For a copy of the Official Rules governing this sweepstakes, send a self-addressed, stamped envelope (WA residents need not affix return postage) to: Extra Bonus Prize Drawing Rules, P.O. Box 4590, Blair, NE 68009, USA.

SWP-H1294

Fifty red-blooded, white-hot, true-blue hunks
from every State in the Union!

Look for MEN MADE IN AMERICA! Written by some
of our most popular authors, these stories feature fifty
of the strongest, sexiest men, each from a different state
in the union!

Two titles available every month at your favorite
retail outlet.

In December, look for:

NATURAL ATTRACTION by Marisa Carroll
(New Hampshire)
MOMENTS HARSH, MOMENTS GENTLE by Joan Hohl
(New Jersey)

In January 1995, look for:

WITHIN REACH by Marilyn Pappano (New Mexico)
IN GOOD FAITH by Judith McWilliams (New York)

You won't be able to resist MEN MADE IN AMERICA!

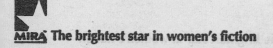

If you enjoyed the Matchmakers by

DEBBIE MACOMBER

Here's your chance to order more stories by one of
Harlequin's beloved authors:

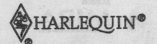